OPENING MOVES

'THE FIRST BOOK IN THE RED GAMBIT SERIES'

COLIN GEE

1

Opening Moves

The First book in the 'Red Gambit' series

12th JUNE TO 13th AUGUST 1945

WRITTEN BY COLIN GEE

Series Dedication

The Red Gambit series of five books is dedicated to my grandfather, the boss-fellah, Jack 'Chalky' White, Chief Petty Officer [Engine Room] RN, my de facto father until his untimely death from cancer in 1983 and a man who, along with many millions of others, participated in the epic of history that we know as World War Two.

Their efforts and sacrifices made it possible for us to read of it, in freedom, today.

Thank you, for everything.

The 'Red Gambit Series' novels are works of fiction, and deal with fictional events. Most of the characters therein are a figment of the author's imagination. Without exception, those characters that are historical figures of fact or based upon historical figures of fact are used fictitiously, and their actions, demeanour, conversations, and characters are similarly all figments of the author's imagination.

Overview by Author Colin Gee

The general concept of these books addresses the fears of war-weary nations in 1945.

The World War was drawing to a close, with solely the Empire of Japan to vanquish and yet, in the hour of triumph, the European victors stood facing each other across the ravaged terrain of their former German foe, not in friendship, but in worry and suspicion.

There was a genuine fear amongst allied servicemen and public alike, that the communist Red Army, much lauded during the years of the struggle against Nazism and so very obviously capable and professional, would continue its crushing advance to the shores of the Atlantic itself.

On the Soviet side, similar concerns and fears were realised in different ways, as all that could be seen was a relatively unclouded group of capitalist nations posturing and dictating to a Rodina that had spilt so much blood in everyone's name. As I progressed in my research, I found a number of things that could have given the Soviets reason to doubt the alliance and to feel threatened. Much of what is set before you in the lead up to the conflict has a basis in fact.

Neither side's soldiers wished for more combat, for most had seen enough to last a thousand lifetimes. Despite that and, somewhat perversely, it seems that it was the Soviet soldier who was more prepared to continue against former allies, despite the immense sacrifices he and his Motherland had already endured. Political indoctrination played a great part in that obviously, as much about Western Europe and America had been criticised and held as false.

That what developed became known to all as 'The Cold War' is an historical fact. However, what could have happened is laid out in these books, as if the reader is taking onboard a factual account of those difficult days. Indeed, much of the book, leading up to hostilities is based upon accepted facts, probably more than the reader might care to believe.

It is not my intention to do anything other than to illustrate that there are no bad peoples, just bad people. It is my hope that the reader will be able to see the strengths and weaknesses of the characters and be able to appreciate the qualities each brings forth, regardless of the nation or group to which the individual belongs.

We must all give thanks that it never happened, but may possibly wonder what might have come to pass, had it all gone badly wrong in that hot European summer of 1945.

I have deliberately written nothing that can be attributed to that greatest of Englishmen, Sir Winston Churchill. I considered myself neither capable nor worthy to attempt to convey what he might have thought or said in my own words.

My profound thanks to all those who have contributed in whatever way to this project, as every little piece of help brought me closer to my goal.

This then is my offering to satisfy the 'what if's' of those times.

[For additional information, progress reports, orders of battle, discussion, freebies and interaction with the author please find time to visit and register at one of the following:-

www.redgambitseries.com, www.redgambitseries.co.uk, www.redgambitseries.eu,
Also, feel free to join Facebook Group 'Red Gambit'.]

Thank you.

I have received a great deal of assistance in researching, translating, advice and support during the two and a half years that this project has run so far. In no particular order, I would like to record my thanks to all of the following for their contributions.

Gary Wild, Jason Litchfield, Mario Wildenauer, Pat Walsh, Elena Schuster, Stilla Fendt, Luitpold Krieger, Mark Lambert, Greg Winton, Greg Percival, Loren Weaver, Brian Proctor, Steve Bailey, Bruce Towers, Victoria Coling, Alexandra Coling, Heather Coling, Isabel Pierce Ward, Ahmed Al-Obeidi and finally BW-UK Gaming Clan.

One name is missing on the request of the party involved, who perversely has given me more help and guidance in this project than most, but whose desire to remain in the background on all things means I have to observe his wish not to name him.

None the less, to you my oldest friend, thank you.

Wikipedia is a wonderful thing and I have used it as my first port of call for much of the research for the series. Use it and support it.

My thanks to the US Army Center of Military History website for providing the out of copyright images.

All map work is original, save for the Château outline which derives from a public domain handout.

If I have missed anyone or any agency I apologise and promise to rectify the omission at the earliest opportunity.

This then is the first offering to satisfy the 'what if's' of those times.

Book #1 - Opening Moves [Chapters 1-54]

Author's note.

The correlation between the Allied and Soviet forces is difficult to assess for a number of reasons.

Neither side could claim that their units were all at full strength and information on the relevant strengths over the period this book is set in is limited as far as the Allies are concerned and relatively non-existent for the Soviet forces.

I have had to use some licence regarding force strengths and I hope that the critics will not be too harsh with me if I get things wrong in that regard. A Soviet Rifle Division could vary in strength from the size of two thousand men to be as high as nine thousand men and, in some special cases, could be even more.

Indeed, the very names used do not help the reader to understand unless they are already knowledgeable.

A prime example is the Corps. For the British and US forces, a Corps was a collection of Divisions and Brigades directly subservient to an Army. A Soviet Corps, such as the 2nd Guards Tank Corps, bore no relation to a unit such as British XXX Corps. The 2nd G.T.C. was a Tank Division by another name and this difference in 'naming' continues to the Soviet Army, which was more akin to the Allied Corps.

The Army Group was mirrored by the Soviet Front.

Going down from the Corps, the differences continue, where a Russian rifle division should probably be more looked at as the equivalent of a US Infantry regiment or British Infantry Brigade, although this was not always the case. The decision to leave the correct nomenclature in place was made early on. In that, I felt that those who already possess knowledge would not become disillusioned and that those who were new to the concept could acquire knowledge that would stand them in good stead when reading factual accounts of WW2.

There are also some difficulties encountered with ranks. Some readers may feel that a certain battle would have been left in the command of a more senior rank, as well as the reverse case, where Seniors seem to have few forces under their authority. Casualties will have played their part but, particularly in the Soviet Army, seniority and rank was a complicated affair, sometimes with Colonels in charge of Divisions larger than those commanded by a General.

It is easier for me to attach a chart to give the reader a rough guide of how the ranks equate.

Fig#1 – Table of comparative ranks.

SOVIET UNION	WAFFEN-SS	WEHRMACHT	UNITED STATES	UK/COMMONWEALTH	FRANCE
KA - SOLDIER	SCHÜTZE	SCHÜTZE	PRIVATE	PRIVATE	SOLDAT DEUXIEME CLASSE
YEFREYTOR	STURMMANN	GEFREITER	PRIVATE 1ST CLASS	LANCE-CORPORAL	CAPORAL
MLADSHIY SERZHANT	ROTTENFUHRER	OBERGEFREITER	CORPORAL	CORPORAL	CAPORAL-CHEF
SERZHANT	UNTERSCHARFUHRER	UNTEROFFIZIER	SERGEANT	SERGEANT	SERGENT-CHEF
STARSHIY SERZHANT	OBERSCHARFUHRER	FELDWEBEL	SERGEANT 1ST CLASS	C.S.M.	ADJUDANT-CHEF
STARSHINA	STURMSCHARFUHRER	STABSFELDWEBEL	SERGEANT-MAJOR [WO/CWO]	R.S.M.	MAJOR
MLADSHIY LEYTENANT	UNTERSTURMFUHRER	LEUTNANT	2ND LIEUTENANT	2ND LIEUTENANT	SOUS-LIEUTENANT
LEYTENANT	OBERSTURMFUHRER	OBERLEUTNANT	1ST LIEUTENANT	LIEUTENANT	LIEUTENANT
STARSHIY LEYTENANT					
KAPITAN	HAUPTSTURMFUHRER	HAUPTMANN	CAPTAIN	CAPTAIN	CAPITAINE 1
MAYOR	STURMBANNFUHRER	MAJOR	MAJOR	MAJOR	COMMANDANT
PODPOLKOVNIK	OBERSTURMBANNFUHRER	OBERSTLEUTNANT	LIEUTENANT-COLONEL	LIEUTENANT-COLONEL	LIEUTENANT-COLONEL 2
POLKOVNIK	STANDARTENFUHRER	OBERST	COLONEL	COLONEL	COLONEL 3
GENERAL-MAYOR	BRIGADEFUHRER	GENERALMAJOR	BRIGADIER GENERAL	BRIGADIER	GENERAL DE BRIGADE
GENERAL-LEYTENANT	GRUPPENFUHRER	GENERALLEUTNANT	MAJOR GENERAL	MAJOR GENERAL	GENERAL DE DIVISION
GENERAL-POLKOVNIK	OBERGRUPPENFUHRER	GENERAL DER INFANTERIE*	LIEUTENANT GENERAL	LIEUTENANT GENERAL	GENERAL DE CORPS D'ARMEE
GENERAL-ARMII	OBERSTGRUPPENFUHRER	GENERALOBERST	GENERAL	GENERAL	GENERAL DE ARMEE
MARSHALL		GENERALFELDMARSCHALL	GENERAL OF THE ARMY	FIELD-MARSHALL	MARECHAL DE FRANCE

* OR ARTILLERY, PANZERTRUPPEN ETC

1 CAPITAINE de CORVETTE 2 CAPITAINE de FREGATE 3 CAPITAINE de VAISSEAU

ROUGH GUIDE TO THE RANKS OF COMBATANT NATIONS.

Fig#1a- Map key to military icons

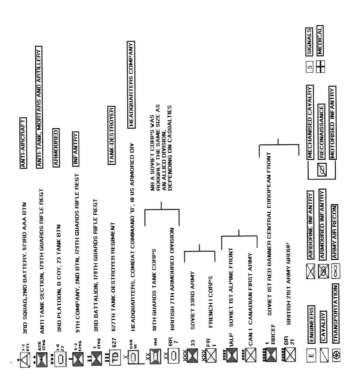

3RD SQUAD, 2ND BATTERY, 573RD AAA BTN — ANTI-AIRCRAFT

ANTI TANK SECTION, 179TH GUARDS RIFLE REGT — ANTI-TANK, MORTARS AND ARTILLERY

3RD PLATOON, B COY, 23 TANK BTN — ARMOURED

5TH COMPANY, 2ND BTN, 179TH GUARDS RIFLE REGT — INFANTRY

3RD BATTALION, 179TH GUARDS RIFLE REGT

627TH TANK-DESTROYER REGIMENT — TANK-DESTROYER

HEADQUARTERS, COMBAT COMMAND "B", 10 US ARMORED DIV — HEADQUARTERS COMPANY

10TH GUARDS TANK CORPS

BRITISH 7TH ARMOURED DIVISION

NB A SOVIET CORPS WAS ROUGHLY THE SAME SIZE AS AN ALLIED DIVISION, DEPENDING ON CASUALTIES

SOVIET 33RD ARMY

FRENCH I CORPS

ITALP SOVIET 1ST ALPINE FRONT

CAN 1 CANADIAN FIRST ARMY

RBCEF SOVIET 1ST RED BANNER CENTRAL EUROPEAN FRONT

BR 21 BRITISH 21ST ARMY GROUP

ENGINEERS

CAVALRY

TRANSPORTATION

AIRBORNE INFANTRY

ARMOURED INFANTRY

ARMY AIR RECON

MECHANISED CAVALRY

RECONNAISSANCE

MOTORISED INFANTRY

SIGNALS

MEDICAL

Fig#1b- Map of important European locations

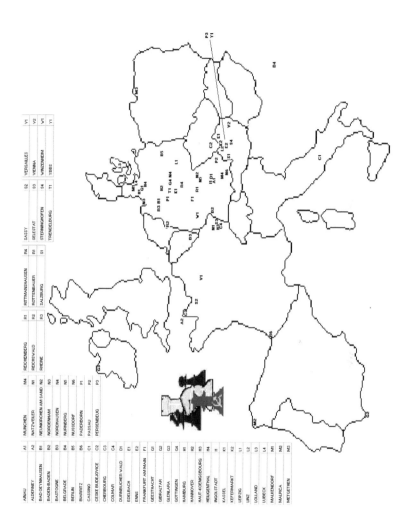

Book Dedication

'Opening Moves' is dedicated to a man who exhibited the very highest level of courage and bravery under fire in one of the truly exceptional stories of World War Two.

I cannot begin to comprehend the metal of a man who exposes himself to enemy fire holding nothing more than a set of bagpipes. So to you, Piper Bill Millin, my humble admiration and thanks for your service. May you rest as peacefully as your love of the Pipes will permit.

Although I never served in the Armed forces, I wore a uniform with pride and carry my own long-term injuries from my service. My admiration for our young servicemen and women serving in all our names in dangerous areas throughout the world is limitless. As a result, **'Help for heroes** is a charity that is extremely close to my heart. My fictitious characters carry no real-life heartache with them, whereas every news bulletin from the military stations abroad brings a terrible reality with its own impact, angst and personal challenges for those who wear our country's uniform. Therefore, I make regular donations to **'Help for Heroes'** and would encourage you to do so too.

Table of Contents

16

19

The Foreword

This is a work about men and their capacity to endure. I hope it is balanced and even, just telling how it was for the soldiers of both sides who fought and died in those troubled times. The references, evidences and memories that I have been able to consult have been strangely both starkly detailed and sketchy, in equal measure, possibly because the mind can be very selective when it wishes to be.

So I have tried as best I can to tie in personal contributions with the general military and political facts we all now accept. I admit that I have tried to tell little of the politics, save those details that I have considered essential and concentrated upon using the personal details and evidence to weave the story of those awful times in a way that best shows the reader what incredible men and women all our grandparents were.

It is a fact that bravery knows no national boundaries and that the other side always have their honourable and courageous men too. I hope that I have reflected that and done due honour to all those about whom I have written.

My prime interest has always been the World Wars, probably because I grew up with their first-hand effects upon my family. The Great War laid my family low, my great-grandfather's three brothers and two cousins, permanently entrusted to the soil of France, from where none returned; there were no tales of heroism or of horror brought home from the front in the Great War.

Whereas, for the conflicts of 1939-1945 and 1945-1947 stories abounded, tales of great-uncles and family friends who perished in the sands of North Africa, fought in the waters of the North Atlantic, were enslaved as prisoners in the jungles of Burma, or who died violently on the farmlands of Germany. I would polish an array of medals for my Granddad on the occasions he ventured out for reunions and events and I often listened to the conversations of old men around tables on a warm summer's eve, when stories of those times came alive in their words.

27

I always wanted to write something; not just something to satisfy my own desire for the immortality of a writer, but something that would pay tribute to the good and brave of all sides who fought and died in those difficult years.

I suppose I was destined to write this particular book. By accident, happenstance or coincidence I came into possession of the knowledge with which to construct this account, varying from the writings of participants, through official documentation that I hunted out, onto personal interviews with surviving combatants or their families.

Synchronicity took over, that turn of events that make that of which you mused possible, if not likely, as Madame Fate started to weave her web over me, delivering into my possession the means to do something really special.

The first set of memoirs that came into my hands were those of SS-Sturmbannfuhrer Rolf Uhlmann, formerly of the 5th SS Panzer Division "Wiking" and whose exploits in the conflict are now the stuff of legend. A hand written personal journal of his war, that remained unpublished, was offered to me to consult by the woman into whose hands it had been entrusted, on the explicit understanding that I would faithfully reflect its contents. This I now do, Krystal, in tribute to both of your men, so lie easy in your eternal rest.

It was my privilege to meet with the family of the legendary SS-Standartenfuhrer Ernst-August Knocke, who were able to furnish me with private papers and anecdotes as told them by their husband and father. It was they who secured me an introduction to a secretive and proud group of men who were vilified in the days after the German surrender, despite the sacrifices they made in the name of their country. To all of you, my thanks, but especially to Anne-Marie, his wife and a woman I greatly admire.

On my first trip to Russia, an official research visit to some of Russia's Military museums, I was approached in my hotel by an old gentleman, who knew surprisingly much of my purpose. He offered to loan me an unpublished document written partially by Colonel [Polkovnik] of Tank Troops Arkady Yarishlov, referring to his role in the Great Patriotic War from 1941 through to its bloody end, when it was

28

entrusted to one of his comrades. That comrade then gave me the responsibility to use it wisely and ensure its main author received the laurels he truly deserved. I hope that I have done so and honoured a brave man. To Stefan, who completed the writings, translated them and filled in missing information, I thank you for seeking me out and entrusting me with those precious documents and the story of a true soldier.

Gaining access to the fourth set, namely the soon to be published memoirs of Vladimir Stelmakh, was more bizarre. A shared moment with an old man looking at a famous battle-damaged tank in the Kubinka Museum led to an enduring friendship and access to the kind of intimate information historians can normally only dream about. In particular, your intermediary work with the family of one of the Soviet Union's greatest General's and heroes, Marshal Zhukov, and the incredible documents they permitted me sight of. Without your direct support for my cause, much of the important events in Moscow during September 1947, one of the most remarkable elements of the history of World War Three, would never have been fully known. Thank you my friend.

The fifth set I had access to all the time, but never knew it. My grandfather, Major John Ramsey, was something of an amateur writer and left many papers relating to his wartime exploits, typically penned in a self-effacing fashion, as befitted the modest man he was. My grandmother casually told me of their existence over roast pork one Sunday, shortly after I returned from my first trip to Russia. It never occurred to her to offer them beforehand and never occurred to me that such things existed. Of his actions, we British know much already. Thank you Nan. If only I had been old enough to understand the nature of the medals I diligently polished!

Last but one are the papers and letters of General de Division Christophe Lavalle, soldier of France and officer of the Légion Étrangère, who escaped the conquest of his country and found ever-lasting glory at Bir Hakeim and beyond with his beloved legionnaires. It was his relatives who were able to smooth my way into the records of the Légion Étrangère, without which access, much of this story could not have been properly told.

Lastly, came the documents of and recorded interviews with Brigadier-General Marion J. Crisp, US Paratrooper, who carried his carbine from D-Day to the final battle and upon whom fell a terrible responsibility in those last bloody days.

The intertwining of their war is remarkable and will be revealed as the text progresses.

I was able to piece together the last mission of Flight Sergeant Andrew McKenzie VC, using only enemy accounts and squadron records, but what he achieved is well known today and I have just added a little meat to the bones of what this bravest of men did one wet and windy autumn day. I am proud that my research was able to ensure that his incredible bravery and self-sacrifice was finally rewarded.

During my research, I came across many tales of heroism and sacrifice, but one will be included here because it was the wish of his opponents that he should be so acknowledged. Without that wish and the accompanying testimony of his enemies, as in the case of McKenzie, the actions of Starshy Serzhant Ivan Alexeyevich Balyan would have been secret for eternity. Thanks to his enemies and their professional admiration for what he achieved, his story will be written here and, on reflection, his Motherland may wish to afford him the honour that his sacrifice demands.

It was beyond me to be able to get access to the records of the former Deuxieme Bureau, but I was able to interview some former employees 'off the record'. I thank them for their invaluable assistance and admire their courage by risking much to ensure some worthy people get the recognition they deserve.

With the help of all these documents, the personal memories of the above and others, I have been able to put together a story of the last two years of World War Two, or as they are now known, World War Three, years that cost many lives and that left such an indelible mark on those who fought, no matter what the colour of their uniform.

I need not overly set the scene, for the events up to the German capitulation in May 1945 are well known and well documented. Europe was in ruins after the armies of many

30

nations had rolled over it. The world waited for the end, as the relentless steamroller of the United States of America's industry continued to roll over weakened Japan.

In those heady summer days of July 1945, the Allied and Soviet armies in Europe licked their wounds after their trials against Nazi Germany, whilst the politicians bickered and argued over the small print of victory. Niggles between allies started to become more serious and tolerances became fragile. Agreed boundaries became points of argument; ground taken at the cost of a comrade's life is not easily given over to another and, in four instances, shots had been fired and deaths occurred. None the less, life suddenly felt good for most, for they were unaware of the agendas of the powerful, and men who had been fighting, in some cases since 1939, could look up and feel the sun on their faces and not feel afraid that death would visit them that day.

It was the pause, but they didn't know it.

Do not rejoice in his defeat, you men. For though the world has stood up and stopped the bastard, the bitch that bore him is in heat again.

Berthold Brecht

Chapter 1 - 'THE DECISION'

0748hrs Tuesday, 12th June 1945, The Kremlin, Moscow, USSR.

It was a simple piece of paper. What complicated the day greatly for the reader was the information typed upon it, words that had been days in transit from their source, half a world away, until now, when they were produced in front of the General Secretary of the Communist Party of the USSR's Central Committee.

Clad, as always, in his simple brown tunic and trousers, he frowned deeply, re-read the information and then looked up at the man standing at the other side of the impressive Tsarist wooden desk.

'So, Lavrentiy. Are we sure of this?"

The man, short and prematurely balding, removed his wire frame glasses and, withdrawing a white cotton handkerchief from his suit pocket, studiously polished them. Such was his habit when he was considering his answers very carefully; a practice that was very wise when dealing with the General Secretary, even for a man as powerful as Lavrentiy Beria, head of the NKVD.

"You know that with this agent and agent Gamayun, we have properly infiltrated their inner project and extracted much information to aid our own research, Comrade. Alkonost is an ideological agent who has been 100% reliable and I do not see any reason to doubt a report now."

The General Secretary leant back in his modest chair and drew deeply on his pipe, looking around his place of work and thinking.

"They are that advanced?"

32

"It seems so, Comrade."

"We have received no notification of this from our other assets?"

"None whatsoever, Comrade General Secretary. All have been quiet for some time and our messages go unanswered. Not unusual for any agent and certainly not those within Manhattan. We have directed them to take no risk unless the information is crucial, particularly 'Gamayun' and 'Alkonost'."

The office was capacious and reasonably furnished, the most important and imposing piece therein being a huge table set centrally. Some trappings of Imperial times could be seen hung on the wall, but for a man in his position, the room could have been thought of as comparatively austere, when viewed side by side with the other chambers of the old palace. None the less, the power was wholly focussed here and in particular in the person of the man puffing away thoughtfully on his simple pipe.

"Some light, Comrade" was the implied instruction, accompanied by a gesture with the smoking stem, aimed towards the nearest heavy velvet curtains.

Beria walked to the window and opened the long curtains. Sunlight streamed in, causing them both to squint until they grew accustomed to its brightness. He paused briefly at the window, looking down on the Kremlin walls, where a detachment of his NKVD troops was being inspected by a young and extremely keen major.

It was nearly eight in the morning, but both men had been working for some hours already.

"Our own project Lavrentiy? I assume we have made no great headway since your last report?"

This was a subject of embarrassment to both of these men. The possibilities of fission research had originally been ignored by Stalin, in favour of other, more understandable concepts. The first warnings that the Motherland was years behind in something extremely important were from Georgy Flerov, a notable Soviet nuclear physicist. He pointed out that, despite the discovery of fission in 1939, the West's scientists published no further papers. This suggested that they were

33

working on an atomic programme that was being kept secret. Assets in Britain sent further information, confirming the existence of an American Atomic Research project and so the USSR had commenced her own atomic programme in September 1942. Until then, it had not been considered important enough, an opinion that both men had held, quickly discarded and now bitterly regretted.

"Nothing too dramatic, Comrade Secretary. I am satisfied that the scientists and technicians are working flat out and there is some progress by other, unexpected means, as well as the information gained by our agents in place. We have made some interesting advances in the physics with Serov's interrogation of the Germanski scientists and the facility that Rokossovsky so kindly delivered intact, has yielded more useful pieces of the jigsaw. Of course, the oxide we discovered in Oranienberg and Glewe will greatly assist our progress, particularly as I have it on good authority that it is already of the correct grade. The information Agents Alkonost and Gamayun have been supplying has greatly assisted the programme, particularly with the previous two reports we were sent, which seem to have allowed us to make good advances, Comrade."

Rummaging in his briefcase, Beria produced a small file containing a technical brief, authored by one of Russia's most eminent scientists.

"Here we have Comrade Kurchatov's recent report on how the information on the use of purified graphite and method of isotope separation, supplied by our pet German scientists, has greatly assisted progress and will undoubtedly bring forward our own completion date. I asked him to put it in simple terms that I could understand."

Passing the file forward Beria knew better than to look too smug, especially as that was not quite what he had said to Comrade Kurchatov.

"We also have other agent assets, code names Mlad and Kalibr, both at the Amerikanski facilities and we hope for more information from them, but we have again been unable to get messages through to them and have received nothing for some months. In any case, they have been of limited value to date."

Wishing to be as upbeat as possible, Beria concluded positively.

"Comrade General Secretary, if we were to acquire no further information from this time forward, we would anticipate having a weapon available for testing by mid-1948, possibly sooner."

Stalin automatically deducted a few months from that, as everyone always hedged their bets when it came to timings. Placing his pipe to one side and lighting a cigarette, he read the document, understanding little and took the copy intended for him before handing the rest back.

A significant piece of information included in one report was that scientists working on the American project had started to feel that this technology should be shared, not become the province of a single state or alliance, war conditions aside.

"Of note to me is this comment from your agent, regarding attitudes amongst the American scientists in New Mexico. What plans do you have to make use of this new wave of feelings, Lavrentiy?"

This question was obviously anticipated and so the answer flowed freely.

"That greatly depends on what the GKO directs, Comrade General Secretary," knowing full well that the State Defence Committee, as it was known in full, would do pretty much what they were told, or receive a one-way trip to a basement room in the Lubyanka.

"At this time, we have solely an intelligence gathering operation and if we are to remain as that, then these assets will be carefully stroked into place and we should gain more information to accelerate our own programme. If it is decided to take the different route previously discussed, then some physical interference with the American project will definitely be possible with the existing agents. At our present assessment, I have discounted that on the basis of risk to our agents in place, against the quality of information we receive."

A moment's pause to mentally check his lines.

"Greater sabotage would probably be possible with this new development, provided recruitment was carefully done. That recruitment will take time, time that we do not have."

Despite the secure nature of his present location, Beria could not help a swift conspiratorial look around before speaking in a quieter voice.

"On the time scale we are still considering for Kingdom39, I think there is insufficient time to involve these new possibilities."

More puffs on the cigarette, this time lighter in nature, but decidedly more urgent.

"I agree, Comrade. The Americans are more advanced than we thought. How can that be, without your agents knowing of it sooner?"

Although he knew the answer, Stalin asked anyway, for he liked to keep people on their toes.

"There are at least three separate major sites where research continues, certainly more, plus the capitalists use compartmentation, Comrade General Secretary. Separate sides of the project develop away from each other and then the finished projects are brought together, unless there are issues that encroach on another's development. Our agents have limited access to information in their roles, so we have been lucky that these scientists have been loose-tongued over dinners and games of chess, or we would not have found out much of what we already know."

Stalin interrupted with a light gesture of the hand.

"In any case, that is not important. What is important is how we respond. What are our options?"

Even though he had this part of the conversation with himself a number of times in his own office, it was still a very delicate moment for the head of the NKVD.

'The options we should consider are these."

A nervous clearance of the throat and the chairman of the NKVD commenced.

"We can abandon Kingdom39." Stalin's face remained impassive and Beria continued. "I do not see that as an acceptable alternative."

36

He received no clue from the General Secretary's facial expression or posture as to whether he was being well received, or if each point was to be discussed in turn, so Beria decided to carry on regardless.

"We can delay it until more favourable conditions exist. However, the re-establishment of a working German puppet state would be more likely, with the attendant problems that that would bring us. At this time, the capitalists are burdened with millions of German prisoners and still more refugees, all of which works in our favour. The German is cowed and beaten and out of the equation, but not indefinitely so and it is an essential of our operation that no large-scale organised German resistance is possible, so the reasons for deciding our present timescale were sound and remain so. This new information introduces nothing to encourage delay in military or political terms, especially as our negotiations with the slant-eyes would appear to be bearing fruit."

The gentle nodding from the dictator was all Beria now needed.

"Our country and people are on a war-footing. Our army is in the right place and at its peak. So is our ability to produce the goods of war. Our maskirova so far is working and effective already and merely needs to be increased when it is decided to pursue this venture."

Now he knew which way the land lay, he reached deeper into his briefcase and passed over a detailed synopsis of some recent messages.

"I have here reports from agents across Europe indicating poor morale amongst western allied troops; homesickness and the like. They are less capable of sustaining casualties than we, which is proved, Comrade." That was a statement that meant very little, for it mattered not a jot to either of them how many casualties were sustained in the course of achieving their goals. Even if a million more mothers cried tears of loss, it would be as nothing.

"Some of our military personnel have fraternised with them on my orders, attended exercises, exchanged pleasantries and watched their soldiers perform badly, indicating inexperience, or lack of combat ability."

"The Amerikanski particularly have issues. Some of their soldiers are of good quality, of course, but if you see page fourteen onwards, you will see an appreciation of the abilities and readiness of all units, theirs and the other allies. We have gained quality intelligence on every single divisional sized unit in their order of battle, Comrade General Secretary."

Searching his memory, he continued.

"The Amerikanski paratroopers are particularly good but are few in number, Comrade, a mere three divisions only." And that was the first item of information that was not accurate, for there were actually five in existence at that time."

"Again, some of their tank and infantry divisions fought well, but many are relatively untested and of average quality. Remember the new division that the Germans captured during their Rhine campaign?"

Stalin searched his memory and found the information needed. A brand-new division, '...was it the 106th...?,' had been placed on front-line duty in the Ardennes and had surrendered wholesale to the Germans during the Battle of the Bulge.

"Also remember, when they first arrived in Africa, their number one infantry division turned tail and ran when the Afrika Korps attacked them at Kasserine," the accompanying chuckle was soft, but Stalin didn't miss it.

"The Amerikanski rely on numbers and firepower to achieve their victories, but they are soft, Comrade General Secretary. We have numbers. We have firepower. We are not soft as they are soft."

A swift glance down at the document brought forth further information.

"Their Marine Divisions have quality but are all concentrated against the slant-eyes, so are of no concern to us at this time."

"The British and their crony states are bled dry. They can fight, but they are weakened and cannot stand against us for long. That island of theirs will be a different matter of course, but we will develop the means to cross the divide in time."

Almost as an afterthought, Beria added, "With only a handful of divisions, the useless French can be discounted, obviously."

And with a shared nod of heads, a once proud nation was dismissed as an irrelevance.

The file returned to Beria, minus Stalin's copy.

"In any case, our proposed arrangement with the slant-eyes will ensure that the Allies must all dedicate resources to the Pacific, no matter what the demands of Europe."

Stalin looked unconvinced on that point and pressed Beria.

"Will their presence be enough alone, Lavrentiy? They have virtually no ability to project power or threat any more. Their navy is almost destroyed, their air force crippled and their army lacks decent weapons. They have only manpower and spirit, as I see it. I do not think those will fix sufficient Allied forces in place."

Beria felt triumphant inside as he produced a proposal document from his deceptively capacious case.

"This is a matter on which you have expressed reservation before, Comrade, so I have looked into it and believe that this proposal might meet your concerns."

This file required time and another cigarette to examine properly, so Beria stealthily shifted back to the window in time to see the inspection parade dismiss.

The wait was interminable.

Something obviously jumped out of the page.

"You wish to concede our claim on the Kurils permanently, Comrade?"

"Not permanently, just for now, Comrade General Secretary, purely as a sugar for the Japanese."

A dramatic frown sufficed as a reply and Stalin returned to his reading, frown deepening, mouth opening further, as he progressed through Beria's proposal document.

"We sign a peace treaty ending all territorial disputes? All disputes, Lavrentiy?"

"Yes, Comrade General Secretary, in order to secure their compliance and support, we must sweeten the pill. What we choose to do when Kingdom39 is complete is another matter."

Stalin stopped in his tracks, his mind obviously working hard, eyes fixed on Beria.

Tension.

Stalin's face then softened and the tension evaporated as quickly as it had arrived.

"True, true".

Stalin lapsed into silence, his frown departed and he consumed the rest of the document.

"We simply do not have the capability for this grand design, Comrade. It is an excellent proposal, but surely it would make inroads into our stocks of all materials?"

"I believe we can manage it, Comrade, particularly as we have already decided to place many third and fourth stage assets in that region as part of the maskirova." Beria thumbed through his copy quickly.

"If you look at the suggestion laid out on page 17 and addendum F, you will find an intriguing proposal."

"By moving the equipment detailed in addendum F, we can increase the firepower and ability of their forces, without affecting our own, all without raising suspicion from our 'allies'. Indeed, my office feels we will profit logistically by removing these assets from our own rosters."

Sitting back in his chair, pipe between his lips, the General Secretary said nothing. Beria waited.

"You may present that," returning the document, still with his copy attached, "To the GKO today. We shall see what they think of it before I give it my support."

That was code for, '*I am distancing myself from this at the moment, but you stick your neck out and I will jump on the bandwagon and grab the reins if it proves successful.*'

Not uncommon for the General Secretary.

"Moving back to our alternatives, Comrade, I will reiterate."

Stalin held up his hand and stopped Beria dead in his tracks.

"Before that, Comrade, has there been re-assessment of the air and sea situation?"

40

"No substantive change, except an increase in the number of jet fighter aircraft that are becoming available to them, so just the words of caution, as always, Comrade. Their Air forces are superior in every department and planning addresses that with pre-emptive attacks and strikes by partisans and special forces. Additionally, it is imperative that the specific paratrooper sub-operation Kurgan, detailed in Kingdom39, addressing the threat, is fully supported, given all the assets needed and prosecuted with the utmost vigour."

Beria paused as Stalin lit another cigarette.

"Obviously, Kurgan will be very costly."

"Obviously. That was always the case, Lavrentiy. Proceed."

"Naval power bears no comparison, but this will not be a war of Navies. The Black Sea Fleet should ensure no incursions into our waters there, because of the narrow Dardanelles approach. Politically, we see no shift from Turkey to either side and we would expect their national waters to be honoured by the capitalists. We will, of course, be making our own overtures and issuing assurances to them."

Stalin acknowledged that with a gentle nodding, although in his mind the word 'assurances' was replaced by 'threats'.

"The Baltic will be an issue until such times as Denmark is ours, when that avenue will be closed too. Until the military plan is submitted we will not know how soon that may be, but my staff anticipate that Denmark could be ours within 3-5 days, Comrade. We also have a plan that should ensure the Baltic is sealed and secure in the interim. The Swedes will definitely not get involved and most certainly have power to ensure no incursions into their waters by either side."

"In more northerly waters, I believe we have nothing to fear, because any hurt would be minor and a simple distraction. We would also have the fallback of our suggested later intervention in Norway, should it be required, although the continued presence of organised German divisions in country cannot be ignored. Our proposal for the slant-eyes would distract from any attempt on our Siberian waters."

41

'So, Air Force aside, it is their armies that will pose us most problem, Comrade."

Beria adjusted his tie and made his pitch.

"We can abandon, we can delay, or we can proceed. If we proceed, I see no alternative but to risk our agents in place and cause as much damage to the American Atomic programme as is possible. If that can delay their project until 1948, then we will be on an even footing in that regard and there will be no more threat. By 1948, we will have long finished what we started in Europe. I believe that the capitalists are weak and one kick will bring the church down around them. We seem now to have the probability of recruiting more assets in Manhattan, even if our present agents are lost to us. We will never have a better opportunity, Comrade General Secretary."

And so there it was; Beria had firmly nailed his colours to the mast.

The dictator looked hard into Beria's eyes, almost as if trying to read his innermost thoughts. Even a powerful man like the head of the NKVD felt intimidated by that stare, but dare not look away.

"Very well, Lavrentiy. I agree with you. So let us see what wisdom and guidance our comrades bring later on. Thank you."

Stalin reached forward and spoke briefly into the ornate gold phone.

The two men sat in silence until the tea and sweetbreads had arrived and the orderly, actually one of Beria's NKVD spies, left the room. Beria poured and handed the delicate cup to Stalin.

"I think you should prepare the order for your agents Lavrentiy, just in case."

Delivered in a deadpan style, but there was mischief there for sure, which Beria acknowledged with a rare smile.

"It will be ready for immediate dispatch after the GKO meeting Comrade."

The order was already prepared and in his briefcase.

"Good. Now tell me more of this plan for the slant-eyes."

42

1542hrs, Tuesday, 12th June 1945, The Kremlin, Moscow, USSR.

At 1542hrs precisely, the members of the GKO departed from the committee room where they had met. If anyone had been watching their arrival and subsequent departure, they would have noticed a defined variation in mood.

The men leaving wore gaunt and set expressions, appearing burdened, almost as if the weight of the world had been placed upon their shoulders.

At the same time as they left the Kremlin, a small message was starting its journey down the line to a number of Soviet agents throughout the whole US Atomic project. The message was simple.

'Priority 7. Prepare to damage/destroy Manhattan within 72 hours of receipt of codeword "Napoleon". Codeword 'Wellington' when ready to proceed. Imperative be ready to expedite by 6th July latest.'

*First say to yourself what you would be; and then do what you
have to do*

Epictetus

Chapter 2 – THE SPY.

2241hrs Saturday, 16th June 1945, Scientist's Residential Block, Los Alamos, New Mexico.

Mathematician Perlo opened the letter, ostensibly from a cousin in Washington, with whom, the FBI had noted, there was regular correspondence. Waiting until privacy was assured, a small geometry reference book was taken from a bedside drawer and an exercise in decoding commenced.

The message was as clear as it was surprising, if not terrifying. A slightly trembling hand sought and found a bottle of bourbon and a large measure was consumed to steady the nerves.

Quickly reverting to proper field craft, the textbook disappeared back into the drawer and the decoded message was burned, a chesterfield being lit from the burning embers to cover the fumes. The pad was checked for impressions from the soft pencil used, but none was apparent. None the less, the top two sheets followed the message into the ashtray. Lastly, a brief note was penned to the cousin, using a simple phrase that would acknowledge receipt and understanding to the recipient, actually an undercover communist agent working for the Turkish Embassy in Washington.

Another chesterfield was lit, this time for pleasure, and Perlo lay back on the bed and prepared to spend a restless night wrestling with the technical issues of effectively destroying years of scientific work.

The mathematician's security access did not cover the physics labs, engineering and assembly areas, so how could successful sabotage be undertaken?

When morning came, Perlo was no closer to knowing how to damage the important work.

About the only decision reached in the restless slumber Perlo had experienced was that to damage the project irreparably was virtually impossible. The project had assembled the world's finest minds and any damage that was inflicted would be purely temporary.

Sitting on the side of the bed, naked and red-eyed, Perlo reached across for a pack of cigarettes, lit up and drew the heavy smoke into expectant lungs. The dawn sun suddenly broke through the window, bringing light and also bringing with it the germ of an idea.

Perlo's face started to come alive as the suggestion grew further. Bringing the lighter up, level with narrowed eyes, a simple flick of a finger brought it to life, its yellow flame steady in the breezeless air, suggesting the resolution of the problem.

'The world's finest minds,' words that echoed in the mathematician's mind as it devised the way to damage the important people.

*Hegel was right when he said that we learn from history that
man can never learn anything from history.*

George Bernard Shaw

Chapter 3 –THE FRENZY

1100hrs, Monday, 18th June 1945, The Kremlin, Moscow, USSR.

The simple message to return for briefing and consultations had gone out all over Europe, two days before, arriving on a Saturday lunchtime and spoiling the plans of a number of very senior military men; Marshals of the Soviet Union mostly. The same message had gone eastwards a day earlier. When such a summons was received, it normally spelt either death or promotion. Marshal was virtually the pinnacle of Military advancement in the USSR, so some in that rank feared the worst. But still they came, flying into Vnukovo Air Force base and making the short journey to the seat of power in staff cars sent specifically for the purpose.

One by one, they arrived, until the chosen meeting place was full of senior officers and their aides. Cigarette smoke filled the room and whilst some of the talk was of wives, daughters and mistresses, or a son needing advancement in someone else's area of responsibility, the conversation eventually turned to the one question no-one could answer but, about which, everyone was prepared to venture an opinion. Why on earth was every senior commander from the entire Red Army and Air force assembled in this room? The interestingly small numbers of naval seniors present fuelled speculation further.

Some still expected a squad of heavily-armed NKVD to rush in and spray the room with bullets, but most appreciated that something very momentous was about to be revealed.

An NKVD Major-General entered the room at the allotted hour of eleven o'clock precisely and sent the aides away, leaving solely their bosses, who submitted themselves to the requests of the NKVD officer and followed him into the larger chamber from which he had emerged.

Another room from the bygone age of the Tsar's, gold leaf still shining on ornate cornicing and wooden wall panelling polished to a deep velvety glow by generations of servants. Some of the art works hanging on the walls, or displayed on marble plinths, represented an entire tank regiment in rouble value. It would be fair to say that most there failed to appreciate the beauty and opulence of their surroundings, especially once they saw the entire GKO assembled on a podium at the end of the former music room, with the General Secretary sat in the middle, silent and coiled like a snake about to strike.

Directed to their designated places on the arranged seating plan, Marshals and Generals alike sat down and were presented with a simple folder. The name in large bold type on the front cover gave more than one a moment of mirth, but not one that survived a withering stare from Stalin or Beria. They knew better than to open the file yet, but it did not stop their minds from working hard to fathom the meaning of the title. There were only two officers present that did not search for the link between their presence here and the title of the folder. Those two were GRU Generals who were intimately familiar with the documents it contained.

A nod from Stalin and the Deputy Commissar for Defence stood.

The room immediately hushed and the officers waited expectantly.

Nikolai Bulganin stroked his goatee beard for a second and then spoke in a deep, gruff voice.

"Comrades, you have answered the call to come here and you will now learn of the part each of you will be required to play in shaping history." That certainly got their attention, especially as most felt they had already played a useful part in shaping a positive history for the Motherland and, for that matter, the world.

"The German is defeated and cowed, half his lands and cities are ours and we will bleed all we can from them in reparation for their bloody unprovoked attack on our Motherland. That is our right."

The surprising spontaneous, but light, applause died a swift death as a silencing palm was raised.

"But comrades, we cannot rest there whilst others go unpunished for their aggression and treachery. Part of Germany is still free, occupied by the capitalist states; the same capitalist states who prevaricated, doing nothing of worth, whilst you and your men bled in 42, 43 and half of 44."

That drew a few nods and sounds of agreement. A raised hand again brought silence and Bulganin continued.

"Yes, the Capitalist Allies initially fought hard against the German and soon they broke them, those pitiful few divisions that faced them," Bulganin qualified in a dismissive tone.

"We fought for every metre of land, ours... and theirs... and paid in blood! Whereas these Western Allies, these democratic nations... Ha! ," Bulganin snorted his disgust, "They were welcomed with open arms into the German lair, the green toads surrendering in their thousands, whilst they fought us tooth and nail."

More noises of agreement from the group and again the hand was raised.

"The capitalists have lordship over the better half of Germany and have constantly threatened and tried to bully our Motherland, over our agreements to withdraw to some apparently agreed lines on a map," his voice rose, "Expecting us to concede ground rich with the blood of our troops!"

"We have responded to our agreements and relinquished some territory, as they have," he conceded, "But they still sit on lands won from the German at great cost, not to them, but to us!"

With a solemn shake of the head, Bulganin almost reluctantly continued.

"Berlin, bloody Berlin. How many of our son's hearts were stilled in those streets, eh? Streets made sacred with our Soviet blood! And yet, we have ceded vast portions of the city to honour our agreements."

The diatribe was having its effect and some of the ensemble were becoming agitated. Stalin sat inscrutably and observed the emotion build.

"What they gave up to us does not measure against our own concessions!"

Bulganin's voice continued its ascent in both pitch and volume.

"That is not right and must be, will be, changed. However, they refuse our requests for change; refuse our reasonable suggestions for further developments. The Nazi lackey Spain should be brought to heel but no, they refuse to remove this blight, despite the fact that they fought us and killed our soldiers!"

His disgust was evident.

"Italy, whose soldiers fought us on the steppes, is now a partner, an ally! It should be ravaged and made to pay, its coffers emptied to recoup the payment we have made in blood, but no, the Western Allies now venerate them as allies, because they switched sides when the writing was on the wall! Govno!"

A pained expression swiftly took hold of his face.

"France, vanquished, humiliated and crushed is somehow now an equal partner?" A look of disgust spread across Bulganin's face swiftly becoming a sneer. "A sharer in Berlin and German territories? For what? As a reward for years of Vichy cooperation and service to the German toads? Mudaks!"

The informed observer would have been amazed at Bulganin's delivery and the effect he was having on everyone present. The man's passion was evident.

"Land bought with the bodies of our comrades cannot just be handed back to those who are not fit to lick their boots! Not without proper acknowledgement of their efforts!"

Three of the officer group stood and shouted their opposition to such handovers, before calming down and resuming their seats.

"Your revolutionary spirit does you credit, comrades, so you will not permit this injustice to stand, this I know."

"Now we have discovered why these Western Allies act as they do, for there is something else here; something called treachery!"

Bulganin looked at Beria, who fished inside his briefcase and took out a simple folder. It passed theatrically from hand to hand until it ended up with Stalin. Casually and without flourish, although it was a trump card in its own right, the file made its way to Bulganin, who removed the first sheet and brandished it to his military audience.

Bulganin's voice began strongly.

"Our own sources inside the British bureaucracy have provided Comrade Marshal Beria with some interesting information."

As Stalin relit his pipe noisily, Bulganin continued.

"It would appear that Churchill ordered a military study on invading our territories," interrupted by a deep breath, "In May."

Everyone focussed on Bulganin immediately, making a perceptible wave of heads throughout the room.

"Yes, Comrades, May! The treacherous English bastard was about his tricks quicker than we thought."

Some very serious and capable military muscle suddenly felt very much betrayed and exceptionally angry, which was the whole purpose behind the style of the presentation.

He held aloft the document he had been passed, and all eyes automatically shot to it.

"Operation Unthinkable it is called, named in an effort to deflect us should we find out about it I expect."

Bulganin's voice rose to almost a shriek, punching out his words to huge effect.

"Over forty capitalist divisions to attack us in Northern Germany, striving for the Baltic. Our Allies, Comrades, our dear... trustworthy ... Capitalist ... Allies!"

Voices from the floor were raised in disbelief and anger at this apparent backstabbing and many normally calm men became very agitated.

Bulganin waited for the furore to subside, hands on hips, staring wildly at his willing audience.

He picked up his folder and indicated its contents with a scowl.

"Reports here of the best general they have, George Patton, speaking out against the de-Nazification of Germany and preaching of the threat posed by Communism....Mother Russia.... US! He has even urged his commanders to attack us before we grow too strong!"

The howls of the betrayed filled the air and were not easily brought under control by an increasingly agitated Bulganin.

"Their transport of troops home has greatly slowed, despite their assurances that they would start to demobilise. Only those to be sent to the Pacific to fight the slant-eyes now leave Europe!"

He took a very obvious moment to compose himself before continuing.

"Comrade Polkovnik General Pekunin's agents have also discovered more treachery in the Western Allies; treachery that you will not believe, comrades!"

"They, the useless French Military that is, plan to employ defeated German soldiery in their army to fight in Indo-China against our communist brother, General Ho. At the same time, in an operation laughably called 'Apple pie', the American leadership are courting German Generals and their main topic of conversation is us!"

A furore of angry words burst forth upon the room and this time it needed Stalin himself to thump his hand repeatedly on the desk to bring the group back to some sort of order.

Bulganin nodded appreciatively at the General Secretary before turning once more to his incensed audience.

"The Americans have an operation they call 'Paperclip', which is channelling every German scientist who worked on the Nazi's rocket programme into working for them! Nazis making rockets for the Americans! To what end, I ask?"

More anguish poured forth from the military.

"Comrades, you must stay calm, as your leadership has stayed calm. There must be no action in anger or haste."

Wise heads and hot heads alike, nodded at those sensible words.

It was to a silent room that the punch line was delivered.

"After much consideration, it has been decided that the Motherland will not bow to these threats. We will retain each and every metre of soil we now hold and there will be no more negotiations, no more concessions. Our existing agreements with the Western Allies are dead."

There were many hearty claps to honour that decision.

"Our leader," he indicated Stalin, with an expansive gesture, "Also knows the people and the party, will not accept this treachery and has planned for the day when we will oppose it and cast it aside."

"In your hands you possess the plans by which the Motherland will overcome these travesties. The memory of all our comrades who gave their life's blood will be honoured and our country will be properly rewarded for destroying the threat of Nazism forever."

Bulganin held up his folder and moved it around so the title could be easily seen by every man. Once satisfied that all had read what he held, he continued.

"Our leader's little joke, for this is one fairytale that will come true for us, but will become a hurricane visited upon the capitalists and their lackeys."

Even with the passion of the moment, some laughs were still forced, for the older, wiser officers knew they were about to be immersed in another sea of blood and fire.

"Comrades, let us begin."

1724hrs Monday, 18th June 1945, The Kremlin, Moscow, USSR.

The meeting had commenced at approx 1103hrs. By the time it finished, at 1724hrs, every question had been answered and the overall political plan was accepted. Actually, nearly every question, because one extremely important question had not even been raised, much to the surprise of every military man present.

No one dared to ask.

The military translation of the document into formal planning would take some time. Reorganising the Soviet Military Fronts into the new formations would take weeks by itself. The Marshal responsible for the largest Front in the west suggested eight months to prepare, whilst others felt it was possible in six.

Professionally, the Generals and Marshals felt the political plan good and fully understood the reasoning behind it. The evidence of the Western Allies' own provocations was damning.

It was the timing that caused the major problem. So much to organise. A logistical nightmare that only time could assuage, or so their collective experience told them.

Stalin had said nothing, allowing his Deputy to field all the questions, with additional clarifications sought from Beria and, on two occasions, Colonel General Pekunin of the GRU.

Until the question of preparation was discussed.

As possible timescales were being thrown around by the Marshals, Stalin quietly rose from his chair and slowly walked round to stand in front of the table, adjacent to his Deputy. That was unusual and, during his short journey, the voices trailed away until there was only silence and the sound of his footsteps.

The room held its collective breath.

Stalin looked directly at the Marshal who had advised the longest preparation period.

"Comrade Marshal, eight months is preposterous. Six months", he pointed directly at another senior man, who had first touted this time scale, "is wholly unacceptable."

There was no argument. They now knew that Stalin has his own fixed agenda.

"The moment to strike is now," he punched his fist into his hand in emphasis, "And the more we delay, the better prepared the Western Allies will be."

He held up his file. All eyes were drawn to it.

"You have read and discussed the contents. Comrades Beria, Bulganin and Pekunin have answered the specifics of your enquiries and you have accepted their reasoning and information. The maskirova is already in place and working and, even as we speak, we move forces eastwards, in line with our agreements with the capitalists, armies that can be diverted, following the plan cited in the section covering the involvement of the Japanese."

He lowered the folder in a style not dissimilar to a headsman's axe descending.

"We have all we need... and the time is right."

Stalin turned and walked back round to his seat, tossing his folder noisily onto the table.

"This is no fairytale, Comrades; this is reality."

He took his chair by the back and pulled it out.

"I will expect detailed plans ready for presentation and approval when this group next convenes, on 2nd July, with a view to executing the attack at the earliest favourable moment after that."

The General Secretary sat down and relit his pipe, appearing about as unconcerned as if he had just ordered a light lunch, rather than instigating Armageddon.

There was nothing but stunned silence.

Stalin looked around him, expecting some comments, but there were none, so he continued puffing gently as his eyes swept the room.

His voice broke the strained silence.

"Place your units in the charge of your deputies, if you must, but work hard and give the Motherland a plan for victory. There will be no excuse for not being ready, Comrades, none whatsoever."

No one present doubted that, but such a short period of time to plan such a huge enterprise?

One Marshal, his shaven head already full of orders and maps, stood and waited to be recognised.

Stalin acknowledged him with a gesture of his head.

"Comrade General Secretary, as you say, the political plan is good and the timing is right. We can and will present the military plan, but we lack two vital details."

This was the one thing that had, for some reason best known to the General Secretary, been omitted from the documents.

"Yes, you are right, Comrade Marshal. The details of who will command and oversee Operations."

"Yes, Comrade General Secretary."

"Those decisions had not been reached until today."

Looking around at the rest of the GKO, Stalin received the expected nods of assent from all, even though only Beria and Bulganin knew which names were to follow.

"The command of the Far East Front will be placed in the capable hands of Comrade Marshal Vasilevsky." The recipient acknowledged his appointment by standing up and clicking to attention.

"Command of the newly created Red Banner Forces of Soviet Europe will fall to......"

Stalin's voice trailed off and he slowly, almost theatrically, looked around the room, most officers managing to avoid his eye as his gaze swept over them before returning to the standing Marshal who had posed the question.

"Well, you of course, Comrade Marshal Zhukov. Who else would we entrust this great venture to, but Georgy the Victory Bringer?"

The tragedy of war is that it uses man's best to do man's worst.

Henry Fosdick

Chapter 4 –THE INFORMATION

2350hrs, Thursday, 28th June 1945, Scientist's Residential Block, Los Alamos, New Mexico.

Emilia Beatriz Perlo was always in demand. She was twenty-five years of age and had all the classic Mediterranean beauty associated with her lineage, from smouldering hazel eyes, framed by heavy eyelashes, shoulder length jet-black hair that hung in natural curls, through to a full and extremely curvaceous body, all of which made Emilia the subject of much attention and desire amongst her fellow scientists.

Her speciality was algebra and, in particular, algebraic geometry. She was outstanding in her field, even at such a young age. Perlo's abilities within the field of Mathematical Physics meant that she stood out in a peer group of outstanding talent.

Having been sent from her native Spain in 1934, when her family realised the civil war coming, she lived with her Aunt in Washington DC, entering the American education system as a regular student. It was not long before her incredible talents became noticed and she was nurtured through higher education and into a government programme.

She was nineteen years old when she received the news that her father had been killed in action, fighting alongside the Nationalist forces during the Battle of Teruel on 21st February 1938.

She was twenty-one years old when her aunt sat her down and told her the truth.

Her father was not a nationalist, but was a communist, who had sided with the Republicans. He had remained as a spy inside the Nationalist forces, supplying information to his communist commanders and risking his life daily in the process.

In an awful twist of fate, he was accidentally shot by a nationalist soldier when returning to his encampment after clandestinely contacting another republican agent with vital information. The nationalists honoured him with a full military funeral, as befitted his major's rank and status, whilst the Republican hierarchy mourned his passing and the loss of intelligence they would now sustain.

Her aunt spoke of so much more; of ideals, of politics and of a future classless society where all were of equal status and worth and she wove such a spell that the young Emilia was swiftly hooked into the communist ideal.

More than that, her Aunt cultivated the darker side, the like of that which had been Emilia's father's domain in his final years. Again, this appealed to the young woman and she found pleasure in hiding her true feelings from everyone, save her aunt and older cousin, Victoria. Indeed, it appealed to her ego, to be clever enough to hide what was true from those around her. Recruitment into the shady world of espionage followed, in keeping with her cousin and aunt, who both clandestinely served the Red Banner. She learned much from her relatives and the gentlemen who came calling. To the outside world, they were probably suitors for the young women's favours. They always brought flowers or candy but in reality, they were communist agents, charged with the task of secretly preparing the young Emilia for a life of espionage.

Educationally, her progression under the guidance of the US state was impressive and she was offered a senior place in a government research programme on her twenty-second Birthday, two days before the attack on Pearl Harbor.

She moved from project to project, gaining trust and, more importantly, higher clearances, as her credentials were carefully scrutinised, checked and re-checked. The fact that she showed no interest whatsoever in politics was noted. The fact that one of her two living relatives, both of whom resided in the US, was employed as a laundress in the Turkish Embassy was not considered unusual.

Victoria Alejandra Calderon was twenty-seven and had no adverse history; her name only appeared in a file associating her with a US Air Force major, since killed in an accident in the Philippines during June 1941. The other, her Aunt, Marta Alejandra Calderon, worked as a sales clerk in a local shoe shop, housed in a building mainly used by a clothier's business, belonging to a Michael Green, a gentleman of slight interest to the FBI, for no other reason than he met with many military men in the course of his work.

Notes indicated suspicion of some relationship between Michael and Marta, but none was confirmed. Maybe Green just bought a lot of shoes, surmised one annotation. Another stated that he fulfilled private uniform contracts for senior army officers, based in Washington, contracts including the provision of shoes. In any case, neither he nor the women were of concern to the FBI and therefore, by dint of association, neither particularly was Emilia, until she was slated for Manhattan.

Perversely, it was any communist links that were considered more of a threat and prioritised accordingly. Her father's service with the Nationalists was explored, but his clandestine belief in the Republican cause was not uncovered.

The Nationalist link did still cause some concern to investigators and, for a while, it was touch and go as to whether her higher security clearance would be passed.

Emilia applied for US citizenship on her twenty-third birthday, which actually helped clinch her security clearance and she was soon moved to the secret facility at Los Alamos, New Mexico, wherein "Manhattan" was making huge strides forward in the understanding of fission.

As agreed with her aunt and cousin, there would be no coded exchanges for six months, regardless, as her letters were bound to be scrutinised carefully, which they most certainly were. They were just full of the things that girls speak of to each other and the FBI must have been sick to death of reading about dresses, make-up and boyfriends. Which was most definitely the plan.

Long before that self-imposed time was up, her risk category was downgraded and Emilia had become less of a priority, but the women stuck to the agreed time scale, so it was late 1943 before Victoria started to receive information from her cousin.

Because of Emilia's existing 'professional' contacts, a more complex system of reporting and ordering had been set up to protect all involved. There was delay as a result, but even Beria felt it was safety first with this asset. There were occasional doubts about the security within the Soviet Embassies, so those premises were avoided as much as possible, as was the case with every important Soviet agent at this time.

Whatever came in from Emilia was decoded by Victoria and re-encoded, very precisely, with her own special cipher. The new message was then passed to her aunt, who secreted it within a shoebox purchased by her contact, Iskhak Akhmerov, the resident illegal in America, also known as Michael Green.

He then further encoded it in the appropriate NKGB code and then passed it to Hakan Ali Hakan. Hakan was a Turkish intelligence officer who gave his loyalties to the communist ideal and who, in his turn. further encoded the message, this time in an ancient Turkish Intelligence cipher and forwarded it to the Foreign Ministry in Ankara.

Here it landed on a desk in the American business section, marked for the personal attention of one Teoman Schiller, son of a First World War German officer, who happened to be good communist, as was his son. Schiller then passed it, by dead drop or brush pass, to Vice-Consul Konstantin Volkov of the Soviet Embassy, who decoded both the Turkish and NKGB codes before encoding again, this time in NKVD code. He was Deputy Head of the NKVD in Turkey and knew exactly what it was that he was handling. He tried to break Victoria's special cipher, for professional satisfaction as well as for his personal insurance policy, but he had been able to understand very little of its content, despite his best efforts. He sent the NKVD coded version on its way across the Black Sea, from where it speeded to Moscow.

There it was decoded by a senior cryptographer using the NKVD code and Victoria's special cipher and the translated version was then placed in the hands of the head of Soviet Intelligence services, namely Lavrentiy Pavlovich Beria.

It was by this method that Emilia Beatriz Perlo, known as Alkonost, had dispatched the report that arrived in Beria's hands on the 12th June, the first that made the USSR aware of the advanced nature of US atomic weapon construction .

The arrival of the petite Minox camera had been both a bonus and a challenge.

All mail for the personnel at Los Alamos was addressed to PO Box 1663, Santa Fe, New Mexico, which meant that at least once a month she took an official excursion with the mail run to the market in the Plaza around the Palace of the Governors. This had been communicated to her cousin via letter as a possible exchange point, even though she and her fellows were always accompanied by security staff. As secretly directed in her cousin's latest letter about Washington fashion, she made her way to an eye-catching stall buying and selling clothing and fabrics, investing $16 in a flowing ivy green dress with an extravagant and gaudy decoration on the shoulder. Her minder thought to himself how gorgeous the Spanish beauty would look in it, especially with that low cut front. He would lose the decoration himself as it just did not look right, but Emma waxed lyrical about how she loved it, so who was he to comment.

On her return to Los Alamos, she carefully examined the dress and quickly discovered the Minox miniature camera and film within the decoration. The bonus of it was that she could be swifter in her habits, photographing, rather than sketching or writing, reducing the risk of discovery. The challenge was to find a place to secrete it, but she had previously discovered a small void behind a loose tile in the pedestal of her shower, which she hoped would be perfect and it was. A swift 'grouting' with toothpaste and the tile looked no different to those around it. Emilia immediately determined that it would never venture into the complex with her, but would be solely used for sessions such as this evening, in the comfort of her own bedroom.

The sex had been average at best but, as was her habit, she moaned and screamed her way through the brief session before collapsing on top of her spent lover as if he was her best ever.

It was not the first time she had slept with this one. He certainly was a looker and had the equipment, but no expertise in using it. *'Well, there are other fish in the sea,'* thought Emilia, but not any with the knowledge that this one possessed, and not that were sufficiently senior within the project and crossed all the boundaries not open to her. He also carried a secretary's notebook in his back trouser pocket wherever he went, contrary to regulations, in which he jotted notes when a thought occurred, or swiftly recorded a fellow scientist's idea to think through more carefully later.

Emilia had slept with a number of members of the Manhattan Project; actually quite a number. Always those she felt she could extract information from or those who, like Irving Zbrynevski, carried a notebook or diary in which they were often indiscreet about their work. Sex was a bonus if it was good.

The last time Irving had been permitted to sleep with Emilia, she had discovered drawings of geometric shaped explosive charges with extremely precise measurements annotated alongside, so she was keen to see what new entries there were tonight.

His orgasm would probably have knocked him out for hours anyway, but to be on the safe side, Emilia had plied him with a bottle of Bourbon too. The empty lay on the carpeted floor, testament to his capacity. He slept on his back, arms and legs splayed like the Vitruvian Man. A gentle, almost feminine snoring, marked him as out for the count.

A quick check of the clock reminded her that it was nearly two in the morning and if she wanted sleep, she best get moving quickly.

The camera retrieved and made ready, she extracted the notebook from Irving's trousers and quietly pulled the door of the toilet shut behind her.

From memory, she turned to the page she had last read a week ago, turned the paper over and skimmed the first new entry for anything of note. Frustratingly, it was solely a list of things to do around his own living quarters. The next page was more fruitful, with some complex electronic circuitry, most certainly in the hand of another, possibly trying to show Irving what he had been talking about. A swift click of the button and it was captured by the Minox. Another shot to make sure the image was captured, just as she had been taught.

After that, there were a few pages of notes on what looked like physics and a page of doodling, followed by some amateurish pictures of female breasts.

'Pervert.'

No picture of that was necessary.

Another turn of the book and then the Holy Grail gazed up at her from the paper.

Emilia was looking at an impressive sketch of an atomic bomb, apparently called 'Little Boy', accurate dimensions boldly recorded and with precise annotations on critical masses.

The camera rolled four times on that and she felt the perspiration trickle down her cleavage, although the bathroom was cool enough.

On the next page was a list of 'favourite women'. Emilia had no interest in that, so failed to notice she had made number three.

She stopped dead when she turned the next page over.

There in a bold hand were the words '16th create a rainbow, 17th all go home.'

'Create a rainbow' was an expression she had heard a few times. It was an insider's jokey comment about the expected visual effects of a full Scale explosive fission reaction.

She took no pictures. There was no point. She understood perfectly. Suddenly, the sweat dripped off her as she stood naked, digesting the enormity of what she had just read.

Thinking quickly, she re-hid the camera and unlocked the bathroom door, slipping quietly back into the bedroom and returning the book to Irving's trouser pocket. Ensuring everything was at it was before, she quietly ran the hot tap until warm water came out. A quarter glass was enough and she moved to the bed and lay down. Pulling back the sheet, she made a swift movement and the liquid was spilled on the mattress around Irving's groin. Putting the glass on the floor by her side, she rolled back to Irving and started to violently shake him.

A sleepy Irving moaned "Wassup honey? You want more? Huh baby?"

The tone of the reply quickly made him aware that not all was rosy in the garden and that his services were not to be needed again that night.

"Get out, you dirty bastard! You've peed in my bed! Go on Irving, get out!"

His hand shot down and was greeted with warm dampness.

"Shit! Ok honey... quiet... shit... I'm sorry... oh gee... sorry."

Every lean to recover an item of clothing, or bend to hook out a shoe, was punctuated with an apology. Emilia would have found it comical, had her mind not been consumed with more pressing matters.

"Please don't tell anyone, Emmy. It musta been the Bourbon, honey. Sorry"

He vacated the room, having dressed in record time and hurried off before his embarrassment overcame him.

Emilia, still naked, threw back the sheet to allow the air to dry the bed, then she grabbed a robe and a chesterfield.

Sitting quietly in her private space, she analysed what she had just discovered. Less than four weeks ago, she had found out that the project was more advanced than anyone thought. Now she held proof that, less than three weeks from today, the project would test an atomic device. She had heard the talk but it had always seemed months off, possibly years. Yet here was a simple comment in a notebook that she knew was confirmation that the Manhattan project was about to go live.

"Fucking hell!"

This needed to go out straight away and so she sat to her desk, brought out her text book and wrote a lovely girly

63

letter to her cousin. She even referred to the unfortunate nocturnal urination of her drunken lover, just in case anyone still read them, which of course they did. The film would go out next time she took a trip over to Santa Fe, but this had to go out tomorrow. She also included one other word.

'Wellington'.

The superior man is modest in his speech, but exceeds in his actions.

Confucius

Chapter 5 – THE LEGIONNAIRE

0712hrs, Sunday, 1st July 1945, Bad Kreuznach, Occupied Germany.

In a world of the toughest men, he was an enigma. Slight of figure, balding and of modest height, he could have easily been ignored if he crossed someone's path wearing civilian clothes, although the tell-tale signs of bearing and fluidity of movement would be there for those that knew of such things. In his uniform of Colonel in France's famous Foreign Legion, he presented a figure of awe and reverence to his troops and of total professionalism to all others.

Unlike many of his countrymen, Christophe Lavalle had fought long and hard, never surrendered and had preserved his nation's once-proud military tradition, at a time when it lay in the dust and was trampled by jackbooted feet.

Initially serving with 1st Regiment Étrangère Infanterie, in the hot and unfriendly surroundings of a frontier fort in Algeria, he distinguished himself sufficiently in the desert skirmishing to be promoted to Lieutenant. On the declaration of war, he was transferred to the mainland, to provide experienced officer leadership for the brand-new 11th Regiment Étrangère Infanterie.

His military career nearly ended when, as a Capitaine in the 11th REI, Stuka dive-bombers attacked his convoy on its way forward in 1940. Unlike many of his men, Lavalle escaped to join his Regiment, just in time for it to be savaged and retreat once more, as German columns raced around any pocket of resistance.

During one brief rearguard action, Lavalle had been felled by an explosion and was left for dead by his comrades. Coming to, dazed, disorientated and behind enemy lines, he gathered his wits and what supplies he could find on the battlefield and moved towards the nearest positions in which he believed friendly forces were positioned.

With immense determination and not a little luck, he reached British lines and had his wounds tended. His arrival preceded yet another Stuka attack and in the subsequent German infantry assault, he was pressed into action alongside the men of a famous Scottish infantry regiment, as he could still hold a rifle.

On one occasion, he personally rallied a group of six men and counter-attacked, retaking a machine gun that was brought back into play with great effect. Two hours of sustained fighting saw him wounded once more, so he was packed off with some retreating medics and successfully evacuated across the channel to fight another day with De Gaulle's Free French. The British officer commanding the jocks found time to record Lavalle's actions on that day and so he found himself invested with the Military Cross by his allies. Not to be outdone, his own superiors honoured him with the Croix de Guerre.

It was at this time that he was given a transfer into the newly formed 13th Demi-Brigade Légion Étrangère and, despite a negative start, he never looked back, leading his troops through many bloody campaigns.

Still recovering from his wounds, he developed a severe chest infection and so was considered unfit for full duty, missing the excursion of the 13th D.B.L.E. into the Arctic waters around Norway. On the Legion's return, he heard tell of the fighting qualities of the German paratroopers and mountain troops, before the collapse of resistance elsewhere in Norway had forced the Legion to escape back to England.

In December 1940, 13th DBLE arrived in the French Cameroons and then moved onto East Africa, to assist the British at the battles of Keren and, most especially, Massawa.

It was perhaps one of the war's most tragic episodes, that the Legion brigade to which Lavalle belonged was pitted against the Vichy 6th REI in the Syrian hills at Damas. Here, legionnaire killed legionnaire in extremely fierce fighting, despite many men knowing each other as former comrades and friends. 13th DBLE triumphed and, at the end of the campaign, many former 6th REI members volunteered to form a third battalion in Lavalle's unit.

For his valour in this awful action, Lavalle received the Croix de Guerre's Silver Star citation

In May 1942, Capitaine Lavalle led his legionnaires in defence of Bir Hakeim in the western desert, resisting the advances of the Italian Armoured Division 'Ariete' and winning the Medaille Militaire for his leadership and personal tally of four Italian M13/40 tanks. All four vehicles were stopped just in front of his command bunker, using a Boyes anti-tank rifle, taken from a dead legionnaire.

Supporting RAF bombers mistakenly attacked the wrecked Italian vehicles on May 29th, thinking they were in fact still live and Lavalle was wounded in the head by a bomb fragment. He was unable to be evacuated because of the siege nature of the battle and, despite medical protestations, he continued to lead his unit in fierce fighting, particularly against the 90th Leichte Afrika Division. Lavalle finally withdrew his unit in good order on the 11th June, along with the rest of the Brigade. It was generally accepted that the defence of Bir Hakeim enabled the later successes, starting at El Alamein.

Lavalle excelled in combat, both personally and in a command role and was considered a natural leader; a man who would be followed anywhere by the professionals he led. This was recognised by his superiors and a further step up the Croix de Guerre ladder came with the award of the Bronze Palm. He was promoted to the rank of Commandant and this promotion was welcomed by every man who served under him, for fighting soldiers like to be led by competent men.

Combat continued into Italy, as part of the US 5th Army, with a sobering stint in the attacks east of Monte Cassino, made in support of 3rd Algerian Division. A bloody but necessary attack on an MG42 position nearly proved his end, when his uniform was riddled with bullets, all but two of them missing him completely. The sole strikes hit his left hand, carrying away two fingers and, once again, his head, knocking a lump out just above his desert wound and plunging him into instant unconsciousness.

He was stretchered off the battlefield and began four months of recuperation, receiving the silver-gilt palms to his Croix de Guerre from his own General and the Silver Star from the US Army Commander, whilst still immobilised in his hospital bed. This battle, more than any other, scarred Lavalle, for far too many of his old comrades would remain forever in the soil of Italy and most of them died on those fateful days in late January 1944, when the mountain troops of the Wehrmacht demonstrated just how tough they could be and that they were no respecters of reputations, not even the Legion's. Lavalle had fought many enemies, but none were as tough as the 5th Gebirgsjager Division during those few bloody days in Italy.

As part of the 1st Free French Division, he took his Battalion ashore, landing in Southern France with Operation Anvil in August 1944. Lavalle managed to duck his next promotion for as long as possible, but the new rank caught up with him when he was wounded again after the campaign moved into the assault on Germany proper, when his battalion was one of the few French units to see serious action.

During the Battle of Colmar, he was shot during a ferocious fire fight with the Waffen-SS, this time a rifle bullet in the thigh and the powers that be swiftly took the opportunity offered. He was permanently transferred from his beloved legion regiment and, after recuperation, received his Colonelcy and was required to serve as a staff officer in the headquarters of the First French Army. On his first day of full duty, he was paraded before an immaculate honour guard of his former legion battalion to receive his Knight's rank Legion D'Honneur. Truly, he had become one of France's most decorated combat soldiers.

As with all things he undertook, Lavalle did his best in the staff job, but it was not what he had joined soldiering for and so he had additional reason to be pleased when the German surrender came. At the cessation of hostilities, he was stationed in the Stuttgart area and immediately the soldier's talk was of Indo-China and use of the Legion there. So, expectantly, he applied for command of a unit destined to be sent there, but was refused.

He was instead swiftly transferred to a special and decidedly clandestine French intelligence group, based in Ettlingen and given a briefing by no lesser person than the Army Commander himself. The new group's task was to trawl through the German POWs, rooting out those whose excesses made them too hot to handle, but offering more soldiering to those felt acceptable and suitable. Any appropriate German, who considered a French Foreign Legion uniform and a communist guerrilla bullet were preferable to languishing in the hellholes set aside for them, would be invited to join the Légion Étrangère and be spirited away to North Africa for training. The others would continue to rot in the Rheinweisenlage, or similar hellholes, until the Allies decided what to do with the hundreds of thousands of German prisoners in their hands.

Far from being boring and routine, Lavalle found it enthralling work and put his all into ensuring France could rely on his selection of legionnaires for Indo-China.

The interrogation of one former Hauptmann of the Gebirgsjager had proved enlightening, as he had been part of the bloodbath in Italy that had left such a mark on Christophe. There was no animosity, just professional courtesy and mutual respect. Once the German realised that he was facing one of the legionnaires who had spent their blood so profusely in that struggle, he opened up much more. The handshake at the end was firm and sincere and Hauptmann Renke went off to do his bit for the Republic.

Today would be different for Lavalle. He was venturing into almost exclusively SS territory, for they were the main occupants of the camp outside of Winzenheim. Of course, he had already met some of this particular breed and found them to be at both ends of the scale. Rabid fanatics, who still expected the Fuhrer to rise up and smite down the enemy, to those who were good soldiers, who had given their all militarily and just wanted to go home.

What set them aside from the run of the mill Germans was their spirit and intense comradeship, still strong and intact, after all the desperate combat and loss they had sustained, followed by the privations of captivity. The German was a strong beast in any case, but the Waffen-SS, particularly, had a

69

comradeship as deep as his own legion, if not more so. No light admission coming from a legionnaire and one that troubled him often.

The previous afternoon, a very senior officer of French Military Intelligence, an Alsatian like himself, had visited the office with clear instructions for Lavalle. His task today was to recruit soldiers into the Legion as usual, but firstly to meet a hugely respected enemy and make a very different suggestion, contained within an envelope in his tunic, the contents of which were no less incredible to him now than when he had read them the day before. Translating them into German, he had laboured hard to try to understand the full implications of the document but, by his own admission, had probably failed.

Having spent a restless night in the Hotel Michel Mort, in sleepy Bad Kreuznach, he was not looking forward to the short trip in his Citroen staff car. Not the fault of the hotel, as his thigh wound was often quite aggravating. None the less, he would perform his duty, for his work was important to the interests of his humiliated country.

In that thought, Lavalle was absolutely correct, although he could never even dream that today he would be involved in a matter with such far-reaching consequences.

It's choice, not chance, that determines your destiny.

Jean Nidetch

Chapter 6 – THE LEGEND

0917hrs Sunday, 1st July 1945, Winzenheim Camp [Rheinwiesenlager], Occupied Germany.

SS-Standartenfuhrer Ernst-August Knocke cast a spell wherever he went, be it on his own comrades, or on those detailed to guard the prison camp, full mainly with members of the SS, combat soldiers incarcerated alongside those who had spent their war at a desk, or in a concentration camp.

What immediately set him aside from every other German there was the fact that he strode around the camp in full black panzer uniform, complete with those tangible marks of years of bloody intense combat, from his Great War Iron Cross First class, awarded for his heroic defence of a trench position, through to the Knights Cross with Oak leaves and Crossed Swords at his throat, the last personally presented by Adolf Hitler. Underneath the Knights Cross was the 'Pour le Merite', or Blue Max, also of Great War fame, which the young acting Oberleutnant Knocke had won two days before hostilities ceased and which had not been confirmed until 1929. These awards and insignia had not been looted, as was the norm and he was held in the very highest esteem by those who imprisoned him there, particularly the camp commandant. The French Colonel had once served with the Vichy Forces, but had been forgiven sufficiently to be placed in charge of the abhorrence that was Winzenheim camp.

Knocke was the third ranked officer presently in the camp, but the other two above him were held in virtual contempt by the combat troops, who deferred to his authority on all matters. Because of the respect they held him in, they continued to march and drill on his orders and the exercise sessions were rigorous and long. Thanks to his efforts, his combat troopers kept fit and healthy, whilst others, less prepared, succumbed to disease and the melancholy of the unoccupied mind. All in all, there were one thousand and thirty-eight members of the SS in the camp, of which, over half had once been SS combat troops. Add in two hundred and one members of the Wehrmacht and Luftwaffe and a camp fit for habitation by five hundred and forty souls was crammed with one thousand two hundred and thirty-nine prisoners.

In a nutshell, Knocke was a legend on both sides of no man's land. An energetic forty-seven year old who had seen time in the trenches of the Great War, he departed from the beaten German army at the end of hostilities, surviving the great German depression with work as a night watchman and baker. The full recognition of his Great War service came in 1929, when the Pour-le-Merite was belatedly presented to him and with it came an opportunity to join the Wehrmacht; to be a professional soldier once more.

He joined the rising National Socialist party in 1934.

In February 1941, he transferred from the Wehrmacht into the Waffen-SS and from that time he never looked back. He had served with a number of Germany's elite SS divisions, rising from Untersturmfuhrer with the Leibstandarte-SS, through to Standartenfuhrer in SS-Das Reich, with command appointments in every SS Panzer Division but SS-Frundsberg and SS-Hitler Jugend.

Panzers were his main tool and he was a master craftsman. Employing his metal leviathans correctly at all times, he successfully completed mission after mission, butchering the massed Soviet ranks with precision and sweeping the field with his meticulous manouevrings and instinctive judgement.

Wherever he had gone, he took victory with him, even if his contribution could not stem the tide elsewhere.

His final command had been immolated outside Vienna, but not before successfully counter-attacking once more and inflicting huge losses on the Soviet army.

The division had then virtually ceased to exist and Knocke had tried to proceed back to Berlin, directed by orders from someone who clearly did not understand the transport situation.

He had fallen into the hands of the French Army two days later.

The young North African soldiers who captured him had obviously been in awe. They did not even remove his handgun, which fact caused some consternation with the French regular army Major, who was confronted by a loaded Walther P38 when Knocke handed it over before his interrogation. In truth, he might still even have it on his person now if he had not taken it from its holster himself and placed it on the table. Money could not have bought the look on that officer's face and Knocke delighted in telling the story often.

In his mind, Knocke appreciated that Germany would still need soldiers and so he trained his men in the arts of war as he knew them. From veteran to new trooper, he set in place a continuing tactical training programme, often using stones or pieces of wood to represent tank tactics and formation manouevre on the floor of the barracks. He reasoned that even the French might object if he did so openly in front of the guards.

Because of his teachings, many a young man in his captive audience acquired knowledge that would stand him in good stead, should there be further bloodshed in Europe.

Unfortunately, Knocke could not continue as he would have wished today, for he had been requested to attend the administrative block for clarifications. That was code for interrogation about wartime career's and, most importantly, where he had been and whom he had killed.

Well, that was the day gone then, Knocke mused, for he had been many places and killed many enemies.

Human beings, by changing the inner attitudes of their minds,
can change the outer aspects of their lives

William James

Chapter 7 – THE MEETING

0925hrs Sunday, 1st July 1945, Winzenheim Camp [Rheinwiesenlager], Occupied Germany.

Lavalle had seen a lot of German officers by now and felt that nothing was going to surprise him anymore. From the 'seig-heiling' stiff-backed fanatics, through to those whom awful experiences had cowed; they had all been across his desk and received his personal interrogation and decision.

His task was simple.

Regardless of the previous years of war and what had been done that was regrettable, find men who would wear the uniform of his beloved legion and who were prepared to honour the legion code; men who could bring soldierly qualities to the struggle against the communists. What his country needed now were soldiers of quality and no one could refute the fact that the Germans had them in large numbers, many of them desperately clinging to humanity in Allied prisoner of war camps, the length and breadth of Europe.

Rumour had it that there were over five million Germans presently in captivity, less the sixty-three men Lavalle had thus far found to ply their profession further afield, in the jungles of Indo-China. Most of those were either on their way to, or had arrived at, the Sidi-bel-Abbes headquarters of the Legion.

That the struggle for which Lavalle was recruiting was exclusively against the communist, meant that he had only had three suitable candidates turn away from the offer he put on the table, for one thing each and every German understood, was the communist threat.

So, here he was in Winzenheim, one of the Rheinwiesenlager, the set of camps hugging the Rhine,

74

aberrations that were rapidly acquiring a reputation as hellholes for their occupants.

The large room set aside for his 'interrogations' was classically devoid of any charm. Concrete walls, white-washed and bare, save for an electric fan high in one corner that soundlessly agitated the air. Windowless and poorly lit, the only furniture being the two chairs and a battered, but serviceable, table placed centrally, topped off with an electric lamp and an ashtray.

He sat down at the table and reached for the file on top of the pile. This file had drawn his attention the moment it arrived in his office, for it was one of very few which were red and one of only six he had seen that had a blue ribbon around it. That made the person described therein very special indeed. This man was also the reason Lavalle was conducting his business on a Sunday, when the rest of the section was off enjoying the high-life in Karlsruhe. The name on the file had been known to Lavalle long before his involvement with the clandestine operation that brought the document into his possession.

He had read it previously, of course, three times in fact and fascinating reading it was too, now supplemented by additional witness statements from German prisoners and with some newly arrived Soviet Intel files adding to what the allied intelligence services had scrounged up during six years of war. The man described in these pages was a real legend, both in his own army and in that of his enemies, which was a rarity. Rommel had achieved it, of course, but this man had fought his war exclusively in Europe and most of it in the bloodbath that was the Eastern Front.

The door opened and the guard gestured the arriving prisoner inside.

Lavalle looked up and his immediate reaction was to stand and salute, a reaction he only just managed to suppress in time, although the man who stood opposite him saw the faint twitch of movement.

The German in front of Lavalle was the most impressive soldier he had ever seen, the more so as he was

75

stood at the attention in immaculate full uniform, his medals shining and resplendent, eyes calm and firm.

He invited Knocke to sit, which Ernst did with a lithe and graceful movement.

The lack of any formal introduction from his interrogator was not lost on Knocke.

Lavalle opened the folder and, in perfect German, read aloud through the family details, list of unit assignments and general service record, pausing only to confirm a date here, an award there.

"Well, you seem to have been very thorough," ceded Knocke, after ten minutes of solid listening.

"You even have my two weeks at Zossen recorded, which was extremely secret and not even my divisional commander knew I had been there. Also, I congratulate you on your mastery of my language".

"Thank you, Herr Knocke. I am from Alsace, of course. Now, let me be frank and get to the point. My main purpose is normally to interview members of the defeated German army, with a view to recruiting them into the Foreign Legion and sending them to fight for France in Indo-China. You are not seen in that role, partially because of your age, but partially because of your speciality being with tanks."

"War is a young man's business for sure, Herr Oberst, and panzers are not a jungle weapon," and delivered with a quizzical inflection, "So, why am I here?"

"That is a good question."

Lavalle brought out his Gauloise cigarettes and offered one up. Ernst did not comment on the fingers missing from the hand holding the packet. Veterans did not do such things. When both men were enjoying their first puffs, Lavalle continued.

"I am here because it would seem that you fought a fair and chivalrous war and are not tarnished with excesses, such as are some of your countrymen. Neither are you in anyway directly involved with the extermination camps."

Lavalle straightened a little. "Had you been so involved then we would be having a very different conversation right now. Instead, I am here to make you an offer. Many of your comrades find the lure of fighting communists too much to resist, some wish to hide in the legion to evade responsibility for what they have done and others sign up simply because they have nothing better to do. I do not see you agreeing to serve France, in any capacity, for any of those reasons, Herr Knocke. Not even ego, I suspect", which was said in such a way as a listener might think it was also a question.

Knocke shifted slightly and delivered a gentle riposte, in a tone that made Lavalle understand the force and personality of the man opposite him.

"I can assure you that the Russian front afforded no room for ego, Herr Oberst."

"Permit me to rephrase that," Lavalle countered softly, after a respectable pause.

"You have skills, skills that my country and others might need to draw upon. Sat opposite us are millions of Russians and already there are problems brewing. Across the world, communism is taking further root. Who knows where the next Hitler or Mussolini will rise?"

"Or Stalin?"

"Or Stalin, Herr Knocke, indeed, or Stalin."

Lavalle offered his cigarettes again and when both men had eagerly drawn the rich smoke into their lungs, he continued.

"This war is over and you will not take to a uniform again to oppose the enemies of your country, or mine for that matter. You will not bear arms again, I am sure, but you have priceless knowledge and skills. I do not understand precisely where you would fit in within the greater scheme of things, but I do know that you will not be allowed to fade away and that you will be asked to bring your skills to serve again."

'So, basically, you have nothing to offer me and no idea of what you might want me to do. How can I refuse?" with a chuckle that fell short of amusement.

"Au contraire, Herr Knocke. I am empowered to offer you and a selected group, removal from this facility within the week, unofficial paid employment based in pleasant

77

surroundings and a guarantee that you will not be asked to do anything that would harm your comrades or country."

"A lot is expected with little by way of definite information. I cannot entertain any advance from an enemy of my country, in any case."

"We are no longer enemies, surely that is clear?" Lavalle left that hanging in the air, but received no acknowledgement from Knocke. "The war is over, the peace is signed. We must all now stand together in the face of the communists."

Knocke leant slightly forward.

"As we Germans were saying for years; years in which we stood alone against them! We have already shed much blood and suffered much loss and I saw too many of my men die in the cause you now conveniently wish to champion. You have just read out that I grew up in a small village called Metgethen, Herr Oberst; does that mean anything to you?" The emotion was controlled but none the less there, and again the force of Knocke gave Lavalle pause his reply was obviously sincere and heartfelt.

"Yes, I know of Metgethen, Herr Knocke, and I am truly sorry for your loss, but you know as well as I do that Nazi Germany could not have been allowed to stand and that the Western Allies could not have fought alongside a nation driven by Hitler and his band. I have been to a quiet but dreadful place called Natzwiller-Struhof, where the reasons for the need to remove Nazism were made very clear to me, by my own eyes. There are other, much more awful places that I have not seen, but about which I have heard nightmare stories. The people of a nation always pay the price of the policies laid down by its politicians and undoubtedly Germany has suffered much in that regard, that is true."

Lavalle placed the envelope he had been holding gently on top of the folder.

"Surely, Herr Knocke, you must see that the best hope of salvation for your homeland, your Fatherland, lies with a joint approach, to prevent the spread of communism westwards. What happened at Metgethen is still unclear, but what I do know is that none of us wants that to be visited upon any other village, town, or city. That surely must be something for you to consider? It's too late for you to act in preservation of your own family, but you can assist in protecting the rest of your country and, in so doing, preserve mine too. You have skills and knowledge, which may become much in need."

Such a speech required a considered response and so Knocke paused to order his thoughts before replying.

"Again, I have to say that a lot is expected with little information to go on. I will grant you that we may no longer be active enemies, but don't expect that a political end to the war will just make our enmities go away over night."

Lavalle assessed Knocke's response as much in his poise and tone as in his words. It was obvious to Knocke that the Frenchman's mind was working out the next move. It was equally obvious when the decision was reached.

"You have said enough for me to go further."

Lavalle took up the envelope that had appeared in his hands previously.

"I am permitted to show you this document and solely request that if you do not wish to be associated with the project outlined in it, that you do not speak of it further. I am empowered to make certain threats in that regard, but out of professional courtesy, my understanding of their pointlessness in your case," he looked Knocke directly in the eye to stress his earnestness, "And through personal choice, I do not. I will ask for your word, as an officer."

Knocke digested the words and understood that, in Lavalle, he was encountering a soldier such as himself. Between two such men, honour still had a place.

"That is given, Herr Oberst."

The envelope changed hands and Knocke read the title.

"Colloque? This means what exactly, Herr Oberst?"

"Ah, apologies, Herr Knocke, my error. In your language, it would say symposium. "

A few moments pause hid a burst of deep thinking by Knocke, ended solely with a softly spoken "Danke", as he extracted the contents, one translation set in German, the original in French, reading slowly and without expression.

79

Once finished, Knocke obviously saw the signatories authorising the symposium, checked the original French copy and looked directly into Lavalle's eyes, uttering a soft "Mein Gott". He then re-read the entire four pages three times, before returning them to the envelope and handing it back to an expectant Lavalle, whose cigarette packet once more disgorged two cigarettes.

"Are you aware of the contents of that document, Herr Oberst?" Knocke asked in a way that almost defied the contents to be true.

"I am, as I typed the German language translation you have just read and so miserably failed to place a proper translation on its cover, for which I apologise again. I do not profess to fully understand the words I wrote, nor their implications for France, Germany, Europe, or you, for that matter, Herr Knocke."

Gentle nodding of the head acknowledged acceptance of Lavalle's comment and then Knocke merely closed his eyes and withdrew into thought, his fingertips extended against each other, as was his want when deep in contemplation of a problem.

Obviously much was rattling and rumbling through Knocke's head, so Lavalle wisely decided to let him work through the dilemma without interruption.

The wait was interminable.

Another cigarette was lit and Lavalle placed his pack and lighter within reach of Knocke, but said nothing, not wishing to interrupt him in such deep thought.

After what seemed like a lifetime, Knocke nodded to himself, almost imperceptibly, his eyes opened and he looked directly into Lavalle's, who once again felt the power driving the man.

"I will not do anything that will go against the wishes and needs of my country, or my comrades, but I will, in principle, concede that the menace of communism is one that we would be better fighting together, rather than separately. Your timing is less than impeccable for me as a German, this you will understand"

Lavalle's subtle inclination of the head said all that could be said on that matter and he gestured to his cigarettes.

"Danke, Herr Oberst" and Knocke took and lit one swiftly, drawing in the pungent smoke before continuing.

"I confess to being intrigued by the concept outlined and can see probable benefits for my country. If I commit to this largely unknown exercise, will I be permitted to leave and return here if it contradicts my beliefs or values?"

"To that I can give a qualified yes, Herr Knocke. I am told that you, any of you, will not be forced to do anything that you do not agree with and that anything you do will be entirely voluntary. I cannot guarantee that you would return here in the event that you quit the group."

After the briefest moment to digest that reply, Knocke responded, "In which case, on the limited information you give me and on that understanding, combined with the contents of that document and the signatory, I accept."

"Then we would please ask that you do not speak of this, except to the six men whom you will select to fulfil the criteria within that document and even then, we would ask that you tell them as little as necessary to induce them to attend. Please appraise Colonel Frisson as soon as you have your men and he will make the arrangements for them to be interviewed. Please understand the criteria that we have for such matters and do not request to employ someone who would be unacceptable to us, no matter what their credentials."

"I understand perfectly. Firstly, I will need eight and I request two named men who are not within this camp, if they remain alive?"

"We anticipated this, so yes, you may, on both counts." Lavalle pushed forward a pencil and a notepad. "Please put their names and units down there, so we may investigate as to their whereabouts. We can offer no guarantees, but if they are alive and satisfy the criteria, then we will do our best. The British are not being too helpful at this time, unfortunately"

A swift eight lines of script and the notebook and pencil were back in Lavalle's possession.

"There are the names of all the officers I will require for this undertaking, Herr Oberst."

Both men stood and exchanged a natural and respectful handshake before Knocke was returned to his comrades.

"I always wanted to visit Biarritz in happier times. Hopefully the war has not left too deep a mark upon it?"

Lavalle deflected the obvious probe.

"There was little left unmarked in the war, as both of us know too well. Goodbye and good luck, Herr Knocke."

"Auf wiedershein, Oberst Lavalle," was Knocke's well-timed final statement, as he disappeared from sight.

Lavalle smiled to himself and wondered how the German had acquired that piece of information. He immediately vowed that if he ever met Knocke again, he would never underestimate him. Not that he would meet him again, for Knocke was now, officially, in a very different world to his own.

He felt the sudden weight of that envelope in his pocket and understood why the signatures had the same effect on Knocke as they did on him, when he first saw the document.

A quick note was written and handed to the summoned orderly, for forwarding to the waiting dispatch rider, just to confirm to his boss that Colloque Biarritz had been successfully initiated.

Another note was dispatched shortly afterwards, destined for Colonel Frisson, containing the names of six special prisoners for interview over the following week.

Settling back down, he reached for the next file and waited for the former SS Hauptsturmfuhrer Richter of pioneers, who was next in line for a one-way ticket to a swift death in Indo-China. If he so chose, of course.

Demoralize the enemy from within by surprise, terror,
sabotage, assassination. This is the war of the future.

Adolf Hitler.

Chapter 8 – THE BOMBSHELLS

0755hrs Monday, 2nd July 1945, The Lubyanka, NKVD Headquarters, Moscow, USSR.

When it first hit Beria's desk he read it incredulously and immediately ordered another translation done, just to check. Thirty-five minutes later, the senior cryptographer arrived back in his office, holding the second version.

Comparing the two, it was immediately apparent that they were identical in every way.

'*[priority code] GCG*
[agent] Alkonost
[date code] 280645c
[personal code as an authenticator] FB21162285
[distribution1] route x-eyes only
[distribution1] AalphaA [Comrade Chairman Beria].
[message] first test imminent indicator A+ on 160745c Confirmation type2 via Moth 050745c. Wellington. Freya-North.
[message ends]

Message authenticates. Codes for non-compromisation valid.

ORIGINAL RECEIVED 06:16 2/7/45-B.V.LEMSKY
SECOND DECIPHER 07:31 2/7/45-B.V.LEMSKY'

"No possibility of mistakes, Comrade Academician?"

"None at all, Comrade Chairman. I have even tried predicting an error in encoding, but nothing produced sensible decodes. The message, as you see it, is the one that was sent, Comrade."

"Thank you, Boris Vissarionevich."

The cryptographer left the room and Beria was alone with his thoughts.

Automatically, his glasses were in his hand and the gentle polishing motion began. He looked at the clock.

Eight am.

After a short pause, he leant forward and picked up his phone. It was immediately answered by his secretary.

"Danilov, put me through to the old man immediately."

As the connections and requests were being made, Beria drank some tea and waited patiently. A gruff voice brought him from his momentary daydream.

"Comrade Chairman."

"Comrade General Secretary. I have a report on my desk that you will wish to see urgently. May I come over now?"

"Can it not wait until the meeting later, Lavrentiy?"

Stalin seemed to be in a good mood, maybe because of what the day held for him, but now that mood was about to be darkened.

"I believe not, Comrade. It is an Alkonost report and of some considerable urgency."

The pause was brief as Stalin mental processes worked out the identity of the report writer and realised the possible significance.

"Twenty minutes, Comrade Chairman."

Before Beria could reply, the phone went dead and he replaced his handset gently to hide his annoyance. Picking it back up, he had a mere second to wait before he was speaking again.

"Danilov. My car now, please."

Picking up the two decoded messages, he placed them inside his briefcase along with the three other files he had consulted that morning and left the office.

0840hrs, Monday, 2nd July 1945, The Kremlin, Moscow, USSR.

Less than an hour beforehand, the same piece of paper had been presented to Beria. Now, here it was, in the hands of the General Secretary. Stalin's reaction was initially calm.

"Let us look at this separately. Firstly, we have the codeword we expected. With 'Wellington,' we know we can now, at minimum, disrupt the American programme."

Beria impatiently nodded in assent, although that was not quite what it meant, wishing to move on to the section that caused all the consternation.

"We were first informed some few weeks ago that their project was more advanced than we first suspected. That is why we have set in place the mechanism for our agents to commence delay or destruction, on our order, is it not?"

"Yes, Comrade General Secretary."

Stalin rose and placed his hands on the desk, knuckles supporting him, as he leant forward. His anger was now wholly apparent and his voice rose.

"Now, some few weeks later, we discover that the capitalist bastards are a handful of days from testing the real thing?"

Reaching the highest volume, Stalin screamed, "How the fuck can that be, Comrade?"

Beria was unable to answer with fact, so said nothing.

"Some bastard will be counting trees for this!"

Stalin sat back down with a thud and picked up his pack, fumbling for a cigarette. He sought out a match and ran it down the desk in his anger, puffing agitatedly, until a sudden calm descended upon him as quickly as his anger had risen.

"Last time we spoke of this agent, you quoted 100% reliability, Lavrentiy, 100%."

Having weathered the brief but extremely dangerous storm, a relieved Beria spoke with assurance. "Alkonost has never let us down, Comrade General Secretary."

"Let us hope that continues. Send the preparatory action code immediately."

85

Stalin paused to wrestle with an issue in his mind, which he swiftly resolved.

"The other agents must also be ordered to prepare to act. Even though we have not heard from them, send the code to prepare to all your agents within Manhattan."

Beria nodded his assent and, deciding to hold on to the other files until later, made to leave the room.

"Tell me, Comrade. This agent, Alkonost. What sort of man do we pin our hopes on here?"

Replying with extreme care for the benefit of the microphones, Beria paused before the door and turned.

"This agent is in the right place, Comrade, and there has never been failure. Alkonost will do well enough. Until later, Comrade General Secretary," and with a nod of the head he was gone.

Outside the room, Beria walked through the building, gently unburdening himself of the stresses of that meeting. As he climbed into his car to make the journey back to his office, he could not help but smile. What would the Boss say if he knew that the fate of Kingdom39 and more, was in the hands of a twenty-five year old woman? The smile faded as quickly as it arrived, as the possibility of Alkonost failing made its presence felt in his head. In that event, the age and gender of the agent would not matter to Beria, for he would be long dead.

1100hrs, Monday, 2nd July 1945, The Kremlin, Moscow, USSR.

At 1100hrs precisely, the group convened again, this time in Stalin's office. By prior agreement only Marshals Zhukov, Vasilevsky, Chief Marshal of Aviation Alexander Novikov and Admiral of the Fleet Hovhannes Stepani Isakov were present, along with their closest staff. On the other side of the table were the full GKO and, standing to their immediate left, the GRU Polkovnik-General, Roman Samuilovich Pekunin.

Zhukov, resplendent in his full uniform and every inch the soldier, made the full presentation himself, needing his staff solely to place maps on the table in front of the General

Secretary and other GKO members, to make marks on a chalk board placed on an easel at one end of the table, or occasionally to quote a figure or two from the addendums to the master copy of the now ready version of plan Kingdom39.

The planning was incredible and complex, covering everything that could be possibly imagined. The requirements for operational security prior to and after the attack were extreme. Maskirova was of prime importance, up to the moment that the tanks started to roll in Phase#3, because any advance warning could turn the plan from a triumph into a disaster. Some was already in place, but much more would be needed.

Without a doubt, the destruction of the Allied Air forces was key to the success of the plan, but even with the excellent planning laid out before them, the price of that destruction would be extremely high for some of their own young men. To the GKO members, it was but a bill to pay and a fair one at that. Unusually for Soviet Doctrine, a broad front attack had been chosen, but unlike with Rokossovsky in 1944, Stalin did not challenge the plan. The reasoning was, after all, clear and understandable and matters would probably revert to accepted doctrine within the week.

Once the doors had been closed and the guards posted, no one was permitted to enter the room, on pain of death, so there were no orderlies to bring drinks to the occupants. They had to get their own and choose from a selection of snacks that had been placed there before the conference convened.

Vasilevsky placed a tea before Zhukov, who acknowledged the gesture, paused in his presentation and consumed it swiftly. Many others took advantage of this lull and went to get their second or third such drink and it was Stalin who brought the room back to order again and the presentation continued.

It was gone 1400hrs before Zhukov finished the main army plan and invited Air Force Marshal Novikov to put over the role his forces were to play.

Following him came Isakov, the Navy's Chief of Staff, recently having left the hospital where wounds from a 1942 German air raid on Tuapse had confined him.

The clock above Stalin's desk showed 1522hrs, when Isakov's final word of presentation was spoken and so Zhukov summed up.

"Comrades, you have set the Red Army a task and we have presented you with a plan that will complete that task in the timescale you require. As with all such plans, nothing can be taken for granted. Provided our maskirova is successful, particularly plan Chelyabinsk, we will achieve ground forces surprise. Provided their Air Forces are taken out by Plan Kurgan and the other elements, then no one will have air superiority unless, of course, it is us."

He took a discernably deeper breath.

"That will ensure that ground superiority will be ours for sufficient time to complete all phases presently proposed and, probably, the additional possibilities within the Iberian Peninsula and the British Isles."

"Casualties will be huge on both sides and losses in materiel extreme".

Zhukov left that hanging, in the faint hope of seeing some tinge of regret from the faces looking so intently at him. He saw none and, of course, never really expected otherwise.

"Our planned sabotage operations only need to be 50% successful to have a marked effect upon allied resistance."

"A word of caution though, Comrades. We must expect sabotage in our own rear areas, increasing as we advance deeper into their territory. In addition, the Army will have little manpower to spare to guard against saboteurs in the territories we presently hold, because we will be advancing. We must have assurances from the NKVD and other security forces, that our logistical tail will be secure."

Beria was half listening, but fully missed the pause. Slowing becoming aware that he was the centre of attention in a silent room, he replayed his memory, seeking out Zhukov's words.

"Comrade Marshal, the security forces of the Motherland will ensure that the Red Army is protected from back-stabbing saboteurs."

"Thank you, Comrade Chairman."

"Comrades, that is plan Kingdom39. We can implement it within sixty hours of receiving the order and we can be ready to execute it any time from 18th August."

After such a display, Zhukov merited applause and a rest, but neither was forthcoming. No one spoke, as it would fall to the General Secretary to make the first comments.

Stalin took centre stage.

"Comrades. I must congratulate you on this plan. The Motherland will be proud of you when you execute it successfully and the capitalists are driven from Europe."

"The points made are noted and we will talk on them further. The Party will throw everything behind the Army, Air Force and Navy to ensure victory."

"NKVD units will respond to all reasonable requests from Army Commanders in order to prioritise defence of logistic routes. Comrade Beria will liaise with you to ensure that happens smoothly."

"It also happens that the Comrade Chairman has anticipated some of your needs for rear-area security and has prepared a document for consultation."

Stalin paused to permit Beria's aide to hand around a folder. Whilst they were being distributed, Zhukov, as was his recent habit, mentally checked through his headquarters staff to work out who was the NKVD spy whose reporting back allowed Beria to be so prepared. Not that, in this instance, it was a problem. In fact, all the better for the success of the mission. This time.

The document detailed actions to be taken in the lead up to the attack by D-minus, rather than by date. It was actually very impressive and would probably cover all eventualities, some not even considered possible by the army staff's. One section in particular caught most eyes, but no one said a word. Even though the numbers were considerable, mass murder was less remarkable now, given the preceding six years.

Zhukov swiftly took in the major details.

"Most efficient, Comrade Chairman."

Beria accepted the words, no matter how negatively they were intended. "Our staffs will sort out the finer details immediately".

"Comrade Marshal Novikov. The Air Force's part in Kurgan is exceptionally important. Transports aside, the figures for the initial element of the attack are impressive. We have concerns over whether there are sufficient correctly trained personnel to do as you outline here."

Stalin jabbed the open folder in his hands.

"Comrade General Secretary, for some it is a case of refresher training. For others, it is just familiarisation. As we do not intend to use these capitalist assets regularly once open combat has started, then a lesser degree of skill is acceptable, offset against the surprise element involved. Personnel would then return to their normal units and aircraft."

"Very well, Comrade Novikov."

Stalin spoke out again, this time addressing his comments directly at Zhukov.

"We are concerned about the assets you are committing to Plan Kurgan. As you say, Comrade Marshal, this is a key part of the overall mission and must not fail. Why do we not employ more troops in the first mission?"

"That is a simple matter of transport capability, Comrade General Secretary. We do not have the capacity to take more than the numbers presently committed. We have set aside 10% of our transport aircraft to allow for breakdown and other problems. It would not be advisable to eat into that safety margin"

"I see. And we cannot obtain more capacity in time?"

Marshal Novikov raised his hand at this point and was immediately noticed and Stalin gestured to him to speak.

"Comrade General Secretary, I believe we can supply additional capacity if we transfer units from our maskirova operation in the East. In my estimation, that would permit an increase in carrying capacity of around 30% to 35%, whilst maintaining the 10% cushion required by Comrade Marshal Zhukov." Vasilevsky remained impassive as his own operational plan, Diaspora, was partially dismantled by others.

"I can work on that and get more precise figures."

Maskirova, the act of deception, is a sacred and necessary thing for the Russian psyche and to lessen it, or remove assets from it, is rarely well received. In this case,

Novikov was offering a solution to the shortfalls of plan Kurgan that could not be ignored for a 30% increase in capacity. It was clear that the Air Force Marshal had more to say, so he was given the floor again, although Zhukov and a number of others were wondering why the Air Force hadn't spoken about this before.

'Perhaps to ensure the GKO was given every opportunity to appreciate the Air Force's role as well as the Army?'

Zhukov dismissed the thought immediately, as Novikov was a professional. Anyway, he had offered an excellent solution to the problem and there was more to come.

"In addition, if plan Diaspora is initiated without the airborne element for the first week then I anticipate an additional 20% increase in capacity for Kurgan, that is to say a total of 50%. Once that is completed, we will have no need for our resources to be stationed in Europe in such large numbers and they could be transferred back to Diaspora in suitable numbers to make up the shortfall within approximately eight days of release."

Stalin was actually quite impressed and clapped his hands three times.

"This is a good plan, Comrade Novikov. If Comrade Vasilevsky has no objections, then Comrade Zhukov will recalculate using your suggestions and upgrade plan Kingdom39."

Vasilevsky paused to gather his thoughts before speaking and in so doing, lost the opportunity.

"Comrade?" enquired Stalin.

Beria obviously had something to say.

"I can confirm that my own staff's calculations indicate a definite 35% minimum increase in capacity if the assets are transferred as indicated by Comrade Marshal Novikov. More to the point, he is too modest to say that if the forces from Diaspora are also employed, that there is a 50% increase in capacity. It will be much nearer a total of 60% overall. The eight day catch-up period is wholly accurate."

Novikov nodded impassively, as Beria managed to illustrate that Novikov's staff was thoroughly penetrated by

NKVD spies and that everything the Marshal had said was already known to the men in front of him. Such were the games that great men played. He exchanged a knowing look with both Zhukov and Vasilevsky, who could offer no consolation, save silent understanding.

Admiral of the Fleet Hovhannes Stepani Isakov stepped forward.

"Might I also suggest that some of the assaults planned within Kurgan can be carried out equally well by naval units delivering troops or marines, as some locations lie close to shorelines, particularly in Northern Germany, Denmark and Italy."

Yet more unexpected assistance, this time from the Navy. Such assistance had not been available when it was first enquired about, so something had obviously changed. Zhukov mentally played with the new possibilities.

"We have surmised that we can free up approximately 3%-5% of the transports on the night of Kingdom."

On that assurance, Beria was strangely ill informed, merely surmising that the Admiral's stated figures were about right. Beria would speak with Rear-Admiral Batuzov later and enquire why that piece of information had not come to him in the last report.

Others in the room envied Isakov for his obvious lack of an NKVD informant on his staff. Isakov impassively listened as Beria tried to sound prepared and was the only one there who knew he had not planned it, having just thrown it in on the spur of the moment, so as to be seen to contribute. Mentally, he had quickly checked off what was possible and decided that he had not claimed too much. It would work.

"Excellent again, Comrade Admiral. At each turn we find solutions."

"Comrade Marshal Zhukov will look at the new capacity and revise plans for Kurgan to ensure full success. Both Air Force and Navy will liaise with Marshal's Zhukov and Vasilevsky, to establish the effect of these new suggestions."

"Now, before we proceed with briefing for Plan Diaspora, remove all of this," Stalin cast an expansive arm gesture at the paraphernalia of Kingdom39, "So that we may include our guests."

The documents and maps disappeared in record time. Stalin exchanged subtle nods with Beria, who picked up the phone.

"Show our guests in."

The gilded doors swung open and in strode the diminutive figure of General Michitake Yamaoka, respectfully tailed by the larger Vice-Admiral Kenji Asegawa.

Beria was discretely handed a folder containing two messages by the escorting NKVD General. Marshal Vasilevsky made the introductions, introductions accompanied each time by deep bows from the Japanese Attachés. Only one present noticed Beria's subtle reaction as he read what he had been passed.

"So, now we can proceed." Stalin's irritation with the Japanese time wasting was hidden, but only just.

"Comrade Marshal Vasilevsky?"

Vasilevsky proceeded to talk through the planning for the Far East operations, adjusting as best he could for the absence of the airlift capacity, now dedicated to Kingdom39. Yamaoka and Asegawa both noticed the differences from the briefing they had been expecting, but decided now was not the time to discuss where the airlift capacity had gone. That the Soviets were going to move in Europe was known, and it was hardly surprising that they did not wish to share the operational details with their new allies, as yet.

Surprisingly, Vasilevsky and his staff had found that the original concept and outline by Beria was actually quite sound in reasoning and certainly achievable. Professionalism required that they improve upon it and they did that exceptionally well. Nodding assent from politicians was commonplace, but the inclination of the head and nod that he received from an impressed Zhukov was welcome professional acknowledgement that the plan he laid before the GKO was indeed excellent.

"The support received from the Imperial Army has been superb and the details of this plan have been worked out in complete consultation with General Yamaoka. If this is approved by the GKO, the planning document will be taken to Manchuria, where General Yamaoka and Admiral Asegawa will present it for ratification. I have ordered Comrade General Savvushkin and his staff to accompany them."

"Might I also say that Admiral Asegawa suggested the bold naval plan, in partnership with Comrade Admiral Yumashev."

Asegawa bowed deeply to the GKO and Stalin motioned to his NKVD chairman. Beria spoke directly to the Japanese Military Attaché.

"We would welcome your views on this plan, General."

More bows and Yamaoka stepped forward.

The painfully small general was never a man to waste words and so, instead of the lengthy appraisal the room was expecting, he spoke but two sentences.

"General Secretary, it has been an honour to be fortunate enough to consult closely with Marshal Vasilevsky and his staff during the planning and I have been completely impressed with their professionalism and daring. This plan is wholly acceptable to me and I will commend its adoption, without alteration, to the Imperial High Command."

The deepest of bows both terminated his statement and took everyone by surprise.

"Thank you, General," Beria, slightly thrown, suddenly found himself speaking well before his imagined time, "Then there remains one matter to establish and that is the moment of execution. Comrade General Secretary?"

Stalin rose once more.

"Indeed, Comrade Chairman. We have exhausted this for now and we must congratulate all our Comrades who have laboured to provide us with the means to achieve our Motherland's goals."

Stalin tamped his pipe and drew heavily, puffing out thick smoke, which almost seemed to target the two Japanese officers.

"And so, when do we anticipate commencing?"

As was his habit, he looked around the GKO members for assent with what came next. The normal set of compliant nods was given, although they did at least know what Stalin was going to say this time.

"The new arrangements for Kurgan must be factored in and done quickly. The effect of change upon Diaspora must also be reflected and changes made. In both cases, you are authorised to immediately commence the movements necessary to get your forces in place, in line with all the plans submitted. This has absolute priority and all your efforts should be directed into preparation. You should prepare to execute both plans from the 3rd August. Please return to your respective headquarters, Comrades"

There were no groans, no sounds of dismay, nothing.

Nevertheless, each senior officer present, inwardly sank at the timescale forced upon them, none more so than Isakov, who had recently made a claim that he had no idea if he could back up.

Vasilevsky who, as yet, had not worked out the effect of loss of transport aircraft on his plans, was silent, but in despair.

Zhukov, as ever, took the bull by the horns.

"We will be ready, Comrade General Secretary."

"Yes, you will, Comrade Marshal."

1545hrs, Monday, 2nd July 1945, The Kremlin, Moscow, USSR.

The military men had all gone, the GKO had gone its separate ways. That left Bulganin and Beria accompanying Stalin and, at his request, taking a slow walk back to the General Secretary's office.

Once inside, tea was brought in and the men discussed the course of the day. The joint opinion was that it had gone well.

However, there was one matter that irked Stalin.

"Comrade Chairman, your messages. It is rare that news has such an effect upon you and I assume you have something to share?"

Stalin had not missed Beria's earlier discomfort after all.

95

"Yes, Comrade General Secretary. More agent messages from Manhattan."

Beria passed one over without another word and waited for the storm.

'*[priority code] DDX*
[agent] Gamayun
[date code] 260645d
[personal code as an authenticator] EX644007XE
[distribution1] route x-eyes only
[distribution1] AalphaA [Comrade Chairman Beria].
[message] Wellington. Weapon test 1607, strength A+ Confirmation type1. Diagram of bomb fat man en route via Tiger soonest. Load-Eels.
[message ends]

Message authenticates. Codes for non-compromisation valid.

RECEIVED 11:14 2/7/45-B.V.LEMSKY'

The storm did not arrive.

"Your interpretation of this, Comrade Beria?" No storm, but the cut in Stalin's tone was noticeable.

"Confirmation of the date of test, certainly, Comrade. We now have two names for a bomb, which implies two bombs. This is not news as we know the Americans are working on both uranium and plutonium projects." That it actually was news, and also not actually good news, was truer.

"On the positive side, we now know Gamayun is still active and he has received our order, as he acknowledges with 'Wellington'. Our chances for interference with their project have increased."

"Then why did you react so, Comrade?"

"Because I learned this morning that we may have some difficulties with secure communications, particularly with our Washington Embassy, through which this message was unfortunately routed."

Stalin looked pointedly at Beria, in a way that conveyed that this was not news to his ears.

96

'This possibility was only uncovered last night and was acted on immediately. It would probably have been too late for this message."

Stalin's gaze did not falter, drawing Beria into further commitment.

"I have my best staff interpreting our intelligence on this, but, as a precaution, all NKVD codes have been changed and new routings established."

In an effort to end with something upbeat, Beria hastily threw in an assurance.

"Our Manhattan agents all have lines of reporting that would remain uncompromised in any case, some because their own needs have dictated more complex methods of exchange."

He indicated the message still held in the General Secretary's hand.

"That message should not have gone through the embassy and we have identified the error and corrected it."

Everyone present understood that referred to an individual, as well as what corrected meant in this instance.

As was the case, many a time, Stalin's words were more order than question.

"You will confirm for me that there is no suggestion of Army codes being involved and absolutely no possibility of Kingdom39 being compromised."

Beria answered with a conviction he genuinely felt.

"Absolutely not, Comrade General Secretary. There has been no compromise of NKGB, GRU, or Army codes. Of that we are sure."

"The party will hold you to that, Comrade Marshal."

Stalin sat back in his chair.

"And the other?"

Beria extended a hand containing the other agents report.

Stalin read it slowly and was visibly agitated by its contents. Bulganin's eyes silently questioned the NKVD chief, who was furiously polishing his glasses.

Stalin passed the paper to Bulganin and lit a cigarette.

Bulganin digested the words.

'*[priority code] ZZZ*
[agent] Kalibr
[date code] 250645b
[personal code as an authenticator] OV322628BK
[distribution1] route x-eyes only
[distribution1] AalphaA [Comrade Chairman Beria].
[message] Reassigned Alamagordo NM. At O.R. material produced sufficient for 4 weapons max. Strength A. type-2. Wellington not possible. End-low.
[message ends]

Message authenticates. Codes for non-compromisation valid.

RECEIVED 11:26 2/7/45-B.V.LEMSKY'

"Four? Enough for four, Comrade?"

Beria replaced his glasses.

"Admittedly, we expected material enough for three maximum. One for test purposes as we have confirmed. Two for offensive purposes against our slant-eyed comrades, also confirmed by the GRU's asset in Washington. We can already sabotage the facility, as we know, without Kalibr, so this will not alter anything, Comrade General Secretary."

Stalin looked unconvinced, so he pressed on.

"Our intelligence is good. I concede, we only recently discovered how advanced the project was and that they approached testing, but we now know for certain what assets they have and we have known for a long time what they intend. We have agents in place awaiting orders to damage the project. Our security is intact, despite the Washington routing problem. That the Capitalists may have additional material for another bomb does not change anything. I see no cause for concern here, Comrades"

Beria finished with a confident flourish of the hand.

Stalin took the message from Bulganin and read it once more.

With an expansive gesture, he fired the message across the table at Beria and it slid, almost menacingly, dropping onto his lap with all the weight of a death warrant.

98

"The party will also hold you to that, Comrade Marshal."

Beria stood as if to leave.

"One last thing, Comrade."

Beria waited.

"Do not send the preparatory code to our agents."

The NKVD Chairman, missing the point, drew breath to remonstrate.

Stalin held up his hand and with a lightness inappropriate for the moment, he added, "Initiate Napoleon immediately."

Destiny is no matter of chance. It is a matter of choice. It is not a thing to be waited for; it is a thing to be achieved.

William Jennings Bryan

Chapter 9 – THE RELOCATION

0235hrs Friday, 6th July 1945, The Château du Haut-Kœnigsbourg, French Alsace.

Colonel Frisson had been remarkably efficient and organised the segregation of the seven selected German officers. It would have been preferable had he exercised some thought, as his efficiency obviously telegraphed the impending departure of Knocke and the others to every German in the camp. Initially, rumours of trial and execution abounded, but a message was smuggled out through an easily bribed French-Alsatian soldier.

The prisoners were relieved to hear that the seven were not harmed and were just relocating to another base for further debriefing.

The interview between Knocke and Lavalle had taken place on the Sunday; those with Knocke's named candidates were satisfactorily concluded over the next four days. Perversely, the French had chosen Biarritz as the name for their symposium as it was not associated with Alsace, which was the symposiums actual location. Perhaps because it would all appear wholly French if, heaven forbid, news of it came out.

And so it was that Knocke and his comrades found themselves en route by truck to a secret location within Alsace, not to Biarritz in the south-west of France. It was the early morning of Friday 6th July 1945. The significance of that date brought a wry smile to some of the faces in the back of that truck. Two years previously, many of the group had been involved in the bitter combat in and around the Kursk Salient and each man wrestled with memories of comrades lost in those dreadful days.

They passed incognito through the growing dawn, crossing from Germany into Alsace, on their way to a sleepy

100

little hollow called Orschwiller and their meeting with destiny and Colloque Biarritz, at the Château du Haut-Kœnigsbourg.

Elsewhere in Europe, three other such groups were assembling in comparable secrecy, in and around Hamburg, Paderborn and Frankfurt. All three comprising similaly tried and tested men who had also agreed to provide the unique services of the secret symposiums. The first two locations housed German officers of similar stature and rank to those assigned to 'Biarritz'.

Frankfurt was different, graced with General grade officers of all nations and concerning itself with higher matters.

However, all four were dedicated to the single purpose; that of educating the Western Armies in the fine art of fighting their erstwhile allies, the Red Army.

I would rather have a mind opened by wonder than one closed by belief.

Gerry Spence

Chapter 10 – THE KAMERADEN

0720hrs Saturday, 7th July 1945, The Château du Haut-Kœnigsbourg, French Alsace.

The previous day, the lorry had taken them straight to the Château, where all seven were subjected to an intense medical examination, conducted sympathetically for a change. All were given vitamin supplements and, in one case, some penicillin tablets had been prescribed to address a throat infection. Each was then afforded the opportunity of a hot bath or shower, an opportunity that was universally accepted.

The rest of the day had seen the group casually escorted around their impressive new home and given the full guided tour by Patrice Dubois, a young officer of the French Naval commandos. During the tour, he also pointed out the strengths of the security arrangements put in place for the symposium. None of the group failed to notice the very obvious fact that a considerable amount of the security faced inwards and was for an entirely different, but not unexpected reason. None of them had any doubt that was part of the purpose of this "impromptu" tour.

In the northeast corner of the lower courtyard, silent kennels caught everyone's eye, for German soldiers love their dogs and this group was no exception. The four large and obviously recently built pens, held three German Shepherd dogs of considerable size. One hound was obviously out being exercised, or doing its duty. Resisting the urge to approach closer, the group moved on to the Little Bastion.

Fig#2- Main plan of the Château

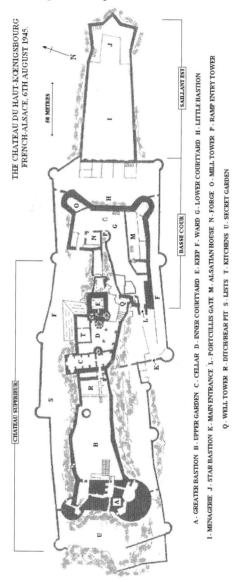

THE CHATEAU DU HAUT-KŒNIGSBOURG
FRENCH-ALSACE, 6TH AUGUST 1945.

50 METRES

N

CHATEAU SUPERIEUR

BASSE COUR

SAILLANT EST

A - GREATER BASTION B - UPPER GARDEN C - CELLAR D - INNER COURTYARD E - KEEP F - WARD G - LOWER COURTYARD H - LITTLE BASTION
I - MENAGERIE J - STAR BASTION K - MAIN ENTRANCE L - PORTCULLIS GATE M - ALSATIAN HOUSE N - FORGE O - MILL TOWER P - RAMP ENTRY TOWER
Q - WELL TOWER R - DITCH/BEAR PIT S - LISTS T - KITCHENS U - SECRET GARDEN

The Château was impressive as a structure in any case, many different levels built into the solid rock on the site of the old fortress that had overseen the area, in one form or another, since the 12th Century. Standing on the eastern edge of the summit, at a height of over seven hundred and fifty metres, it was the dominating feature for many miles around. The narrow approach twisted and turned, by both military design and constructional engineering requirements. Indeed, the previous evening they were twice aware that their transport grated along rock or wood on sharp turns and narrow squeezes.

It sat on a stark promontory, open to the elements, but that was a godsend on hot summer's days like today, when breezes ventilated the Château and created a very pleasant environment. From positions around the battlements and especially from the imposing high tower, there were all-round expansive views across the Alsace plain.

The Château was strategically positioned, so had seen its fair share of bloodshed and had fallen to assault on more than one occasion. Not that any assault was a possibility any more, with peace in Europe, but one hundred and twenty aggressive looking and well-armed French commandos would, in any case, call a halt to any belligerent incursion.

During the Thirty Years War, a Swedish army had laid siege to, taken and razed the castle to the ground, since when it had fallen into unoccupied decay for over two hundred years, until efforts were made to rebuild it in 1882, which failed for lack of funds.

The city of Selestat, which owned the Château, offered it to the German monarchy and so it was that the impressive reconstruction of the present Château was started at the turn of the century, at the behest of the Kaiser Wilhelm II. That was probably one reason why the French nation did not take it to their hearts so readily and which national reticence made it an ideal secret location for 'Biarritz'?

Their hosts had provided a veritable mountain of American "Chesterfield", "Camel" and "Lucky Strike" cigarettes, as well as 'Gauloise' and 'Gitanes', which were seized upon by everyone. A nice touch were the quality Colibri lighters, each man's name perfectly engraved in the solid silver cartouche. A splendid evening meal of venison and light conversation, followed by an early night, was about all they could manage.

Fig#3 - Château first floor plan

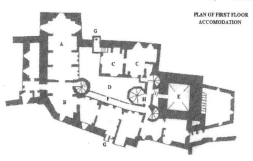

THE CHATEAU DU HAUT-KŒNIGSBOURG
FRENCH-ALSACE, 6TH AUGUST 1945.

PLAN OF FIRST FLOOR
ACCOMODATION

A - ARMOURY   B - TROPHY ROOM   C - MARSHALL'S CHAMBERS   D - INNER COURTYARD   E - KEEP
F - WOODEN GALLERY   G - LATRINES   H - OCTAGONAL STAIRS

Comfortable and content with his small medieval style bedroom, complete with four-poster bed and embroidered wall hangings, it took little time for Knocke to undress, clean his uniform and swiftly descend into his dreams. Woken gently from the best sleep he had experienced for months, if not years, Ernst-August washed and shaved at an old wooden wash stand that looked like it might have accompanied one of the previous occupants on the early Crusades. Then, as the new French orderly had requested, he made his way to the dining room for breakfast.

Immediately losing his bearings, he took a wrong turn from his bedroom, the former Empress's Chamber and found himself descending the spiral stairs, before being rescued by a passing orderly, who directed him along the first level walkway, to climb a different spiral staircase leading to the dining room. On arrival at the top of the stairs, he greeted two of his comrades warmly, immediately noticing that their uniforms had been replaced by civilian suits of a superior cut in a fetching dark grey and pinstripe, which, if not a perfect fit, were both close enough. Yet again, he had been left with his uniform. Both men lacked enough meat on their bones to make the suits sit perfectly, but if the standard of hospitality continued, then that would soon be remedied.

Fig#4 - Château second floor plan

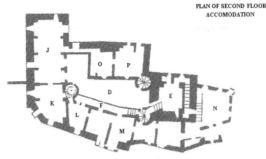

THE CHATEAU DU HAUT-KŒNIGSBOURG
FRENCH-ALSACE, 6TH AUGUST 1945.

PLAN OF SECOND FLOOR
ACCOMODATION

J - KAISER'S HALL [DINING ROOM] K - LORRAINE CHAMBER L - CHAPEL M - DRAWING ROOM N - STUDY
O - EMPRESS'S ANTECHAMBER P - EMPRESS'S CHAMBER F - WOODEN GALLERY D - INNER COURTYARD E - KEEP

0857hrs, Saturday, 7th July 1945, Château du Haut-Kœnigsbourg, French Alsace.

And so it was that the group came together on the morning of 7th July, refreshed and more than ready to enquire as to the purpose of that which they had committed to. Unlike the previous evening, when the galleried dining room belonged solely to them, the flags and the orderlies, they were now joined by a stranger clad in an impressively cut lounge suit.

Seated at the head of the long wooden table was an imposingly large Frenchman. He was deep in discussion with Wolfgang Schmidt, Knocke's former Chief of Staff, until recently an Obersturmbannfuhrer in the 2nd SS Panzer Division. Another comrade from Das Reich walked in from the stairs, distanced respectfully behind Ernst, a position Dr Jurgen

Von Arnesen had occupied on many occasions when he served as a Sturmbannfuhrer in the Panzer-Grenadiere's of Knocke's division.

The Frenchman, solidly built and seemingly about forty-five, rose and bore down upon Knocke, extending his hand and speaking in accented German.

"Herr Knocke, welcome. Georges De Walle, at your service. I trust you slept well?"

"I slept very well, thank you, Monsieur De Walle".

The hands shaken, certainly warmly for the Frenchman's part at least, the ballet of first introductions took place.

"This is Von Arnesen... and this is Rettlinger," Knocke first motioned to his right and then indicated the second officer he had met at the top of the stairs. "I have little doubt you know that anyway and are intimate with every personal detail of this assembly".

More handshakes.

"Gentlemen, welcome. Forgive me, Herr Knocke, but you are, of course, quite right. No introductions are necessary, save my own... and I will do so properly after we have eaten."

"Please sit and enjoy breakfast" and Knocke was ushered to sit opposite Schmidt at De Walle's left-hand.

On his way to the seat, Knocke acknowledged every member of the group.

An orderly appeared by Knocke's right hand, waiting for some indication of his requirements. "I can recommend the cooked breakfast here. The English may be awful at most things culinary, but they do have the right idea when it comes to mornings, not that most of my countrymen would agree."

A modest ripple spread through the ensemble, indicating that everyone was, if not totally at ease, sufficiently relaxed to recognise a weak attempt at humour.

A simple nod to the orderly and the preference was relayed to the cooks ensconced in the newly created facility crammed into the Spartan lower kitchens.

"My apologies, Herr Knocke, but for some reason your orderly could not bring himself to remove your uniform last night. He has been replaced and a comfortable suit is waiting in your bedroom at this moment."

Knocke looked up at the Frenchman and considered his response.

"I would wish to retain my uniform for appropriate occasions obviously, but am happy to wear a suit, if we must all do so."

"I did not mean to remove your uniform and not return it. I meant for its cleaning, Herr Knocke. All uniforms will be returned to you, as I have no instructions to the contrary. Here there is no dress code of uniform or non-uniform," and with a chuckle, "Although it intrigues me what would happen if the intended meetings of this symposium go ahead as planned and convene with all of you wearing the uniforms of our former enemy. I can see that adding a certain edge to proceedings. I will think on that some more".

"In that you have most of us at a disadvantage… Monsieur?" The word hung there, like the enquiry it was.

"In good time, Herr Knocke, all in good time. Please enjoy your food."

As if by magic plates appeared before the ensemble, containing everything they had ever heard fitted into an English breakfast, except four times as much. Clearly, this Château was not affected by rationing. Coiled sausage with the girth of a bazooka, sliced bacon just the right side of crispy, stacked high and covered with two huge fried eggs, grilled tomato, deep fried baguette and huge mushrooms, cooked whole and laid on the plate with their caps upwards and filled with sliced fried potatoes. The smell was incredible and De Walle consumed his avidly, as did every officer at the table, with scarcely anything spoken apart from a word of pleasure here, a word of agreement there.

The plate clean, save for a smear of grease and yolk, Knocke leant back and, dabbing his mouth with a silk napkin, stifled a belch, a feat similarly attempted but abjectly failed by Amon Treschow, immediately to his left. The loud bass note penetrated every recess of the grand Kaiser's Hall.

"Typical Luftwaffe," ventured Knocke with a grin, flipping his lighter and drawing heavily on a camel, which was followed by less delicate ribbing from the rest of the group. Treschow, ex-Hauptmann, was a popular man amongst his peers, mainly because he was slightly mad, or at least that was the considered opinion of his friends and the Luftwaffe doctors who had tried to ground him since early 1943. More accurately, the doctors had considered him totally mad! He somehow managed to dodge them and continued to fly combat missions in a ground-attack role specialty that claimed every other pilot in his squadron and all their replacements. What Treschow didn't know about that witches art was not worth knowing, which was why Knocke had asked for him.

Next to him was Jakob Matthaus, the quiet anti-tank gunner. The former Major had huge experience against Soviet rolling tank assaults during his service in the German Army's premiere division "Großdeutschland".

Seated opposite him was Bruno Rettlinger, former Sturmbannfuhrer of the 6th SS Gebirgsjager, who had intimate knowledge of cold weather combat and, in particular, dealing with Soviet ski troops in harsh arctic conditions. He was the biggest character in the group and "DerBo", as he was universally known, gave Treschow the most ribbing for his "pig-like manners". However, the deadpan delivery and precise timing of Matthaus's line "maybe pigs can fly after all" hit the right note with everyone, especially DerBo.

To Rettlinger's right was the youngest of the group, Walter Olbricht, a skilled army Hauptmann of engineers. An officer whose pre-war talents extended to the design and construction of public works and whose operational war experience covered the total destruction of public works and anything else he put his mind to. Alas, this included his left arm, lost in a premature explosion caused by sub-standard explosive, during his failed attempt to destroy a bridge over the Gniloy Tikich River, during the Tscherkassy pocket escape.

He was also Treschow's deliverer from Rettlinger's wit, when he drew attention to the fact that DerBo's moustache contained enough breakfast for a mid-morning snack. It didn't, but no one cared.

Von Arnesen, ex-SS-Sturmbannfuhrer of Das Reich's Panzer-Grenadieres and Doctor of History, completed the

109

group, the sole non-smoker, although he had, of course, grabbed his share of cigarettes through habit.

De Walle slowly stubbed out his own Gitanes Mais, stretched and focussed on the next part of the day.

"Gentlemen," sitting stiffly upright and with a pause to permit the humour to fall away, "To business".

"My name is Georges De Walle and you might by now have guessed that I am from Alsace. My rank is given as Colonel in the Army of France, but you will all understand in a short time that I have not been on a battlefield as you know it for many a year and that my field of expertise resides in other, darker places." As befitted his present calling, the lies slipped easily from his mouth.

"The name of my organisation is very complicated to remember, so most of us still think of ourselves as Deux's. That is to say, the former Deuxieme Bureau." He left that titbit to hang in the air for a while and it was Rettlinger, still wiping his moustache with his napkin, who took up the unspoken thoughts of those present.

"Military Intelligence?"

"Just so, mein Herr."

De Walle stood and moved to one of the huge square stone columns that lined the dining room and paused, which silence was punctuated by a sudden soft straining sound from one of the huge chandeliers hanging in the ornate ceiling.

"I know you have been given certain assurances by Colonel Lavalle, Herr Knocke. These assurances I confirm, here and now, and on the basis of this previous agreement, you have come here and brought your comrades with you. Colonel Frisson informs me that you have not confided any part of this in these gentlemen. He also informs me that you resisted his attempts to find out what exactly was behind the removal of German officers from his camp."

De Walle could not bring himself to criticise a French officer in front of Germans, but he considered Frisson a fool and an ex-Vichy fool at that. That the Colonel was always watched went without saying.

"From what I have heard this morning, these men are keen to discover what exactly it is that they have followed you

110

so blindly into." Knocke made to comment but de Walle continued quickly, moving back to his place, but not sitting.

"Please, Herr Knocke, understand that these men have followed you here on trust and respect for you as an officer and man. That is to be admired and I salute all of you." A simple nod of the head to the group gave sufficient pause for De Walle to sip his coffee before continuing.

"There will be no written contract between us and officially this group will never exist. The commandos stationed here are to provide complete security for this site, as well as to ensure that all of you remain here to fulfil the terms of this agreement. Once the symposium is complete, each of you will be returned to any part of Germany, or Austria, or actually anywhere you choose within reason and given every assistance to start a new life away from any stigma or investigation. That is our promise to you and your presence here is taken as agreement to all that will now come to pass. Your faith in Herr Knocke's judgement is not faulty, I can assure you, gentlemen. I must stress that we continue on the strict understanding that this symposium is never spoken of outside this facility and remains a state secret."

Looks were exchanged by all except Knocke, who remained firmly focussed mentally on De Walle's words, understanding precisely what lay behind them.

"Your purpose is to employ the expertise you have acquired in battle against the Red Army and devolve that to allied officers who will visit here. Once the other two gentlemen that have been asked for arrive here, this symposium will consist of nine former German officers," to Knocke, the 'former' stung badly, "Who have expertise in every field of combat, most of it hard won on the Eastern Front.

A click of his fingers and an orderly appeared with nine blue-card folders, each named for one of the men present. Knocke looked at the two folders that lay unallocated in front of De Walle's seat. The names of Kuno Von Hardegen, until recently Oberstleutnant of the Panzertruppen, and Christian Menzel, former artillery regiment Oberst, cousin to Knocke's wife, were plain to see. Schmidt processed the names immediately and nodded lightly in acknowledgement to

111

Knocke, even though his precise mind had already seen the names on two Colibri lighters waiting for the new arrivals.

"Please read the outline carefully. You will obviously wish to decide whether you intend to become part of this enterprise in the first instance. If you wish to return to your former surroundings, we will do that immediately. If you wish to remain, then please look at how you feel this group can address the stated requirements and, on my return, we can discuss how best to undertake this exercise. I will leave you alone for now as I have business elsewhere. I hope that your two absent comrades will be here by the time I get back. Unless there are any immediate questions gentlemen?"

A silent chorus of shaken heads was sufficient to excuse de Walle from the room, as each man immersed himself in the document that outlined the remit of Colloque Biarritz. Again, lighters summoned forth flame and the dining room became a fug of blue smoke.

Even though he was aware of its content previously, Ernst was still the last to finish reading and he looked up a number of expectant faces, with the exception of Von Arnesen, whose doctorate in history drove him to examine the Hohenzollern and Hapsburg standards hanging on each stone column. The fact that the Château had once been known as 'Staufenberg' was something Von Arnesen felt he would keep to himself, for the moment. It did not seem appropriate given, what was about to be proposed.

As they had waited for Knocke to finish, the others relaxed and took in the surroundings, the ornate wood panelling, painted walls and ceilings, each eye eventually being drawn to the ceiling and its central feature, an Imperial Eagle.

The sharper eyes were able to make out the inscription 'Gott mit uns' in the aureole surrounding the eagle's head.

A polite cough brought all back from their reveries and to the business in hand.

"Well, Meine Herren, now you know. We are here to play teacher to the men that conquered our nation. Yes, Jurgen", he held his hand up to silence the obvious comment forming on the lips of the returning Von Arnesen, "We all know that the Western Allies did not and neither could they

112

have done, but that is how they view themselves. And that is the crux of this as I see it. They are not a threat to our Fatherland, not in the way that the communist is... and this proposal, this symposium, this... Colloque, gives us an opportunity to instil some of our fighting values in the Western Allies, values that stood all of us in good stead during the difficult years in Russia."

He stood very carefully and walked to the window next to the fireplace. With his back to the group and oblivious to the countryside of Alsace spread out before him, Knocke carefully tugged at his tunic and straightened his uniform, before turning to continue.

"When this matter was first put to me, I had little time to consider, but my inner feeling, my blood feeling, was that it was a good thing to do for Germany. I have had much more time to consider this than you have, obviously, but I promised not to reveal the nature of this group before the correct time. My apologies."

"We have known each other as soldiers in troubled times and relied upon each other on more than one occasion, either face to face or," he acknowledged Treschow, "More distantly, but equally professionally reliant."

"I am wholly comfortable with doing this and believe it will serve our country better than rotting in some prison camp, regardless of the route that history takes from this point."

Around him, positive noises came from every man.

"However, think on this, kameraden. Some of you have fought these Western Allies. How do you think they would do against our communist opponents?"

That question was left hanging in the air, as each man mentally wrote off the Western Allies in a direct confrontation with the Russians.

"Indeed, menschen, indeed," said Knocke, calling a halt to their imaginative mental destruction of the western allied armies, "So it would be much in Germany's best interest for our 'new' allies to be better prepared to fight the mutual enemy. If we can use what we have learned and preserve what is left of our Fatherland, then we can only be serving our country and honouring our fallen comrades."

De Walle, listening to the exchange from the ornate wooden musicians' gallery, smiled to himself. His estimation of Knocke was correct and France had her Colloque for sure. He would not need Dubois to undertake the clean up that was the contingency for non-compliance. He quickly wondered if any of the Germans had considered such a possibility.

"You can see from that brief that our hosts desire a formal structure prepared for examination by 1400 tomorrow." Even though everyone had read the document, it didn't stop a few knowing grins being exchanged, especially those who had worked alongside Knocke before.

"Kameraden", the punch in that made each man shoot to attention, quite as Knocke intended.

"There is no pressure to stay or to involve yourselves in this. I will remain and undertake this, because I believe I serve my country as well as I can at this time. Please consider this and inform me of your decision as soon as possible."

With the exception of Rettlinger, each man's heels clicked automatically and each man's eyes confirmed his commitment when contact was made. Except Rettlinger, the only man there, other than Knocke, who had fought the Western Allies in recent months, which period had seen him bury both his best friend and his brother-in-law, killed by American artillery and aircraft respectively.

"Ah yes, Bruno, for you this is a more difficult commitment. You must think it through more, perhaps?"

"Not necessary, Standartenfuhrer. I was just thinking of Hans and Josef and not fully concentrating on your words. My apologies, sir," and Rettlinger followed suit, clicking his heels, once more under control.

De Walle risked a look down around the stonework and made a mental note to watch that one very carefully.

In the background, the sound of a light vehicle approaching grew in volume, but not enough to cause Knocke to raise his voice.

"Then let us have coffee and start to plan for the work ahead. Danke, kameraden. You have your symposium, Colonel."

De Walle heard the words and automatically looked down through the ornate balustrade, straight into the steely eyes of Knocke.

The Frenchman nodded and made another mental note. Lavalle's briefing document was right. Never, ever, underestimate Knocke.

As coffee was taken, the two missing members of the group arrived and were ushered into the Kaiser's Hall.

Both men were warmly welcomed, given their folders and time to read them. Cigarettes appeared again and were greedily consumed by the newcomers. As they studied carefully, they occasionally paused, either to look at one of the ensemble or to consume one of the array of sandwiches that had been set before them. When they were done, they listened. Knocke's obvious commitment to the programme, as with the others present, was sufficient for them to agree involvement.

The requested writing materials arrived with the new officers and the symposium started to put together the way it would work. Lunch was taken in snatched bites in between discussions, as each group of two officers wrestled with their own issues, as dictated by Knocke, who moved easily between the groups. Once one group established a programme, it was critiqued by another group, usually over a cigarette, until slowly a format took shape that satisfied the military requirements of the Western Allies and the professional requirements of the Germans.

It was mid-afternoon when de Walle ventured into the room to find out how much progress had been made. His question drew a familiar wry smile.

"We have a format on which we are agreed, Colonel. One that fits your requirements, although we have felt it necessary to alter some matters and have included Kreigspiels as essential learning opportunities for all participants."

De Walle smiled at the inclusion of the famous German wargame training.

"The training package we present will ensure your commanders leave here with valuable knowledge, in the event that our enemy, our mutual enemy, attempts to spread communism even further across Europe."

In his hand Knocke held a modest sheaf of paper, neatly hand-written, outlining the format. De Walle was surprised and actually checked his watch to confirm that in just over five hours these Germans claimed to have sorted out the entire Symposium. That was singularly impressive, provided it was fit for purpose, he cautioned himself, although somehow he never doubted that it would be precisely what had been intended, when the concept of the symposia was first considered last Christmas.

"How long will it take you to present this, so I can make a judgement, Herr Knocke?"

Without stopping to consider his answer, Knocke indicated seven minutes, but did permit a subtle, but none the less ,very apparent grin to alter his face.

"Impressive, mein Herr, very impressive" said De Walle genuinely and again underlined his mental note on not underestimating the soldier in front of him.

Another look at his watch reinforced a decision he had just reached.

"I suggest that we take a break now so that you gentlemen may enjoy the grounds, or take some rest. It is now 1512, so I suggest that we enjoy our dinner, which I will arrange for 1900 sharp and then, once we are rested and comfortable, the presentation may be made."

There were no dissenters and so, with their official business done, the group visibly relaxed.

"I will arrange for Dubois to take you two gentlemen," indicating Von Hardegen and Menzel, "And show you around our little Château. One more thing, Herr Knocke. If I may take the document, I will arrange for our clerking service to type it up and have copies ready for 2000 hours." The papers changed hands without a word.

"I will have the armoury set up for our after-dinner work. I think that will suit us nicely. Until dinner, gentlemen"

"Until then, Colonel."

116

Once De Walle reached the 'clerks' office, within the middle level of the Château, he sat on a desk and started to read the document and without comment passed each page in turn to the stunning woman sat at the typewriter, who swiftly transformed the written word into roman text in carboned triplicate.

Anne-Marie Valois was a tall brunette, twenty-six, extremely and classically beautiful, as well as being the deadliest shot with a pistol De Walle had ever met. Typist was a role she slipped into solely because she could type, whereas her mind had all the sharpness of a successful intelligence operative and her physical abilities in matters other than typing were impressive. Like all four senior members of 'Deux' who worked in the Château, she was cleared for any secret of the state and she knew where all the skeletons were buried. She had even buried some of them herself.

Valois' weapon of choice was the Walther P38 German army handgun but, unlike most pistol specialists De Walle knew, she spent time with all different types, learning the subtleties of each in turn.

By the time he had finished reading, he was convinced that the symposium would have great value, if the attendees permitted themselves to be taught of course.

Anne-Marie, publically his personal secretary and privately, de facto bodyguard, had similarly finished, but repeated the exercise until six originals and twelve carbon copies lay in a neat pile, ready for their respective destinations. As she worked, De Walle speedily typed out his own letter on an adjacent machine, matching the woman for speed and accuracy.

When both had finished, the room was suddenly silent.

Valois arranged her copies and placed them on de Walle's desk.

"Impressive."

117

She patted them gently and moved to the stand where she poured a Perrier for herself and her boss.

De Walle could not help but agree with Valois' simple assessment.

"Very much so. However, on another matter, Rettlinger may not be as committed as the others. Let everyone know please, Anne-Marie."

"Yes, Chef."

Four typed originals and eight carbons were placed in an envelope, complete with the hand-written original, ready for delivery to the armoury. One triplicate set was then given its own envelope and also included was De Walle's letter, all then handed to a dispatch rider, summoned specifically for the purpose. He knew his destination and so immediately left the Château, safe in the knowledge that, his Sergeant permitting, he would enjoy his girlfriend in Baden-Baden later that evening.

The final set of documents went into a small but impressively secure safe that had recently been fitted in the same office.

With the carbons in his hand, De Walle strode down the Hexagonal Stairs into the inner courtyard area and approached a small brazier, burning lazily adjacent to the stone water cistern. Within a second, they were alight and would never give up the secrets they contained.

Great ability develops and reveals itself increasingly with every new assignment.

Balthasar Gracian

Chapter 11 – THE SYMPOSIUM

2000hrs Saturday, 7th July 1945, The Château du Haut-Kœnigsbourg, French Alsace.

Dinner was excellent and the symposium members had eaten heartily, as well as availing themselves of a pleasant bottle of Edelzwicker. More than a bottle, if the truth was known, although Knocke had but one glass. As the dining room was cleared around them, the party moved downstairs into the armoury and eased themselves into the comfortable chairs arranged there. Around them was the paraphernalia of wars past, from halberds and pikes, swords and crossbows, through to uniforms and suits of armour.

De Walle took his allotted place, sitting at the front.

Knocke stood, as imposing as always in his black panzer uniform and waited for everyone to settle. The evening sunlight softly illuminated the stained-glass window at his back, its armour-clad figure overseeing proceedings.

"Meine Herren, you may smoke if you wish." A suitable pause later, he launched into his delivery from memory. "I will begin. Colloque Biarritz is a programme devised to provide experienced input on Red Army tactics, across a range of disciplines, to officers of the Allied armies up to and including, Brigadier-General rank. The brief stated that the requirement was to deliver as much knowledge on Soviet tactics, specifically relating to ground combat and Soviet response and behaviour in combat as is possible in five days, to a group of allied officers, not exceeding eighteen. To do that successfully, we are expected to deliver lectures." Knocke's voice took on the slightest of edges. "This is most unsatisfactory as a standalone method of learning and, in our view, must be accompanied by practical exercises, or Kriegspiels. In order to focus the candidates on the task to hand, it is proposed to clarify their learning needs and overcome their natural reluctance to accept input from such as us, by conducting a gaming exercise. This will make each candidate more open to the concept that he has something to learn here. That is important."

And for the first time, Knocke displayed a small element of humour, albeit laced with the certainty that comes with absolute confidence in your own and others ability, "We are assuming our victory in the first round of Kriegspiel obviously".

De Walle suddenly felt everyone focus on him but controlled himself to an acknowledging raised eyebrow and no more reaction than that.

"The specifications of four different all-arms scenarios will be available as soon as we are in possession of military maps of any area you choose. We suggest that we are given maps relative to the regions of origin of the candidates attending, again to help focus their minds on the task in hand."

"We recommend that attending officers have a balanced skill and qualification range and definitely come from a good balance of arms. For example, it would not be advisable to have fourteen artillery officers and four from supply attend this course on the same cycle."

A gentle nodding of De Walle's head indicated that had already been considered, but he logged the thought as it would not hurt to confirm it.

"We will then undertake a rolling programme of lectures, delivering to two to three candidates at a time, each of us dealing with Soviet tactics and doctrine in our area of specialist knowledge and, of course, how to defeat them. Each is a stand-alone lecture, so the order they are given in should not matter, therefore ensuring we can all be employed at the same time, giving more time for other matters.

"To clarify," and proceeding without visible thought, Knocke reeled off everyone's remits, 'Schmidt – Soviet divisional and corps set-up, logistics and control, Dr Von Arnesen – Soviet infantry tactics, Treschow – Soviet air force ground attack and close air-support tactics, Matthaus – Soviet tank tactics as applicable to infantry, Rettlinger – Soviet

120

infantry cold-weather tactics, use and capability of ski and mountain troops, Von Hardegen- Soviet tank and anti-tank tactics, Menzel – Soviet artillery tactics and myself – Soviet military weaknesses. There is an absence in that list of a delivery on Soviet paratroops. Unless you possess significant intelligence to the contrary, it is our understanding that most Red Army paratrooper units that were jump qualified have committed to land action and can therefore be discounted. It is an obvious omission from our brief. In any case, we do not have the knowledge base here on that subject. If that needs to be addressed, we can supply the name of a suitable addition to this group." Another quick note made it onto De Walle's mental list.

"Perhaps lecture is too strong a word, as this will be done as an informal face to face discussion and dissection of the enemy's methods of war."

A subtle change in Knocke's posture clearly illustrated the importance the man placed on his next words.

"It is absolutely essential that discipline is maintained during the symposium and the absence of assurances in your documentation is noted, We request that each and every candidate is made to understand that we undertake this as volunteers through choice and have not been coerced. Also that our reasonable requests should be observed and all members should be correctly treated. We accept that it would be too much to ask for rank structure here."

Knocke paused and waited for an indication of understanding.

Very carefully, De Walle spoke to the wider audience.

"Every allied officer attending this Colloque, regardless of his rank or nationality, will be informed that he is required to treat you and your comrades with full courtesy and afford you the respect due to proven fellow professionals. Neither you nor I, gentlemen, would expect to give or receive less."

It was a fair answer and so Knocke proceeded.

"The specifics of each officer's lecture have been discussed already and we estimate a maximum of two and a half hour's for any session, including questions and answers."

Looking around at his assembled comrades in a way that challenged them to fail to measure up to that, Knocke went on.

"Whilst we have already moved forward with the lectures, as you will have seen from the initial document, we need more time to complete in full detail. The final specifics of those lectures will be available in hand-written form by 1300hrs tomorrow, but we understand that your requirements may not necessarily be those we anticipate and so change may occur, once the symposium has had the opportunity to review."

"Given that candidates arrive by 1000hrs on the first morning, we can safely assume that we will be able to commence by 1030 hrs. This permits an introduction to the aims of the symposium and to the personnel running it, namely us."

Again, De Walle noticed the slightest change of posture as the German spoke.

"We request that we are permitted to wear our national uniform for this initial portion, political insignia removed, of course, as we see it as a useful tool to focus the minds of those attending, establishing our own credentials, as well as adding a certain edge to the afternoon's Kriegspiel. In that regard, we have prepared a listing of each officer's decorations and uniform requirements, included in the package as addendum A."

Knocke drove swiftly on from this startling group request, in such a way as it was very obvious that it was a considered and non-negotiable statement of requirement. De Walle had read it earlier, but still found himself perturbed by it.

"Dinner will be taken early and the candidates will be debriefed immediately afterwards."

"The next two days will be intensive lectures, with reasonable rest periods in between."

A dry tickly cough gave a moment's enforced pause.

"The fourth day will be dedicated to a detailed re-run of the Kriegspiel. We will employ standard Soviet doctrine, as taught to our candidates and see what they have learned. Again that will be heavily de-briefed."

Once more, the humour surfaced. "This time we would expect your officers to be much improved and victory would not be taken for granted".

Knocke theatrically gestured for a drink. A sip on the water, instantly offered up, gave him an opportunity to leave that comment dangling in front of De Walle.

"Danke, Menzel. On the final day we will address specifics issues that will have come to our attention during the week, as each man will bring his own special needs and issues to this symposium."

"Generally, we consider it important that we and the candidates are permitted to mix openly at all times, once the initial Kriegspiel is completed, for meals, refreshment breaks and any off-duty times. We feel it is important that no alcohol is consumed until dinner and not even then if, for some reason, there is business scheduled for afterwards. It is accepted that there may be displays of bad feeling linked to the recent war, but they must be met head on and not be allowed to interfere with the symposium's objectives. If a candidate becomes so disruptive that we ask for his removal, we fully expect that officer to be immediately relieved and dealt with appropriately by his own commander."

"As you have requested our feedback on your personnel, a full report on the ability of each man, as well as analysis of his performance during the symposium, will be made available to you by Saturday at 1300hrs. This will contain individual comments from each of the officers here, relative to their own area of expertise and my overall assessment."

"For this to be of value, these reports will be wholly accurate and not dressed to prevent damage to an individual's personal feelings or professionalism. They will also be based solely upon performance, not character or conduct during the week, unless either of those have a direct effect upon performance. We would expect to receive similar reports on our own performance from those attending."

"Saturday afternoons should be used to critique the symposiums content and structure, to highlight areas of improvement and issues for change."

Looking at the Frenchman, Knocke deliberately emphasised his next sentence.

"In order for this symposium to run successfully for the long term, we request that we be permitted Sundays without official duties and, in essence, make that non-negotiable."

A wry smile and a nod of acceptance were sufficient. Being French, the concept of only one day off a week was horrifying. De Walle and his superiors had anticipated a full weekend of leisure.

"A detailed timetable of symposium events has been compiled and is included in the documentation before you, labelled as addendum B."

"As a personal request by four of my officers, at addendum C, you will find a list of German nationals who are relatives. We would consider it an act of friendship if you could attempt to establish the well-being and whereabouts of those named."

This had not been in the document De Walle had previously read and he was not ready for the words, nor for that matter, the list offered to him by Schmidt. The proffered paper was accepted with the faintest of nods.

With a small, but none the less noticeable exhalation of relief, Knocke concluded.

"Danke. Colonel?"

"Indeed Herr Knocke, indeed," and De Walle stood and moved slowly to Knocke's side.

"Gentlemen, your efforts so far have proved to me that the right men are here to do this job. On your request for family information, we will do what we can, my word on it."

"Your outline for the symposium," he flourished the document and bowed his head swiftly in acknowledgement, "Is thus far excellent and nothing that you have laid out gets anything but approval from me, with two possible exceptions. On the matter of uniform, that spectre raised itself the other evening and I have given it some thought. I am not a military man, so my thinking may be flawed, but I can see some value in it, as obviously can you. Others may feel differently, so I will seek advice from a higher authority on that one. On the matter of mixing, I can see pitfalls there, ones that you will most certainly appreciate. However, I understand the purpose of that proposal and can see additional benefits, provided there is no provocation by either side, intended or otherwise. Again I will seek others input before we decide upon that."

"Everything else here I am empowered to approve, as far as I can, but understand that a copy of your documentation is presently in the hands of the man that will ultimately accept your proposals, or he may request…err, yes, request change of you". The momentary stumble was caused by the mental image of the French General requesting defeated German prisoners to do something he would order anyone else to do on a whim. If it came, it would not be a request and, judging by the faces, not one of the Germans thought otherwise.

"Thank you for your efforts, Gentlemen… and if I may," indicating to a waiting orderly, who had somehow appeared at the absolutely correct moment, "I ask you all to accompany me back to the Kaiser's Hall."

The company took the short journey up the spiral stairs to the dining room, where a silver tray, glasses and bottle lay awaiting their arrival, all twinkling in the light of the roaring fire that warmed the room splendidly.

"A toast to our venture, one for the benefit of both our countries." De Walle grabbed the bottle displaying the label to everyone close by. "A fine bottle of cognac, which the concierge here assures me was laid up on completion of the renovations in 1908. I had to threaten life imprisonment for him and his family to secure the rights of consumption on the contents obviously".

A faint wave of laughter spread through all, although the comment served to remind everyone of the power of the affable Frenchman.

Glasses filled and raised, De Walle ventured the toast and was immediately followed by a chorus from the others.

"Biarritz!"

Cognac bit into throats, warmed bellies and the glasses smashed into the fireplace as the tradition toast was taken, a toast that marked the start of something that was to have more significance than anyone could ever have imagined.

*No matter how enmeshed a commander becomes in the
elaboration of his own thoughts, it is sometimes necessary to
take the enemy into account.*

Winston Churchill

Chapter 12 – THE PROVOCATIONS

1250hrs Monday, 9th July 1945, The Kremlin, Moscow, USSR.

During the German War, the work done at Bletchley Park in England had been extremely useful. The Germans had no idea that the Allies could read their private communications and that fact alone had shortened the war considerably.

Of course, the Soviet Union had its moles. Some had been motivated by a sense of equality; in that what was known by some should be known by all fighting the German. Others were politically inclined towards the Motherland anyway. One particularly productive source worshipped on the altar of the pound.

Information filtered out to the Soviet Union and, on occasion, made a major difference.

Whatever the motivation of each mole, since the surrender there had been a huge cut in message traffic and what had been sent had been worth comparatively little. It was with some surprise that, having been summoned to Stalin's office, Beria should be confronted with something of considerable interest originating from that sleepy corner of rural England.

"Well, Comrade Marshal?"

Pekunin, the GRU officer who had brought the message to Stalin, remained impassive as the head of the NKVD floundered in front of him.

"We knew for certain that some German Generals were being courted in some way, as was announced to the military group some while back. Apple Pie is the name they use, as you will recall. However, my own sources have no definite knowledge of these groups Comrade General Secretary. Rumours abound, of course, but I would not bring unsubstantiated talk to your office. I deal in facts, as do you, Comrade General Secretary."

It was a reasonable dance, but did not cover the fact that the GRU had hit the target long before the NKVD. It was a rare triumph for the senior GRU General and he silently savoured every second as Stalin spoke directly at Beria.

"GRU assessment of this information is that these groups may pose a threat. That their existence shows, at minimum, deep suspicion and, at worst case, aggressive intent by our former allies. They could also be used as a possible rallying point for any organised German force once Kingdom39 is initiated. Your assessment?"

Stalin sat back, aware of Beria's discomfort.

"I can only agree with the interpretation of my GRU comrades and congratulate them on their diligence." Both listeners knew how much that hurt the head of the NKVD, who was already promising himself a none too pleasant conversation with his top insider in the GRU.

"In my view, we should eliminate these groups as soon as is practicable," using the prospect of definitive action to mask his hurt.

Beria paused and conceded, "However, we cannot do so before the initiation of Kingdom, so it must be part of the initial assault plan."

"And your reasoning for that is what, Comrade Marshal?" Stalin purred reasonably.

"Simply that we have beaten the German and he is cowed. A further assault on the remainder of his country, complete with destruction of the armies and air forces of his newfound friends should be sufficient to keep him cowed. We have not considered the German entering the fight in numbers and organised, having always believed the large number of refugees and POW's would prove a huge encumbrance for the Western Allies."

He indicated to General Pekunin and the message was passed to his expectant hand. Beria picked up where he had left off.

"A possible rallying point....I agree. A beacon to the German soldier that his new friends accept him not as a beaten enemy, but as a soldier who can advise them on how to fight us. We must strike these groups," Beria inclined his head to take in a particular word on the page, "These symposiums, and strike them hard. They must not stand, Comrade General Secretary. But we cannot do so before Kingdom initiates, or we risk alerting the Western Allies unnecessarily."

"Tea, Comrade Pekunin." Stalin was not offering, as Pekunin well understood and he immediately moved to pour three cups.

Stalin tapped out his pipe on his hand and dropped the ash into a bin. Deep in thought, he refilled his pipe and, once satisfied, relit it and drew deeply.

"Comrade General Pekunin. I believe that Marshal Zhukov's Chief of Staff is in Moscow, visiting your department at the moment?"

"It is so, Comrade General Secretary."

"Have him attend here at 4pm."

"I will tell him myself Comrade Gen...."

Stalin cut in.

"Then please do so now, Comrade."

Pekunin saluted and turned on his heels, marching out of the room, his victory over Beria slightly blotted by his obvious early dismissal by Stalin.

"The GRU put one over on you there, Lavrentiy," taunted Stalin, once the large double doors had closed.

"We both serve the party and the Motherland, Comrade General Secretary, so I am content."

"Quite so, Lavrentiy," with a grin the like of which Beria had never seen before.

His inner voice whispered to him.

'*The Georgian bastard enjoyed that.*'

"Your plan for the rear-areas included security measures for German officer prisoners. I suggest that you implement a broader consideration to include those in the territories we will occupy once Kingdom commences."

"It will be done, Comrade."

"You suggested assassination of certain generals immediately prior to the attack. I do remember Comrade Zhukov rejecting that, as he would rather fight those he knew

128

and felt were less capable, than be surprised by someone new who could possibly perform well."

Beria smarted again. It had been a good plan and had been rejected out of hand.

"I suggest you revive and modify that plan and target these," Stalin picked up his copy of the report and read a section again for confirmation, "Symposiums Hamburg, Frankfurt and Paderborn with the resources you had set aside for that purpose. See what assets you can provide to assist Marshal Zhukov."

As a father comforting a son, he added.

"I will speak to him about adopting the assassination plan as you submitted. It appeals to me."

Stalin looked up at the clock.

"It would appear that you have three hours, Comrade Marshal. Your submission will then go to Zhukov for incorporation into Kingdom39."

1600hrs Monday, 9th July 1945, The Kremlin, Moscow, USSR.

When all were assembled, at 1600hrs precisely, Stalin took centre stage.

Zhukov's Chief of Staff awaited his pleasure.

"Comrade General Malinin. There are small but important additions to the plan that the GKO wishes inserted into Kingdom39 immediately."

Malinin stiffened automatically.

"Firstly, Marshal Beria's assassination plan will now be included, as originally put forward. That is on my order."

There was absolutely no argument on that score.

"Secondly, Comrade Pekunin will brief you on a new development."

Beria had to concede it was Pekunin's right, so he did not bristle as Stalin had hoped.

Pekunin outlined the intelligence received from the Bletchley Park agent.

When he finished presenting the revised version, adapted to protect his source, he stepped back again. "Comrade

129

General, you will understand that we must deal with the potential threat of these symposiums and so Comrade Marshal Beria's original assassination plan has been expanded. Comrade Beria has the details."

From the briefcase, five documents were produced, one for everyone present.

"Comrades, this is Plan Zilant, a small but very necessary plan. Comrade General Pekunin will liaise with you to ensure you are kept up to date. You will see we are still lacking some important pieces of information, but those must and will be delivered."

At that moment, he looked at Pekunin, who understood the message loud and clear.

"The sole assets already tasked in Kingdom that are required for this plan are transport squadrons, which the GKO will authorise removing from the operational transport reserve, plus a single third wave formation, curiously tasked as ground infantry, whereas the unit is qualified for what we have in mind. Namely," unusually Beria had to consult the document, "100th Guards Rifle Division 'Svir', which is airborne in all but name."

Malinin knew that obviously, which was why it was lightly tasked only in phase three, in order to keep an ace up the sleeve.

"The commanding officer," again the swift consultation by Beria, "Mayor General Ivan Makarenko, has already been instructed to liaise with Comrade Pekunin, to get as much up to date information with which to construct a operational format for Plan Zilant."

The obvious breach in protocol was ignored.

Stalin stood up and spoke forcefully.

"I want this plan included in Kingdom39 by Friday and I want these bastards dead."

I know that you believe you understand what you think I said, but I'm not sure you realise that what you heard is not what I meant.

- Robert McCloskey

Chapter 13 – THE MISTAKE

1140hrs Tuesday, 10th July 1945, The Khavane Erbil, Istanbul, Turkey.

Konstantin Volkov was an unassuming man of indeterminate age, which made him perfect for his role. He was deputy Vice-Consul in the Soviet Embassy in Istanbul, Turkey, or at least that was his official title. What actually consumed most of his time was being Deputy Head of NKVD in the country, although he had simply had enough of that post and was looking for a way out.

For some time he had been gathering intelligence from messages that passed through his hands, steadily building up a portfolio of information from agents across the globe for his 'insurance policy', a stock of restricted information with which to attract foreign intelligence agencies to 'look after' him.

A secret meeting had been arranged with a member of the US mission, scheduled for the 5th July, in order for Volkov to make his play. The two men secreted themselves deep in the rear of a modest coffee shop and, once the identity of the American had been established, immediately got down to details. Wreathed in thick tobacco smoke, Volkov gave his starting position. In exchange for $27,000 and political asylum, he would hand over the details of numerous Soviet agents in Turkey and Britain. The American, actually a very out of his depth young Marine Captain, offered nothing, but promised to report back to his superiors and then bring Volkov the reply.

To be frank, the offer was not taken seriously and, in any case, Turkey and Britain being riddled with Soviet agents was not a huge concern for the Marine's boss, an ageing US Army Lieutenant Colonel, soon to retire on health grounds.

None the less, the man was still professional enough to send the young Captain out for another clandestine meet five days later, this time with a request for proof and, more to the point, proof that was of value to the United States.

The Captain arrived first and Volkov arrived shortly afterwards. Expecting an answer to his question, he was extremely surprised and very upset to discover that he would not be offered what he wanted during this meeting.

There was nothing he could do except try and satisfy the requests put to him.

Fresh in his mind was a message that he had encoded for sending via his Turkish contacts and so he spoke of it. He assumed this eventually went to the Turkish Embassy in Washington but knew no more. The contents were also unknown to him, but he was conscious of the fact that it was an extremely important agent, for whose messages, incoming or outgoing, he was to be brought into the embassy, no matter what time of day or night that a message arrived. The young Captain made written notes, which made Volkov very uncomfortable.

"Enough!" he hissed. "Remember what I tell you. No writing."

"OK, sir." He made a point of dramatically finishing the sentence he was writing. "Anything else I can pass on to my boss?"

"Just that there is much concern that you may have broken our NKVD, diplomatic and trade ciphers, so we are moving to a new code system in the next two months."

"Well, there's not a lot there for my boss to sell this idea, sir."

The more Volkov thought about it, the more he agreed. The Turks would fall over themselves for his info. The British would wet their pants when he revealed what he knew. Why on earth had he gone to the Amerikanski? The answer to that lay with British Military Intelligence. He could not trust them, for they were infiltrated by the NKVD.

His mind wandered back to finding something of import for the moment.

Once, when the route had first been established, he had partially decoded the NKGB version of a message, from an agent AKONHOST. It had made little sense to him, but he did remember one word.

"Manhattan, my Directorate knows about Manhattan."

The Captain looked amused.

"Sir, everyone knows about Manhattan. It's on all the maps."

Both men stood up, one to leave and one to remonstrate, but he then thought better of it. One was resolved to file a relatively useless report with his boss and the other was resigned to the fact that he had made an error approaching the Amerikanski and would now carefully approach the British instead. Very carefully obviously, with conditions of who was to know what and how communications should be managed, but he was sure they would like to know what he knew about the depths to which Soviet Intelligence had them penetrated!

They went their own ways, with neither a shake of the hand, nor another word.

Those who talk on the razor edge of double-meanings pluck the rarest blooms from the precipice on either side.

Logan Pearsall Smith

Chapter 14 – THE REPORT

1035hrs Friday, 13th July 1945, Department of Justice Building, F.B.I. Office, Washington D.C.

The Captain compiled a written report on the meeting that was concise and accurate, even down to the Russian's useless joke at the end of the meeting.

The report was placed on the Lieutenant Colonel's desk on a day that he was on sick leave and so was not processed for forwarding until the following day.

He viewed it with no great interest but sent it with grade 1 priority, solely based on the stuff about code changing.

It was a low traffic day on the 12th, so the report made its way through to the FBI in Washington in record time.

The 'stuff' on code changing arrived and produced a seismic wave at Project Venona, a joint US Army-FBI attempt to decode Soviet communications. Not only was it a heads-up that change was possible, it was also indicative of the fact that the Soviets were sensing an extra pair of eyes reading their private thoughts.

The report took other routes at a more leisurely pace.

It was Friday the 13th by the time it arrived in the FBI building.

Agent Drew Hargreaves had drawn the short straw and was undertaking the communications review occasionally done on the letters of all staff at a certain location in New Mexico.

Having just been wholly bored reading women's talk for half an hour, he was at the coffee machine when a new report arrived. He signed for it, mainly as he was the nearest and could hardly run away in any case, taking it with him into his booth.

134

Something different to run his eyes over before he got back the serious business of reading what the fashion of the moment was.

The report had been sanitised and all hint that it originated from a possible defector had gone. That meant that it held little of substance.

He opened it and speed-read the page, somewhere in his brain noted the word 'Turkish' but did not process it fully, as Hargreaves was compulsively drawn to the final paragraph.

"Sweet Lord on high, sweet lord on high."

His brain raced with thoughts. *'Manhattan; the Soviets know about Manhattan. Sweet lord on high. They know about Manhattan.'*

"Sweet lord…"

His mind flicked deliberately and accessed his memory covering the word 'Turkish' and he read that section more closely.

His left-hand reached out and he re-read the file cover note for the private Los Alamos correspondence he had been reading.

Hargreaves was a god-fearing southern boy, brought up in the State of Mississippi. Crippled in a farming accident at the age of nine, he threw himself into academia, earning top honours in college and subsequently choosing a life of service to the government that had provided his education. He entered the FBI in 1938 and found his niche in intelligence. He was a first-rate analyst and never accepted coincidences.

He also never, ever cursed.

"Fuck!"

And so it was that he held in his right hand a low-level report from Istanbul containing the codename of the most important project his country was undertaking in modern-times, coupled with inference of important spy information going through the same country. In his left hand was a file cover-sleeve that indicated that this particular scientist corresponded regularly and at length, with a cousin employed at the Turkish Embassy.

One telephone call later, the FBI started a minute inspection of the life of Emilia Beatriz Perlo and her family.

135

Others re-examined all the letters exchanged between the family. By that evening, the Agent in charge realised that serious mistakes had been made and, even though some information was still to come from the renewed friendly contact with Spain, there was enough proof in hand to arrest Victoria Calderon and Emilia Perlo.

Recriminations could come later.

Fall seven times, stand up eight

Japanese Proverb

Chapter 15 – THE GERMAN

1230hrs Sunday, 15th July 1945, Soviet POW Camp, Ex-OFLAG XVIIa, Edelbach, Austria.

His name was Uhlmann and he was Waffen-SS.

He had soldiered from 1940 through to the difficult days in early 1945 and had the scars to show for his endeavours in a losing cause. Had he not had his personal effects removed by his captors over the weeks, then the casual observer would have noted that he held his country's highest decorations for bravery, from the Iron Cross second class he had won in Northern France, through to the Knight's Cross placed around his neck for his actions on the Russian steppes. He started as a soldier in the Leibstandarte-SS "Adolf Hitler" and ended his days as an officer commanding a panzer battalion in one of Germany's cream SS formations, namely the 5th SS Panzer Division 'Wiking'.

He was thirty-three years old and his time soldiering had not sat too heavily on him, apart from the occasional stiffness of an old wound, of which he had received more than his fair share. In particular, an unusual thigh wound would often trouble him, but the story of how he had sustained it earned Rolf many a drink, so he endured it with good humour.

In his younger days, his 1.88m frame, blonde hair and blue eyes would have put him on any Waffen-SS recruitment poster and, in truth, he still cut a dashing figure.

Being Waffen-SS meant he got special treatment from the guards. Because he could speak Russian and was therefore valuable, ensured that he didn't get that special treatment as badly as some other SS officers, although rarely a day went by without some new insult or injury being visited upon him by the Bulgarians who policed the camp at Edelbach. There had been some two hundred and fifty-six officers at its peak but a combination of execution, disease, abuse and escapes had

137

reduced that number to two hundred and seventeen. Exactly two hundred and seventeen Rolf knew, for it was his job to know these things and the Germans have never been accused of being inefficient.

It had been two hundred and nineteen at breakfast time, but Maior Nester had succumbed to his devastating infection in the mid-morning and Leutnant Lindemann had been shot at 1136hrs. The memory of that was too fresh. Murdered was more the truth, for no reason other than he was the closest prisoner to that damned NKVD officer, who just wanted to show his girl how powerful he really was.

They all knew Kapitan Skryabin was a psychopath and an asshole, but to do that? His absence on home leave had been a period of relative calm for the inmates, but now he was back. No rhyme or reason, just pistol out, trigger pulled and handsome young Lindemann, former art student of Leipzig, was no more. Another senseless death in a decade of senseless deaths.

The trouble with Skryabin, one camp guard had previously confided in a comrade and was overheard by Rolf, was that he was connected in Moscow and was pretty much fireproof. Uhlmann had no idea who or how highly connected, as it was not the sort of thing you would just up and ask a guard, certainly not the guards in this camp anyway.

He had discussed Skryabin with a few of his fellow officers but there was a general feeling of apathy and depression about many comrades, which excluded in-depth thought and conversation, unless it was talk of escape, home and family. Perhaps understandable, given what had happened over the last six years.

Edelbach was a former German POW camp for the incarceration of Allied officer prisoners, mainly French, with a smattering of Poles, previously known as OFLAG XVIIa. In 1943, it was the site of the largest mass escape of allied prisoners in World War Two, when one hundred and thirty-two men made a bid for freedom through a tunnel on the nights of the 17th and 18th September, escaping in two groups, a day apart, with only two men making the full escape to their native France.

Now the sole occupants of this miserable place were its former proprietors and their new custodians. The previous inmates of Edelbach had been marched away to Linz before the Red Army captured the site, with many failing the harsh physical test and dying right at the end of the war. Most of the barracks were damaged and unoccupied and solely the five blocks that housed Rolf and his fellows remained inhabited from the thirty or so that had been home to thousands of unfortunates.

There were all sorts in Edelbach now, from Nazi political animals through to frontline regulars like Rolf, who cared little for politics and who had fought for country when called, regardless of the regime in charge. Most were from the regular army, the Wehrmacht, with a considerable number of Waffen-SS, some Luftwaffe and even one Kriegsmarine Officer. As was the case with a number of SS officers, Rolf was, or rather, had been a Nazi party member until Germany's collapse, but would confess his membership derived from him being caught up in the euphoria of the early years, rather than any fanaticism or dedication to the cause.

Evidence of the presence of military personnel from France and Poland was to be found in the unusual graffiti in some of the separate blocks. Overall, the forty plus buildings had occupied a site of about a quarter of a hectare in the Austrian Waldviertel. Barbed wire and guard towers surrounded the whole camp, with solely the one way in and out. Dated it may be, its facilities having clearly suffered the abuses expected with four years of service, but it was still very effective at keeping people just where the watchers wanted them. Each remaining hut sat on a concrete plinth, above which it was raised three feet, so that inspections could be done to ensure no tunnels were being dug. German efficiency was turned against them and had caused many a wry smile in discussions. A single central wood-burner provided heating for the whole hut. That was not a problem as the European summer visited them, but would undoubtedly lead to deaths as 1945 drew to a close. Beds were straw paliasses with blankets and it seemed there was never enough of either to go round.

Meals were two a day. Early morning there was a small ration of bread with a thin vegetable soup and evenings brought the delights of more thin soup and the hope of some meat floating in it. The question had been raised a number of times as to what the meat was, so Rolf had enquired but hadn't translated it literally, preferring to keep his comrades in the dark about what they were enjoying so heartily.

Of course, there was constant talk of escaping the camp and going home, but only recently had the talk of escape been harnessed to a genuine fear of safety at the hands of the guards. Treatment had been strangely reasonable initially, when their guards were from a combat infantry division.

Now it was a very different kettle of fish with the new Bulgarian bunch that had not fired a shot in anger and had much to prove. Of course, Ostap Shandruk, the ever-cheerful Ukrainian, had more reason to fear than anyone else did. If his identity were to become known he would be summarily shot. His papers said he was German and that had not yet been investigated. His Ukrainian SS insignia had long ago been discarded and his mastery of the German language, which had guaranteed his promotion in the Galician Division, now helped to keep his identity secret.

Rolf had an advantage over his fellow prisoners, in that he could speak excellent Russian. That made him invaluable to his captors and often he was the only person privy to both sides of interrogations and discussions between the "management" and his own boys. It didn't stop him getting his share of physical attention from the Bulgarians, but his duties often took him within range of food, drink and other objects that somehow found their way into his possession. More than one young man in field-grey had profited from Rolf's activities and received life-sustaining food when at death's door.

His latest acquisitions of Red Star cigarettes and matches were in the possession of Hauptsturmfuhrer Braun, ready for allocation. Braun was the senior NCO in camp and Rolf's former top dog in the panzer battalion of which he was once commander. More to the point, he was also Uhlmann's close comrade and would soon, fate willing, be his brother in law. Both he and Braun had been captured when their battalion,

140

II Abteilung, 5th SS Pnz Regt, had been virtually annihilated outside Vienna on 26th March 1945.

They had managed to destroy everything of use to the advancing Russians as their surviving men tried to make good their escape towards the west. A few days of evasion and they were both finally taken prisoner without a shot being fired, just northeast of Traismauer. Both men marvelled that they had been taken prisoner at all, given their arm of service and insignia, but neither ever spoke of it to the other. It had been a nervous few hours, most certainly and, so Rolf thought, more nerve-wracking than combat,.

After some time, they had been moved off with a few other stragglers, none of whom was from Uhlmann's unit, he was glad to see. A few pioneers and artillerymen from Wiking for sure, but the division obviously had made good its escape.

After being marched around a few different holding areas, he and Braun had come to rest in Edelbach and it had become their home, such as it was. What the future held for all of those incarcerated there was unknown, but, given that the Germany that had laid waste to half of Europe was defeated and that those who had suffered were bound to bay for blood, Rolf felt that it would be long and unpleasant.

He was partially wrong and, unfortunately for many who shared his present fate, he was also partially right.

A promise made is a debt unpaid.

Robert Service.

Chapter 16 – THE UNDERSTANDING

1620hrs Sunday, 15th July 1945, The Kremlin, Moscow, USSR.

The work was still being done in the office of the Soviet General Secretary.

As usual, Beria was there. Less the norm was the presence of Deputy Chairman Bulganin and People's Commissar for Foreign Affairs Molotov, both members of the GKO.

"I can accept the reasoning behind delaying implementation of section 13 of your plan, Lavrentiy, but I see no reason not to send out a warning order to allow our men on the ground to prepare. It is not a small business and we must learn the lessons of Katyn."

A word guaranteed to make Beria recoil. Hardly the NKVD's finest hour, when something that was supposed to be clandestine had made the world's front pages in the middle of a world war. It was a total embarrassment to the Motherland, let alone the NKVD.

Beria folded immediately.

"As you direct, Comrade General Secretary. I will send out the preparation order this evening."

Both other men nodded sagely at the decision to liquidate thousands of helpless men.

"So, until tomorrow's GKO meeting, comrades."

The three departed and walked together to their respective cars.

Beria paused.

"Comrade Molotov, a word if I may."

They took their leave of Bulganin and waited until his car pulled away.

The two men did not particularly like each other.

142

"Vyacheslav Mikhailovich, a word of assistance to you and your family."

Molotov prickled, but he held his peace.

"It has come to my attention that one of your line, your sister's boy, Viktor, is speaking loosely of something he should know nothing about."

Molotov knew only too well that of which Beria spoke. He had stupidly spoken to his wife in general non-specific terms about the upcoming Kingdom39. She in turn had told his sister, who in her turn had confided in her son during his leave. The boy, using his military knowledge, had pieced together a lot more of what was to come. Viktor had spoken to him later and received short shrift. From what Beria was saying, it seemed Molotov's anger had not made a difference.

He had never liked the boy anyway and even more so since he tried using his Molotov's name to attempt additional advancement within the NKVD.

"I have said nothing and will leave it to you to address. No harm is done at the moment. Unless he continues, in which case I will have to act. He is one of my men remember. "

"Thank you, Lavrentiy Pavlovich. I am in your debt and I will address this. I will write to him immediately in the strongest possible terms."

Both men knew that Molotov certainly was in Beria's debt, but only one of them liked it. Beria had left unsaid the fact that it was Molotov who was most at risk for speaking loosely of Kingdom39 in the first place. In the political manoeuvrings of the Kremlin, Molotov would be crippled for some time to come in his dealings with the NKVD Marshal.

"Good night, Comrade Commissar."

"Good night to you, Comrade Marshal."

The superior man, when resting in safety, does not forget that danger may come. When in a state of security he does not forget the possibility of ruin. When all is orderly, he does not forget that disorder may come. Thus, his person is not endangered, and his States and all their clans are preserved.

Confucius

Chapter 17 – THE CANARY

0529hrs Monday, 16th July 1945, White Sands Bombing Range, New Mexico, USA.

The White Sands Bombing range was a desolate place… and hot; so very, very hot. Despite that isolation, or actually because of it, the land had, of late, seen many visitors.

Sat at the top of a one hundred foot metal tower was a gadget; actually, **The** Gadget, for that was what it was called. It was a plutonium implosion device and it was there to be exploded to prove that the technology worked.

Scientists and military alike observed from positions around the site, some officially and some unofficially.

Klaus Fuchs, also known as Gamayun, being on duty, watched from a proper camp, some ten miles distant from the tower. A last-minute change in security procedures had left him with no opportunity to do anything harmful to the project. He hoped that the other agents within Manhattan would be more successful, but his priority was his own survival.

Emilia Perlo, also known as Alkonost, had been enjoying the constant companionship of a reserved, yet handsome, Lieutenant Colonel of US Military Intelligence since lunchtime on Friday. They had excitedly discussed the upcoming test and agreed to take the early morning drive down to see the 'rainbow' in all its glory. Setting off while it was still dark, they had travelled in his staff car to a beautiful spot, roughly fifteen miles southeast of Socorro, parking on high ground, about twenty miles north-west of the device. The driver, she hadn't expected a driver when the idea was first ventured, had parked up almost oblivious to the pair, leaving

144

them to carry their picnic hamper to a vantage point, where they smoked cigarettes, drunk soda and waited for the show.

This officer was new to the camp and Emilia had noticed him looking at her, so the play had been made. He wanted to look round the camp, so Emmy had been his guide for the whole weekend and now here they were. He was too much of a gentleman to accept her barely concealed offer to join her in her bed on the previous evening, but she hoped that he would lose his reserve for tonight.

In any case, they were both here to witness history being made and so she put aside her earthy thoughts, for now, concentrating on looking westwards. His constant attention had meant that she had delayed her plans to sabotage some of the project but, in any case, once the test was successfully out of the way, Emilia was sure access to the accommodation block she intended to destroy would be easier in the euphoria.

At approx 0530hrs, the gadget was detonated.Or rather it wasn't; or actually it was, but didn't.

Either way, there was no spectacular demonstration of fission. What transpired was colloquially known as a fizzle. Those paying close attention would see something, but not the anticipated spectral rainbow and vast explosion. The device did explode, but mainly spread its plutonium around the local site, which brought its own problems for the team who had to decide what went wrong.

It would be some weeks before a proper investigation would begin. Until then, the scientists struggled with their figures and calculations and progress was virtually halted.

Gamayun knew immediately that something had gone wrong and celebrated inwardly that another agent had clearly managed to somehow tamper with the device.

Alkonost knew only that the expected show had not arrived on the allotted hour and started to wonder the same, but she and the officer stayed where they were for some time anyway, just in case it was merely delayed.

All over the Manhattan Project, there was disbelief and immense disappointment for months, possibly years of wasted work.

2013hrs Monday, 16th July 1945, Scientists Accomodation Block, Los Alamos, New Mexico, USA.

Disappointingly, Emilia had been forced to drink alone, as her handsome escort had cried off at the doorway to her block earlier in the evening, pleading tiredness as an excuse for his swift departure.

After a couple of bourbons, Emmy decided that she had best stop drinking for the moment, as she obviously needed to compile a report for her cousin.

Out came the necessary items and she steadily went to work, putting together a nice letter to Victoria, talking about the weather and the handsome young officer who clearly wanted her so badly.

Letter finished, she sealed it in an envelope, addressed it and placed it on the small table by her door.

The knock on that door took her totally by surprise, more so because she heard the voice of her newest potential lover calling her name. The evening may not be so bad after all, she thought, as she placated him with a reply and rushed to secrete her book, swiftly scanning the room to make sure that no clues lay open to scrutiny.

She opened the door, having quickly checked her hair and lips. That she was in her underwear was of no concern to her.

"Well hello, Karl. Changed your mind, honey?"

As wonderful as Emilia looked in her stockings and lacy bra, Lieutenant Colonel Karl Da Silva was there for another purpose. In fact, he had been rushed to the facility on Friday morning purely for that single purpose.

All of Emilia's senses lit off in one second, as Da Silva walked wordlessly into the room, followed by a civilian whom she knew was an FBI agent based on site. She had even tried to bed him once, but his preference for other pursuits had terminated her attempt.

'*Military Intelligence*' was ringing loudly in her mind and she inwardly screamed at herself.

'*He's Military Intelligence, you stupid fucking useless bitch!*'

146

The thought cut to the heart of her. She had just accepted it because MI officers were in and out of the area all the time, sniffing around the scientists. How could she have been so stupid?

"Please sit down Miss Perlo."

She did as she was told and reached for the bourbon. Da Silva neatly fended her hand away from it, took it up and placed it away from her reach.

"I think not, Emilia. You will need a clear head."

Da Silva looked around, grabbed her robe, threw it to her and took a chair opposite. The FBI agent took out a pad and sat on the bed. It was mainly for show, as the room had been extensively wired when Da Silva had ensured Emmy was absent for sufficient time during the previous evening. It had taken them about five minutes to find where she hid her camera.

Tape-recorders were already rolling.

"Now, you know why Agent Manzoni and I are here."

He held up his hand automatically.

"Please don't bother with denials or reasons." He suddenly realised that no immediate denial had sprung forth from Emmy's mouth and that the woman in front of him had already crumbled inside and would be ripe for his purposes.

He continued more softly. "We just want to know everything, from the very beginning, leaving out nothing."

"Before you begin, understand that at this very moment, other security officers are having similar conversations with Cousin Victoria and your Aunt Marta."

That actually wasn't true but the leverage wouldn't hurt.

"You have no one you need to protect and nowhere to run. Your future depends on what you do and say here. Do you understand?"

No words came, just a simple frightened nod, as every essence of confidence and assuredness drained from her and she became nothing but a frightened child confronted by the bogeyman.

"So, your story, from the beginning, Emilia."

And a very illuminating story it was too.

Human beings, who are almost unique in having the ability to
learn from the experience of others, are also remarkable for
their apparent disinclination to do so.

Douglas Adams

Chapter 18 – THE INTRODUCTION

0700hrs Monday, 16th July 1945, The Château du Haut-Kœnigsbourg, French Alsace.

During the previous week, it had been hectic at the Château. The kitchens had been taking deliveries every day and completely new rooms and buildings were springing up all over the Château. Where once there was a dark and dank cupboard, now there was a compact space, with everything the occupant needed to carry out the job. There was now a staff of twenty-seven on site, not including the security detachment.

The guest accommodation was swiftly transformed to take a possible twenty visitors. The entire symposium noticed that two of the 'suites" were of a standard fit for a king and made assumptions that someone above Brigadier-General rank might be making an appearance.

The Alsatian House in the lower courtyard was made ready to receive more allied officers, as the guest accommodation in the Château proper, simply could not be laid out adequately.

Care was taken not to damage any of the venerable fittings and fixtures, but everywhere new walls sprung up, as rooms were compartmented for privacy.

The menagerie enclosure in the Saillant Est section now contained new wooden huts, into which the Commandos had moved without rancour, the huts being well appointed and benefitting from showers and wind proofing. The central Basse Cour area was mainly set aside for staff and guests.

Fig#5- Chateau - Biarritz modifications

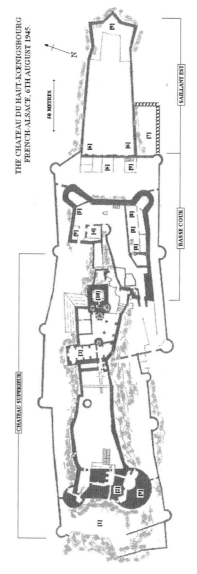

THE CHATEAU DU HAUT-KŒNIGSBOURG
FRENCH-ALSACE, 6TH AUGUST 1945.

50 METRES

N

CHATEAU SUPERIEUR

BASSE COUR

SAILLANT EST

[1] - NEW SLEEPING ACCOMODATION CONSTRUCTED FOR SYMPOSIUM MEMBERS.   [2] - CONVERTED INTO OFFICE FOR SYMPOSIUM AND RESIDENTIAL ACCOMODATION FOR DEUX STAFF.

[3] - FOUR CLASSROOMS BY DAY, CLUB AREA BY NIGHT.   [4] - COMMANDO COMPANY HEADQUARTERS [FIRST FLOOR, DUBOIS' SLEEPING QUARTERS.   [5] - DOG PENS

[6] - NEW ACCOMODATION FOR COMMANDO COMPANY. [7] - SECURE VEHICLE COMPOUND   [8] - VISITING OFFICERS ACCOMODATION [9] - MILITARY STORES   [10] - STORES

149

The symposium members had been moved into the Secret Garden in the Château Supérieur, where they enjoyed similar quarters that also satisfied the new requirement that they be kept aside from the Allied officers, at least until after the first morning. The Deuxieme Bureau staff moved into the adjacent Grand Bastion where less grand but extremely comfortable conversions had been put down by a team of carpenters, creating bedrooms where once shot was stored, or cannon stood.

Fig#6 - First floor - Biarritz Modifications

THE CHATEAU DU HAUT-KŒNIGSBOURG
FRENCH-ALSACE, 6TH AUGUST 1945.

PLAN OF FIRST FLOOR
ACCOMODATION

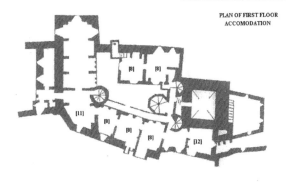

[8] - VISITING OFFICERS ACCOMODATION [11] - SYMPOSIUM GENERAL OFFICE [12] - ORDERLIES ACCOMODATION

The cellar had become multi-purpose, by day divided into four distinct classroom areas, by night filled with comfortable furniture and livened by the sounds of men sampling the local brews.

Whilst the disjointed nature of the facilities was not ideal, once everyone grew confident in the layout, the Château was more than suitable for the task.

Ever a people of routine, it had become accepted practice for the symposium's exercise to be taken around the walls of the Château Supérieur and, occasionally, the Basse Cour, often being joined by De Walle and Valois. Pleasant and

150

extremely attractive as she was, it occurred to all that she was not a woman to be trifled with, which suited Anne-Marie just fine, because they were absolutely right.

Fig#7 - Second floor - Biarritz Modifications

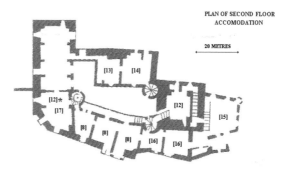

THE CHATEAU DU HAUT-KŒNIGSBOURG
FRENCH-ALSACE, 6TH AUGUST 1945.

PLAN OF SECOND FLOOR
ACCOMODATION

20 METRES

[13] - FEMALE 'DEUX' AGENTS ACCOMODATION [14] - VALOIS' ROOM [15] - DE WALLE'S ROOMS [16] - 'DEUX' OFFICES

[17] - SYMPOSIUM GENERAL OFFICE [8] - VISITING OFFICERS ACCOMODATION [12] - ORDERLIES ACCOMODATION

[12]✷ ORDERLIES ACCOMODATION [MINSTRELS GALLERY.]

On the Thursday morning, Valois had attended breakfast and provided Menzel with the information that his wife and son were both alive, well and living with her sister in Bonn.

In almost tearful relief, Menzel took her hand and thanked Valois, already mentally writing the letter he would send them that very morning.

For Von Arnesen and Knocke there was no news at all.

Each day the group had gathered and gone through everything in the minutest detail, or at least everything that could be so examined. The intangibles of ability, personality and character, they were unable to predict.

Initially, Knocke had carried the group with him because of who he was and their complete faith in him. Certainly now, each man, in his own right, was full of

151

enthusiasm for the task and actually relishing the challenges ahead.

No one had any doubt that there would be challenges.

Monday morning, 16th July 1945, arrived in the superb early morning sunshine of a promising European summer's day. The symposium members gathered for breakfast at the agreed hour of seven, avoided the dining hall and were served in a room in the Grand Bastion thathad been converted into their private offices. Alone, for a change, as De Walle was elsewhere tying up some loose ends with Capitaine de Frégate Dubois. The conversation was light and easy, although they were always status conscious in some way, despite the fact that this morning all wore civilian clothes.

At Knocke's suggestion, they avoided wearing their full uniforms as, and with unusually direct humour for Knocke, DerBo's track record with egg yolk would ensure the visiting officers would think they were attending a chicken farming course. Humour aside, it was a fair point and, in any case, a shirt was just fine and nicely comfortable, as the sun's rays streamed in through the open windows bringing the summer's warmth to all as they ate.

The plan for the immediate morning had been agreed and rehearsed previously, as everyone was conscious that first impressions would be everything and much of how the week went would be determined by those initial minutes.

In front of each man was a list of the candidates on this first symposium, complete with a synopsis of his life and career. The mix of arms of service seemed just right and there were some veteran soldiers in the group. The inclusion of the two American and two British Officers had been a surprise. De Walle had explained the existence of the two other similar Colloques, the British one at Hamburg and the American facility just outside of Paderborn and how there would be officers exchanged between national groups. This was done partially on a goodwill basis, but also to try to ensure symposiums did not slip into one specific national mindset, a point that Knocke conceded had not occurred to any of them.

It was at this time that the group learned of the existence of a special symposium at Frankfurt, for General

152

Staff and higher formation commanders, run by the Americans. De Walle had verbally run through a list of German officers attending that one and it was like a who's who of the Wehrmacht's best generals, although it was obvious that no SS senior commanders were named.

The list of officers in front of the symposium was less impressive but, as coffee arrived, conversation focussed on one name in particular; that of an American Major. In honesty, few American officers became well known to the German soldier, in the way that a Zhukov, Montgomery, or Rommel did to their foes. This officer was no exception, but they were still all drawn to the American by the name of Hardegen, a Major in an American armoured division. They determined to test his mettle and see how well he compared to his namesake.

Breakfast over, the group stood and, almost as one, instinctively turned to Knocke for some final words. But he merely clicked to attention, nodded and proceeded out to his bedroom, to dress and prepare for the first meeting.

0957hrs Monday, 16th July 1945, The Château du Haut-Kœnigsbourg, French Alsace.

The Armoury buzzed with conversation. The suits of armour were now slid back against the walls, standing silent witness to what was to come. It had been decided that this was the most suitable place in which to undertake the difficult task of introducing the pupils and teachers.

Officers from France and Britain mixed well from the start, the two Americans keeping more of their own company initially, but soon drawn into the group of fellow professionals. Sixteen officers, from Major to full Colonel, were on display, with experience of combat from the Middle East through to the icy waters of Norway. Much of the small talk turned to the ancient weapons on display and how much more effective the art of dealing death had now become.

At 0957hrs precisely, a group of six immaculately turned out French commandos marched noisily into the room and took post, one on each quarter and the remaining two either side of the entrance. Their equally smart officer waited for

153

them to finish their dressing, before taking post in front of the small podium that had been erected at the far end of the armoury hall. Standing there at the attention position, flanked by silent armoured men-at-arms from centuries past, he cut an impressive figure.

Without instruction, all the candidates moved quickly to their seats, but remained standing. It was all part of the stage management, planned to the minutest detail by Knocke and De Walle. The latter strode confidently in, wearing the dress uniform of a Général de Brigade of French General Staff, laden with more medals than most had ever seen. The smile on his face was partly for the dawning of this momentous day and partly because none of the symposium knew of his real status and rank and it would be a surprise for all, especially Knocke. As De Walle marched in, Dubois relocated to the right side of the podium. The commando officer saluted him crisply, which salute was extravagantly returned and De Walle took to the podium.

The officer group was silent and focussed on him.

"Gentlemen, welcome. In particular, our distinguished visitors from His Majesty's Brigade of Guards," his words were accompanied by a formal and professional nod, which was returned by both British Majors, "And two decorated members of the United States Army," followed again by a nod of acknowledgement, which was accepted with a mumbled word or two.

"You are the first group to attend this facility and are therefore privileged to be the first to take advantage of the opportunity of learning that it represents. This will not be easy, neither will it be conventional, for we are in uncertain times and need to try new methods."

"The pre-requisites for attendance here are that you must have seen active service, will remain in command of your respective units for at least the next year and are identified as suitable for promotion. You will appreciate that many of your peers fit those criteria, so it is essential that you do not waste the opportunity you have been given here, this week."

De Walle let that hang in the air for a while before pressing on.

"Your instructors have the highest credentials for this symposium, with ranks ranging from Captain to full Colonel. They will treat you with respect at all times and they will be treated with respect at all times. Regardless of what harsh lesson they hand to you and believe me they will, you will learn a great deal here, if you are prepared to accept that those who are here to give you the knowledge, have acquired theirs under very difficult circumstances and know what they are talking about."

There was no perceptible shift in his posture but suddenly De Walle seemed to be a foot taller and bordering on sinister, his voice taking on an edge of extreme seriousness.

"Understand this, Messieurs, we cannot afford to carry people who do not contribute or are disruptive. If an instructor requests that one of you be removed then there will be no appeal, no discussion and no delay. You will be gone, along with my written report on you and a guarantee of personal attention from a number of very important people who will not have your best interests at heart".

A snigger punctuated the intended silence.

"That was not humour, gentlemen; it was a statement of fact."

His eyes bored into the culprit, an American Major, who got the message loud and clear.

The moment passed and De Walle relaxed back into his presentation again.

'So, why are you here and what are we about to do? The questions that all of you have been asking yourselves, in one way or another, since you got your joining papers."

"It will come as no surprise to you that relations with our Soviet comrades are strained at times. Some of you will already have experience of provocations and regrettable incidents." At least three officers nodded enough to be instantly noticeable.

"We have no reason to believe that our alliance will fail, but we would be foolish not to prepare for such a failure before it is too late."

A wave of realisation spread through everyone in the room and an anticipated boring week of army lectures on dealing with refugees, or similar, disappeared in a few well-chosen words from De Walle.

"I will remind you that you may take away the lessons of this symposium, but not the purpose or location of it. You may not directly speak of it, to anyone, ever."

The silence and anticipation pervading the room was stifling.

"Gentlemen, you have all fought the Axis powers, in some cases since 1939 and fought well, learning and evolving tactics through experience and, at times, other's mistakes. It is the considered view that we would not have that luxury should the communists choose to attack us here, in Western Europe. Therefore, we propose to use this symposium to give you the means to fight well again against a new enemy, should you be called, means that can be trusted, as they are the result of other's learning, experience and mistakes."

The tension was immense, as some of those present grasped the true meaning of the words.

Commander Dubois strode one pace forward, smashed his heel to the stone floor, startling even the experienced combat veterans in the hall. With a voice loud enough to be heard some considerable distance away, he roared "Room, room Atten-shun!"

The sound of feet slamming into stone was combined with the groaning of the heavy wooden door at the rear of the hall, as it was pulled open by the two commandos stationed there for the purpose.

The hinges had been left un-oiled to increase the dramatic effect.

Immediately, the sound of feet, marking time in perfect synchronicity, invaded the expectant silence

De Walle had seen it before, as had Dubois, for the act had been carefully rehearsed, although, granted, on those previous occasions not all the props had been to hand. What both saw now reminded them of the mettle and worth of the symposium members.

Through the hall, the sound of marching feet gathered volume and reverberated as, without verbal command, Knocke sent in the members of "Biarritz".

The echoes of their precise steps, reflected off the stonewalls, grew in volume, until it seemed to some that a regiment was bearing down upon the occupants.

De Walle noticed the looks on the assembled faces as it became apparent to all that a squad of eight German officers was marching to the front, to take a position in front of the podium. Some faces were incredulous, some were shocked and one or two were darkened by hatred. The barely audible Texas-twanged comment of "they're fucking krauts" was totally unnecessary.

The eight officers, resplendent in full uniform, complete with medals, belts and headgear, split precisely in front of the podium, forming four either side, with their backs to the candidates. On an unspoken command, they turned and took a position of attention, facing the bewildered group, their eyes focussed on something distant.

In front of them, the Allied candidates seemed confused and unsure of what their reaction should really be. The array of awards on the German officer's uniforms was indicative of huge experience, personal bravery and, most certainly, competence.

Nevertheless, they <u>were</u> German uniforms and some were even SS, although all noticed the absence of the National Eagle, the flags of Germany and France, embroidered into a curious badge, being worn in the eagle's stead.

All of that being said, they were not prepared for Knocke.

Again, they became aware of the rapping of boots, a single set of precise military steps marching down the centre of the room. A man in black uniform passed, stopping in front of the podium and saluting De Walle formally, in the accepted style. Knocke, with no overt surprise, noted the Frenchman's uniform and rank, then mounted the podium and took the central position, ceded to him very deliberately by De Walle.

He turned and paused the required time before his leg shot out into the 'at ease,' in precise timing with that of his men and Dubois, as all assumed the position.

It was De Walle's idea that he should now pause and let the vision of his presence and bearing take some effect, before delivering his most important words of welcome.

For a man who had faced the perils of the Russian Front, it surprised Knocke that he was actually nervous, but he felt confident it would pass.

"Gentlemen, welcome to Symposium Biarritz. Please be seated"

It was an innocuous start, but an extremely important one, especially as every man before him instantly sat on the direction of a German officer, displaying response and acknowledgement of Knocke's authority, whilst quietly remaining focussed on the immaculate soldierly vision to their front.

"My name is Knocke, formerly a Colonel of tank troops in the Army of Germany. General De Walle informs me that any further introduction is superfluous, as you will all know of me. The other officers before you have also served in different areas and achieved different things and they will be introduced shortly."

"What we all have in common is that we have met the Russian and we have killed him in great numbers. He is a deadly enemy, an implacable enemy, who possesses infinite resources and manpower. His methods are ones you have not met before and the purpose of this symposium is to give you input that will allow you to make informed judgements, in the event that your home countries go to war with the Soviet Union."

A statement like that requires a period of silence to let it sink in, so Knocke halted and watched realisation spread across the faces in front of him.

"We have skills and we will teach you willingly, for communism threatens what is left of our homeland, just as it threatens yours, no matter how far away you may live. Yes, we were defeated by the Russian, but do not imagine for one moment that was because we lacked the skills to beat him, for we did not and, importantly, do not."

"We are here because we volunteered for this and we believe in the aims of this symposium."

"You may not like us and we must accept that. But what we will not accept is failure and so we must <u>ALL</u> set aside our personal feelings", the emphasis on 'all' was very marked on each occasion, "And <u>ALL</u> remember that our time here, yours and ours, serves the greater purpose of protecting <u>ALL</u> our countries, if the worst fears are realised."

And, in a change of tone that sounded more like conversation, Knocke concluded, "For my part, I believe it is not a case of if, but when."

"General De Walle?" Knocke enquired, as he smartly stepped aside to relinquish the prime position.

It had been decided that too much at the first encounter could prove counter-productive, so it was planned that Knocke's delivery would be the end of the beginning and the introductions of the rest of "Biarritz" would occur once the shock had worn off.

However, De Walle had decided to have a small departure from the rehearsed performance and started into it.

"Before the symposium members leave us and I invite your questions, I must say this."

Knocke remained looking straight ahead, as did the rest of the Germans, but De Walle could sense some confusion in the change. This time his mental note was a plus to him for putting one over on Knocke. His inner smile worked its way to his face before he realised it, but he kept it there in any case as it was appropriate.

"The men stood before you today were your enemies. This time last year, you would have tried to kill them, as they would have tried to kill you. Today, our fight with them is over. Yes, they were beaten and they surrendered to the allied forces, with their country occupied and their army destroyed."

He knew that would hurt Knocke and his men, but felt it needed to be said.

"Mark my words, Messieurs. They did not lose through their inability, or a lack of courage, or of skill. All of you here have fought them and will know the worth of the German soldier; a soldier who is as good today as he has always been. If you doubt that then I suggest that you take a long hard look at Colonel Knocke."

159

"A long hard look." A statement, the delivery of which, dared the listener to look away for a second.

Eyes scanned Knocke from head to foot and they understood.

"All of you knew the name Knocke before it was spoken here today. Why? Because the man is a legend, a legend earned in the harshest schools of combat and a legend from whom you now have the opportunity to learn."

"Major."

Again, the crash of Dubois' boot on the stone slabs startled some, as he called the room to attention. The response was instant and De Walle, acknowledging Knocke's salute once more, knew that they had done well.

The precision continued without orders, as Knocke marched between his men and each moved off in perfect step, in turn, until the group was again in column and well out into the hall.

The door whined in protest as it closed and then shut with a theatrical bang. Dubois shot his foot out into the at ease position and De Walle looked quizzically at the stunned men in front of him before posing a challenge to the ensemble with the simple line.

"Any questions?"

To his great surprise, there were none.

Moreover, in the brief history of Symposium Biarritz, there never ever were.

In the trophy room outside, the closure of the door signalled the halt of the symposium's march. Knocke dismissed the parade with a quiet flourish. All relaxed and grins were exchanged.

"Danke, Kameraden. I think that went well. Now the real work begins."

160

All our knowledge merely helps us to die a more painful death than animals that know nothing.

Maurice Maeterlinck

Chapter 19 – THE ERRORS

1103hrs Saturday, 21st July 1945, The Kremlin, Moscow, USSR.

Beria held the message out to his leader, unable to conceal his glee. Stalin did not take it, but read Beria's mind and posture instead.

"So, your agent is not lost to the Motherland, Lavrentiy?"

It was not a question. Beria felt deflated that he was so transparent to the General Secretary.

"It would appear not, as authentication code is correct and there is no compromisation indicated."

"Therefore we can assume the Turkish difficulty has not affected Alkonost?"

"I would say not, but we are in the process of finding out exactly what our issues may be."

"Keep me up to date." Stalin moved on.

"So your informed view of this message is?"

"Confirmation of the failure reported by two other agents, Comrade General Secretary, plus additional news of some note that will need confirmation."

Stalin looked up and took the paper, running his eyes over it, greedily consuming the contents. Even the dictator could not hide his happiness with the contents.

The message read:-

'*[priority code] SDD*
[agent] Alkonost
[date code] 160745c
[personal code as an authenticator] FB21162285
[distribution1] route x-eyes only
[distribution1] AalphaA [Comrade Chairman Beria].

161

[message] test failed. A+ self observed. Reliable reports B+
many scientist deaths. Train-Snake.
[message ends]

Message authenticates. Codes for non-compromisation valid.

RECEIVED 09:19 21/7/45-B.V.LEMSKY'

"So this failure, Lavrentiy? Our agents, or their inefficiency? Do we know?"

"Neither Alkonost, Gamayun, nor Kalibr reports indicate action on the part of the agent, but all three messages have been brief. It's possible that it could be modesty on the part of an agent, of course, but I would have expected credit to be claimed, however brief the message."

After a moment's thought, Beria offered a plausible explanation.

"I can imagine there's much consternation in the Amerikanski project, so, possibly, our agents have sent short messages for their own security."

"Only Alkonost mentions casualties, but the reliability seems reasonable. We will know more later."

Stalin pushed a little harder.

"So, I was correct? No need to trouble our military after all?"

"That would appear to be so, Comrade General Secretary. Their project is now stalled and, if the report of casualties is true, then we may even find our own research proves fruitful before theirs. That's a thought to sustain the revolutionary heart, Comrade!"

"Indeed it is, Comrade Marshal," and what passed for a laugh escaped the dictator's lips.

Recently, Beria's position had been cosmetically changed from Chairman to Marshal and he had difficulty getting used to the idea and the uniform, for that matter. The suit he wore today made him feel more the part.

"Now, I must receive a delegation from the Ural's factories. A necessary evil."

162

"I will inform your staff that you are free on my way out, Comrade General Secretary."

Beria did so as he passed through the anteroom, his mind already wrestling with his next problem. Hopefully, Comrade Philby's timely Turkish present was already singing, but it was already clear from Philby's report that no information had been handed over. Therefore, Beria's men were just going through the motions of interrogation, before disposing of the traitor.

Actually, by the time Beria had the thought, Volkov's body was already stiffening, his interrogation and torture completed in record time, as his liaison with the British was already well-documented. He took the crucial secret of his fruitless liaison with the US with him to his cold and silent grave.

They simply hadn't asked that question.

1400hrs Saturday, 21st July 1945, The Château du Haut-Kœnigsbourg, French Alsace.

It was on this morning that Anne-Marie Valois broke the news to Von Arnesen that his son had been killed in the fighting during the last days of resistance in Berlin. There remained no news of his wife.

At precisely 1400hrs, Knocke and De Walle adjourned to the Frenchman's private office to discuss the submitted reports for the first week of the symposium. Overall, it had been a huge success, with the allied soldiers accepting the input of the Germans, grudgingly at first, but with increasing thirst for knowledge, as they began to appreciate the abilities and experiences of their teachers.

Both Kriegspeils had been Symposium victories, but the second had been a remarkably close run thing.

The sole problem had been the arrogant and mouthy American Major, Parker, who constantly tried to undermine the sessions with snide comments, despite being verbally slapped into place by his peers. His lack of humility in the august company he kept that week, caused more than one of his fellow officers to take him to one side.

The report on his attendance accurately reflected his conduct and, more damningly, his lack of tactical ability. It was sent to his Divisional Commander, complete with the note of abject apology, handed to De Walle by a very embarrassed Major Hardegen, also of the 4th US Armored Division.

Hardegen was at the other end of the scale to Parker. Quiet, unassuming, but exceptionally competent in the military arts and Knocke and his men were glowing in their praise for the man's ability. Together with Commandant St.Clair, of the 1e [Premiere] Division Française Libre, Hardegen had received the best possible report Knocke felt he could give.

De Walle reasoned that it was important for the symposium members to feel their reports were being properly viewed, so he followed the progress of Parker's negative evaluation all the way.

Over breakfast the following Saturday, he announced that the Major had been transferred from his combat division, with a loss of seniority, into a training battalion due to undertake strenuous retraining exercises.

Whilst that only elicited nodded responses from the ensemble, De Walle knew the news had the desired effect upon his present company.

As he ate his mountain of food, he was satisfied that the Parker problem had been properly addressed.

Unfortunately, an embittered Major Parker still had a part to play in the future of Symposium Biarritz.

Courage, above all things, is the first quality of a warrior.

Karl von Clauswitz

Chapter 20 – THE RUSSIAN

0655hrs Monday, 23rd July 1945, Hotel Neese, B.O.Q. Building, Div HQ, '15th' US Armored Division, Schlangen, US Occupied Germany.

He stood tall and looked in the mirror and liked what he saw. By his own people's standards, he was handsome, but that wasn't it. Neither was it the muscle-bound frame, jet-black hair and piercing green eyes. It was the uniform of Lieutenant Colonel in the Red Army tank troops and the medals upon it, that gave him satisfaction. Medals that reflected the years of hardship, blood and loss, that accompanied him from Poland in 1941 through to his final battle, in the fatherland of his hated enemy. The rising sun played across his awards, twinkling off them with each breath he took.

His eyes fell upon the 'Hero of the Soviet Union' award that sat apart from and above the rest and, as always, his thoughts went to Alexei and his crew. On his neck above the medal was a scar from that encounter, showing how close the distance between life and death is really measured, as was always the case, his hand rose to seek out the blemish.

The doctor had told him that, in this case, the distance between life and death was about three millimetres, for that was how far the small shard of metal had been from his jugular.

There were other scars and stories to go with them, of course, but none brought back so many ghosts as that one.

He had been Captain Yarishlov at that time and his position at Bilashi, on the northern edge of Kharkov, had been fallen upon by Hausser's SS. Little had been said of it in the Motherland, for it was a stinging defeat at a time of repeated victories, but Arkady knew the human cost of the affair only too well.

He had been ordered to hold the ridge created by the raised railway line by Major Petrenko, dear, cowardly, spiteful bastard Major Petrenko, in order to give time for the rest of the 2nd Guards Tank Corps to prepare a defensive position, around Hoptivka to the north. With a handful of infantry, anti-tank gunners, mortar men and his own T/34's, Arkady had resisted the SS for hours, throwing back attacks from tanks, panzergrenadiers and assault guns.

During the course of the action, Yarishlov received a bullet nick to his calf, a small, but heavily bleeding wound that made him hobble. He received his second wound when he ran at full tilt and threw himself into a trench to avoid incoming mortar rounds. The wound this time was a cracked rib, from accidentally landing on a wooden ammo box, the corner of which penetrated the skin and hurt like hell.

The memento at his throat was picked up from a bursting 105mm high-explosive shell, which destroyed the last Zis-3 anti-tank gun and put its brave crew beyond burial. It had stung for sure and bled like a waterfall, but had not incapacitated him. He ordered the last smoke shells, from his mortars, laid down to cover the withdrawal of his scratch force, as a runner reported their Corps regrouped at Zhuravlevka.

The three surviving senior NCO's moved out and relayed the order to fall back, which order was obeyed immediately, but not without casualties, as the shells continued to fall all around the position.

Senior Lieutenant Alexei Gurundov, commanding the last surviving tank, passed the orders to his crew and the scarred T34 disappeared deeper into the wood in which it had been positioned.

Alexei had taken a final look back, which was fortunate for Yarishlov, as it coincided with the blood loss finally taking its toll and his collapse on the reverse slope of the small hillock on which his command post had been situated. A swift order to halt and Alexei was out of the tank, running for all he was worth, towards the prone form of his commander. Both men had been together since the first bloody days of 11th Mechanised Corps and had been drawn closer by shared hardships and loss, as had many comrades of all nations in those difficult years. Fortunately, the lee of the hillock isolated Gurundov from observation, but the shells were still a problem.

If it had been the other way round, things might have been different, for Gurundov was a bear of a man and Yarishlov was relatively slender. Swept up onto the shoulder, Yarishlov was carried from the field like a roll of carpet, with the safety of the wood reached just before enemy infantry stormed the now abandoned command post. One sharp-eyed SS trooper put a few shots after the pair, but nothing came close and Yarishlov was hauled up on top of the tank by willing hands.

The T34 set off along the track once more.

Eventually, the tank made it back to the next defensive position and the crew took a break, not before they placed their wounded comrade in the hands of the medical service.

Arkady was very weak from loss of blood, but had regained consciousness during the escape, not enough to talk, but enough to listen and certainly enough to drink thirstily from the proffered canteen. He had remained laid on the top of the turret, held in place by Gurundov and his loader, as the tank had bounced along in its search for safety.

As Gurundov laid Arkady on the stretcher, their eyes met, held and unspoken words went between them. Unspoken words of comradeship, love, thanks, fear, hope and warning.

The only words that came were Alexei's.

"Take care, old friend," as he touched Arkady's shoulder and then stepped back to let the medics do their work.

Within three hours, Alexei Gurundov and his crew were statistics; another tank crew immolated in the pursuit of victory. In their case, destroyed by the arrival of a large calibre artillery shell, which landed in their laps as they sat at rest, away from the front line. Their tank was found flipped over, decorated with a grisly mulch of human remains, but was soon recovered and fought on later. The men were never 'officially' found; four more sons of the Rodina, forever lost.

The verbal report given by the departed Gurundov and corroborations from the Starshina of the Mortar Company and Kapitan of the anti-tank unit, were enough to ensure that

167

Arkady received one of his country's most meaningful bravery awards.

Gurundov's death was not known to Yarishlov until the day Major Petrenko visited him in hospital, to inform him of his impending award. Had it been done more sensitively then perhaps, just possibly, Yarishlov would have taken it better, but Petrenko threw the titbit of information at Arkady as he started to leave, turning pride at the recognition of his actions into the abyss of sadness associated with the loss of a close comrade. Petrenko was never one to endear himself to those around him and under him, but he excelled himself that day and would have paled had he read Arkady's mind as he walked out of the hospital.

One week later, to the hour, Captain Yarishlov was presented with his award, by no lesser person than the Bryansk Front Commander, General Maks Andreevich Reiter. He was one of a number of soldiers honoured at the ceremony, some front line swine like himself, others, rear-echelon personnel, who got their piece of metal for who they knew, not what they had achieved. That was, and is, the same in armies all over the world and will never change.

Of Arkady's rearguard force, only four men were left alive. Himself and the Starshina of mortars, who would never fight again, leastways not until the Rodina needed one legged-soldiers desperately. The gunner's Kapitan and one seventeen year old anti-tank soldier were also on the line of recipients.

The Latvian Starshina, Artur Gaudins, got his in hospital, just outside Belgorod and he felt it was a fair exchange, all said and done. His leg for a shiny award and the promise of continued life with his family, away from the horrors of the front.

Anti-tank gunner, Kapitan Yuri Lapanski, proudly received his award from his Corps Commander and posed for Pravda photographs, looking every bit the Soviet Model soldier, the day before he coughed his life out, struck in both lungs by fragments from a short round, fired by friendly artillery.

The younger man, one Boris Orlov, revelled in his award and the celebrity status which accompanied it, for few

168

anti-tank gunners survived after killing a German tank or two and certainly a gunner who had been the sole server of his weapon and still managed to slay seven armoured vehicles was unheard of. He rode his luck for most of the war, strangely failing to destroy another enemy vehicle, despite being in numerous actions. Orlov died, impaled on the bayonet of a teenage paratrooper, during a vigorous German counter attack in East Prussia in '45.

Arkady mused.

'All those thoughts, inspired by the simplest gaze at a piece of treasured metal.'

So, many dead comrades later, Arkady and his troops now rested on the quiet outskirts of sleepy Springe, in Lower Saxony, directly opposite their erstwhile American allies, enjoying their occupation duties in the homeland of those that had done so much harm on their own native soil.

And so now he stood ready for his meeting with those same Americans. He was to be shown the manoeuvrings of a US armored division and, as his American hosts would hope, be impressed with the projection of power it represented and, as his commanders would hope, gather useful information on unit strengths, personnel capabilities,and tactical weaknesses.

Perversely, Arkady had first-hand knowledge of the Americans tanks from the lend-lease scheme. Britain, Canada and the United States, had provided his country with tanks and vehicles, in order to help carry the fight to the Germans whilst the Western Allies did little by way of direct action. He had lost a Sherman, knocked out from underneath him by a panzerfaust, so he was painfully aware of their weaknesses, not as painfully as the members of his then crew, who would bear the scars and torture of their burns until their final day.

Generally, American tanks burned very well.

Before more memories flooded over him, Arkady left his room and walked to the waiting staff car for the drive to Paderborn.

Regard your soldiers as your children,
And they will follow you into the deepest valleys.
Look on them as your own beloved sons,
And they will stand by you even unto death!

Sun Tzu

Chapter 21 – THE HERO

0655hrs Monday, 23rd July 1945, Former SS Panzer Training Centre, Paderborn, US Occupied Germany.

He was the genuine article.

Major John Ramsey VC, DSO and 2 bars, MC and bar, was a real gold-plated military hero, much loved by his country and his men. His country loved him from the first moment he had come to their attention.

Leading his Scottish infantry in the Western Desert, in a desperate, yet successful, defence of a forward position at El Alamein against counter-attacking Italians, he earned his first Military Cross for leadership and personal bravery, some said, a hundred times over. It was followed swiftly by his first Distinguished Service Order, awarded for the successful repulsing of German infantry assaults at Wadi Akarit. His men loved him because he was a superb leader, genuinely concerned for each and every soldier under his command and keen to bring every one back home in one piece, whilst knowing that he would never do so. He asked his boys to do nothing he wouldn't do himself and more than one of his jocks owed their life to him, whether they were dragged back wounded from exposed positions, or preserved by a timely intervention in the heat of combat.

A bar to his MC arrived in the mountains of Sicily, the second award of a DSO during the night attack at the Gerbini railway station* in Sicily and his third award of DSO for actions under fire in the action at Hives, during the Battle of the Bulge.

170

There was a school of thought amongst his peers that Ramsey should have been the first triple holder of the VC, but that award fell to him only once, earned superbly at the cost of a quartet of minor wounds in the gutter fighting that was the Reichswald assault. He destroyed two MG42 positions with grenades and killed the three surviving gunners with nothing more than a commando knife, as his Sten gun had been smashed by a round when he charged forward. He would have gladly traded that award and all the others for the lives of the nine young men of his command that those machine guns had claimed that February afternoon at Hekkens.

His solid and athletic twenty-five year old frame had sustained a score of wounds, on battlefields from Europe to Africa, through the Mediterranean and back to Europe, both before and after the French occupation.

When the dark cloud of war fell over Europe in 1939, he was a young officer, newly arrived with his unit, and it was not long before he took them off to fight in France. Since then and the miracle escape from that conquered land, Ramsey had been constantly in action in theatres across the spectrum of combat and had received more wounds and injuries than most could cope with and he cared to remember, but he always healed fast, so he was soon back in the thick of it all.

His final knock was at the hands of a fourteen year old Bund Deutsche Madel sniper, on the road to Bremerhaven, whose efforts rewarded Ramsey with a wound that bled like a hosepipe, along with a cracked collarbone, and brought the fanatical German girl an instant and violent Valhalla, in the shape of vengeful Scottish bayonets.

Since that last action in Nordenham, Ramsey had been on the mend and his unit withdrawn from serious action, facing only minor skirmishes with remnants of hardcore Germans. Skirmishes still deadly enough to put two of his good friends in early graves for no great purpose.

Now he was to return to his unit, in sufficient time to be reacquainted with his boys, prior to their returning home to Blighty for garrison duties in Edinburgh and possible subsequent redeployment to Palestine or Greece.

171

Himself a regular soldier, Ramsey would remain in the post-war army and, by dint of his many decorations, no doubt carve an illustrious career and achieve the highest ranks. A date at the Palace for the investiture of the Victoria Cross was to come, but the ribbon sat proudly on his chest, as was his right.

However, for now, all he wanted was to be back home and spend some time with his family in the peaceful Berkshire countryside and the opportunity to discover exactly what the freedom of the borough meant in his home village of Hungerford.

In the meantime, there were other duties and so he made sure he was immaculately turned out for the tiresome yank tank display, to which he was committed for the entire day, because of the inconvenient absence of his CO in Bruxelles.

Still, he thought, going home would come soon enough.

Somehow our devils are never quite what we expect when we meet them face to face.

Nelson DeMille

Chapter 22 – THE BROTHERHOOD

1430hrs Monday, 23rd July 1945, Former SS Panzer Training grounds, Paderborn, British Occupied Germany.

Without putting too fine a point on it, most officers there had probably already seen enough tanks to last a hatful of lifetimes. None the less, here they were, basking in the sun on the top of a steep hill in the middle of German nowhere, watching the '15th US Armored Division' exercise and had been since 1115hrs precisely.

From a distance, the casual observer would just see a bunch of soldiers, lacking in animation, with some more bored than others. However, closer up, even the uninitiated would be able to see different uniforms and realise that officers of a number of nations were gathered together.

The exercise was American run, despite the location being in the British-held portion of Germany and so the greater number were clearly US officers, mostly from other units, as the relatively inexperienced members of "15th Armored" struggled not to make fools of themselves in front of people who had actually done it all under fire, on more than one occasion.

Occupying the top of the hill was the young US Senior Officer, a Major General, holding court with a Soviet Army General of Cavalry old enough to be his father. Both had their entourages in place, alternating between making positive sounds to anyone who was in earshot and pouring coffee from huge flasks sat next to the largest mountain of sandwiches anyone had seen this side of the invasion of Poland. As in all these things, there were sycophants and kiss-asses plying their trade, but there were also some serious officers there, wishing to learn, or at least observe the exercise properly.

The first scenario had been a hasty attack against a fortified hillock, well defended by anti-tank guns, infantry and artillery. Experienced observers from the US, UK and Russia conceded that the attack had gone reasonably well and might even have triumphed, had there been real lead and explosive in the air.

The second exercise was nothing short of a shambles, to all except the Divisional Commander, his staff and the Russian cavalry general, for that matter, or so it seemed. In the first instance, any fool could see that gathering tanks in one place, open to observation as they were, would just invite a barrage of artillery in short order. The umpires had a field day with that part. Even if that had not happened, then the choice of attacking up and over a small but pronounced ridge was not sound, as it displayed tender hull floors to any anti-tank weapon in the vicinity. More vehicles were 'removed' at this point.

"At least the umpires are competent" was the acid aside from a British Brigadier, whose insignia indicated that he had his roots in a distinguished cavalry regiment and now had a command in 11th Armoured Division.

To be frank, it was embarrassing. The route the US Regimental commander had selected was nothing short of madness, as even the observers on the hill could see the ground turned to a marsh by a weekend of heavy rain. Sure enough, a large number of tanks bogged down, including the presentation company, comprised of the latest M26 Pershings.

Another of these vehicles was positioned at the bottom of the observer's hill, so that they could study it close up and even get in it if they chose, via the set of wooden steps provided. Two young Soviet junior officers were already taking in every detail, inside and out. Both would submit comprehensive reports upon their return. A number of the staff officers chose to have photos taken, standing in the commander's cupola, already mentally shooting a line to their friends stateside about their time rampaging across the German countryside, sweeping all before them.

The third exercise had apparently been planned as an armoured wedge attack, but it would never start, unless the debacle of the second attack was sorted out and no one seemed in a position to get to grips with it.

One US staff officer tried to climb up onto the M26 and suddenly howled with pain, jumping back like a scalded cat. Sucking on a finger, he complained to the Captain with him that he had broken a nail.

Two other men, one English, the other Russian, had drifted away from unsatisfactory company and now stood together, close by. They exchanged glances. Although they spoke no words, their eye contact spoke silent volumes and they shared a professional smile.

To date, generals and cronies apart, there had been little mixing, but, with the awkward silence broken by the American officer's misfortune, the two struck up a conversation.

The Englishman saluted, which the Russian smartly returned and stuck out his hand.

"Good day to you, Colonel. John Ramsey, Major, The Black Watch, 51st Division."

"Comrade Major," acknowledged the Colonel with the slightest of grins and he shook the offered hand firmly. Ramsey's relief at finding an English speaker was very evident.

"Colonel Arkady Arkadyevich Yarishlov, Red Army Tank Corps."

With a swift toss of the head, Ramsey ventured "Two different types of officer here today, Sir."

"Yes, I agree. Let us hope his nail to be fine in the morning, Major."

Ramsey had always thought of the Russians as a humourless lot, so the comment caught him unprepared and he laughed aloud.

"Indeed, Sir, or the division will grind to a halt."

"I think it will have done so already, Major."

And so the professionals broke the ice at the expense of the amateurs and walked, by some unspoken agreement, to a more private place, strolling silently along a small well-worn path, until stopping adjacent to a large rock.

"You speak excellent English, Colonel. Cigarette?"
Not the first time Arkady had been told that and always in such a way as it seemed a question as to how.

He was happy to supply the answer.

"Thank you, Major. When I was in Military Academy, I were tasked to draw up a total presentation on the Battle of Waterloo. I had to learn English to read the books. Do you know of this battle, Major?"

The unintended humour of that question, timed with a deep draw on his cigarette, caused Ramsey to cough violently.

"I am aware of it, Colonel. We and our German cousins gave the frogs a damn good hiding as I recall."

"I'm sorry, Major. Frogs? I am not …err… understand."

"Ah, so sorry. It is our pet name for our French allies, Colonel."

"Ah yes, I remember now. But why?"

"Something to do with their culinary habits I believe."

Unfortunately, that was also wasted on Yarishlov.

"What is culin-airey, Major?"

"I was talking about the things they eat, Sir. Rumour has it, they eat bits of frogs, such as the legs, Colonel."

"A uncivilised nation indeed, Major, also, my apologies."

No matter how many times it happened, Ramsey could never get used to it. Yarishlov came to full attention and saluted the British Major again, because of the small piece of ribbon on his left breast.

The salute returned, Ramsey ventured "Thank you Colonel. I suppose that you also learned of that little custom from your English studies?"

"I study some more than Waterloo, Major. You are the first VC medal man I have see".

Within the British and Commonwealth forces, any holder of the VC was saluted first, regardless of rank, as an acknowledgement of the importance of the award.

"There are a few about, Sir, certainly a number more since all the unpleasantness started in thirty-nine. You are not without your own awards I see. I suppose we also know that we

176

wear them because we were fortunately seen to do what we did, or were just plain lucky, and that countless others who deserve the same went without recognition."

Yarishlov did not ask about the words he didn't understand because he identified with the spirit of what he knew the Englishman was saying.

"Yes, you are right; mine each having memories, all of which are bad, but they also remind me of comrades and friends I have bury."

A second of silence and a slow knowing nod, "Yes Colonel, I know exactly what you mean".

A nod was returned. Surprisingly, the following silence was not awkward, just two men in inner reflection, with understanding of the other's experiences and both with their own private hells.

Ramsey broke the moment.

"I think we might get back to the group now, Sir. It seems that a decision has been reached. End of business for today, by the look of it".

Yarishlov swivelled to stare uphill and turned back to Ramsey with a beaming smile on his face. "Good. I have had enough of watching these American tanks now. It has been good to meet you, Major Ramsey. I wish you luck for the future."

"As I do to you, Colonel Yarishlov. I hope our future is brighter than some people seem to think."

Yarishlov had started to move, but this comment brought him to an immediate halt.

"What do you mean, Major? The Germanski is defeated, is he not? Soon we go home!" He slapped Ramsey on the shoulder, in a way that was as wholly acceptable to comrades in the Russian tank force, as it was unacceptable to British army officers. In particular, British army officers who recently had a rifle bullet dug out from the same area. It hurt like hell and Ramsey could not help but yelp.

Yarishlov looked appalled. "My friend, I am sorry. You hold yourself well. I did not know."

"It wasn't much but you know how it is. The small ones hurt like hell, Colonel".

"They all hurt, Comrade," stated Yarishlov with a smile, evenly and with the knowledge and conviction of a man who had experienced the full spectrum of what battlefield wounds had to offer.

"I am sorry. What was it?"

"Sniper in Nordenham, just before the end. Nothing serious, Colonel".

"Then we move on. What did you mean?" The imperative present in the first question had gone, but the answer was still expected.

"I mean that relations between the allies and your country seem a little strained at times and there is some worry that your country may wish to aggravate matters more. After all, look at the issues we are facing with moving to the correct demarcation lines."

"I know little of the....aggravation," a moment's pause to receive a confirmation on pronunciation, "Major Ramsey, but I do believe that some people have done some stupid things on both sides."

Ramsey could not argue with that, so accepted it.

Yarishlov ploughed on.

"I know there have been difficulty to withdraw some of our forces, particularly in the Austria area. The Germanski was very good for wrecking, as you know. The train lines are not good. My own unit has had equal difficulties." A dismissive wave of the hand said all that Yarishlov had to say on that point.

"As for the rest, it is just politicians hot wind, is it not? None of us front animals want to start the dance again. Forget it, Major, the Soviet Union is your friend, truly."

And to be honest, Ramsey believed that this Russian meant what he said and believed what he said. However, what he had heard on official briefs plus, his Battalion Commander's confidential chat about his experience at the Hamburg Symposium, had made him worried that something was coming and it was not going to be good. Maybe this Colonel just didn't know, or was he a damn good liar?

"Come, Major, I am taking dinner in Schlangen with the generals and I need to practice lying, so I can tell the Americans how good they are."

Given Ramsey's last train of thought that was not the best thing Yarishlov could have said and he felt a momentary coldness in his stomach.

The Russian looked around and pointed.

"Let us talk to those officers there so I can get my lies practice right."

It was the grin that did it, splitting the Russians face from ear to ear and the coldness went as quickly as it had come. They strolled leisurely forward towards a group of American officers.

"I'm afraid I can only lie so much, Colonel. I may have to answer a call of nature if it gets too bad."

"What is call of nature, Major?"

"Too much coffee Colonel, a man must walk off alone to get rid of it."

"Ah, you need piss, yes?"

"Well not yet, sir, but I may do if the Americans ask too many potentially embarrassing questions."

"I think I understand that. A good plan. Perhaps I should have some more coffee first?"

Ramsey liked this man, although something told him he really should not. One of the Americans moved forward and a Texas-twang cut through his thoughts.

"Ah, Lootenant Colonel Yarslov, I hope you enjoyed the display we put on, sir?" The casual salute was only just on the right side of acceptability, whereas Yarishlov's return was as impressive as earlier.

"Yes, thank you, Major?"

"Parker, Nathaniel T, sir."

"I learned much. May I introduce Major Ramsey of His Majesty's Black Watch?"

The two Majors exchanged salutes that confirmed the lack of respect in the salute given to Arkady. Neither did the American honour the VC, although that was not an issue for the holder in any case. Yarishlov noted the immaculate nature of the man's uniform and the vast array of medal ribbons on his chest.

"It's a shame we had to curtail the day, sir. We had a real peach of a run organised for number three." If he could have puffed himself up any more, then the American would have exploded in a second. "Designed it myself, sir. Armoured wedge attack over open ground, with artillery rolling only one hundred yards in front of the van. Would have been a real show for y'all."

"Another time, Major, another time."

Words that were meaningless, for Yarishlov had already promised himself never to attend another of these nonsenses if he could possibly avoid it.

"Your General enjoyed the two we ran though. Very complimentary, sir, very complimentary."

"Then you should be pleased, for the General is a man of great experience and knows what he is talking about." The General did indeed know his trade, which was why Yarishlov knew the General must have practiced his lying too."

"Excuse me," swiftly saluting both, "I need to answer a call of nature," and Ramsey was quickly gone.

"He means he needs piss, Major," confided Yarishlov, in the style of a teacher back in his old school.

"Musta needed it badly, that's all I can say, Colonel." Gazing with scant interest at a retreating Ramsey, he ventured an opinion.

"Looks a bit weak in spine to me."

Yarishlov looked directly at Parker, face smiling, eyes not.

"That being caused of bullet from a fascist sniper, Major."

He turned his gaze in the direction of the disappearing Englishman.

"He also wears the Victoria medal, so his spine is not being so weak. You might not have see that. Anyway, it have been too much coffee for him I thinks, Major."

"So he's been around the block too. Medals everywhere around here," dismissed the American, actually annoying Arkady.

180

"Anything I can help you with before we move off, Colonel?"

"Are the tank recovery team well practised, Major? They seem to be taking their time down there," swiftly changing the subject to mask his strange feeling of hurt for the British Officer and indicating a field of bogged-down armour and half-tracks with a gesture of his left arm.

"No, sir. We sprung this on them as a surprise exercise. Part of the plan. It will take them a'whiles to get the vehicles back online."

Yarishlov could not suppress the amusing thought about who had been practicing lying the most, for the American was being outrageous.

"Not same Sherman tanks to the one's I had used, Major."

"Indeed sir? I believe we sent you quite a few and I'm sure they made all the difference. The Sherman is a good horse with plenty of firepower. Equal of the panzer in my view, Colonel."

Which it certainly was not, but Yarishlov wasn't going to argue with the man's obvious lack of hard-won expertise on enemy armour, no matter how outrageous he was being. His view of Americans was nose-diving by the second.

"Still y'all had a good day. Makes a nonsense of all the talk, doesn't it?"

"What talk might that be, Major?" the annoyed Russian was already preparing a similar response to the one Ramsey had received earlier.

"I mean all this nonsense about you maybe planning an attack on us, Colonel. Spent a whole week in some French castle with some ex-kraut officers. Learning about your tactics, just in case. Their top dog was ex-SS too". The Major deliberately hawked and spat, solely to impress Yarishlov.

"Bastards got me transferred from my unit because they couldn't deal with the fact that I was better than them." The bitterness in his voice was extreme. "Cost me my bird for some time to come."

Yarishlov clearly did not understand.

181

"My bird," tapping his collar, "Lieutenant Colonel's rank. Won't get that because of the attitude problem they reported I have."

Yarishlov had a look on his face that Parker interpreted as support, but that was actually something entirely different.

"Anyway, whole thing doesn't scour at all. Waste of time. We all kicked the krauts out, so why would we start on each other? Reckon it's the goddamn Nazis agitating myself. Goddamned symposium nonsense. Hell, we've even got one of our own too!"

Parker let out a huge sigh.

"It's enough to try the patience of a saint, Colonel."

Parker extracted his Lucky Strikes and proffered the pack to Yarishlov, who declined.

Parker lit up.

"Still, I'm having a week's furlough in the south of France soon as I can. Colonel, Biarritz, you should go there some time, sir. Hell of a place for a man to relax."

The Major just let it all come tumbling out without a care in the world. Had he looked more closely, he would have realised that a Russian Lieutenant Colonel just had his antenna twitch. But he didn't, so he had no idea that the Russian was making a mental note that this 'Symposium" was something he had to write up in his report, on return. He also missed the look on the face of a Black Watch Major, returning from his unnecessary call of nature, wondering incredulously whether he had just heard what he thought he had heard.

"I may well do, Major," was about all Yarishlov could say, as he processed the look on the approaching Ramsey's face.

'Something is wrong, but what is it?'

"Did you see much action, Colonel?" was about the most stupid question the fool could have asked, but it didn't stop him from asking it.

"I saw a few battles, Major, enough to satisfy my childhood desiring for such things."

"We saw quite a bit ourselves, of course," which both Russian and Englishman knew was a crass lie, for both had

182

discovered that the soldiers present had only been in Europe since early March and at a time when the German was surrendering to anything that came from the west. It was different for the Russians, of course. Their final days of combat had seen the bloody Armageddon of Berlin that had cost so many lives.

However, both men's thoughts were still in turmoil. Ramsey working out what had been said; did he really hear the words "Biarritz" and 'symposium"? Yarishlov replaying the event and trying to decide what exactly had happened.

"Anyway, Major, now I must have piss of nature too. Goodbye and thank you. Major Ramsey." Salutes exchanged and Yarishlov was gone.

Ramsey struggled to find a way to approach the matter without going at it head-on. So he did. "Did you tell the Russian about the symposiums, Major?"

"Hell no, just told him we get a whole load of boring lectures, that's all."

"And Biarritz? You mentioned Biarritz."

"That's where I'm going on furlough next week, Major. Just told the Colonel that he might want to go there someday."

Ramsey could not help but think the very obvious thought that the Russians might well want to go there one day, in something painted green, but resisted making further enquiries. He would have to mention this in his report anyway, so he would leave it for now. What Ramsey did know was that both words appeared on his top secret joining orders for 6th August, for a week of special training. Secret was a word he understood and clearly the yank did not.

None the less, he took further stock of the young Texan in front of him and his eyes were drawn to an ornate emblem on his chest.

"May I enquire what that is for, Major? It is very grand and must be important indeed."

The American swelled and puffed out his chest.

"I got that for being second in my class at the Texas Military Institute, Major. That reminds me. The Colonel said you have the Victoria Cross. What did you get that for?

"For being first in my class in the School of the Reichswald, Major. There were no prizes for being second. Good day to you."

And with a salute that Ramsey had never meant less in his entire career, he strode off towards the Brigadier and his staff.

1602hrs Monday, 23rd July 1945, Former SS Panzer Training grounds, Paderborn, British Occupied Germany.

Yarishlov joined up with the Soviet entourage as they prepared to return to Schlangen for a dinner with the American Staff. He was beckoned forward by the general.

"Ride with me, Arkady Arkadyevich, ride with me and tell me your thoughts."

"Yes, Comrade General," directing his own staff car to follow without him.

As the Mercedes-Benz, which had been appropriated some weeks before hand, started off on the short journey, Yarishlov was encouraged to speak his mind.

"I believe that the unit we saw today is extremely inexperienced, unless the Americans are deliberately misleading us. I am not sure they are that clever."

"You are right, Colonel, they saw little action. We have no intelligence on a 15th Tank Division in any case, but we know the men have been in Europe for only a few months. However, it is not important. What is important to me is what you think of them?" The strange emphasis on the word 'them' caused Arkady a moment's puzzlement.

He replied with the truth as he saw it.

"They have neither the skills nor the equipment to function properly in the field. Their experienced units simply have to be better than these we have seen today, or the green toads would have devoured them in an instant. The new Pershing tank looks nice, but it floundered in modest mud, as you saw."

"Indeed. Whichever officer directed that second assault would be counting trees in Siberia now, if he were one of mine."

184

"One of yours would not have done such a thing, Comrade General," stated Arkady with total conviction.

"But what of them, Arkady? What of them?"

"I spent some time with a British Major. He is a professional, for certain, Comrade General, as were the other British I saw." He paused just long enough to consider the next statement. "The Americans I spoke to were fools. I saw not one man there who I would trust on my right-hand in combat, Comrade General."

Arkady felt as if his words were a catalyst to something, but he didn't know what.

The General smiled and merely spoke, softly and with certainty, "Fools indeed, Arkady."

The American units had been running field exercises at Paderborn the whole week before the Soviet visit, in an effort to get combat effective. They were actually a conglomerate of newly arrived formations, as yet unassigned to any division, but it had been decided to place them under the fictitious umbrella of the 15th US Armored Division, purely for the purpose of masking their true identity. Had they been veteran US tankers, perhaps the reports that went back to Moscow might have said something very different.

A moment of luck, good or bad, often plays a greater part in our destiny than hours of design.

Ernst-August Knocke

Chapter 23 – THE REPORTS

1430hrs Wednesday, 25th July 1945, Soviet Military Intelligence Headquarters, Schloss Gunsdorf, Leipzig, Soviet Occupied Germany.

The reports written by Yarishlov and Ramsey held much the same information. Firstly, that the American tank exercise had been an utter shambles. Both explained the reasons why, although Yarishlov's expertise in tank combat made his submission more detailed in that regard. Secondly, that the American officers either did not realise it had all gone badly wrong, or were delusional, or lying, or a combination of those. Thirdly, an American officer had made direct mention of the word 'Symposium'. Ramsey's report also included the word 'Biarritz' and the US officer's identity.

He submitted it to his Colonel's office, from whence it was sent to Brigade headquarters. The Staff Sergeant, responsible for compiling the daily bulletin for the Brigadier's ADC, started to read it, but was disturbed by a package delivery to the office. He put the message down and returned to it, only to find that a large area was smouldering where he had placed the paper over his cigarette. In a panic, he dowsed it with tea, screwed up the document and stuffed it in his pocket, disposing of it down the latrine as soon as possible.

In Yarishlov's report, this 'Symposium' in a French castle was identified as something that he felt was important and he also mentioned that he felt the British Major, who had overheard part of the conversation, looked concerned by it. The whole conversation with the US officer was recorded reasonably well. Even though Arkady wondered if he was making an elephant from a fly, his professional senses had lit off at the time and he had to trust them.

186

That report ended up in the office of overworked GRU Colonel General Pekunin, whose staff was presently tasked with interpreting intelligence gained on the Western Allies and compiling detailed reports for the GKO. The inclusion of certain key words meant that some reports ended up on his desk. In this case, the word 'symposium' was familiar to him and he immediately summoned another GRU officer to his office.

"Ah, Comrade Nazarbayeva, this may be of interest to you. Full analysis on my desk in four hours."

Apart from looking up briefly to check it was the Kapitan he had called who came in, the General never lifted his eyes from the file before him. Tatiana took the proffered report and left the room, but not before she had caught the words "Kingdom39" on the file that the General was finding so captivating.

Tatiana Sergievna Nazarbayeva understood that perfectly and smiled, for she was a mother who had read to her four sons, and to Russian children the 39th Kingdom was where all good fairytales are set; in a land far, far away.

Nazarbayeva was forty-six years old and strikingly beautiful for a Russian woman. Rich black hair and piercing brown eyes brought her many admiring glances from senior officers but, despite numerous advances, she remained loyal to her husband Yuri, a combat infantryman with a Guards Corps.

She had once been a fighting soldier with a mortar unit in the Crimea, fighting through the difficult retreats, right up to the crushing defeat on the Kerch Peninsula in May 1942. During heavy fighting, she had picked up a Mosin rifle on occasions to clear direct pressure on her unit and was credited with seventeen kills in an hour, outside Osovyny, when the panzer-grenadiers of the 22nd Panzer Division had pressed her unit hard.

As her company's position was about to be overwhelmed, she counter-attacked single-handedly with grenades and a pistol, driving off the Germans with heavy casualties. One souvenir of that bloody time was kept well hidden and few ever noticed the slight limp, caused by the absence of half of her left foot; the only serious injury she sustained during her time in action. She was the last wounded soldier loaded on the last boat to escape the debacle, a defeat that saw the rest of her unit disappear into German captivity.

It had taken her some months and use of a special metal ankle strap, to learn to walk with anything approaching a normal gait.

Despite the constant presence of her limp, the other souvenir of those desperate times attracted much more attention.

She was the second woman to receive the Hero of the Soviet Union Gold Star and she wore it with pride.

None the less, many wondered if she had secured her present position by use of her obvious charms, but that was not how she had advanced to become a respected Captain in the GRU. Her rank and status were achieved through her abilities and excellence at her job.

It was no surprise to Pekunin that, three hours and forty-seven minutes later, she placed a comprehensive and detailed report in front of him, which now surmised that there were four symposium operated by the Western Allies, not three as Russian Military Intelligence first thought.

Their purpose was already known through other means, but this was the first sniff of a possible French-run facility so far. Given the placement of the other three known symposium, it seemed likely that the French would place theirs in Alsace, Franche-Comte, or Rhone-Alpes. If the French symposium followed the same rules on the national identity of attendees as the others did, then the most likely location for the travel convenience of US and UK officers would be Alsace. A list of castles and other similar structures in Alsace was attached, complete with suitability profiles, where information had been available.

There was also more confirmation of the Western Allies 'apparent belief that an attack would take place.' Also of note was that there was no record of a 15th US Armored Division on the order of battle for the Western Allies, so either it was another unit masquerading as part of some sort of

American 'maskirova', or it was a new formation. Given the appreciation within the report, it was felt most likely to be a new formation and a poor one at that.

To round off the report, a list of possible German officer candidates of Colonel rank or above known to be in French captivity was attached. Admittedly, the list ran to over two hundred names, but Tatiana had asterisked seven who she considered the most likely candidates. Six of them were SS and number two on the list was a name of some considerable repute. Also attached was a copy of the French Military Intelligence request for information on a list of German officers. Some names appeared in both lists and Tatiana had cross-referenced them. There was also reference links to three other GRU files relating to numbers two, five and six. Those were not to hand, but the report indicated that copies had been urgently requested from the GRU department covering the former East Prussia. It was an excellent report and wholly accurate.

Pekunin placed it in his briefcase with the intention of reading it again on his flight to Moscow. If it was all that he thought it was, then it was about time Tatiana received her next step on the promotion ladder. In the meantime, instructions were issued to act upon its contents.

How many things apparently impossible have nevertheless been performed by resolute men who had no alternative but death.

Napoleon Bonaparte

Chapter 24 – THE EXECUTIONS

1210hrs Friday, 27th July 1945, The Kremlin, Moscow, USSR.

There were always minor details to confront and review, even for the powerful and great.

As the date approached when Kingdom39 could go live, more problems presented themselves.

Rigidly, the GKO stuck to their requirement of the 3rd August and faced down every request for delay from Zhukov and Vasilevsky.

The previous day, GRU reports had been forwarded from all over the former Germany and landed on Pekunin's desk in Gunsdorf. Nazarbayeva and her staff had collated the facts and Pekunin was able to send specific instructions for his agents in Western Europe before he left his office to fly to Moscow.

Beria and Stalin had been celebrating the undoubted advantages that their plans had secured, as a result of Churchill's removal from power in the UK General Election, confirming Stalin's view that such democracy undermined a country's stability and welfare.

Their crowing was interrupted when Pekunin arrived bearing bad tidings.

The contents of that report had been discussed, and they all now sat in the General Secretary's office, waiting for the arrival of another.

The telephone rang and a brief message was relayed.

Stalin did not even acknowledge the caller and returned the handset to its proper place.

The doors opened and in strode Major-General Ivan Makarenko, commander of the 100th Guards Rifle Division 'Svir'.

He stood before Stalin for the first time, but, unlike many, he seemed unafraid.

"Comrade General, how is the planning for your task going?" Stalin obviously knew, but he had chosen to approach this man differently.

"It is complete, Comrade General Secretary. Comrade General Pekunin was able to supply the last piece of the jigsaw two days ago." That the last piece of the jigsaw was the precise location of Symposium Paderborn and the strength of its military presence went unsaid. For Pekunin, it had been a close run thing and Beria had enjoyed watching him sweat before he passed on the information his NKVD agents had acquired, just in time.

"We now practice mock attacks upon targets chosen because of the similarities to the symposiums. In three days, we will be ready, Comrade General Secretary."

Beria questioned the statement on behalf of all the listeners.

"Three days, Comrade Makarenko? Surely you will need longer?"

"That is not the case, Comrade Marshal. Once we had the precise locations, we need only to have some knowledge of the area and target. The more time we have, the better, but we will be relying on surprise and firepower. That will not increase with time, so three days will get the basics into my boys."

That was quite some speech and marked the fact that this was Makarenko's first time in his present company.

"Why then, are you here in Moscow and not working with your division, Comrade?"

Makarenko straightened and spoke with real emotion.

"Colonel Erasov, my second in command, was killed in training, Comrade General Secretary. I am here to honour him when he is buried today. It is my wish to tell his wife and four sons how proud they should be of their father, who fought from the first day that the Germanski violated the borders of our Motherland."

191

Stalin nodded and spoke softer words. "Tell his family that the party feels their loss." Despite the difference in tone, there was no warmth or sincerity there.

"Thank you, Comrade General Secretary, I will."

"We will not delay you further, but do not dally here in Moscow. There is a new development. Comrade General Pekunin?"

Stalin indicated Pekunin and lit up a cigarette.

The GRU General addressed Makarenko directly.

"News has reached us of a new symposium; one run by the French. It too must be eliminated. All we know for now is that it is probably in Alsace. Comrade Marshal Beria and I have assets working tirelessly to locate it. In the meantime, you must change your plan to include this new location and allocate the necessary forces to its total destruction."

Makarenko's face had grown cold.

Handing over a folder with all the new information, Pekunin spoke with conviction.

"I know you can do this, Ivan Alexeyevich... and you know I will have that information as soon as I can."

A nod to Pekunin, a salute to his commander and Makarenko strode from the room.

From the first moment he had been handed his orders, he knew it was a suicide mission. Projections for his troops to fall in with advancing Soviet columns were unrealistic and he knew his troopers were mainly going to death or captivity.

Moreover, that was with only three targets. He mused fatalistically.

'Now, at least, death would come quicker.'

As Makarenko departed, those remaining turned to other matters. Stalin spoke directly to Pekunin, but with words intended for both senior men.

"The location of this new French operation. We must give Makarenko his three days."

In the intelligence world, acquiring information was rarely done to timescale, but, in Stalin's case, he didn't care, so he laid out the requirement anyway.

Beria unexpectedly came to Pekunin's rescue.

"Comrade General Secretary, I have all of my assets in the area focussed on this one task. By sharing information with our GRU colleagues we are removing possible locations from the list each hour."

Beria looked at Pekunin, who took up the baton.

"Comrade Marshal Beria's staff and mine have managed to reduce the possible locations down to a manageable number and we have both dispatched agents to investigate the remaining potential locations." Beria risked a swift glance at the GRU man, because even the number left would take their agents days to check thoroughly, unless they received something that would allow them to focus specifically.

"We have acquired much intelligence these past months, when our officers have mixed with the Western Allies, as the capitalists have loose tongues. GRU and NKVD officer numbers have been substantially increased for every official liaison, to assist in intelligence gathering, but we must be careful to avoid causing suspicion for our Allies."

"However, as part of our plan has been to reduce these liaisons for own operational security, as well as causing and provoking minor incidents to keep both sides more apart, there has been less opportunity for this sort of intelligence acquisition."

Pekunin was very careful to keep his voice neutral in that delivery, as those mainly responsible for the plan to reduce interaction between the armies were listening to him now.

"The shooting down of the RAF aircraft yesterday evening will greatly affect relationships, as it was planned to do, but will certainly reduce the effectiveness of the liaisons in providing us with information, most certainly with our former comrades from Britain and her cronies."

Pekunin handed the baton back to Beria.

"However, our agreement with the Western Allies, regarding specific German prisoners is holding and we have three groups touring their prison camps looking for war criminals. From Comrade Pekunin's reports we have established some likely names for the symposium personnel and have yet to find any in the allies' camps."

"That, in itself, is disturbing, Comrade General Secretary. We would have expected to find some of the names on our list by now."

Stalin was inwardly amused, as the two intelligence leaders presented a unique united front, mainly for his benefit and, as it suited the Party's purpose, he would say nothing to disrupt it.

Beria concluded.

"In any case, we are sure to find something of note during these visits and liaisons, as well as through our own direct efforts. As you point out, correctly, it is just a matter of time, Comrade General Secretary, but we must give Makarenko his three days."

"Very well, comrades, we must move on. But first, tea"

The normal procedure of phone and orderly followed.

When the three of them were alone again, Stalin puffed deeply on his pipe and spoke.

"Comrades, have the order for Operation Sumerechny [*Twilight*] sent out today for implementation immediately. I want the bastards out of the way, or in the ground, as soon as possible."

Although neither of the other men was surprised, they exchanged glances.

Sumerechny was the codename for phase thirteen, the mass movement of German POW's and general execution of officer prisoners.

Beria spoke first.

"We have made a further assessment, Comrade General Secretary. Using the rolling stock that is bringing our forces to their rallying points to remove the prisoners, we can have most of the problem resolved before Kingdom initiates. Combined with those numbers, for whom we intend different disposal, I anticipate the whole eastern area will be cleared, one way or another, by Day+8, provided there are no increased calls on NKVD or GRU troops in the interim. We have designated certain German prisoner groups as worker groups, who will perform the labouring tasks required, before they too join their comrades."

194

"Comrade Marshal Beria and I have already agreed that we can transfer additional assets from our units in the Ukraine and elsewhere, if necessary, allowing for the fact that that would slow down the resettlement programmes there."

Looking at Beria for support, Pekunin continued.

"We have not actioned this yet, but it is in line with your edict on priorities."

It was only a few seconds silence as Stalin thought it through, but it seemed longer to the GRU officer.

"The Ukrainian monkeys can wait a while longer. Transfer the assets, if it becomes necessary, ensuring sufficient left in place for security. I don't want those damn Slavs starting anything that could damage our western operations."

It was as easy as that. A decision that was to move uncountable numbers of men hundreds of miles and condemn thousands of others to instant death.

The orders flowed around Europe and by midday on the 28th, large contingents of German prisoners were moving eastwards. Driven on foot by their guards, most were glad to be leaving their accommodation, but all shared the trepidation that accompanied a clear move to the east and away from their homelands.

Other groups of Soviet security troops were tasked very differently and the killing started.

Military officer figures, Captain had been selected as the lowest rank to be liquidated, were herded away from the large groups on some pretext.

The plan was simple.

Move the German prisoners away from the logistical routes so they could not cause problems. Use the returning transport to expedite the move swiftly. Kill as many German officers as possible.

Katyn had been cited in Stalin's office and it was a fair comparison.

From camps the length and breadth of Soviet occupied Europe, columns of men were on the move, whilst assassination squads worked feverishly before moving on to the next assignment.

As was bound to happen, some camps realised what was happening and there were outbreaks of rebellion. In such cases, five in total, everyone was killed out of hand. In those five camps alone, seven thousand prisoners were efficiently murdered. Flamethrowers were employed to burn the bodies in their huts, after the surviving prisoners had stacked their comrades and then were shot in turn.

One incident outside of Ostrava saw a column of nine hundred and fifty prisoners denied use of the bridge over the Opava River.

Men who had been run into the ground for hours previously, were forced into the water in a bid to reach the other bank. Comrade struggled to help comrade; those who could swim attempted to assist those who could not, through lack of ability, emaciation, exhaustion, or injury. They drowned in their hundreds.

Less than two hundred men formed on the other side and of them, only one hundred and twenty-six made it to the railway line, the rest falling dead or dying en route.

About two thousand men who crowded into a modest steamer were lost in the Baltic, when it ran into a floating German mine off Danzig.

Trains crammed with prisoners flowed eastwards in the daytime and back again at night, filled with very different cargoes.

Some trains hauled only bodies to special sites, where they were swiftly interred and all traces removed.

It was murder on a huge scale.

Some have been thought brave because they were afraid to run away.

Thomas Fuller

Chapter 25 – THE BOY

1210hrs Friday, 27th July 1945, Tank Laager, Stendal, Soviet Occupied Germany.

He was the product of his country's military machine, twenty-two years of age, finely honed, schooled in war and all it's intricacies and yet, both fortunately and humiliatingly, he had seen no combat. Short and thin, he was unassuming to the eye, but had abilities that were apparent to all those who taught him during his formative years.

Selected for the officer training as much because of his connections as for his obvious talents, Junior Lieutenant Vladimir Stelmakh had eventually been given command of a brand new development in Soviet armour, namely the Iosef Stalin III. A beast of a tank, some of his peers and one of his class mates had ridden them into action in a small skirmish south of Berlin, quickly immolating two tired old Panzer IV's and a battery of 105mm Flak guns, without a shot being fired back at them.

Yet more of his friends had been dispatched across the country, to serve in the upcoming Manchurian Operation, but he, both to his chagrin and relief, still languished in barracks outside the German capital.

Son of a distinguished Red Army General, a man of impeccable political roots, as well as of the highest military credentials, Vladimir had done all the things a good up and coming member of the party should do. Meetings attended, works carried out with the Young Communists, forever earning the praise of those who now watched over his progression.

His father had met his death at the hands of the Luftwaffe, on the South-Western Front near Kalach in late 1942, leading his troops from the front in one of the many desperate counter-attacks of those fraught times.

The full nurturing of Vladimir's career meant he was not thrown into the final days and was extended the honour of serving with the 6th Guards Heavy Tank Breakthrough Regiment, 12th Guards Tank Corps, equipped with the revolutionary IS-III, ready to engage the heavier German tanks on even terms with a vehicle of excellent armour defence and hitting power.

Whilst it was an honour to be selected, it was a double-edged sword, because, as the son of a holder of numerous of his nation's highest awards, Vladimir would obviously need to claim some glory of his own, if he was not to fall forever under the shadow of his predecessors. Even his grandfather had, in the Czar's time, won fame and accolades in the Great War, although the final and highest accolade had admittedly also been accompanied by untimely death.

The prospect of serving in the crushing of Japan's Manchurian army had similarly raised his hopes, which were crushed in turn and he remained behind, as classmates and comrades took their tanks off to fight in the final battles of the war in the east.

It was difficult for him to wholeheartedly indulge in the European victory celebrations with his comrades, when all that sat on his chest were his political awards, not one earned for risking his life in combat, or leading his troops in swift victories.

The majority of his unit were veterans, survivors of many bitter clashes with the hated panzers, those whose wits had preserved, skills had saved, or lady luck had plucked from certain death. They had meted out their share of destruction upon the Germans and carried the rewards of their bravery on their uniforms, as proudly as they bore the scars sustained earning them underneath them. Alongside them, Vladimir felt equally shamed and relieved, as there was nothing he could do to rectify the situation, so he would probably forever be bereft of evidence of his prowess in combat and his commitment to the Motherland.

The American officers with whom he often enjoyed off-duty time, had no idea the metal on his chest came from non-combat achievements, so, with them at least, he could relax a little. That was perverse, for they represented a system as much despised as the National Socialist system that had brought his Motherland so much death and destruction. The capitalists had been useful during the patriotic struggle, that was true, but their system was corrupt and would undoubtedly fall in time.

Whilst others found the Western Allies offensive and considered them as much an enemy as the Germans so recently crushed, Vladimir found solace and comfort in their company, solely because they had no idea of his failure to contribute to the event of the century.

In his duties, he was impeccable, training to the highest standard, preparing his troopers for a battle already over. He learned the intricacies of his new tank in depth and was quick to pass on his knowledge to all his men.

His crews loved him, all the same, recognising the hurt in him, alongside the extraordinary abilities of the natural born leader. They strove to be the best they could be, partially because memory told them they had needed to be and partially to make their leader proud of what he had made them into.

If the hated Germans rose again, then the heavy tank platoon commanded by Junior Lieutenant Vladimir Stelmakh would walk tall on the battlefield and give such an account of itself that his name would eclipse that of his forebears.

However, he knew that the German was a vanquished foe and that he would never take his men into glorious combat and, for that, he was both sorry and happy, for Vladimir was a coward.

I like to see a man proud of the place in which he lives. I like to see a man live so that his place will be proud of him.

Abraham Lincoln

Chapter 26 – THE PARATROOPER

0705hrs Monday, 30th July 1945, Château du Haut-Kœnigsbourg, French Alsace.

He was twenty-five and home was a thing of distant memory for Captain, Acting Major, Marion J Crisp of the 101st US Airborne Division. It would have been even more distant if his application to join the newly formed 13th US Airborne Division had been approved, for that unit was being prepared for the invasion of the Japanese homeland. That would be no brief encounter and certainly no picnic.

However, others had been chosen in his stead and so he was now resigned to either joining the slow but steady stream of US service personnel returning to their own country after service overseas, or remaining on the continent to police the remains of Europe.

Neither seemed a rosy prospect.

Crisp had joined the army to fight, for he saw, across the Atlantic, the growing Nazi threat to his country, if not realistic now, then certainly for the future. With the Japanese attack had come a focus elsewhere. He resolved to seek transfer to a combat unit destined for service in the Pacific, until the formation of the paratrooper units caught his eye and assaulted his senses with tales of glory, action, élan and professionalism and he was hooked.

After completing his training, Crisp was given his platoon and he took them across the Atlantic to train and prepare for combat. Billeted outside the small Berkshire village of Hungerford, close to the Wiltshire border, Crisp brought his men up to and beyond excellence. Skills were honed in manoeuvres through the green fields and country lanes of England. His utter professionalism and drive pushed him to the

200

forefront of a unit of similar professionals and his silver bar came quickly.

It was as a First Lieutenant that he made the D-Day jump with the 501st Airborne Infantry, Charlie Company, 101st US Airborne Division.

On that bloody day, he had earned his Silver Star rescuing, under fire, the dying pieces of a man that had once been his Captain and leading the remnants of the company in successful action against a German paratrooper force. Paratrooper fighting paratrooper always carried a special meaning and ferocity and that combat had left him with less than half the men he had jumped with still on their feet. His first purple heart was nearly the last award he received, for the bullet that creased his head would have ended his life if it had been an inch to the left.

Acting as infantry for many weeks after the initial assault, his paratroopers engaged the cream of Germany's forces and gave good account of themselves, in particular, dishing out some heavy punishment to the 17th SS Panzer-Grenadiere Division and, in turn, receiving a mauling at the hands of the 2nd SS Panzer Division.

After being withdrawn to England for recovery and the integration of reinforcements, some lunatic had come up with the nightmare plan of Market-Garden and again he dropped with his men into German territory. Fate dealt him a heavy blow and he was unfortunate to break his leg on landing. He never fired a shot during the operation and never saw a German. His company went forward to battle, once more confronted by SS panzer troops, but this time they fought only to a bloody draw.

He returned to the unit before his leg had properly healed, just in time for the move forward to Bastogne, during the Battle of the Bulge. It was here that the Distinguished Service Cross was earned. During an engagement with the 9th SS Panzer Division, the young Captain, still inhibited by his damaged leg, ran, crawled and stumbled through a storm of fire to successfully destroy three German panzers with his bazooka and crowned that by using a discarded MG34 to destroy a German platoon that was outflanking his own position.

There was a school of thought that he earned that 'medal of medals' more than once in those cold and bitter days, as his inspirational leadership, guts and determination, carried his unit through some terrible times in the face of everything that the enemy could throw at them.

His conduct in the drive into Germany proper had brought him a second DSC, for taking the village of Nussdorf single-handedly. He drove into the fortified position alone, in a jeep, parleying with the garrison commander under a flag of truce. Legends were built around what he may or may not have said to that SS Major, but the fact that three hundred and forty heavily armed SS diehards gave themselves up, without so much as a bun thrown, was huge testament to the personality of the man.

The German surrender had found the unit in Southern Germany, on the Austrian border, near Berchtesgarten. Most of the paratroopers who had survived heaved their collective sighs of relief and awaited their passage home, for they were certainly assured they would be amongst the first. Some, like Crisp, volunteered for the Japanese assault, but were not afforded the opportunity to transfer into the newly forming airborne units. Some, unlike Crisp, got their orders and were already on their way to death or glory in warmer climes.

The 501st was separated from the division and settled into France for retraining, prior to being shipped to the Pacific in its own right, after the assault.

Which brought him round to today, Monday 30th July 1945.

He stood in front of the ornate full-length mirror and adjusted his tie, before working his experienced eye over his uniform from head to foot. With a nod of approval to himself, he walked to the window and looked out over a stunning view, vineyards and villages spread out as far as the eye could see.

A check of the newly installed wall clock, which had ticked relentlessly through the still of the night, indicated that breakfast time was already upon him, his first meal since his late Sunday evening arrival.

One last look of appreciation for his baronial surroundings and he left the room, in search of the mess hall.

202

At the bottom of the hexagonal stairs, he found no clues, but luckily an orderly emerged from the kitchens.

"Excuse me. Could you please show me to the mess hall?"

"Of course, Commandant, follow me if you please." Crisp was conducted back upstairs and shown into the impressive stone columned dining room, wherein sat a number of allied officers, eating large breakfasts and chattering incessantly.

His eyes took in the officers, none of whom noticed his arrival. Twelve French and four Brits, with solely one other in the uniform of the US Army.

And so it was that the last member of the third class sat down for breakfast in the grand dining room of the Château du Haut-Kœnigsbourg.

Fortune brings in some boats that are not steered.

William Shakespeare

Chapter 27 – THE CHANCE

1659hrs Monday, 30th July 1945, Bossong's, Quai de Pêcheurs, Selestat, French Alsace.

Whilst the great men sat in the Kremlin and made decisions affecting the lives of everyone on the planet and allied officers listened to the sage words of Germans in the symposiums, a conversation took place in a vintners in Selestat.

Bossong's was an old shop, a symbol of a bygone age, but it still served its purpose well. Ancient wooden shelving, created specifically for housing delicate vintages, surrounded the open central area, where stood a tall table, complete with all the paraphernalia associated with the tasting of fine wines.

The layer of dust and mulchy smell were all part of the image, as were the huge oil lamps that cast their flickering shadows around the room.

A gothic style wall clock loudly chimed five o'clock in the afternoon, completing the scene.

The owner had continued trade as well as he could over the German occupation and, with the coming of the allies, had recovered some of his considerable hidden stocks to sell to the allied liberators at a fine profit.

Loose tongues had immediately wagged and a requisition order from the French Army had arrived, born by a smartly turned out French Commando officer, reducing his best Alsatian stock to a bare minimum. Admittedly, he would be paid, but not at the rate he was securing from the allied officers who presently frequented his establishment.

One such, a Polish liaison officer with the French First Army, had visited for his regular bottle of Trimbach, only to find the owner sympathetic but not forthcoming.

Despite the fact that the previous Friday there had been well over a hundred bottles available, today the owner had none for sale.

"But Monsieur, surely you can find a bottle for me? I have promised my girl some of your fine Trimbach."

"Commandant, I regret I cannot, even for a good customer such as yourself. I have none available and neither do I have any Edelzwicker either, for both supplies have been requisitioned by the Army of France."

The Polish Major leaned forward, inviting the proprietor into conspiracy.

"Surely they would not miss one bottle, Monsieur Bossong?"

The owner looked up at the doorway, even though he knew no one was there.

"Commandant, again I regret, but I have signed a document and must deliver them all to the Château, where they will be checked in. The figures are precise."

The owner consulted a document on the desk.

"One hundred and six bottles of Trimbach and fifty-eight bottles of Edelzwicker, all by tomorrow afternoon. I have even been given a permit and military transport has been detailed to arrive here at 2pm tomorrow. For me to be paid, I must ensure they are all checked in at the Château."

The owner wrung his hands in the manner common to all those of subservience over the ages.

"Forgive me, Commandant, but I cannot appropriate one for you, as I will not risk the wrath of 'Deux'. Please feel free to select another wine and I will sell it to you at cost, as a token of my apology."

The Major grunted acceptance and looked over at other wines arranged in a large wooden rack down one long wall. He studiously picked up a particularly good Moselle and chose his words carefully.

"Surely one soldier looks like another in our uniforms, Monsieur. And besides, French Military Intelligence is all over at Baden-Baden, with their top brass."

The Moselle was returned, in favour of a dusty Liebfraumilch.

"Commandant, I experienced the pleasures of the Gestapo and their agents crawling around here for nearly five years during the occupation. I know the type intimately. The man with the infantry officer was Deuxieme Bureau."

The Liebfraumilch was returned and the Moselle reselected.

"Maybe some General has a party planned then eh? In any case, I have to get moving. May I have this one, monsieur?"

The Major passed the bottle and its label drew the admiration of the proprietor.

"An excellent choice, Commandant. If you will give me a moment."

Etienne Bossong turned around to the rear bench, where he wrapped the wine in embossed tissue paper and included his card.

As his back was turned, the Major leant forward and scanned the signed purchase documents.

The details went swiftly into his mind and his stance was apparently unchanged when the bottle was passed to him.

"On my account, Monsieur?"

"It shall be so, Commandant. Good night, sir."

"Bon nuit, Monsieur Bossong."

Hiding his disappointment, the owner withdrew his ledger and entered a further sum on the growing account of Major S.Kowalski.

Outside, Stanislaw Kowalski mentally processed his day so far, as he made a few swift notes in a small pocket book.

Having taken leave, he had signed for a jeep and spent the day driving around Northern Alsace sightseeing, paying particular attention to large buildings, such as castles and Châteaus. After eight hours of the Alsatian countryside, he decided that he had done enough for one day and he had gone to get a bottle of fine wine, prior to taking his woman rowing on the River L'ill.

Now, by the strangest coincidence, his evening plans would change. That which he sought all day appeared to have dropped into his lap by chance, although the following day, Kœnigsbourg would have been his first enquiry. He smiled to himself and mused that if you wrote it in a story it wouldn't be

206

believable. Anyway, for whatever reason, Madame Fortune had smiled.

Obviously, Irma now had to wait, as he would take a drive over to Orschwiller and see if he could definitely confirm this 'Biarritz' at the nearby Château, before passing the information on to his contact. Sergey Andreevich Kovelskin was the name he was given at birth and he was an Officer of the GRU, born and bred on the banks of the Volga.

Little did we guess that what has been called the century of the common man would witness, as its outstanding feature, more common men killing each other with greater facilities than any other five centuries together in the history of the world.

Winston Churchill

Chapter 28 – THE DATE

1410hrs Wednesday, 1st August 1945, The Kremlin, Moscow, USSR.

Despite his seniority, Pekunin had little doubt as to his fate if neither his nor Beria's assets came up with the information on the French Symposium.

Soon, he would have to return to his GRU section within Zhukov's Headquarters but, for now, he hung on in the hope that the information would come through.

Having signed and sealed the paperwork to promote Nazarbayeva to Major, he was taking a constitutional early afternoon walk around the Kremlin complex when he saw the commotion caused by a running man. His immediate reaction was to brace himself and go out with dignity, until he realised the uniform was GRU and that the running figure was his Communications Starshiy Leytenant.

He knew what information was in the man's hand before the breathless report tumbled out.

Now he could give Makarenko his three days and maybe, just maybe, grow old with his grandchildren.

The entire GKO and the now fully involved STAVKA were assembled and had spent a long afternoon and evening reviewing the military plans, hearing the refinements, the enforced changes and the myriad of problems that accompany mobilising two large military forces in as secret a way as possible. Marshal Zhukov was also present, Vasilevsky being absent because of the distances and time scale involved.

Three new reports had just taken everyone's attention, but were now resolved. The first information, namely the location of the French symposium, was welcomed, but not everyone saw it as essential in the way that Stalin did. None the less, no one was foolish enough to question the General Secretary's new pet project.

The second was a portfolio of photographs and a short movie reel depicting American and British armoured vehicles attacking Russian troops in Berlin, set against a backdrop of recognisable landmarks. To be used as part of the international justification, if required. No one would be able to tell that the vehicles were lend-lease Shermans and Soviet manned, or indeed that the photographs were already a week old.

Thirdly, and of greater concern, was the shooting down of another British Mosquito reconnaissance aircraft over Soviet territory.

The diplomatic channels would soon be buzzing and Molotov was already on his way to his office to prepare soothing and placatory messages, promising to investigate and punish the offenders. Of course, there would be an advisory to keep away from Soviet airspace included. The Mosquito had been deliberately shot down, as it was about to wander over a sensitive assembly area in Northern Germany. Whilst these areas were cunningly concealed, there were no chances taken. The two-man crew would be returned to the British, once the remains had been recovered.

The meeting had been going for some five hours and there now seemed to be nothing of note left to discuss or decide upon.

Except for one small matter.

Stalin stood and tapped his pipe upon his table to call order, sending a few sparks across the paperwork and maps near his right hand.

"Comrades, we have laboured long and hard to ensure that our plans are the best they can be and to ensure success in this great venture."

The stem of his pipe swept the room in an expansive gesture.

"We can all be proud of the service we have done for the party and Motherland."

He locked eyes with Zhukov.

"So, now we must decide whether we draw back from the path we have planned, or if we proceed with all our might."

To the casual onlooker, it could have seemed that Stalin was indeed undecided, but no one there believed other than he was committed to the attack and was merely trying to detect weakness around him.

"Zilant-4 preparation will take three days," he held Makarenko to his word on that, "And nothing else we have discussed here today will take more than a few hours of staff work to resolve."

"Our timescale is on track. The secret forces for Diaspora and Kingdom39 are either in place, or en route. Our new allies are also prepared and committed."

His voice started to grow in volume and power of delivery.

"There will be no better time; no period when we are stronger and none where they are weaker."

He acknowledged Beria with an uncharacteristic hand on the shoulder.

"Comrade Marshal Beria's agents have removed the immediate threat of the American atomic research project."

Stalin moved slowly around the room as he spoke, making eye contact with each and every man in turn.

"The capitalists are soft and war-weary. They do not have the stomach for further losses."

Behind him, Zhukov paled unnoticed.

"They are burdened with refugees and prisoners. The German state is on its knees and will never be more easily destroyed for ever than it can be now."

Returning to his position at the head of the table, he turned and relit his pipe.

"So I say, we must not let this opportunity pass, or we will be judged poorly by history. We must not be judged to have been found wanting."

Puffing gently on his pipe, the General Secretary sat down and waited, observing the strange spectacle of a group of powerful men exchanging looks in total silence. His observations of their collective behaviour in those few seconds confirmed his views on who had and who did not have, the stomach for what was to come.

Beria, as was usual, was the next to speak.

"The reasoning is as sound now as it was when we first started this enterprise." His face turned to Stalin and he drew himself almost to a position of attention. "I, for one, will not be found wanting by history, Comrades. I say go."

Bulganin was next.

"Comrades, our planning is perfect, our maskirova, excellent. Their weakness is at its height. The Rodina would never forgive us if we held back now."

And then came a steady procession of positive words, until only Zhukov had not spoken.

Stalin looked up at the proud Marshal, silently inviting him to speak.

"Comrade General Secretary, Comrades. I am a military man and know little of politics. In those matters, I am guided by those who have the ability and expertise to judge. To my uneducated eye, the political considerations for this mission are proven."

He took the plunge.

"As a soldier, I have fought for the Motherland these last four years... and years before them too... and the sum of those years has seen death and destruction on a scale none of us could ever have imagined."

"Our planning gives us the opportunity to fight on the soil of our enemies and not on our own sacred land and so we will not see similar deaths to our own people, such as were wrought by the Germanski invaders."

He took out a document.

"As part of the necessity of military planning, I have had to project losses amongst ours and our allied forces, on a best, middle and worst case scenario. It is right that I share these figures with you. You must have this information, because you know best how we may replace these losses and remain combat effective."

211

This was very dangerous ground for Zhukov and everyone in the room knew it. More than one sideways glance was made at the impassive Stalin, whose sole response was to tug gently on his pipe and stare.

"In our best case, casualties amongst military personnel would be between two and four hundred thousand up to June 1946, allowing for Pacification of occupied territories and without the Iberian option. That is solely within Europe. Their casualties should at all times mirror ours. I make no reference to any civilian casualties in the affected countries."

"Middle case indicates five hundred to eight hundred and fifty thousand, with plans being protracted beyond the expected completion dates, again without Iberia and including Pacification."

"Worst case scenario extends our completion dates further and will probably entail 1.2 million plus casualties."

Almost as an after-thought came a statement, which many thought would probably save his neck.

"If our casualties are high, theirs will be similar in proportion. They do not have the political will to sustain extreme loss, certainly not as we do."

That the last comment was not necessarily glowing praise for the present assembly was missed by everyone.

Stalin stood abruptly.

"Comrade Marshal, lives lost in the protection of the Motherland are lives well spent. That has always been the case."

More than just Zhukov felt fear at the tone.

"The key question is not how many will die, but will they die in vain."

His hand smashed down on to the table with a sound not unlike a gunshot.

"We have given you the outline and you have given us the plan. Yours is the responsibility. To bring victory and deliverance from capitalism to the Rodina is the task of the Red Army."

His arm shot out and a thick finger pointed straight at Zhukov, emphasising the middle word, "Under YOUR leadership!"

That message was loud and clear. Responsibility equalled firing squad if things went wrong.

"So, Comrade Marshal Zhukov, are you capable of delivering victory?"

Zhukov snapped to attention.

"I can, and will, defeat the Western Allies militarily. Kingdom39 will succeed, Comrade General Secretary."

Stalin gently nodded, but without taking his hardened eyes from Zhukov, assessing him, reading his resolve and commitment.

"Very good, Comrade Marshal."

His eyes flicked away and the danger was gone. Others now met his gaze, but Stalin's eyes had softened from the extremes of the last few moments.

"So, we are all agreed. We will initiate the operation as discussed?"

The unusually genuine quizzical tone caught a few by surprise and their nods were deeper and more rapid.

Turning around to focus on Zhukov once more, Stalin gave the order.

"Operation Kingdom39 is fully approved and will commence at 0530, on 6th August."

Thus ended the pause.

It had been Beria's idea to use the BBC to spread the information throughout Western Europe and so the radio stations evening broadcast carried the unexpected, but extremely important news, that Soviet Ministers Bulganin and Molotov were to visit London and Paris in the week ahead, starting with a fight to London, arriving on the morning of 6th August.

From the Atlantic coast of France to the Baltic Sea, a number of resolute young men noted that date and consulted their orders, confirming with a mixture of trepidation and excitement that the inclusion of Bulganin's name indicated dawn minus fifteen minutes on the stated date.

Better to fight for something than live for nothing.

George S. Patton

Chapter 29 – THE CAMP

<u>2154hrs Friday, 3rd August 1945, Soviet POW Camp, Ex-OFLAG XVIIa, Edelbach, Soviet Occupied Lower Austria.</u>

Like many things in war, or peace for that matter, what happened that Friday evening was neither planned nor anticipated. An event invited them to act and act they did.

For six days now, most of the prisoners had been marched out of the camp as dawn gathered itself, in order to dig huge anti-tank ditches all round the site, for Soviet military exercises, returning only when the light was failing and overseeing was becoming difficult for the guards. Everyone was weary, including the Bulgarians, so sleep became the favourite and most welcomed activity for everyone. Seven men had succumbed on the fourth day and were buried in a shallow grave outside the compound. Even the frequent firing of the Soviet military exercises, rending the still nights of the last few days, did not overly disturb the prisoners slumber. Tonight, any gunfire would have to compete with a Central European thunderstorm of biblical proportions.

Eavesdropping guards' conversations during the day, Rolf Uhlmann became aware that many of the Bulgarians intended to visit nearby Allensteig that very evening. Skryabin had called for a celebration, as it was a popular officer's birthday. A stash of German brandy had been uncovered, so the Bulgarians had decided to get drunk and visit the fraternisation centre for a little bit of female company.

That the guards were going to be low on numbers was the main subject of conversation over the evening meal, but little more was said, as there was no escape kit available, leastways, none worth a damn. The recent previous effort had reduced their limited resources and it would take some time to gather more items suitable for purpose. Escapes required planning to be successful and, as far as they were aware, unsuccessful escapees did not get a second chance with the NKVD. Obviously, the fact that all were exhausted also played its part.

More of note at the time was the fact that the inexperienced Bulgarians were quite happy to troop off two kilometres away and leave a few men guarding their charges. Thoughts turned to future planning, if such an event should happen again.

Still, some of Rolf's fellows amused themselves with the thought that the driving rain and high winds would at least curb the guard's enjoyment of their night out.

Life and death are balanced on the edge of a razor.

Homer

Chapter 30 – THE AIRCRAFT

2155hrs Friday, 3rd August 1945, Airborne approx 400 ft above Soviet Occupied Lower Austria.

Junior Lieutenant Marina Budanova was lost and frightened. Her present mission with 586th Fighter Aviation Regiment had gone very wrong and was getting worse with every passing second. Where her comrades had got to, she had no idea. All she knew was one moment they were there and the next she was flying alone in the vastness above Northern Austria. and in the failing light of a very stormy European evening.

There had been no prediction of the extent of the foul weather that was presently buffeting her Yakolev-9 fighter aircraft and certainly no prior indication that her compass and radio would both pack up. Her knowledge of the area was limited, as she had only arrived at the airbase in Znojmo last week, so she desperately unfolded her map, in the hope that she could pick out some recognisable landmark on the ground.

She was unpopular with her comrades, more for her apparent inefficiency than for her mixed Polish-Russian parentage and gruff, unapproachable manner. Already reprimanded by the Regimental Commander, Budanova could not afford another black mark so soon and was rapidly becoming hysterical in her search for guidance home.

The storm was becoming more intense and it was increasingly difficult to see the ground, so Budanova, like the inexperienced young pilot she was, dropped lower and lower until vision was restored.

A flash of lightning alerted her to the presence of a body of water on her port side, so she frantically searched the map.

The body of water in question was the modest Stadtsee, not that it made the slightest difference for Budanova.

216

Desperately, her eyes swept the sheet for nearby airfields on which she could land swiftly, before the failing light died completely.

In any case, her panic had already condemned her, because her altitude had almost completely gone by the time she ripped her eyes away from the map and realised that her death was approaching as quickly as the ground that filled her vision.

A superhuman effort on the stick and an increase in engine revs could only buy her a few extra seconds of life.

Both were instrumental in saving the lives of scores of others.

Budanova was vaguely aware of buildings ahead as she desperately sought height, but her aircraft snagged overhead wires and she was dropped into the ground at speed, landing exactly flat to the earth and skimming at well over two hundred miles per hour, despite the destruction of the propeller.

The aircraft ploughed through some wooden buildings and was then flipped over by a number of stout poles.

Upside down, the last thing Budanova saw was the canopy disintegrate and the metal framework start to gather up earth like a shovel, as the aircraft continued to expend its energy in forward momentum.

The scraping effect of her smashed canopy slowed the aircraft's passage, but held no advantages for Budanova. She died a painful, but reasonably swift death, broken, crushed and suffocated in her cockpit by the heavy press of gathered earth. She did not feel the heat when the now stationary aircraft started to burn around her.

Too late to fight in the war, she had merely become a statistic in the peace, but was the catalyst to something that had very far-reaching consequences.

The secret of success in life is for a man to be ready for his opportunity when it comes.

Benjamin Disraeli

Chapter 31 – THE OPPORTUNITY

2155hrs Friday, 3rd August 1945, Soviet POW Camp, Ex-OFLAG XVIIa, Edelbach, Soviet Occupied Lower Austria.

Uhlmann and Braun stood closely together, sharing a cigarette and talking about Braun's wife to be. Krystal Uhlmann, Rolf's sister, had been immediately attracted to Braun and the feeling was mutual. For convention's sake, the relationship had been kept secret, or Braun might have had to leave the unit, but neither man permitted their future ties to interfere with their professional soldiering or relationship.

Now, whilst they enjoyed a quiet smoke away from the rest of their comrades, they could relax and talk about the future as friends. It was very necessary for everyone in the camp to talk about the future that they imagined for themselves, even though their immediate future held no great promises.

"And of course, you have strictly honourable intentions, don't you?" teased Uhlmann.

"Obviously, or I wouldn't have proposed to her, Herr Sturmbannfuhrer," which was couched in disrespectful tones, such as these two friends often used when alone.

"And obviously she is smitten with you, for reasons that presently escape me," stated Uhlmann enquiringly.

"I rather suspect she fancied having a genuine military hero in the family, for a change," which riposte was accompanied by a huge grin as the point was scored.

"Asshole NCO's. My life has been ruined by asshole NCO's," and Uhlmann aimed a playful swipe at Braun's head, careful to miss the still dressed site of his most recent wound.

"Seriously, Johan, where will you both live once this mess is all resolved?"

"I rather suspect England, Rolf"

"England?"

"I have family there and it may be that Germany will not be a place for us in the years ahead."

"Yes, agreed, but England? Near your sister, I suppose. And yet you take my sister away from me?"

"Whoa friend! Don't imagine that it is me imposing my will on your Krystal, will you? You know she knows her own damn mind and if she wanted to go to the South Pole it would be me following her like an obedient dog!"

A nodding Uhlmann saw the opening and went for it, grinning like a Cheshire cat. "I've often thought of you that way myself, Johan"

The draw acknowledged with a shared smile, a second cigarette was brought forth and passed between the two.

Their comfortable silence was interrupted by Braun, who held up his hand, obviously listening hard above the sound of rain and wind that relentlessly buffeted the lean-to in which they had secreted themselves.

Very quickly, Rolf also became aware of the sound of a low-flying aircraft and became uncomfortably aware that it was certainly very low and getting a lot closer.

"Aircraft... and damnably low at that," Rolf confirmed to Braun.

Before either man could really react, the sounds of the aircraft became more urgent and loud and then quickly changed into the recognisable sounds of destruction and death that accompany crashes at speed.

'Schiesse! It's hit the camp," shouted Rolf and they both sprang forward into the driving rain.

As both men ran in the general direction of the noise, they were too late to witness the demolition of the guard hut and swift unheralded death of its occupants. They did manage to see the aircraft flipping over and the subsequent destruction of over one hundred and fifty metres of fence, before the wreckage ground to a halt and started to incinerate the hapless occupant.

Neither man was ever slow to act, but the enormity of the possibility presented to them took a few seconds to sink in.

"The fence is gone Rolf"

219

"The guard hut's gone too. What do we have to lose? Let's do it!"

It was an opportunity to seize and they both ran, shouting for all they were worth, desperate to rouse their comrades to the risky, yet tantalising possibility, that had literally fallen from heaven.

Prisoners magically appeared, running hard, the spectre of freedom driving every man. Strangely, some brave souls attempted to rescue the pilot, although they quickly realised it was a fool's mission.

Still others overpowered the two guards that remained, transfixed by shock, at the main gate, spared by about two metres when the Yak drove in next to them.

Other guards were positioned in the towers and, recovering from their own shock, the shots cracked out, immediately dropping two men in their tracks. But by now the chance of escape drove every German in the camp and they surged towards the huge rent in the wire, and beyond.

Their headlong flight was accompanied by an impressive display of thunder and lightning, which gave the whole scene a Wagnerian aspect.

As the group containing Rolf and Braun crossed the destroyed fence, Rolf shouted to them.

"Grab anything you can, Kameraden, but don't dawdle; food and weapons, anything of use."

Rolf, Braun and a few others, slowed sufficiently to claw and grab at various items thrown from the guard hut, but no one stopped to admire the handiwork of the Russian fighter, or lament the red grease that had once been the readiness guard detachment.

As the Germans tumbled out of the compound, some were dropped by rifle fire and a belatedly employed DP28 light machine gun. By the end of the break out, some twenty-three POW's had paid the ultimate price for their attempt at escape. Those not killed outright were subsequently dispatched, either with a bullet in the brain, or by a bayonet. In all, about one hundred and fifty Germans made it out of the killing zone and fanned out into the surrounding woods, forming small groups and starting to disperse in all directions without command. Rolf

220

and his faithful NCO struck out to the north, in company with fifteen others. After five minutes of frantic scrambling, a quick halt was called, to establish where they thought they were and how best to make it back to their homeland. As the group struggled to gain their breath, the constant sound of gunfire punctuated the night.

"I don't know this area at all. Anyone here have local knowledge?" panted Uhlmann. Shandruk was in the group and could obviously contribute nothing, but two Austrian Gebirgsjager spoke up and felt able to take the group forward with their knowledge, suggesting that the railway to the north offered the best chance of escape, or at least the best chance of clearing the area at speed. Certainly of late, the prisoners had become aware of trains at all hours, so they reasoned there was a good chance of getting away from Edelbach onboard one, before the Soviets became too organised.

A quick inventory of their possessions yielded some surprising items. Shandruk had the prize with a Tokarev pistol and belt that he had grabbed as he ran. Others brought forth two bread bags stuffed with various foods, none of which were the regulation bread, which made Rolf smile. An SS Kavellerie Untersturmfuhrer had recovered a canteen that was full to the brim with vodka. Rolf had managed to snatch a binocular case, only to find it contained cigarettes.

"Not what I had hoped for, menschen, but with good value, none the less," he ventured and received the odd grin and nod.

"Just you left then, Braun, What delights have you brought to the party?"

Braun looked exceptionally smug, for he had lifted what he thought was a map case. In fact, a cursory examination showed it was just a bag containing the camp guards personal mail, with not even a single official envelope in sight to ease Braun's obvious pain. Upset that his contribution had yielded nothing of value, he loudly determined to hang on to the letters, for no other reason than to wipe his good German ass, much to the amusement of the others.

"Don't worry, Braun, we didn't have much time to select the sweetest items and at least you'll have a clean arse

221

for a few days." None the less, despite the obvious humour of it, Braun was less than happy that his efforts had been fruitless. That he had the only cigarette lighter in the group was his salvation as he saw it.

"Ok, Kameraden." He addressed the officer with the vodka.

"Untersturmfuhrer, one nip each to warm the heart. You will oversee this, please."

A quick 'jawohl' and the process started.

"The food will be divided into three amounts, one for each of the next three days. We will eat now so we have strength before we run further, but quickly, kameraden, quickly."

So, with a decent yet small and hastily consumed supper and a warming jolt of vodka in their bellies, they started out north-west, heading for the nearest rail line as the Austrians suggested. The tobacco would be saved for later.

As they accelerated away from the camp that had housed them, they were unaware that many of their former comrades were dying; both those who had made the bid for freedom and those who had failed to act upon the opportunity and remained within the camp, probably more from fear than sloth.

Those caught in flight were mown down without mercy or thought for recapture, as the Bulgarians flooded back to the camp. Those remaining inside the wire fared no better. Their guilt immediately established, all forty-four were dragged outside and swiftly executed, their bodies being arranged around the broken fence, in order to show how well the guards had behaved in stemming the flow of escapees.

It served little purpose, for within the next hour, the surviving Bulgarian guards were also rounded up and summarily liquidated by the detachment of NKVD stationed at NeuPolla, which had eventually responded to the garbled radio summons from the camp commandant. His Major's rank didn't save him either, for despite his protestations, the recently returned NKVD Captain Skryabin blew the man's brains all over the wall to save on the time and expense of a mock trial and probably to cover his own complicity in events.

222

The telephone lines had been brought down by the first contact of the Yak and their destruction did much to inhibit the immediate organisation, but, even so, resources were slowly brought to bear to contain the escapees.

NKVD and regular army units were mobilised and by the end of the night, some thirty-five hundred Soviet troops were involved in the search. Ninety-seven Germans had already been apprehended outside of the camp and all but three of them were summarily dispatched with a bullet in the head or a bayonet. The unlucky three were nailed to telegraph poles in Zwinzen, left to die a lingering death, as examples to the local community.

2302hrs Friday, 3rd August 1945, Gopfritz am der Wild.
Soviet Occupied Lower Austria.

As the Russian search effort was still in its infancy, Rolf's group continued to strike out for the possible safety of the railway line, both helped and hindered by the hammering rain and winds. Speed was of the essence, as it was decided to put as much distance as possible between the camp and the group, before Soviet security efforts were fully organised. The two Austrians constantly consulted about direction, but the trail was blazed by a young officer of the Brandenburgers, whose field craft in such matters made him the obvious choice for the role.

They stumbled across the line and followed it northwards, hugging its eastern side as they progressed further away from the camp. There was a narrow escape at a crossing point, when the group unfortunately timed their sprint across the road with the arrival of three trucks, full of Soviet infantry.

That they were not seen was probably more down to the driving rain dampening the spirits of the Russians than anything else.

The group made speedy progress, following the rail line around in a long curve, until it finally ran almost southeast and disappeared into a village.

Rolf made the decision to cross to the north, at a point where rail line and road were most adjacent and the group swiftly made their way over.

Not a moment too soon, as more Soviet infantry, supported by some of the hated NKVD, arrived from the northwest and started to drop off sections of soldiers to form a physical barrier against anyone coming from the direction of the camp.

Immediately, the blocking deployment bore fruit.

South of the railway line, two German prisoners, one of them an old comrade of Rolf's, were caught in a vehicle searchlight. Shouts and rifles rang out simultaneously and one man dropped like a stone, obviously shot in the head. Rolf's comrade tried to drag the wounded man to cover, but both were shot at point blank range by a young submachine gunner, eager to be able to tell his family that he had killed his Germans.

Whilst it was unfortunate on both slain prisoners, it was extremely fortunate for Rolf and his men, as the young officer in charge of the group oriented his troops all to the south, on the supposition that his men had killed the first arrivals.

Rolf's group moved silently away in the opposite direction, crossing swiftly over another railway line that snaked into the darkness, northwest from their position, its rails picked out by the increasingly frequent lightning.

Silently, but swiftly, the group moved through the gardens and back ways of Hauptstraße and Nordrandweg, the good Austrian people staying firmly in their homes, as gunfire mixed with thunder in the night.

The escapees gathered together in an overgrown walled area between Nordrandweg and the rail line, right opposite a junction spot, where the single line became three and then five, until there was enough illumination to make out a small rail yard.

It was immediately apparent that there was little military presence in the area. With the exception of a GAZ jeep and Studebaker truck parked up outside an obvious headquarters building in Bahnhofstraße, no signs of danger were apparent, so it might be that the driving rain was more in their favour than they first thought.

The group hid up and surveyed the scene. Apparently, the village was called Gopfritz an der Wild, but no one, not even the Austrians, were any the wiser for knowing that. As they examined the lie of the land, the sounds of an approaching express reached their ears and before they knew it, a sixteen car military freight train hammered straight through and off into the darkness, bound west for places unknown.

A swift appraisal of the illuminated area indicated that a small train of one engine, eight freight cars and a passenger coach, was on a siding, ready to roll eastwards. Another, of fourteen freight cars and a very obvious ex-German quadruple anti-aircraft gun, carried on a sand-bagged carriage, sat on the other side of the triple tracks, pointing to the west. The flak gun wagon was worryingly close to their position, although there was no sign of its crew.

What was of considerable interest was the fact that the eastbound train's engine was busy puffing away. The priority was still to put as much distance between them and the camp, so it was quickly decided to go for the smaller train and head east. This suddenly became an imperative as Rolf observed figures around the engine climb aboard and the train started to slowly puff its way forward to the points.

'Schiesse, no time for stealth, Kameraden! Go hell for leather for that train. Move!"

Frantically, the group leapt the stonewall and charged headlong towards the rearmost freight car. Its doors were only partially open. Swiftly realising the error, Rolf adjusted to the second car ,as its doors were gaping invitingly.

Fortunately, the train slowed slightly before reaching the points, as they needed to be manually switched. Unfortunately, they were operated by a beast of a man, wearing Soviet uniform and sporting a PPSH sub-machine gun.

The lithe and wiry Shandruk was first up and into the second truck, immediately offering his hand to others. Man after man piled in, but the train started to gain momentum as it moved onto the main track and drew the desperate group ever closer to the Russian guard. One man even managed to get through the slightly open door of the rearmost truck, but it was quickly obvious that some would not get aboard in time and they selflessly scattered away from the track before they could be spotted.

One of the Austrians just failed to gain the truck and fell badly, twisting his ankle. A comrade stopped to help and together they struggled towards the temporary safety of a small platelayer's hut, adjacent to the main line on the westbound side.

Unfortunately for them, the last truck just cleared away from the Russian giant as a lightning bolt illuminated the area and he was immediately aware of two men moving through the rail yard. Shouting a challenge at the top of his voice, only the two fugitives he concentrated on heard him. The burst from the submachine gun drew much more attention.

The young gunner, supposedly standing guard on the anti-aircraft truck, emerged from beneath his tarpaulin and saw at least eight men milling around the yard. The SVT40 automatic rifle by his side was quickly brought up, aimed and ten shots were rapidly fired off.

The first shot struck a mark and the Austrian fell dead, as the round took him full in the neck, wrecking both his windpipe and jugular vein in a fraction of a second.

Rounds two to seven went wild, although round five did take out one of the yard lights.

By the time the eighth bullet left the barrel, the young gunner was bringing the weapon back down and under control, that round removed the left knee of an SS Untersturmfuhrer of Kavellerie, running beyond the struggling pair.

Round nine hit the track and ricocheted into the already dead Austrian.

Round ten took the would-be rescuer in the left thigh, dropping him to the rain-soaked ground. As he sat there, looking at his pumping wound, he fatalistically understood that his destroyed femoral artery meant he would be dead long before anyone could even think about a tourniquet. And so he was, lying back onto the ground, as blood loss overtook him and death came to him in seconds. By now, the yard was mayhem and the other prisoners sought any cover possible, as more Russians arrived from their shelters, adding to the force trying to find the escapees.

Other evaders had also made it northwards to the yard and they further added to the confusion.

Despite the stormy conditions, they were all swiftly hunted down, with only the wounded Untersturmfuhrer left alive to tell the tale.

In the morning, the guard commander would display the sixteen corpses and hand over the wounded prisoner to the NKVD officer who led the arriving guard detachment. He was given assurances that no German had escaped and that the only ones who had entered the yard lay before him. In a wish to escape blame and to make themselves look good, the guards immediately took the heat off Rolf and his comrades. In a time when acts of bravery went unrewarded and he knew his comrades would never know of it, the painfully wounded Untersturmfuhrer did not disclose the escape of some ten of his fellows, even when his other knee was rearranged by a heavy Nagant bullet at close range, followed by his elbows and his genitals. Mercifully, he was unconscious when the officer was finally satisfied and the fifth bullet took his life.

The vodka he once carried had been consumed instantly by his captors.

*It is better to do one's own duty, however defective it may be,
than to follow the duty of another, however well one may
perform it. He who does his duty as his own nature reveals it,
never sins.*

The Bhagavad Gita

Chapter 32 – THE RAILWAY

0002hrs Saturday, 4th August 1945, On eastbound train, Soviet Occupied Lower Austria.

Even as the escapees were being hunted down all over the yard, the little train and its exhausted cargo slowly chugged its way eastwards, away from the immediate danger of detection. Rolf and Braun exchanged looks and the blowing out of the latter's cheeks indicated how close he felt it had been for all of them. Rolf took a moment and looked around his exhausted comrades.

"Is everyone ok here?"

The hope in his voice very evident. It was quickly established that no one in the wagon was hurt.

Uhlmann took further stock of their possessions and discovered they had lost one of the bread bags, as well as the canteen of vodka. A setback for sure.

"Relax for a while, Kameraden. I must think this through. Braun, Moeller, keep watch."

The two selected men took one side each and those who wanted a cigarette took advantage of the journey to enjoy a smoke. The truck was soon filled with tobacco smoke and lightly snoring men. The hypnotic sound effects of the rain and rail track produced a general feeling of well-being in all of them and it was almost relaxing, except for the small points that it was the dead of night, stormy and they were being hunted.

As the minutes ticked by, those in the wagon started to become aware of the presence of particular odours, odours that most identified with death, namely, faeces and blood. As they looked around the wagon, the dark was occasionally banished

228

by a lightning bolt, or a passing station, not much, but sufficiently for all to be aware that this wagon had been used to transport the dead and that each bore, on his hands and uniform, tokens of the former unfortunate occupants of the wagon.

Just over forty minutes after leaving Gopfritz, the train slowed down and crawled into a small town, some twenty or so miles down the track, east of the drama in the rail yard. Pulling off to the left, the train drew to a halt on a short spur, three hundred metres short of the station platform; which platform was dotted with Soviet military personnel. The fact that they were there and not hiding from the wind and rain caused some initial alarm, but there appeared to be no interest in their little train.

As if thrown by a single switch, every light in the vicinity was extinguished, the sole illumination being the occasional, but now distant, flash of lightning. Every prisoner was wide-awake and the tension in the wagon rapidly approached unbearable. It was impossible to tell if there were soldiers moving around them, so Rolf decided they should stay put. His mind immediately started to wander to the possibilities that lay open to the group, if they were discovered.

Moeller the Austrian suddenly became animated and pulled one of the others over to keep his lookout, then quietly approached Uhlmann with some news.

"Herr Sturmbannfuhrer, I am familiar with this town, or at least, I know a little of the railway here."

That obviously got Rolf's full attention and he was suddenly more focussed.

"This is Sigmundsherberg. The other side of the Bahnhof there is a junction, which splits in three directions."

"Don't tell me Moeller. Berlin, Munich and Hamburg by any chance?" It was said loud enough to draw smiles from all in the wagon, his weak attempt cut through some of the tension that was peaking, as all waited to hear Moeller's words.

"Simply put, Herr Sturmbannfuhrer, left or straight ahead ,we are in trouble. Right, we can cope with. From memory, left goes to Wien and all places east. Straight ahead can also get you to Wien, amongst other places, but also can

229

take you south through the passes and into Italy. Right...," the voice suddenly almost soft with emotion, "Right can take us to München, or on to Salzburg."

Rolf rubbed his chin slowly and nodded gently at the man in front of him.

Placing his hand on his shoulder, he chose his words carefully.

"Then we must trust in our luck that we go right, for all of us need to go home, Alois. Salzburg is home for you, yes?"

"Yes....it's been so very long since..." Moeller's voice trailed off as his mind wandered to happier times.

Rolf clapped his hand on his shoulder and smiled.

"Then we will go to Salzburg and have done with it."

Moeller, out of his short reverie, grinned and nodded.

"Zu befehl, Herr Sturmbannfuhrer," and moved back.

Moeller resumed his guard and was the first one to warn of an approaching train. The escapees kept their eyes firmly on the surrounding area, but still saw no one looking remotely interested in their little world. Uhlmann estimated the time to be about 1am and it seemed reasonable to expect about four more hours of darkness before the dawn broke upon them in its full splendour. He still believed that it was still safer to stay put than to move off.

A whispered warning prevented everyone from jumping, as the door was gently slid back and Krantzschen, the man who had made it into the rear wagon, joined the group. He brought Rolf's attention to the fact that two other trains were pulled over, almost as if waiting for something more important to pass by.

Which they were, of course, and that fact came home to all the watchers as the train Moeller had heard approaching slowly steamed past from the direction they had come and took the right hand track, which they hoped was heading towards Salzburg. Rolf was about to state that this was a good sign, as it was likely they had been pulled over to let this one past.

He never made that comment.

What was carried on that train gave the watchers a moments pause. All of them had sufficient time on the Russian front to recognise the shape of Russian T34s, even when buried under canvas tarpaulins on a dark night. Moreover, a train with twenty-one aboard was not moving about without reason. Twenty-one tanks represented a full Soviet tank battalion and moving a force like that was not done for the hell of it. It had purpose. Hardly had Rolf started to digest what he had seen than another train followed the same route. The unmistakeable shapes of twenty-one more T34's slid by, immediately followed by yet another trainload, but this time carrying twenty-one IS-II types, a Soviet heavy tank, with a beast of a 122mm main gun.

Three trains, five minutes apart, became six, then eight and finally the incredulous Germans spent nearly an hour witnessing seventeen trainloads of Russian materiel, from tanks through artillery and onto troop transports, heading south-west down the track. One Katyusha had been wholly visible, as its protective tarpaulin had been carried away into the night.

By the time the last train had passed, the waiting group of locomotives started to show more signs of life and the nearest one to the junction slowly pulled forward with its load. Its progress was watched intently, so that the Germans could gauge what was likely to happen, when it became their turn. The large number of uniforms around the Bahnhof and surrounding area started to dwindle and none of them seemed remotely interested in the train now moving through the junction.

The most important factor was now which way their train would turn. Any direction but southwest would bring a completely new set of problems to the escapees, but their luck held.

As their train moved through and onto the south-west line, Rolf risked a better look and was struck by the fact that, had he not witnessed it with his own eyes and known differently, he would now be looking at an apparently unimportant piece of railway network. Certainly not one that merited the attention of at least eighty heavily armed Soviet troops on a wet night such as this. Something was happening here and alarm bells were still ringing in his head.

He moved back into the truck and found a number of others waiting expectantly.

"What the hell's this all about, menschen? The war's over and yet we see secrecy like this. What we have witnessed here is important enough to pass on, although, in truth, I'm not totally sure who we should try to tell, or what we would say."

A number of quiet laughs accompanied Rolf's obvious humour, for they all knew the answer to that. However, Shandruk put it into words.

"Maybe it is just manouevre, maybe not. Either way, it is something the Russian wishes to conceal, therefore we have a duty to speak of it and surely it must be the Americans we go to?"

"And be imprisoned again?" came Braun's angry words, echoed by one or two others.

"Quiet now, Kameraden."

Rolf gave a moment for all to settle and focus solely on him.

"Such decisions, we cannot presently make. We must focus on escape, for it may be that we won't be able to exercise choice over which enemy, or friend, we next encounter".

It was a fair point and making light of the situation obviously eased the immediate tension. Rolf continued after a pause.

"What we must agree is not to speak of it to the communists, if we are taken. For I think if we did, we would guarantee a bullet in the head for each of us. So, let's now concentrate on getting out of the Russian area and into whatever of Germany is left to us. Agreed?"

No voices rang out, just nods of agreement, and the group just went back to what they had been doing.

Krantzschen sidled up to Rolf, his voice low.

"The other carriage is exactly the same as this one, Herr Sturmbannfuhrer. A fucking charnel house."

There was a distinctive whistle to Krantzschen's voice, caused by the absence of his two front upper teeth, both victims of a vehicle accident in the Ukraine.

He looked to see if anyone was watching and covertly slipped a piece of cloth into Rolf's hand.

"I found this jammed in the door runner. I think it was what was preventing it from moving."

Even before Rolf's eyes took in exactly what it was, he had a fair idea of what Krantzschen had pressed into his hand. He swiftly summoned Braun for his lighter and a quick flick of the wheel was sufficient for them to see a Major's epaulette, with its pink Panzer waffenfarbe trim quite clearly.

The three of them exchanged looks.

With that one object, all became clear to them.

They had not been digging tank ditches.

The gunfire at night was not part of Russian military manoeuvres.

The increased numbers of trains were not bringing cargoes, but German bodies from far afield.

Rolf quietly and solemnly slipped the epaulette back into Krantzschen's hand and squeezed it around the material firmly. Both Braun and Krantzschen immediately understood that the matter would not be discussed further. Krantzschen slid it back into his pocket for later disposal.

The train progressed slowly through the silent and dark countryside, passing occasionally through sleepy villages, the names of which were softly called out by the watchers.

Breiteneich.

Horn.

Rosenberg.

The names kept coming.

Another scare occurred as they ground to a halt in a larger siding area, in order to permit another four trains to pass by, these being mainly blacked out passenger coaches. However, there were enough glowing cigarette ends clustered on the ends of each coach to safely assume that each carriage was crammed with combat troops. The Russians followed the previous routine and extinguished all lights in the area, but this time, had them all back on by the time the fugitive's train clattered through. The station was Krems-Donau and according to the platform clock, it was 0223.

The little train rattled slowly on and those looking out of the left-hand doorway absorbed the comforting vision of the dark waters of the Danube, slowly flowing eastwards.

At Groisbach, their train slewed into a siding and the whole secretive process was repeated, this time with five trains passing slowly by, their military cargo all too apparent.

The final time they were forced to concede the track to military trains, they were just west of Marbach and this time only three trains moved past them.

Sunrise was seemingly delayed by the rain, but the gradual arrival of the morning sun seemed to turn off the tap and both wind and rain disappeared in an instant.

After a longer than normal delay, their little train slowly started chugging its way onwards and, now that there was sufficient natural light, Moeller tried to draw a map in the dirt on the wall of the truck, to help them all work out where they were and where they were going. Four men were detailed to keep an eye open, especially as the train had slowed down and was making extremely slow progress now.

Kloss, the Kradschutzen Leutnant, positioned at a hole on the offside front corner, swore audibly, then called Rolf to him with some urgency. The hole was large enough for two to look out of and so they both had a grandstand view of a heavily camouflaged railway siding within a wood, adjacent to the mainline. Both noted that the trains that they had seen slide past them that very morning were concealed under the vast green awnings.

Of as much interest was the fact that there were at least forty such trains in total, parked in what was rapidly appreciated as a huge area of clear land that was intended to represent woodland. Certainly, any aerial view of the site, would see nothing but a vast wooded nature reserve for birds and deer and no aerial observer would have any idea of the huge amount of tanks, guns and men underneath the canopy of natural leaves and camouflage netting. Large numbers of Russians were moving about the area, obviously stretching their legs, or off to enjoy an early breakfast. Kloss pointed out a cooking facility that produced no smoke, supplying a line of eager riflemen and tank crew.

It was also apparent that the Russians even removed the spur of rail track that led into the sidings, as Rolf glimpsed a pile of track under a roof, constructed on a cunning structure that was supposed to look like a cottage from above. At the other end of the site, a similar building had been erected, obviously where the track was stored, prior to being put in place to permit the trains to continue their onward journey. The switchgear for the dismantled points clearly lay under some false bushes constructed adjacent to the track.

In total, the watchers considered that they had just seen the entire tank, anti-tank and artillery strength, of a Guards Mechanised Corps, parked up trying hard to look like a harmless Austrian wood. That was being done for a reason.

Uhlmann consulted with the Brandenburger and a 12th SS Division staff Hauptsturmfuhrer, both of whom had intelligence credentials.

It did not take them long to arrive at the conclusion that what they had seen was a clandestine all-arms attack force, moving up towards its start position; wherever that may be. The lack of visible facilities to disembark the vehicles made them believe that the final destination was further forward. In addition, no facility such as that secret area would be built just for training purposes. That was something put together for the real deal.

The inescapable conclusion was that the Soviet Union was about to carry the war forward and assault the other half of Germany and probably beyond. Bringing in the Austrian, the conversation continued, regarding where exactly the Russians intended to attack, but quickly moved into how this might affect their possible transit into a zone held by more friendly and understanding enemies and then, by natural progression, came once more to their obligation and duty to pass on this knowledge.

By common assent, after long years of combat in the name of Fuehrer, Fatherland and Folk, their temporary respite as prisoners was brought to a stunning halt. Without a doubt, they did now have an obligation to carry this news to the Western Allies, in order to protect the part of Germany that lay under their control. Any German government that now existed would be bound to resist the Russians and certainly would assist the Americans and British in any way they could, if only as the lesser of two evils.

Rolf called on everyone to listen in and summed up the situation in a few direct sentences. To the credit of every man present, they all instantly understood the responsibility they held; to get through with this intelligence, no matter what.

The moment of decision was interrupted by the jolt of their train as it came to a halt. The watchers quickly allayed any fears and reported nothing of concern. One even spotted the name of the town on the front of a shop some way off.

It was Persenbeug, a fact reinforced by the lofty presence of the grand Schloss Persenbeug, perched atop its rocky outcrop, with its well-known, almost eastern style dome, crowning the grand tower, on which the clock indicated 0520 hrs.

Schloss Persenbeug was directly to the south of the small siding in which their train had stopped. Unchanged from the pictures most had seen of it, its sheer white walls and red roves, stood guard over the mighty river that ran alongside it.

The sweetness of seeing such a welcoming structure was swiftly lost, as Braun urgently informed the group that the engine was being uncoupled. They had reached the end of the line.

236

Desperate affairs require desperate measures.

Horatio Nelson.

Chapter 33 – THE RAILYARD

0920hrs Saturday, 4th August 1945, Persenbeug, Soviet Occupied Lower Austria.

In the wagon, the summer temperature, combined with its effects on the detritus of the former occupants, was making the atmosphere unbearable.

There was little by way of Soviet military traffic, but there was enough sporadic movement to keep the group tucked away in their hiding place whilst they formulated a plan.

Save for the four watchers, they huddled together, deep in discussion. As Braun listened, he opened letters from the mailbag and used both envelope and contents to remove 'unsavoury' items from his clothing and footwear.

"I agree that we cannot sit here forever, Kameraden, that's for sure." The last of their cigarettes was being passed from hand to hand. The foodstuffs had long gone.

"From what we picked up during our time in the camp, we cannot be that far from where the Allied lines are, or at least, were."

In the habit of men throughout the ages, Rolf grabbed his chin and thought hard.

"We must split up into small groups and try to make our way to the Allies with the information we have. That duty is definitely clear."

Even Braun nodded along with the others, his previous concerns having been thought through now.

A moment of pause was thrust upon them as a flight of Soviet single-engine fighter aircraft raced overhead. Rolf waited for the sounds to fade before continuing.

"Moeller, you know this area best of all of us. What alternatives do we have?"

"Herr Sturmbannfuhrer, we have few alternatives, as I see it. Bear in mind, kameraden, it's some time since I visited here. Firstly, there's the obvious one of the railway on which we presently sit. Without a doubt, there will be other traffic in due course, going the right way. Over the other side of the Donau, there's another track; I think it's a place called Ybbs, which could take us to Salzburg, but equally into Northern Italy, or back in the direction of Wien. Into Italy should still see a meeting with the Allies, obviously."

His face split into a grin, in an effort to lighten the moment.

"Obviously, crossing the river will not be without its interesting moments!"

There were some smiles, but mainly inner thoughts on the prospects of swimming a river in their condition, or having the audacity to cross a bridge that would undoubtedly be guarded by watchful Soviets.

"There is always river traffic; boats plying their trade, up and down."

A grateful puff on the last cigarette doing the rounds and he continued.

"Road is a possibility, but would not be without its problems, particularly with security obviously."

"Lastly, there is always walking to fall back on, but I'm sure we are a minimum of twenty-five kilometres from the probable border, as we understand it, so not for the faint-hearted.

Uhlmann nodded his appreciation.

"Thank you, Moeller. So, unless anyone wishes to steal a plane and fly out of here, that's the options."

Discussion quietly followed, as each man made a play for his preferred choice. Surprisingly, agreement was reached quite quickly.

Walking and the road had no takers.

Moeller and three others would take their chance on crossing the river and finding a train direct to Salzburg.

Olsen, the 12th SS Hauptsturmfuhrer, the Brandenburger Leutnant and one other, would go for another train from their present location, heading north-west.

238

All the others opted for the boats and so Krantzschen and Kloss with two comrades would try their luck in one party, with Uhlmann, Braun and Shandruk in the second.

Now all they needed was the opportunity to get out of the small rail yard and into some decent cover.

The group had already spotted some old sheds partially concealed in undergrowth on the Schloss side of the track, but there was a distance of thirty metres to run without a single shred of cover making life difficult.

A watch had been set to try to establish the safety of these sheds and it seemed there was no patrol that looked at them. They were probably safe. However, there were haphazard movements of uniformed men all round the area that did not bode well.

The problem was exercising everyone's mind until Kloss hissed a low warning. German eyes looked through the gaps in the wagon's side and were confronted with the sight Soviet troops assembling down both sides of the main track. In short order, it was possible to see at least sixty Soviet soldiers guarding the rail line. More soldiers could be seen leaving two large huts to the north of the rail line. The activity grew as five old Wehrmacht trucks hove into view and were waved to a halt by the rail guards.

The rain started to fall gently on this assembly, the sky becoming suddenly grey. The area took on a surreal aspect, as yet another summer storm prepared to visit itself upon the locale.

No one thought to question the fact that the Soviets were running their train security in daylight.

Rolf watched as a few men climbed down from the trucks to stretch their legs and enjoy cigarettes and was startled to identify them as German soldiers. Admittedly, it was a difficult light, but the cut of the German panzer uniform was very evident on two of the figures, as was the fact that all bore the signs of blood upon their clothing.

In a moment of pure clarity of thought, Uhlmann understood what he was seeing and what exactly those lorries contained and, more importantly, where the contents were going.

"Listen to me, Menschen. Those Soviets are waiting for a through train and we must move quickly when it passes. We have no time to lose." He gesticulated at the vehicles and shared a knowing look with Braun. "Those lorries are coming to this train to load up."

He gestured to one of the group.

"Get ready on that door. First group out will be Moeller, second Krantzschen, third Olsen and lastly mine. Go on my order. I will observe."

Nods from all, the urgency of Uhlmann's tone inspiring them.

"Quickly. Tidy up anything that might show we have been here," and looking at Braun and his pile of soiled letters and envelopes, "Anything."

Shandruk started picking up the screwed-up letters, stuffing them in his left trouser pocket before stopping dead as some words on one caught his eye. He put that one in his other pocket.

Within seconds, the sound of an approaching train became evident, its noise growing in proportion with the sound generated by the increasing rain.

Again, fortune favoured the Germans, for Mother Nature provided her own additional distractions, as lightning preceded thunder once more.

A train slowly came into view and Rolf prepared to send Moeller on his way with the drop of a hand.

A burst of steam gave Uhlmann the only stimulus he needed to give the signal and Moeller's group bolted from the wagon to the waiting shed. The slow moving train provided another opportunity and Krantzschen's group swiftly followed.

The partially uncovered load on one of the flatbed wagons gave Rolf a moment's pause, but he still managed to get Olsen's group away.

Before he could order his own group out, the train had passed and the Russian soldiers started to disappear in all directions, their duty, for the moment, done.

Braun sidled up closer.

"Did you see those vehicles, Rolf?"

"Ja, I did. Later, Johan, for now we've a big problem."

240

The lorries started up once more and made to move forward, until a single soldier stepped forward to halt them with an imperious hand.

This time, coming from the left as Uhlmann looked, the little engine that had brought them through the night emerged, moving to a position at the other end of the train, ready to be hitched up and take another grisly cargo back to be interred in secret around Edelbach.

"Go!" screamed Rolf, as the engine puffed across the line of sight.

The group bolted for the huts and, in seconds, found themselves face down on the dirt floor of the hut, gasping for breath, surrounded by their comrades, all doing exactly the same thing.

The scared men tried hard to control their breathing, especially as the trucks were now moving again and closing on the wagons.

Uhlmann spoke softly, in spurts between breaths.

"Kameraden, those lorries contain our comrades. They are about to be placed onto the wagons we escaped in. We can do nothing for them, for they are dead."

As if to prove his words, executed German prisoners were already visible through the open wagon door, as the remaining live German soldiers piled the corpses on top of each other.

"It seems that the Russians are killing everyone in uniform. It's not enough for them to win; they must eradicate!"

Uhlmann controlled his speech, as every man was looking straight at him.

"Now we know that we simply must get through to the allies and give them our information."

There was no dissent, only a grim resolution.

"Braun and I both saw something on that last train, which needs to be spoken of. There were American self-propelled guns there," a pause for effect, "M-10's ... with American markings"

Silent looks were exchanged.

"We know the Allies sent equipment to the Soviets. It would seem they intend to use it for mischief, much as our

241

Skorzeny did in Wacht am Rhein. I think it's very important to pass this on."

"Herr Sturmbannfuhrer, there is more."

Attention turned to Shandruk, who did not look up from the soiled letter he was reading as he spoke.

"I'm holding a letter to our beloved Captain Skryabin. Please note the quality of the paper." Shandruk rubbed the edge between thumb and forefinger, as if to demonstrate the paper's superior grade. "My Russian reading is a little rusty, but I'll give you my interpretation of what it says."

Shandruk looked up, waiting for some sign from Uhlmann, who swiftly nodded.

"It is a brief letter, dated 17th July. It speaks of rumours of a loose tongue brought to the writer by someone called Chairman Lavrentiy... and how he will do nothing... provided Viktor keeps his mouth firmly shut from now on... if Viktor must crow then wait until it all starts... even he should be able to manage three weeks... some of the usual pleasantries follow."

Shandruk looked up.

"It is signed by Uncle Vyacheslav."

More than one present let out an incredulous "Schiesse!"

It was known Skryabin was connected, but now it was glaringly and surprisingly obvious to whom. It required no intelligence to work out who the Chairman mentioned was and only modest adding was needed to work out the timescales involved.

"It is soon then, kameraden. We must get the message through quickly."

His eyes took in the awful work in progress outside.

"As soon as it is safe, we must start off from here. Grab some rest while you can. My party will keep a lookout."

The rain suddenly became torrential and talking over it was a danger in itself, considering the proximity of the working party. One bonus of the downpour was the steady stream of clear cool water that flowed through a hole in the roof, from which they quenched their thirsts.

The men made themselves comfortable in the recesses of the shed, whilst Uhlmann, Braun and Shandruk, kept watch, observing the continuing loading of dead in their scores.

Only those three saw the grisly detail conclude, the guards and live prisoners swiftly dive into the attached carriage and the little train, with its awful cargo, start off on its journey to the Waldviertel.

Evening was drawing in when Uhlmann woke his sleeping comrades and, with handshakes and comradely hugs, sent each group on its way.

The antidote for fifty enemies is one friend.

Aristotle

Chapter 34 – THE DANUBE

2255hrs Saturday, 4th August 1945, Ybbs an der Donau, Soviet Occupied Lower Austria.

It was some time since the rain had stopped and, whilst its absence was welcome, it had done an excellent job of masking their sound and keeping the Russians indoors.

Even so, the trio had progressed more than a kilometre from the rail yard, before coming to an abrupt halt.

They had successfully passed by the river bridge, the security on which had made them think long and hard about those comrades who were intent on seeking escape to the other side of the Danube.

As Saturday slipped unnoticed into Sunday morning, they had followed the bank as it curved to the north-west, until they came upon the silent, sleeping camp of a Soviet infantry unit, spread out between the road and the riverbank. Silent and inviting shapes lay tethered to moorings, but while they lay tantalisingly close, they also lay within the patrol of some obviously alert Soviet guards.

Shandruk tapped Braun's arm and motioned towards something set apart from the rest, Braun repeating the gesture to Uhlmann. Thier eyes adjusted and recognised the shape of a rowing boat, albeit lower in the water than any of the others.

The reason for that became apparent as they moved closer to it, for the craft was damaged and had taken on water.

It was further burdened by a Soviet Lieutenant, curled up in a sodden blanket across the central bench, snoring softly. The evidence of his drinking lay witness around his feet, where empty bottles of local beer lay on and around the dead body of a young Austrian girl.

Uhlmann quickly decided to take the vessel and give it a go. With urgent gestures and sign language, he sent Shandruk in to do the grisly work.

244

Pausing only to pick up a large splinter of wood, Shandruk slipped slowly into the water, up to his thighs and moved around to the side where the sleeper had his head. With as little thought as a cat dispatching a mouse, Shandruk clamped his hand over the drunken man's mouth and slammed the splinter into the throat of the Russian four times in quick succession. No sound escaped the officer's mouth as he died, swiftly and meaninglessly.

With no emotion, Shandruk and Braun lifted him from his deathbed and placed him down, partially in the water and partially in the long grass. The dead girl followed, arranged so those who discovered the bodies would plainly see that it was she who had slain her assailant, even as he slid his own knife into her belly.

It was all over within two minutes and the group slid into the water and pulled the sodden boat into the river, quietly pushing out, intent on making the far bank of the Donau.

Using it solely as a flotation aid made sense, as the casual observer would probably see just a leaky damaged boat floating aimlessly by itself.

The current took them back as it flowed eastwards, but they moved slowly out into the middle until they were certainly out of immediate danger, when a brief word from Rolf made them kick out to fight against the flow. As they neared the south bank, they saw a number of boats of all shapes and sizes tied up and were rejuvenated by the possibilities opening up to them. They made for a gap between two such larger vessels and, once in the lee of the large vessels, they permitted the sodden boat to drift away downstream, its purpose served.

It had already been decided what to do, once a suitable craft had been found, so Braun looked around and quickly found a way to get up onto the marina walkway, or at least get a better look around. A handy wooden piling helped him and, within a moment, he was gone.

Uhlmann and Shandruk remained in the water, the latter tightly holding the Nagant pistol he had snatched from the destroyed guard hut at the camp.

0155hrs Sunday, 5th August 1945, Ybbs an der Donau, Soviet Occupied Lower Austria.

Meanwhile, Braun quietly stole upstream on the modest quay, flitting from cover to cover, checking each vessel as he went, until one caught his eye. Or more exactly, the chink of light through a gap in the warped wooden door drew him in.

He slid quietly onboard and stole a glance through the same gap, seeing a large civilian moving inside the modest quarters.

Remaining on his belly, Braun used the fact that he was relatively well concealed to take in more of the quay and general area.

He was still deciding whether this was the right person to approach when he became conscious of something touching the back of his neck. That something was sharp and held in a very firm, unwavering grip.

Speaking in broken Russian, a decidedly Austrian voice enquired casually.

"What do you want Ivan? I have no vodka here. No women. What do you want?"

Without the benefit of seeing who the man was, Braun could only take the gamble they had already decided upon.

"I am an escaping German soldier and I am looking for a boat to take me up river."

If there was any relaxation on the part of the knife bearer, it was not evident to Braun.

"You are about as German as I am. Try again." The accompanying prod broke skin and he felt blood trickle from the wound.

"I am Sturmscharfuhrer Braun, until recently of the Wiking Panzer Division. I have escaped from a prison camp and am trying to get back to Hamburg."

The blade withdrew, simultaneous with a chuckle from the throat of the vessel's Captain.

"You may look round now, Kamerad; this is your lucky day."

Braun sat up and turned around. He was greeted by the vision of a huge one-armed man sliding a dagger back into

246

a wooden scabbard. The leather jacket and cap belonged to the civilian Braun had seen moments before in the cabin.

"Lucky day indeed. I am Pförzer, Hubert Pförzer, and I suspect you and I have shared the same dust in Russia. Until I lost my arm, I was Unterscharfuhrer Pförzer of the Totenkopf Division. Come into my home."

With a huge grin, teeth shining through the darkness, Pförzer took Braun's hand in a vice-like grip of welcome.

Braun hesitated and then committed.

"There are more of us; two more to be exact."

"Then we must get them inside and out of the way quickly. There is a foot patrol along the quay every hour and they will soon be upon us."

Pulling Braun to his feet, Pförzer stepped onto the bank and pulled him physically off the boat. Braun doubted he had ever been in a stronger grip in his entire life.

"Oh and if you ever want to sneak onto a boat, remember your weight will make it shift a little."

"I did wonder how you knew, Pförzer," exclaimed Braun.

With Braun leading, they swiftly moved the small distance to where Uhlmann and Shandruk waited in the water. A whispered warning from Braun helped lessen their surprise and, on instruction, they held up their hands for assistance. Both were equally surprised when they sailed out of the water, extracted by Pförzer's amazing strength.

The Austrian took one look at Shandruk's Nagant and pointed at the water.

"Get rid of that immediately. Let's go, smartly now," was all the conversation from the Austrian, before he whisked them off and into his small but comfortable barge cabin.

The pistol was already on the bottom of the Danube.

Rolf started to speak, but the flat hand held aloft by Pförzer brooked no arguement.

The one-armed giant turned his head to Braun.

"Light," he gestured at the oil lamp and Braun immediately turned it down so that no light would be visible to the approaching Russian patrol.

247

The two bored men strode past noisily and with purpose, which purpose was, fortunately, to get back to their guard hut as soon as possible, not to worry about who could be sneaking around the moored boats and barges.

"We can relax now," commented Pförzer and again he gestured to Braun to adjust the lamp. The huge man busied himself in one corner and then turned around to his visitors.

"My barge is my home," he waved his only hand expansively, "Formerly an iron ore carrier from Linz, but now converted to my own needs."

He clapped his hand on Braun's shoulder and looked at the others.

"So, who do we have here then?"

Both identified themselves and their former unit, Uhlmann receiving a respectful click of the heels.

Pförzer reciprocated and spoke briefly of his service with the 3rd SS Aufklarungs Abteilung, as he sorted under the bench seats for blankets and towels.

A kettle magically started whistling, none of them had even realised it was there and coffee, real, not ersatz, was swiftly thrust into their hands.

All three drank quietly, savouring the wonderful taste. The mugs had seen better days, for sure, their enamel more chipped away than present.

The silence that descended on the group as they drank their fill seemed to turn a little awkward, once the mugs had been emptied.

Pförzer noted Rolf's eyes firmly fixed upon him.

An unspoken question received a proper answer from Pförzer. "Black market, kameraden, black market. I have business arrangements with some fine Russian entrepreneurs hereabouts and with some of our American Mafiosi upriver."

The pot did the rounds again and mug levels were replenished.

After returning the pot, he sat down, stroked his hair into place and picked up his drink.

"Which arrangements are about to help you a very great deal."

With their undivided attention, he continued.

248

"The Colonel here signs my passes. You need passes to move anywhere with the schiesse Russians in control, more so, of late. My passes take me where I need to go, in order to acquire the finer things of life. The Colonel has expensive tastes and I satisfy them."

A pause as his mug was raised.

"He lost his right arm fighting the Italians outside Stalingrad; I lost my left arm at Demjansk in forty-three. Between us, we save lots of money in gloves."

The roguish grin on his face brought out their own smiles and they shared a small laugh.

Shandruk could not hold himself back.

"Truly?"

"Truly. I have at least five right gloves and no left ones."

Not one of them believed the man, but they could not help but smile at his failed attempt to keep a straight face.

A full gulp and, with his mug again emptied, Pförzer yawned and spoke wearily.

"You should be safe here. They don't normally come on here, unless they are picking up stuff for the Colonel. Nothing is due, so no problem on that score. Get dry and grab some sleep. It's coming up to three o'clock, so you can have two hours easily, before I must put you in the hold. You can sleep more in there, provided one of you stays alert."

Pförzer quickly tidied up the mugs, cleaned them and replaced them in the rack, then settled back into his chair and looked at his new comrades, realising that each was already asleep and dreaming of a better world.

At five o'clock he would get them into the hold and then be away to see Colonel Evgeny for his signed passes.

0503hrs Sunday, 5th August 1945, Ybbs an der Donau, Soviet Occupied Lower Austria.

"Waking the dead would probably have been easier," chirped Pförzer, as Shandruk became the last of the three to return to life, all having taken advantage of the safety offered, all having slept deeply.

249

"As soon as you're all ready to move ,we'll get you into the hold while I'm away. It's always locked and it's very secure, so provided you stay quiet at all times, you shouldn't have problems."

He passed a paper wrap to Uhlmann.

"Apple, bread and wurst, is all I have at the moment, but I will be able to do better for lunch, Herr Sturmbannfuhrer."

Pförzer moved out and onto the deck, scanning the area carefully, whilst appearing to busy himself with chores and checks. After a short delay, he beckoned the three out.

Showing them down into the hold, Pförzer whispered, "In the far corner you'll find sacks and sheeting. Very comfortable, I should think, menschen. Leave the boxes and stacks alone, if you please."

Before closing the hatch and locking them inside, Pförzer took another look around.

"I will be back within two hours, kameraden. I'll bring clothes and food with me and we'll leave the quay immediately, if only that we may talk more openly and safely. There's lot of strange stuff going on with the Russians at the moment and I want to get clear of here as soon as possible."

In the darkness, Uhlmann decided to save his precise and worrying explanation of the Russian's behaviour for later.

"No lights, stay silent until you hear me speak directly to you. And for God's sake, one of you stays awake! Alles klar, meine herren?"

Barely audible assent and thanks floated up from the three, already immersed in the total darkness of the hold, and then the locks were in place and Pförzer was gone.

0657hrs Sunday, 5th August 1945, Ybbs an der Donau, Soviet Occupied Lower Austria.

It seemed like the man had been absent but a few minutes, before the sound of the engine, reluctantly coming to life, disturbed Uhlmann. He had stayed awake first, whilst the others slept and then placed Braun on alert, taking his own rest.

250

Two opaque panels in a small central structure, set into the ceiling, allowed a low light to gently bathe the hold, sufficient for Uhlmann to see his comrades.

That Braun and Shandruk were fast asleep, when at least one should have been alert, was not wasted on him, and he had court-martialled men in his unit for the same offence on the Russian Front. The other two started awake as the engine roared with acceleration and he looked at each man's reaction.

Without the need for words, he established that Braun had indeed fallen asleep on guard. In the silence of looks exchanged between fellow soldiers, Braun accepted his blame and his guilt was clearly marked on his pained expression. Rolf inclined his head and raised one eyebrow, in the style of an extravagant silent movie actor. In return, he received a resigned exhalation from the ashamed NCO. There was nothing more to be said.

They became aware that the vessel was moving and so relaxed. After what seemed like an age, the hatch was opened and Pförzer greeted them, as the morning sun flooded into their hiding place. Some clothes were thrown down, along with a brown wrap containing food.

"Morning, Kameraden. Sorry for the delay, but I wanted to pass the bridge before letting any of you out. The day is bright and not a cloud in the sky. No sign of the storms now."

His head withdrew, as he quickly scanned around, before returning.

"Get into those civilian rags as soon as possible. I will put your uniforms over the side later on. When you have done that, we can have you up on deck one at a time."

A further check on the surroundings.

"I normally bring one crew with me, so no-one will be worried to see a hand on deck. Willi is staying at home today."

A huge grin split his face.

"We will have you safe and sound in no time. Watch your eyes."

His hand dropped inside the frame and clicked the switch to the three lights, which immediately illuminated the hold area.

251

The light, even though low wattage, hurt their eyes, as none had been quick enough to react to Pförzer's warning. The hatch dropped back into place.

Recovering their vision, the three sorted through the clothing, made their selections and removed their uniforms, making the final transition from members of the Waffen-SS to civilians with little thought. Their old uniforms were bundled together and tied with twine found on the floor. The contents of the paper wrap were shared between them and they relaxed back in silence, although the hand-knitted jumper Shandruk had selected provided unexpected entertainment, drawing some sniggers, as he wrestled with its overly long arms.

The hatch was raised and Pförzer beckoned to Uhlmann.

"Best we quickly sort out our plan, Herr Sturmbannfuhrer, so you first on deck, I think."

A pack of Chesterfield cigarettes and a book of matches were dropped lazily down, passing Rolf as he ascended the ladder. Replacing the hatch cover, Rolf screwed up his eyes, as the sunlight made its presence felt. As his eyes grew accustomed, he started to take in his surroundings; the wide, steady flowing river and the lush countryside on either bank. For the first time, he noticed the garish paintwork of the barge itself, its mixture of yellow, red and green decidedly heavy on the eye. Gingerly, he made his way into the little wheelhouse.

"Wear that cap, please… and make sure you pass it to the next on deck." Pförzer nodded at a weather-beaten old brown leather flat cap, gently swaying on a hook.

"Part of the uniform. Smoke?"

Rolf nodded.

Pförzer shook out a Chesterfield and lit it, all in one easy motion, offering the pack and lighter to Rolf, gesturing that he could keep both.

In silence, the men drew heavily on the rich American tobacco, the steady chugging of the engine adding an almost mystic quality to the moment. Rolf spotted the two separate small lines, looped at one end, working out that these were what Pförzer attached to the wheel to keep the barge straight when away from the wheelhouse.

Sending his butt over the side, the Austrian looked Uhlmann up and down and chuckled.

"Not quite as smart as your uniform, Herr Sturmbannfuhrer, but certainly not about to attract attention."

"True...true," said Uhlmann, as the realisation that he had worn his uniform for the last time swept over him.

Pförzer leant against the wheel and waved gently at the Captain of a barge moored to the bank.

"So, how may I be of service on this lovely sunny day?"

"Obviously, we must dispense with the formalities, so please call me Rolf if you will."

Pförzer nodded.

"Rolf it is then. Call me Hub."

Uhlmann finished his cigarette, flicking it purposefully into the water and dropped his bombshell.

"We need to report to the American authorities as quickly as possible."

Pförzer's surprise was written all over his face.

"I had expected something different, Mein Herr. Papers for the three of you, cover stories, you know the score, but you actually want to go to the Americans?"

Although Pförzer was a man not fazed by much, it was clear that Rolf had caught him by surprise.

"Then you have something to tell me I assume, mein Herr...err.....Rolf?"

Therefore, the next few minutes were spent in explanation of all that the escapees had seen and understood, leaving out nothing.

"Now I understand, Herr Sturmbannfuhrer. Once again the dance will start it seems, but perhaps this time we will manage to fight with stronger allies."

His wry smile expressed a great deal and was easily understood by a fellow combat soldier.

"I knew there was tension between the Soviets and the Western Allies, but didn't have any idea it was this bad. So, Rolf, when?"

253

"The longer they wait, the more chance of discovery obviously. The hidden laager we saw can only be five kilometres maximum from where we came together. I think soon, Hub, very soon."

"Today is Sunday, tomorrow is Monday 6th August."

A moment's pause for thought.

"As I see it, the first issue is getting through the Soviet checkpoints."

Rolf inclined his head in acceptance.

"That will not be a huge matter for us. I am well known, as I go back and forth often. I drop a bottle or two in the right hands and we will slip through without problem."

He saw doubt in Uhlmann's eyes.

"Rolf, crossing through to the American side will be easy enough with the papers I possess. I also have a few friendly Americans who provide me with good papers for the other side."

His bulk leant against the wheel once more, his hand worked at his chin as he wrestled with the problem.

"None the less, it is the Americans who will pose the biggest threat. If you go to some idiot who is not prepared to listen, or that just imprisons you, then you may find your information becoming 'old news' in rapid order."

The Chesterfields again did the rounds and helped the thought processes.

"We must find a combat soldier preferably, not one of these rear line swine who wouldn't know what to do with what you have to tell them. We must find you someone who will listen," a very obvious idea was spreading through Hub's mind, "Someone who is of high enough rank to get people out of bed on a Sunday."

Rolf's quizzical look drew a response.

"Ah yes, I forgot, you have not encountered our American enemy, have you? They do like their comforts and I would expect that many will be away from their posts, enjoying everything this wonderful country has to offer."

Pförzer used a simple head gesture to draw Uhlmann's attention to a map on the wall of the wheelhouse.

"To our right now is the town of Weins."

He waited whilst Rolf got his bearings.

"We will face inspection at the Freyenstein checkpoint", waiting again whilst Rolf's finger traced upriver to the location, "Where we will have some visitors onboard. So long as two of you are well hidden, I see no problem. I go upriver empty, mainly, so there is nothing unusual."

Uhlmann's finger tapped the map pensively.

"You would agree that we must find the right American, Rolf?"

"Yes, of course, but I can't help thinking that time isn't on our side here."

More searching of the map and fingers running imaginary routes.

"Where are you thinking we might find the person we need?"

"Mauthausen. I happen to know a high-up American Commander, a General no less, is visiting the former camp there today."

Rolf's enquiring face betrayed no knowledge of the name as he searched upriver. His finger came to rest over the spot.

"Former camp?" Rolf's voice asked almost disinterestedly.

"Not a place we should be proud of, my friend. One of the camps where the mass killings took place."

Rolf's head turned, suddenly focused.

An uneasy shift of weight and a sigh revealed Pförzer's discomfort. "The world will stand in judgement on all of us who knew and did nothing and there will be a reckoning."

Rolf nodded.

"One day soon I expect, but if we don't speak out to the Western Allies immediately, that reckoning will be run by the schiesse Russians!"

Again, Rolf's finger tapped the map, this time beating out a rhythm of thought over Mauthausen.

"I also believe that the General will be staying overnight in the area," ventured Pförzer, receiving a grunt from a barely listening Rolf.

"There are few establishments in the area suitable for a distinguished General. I will try to find out, once we get through the Russian checkpoint. I have a suitable contact in Enns, a man who might be able to help us; a frontline schwein."

A gentle turn of the wheel started the vessel on the long right hand bend that would bring them to the Freyenstein checkpoint.

Rolf continued scanning the interior of the wheelhouse and he noticed a modest carved wooden relief of Saint Florian, to the left of the wheel.

"St Florian, Hub? Why St Florian?"

"I was born in St Florian more years ago than I care to remember and he has come to mean more to me than just that."

A new pack of Chesterfields magically appeared and was opened with his teeth before disgorging two cigarettes.

"He is the patron saint of my chosen profession, or at least, the one I chose before the war, when I had two arms."

Rolf looked none the wiser.

"I was a fireman in Linz, until the Anschluss, and then I was caught up in the fervour of the times."

A sympathetic nod said all that could be said.

"Mind you, could have been worse. I might have taken it all the way and joined that bunch of shirt-lifters in the SS Kavellerie, eh?"

Rolf laughed, enjoying the joke at the expense of his former comrades of the 8th SS Kavellerie Division 'Florian Geyer'.

"Here, take the wheel. Keep the same distance from the bank, I won't be long. Oh and if anyone waves, do wave back."

Uhlmann took the wheel, as Pförzer slipped quickly out and to the deck hatch, slipping inside in the blink of an eye.

The vessel was easy enough to steer and he relaxed into the role, pulling gently on the wonderful American cigarette hanging in the corner of his mouth.

He almost jumped as the deck hatch crashed open and Pförzer emerged, carrying a heavy green canvas bag.

Cautiously he looked around, before sending the wrapped and weighted uniforms into their wake. Returning to the wheelhouse, he carefully stowed the bag in a small cupboard. Accepting the wheel back from Rolf, he nodded at the cupboard and grinned. "That's Ivan taken care of when he comes knocking, Mein Herr."

"Vodka?"

"Scotch. Johnnie Walker. Only the best for our communist comrades."

Rolf grunted, again becoming pre-occupied with, almost daunted by, the enormity of what lay ahead.

Pförzer mistook it for envy.

"In my pocket here," he indicated the jacket he was wearing and fetched a flask from its depths, thumbing the spring-loaded cap open as he offered it up.

"Try some of that Kamerad."

Rolf accepted the flask and took a slug.

"Sche..."

Uhlmann was unable to speak and was overtaken by violent coughing.

As the choking started to subside, the grinning Pförzer took the flask back, taking his own tipple, flicking the lid shut and slipping it back into his jacket.

In a voice that sounded not unlike a man who had eaten a bowl of sand, Rolf enquired, "What the fuck is that?"

"That, Mein Herr, is our American enemy's secret weapon! They call it Southern Comfort and I have acquired quite a taste for it."

Pförzer's grinning continued as Uhlmann coughed his way to a clear throat.

"I will remember that for the future!"

Uhlmann could feel the liquid warm his belly.

"Now then, my friend," Pförzer brought them both back to earth.

"We have lost the war. Let us now concentrate on not losing the peace."

257

1147hrs Sunday, 5th August 1945, Ybbs an der Donau, Soviet Occupied Lower Austria.

As the barge approached the checkpoint, Rolf unconsciously moved his hand to the trouser pocket containing the papers Pförzer had obtained for him.

The action was noted.

"Easy, Kamerad, easy. Just take things nice and easy. Speak if they speak to you, obviously, but just leave it all to me and only offer those up if you are approached."

Pförzer paused momentarily.

Rolf nodded, as his eyes took in the scene.

Freyenstein itself did not seem to amount to much at all, pushed up against the Donau by the surrounding hills. A number of small craft, obviously used by the Soviet military, cruised back and forth, intercepting those plying their trade on the river.

His expert eye could see at least four fortified positions on the southern bank, housing what appeared to be Zis-3 anti-tank guns. Rolf knew that, from this point onwards, the left bank was Soviet territory; the right bank belonged to the Western Allies.

Pförzer was conning the barge into the left bank, aiming at a flimsy looking wooden jetty, on which waited a party of Russian soldiers.

The engine was cut, relying on momentum to finish the journey.

He leaned towards Rolf, "When I give you the word, throw them that line near the barrel, up there," he indicated the bow of the barge.

Uhlmann moved forwards and took up the line, in what he hoped was an appropriate way.

The barge slowed to a virtual halt as the current took away the forward momentum and it gently angled into the jetty.

"Now."

The line landed over the shoulder of a waiting soldier, who grabbed it willingly and moved to wind it around a wooden pillar.

Pförzer emerged quickly from the wheelhouse, grabbed the stern line and threw it in one easy motion.

Previously briefed, Rolf picked up a pot of paint and a brush and went to work on the hatch cover.

Another cunning ploy by Pforzer, designed to discourage exploration of the vessel.

Three of the Russians, all officers, stepped down off the jetty and onto the deck. Rolf was amazed to see backslapping and hugging, as they all disappeared into the living quarters of the barge. Pförzer was the last down the steps, green bag prominent in his hand.

Uhlmann had been in many battles and was no coward, but he could not help the familiar stabs of fear that started to gnaw at him, the longer Pförzer was out of sight and he was alone on deck.

He fetched out a Chesterfield and puffed rapidly on it, easing his inner tension.

That was until it was raised again by the sharp sound of boots hitting the deck, as another Russian jumped aboard.

Rolf looked up as a young Soviet Starshina advanced on him with a purpose, the yellow T's on his shoulder boards distinct and new.

His stomach flipped.

The Russian stopped, just far enough away to ensure that no flicks of paint could inadvertently come his way.

"Comrade Boatsman, a cigarette if you please."

Uhlmann was impressed with the flawless German, even if it was a little clinical.

He offered up the pack and the Russian took it, quickly slipping a cigarette into his mouth, lighting it and pausing to examine the pack.

"American."

Not a question; a statement.

"Please, feel free to keep the pack, Comrade. I can get plenty more."

The young Russian nodded graciously and pocketed them.

"Thank you, Comrade Boatsman."

The Starshina walked casually around the deck, taking in everything as he enjoyed the cigarette, even taking care not to flick his ash where it could spoil Rolf's painting.

A peal of laughter sounded out and the below decks party started to emerge into the sunlight once more. Pförzer walked forward, acknowledging the Russian, tossing an empty green bag into the bow area.

Slapping the Starshina on the shoulder, Hub returned to the departing soldiers, seeing them off the barge with more hugs and slaps, carefully avoiding pockets now stuffed with cigarettes and scotch.

Quickly, he disappeared below decks again.

The young Russian threw his butt into the water and looked skywards, relishing the sun upon his face.

"Comrade Boatsman, make sure you do good business this trip, eh?" Rolf looked up and could almost see the pain and fear in the soldier's eyes, "And bring me back something nice, eh?"

Rolf nodded.

Pförzer, emerging from below decks, heard the last statement.

"That we will, Starshina."

He grinned as he thrust four packs of cigarettes into the young Russian's hands.

"Thank you, Comrade Boatsman."

The young Russian moved towards the jetty and went to follow the others, who were noisily disappearing back to their quarters to stash the products of their meeting with Pförzer.

"Starshina Koshevoy, leave it for Starshina Koshevoy."

The young man again stopped and took in the sun's rays, with his eyes closed.

"We'll all have need of something nice in the days ahead."

And with that he was up and gone.

260

Nothing was said by either man until they were safely back underway and out in mainstream again, pushing upriver at good speed. Even Rolf's near-failure to jump back on board, once he had untied the mooring line, raised no comment from either man.

"Soon. It will happen soon."

Rolf could only nod.

They approached the American checkpoint and prepared to go through the same charade.

1313hrs Sunday, 5th August 1945, Ybbs an der Donau, Soviet Occupied Lower Austria.

After passing through the American checks, Rolf returned to the hold, as Braun, then Shandruk, took their turns in the sunlight, the shabby hat changing hands almost as a deck pass.

St Nikola, Grein and Ardogger, all slipped past as the barge drove on.

What was very apparent was that the southern bank of the river, the Soviet side, contained a lot of military positions and hardware, but an absence of activity, or at least the attendant daily activity that would be expected to go with maintaining the positions and equipment.

Uhlmann changed places with Braun, as directed by Pförzer, emerging back on deck after a satisfactory nap in the hold.

In the wheelhouse, Rolf saw that Hub had been busy, for the green bag was again obviously full.

"I will be pulling into shore shortly, Rolf. I have an important contact in a place called Mitterkirchen. If I think it's right, I'll speak to him of our problem."

Within minutes, the barge was tied up on the north bank and Pförzer and his green bag disappeared once more.

In next to no time, he was back.

Rolf did not press him until the barge was safely moving away from the bank.

He slipped into the wheelhouse, but was forestalled by an apparently vexed Pförzer.

261

"He wasn't there."

"Schiesse."

"Indeed, Mein Herr. However, I have discovered something of importance." Rolf looked at Pförzer, but waited, as he knew there was more to come.

"I haven't yet decided if it is a good thing or a bad thing."

The inevitable cigarettes were lit and drawn on, one in thought, one in anticipation.

Rolf waited.

"We decided that we wanted a combat soldier, someone with enough clout to get men out of bed on a Sunday. We may well have hit the jackpot."

Intrigued, Rolf waited.

"The visitor to Mauthausen. He will do, if we can get to him, that is."

Anticipating more, Rolf drew deeply on his cigarette.

"He is the Allied Commander in Austria, General Mark Clark, in person."

Rolf's head snapped up and he immediately choked noisily on smoke forced from his lungs by his exclamation of surprise.

Grinning from ear to ear, Hub leant against the wheel and slapped Rolf's back hard a number of times.

"More to the point, he's staying the night in Enns and there's only one place in Enns suitable for such royalty."

With watery eyes and continuing choking sounds, Rolf listened.

"The Hotel Lauriacum on Wiener Straβe. That's where our man will be tonight and that's where you'll tell your story, Herr Sturmbannfuhrer."

Boast not thyself of tomorrow; for thou knowest not what a day may bring forth.

Proverbs 27-1

Chapter 35 – THE PEACE

2125hrs Sunday, 5th August 1945, Château du Haut-Kœnigsbourg, French Alsace.

Even in the dusky light of a late and stormy European evening, the Château de Haut-Kœnigsbourg was an impressive site.

Having passed through a checkpoint staffed with some relaxed looking commandos, Ramsey took greater notice of his home for the week.

As the Austin staff car moved gingerly up the road, the Black Watch Major could not help himself but appreciate the building from a professional point of view. Even with modern technology, the assault would be difficult and any meaningful defence would put an attacker to the sword, at least from this side of the fortifications.

The east entrance area was obscured by parked vehicles belonging to some French unit, a solid barbed-wire compound further inhibiting pedestrians. The Austin passed through a second checkpoint at the east end of the Château and down a small parallel road that then made a final turn up to the impressive large single wooden door that barred the way into the Château.

A third checkpoint marked the end of the journey.

As his transport rattled to a halt, Ramsey could not help but think of older times, when unwelcome visitors would be received with hails of arrows and streams of boiling oil, until they scaled the battlements, when the hacking off of limbs could commence in earnest.

"We have come such a long way."

"Sorrah Sir?" said his driver, the tip of his tongue sticking out as he concentrated on the manoeuvre to hand.

"Nothing, McEwan, just thinking out loud, son."

263

The young driver looked at his commander and made the wrong assumption.

"Dinnae fret yersel, Major. The week will be gan afore ye know it. Onyways, it isnae that far back tae base."

Deciding not to overly tax his young driver, Ramsey contented himself with an affirmative grunt. The Austin had stopped at the third checkpoint, where Ramsey was invited to disembark. His documentation was thoroughly checked and some casual questions asked, which Ramsey certainly felt were checked off against some list already in the possession of the Officer of the Guard.

"I'll be back for ye next Friday at 1600hrs, Sir. Enjoy yersel... and look after yer shudder."

Internally, Ramsey smiled, for try as he might, he could not imbue McEwan with the virtues of military niceties. That the man was the finest shot the Major had ever seen and possessed the courage of a lion, went a long way with a soldier like Ramsey.

"Indeed, Corporal, thank you. 1600hrs on the dot, McEwan, or no weekend pass for you," he said, with forced sharpness.

The Captain looked up at Ramsey and then McEwan, swiftly reading from the two grinning faces that this was a well-rehearsed act between two comrades. He moved off to the post phone to report Ramsey's arrival. When he was out of earshot, Ramsey spoke again.

"Safe drive home, Mac, and do take it careful round those bends. They will be lethal in the dark, son."

McEwan prepared to move backwards to the hairpin where he would turn his vehicle.

"Ach dinnae worrae aboot me, Sir, il be fine. See ye Friday".

With a swift salute, cut short by the necessity of changing out of forward gear, the staff car was quickly reversed and exited the ramp on its way back to its base.

Ramsey felt a hand on his case and turned to find a smart orderly trying to take it from him. He relinquished his grip, but retained his briefcase and walking stick, his sole eccentricity.

264

A British officer, serving in a senior position, within a jock battalion, simply had to have something to emphasise his Englishness and the black and silver cane was it.

He had purchased it, new, from a Gentleman's outfitters in Glasgow, but a legend had grown and as far as his veterans were concerned it was the very cane carried by Sir Robert Munro at the Battle of Fontenoy in 1745, as presented to their slightly mad Major by clan chieftains. Ramsey did nothing to shatter that illusion. It served a purpose and did no harm. In fact, on two occasions, he had thrown the cane forward, much to his men's horror, encouraging his highlanders to advance when under fire to retrieve the 'prize'.

"Commandant, please follow me."

The orderly moved off and up a rising stone path, before turning left and entering the building, past another small guard station, where both went unchallenged. Ramsey followed the man at distance, taking in as much of his surroundings as possible, climbing the worn stone stairs carefully. Halfway down those steps was an American paratrooper Major, looking extremely dejected.

Ramsey put his cane in his left hand with his case and saluted. The Major, having an eye for certain details, beat him to it, despite his frustration.

"Good evening, Major. I hope that your face is not telling me how bad this place is?"

"Far from it, Major. I just heard your car and prayed it was my own vehicle. I've been waiting here since Friday and transport is supposed to be bringing another officer for tomorrow. I was just hoping he'd chosen to arrive Sunday, rather than Monday. It seems I'll be staying another night."

A hand shot out.

"Crisp, Marion J. 101st US Airborne."

Hands were shaken warmly as Ramsey gave his own introduction.

Crisp ushered Ramsey along after the disappearing Frenchman, who was already up the stairs and moving across a small drawbridge and on, through the Lions Gate.

Both officers increased their pace and made up ground, although more was lost as Ramsey automatically checked the chasm under the drawbridge.

Entering the Well Tower, more steps confronted them, echoing softly with the sound of the disappearing orderly.

"There's no shortage of steps here, Ramsey. It's a bit of a warren to be honest, but by Thursday, you'll be fine."

Grinning back, Ramsey automatically looked down the old well before moving off again, in search of his guide.

Reaching the side gallery of a small courtyard, Crisp spoke quickly.

"When the orderly has you settled down, wander on down to the mess room." He indicated its location with a simple gesture. "Their chow here is superb, Ramsey, and the cellar is very well stocked."

"That is a date, my dear chap. See you then."

Ramsey took two steps at a time behind the orderly, who had not stopped moving forward.

Out through the arches, across the small courtyard and up the hexagonal main stairs to the next floor, where Ramsey was introduced to his bedchamber for the week.

He was no less impressed than the previous occupants, especially as a hot bath was filled and waiting his pleasure.

The orderly, once of the Ritz in London, placed the suitcase on an ornate ottoman at the base of the four-poster bed.

"If there is nothing else, Commandant, I will leave you to your toilette. I shall inform the kitchen of your arrival. May we anticipate you for dinner by 10pm, sir?" The orderly's eyes flicked to the mantle clock as he spoke.

Checking his own watch, Ramsey noted 2135hrs, did the maths in his head and confirmed his attendance.

"Thank you, but no dinner for me. A modest sandwich will be quite fine."

"It shall be as you say, Commandant. If you need anything, just press the button by your bed, sir."

The door closed behind him and Ramsey swiftly undressed and immersed himself in the first bath he had experienced for some months. For him, showers were a necessary evil when the real thing wasn't available.

2158hrs Sunday, 5th August 1945, Château du Haut-Kœnigsbourg, French Alsace.

Having been shown the way by an imposing but accommodating commando Corporal, Ramsey arrived at the cellar, where the pupils and teachers normally gathered to exchange more stories over wine, beer and spirits. On Sundays, the teachers were never there, in order to preserve the impact of the well-practised introduction.

He handed his cane and cap to an orderly and made his way to the low table, where Crisp sat deep in conversation with a British Lieutenant Colonel of Cavalry, nodding in acknowledgement to those other allied officers who looked up as he moved by.

Both rose courteously as Ramsey approached, the eyes of the Cavalry Colonel flicking to the simple maroon ribbon.

No cap, no salute.

Crisp shifted his cigarette into his left hand and extended his right.

"Settled in then, Ramsey?"

Hands were shaken and Ramsey shifted his eye to the man behind Crisp.

"Indeed, thank you for asking, Crisp." Hand extended to the unknown British officer, "Sir."

"THE Ramsey of the Black Watch, I presume? Your excellent reputation precedes you, Major. Cedric Prentiss, 23rd Hussars."

Prentiss affected a typical scatty English gent's accent, but his array of decorations informed Ramsey that the man had seen his own fair share of action.

Prentiss turned and resumed his position in a voluminous and extremely comfortable looking armchair, seeking out his brandy glass and enjoying its contents with great satisfaction.

"Good quality stuff here, Ramsey. Can't fault the frogs for that, eh Crisp?"

"They sure can throw a party, that's a fact, Colonel. I musta put on ten pounds this last week, even with my running and believe me, these hills are murder!"

Prentiss and Crisp shared a small laugh, but Ramsey was confused.

"All week? My joining instructions say I'm here until Friday and I have the battalion boxing championship to referee on Saturday."

"Ah, steady old chap," calmed Prentiss, lighting a Craven A cigarette as he held the pack out to both Majors, who took one on cue.

"Our friend Crisp here isn't staying through choice."

Lighting first Ramsey's, then his own, Crisp stuck his lighter back in his pocket.

"I rather gathered from earlier that you had problems, Major."

"Yes indeedy. My Colonel decided it wasn't errr... prudent, I think he said, to send a vehicle here on Friday and again today. So I'm stuck here until the next man gets here and I can hightail it back in his jeep."

A silver platter descended in front of Ramsey's eyes as an orderly brought his requested sandwich. However, this sandwich would have sustained a family of six for a week. Lean cuts of pork and beef, aromatic sausage, tomatoes, salad and pickled vegetables, were piled high on a warm and delicious smelling fresh baguette.

To the other two, Ramsey's face was a picture.

"Say hi to your first two pounds, Ramsey," laughed a very relaxed Crisp.

Prentiss leant forward. "Fortunately, Crisp here warned me before dinner, so I ordered light. We also took the liberty of ordering the wine for you. A light Moselle to ease your feast down, old chap."

Despite the humour at his expense, Ramsey suddenly felt very hungry. He attacked the plate and listened to his companions pick up where they had left off.

"For myself, I am just glad to have survived this ghastly business, Crisp. Too many good chaps didn't. Still, let's not be maudlin, eh?"

"No, sir. I did feel aggrieved at not going to the Pacific for the assault, but now, I guess it's meant to be and I will just go out there when the army says it's good and ready. And then back home to pick up where I left off."

"Same for me, old boy. What did you get up to before the match kicked off?"

Crisp could never quite get used to the understated British descriptions of the bloodiest war the planet had ever seen.

"I had entered my father's law firm but it isn't for me. Sure, the money was there, but now I think I'll need more in life than just money." Prentiss nodded in agreement as Ramsey tried hard not to choke on a piece of pickled cauliflower.

"Dad'll be none too pleased and that's a fact. Always saw me following in his footsteps, all the way to the court, but not now."

Prentiss waved a summons at an orderly and indicated his and Crisp's empty glasses.

"Two more brandies, there's a good fellow. Thank you."

Again, relaxed back into his chair Prentiss took his turn.

"Same issues with my kith and kin. Father was very much the politician, don't you know. Dead now, poor blighter. Cannot see myself in that line, to be frank. Far too much hot air and duplicity for my taste. Not a career for an honest chap such as myself."

Both men acknowledged the arrival of full glasses and silently toasted each other, which toast Ramsey joined with his exceptional Moselle.

"Our family has an estate in Bonnie Scotland. Rather hoping I can spend my time there, communicating with fellow creatures that neither wish to shoot at me, nor intend to deceive me."

The 'sandwich' was getting the better of Ramsey and it showed.

"Struggling, old chap? Need a brandy to ease it down?"

"No thank you, sir, the wine is quite sufficient. If that is the standard of the food here then I can understand your weight problem, Crisp."

"I'm for dropping the names thing, if that's ok. Call me John."

That was his second name, of course, but it saved explanations.

"Indeed. Call me John too."

All three smiled broadly as they realised the problem.

"Ok, damn it; guess I'm gonna be Marion then," and holding up his hands dramatically, "Yes, there's a story there, ok!"

"Well, far be it from me to stop this heartfelt comradeship from spreading. You may call me Cam in these present surroundings. And there is a story there too, gentlemen."

Ramsey wiped his mouth on his serviette and fell back into the voluminous chair, stuffed to the brim for the first time since he left Blighty.

Suppressing a satisfied belch, Ramsey rummaged in his pocket.

"Splendid. Now then, Marion, you seem to have a story to tell, so fire away."

His Players cigarettes came out and did the rounds before Crisp started.

"Short and sweet version, gentlemen. My father has never touched a drop of liquor in his life, until the day I was born, that is. Unfortunately, he celebrated mighty hard with my Uncle, who then took him down to the County office, to make my birth official."

The two British officers had no idea where this story was going.

Crisp's voice took on the style of an old storyteller, starting into a well-loved anecdote.

"Apparently, Uncle Ralph was propping Dad up and couldn't get much sense out of him. Incidentally, he hasn't touched hard liquor since."

Crisp grinned at the glass in his hand and, taking a sip of his very large brandy, continued.

"The woman clerk was getting mighty uppity, the way Uncle tells it, so he tried hard to get the details from Dad, who was not best placed to be cooperative. Mind you, Ralph is only just a tad more sober than Dad, the way Dad tells it."

Crisp's face took on a serious look.

"Don't forget that Judge John Ryan Crisp, my father, is a man of some distinction and a pillar of the community, which pillar is now, apparently, decidedly horizontal in the county clerks' office."

Prentiss stifled a snigger but still grinned from ear to ear, none the less.

"You see, by this time, Dad was lying on the floor singing, leastways Uncle Ralph says he was singing, but Dad isn't a musical man by nature. Anyway, so there's Ralph on the floor with him, in front of a whole line of people, all with official business in the office, trying to coax the very necessary details of the birth out of a drunken man."

Both now had the amusing image fixed directly in their minds.

"Apparently, there was much annoyance developing with the good townsfolk and Ralph was told, in no uncertain terms, that he should get on with it and get Dad the hell out of there."

More brandy and Ramsey, to his surprise, finished the last of his Moselle.

"And so it was that Uncle Ralph called for silence and asked what the boy's name was."

"Bear in mind now, that there is my Dad and Uncle, lying side by side on the floor of the county office, with a dozen annoyed people leaning over them, straining to hear the not-so-whispered conversation."

Adopting affected drunken whispering tones that represented his father and uncle, Crisp re-enacted the scene.

"What's the boy's name, John?"

"Which boy?" says Dad.

"Your boy," says Ralph.

'My boy?' says Dad.

'Your boy,' says Ralph.

"Ah, my boy, my boy."

"My father spoke my name and the rest is history."

More brandy was consumed as the climax approached.

271

"Marion John Crisp was what my Uncle stated to the clerk."

A pause for full effect followed, perfectly timed.

"Daddy swears he said 'My Ryan'. I've had to live with that ever since."

Neither of the other two heard the second sentence as they were both braying loudly, Prentiss on the verge of choking with glee. They made so much noise that the other officers, mostly French, stopped to see what was entertaining the eccentric British Colonel and his friends.

"Apparently, the listeners were divided on what had been said and an argument occurred. They all decided to stop wasting time and democratically resolved the issue. Majority vote went to Uncle Ralph's version and the rest is a matter of public record. The clerk wrote it down as fast as her hands could do the deed, just to get them all the hell outta Dodge! "

"Wonderful, Marion, wonderful."

Ramsey shook his head, still enjoying the mental images conjured up by Crisp's story.

"That simply isn't true is it...err....Ryan?"

"It certainly is, Cam. You don't think I could make that up?"

His look of innocence was not convincing, but it didn't matter. It was a damn good story.

"So we will go for Ryan, I think. Agreed?"

Prentiss extended his arm and offered his glass forward. The others clinked theirs to his.

"Agreed," spoken as one.

"Right then, sir." Ramsey recovered his poise. "You said Cam?"

"Ah, nothing so fabulous and enthralling as our good friend Ryan here. Merely my initials. I am the possessor of some tiresome names and the family shortened them, for which I am extremely grateful."

"Well, I got the Cedric part earlier. Best you ante up with the rest 'old chap'," said Crisp, obviously feeling the warm spreading effects of some superior French brandy.

"Quite so, Ryan. I am blessed with the names Cedric Arthur Moreton, hence the very simple abbreviation 'Cam'."

272

Both Majors' brains were working overtime with the additional possibilities.

'Prentiss?'

"And before either of you 'gentlemen' goes further into the possibilities of my initials, I should warn you that I make a very implacable enemy!"

Nothing was said, but the grins were loud and clear.

All glasses were now empty and Prentiss again beckoned to the passing senior orderly.

"Three more Brandies, if you please."

The old orderly looked extremely uncomfortable.

"I very much regret, Colonel Sir Lord; I am under orders to govern the intake of all officers this evening. You are now at the limit set by my General and say I must decline to serve you further. Apologies, Colonel Sir Lord. I may serve Commandant Ramsey, of course, and Commandant Crisp may continue, as he will be leaving us."

There was not a lot that could be said about that, not without causing a scene anyway, so Prentiss asked for a Perrier instead.

"Tight ship they run here, it seems, chaps."

"Colonel Sir Lord?" ventured Ramsey.

"Yes, well, very tiresome. Let's not be bothered by it. Sure that damn fellow used to wait tables at the Savoy, you know."

The continuing looks from his two companions stirred him further.

"Oh alright. I am Viscount Kinloss, Sir Cedric Arthur Moreton Prentiss, not really a lord, chaps, or at least, not a proper one."

The additional drinks arrived, but neither Major felt comfortable with drinking the fine brandy in front of an envious Prentiss.

"Well, Gentlemen," Prentiss rose, "I will take a short stroll before retiring to my chamber. I do hope to see you both in the morning," he paused for humorous effect, "My Ryan, but if you are gone, my best regards to you for the future. Pop up and see me in my Scottish seat when you get a chance. I will be easy enough to find."

A hand extended and a firm handshake was shared.

"Thank you, Cam. It's been real fine to meet you, Sir."

Crisp stepped back to let Prentiss pass.

"I'll see you again, Sir."

"Indeed you will, Ryan. As I will see you in the morning, John."

"Indeed, Sir...Cam," Ramsey swiftly corrected himself.

More handshakes and Prentiss took his leave. "Good night, Gentlemen."

"A good man that, John."

"He certainly seems to be, Ryan."

Before the last of the brandy disappeared, Ramsey had a question that was burning away inside.

"So tell me, Ryan. You have done the week here. What's the story?"

Crisp considered his reply, factoring in the closing words of the French Brigadier General, on the last Friday afternoon.

"John, I cannot spoil the surprise, but I will tell you this. You and I are soldiers and both of us have seen combat and all it has to offer. You will meet some more soldiers this week and they will teach you a very great deal about war. This has been a week I will never forget. And that is all I can tell you, my friend."

Both men stood on cue and firmly shook hands.

"I wish you well, Major John Ramsey."

"All the best to you, Major Ryan Crisp."

Crisp returned to his room as the clock was striking midnight and was asleep within minutes. Ramsey followed close behind.

Neither man expected to see the other again. They were both wrong.

Across Europe a line had been drawn. It could not be seen. It could not be touched.

None the less, it was real and it marked a divide.

274

A divide not just between Armies, but also between ideals and philosophies.

The western side of that divide lay at rest, save for a few men patrolling the line, guarding their sleeping comrades and the civilians of liberated Europe.

On the other side of that divide, there was little rest, as men gathered themselves and prepared to unleash hell.

The greater the state, the more wrong and cruel its patriotism, and the greater is the sum of suffering upon which its power is founded.

Leo Tolstoy

Chapter 36 – THE GENERAL

0104hrs Monday, 6th August 1945, Enns, US Occupied Upper Austria.

Finally, the barge nudged into the modest moorings at their destination. After a long journey up the Donau, they had turned into the tributary river, also bearing the name of the city they were about to enter.

Enns was asleep, or so it seemed, the sole sounds of note were now the gurglings of its eponymous river, although the striking of one o'clock by the clock in the famous Enns Tower had only recently faded away into the night.

Uhlmann and Braun were tucked away in the hold and Pförzer left Shandruk in the wheelhouse as he greased the palm of the bored sentry, who immediately slid away to secrete his bottle of Stroh rum, ready to sample later, after he was relieved.

Quickly the group converged on the wooden stage and followed Pförzer's giant frame, as it slid between flimsy wooden structures, before stopping at the door of a solid brick building.

With the padlock removed, Pförzer opened the door and counted the group in before closing it behind him.

It was pitch black inside, but clearly Hub knew his way around and within seconds two candles were burning brightly, granting enough light for the surroundings to become clear. Within the building, whatever it was, for there were no openings, save the one door, the roving eyes saw crate after crate of goods. Bottles of whisky and wine, stacks of cigarettes, smoked meats hanging from ceiling hooks. There were perfumes, nylons and army ration boxes by the dozen.

Rolf picked up an opened bottle of Courvoisier Napoleon Champagne cognac and then marvelled at the dozen or so bottles on the shelf behind it.

"Unfortunately Kameraden, we need clear heads tonight, " said Pförzer, carefully taking the Courvoisier from Rolf's hands and indicating some bottles of Hungarian 'Egri Bikavér' and olive drab cans of Budweiser beer.

A bottle of the 'Egri', or 'Bull's Blood' as it was more commonly known, was quickly opened. Small measures were poured, whilst Pförzer scurried around the storeroom, gathering food, which he set before them on a wooden board perched on a crate.

A reasonably fresh loaf of bread was hacked open and consumed with slices of Liptauer cheese, frankfurter sausages and cornichons. A stone jar of Powidl apricot jam appeared and swiftly became a favourite with Shandruk.

Quickly disappearing into his treasure trove, Pförzer returned with three wristwatches, giving each man one in turn, British Army Vertex style for Uhlmann and Shandruk and a US Army Hamilton design for Braun.

Once the edge was off their hunger and they had settled to more relaxed eating, Pförzer set out his plan.

"As you can see, I am not unfamiliar with the city of Enns, Kameraden."

He pushed the Liptauer to one side and put down a sheet of paper. Pulling a pencil from an inside pocket, he quickly drew a few lines and squares.

Looking up to make sure all were paying attention, he continued.

"This is the Hotel Lauriacum, where tonight sleeps the man we need to see." The pencil switched locations. "Here is the place where my American friend is billeted."

He indicated some lines running back from the billet to the square that obviously represented their present location.

"This is the track I use to conduct my business with him. I think we should be ok getting close to here," he indicated one of the horizontal lines, labelled it 'Basteig' and drew a circle.

"This is a fire damaged house. Deserted. It will be safe enough and we will stop there."

He stifled a small belch with his one good hand.

"Obviously we have the curfew. I have my papers, which permit me to be out. You three do not, so you must shadow me as I walk openly, ok?"

He looked up at Rolf and received an accepting nod.

"Good. I will then go on and speak with my contact. You will be safe there, no problem. However, from that point we have no plan, of course, so we must improvise as we go. My friend will help, if I can make him see the urgency of this."

"And we must go now, I think," Rolf said, putting his hand on Shandruk's shoulder as another slice of bread and powidl was hastily consumed.

Pförzer looked at his watch.

"Shall we, kameraden? Coming up to 0125hrs"

They all took up their watches, winding them and preparing to synchronise.

"On my mark...drei...zwei...ein...mark."

Candle extinguished, the group left the store, pausing only as Pförzer secured it once more.

They stole forward, hiding in the shadows. A jeep slowly laboured down the track, the sound of its approach giving them plenty of warning and time for even Pförzer to blend into the bushes until it passed. Soon, they were all gathered together again in the fire-blackened ruin.

Nothing needed to be said as Pförzer slipped away.

The three huddled together in what used to be the kitchen and waited for his return, ears keenly reaching out to every sound.

The jeep ground its way noisily back from the direction of the river and then the night became silent once more.

With ears straining, the three became aware of the purposeful approach of footsteps coming up the lane from Enns itself. Braun risked a quick look and was rewarded with the unmistakable silhouette of Pförzer bearing down on the building, accompanied by another less bulky, but unmistakably armed figure.

Pförzer strode past, silently gesturing at them to follow and took them further into the blackened ruin, pulling aside a bookcase and indicating steps that obviously led into a cellar.

Rolf wondered why they had not been shown this hideaway at first, but reasoned that Pförzer was just being cautious, in case they had drawn unwanted attention from some passing patrol.

The mysterious figure was last to descend and pulled a heavy curtain across the entrance, keeping apart from the group. Pförzer rummaged briefly in the dark, but soon a lighter brought life to a candle and the whole cellar was gently bathed in its yellow glow, sufficient to see a stack of tarpaulins, life preservers, rolls of telephone wire, signals equipment, box sets of vehicle tools and numerous kitbags stuffed with god knows what, all very obviously formerly US Army property. The sole thing in view that did not once belong to Uncle Sam was undoubtedly the SturmGewehr 44 on a wall mount adjacent to the stairs.

All these things were taken in quickly, because as the group slowly adjusted their vision, they only had eyes for the new arrival, or more precisely, the M1Carbine he was holding and pointing directly at Uhlmann. The man was not tall but he was certainly solidly built, and his shaven head, revealing obvious scars on the line under his cap, made him look all the more threatening.

There was a protracted and extremely awkward silence.

Pförzer broke it.

"This is my good friend and business partner, John. I have told him a little of what you have told me, enough to get him here to listen. Please, now tell him the full story, Herr Maior."

Uhlmann took the cue from that, mentally setting aside any reference to the SS. None the less, he looked at Pförzer questioningly.

"Schwartz speaks our language like he was born here, which he apparently was."

And so Uhlmann began.

279

The muzzle of the carbine slowly dropped, the further Uhlmann got into his story, until the weapon was pointed at the ground and the holder's jaw was almost as low.

The American snapped out of it quickly and spoke in surprisingly good German.

"That is some story, Major, or is it Sturmbannfuhrer?" Even though Pförzer had not complicated matters by telling his partner that they were former SS, the man was obviously intelligent enough to work it out. "Relax; we can do the good guy, bad guy bit later." His outstretched left hand gently waved up and down in a placatory motion.

"I'm sure we would have heard something from Intel on this."

There was no conviction in the statement.

The Major's uniform was clean but worn and he was obviously a combat soldier. Such animals do not always trust in Intel and it was obvious in his eyes that he believed what he had just been told and to hell with the lack of Intel.

"We gotta get this up the line and fast. Hub reckons you need to speak to the General tonight and I have to agree. Gonna be tricky, so I gotta think a'whiles."

The American paused, looking at the three men before him.

"Any of you speak English?"

Braun chirped up immediately and received a nod of acknowledgement from Schwartz.

A moment's hesitation before he turned to the big Austrian. "You got fatigues and such shit in them kitbags, ain't you, Hub?"

A nod and a grin confirmed both that there were uniforms available and that Pförzer had cottoned on to the idea.

Each kitbag held two sets of uniform, from boots through to shirt and tie. Hub rejected the first two bags he opened, preferring the contents of the third and fifth bags. His thinking was that rank opened doors better, so he selected three sets of officer's clothing, making sure that Uhlmann got the Captain's uniform. Size was a good match for both Uhlmann and Braun, but Shandruk needed further rummages before a pair of trousers that suited his smaller frame was found.

280

Three belts and holsters were located and thrown to each man in turn.

In his amused state, Schwartz reverted to his native tongue.

"Hell, but you lot look some stiff mother-fuckers! Lighten up, folks!"

Stiff they certainly were. Perhaps it was natural, given that they were ex-SS wearing another army's uniforms, about to try and break through a security cordon to inform a former enemy General that another former enemy was about to launch a full scale attack at any minute.

Continuing in English without thinking, Schwartz spoke swiftly. "Right, here's the plan. We brazen it out." He spoke almost as if he was thinking it up as he went, with Pförzer mumbling translations for some of the more obscure terms employed.

"I can see the Hotel from my billet so we deploy from there and walk down the strasse, bold as you like. No hiding, no sneaking, just walk right in. If there's shit, then we must have a diversion planned."

A moment's pause as his mind searched for the solution and then a huge smile split the American's face.

"In fact, that's a damn good idea. Hub, you got any damn flares in this goldmine?"

Pförzer opened up the top crate of US Signals gear and liberated a flare pistol.

"Alrighty then, now we're cooking. We agree a time when Hub here sends some of these up and that'll cause the diversion we need. Might even piss Ivan off some." His face revealed his obvious pleasure at the thought.

"The General will be in bed by now and won't be best pleased on being woken, obviously, so people will be dispatched to sort it out for sure."

Schwartz's face clouded and he became serious. He switched to German.

"Only one of you'll be coming in with me, ok?"

The group nodded.

"I guess that ought to be you, Herr Maior, but do understand one thing please."

281

Rolf attentively waited.

"You do anything out of place," he looked around slowly for full effect, "Any of you... I'll blow your fucking heads off."

And none of them doubted that he would do so without hesitation.

Schwartz looked at his watch.

"It's now 0219, so I guess we should be going. Will take but a few minutes for us to get to the billet, not much more to walk to the hotel. Give ourselves a little safety margin in case of delays. Hub, I say you put a load of those damn flares in the sky bang on 0235."

Pförzer grinned, examined the contents of the crate and extracted a box of flares, which disappeared into his pocket.

"Right then, let's move out," and casting a swift eye over the ensemble, "And for fuck's sake, get yourselves looser. You ain't goose-stepping now boys! Hub, 0235 ok? And our business will keep until this shit has gone away. Keep yer head down, old timer," and with that he slapped Pförzer's good shoulder and disappeared up the stairs into the welcoming night.

Time was wasting, but as they took their leave of Pförzer, each man thanked him and shook hands. Rolf was last to go.

"We must hurry. Mein freund, without you we would still be floundering in the Donau, so thank you. In happier times, perhaps we will meet again and share some stories. Until then, as your Yankee said, keep your head down and survive what is to come. Auf Wiedershein, Hub."

"Auf Wiedershein to you, Rolf."

And with a handshake, he was gone.

0223hrs Monday, 6th August 1945, Enns, US Occupied Upper Austria

Schwartz led them forward at a steady pace, openly walking up the narrow lane towards his billet on the corner of HauptPlatz, adjacent to the town's Roman Museum.

All was quiet and there were no further dalliances with patrols. Schwartz turned and ushered them in through a garden entrance at the back of his billet.

Indicating a need for silence with a finger to the lips, he beckoned them forward to where they could view down the street to the crossroads yards ahead.

Using his hand in the universal sign language of the soldier, he swiftly instructed them that the hotel was left at the junction and then down the street, approximately one hundred and fifty yards on the left-hand side. Of course, they calculated in metres.

They stepped away from the dividing fence and huddled close.

A lighter flicked on quickly, reading a watch in the blink of an eye.

"It's 0229 now. If we walk slowly, we should be able to time our arrival with Hub's display."

"Walk in pairs, one pair in front by a few yards, the Maior and me first, you two second. I'll talk in English, you," he indicated Braun, "Do so too. Nothing funny that needs him to laugh, just a story about a girl back home or something."

There was sufficient light for Schwartz to see understanding and compliant nods.

"When Hub does his bit, we improvise and get inside the hotel and improvise some more to get to the General. Good luck to you and may God help us tonight."

Standing straight, he turned to go back into the street and stopped himself.

"Remember, nothing funny and no hurting any American soldiers," as he patted his carbine.

Some whispered assurances and he stepped out into the lane again, closely followed by Rolf and the other pair.

As they strolled into the centre of Enns, the American lit two cigarettes and handed one to Rolf, starting up a conversation about a bland young woman called Emmy-Lou, who was his sweetheart back in the States.

Rolf was aware of a mumbled conversation from behind, as Braun similarly started into some tale of the heart.

283

The first pair arrived at the corner of HauptPlatz and WienerStraße and turned left. Schwartz casually acknowledged a pair of American infantrymen stood next to a buttoned-up 6x6 truck, to the right of the junction, parked in the main square proper. No doubt the rest of the squad was in the back of the vehicle, asleep.

Uhlmann was both relieved and affronted by the lack of professionalism in the soldiers. It would do for them now, but not in the days to come, he concluded.

As Schwartz rambled on further, both pairs turned their eyes to the scene that confronted them.

Outside of the Hotel Lauriacum was a whole lot of trouble.

Eight Military Policemen, looking very alert and undoubtedly more prepared to be interactive than the sleepy infantry by the truck.

An M8 Greyhound armoured car, behind which sat two M20 utility cars. The M8 had crew aboard for sure, a soldier leant idly on the .50 calibre turret MG as he chatted with someone inside the vehicle.

A Plymouth R11 staff car and a Dodge Radio truck were parked up nearest the walking men, but the ensemble was completed by an M24 Chafee tank parked quietly and menacingly further on down, near the next junction past the hotel.

Some simple electric lights were being fed from a US Army generator, ensuring the front of the hotel was bathed in a sodium yellow glow.

Schwartz halted and turned to the following pair, beckoning them closer.

As he asked Braun loudly for a cigarette, he managed to whisper that they had arrived early and needed to delay.

Carefully moving round the group, Schwartz ended up facing the hotel with Shandruk, Braun and Uhlmann both being in the uncomfortable position of not being able to see what was going on behind them.

As the Americans mock laugh was mirrored by Braun, the night suddenly became day as a magnesium flare went skyward. In short order, another followed, then another, the

284

group imagining the one-armed Austrian working hard to load and fire the weapon as quickly as possible.

Rolf indicated, with a jerky head movement, towards the soldiers in the HauptPlatz. The tarpaulin at the back of the lorry had been thrown open and sleepy eyed GI's were slowly dropping out, unsure of what to do next.

In a flash, the way forward became clear.

Schwartz slapped Braun on the shoulder.

"You take command of those boys there and send 'em down to the river to investigate. Slip away and hide up in the garden where we talked a'whiles back. Good luck."

Slapping Braun on the shoulder, he started shouting orders to the same effect in English, gesticulating dramatically, emphasising the urgency of his instructions to his intended audience, the watching MP's.

He turned and strode purposefully towards the hotel, picking out the young MP Officer who was already moving to intercept him.

"Name, Lieutenant?" he asked, not brooking any argument.

"Athabaster, sir. I'm afraid you cannot proceed further, sir." Even though he was young and inexperienced, his confidence rose as two of his MP's stepped in behind him, M3A1 sub-machine guns held in a business-like fashion.

"As you were, soldiers," Schwartz barked at the two MP's, as young and inexperienced as their officer.

"Kill those lights and wake up that damn tank crew. Get them turning over, Lieutenant, and then get these vehicle weapons manned and ready, in case the Fourth Reich has awoken, or Ivan has come a'knocking." He looked back at the radio truck and pointed.

"And I want that radio warmed up, ready to sing for help if this isn't just a fuck up. Clear, Lieutenant?"

Athabaster was clearly confused, faced with clear instructions from a senior officer, balanced against standing policy to maintain the cordon around his general.

He nodded and started to speak, but was ridden over hard.

"I assume you have a detail at the rear?"

"Yessir. Sir…."

The confused MP was immediately cut off again.

"I'll be back in three minutes. Give me these two men," he indicated the clearly perturbed pair, whose M3's were now pointing aimlessly at the pavement as their confusion grew.

"I will organise the rear and then come back. No one is permitted inside until this alert is ended. When I find out which sonofabitch is responsible for this, I'll have his balls, if the General doesn't have them first!"

He strode into the foyer of the hotel, with the two MP's in close attendance, Rolf ensuring that he stayed close.

Of course, he had understood hardly a word, but he definitely understood that he had just witnessed a first class piece of bullying and bullshit.

Fortuitously, the Sergeant in charge at the rear of the Hotel was catching some shuteye, so when Schwartz noisily arrived in his life, there was no room for manoeuvre and he was immediately compliant. Reinforced by the two MP's that had accompanied this extremely loud and aggressive Major, he set about ensuring that the hotel rear entrance could not be stormed by anything less than a battalion of infantry, hoping his efficiency might save him from the Major's wrath.

Schwartz and Uhlmann returned to the foyer and spoke briefly with the night manager, who could see no reason not to tell two American officers which room contained the General.

The two strode purposefully up the stairs and arrived at the floor where the General peacefully slumbered, or at least had peacefully slumbered before a one-armed Austrian had started filling the sky with noisy magnesium light. An extremely loud US Army officer had then shouted the neighbourhood awake and the cacophony was completed when the tank's engine burst into life.

A door with two alert sentries marked the threshold of success and they strode towards it, both wondering how it could have been so easy.

The two sentries stiffened, ready to challenge.

286

Schwartz and Uhlmann tensed, ready to bluster once more.

A door opened and out stepped a bleary-eyed Staff Colonel. Both Uhlmann and Schwartz stopped dead. Neither had ever seen an army officer in pyjamas with rank markings before. If the situation had not been so serious, it would have been comical, especially as they both noticed the night mask pushed up on the forehead and the red satin slippers that completed the apparition before them.

Schwartz took an educated guess based on recent scuttlebutt and got it right.

"Colonel Rhodes, we need a word now."

Rhodes, obviously recently awakened from a deep sleep, tried to kick start his brain and mouth.

Schwartz continued on his mission to harangue the entire security detail.

"You two," he shouted in such a way as to make both men start, "Stay alert, move apart and let no one approach that door. Are your orders clear?"

Both men snapped out an affirmative response and stepped apart, weapons held more aggressively, bright, alert and consciously not wishing to get on the bad side of the vicious looking Major.

Schwartz almost swept up Rhodes and the three disappeared into the staff colonel's room before he could muster an objection, or work out he was being railroaded.

Once inside his room, Schwartz took a different approach.

"Rhodes, this officer and I need to see the General right now. You will take us to him immediately."

Recovering his wits finally, the man blustered.

"Not a hope, Major. If you have a problem out there", he gestured loosely at the heavily curtained window," Sort it and give me your report in the morning. I'll see the old man gets it."

His gaze flicked to the Captain standing behind Schwartz and Rhodes saw danger in his eyes.

"Hold on, who are you two? Identify yourselves before I call the detail."

Schwartz and Uhlmann exchanged glances. Rolf had not understood the language, but the change in tone told him all he needed to know.

The sudden pressure of a carbine muzzle in his chest told Rhodes that he was underdressed for his present predicament. He stole a look at his holster, hanging with his uniform.

"For my part," Schultz softly confided, "I am an American combat infantry officer from the 317th Regiment, 80th Infantry. However, this gentleman is a German officer who's travelled a long way, a hazardous way, I might add, in order to give the General vital information about what's about to happen in Europe, possibly this very night."

Schwartz spoke quickly in German.

"Pass me his holster and sidearm, Rolf."

Uhlmann did as he was bidden and dropped it on the bed alongside where Schwartz was standing. The pretty pearl handle and polished chrome told both of them that this gun was all for show. It was not the gun of a man who expected to go in harm's way.

That view was quickly confirmed as both men could not help but notice the growing wet stain, spreading swiftly across the legs of the Rhodes's pyjamas.

"We're not going to harm you, for fuck's sake!"

Pointing the barrel away from the apparently terrified man, Schwartz gestured with his free hand at Uhlmann.

"I vouch for this man and I've risked much bringing him here. If you'll give me your word that you will take us before the General, then I will give you your pistol and set aside my carbine."

Rhodes switched incredulously from face to face, processing the information, but failing to come to terms with it all.

"We do not have much time, Rhodes. The enemy is coming and the message has to go out!"

As both men waited for a response they heard the unmistakable sound of a round being chambered.

"Nice and easy with the weapon there, Major. On the bed with it…now."

The carbine was cast onto the bed and both Schwartz and Uhlmann automatically started to raise their hands.

"Keep your hands where I can see them and turn around. Clarence, arm yourself."

Uhlmann had no idea who the man in US army shirt, tie and uniform trousers was, although the four shiny stars on his collar lapels of the man stood in the doorway to the adjoining bedroom suggested much. Whereas Schwartz was only too aware of the identity of the man coolly looking down the sights of his automatic.

The main door opened and four soldiers came bursting in. The MP Lieutenant and his two men saw that the boot was now well and truly on the other foot. Weapons were raised and the tension rose dramatically.

The extra man was a staff Captain wearing a shiny helmet and ready to take on the world with his Thompson sub-machine gun.

Rhodes finally had his Colt automatic in hand and did his best to impress everyone that he knew how to use it. Its barrel lay against Rolf's skull behind his right ear.

The General holstered his own Colt, now that the intruders were well covered.

He looked at the Thompson-toting Captain and smiled, partially out of relief and partially because the man's attempt to look warlike was more than comical. Even he had noticed the weapon was not cocked.

"Grice, I want another platoon of men posted here, right now. Contact Colonel Lee and arrange it at once."

With specific orders, the Captain left the room immediately.

It was apparent that the MP Lieutenant had something to get off his chest.

"Report, Lieutenant."

"Sir, the flares were set off by an Austrian civilian, who has been apprehended. Two other men in our uniforms that were with these men," he almost sneered at the two stood there, hands extended towards the ceiling, "Have been taken prisoner. Only this man," he indicated Schwartz, "Seems to

289

have been carrying a weapon. The other three are being held downstairs, under armed guard. Our perimeter is secure, sir."

"Thank you, Lieutenant. We will discuss how these two got this far later."

The young officer winced. It was his watch after all.

"Ok then," the General looked at Uhlmann and folded his arms, weighing up the situation. He had not heard any of what Schwartz had said to Rhodes, but Clark grasped that there was something deeper going on.

"Who the hell are you and what are you doing here and talk fast, son."

Schultz started.

"I am Major Schultz, CO of...."

Clark shot out a hand, palm first.

"I know who you are, son. I pinned a goddamn Distinguished Service Cross on your chest some weeks ago... and that's the only reason I'm stood here now, ready to listen."

The General's eyes narrowed, as his gaze turned to scrutinise the silent one whilst still addressing the major. "You are in deep shit but at least you're kosher. It's this man I want to know about."

"Sir," Schultz ventured, "This officer does not speak English. He is an escaped German kreigie who's risked much to stand before you tonight."

That got the General's full attention and the calm and unfazed demeanour seemed suddenly a little shaken. Pursing his lips, Clarke nodded slowly.

"Do go on, Major."

"This is Sturmbannfuhrer Uhlmann, late of the 5th SS Panzer Division and until recently, a prisoner of the Russians at Edelbach in North Austria."

Although it looked theatrical, it was not Uhlmann's intent, but he could not help but click to attention when the General looked directly at him as his rank, name and former status were announced.

"Sir, if I may speak," Schwartz waited until the senior man gave an acquiescing nod and then continued.

"This man had escaped the Russians and was free, as were those men downstairs, but they have chosen to give up

290

that freedom and risk their lives to come here with vital information, direct for your ears. He has not come to harm you and is unarmed. I know what he has to tell and you must hear him out, Sir"

Majors don't normally use the 'must' word to Generals and escape unscathed, but inside, Clark had to admit that the boy looked fit to burst and it wasn't going to hurt to hear the Kraut out.

After what seemed like an age, the General spoke.

"Alright, son. You two get your audience. Clarence," he looked at the unfortunate officer, "Tidy yourself up and join us."

"Lieutenant?" he queried, looking at the young MP.

"Athabaster, John S. Sir."

"Search these two thoroughly and then post your men outside. No one gets in. Clear? You will then accompany them into my room and ensure that you keep these two under control."

"Yes, Sir."

Clark disappeared into his suite.

A swift search revealed Schwartz's own Colt and a wicked knuckleduster. Uhlmann carried nothing.

The two were ushered into the General's room, where they found him sitting on a desk, leg idly swinging and a mug of steaming fresh coffee in his hands.

"Guess you're going to have to translate what this sonofabitch says for me, Major. I don't need to tell you that this had better be goddamned impressive to keep your narrow ass outta the stockade, son."

"Yes, Sir."

And as the famous Enns tower struck three o'clock, Sturmbannfuhrer Rolf Uhlmann, late of the 5th SS Panzer Division, spoke quickly and accurately of all that he had seen, with Schwartz translating rapidly.

Moreover, by the end of it, Lieutenant General Mark W. Clark was extremely impressed, but he sure as hell wished it otherwise.

Clark was a self-publicist, a trait that had earned him few friends and many critics during his time as commander of the Fifth Army in Italy. His capture of Rome, which many at the time felt contrary to military priority, resulted in a failure to encircle enemy units and ensured the escape of many German divisions. Those same divisions later fought on long and hard, causing many allied casualties. It would always be held against him by many Allied Commanders.

He was famous for ensuring that all communiqués from 5th Army went out emblazoned with his name and that desire for fame, glory and promotion, now worked in favour of the Western Allies, as he started to issue orders. The phone lines were down, but the radio truck could contact half of Europe. He sent out warnings and instructions to his commands all over Austria and Northern Italy. Messages were sent to allied commanders throughout Germany and the rest of Europe, apprising them of the impending storm.

Rhodes, who washed and changed in record speed, had been present for most of Rolf's report and displayed his full usefulness as he wrote out what had been said word for word from memory, presenting it to Clark, who signed off on it, ready for dispatch to his various commands.

Warnings went out all over Europe, cascading from unit to unit, albeit slowly.

The General's entourage swept out of Enns at 0415hrs, heading back towards Salzburg at breakneck speed.

Schwartz returned to his unit to help ready them for the impending storm, Pförzer was released and disappeared swiftly, probably securing his wares from whichever soldiers would come calling. The three escapees were placed in one of the M20's in the column racing back the one hundred kilometres or so to Salzburg, taking Clark back to his command base.

0545hrs Monday, 6th August 1945, Salzburg, US Occupied Upper Austria.

They narrowly missed the commando attack upon Clark's headquarters. Understandably, the General had little

292

time to spare for them, as he set about establishing order amongst his surviving staff. The attack had missed its main target, but despite the warning sent from Enns, many casualties had been caused. Shock seemed to temporarily paralyze those who survived; piteously few, considering a Ranger battalion had been on the road within minutes of receiving the information and had caught the paratroopers on the run-in.

Members of that Ranger unit now viewed anyone and everyone with jaundiced eyes, fingers on triggers. The three German soldiers had been placed under the care of Athabaster, who seemed unsure of what to do with them. He had departed to get instructions, leaving them stood in the care of two of his men.

Things became fraught when Uhlmann, Braun and Shandruk, were challenged by a Ranger Chief Warrant Officer. Despite wearing US uniform, they seemed unable to speak English, except for one who had a distinctly European twang to his words. The two soldiers tried to explain, but the CWO was not in the mood for nervous soldier's bullshitting him, so he shut them both up in short order.

A newly inspired Colonel Rhodes acted as the rescuing cavalry and vouched for the three, before pulling them to one side.

"The General has asked me to thank all three of you again. You have been of great service and many lives have been saved throughout Europe. That will not be forgotten."

Uhlmann did not understand the man, but could not help wondering if this officer was the same one who peed his pyjamas a few hours beforehand.

Braun translated.

"You cannot stay here, so we must escort you back to another facility, where more questions can be asked."

Producing three letters, he passed them on, one to each man. Each was personally signed by General Clark. They were brief in words, but heavy in meaning.

Braun again translated what amounted to a signed personal statement that the bearer was directly associated with the General, who would take a clear interest in their well-being and good treatment at all times, declaring that the bearer had

293

been of great and valuable service to the Allied Armies in Europe in August 1945 and at great personal risk.

"The General's apologies that he cannot hand these to you himself, but he asks me to say that the words are very real and he will honour their meaning."

The two nodded as Braun translated the rest of the letter and Rhodes' words.

Rhodes half turned and nodded to a Corporal holding a bundle.

The man advanced and proffered up its contents.

"General Clark reckoned you might have need of these. Just don't point it at me, Herr Maior."

Braun translated Rhodes' last quip without understanding, but Rolf smiled directly at Rhodes and acknowledged the man's words.

The bundle contained three belts, holsters and Colt automatics.

Tokens of trust from a grateful man.

Each of them took one and buckled it on, feeling a comfort in its presence.

"And for my part, Major, you scared the shit out of me for sure, but I thank you, all of you."

Rhodes extended his hand to each in turn, saving a special firm and lingering shake for Uhlmann.

Still gripping the SS officer's hand, Rhodes spoke without need for any interpretation.

"Hals und Beinbruch, Meine Herren."

They all laughed.

"Hals und Beinbruch, Oberst Rhodes."

'Break a leg' was a common way to wish someone good luck in Germany.

For many, luck was in short supply that night.

CANNON, n. An instrument employed in the rectification of national boundaries.

Ambrose Bierce

Chapter 37 – THE ZILANTS

Early Morning, Monday, 6th August 1945, Airborne over Allied occupied Germany.

The Zilant was a creature of Russian Folklore, most often portrayed as a winged serpent, not that different to the European vision of a dragon.

On this night, there were four such dragons flying through the darkness, all intent on bringing death to their allotted targets; the symposiums.

Men of the 100th Guards Rifle Division "Svir" formed these Zilant groups, which took off from their different airfields in the rear of the Soviet lines.

To the casual observer, the aircraft of Zilant-4 were Douglas DC-3 transport aircraft. Most certainly, they were not, although the Lisunov Li-2's had their roots in the DC-3 and had been produced under licence since 1936, first as the PS84 and then as the Lisunov.

The aircraft carrying Makarenko was a Li2-D paratrooper version, marked to look exactly like a DC-3 of a USAAF transport unit, as were all the others in the same formation, but the other Zilant groups, as with the Kurgan formations, made do with whatever they could that was airworthy and, in some cases not, to get them to where they were going.

Thousands of aircraft were in the air, each with a precise mission, be it the delivery of fighting troops and saboteurs, or to attack ground targets. Zilant-4 had been one of the first groups airborne, rising from Planá Airfield, near the Czech town of Ceske Budejovice. The other three Zilant groups were spread out to the north, each group targeted on one of the symposiums.

Zilant-1, consisting of 1st Battalion, 298th Guards Rifle Regiment, was targeted on Hamburg and the Schloss Ahrensburg.

The 2nd Battalion, as Zilant-2, had a date with destiny at the Schloss Neuhaus, near Paderborn.

2nd Battalion, 304th Guards Rifle Regiment, reinforced with 2 companies of the 1st Battalion, all forming Zilant-3, was concentrated upon Frankfurt and Schloss Kransberg.

Makarenko's group, Zilant-4, consisting of 3rd Battalion 298th and a special grouping of divisional troops, had been handed Château de Haut-Kœnigsbourg and the furthest flight. The remainder of his division was untasked.

Some Allied ground radar stations became aware of many aircraft crossing the new borders and reported in. Some reports were taken seriously, others were not. Some were confused with the intended Molotov flight paths, but in any case, only a handful of night-fighters were sent airborne to investigate. Reports started to filter upwards, but no-one senior enough received warning in time. Partially due to ineptitude on the part of the radar units, but partially because of the successful interference in communications commenced by small groups of Soviet personnel, infiltrated weeks beforehand, for the purpose of wreaking havoc behind allied lines.

Communication infrastructure destroyed during the allied advance into Germany and recently restored, was swiftly destroyed again, along with a number of communication centres and radar warning sites.

Some Soviets were caught in the act and small firefights broke out all over Germany and Northern Italy. The dying started before the sun rose over the morning skyline.

Timed to coincide with all attacks, units of Soviet-manned aircraft arrived over allied airbases at 0530. Those nearest the demarcation lines were mainly visited by Soviet Shturmoviks, PE-2's and their attendant fighter escorts. The airbases further afield got more specialist attention from US built aircraft, sent to Russia under lend-lease and British fighters that had survived the harrowing Arctic convoy run, each in their respective USAAF and RAF colours, but flown by a Russian pilot, sowing confusion with friendly anti-aircraft batteries and responding aircraft alike.

In the first instance, all Soviet air forces were concentrated against the Western Allies airbases throughout Germany and Austria, in an effort to eradicate the weapons that had proved so successful in destroying the German armies in 1944. Operation Kurgan was absolutely vital to the plans set in motion that morning, for whilst the Soviet Commanders had little respect for the armies of the Western Allies, they understood only too well the power of the Air forces of their opponents.

With some cunning, the supposed Paris flight of Ministers Molotov and Bulganin had been used to mask some of the air attacks. The Soviets had indicated five possible routes that the aircraft flight might take, citing security concerns over rogue fascist elements for not confirming the flight plan. In fact, Zilant-4 had flown the southernmost route totally unimpeded. Some allied radar controllers saw what they had been briefed to see, although the numbers of aircraft exceeded expectations. Others already lay dead, with their detection equipment smashed around them.

At times, attacks were met with no resistance and whole squadrons were destroyed on the ground, crews killed as they slept. Some attacks met opposition, as allied aircrew drove their mounts into the early morning sky, dodging the bombs and bullets that sought them out.

It was of little surprise that some responses were poorly aimed and on at least two occasions, RAF Tempests clawed friendly Mustangs out of the sky, sending both the young American pilots to a fiery death.

Airfields near the North German coast and through Denmark, found themselves under ground assault from Soviet Naval infantry, landed in the night from darkened vessels of all sizes and descriptions.

The allied controlled airbase in Berlin came alive with light, as Soviet artillery and Katyusha rockets brought down a huge barrage, destroying every aircraft on the ground and inflicting massive casualties on the base personnel.

In precious few cases were the attackers met fully and equally and, in the space of seventy-five minutes, the western air forces from the Alps to the Baltic suffered grievous casualties in men and machines. In one stroke, a major part of the Allied armies was crippled for some time to come, all for a modest toll in Soviet aircrew and planes.

In other operations, Soviet sabotage and assassination squads had mixed successes. General Clark's warning had proved timely for all but one senior commander targeted, although for General George Patton, it had been a close run thing, the General luckily just missing the attack on his command centre. For French General De Lattre de Tassigny, in his Baden-Baden headquarters, it had run closer, as his slight wounds from grenade shrapnel showed. Perversely, the attack on General Clark's Salzburg headquarters was extremely effective in dealing death and many US military personnel were killed before the situation was restored.

However, the only real success on the part of the assassination squads was in the British sector, at the Headquarters of Bad Oeynhausen, where Field-Marshal Montgomery was severely wounded by sub-machine gunfire, before the Russian attackers were driven off, killed, or taken prisoner.

Sabotage units successfully destroyed ammunition and fuel dumps across Germany and the Low countries. One special NKVD unit even managed to wreck the PLUTO facility at Ambleteuse in Northern France and another sunk two freighters in Antwerp harbour.

In all cases, casualties among the attacking Soviet units were extreme.

The groups targeting the symposiums carried out their missions with varying degrees of success.

Zilant-1, landing surprisingly accurately, in fields to the north-west of Schloss Ahrensberg, swiftly formed and made their attack, overwhelming a strong detachment of British Military police. Within twenty minutes of the first shot, the Schloss was ablaze and every allied officer and all members of Symposium Hamburg were dead or left wounded, to die amid the flames. Few of the attacking paratroopers had perished and they split into small groups, fanning out through the German countryside, intent on further mischief before they were hunted down or teamed up with the advancing ground forces.

At Schloss Neuhaus, near Paderborn, the result was much the same, although one aircraft was downed by anti-aircraft fire and one group of paratroopers drowned when dropped off target into the Lippesee. A company of US MP's defended stoutly, but the Soviet troopers stormed forward, regardless of losses, killing all before them. No allied officers or symposium members escaped unharmed, although a desperate handful of wounded men managed to escape by swimming the moat.

Some remained inside and were hunted down one by one, with inevitable results, but not before one Major from the 82nd US Airborne Division had burst from his hiding place and gunned down the commander and 2-I-C of the attacking paratroopers. Whilst he paid with his life in seconds, almost cut in half by a burst from a PPS sub-machine gun, the net effect was to paralyse the attackers. Instead of fanning out to cause trouble elsewhere, the unit halted as the new commander, an inexperienced young Captain, struggled to gain control. As a result, the Zilant-2 force found themselves besieged, almost medieval style, by arriving US combat units.

Zilant-3's attack was a bloodbath for both sides. Early heavy casualties came to the Russian paratroopers, as they were engaged, both in the air and on the ground, by wide-awake gunners of the 486th U.S. Anti-Aircraft Artillery Battalion, using the deadly US M-16 half-track quadruple .50 cal Maxon anti-aircraft mount. This weapon could put about two thousand rounds a minute in the direction of the enemy and many casualties were simply obliterated in the blink of an eye.

None the less, the paratroopers fought back. Grenades overwhelmed the defenders and the .50 calibres fell silent.

The Schloss was defended by a full company of experienced infantry from the 70th U.S. Infantry Division and it seemed like every window of the three storey structure bristled with weapons.

Russian casualties were murderous.

Some troopers were armed with scoped rifles and they started to methodically work the windows, killing defenders, clearing complete areas to enable an assault to succeed. Finally, the Soviet paratroopers broke into the building and slowly cleared room-by-room, thankful that they had brought additional grenades with each man.

Again, they were ruthless, leaving no man alive, killing even the wounded, be they in uniform or civilian clothing, even as experienced American reinforcements began to arrive.

The battle in and around Schloss Kransberg began to abate, as the surviving groups of paratroops were methodically eliminated, room by room. By the end of it, only ninety-three Russians were left alive of the seven hundred and forty who had dropped on Kransberg and many of them were badly wounded. Of the American defenders, symposium attendees and their German instructors, only three men was found alive, two of which were devoid of any identification, too wounded to talk and close to death. Six allied divisions and four corps had lost their commanders as a result.

"The essence of war is violence. Moderation in war is imbecility"

-British Sea Lord John Fisher

Chapter 38 – THE CHÂTEAU

0401hrs Monday, 6th August 1945, With the Zilant #4 Group, Airborne over Allied occupied Germany.

Makarenko had chosen to go with Zilant-4 for more than one reason. Firstly, it was the assault that the least preparation had gone into and therefore, most likely to need his leadership. Secondly, it was the furthest distance to travel and therefore, the greatest risk of detection en route. Thirdly, it was the most difficult target by far. Fourthly, there was no information on what force was defending the Château. Finally, he had seen the place with his own eyes in the mid-twenties when, as a young Captain of twenty-five, he had visited France as part of a military mission, after the Great War.

As he looked around him at the other nineteen men, similarly confined within the dark red interior of the Li-2 transport aircraft, Makarenko felt an icy hand grip his insides. He remembered how a light-hearted conversation between junior officers in the Autumn of 1925 had become serious, turning to military matters and, more specifically, how to assault the Château. They had concluded that modern weapons would make it an extremely costly exercise indeed.

The General had selected the 3rd Battalion 298th deliberately, as the battalion commander, Lieutenant Colonel Oleg Potakov, was one of his very best officers. Capable of independent thinking and quick in adapting to tactical situations, the old hand had qualities that would be much in demand in the coming action.

The 3rd's troopers were also the fittest of the combat units, again all due to Potakov's regime. This was essential for the assault, as the gradients involved in reaching the Château were severe and would test the strongest and fittest of men, even without the additional load of weapons and equipment.

Not for the first time that night, Makarenko prayed to a god he did not believe in. Thus far, they had not been fired at by ground forces and no enemy aircraft had engaged them. However, unknown to him, his God had already turned his back on him, for the paratrooper battalion's veteran commander and part of his headquarters group were already dead. Their Li-2 experienced catastrophic engine failure and turned into a fireball, trying to land shortly after take-off.

Looking around at his soldiers, Makarenko smiled and tried to encourage a relaxed attitude, whilst all the time filled with foreboding. Smoking was forbidden on the aircraft, not the least of reasons being the two flame-throwers assigned to members of his group, both sitting snugly between the legs of their nervous owners. However, that did not mean that they could not drink and so a bottle of Moscow Crystal vodka was doing the rounds, calming butterflies and bringing a warm glow to otherwise white faces.

All the men with Makarenko were veterans of Leningrad, the Svir River, through to Vienna. None of them expected to survive this night's action, but still they went.

Opposite him was the sleeping figure of his best sniper who, although still a relative boy of nineteen, had taken the lives of over one hundred Axis soldiers with the Nagant rifle he was cradling. Yefreytor Aleksey Nikitin was renowned for his ability to sleep, even in the middle of an artillery barrage but, even so, Makarenko thought it showed great calm to do so on this night of all nights and he envied him the ability to rest.

Makarenko caught the enquiring gaze of a young Senior Sergeant and smiled back with genuine affection. He knew him well, the competent and lionhearted Nakhimov, for he had decorated him with the Order of the Patriotic War [first class] for his bravery, when the 100th attacked over that damn Reichsbrücke Bridge in Vienna. They might still be trying to get over that river now, if it had not been for Nakhimov killing those SS gunners with nothing more than grenades and a Nagant rifle. The hand to hand fighting had been bestial. Bayonets, knives, sharpened spades; all brought their own bloody wickedness. A shudder ran down Makarenko's spine at

302

the thought of the abject terror of that close-quarter fight. His inner voice spoke to him in respect of men long dead.

'*Govno! How those Germans could fight, even when they knew they were defeated and doomed to die.*'

His mind wandered to the calibre of the men with him, similarly doomed, then strayed to the unknown nature of the men they would face this night.

He checked his watch, intimately familiar with the timings of the whole Zilant operation, mentally checking off another milestone, as his group should now be on the final run to target. Given the difficult nature of the terrain on approach, Zilant-4 was designed to arrive before the others, to allow time to get into position for a simultaneous attack by all four Zilant groups.

The vodka bottle arrived back with him, an expensive purchase, obtained during one of his recent visits to the capital and one he shared with his men quite easily. With a smile, a raised eyebrow and a raised bottle, he put the glass top to his lips and swallowed some of the smooth quality vodka. Re-stoppering the third-full bottle, he passed it to the air force crew chief, shouting over the drone of the engines.

"For you and the pilots, as thanks for the ride, Comrade Serzhant."

"Thank you, Comrade General," and no sooner had the words come from his lips than the bulkhead red light illuminated, drawing every single pair of eyes in the aircraft.

"I wish you luck, sir," said the Sergeant, who stiffly saluted and then issued the orders that set in motion preparations for jumping.

As in all paratrooper arms, checking belts and buckles was all-important and the troopers, now standing, went over the arrangements of the men in front and behind.

Parachutes secure.

Weapons secure.

Kit secure.

Hooked up.

The Air Force Sergeant opened the door and all felt the chill of the high-speed air that rushed in.

With a last check to make sure the magazine of his PPSH was firmly in place, Makarenko moved forward to the door and gripped the vertical rails that he would use to throw himself out into the night.

The previous evening, Rispan, one of his Majors, had jokingly asked for a transfer to the Navy and right now that seemed like an excellent alternative.

With no more thought than to understand the meaning of the forceful pat on his back and the now green light in the corner of his eye, Makarenko launched himself into the night sky over Alsace.

0420hrs Monday, 6th August 1945, Zilant #4 Group, Saint-Hippolyte drop zone, French Alsace.

Ideally, he would have liked to put his forces down on the more level and easier ground to the south of Orschwiller, but the distance was too great. Too much chance of the alarm being raised.

Therefore, the drop zone was located to the north-west of Saint-Hippolyte, in an area that was reasonably free of jutting stones and mature trees, but none the less, angled and dangerous. Makarenko had little doubt that some of his young troopers would die in the jump.

Overall, four hundred and ninety-three Russian paratroopers were targeted against the Château, which number had been reduced by the loss of the battalion commander and two further losses, as aircraft aborted through malfunction.

Four hundred and forty-one jumped from their aircraft over France and all made it to the ground, although twenty-seven would never rise again and another forty-six sustained injuries that took them out of the fight.

The dead and injured were mainly gathered together on roughly the four hundred metre height line, near le Luttenbach, a small stream that ran from the heights towards Hippolyte, just west of a small road that led in the direction of the Château.

Leaving a security force and medical personnel behind, Makarenko set off uphill, gathering stragglers to him as he advanced. It was a testament to the air force crews that nearly all his units had been dropped on the correct location and the benefit of that was immediately apparent to the General, as he was quickly in command of a substantial organised force. With the stragglers came more injured, who were either directed or escorted to the aid station by the stream.

As Makarenko moved onwards and upwards, his senior officers gravitated towards him, eager for an update on the plan. In addition, the specially briefed and equipped point party assembled and took the lead.

The absence of Potakov was discovered and a disappointed Makarenko appointed Major Rispan, the able 2IC, to command until the Lieutenant Colonel showed up.

As such, the plan was very simple. Being paratroopers, they could rely solely on what they carried with them and many of the young troopers were laden with grapnels and lines. Others, from the engineer platoon, had explosive charges and detonators. The ever-present sniper rifles would be useful, as ever, but Makarenko's ace in the hole was the mortar unit that hurried along at the rear of the column, having judiciously found every single round possible before joining the advance. Their four tubes would give the General an edge, provided a suitable place could be found to establish them. Field radios were the final essential tool, in order to ensure that the attack was as coordinated as it could possibly be.

Despite all best efforts, over three hundred and fifty men moving through rough terrain in the dark cannot be a quiet affair. And so it was that the advance group had little notice of the presence of a small vehicle, until its headlights announced its imminent arrival, stark against the darkness of the woods. A swift hand gesture and the paratroopers disappeared in an instant, most struggling to control their lungs, as their systems demanded more oxygen.

The men prepared their weapons, but understood the general briefing that no shots were to be fired until the actual assault on the Château got underway. Yet again, the planning had taken into account the need for stealth and a small number of silenced weapons were available. The point party's commanding officer, crouching alongside Makarenko, had one;

305

a Standard HDM .22 calibre pistol. Across the other side of the track, the experienced eye could make out at least two S40 silencer equipped Nagant rifles and Makarenko knew that the Senior Lieutenant Nazarbayev, commanding that group, also had an HDM.

As the vehicle grew closer, Makarenko became aware that they were almost at a road junction and from memory, he could see the map and recall the track running in from the west as the road they were on hair pinned back on itself. Less than four hundred metres from where he stood lay the gateway to the Château.

The vehicle, a buttoned up jeep, slowly descended from the west until it stopped, roughly two hundred metres from the junction. Inside, two lights could be distinguished, one swift in the act of lighting a cigarette, one constant as a torch was switched on. The jeep looked almost primeval, as its split screen, so illuminated, seemed almost to look malevolently upon the hidden paratroops.

By some sixth sense, Makarenko understood the situation and stepped out into the road, calling to two others, switching on his own torch and waving it from side to side. With him stood a relaxed pair of Russian officers, concealing weapons of silent death.

The internal light went out and the jeep started forward towards the group, the driver dipping the lights so as not to dazzle the 'goddamn Frenchies'.

It ground to a halt alongside Makarenko.

The side of the jeep was thrown open and a stocky American officer stepped out. Had Makarenko had the time to study American uniforms, he would have understood the insignia of the 101st US Airborne Division. All he recognised was the rank of Major.

The man stretched and spoke lazily, reaching into the jeep for his map.

"Thank Christ you French guys are out here. I've been driving round for ages, trying to find that damn Château."

He stopped stretching in an instant, suddenly aware that the uniforms were just not right and that there was hostility in the air.

A glimpse of a concealed weapon emerging made him go for his own automatic, but he was dead before his hand made it halfway, two silenced pistols taking his life in an instant.

The driver was only faintly aware that something was not quite kosher, before a second pair of bullets meant another American boy would not be home for Christmas.

Some troopers quickly slipped out of hiding and carried the bodies into the woods.

Nazarbayev extracted the clip and slid two replacement rounds home as he spoke to the General.

"Comrade General. The American spoke of finding the Château. I think he was going there."

Ever the opportunist, Makarenko immediately saw the possibilities.

"Are you sure, young Vladimir?"

A smile and a vigorous nod was all he needed.

The jeep would be their Trojan horse and unlock the gates to Haut-Kœnigsbourg.

Quickly, he consulted his own map and, with his officers, set in place a modified plan.

The main body moved on, ignoring the road and tackling the ascent on a more direct, but less easy fashion, through the woods.

After some delay, the jeep and its new crew, now in American uniforms, took to the road, crossing the track of Makarenko's force twice on its way upwards.

Slowly it ground towards the final bend, to the west of the Château itself, where the up road meets the down road and where the first French checkpoint was located. The assault force gathered to the south-west of the entrance gate. Parties scurried away, cutting communication wires when they found them. Others formed ready to make their own secondary attacks on different sections of the wall, using line and grapnel. The mortar section set up, ready to bring down a barrage on the Château or the road, either to break the defenders, or stop reinforcements in their tracks, whichever was required. A blocking party was positioned on the approach road for just that purpose, with one of the precious radios.

307

The Trojan horse approached the first checkpoint.

A barbed wire framework was across the road, decorated with the universal 'stop' sign. More barbed wire, this time fixed in place, surrounded the site and prevented access, other than by the road. The guard post was completed by a tiny wooden hut and sentry stand, wherein three commandos undertook the most hated duty on the guard roster. As was their habit, the sentry stand was occupied by a single man, the other two finding what solace they could in the Spartan interior of the hut.

0510hrs Monday, 6th August 1945, Château du Haut-Kœnigsbourg, French Alsace.

On detecting the engine sound, the guard rapped on the hut wall, summoning his two colleagues from their game of chess.

The bored commandos immediately slipped into routine, taking up their weapons and moved outside to position themselves either side of the moveable barricade.

The vehicle slowed, its lights dimmed down as it made the last few metres to where the sentry stood, his hand held out to stop further progress.

The last two seconds of the guards lives held no pain or terrors for them, so complete was the surprise of the attack and so efficient was the killing.

Silenced pistols did their work and other men ran from the shadows, some to instantly carry away the dead, some to stand in their stead.

Soviet paratroopers swarmed all over the southern and western sides of the promontory, quietly moving into their attack positions.

Checkpoint #2 was at the eastern end of the peak, again at a point of contact between the 'up' and 'down' roads, barring the way to the Château approach. The small sandbagged position, complete with the traditional stripey pole barrier laid across the road, enjoyed a modest light from the recently installed external system. It was enough to play skat by and the NCO was enjoying a good run of luck with the cards. In any case, this was his game and he viewed his comrades as easy meat. Unlike most of his comrades, the caporal-chef had seen no action and therefore did not understand the need for discipline and vigilance, nor the price that was paid when it was absent. He ran a slack section and had fallen foul of Capitaine de Frégate Dubois on a number of occasions. Not that he cared, for he intended to leave the army at the first opportunity and return to being a croupier in Nice.

Scraping more money in his direction, as he won yet again, he detected the sound of an approaching vehicle. The caporal-chef reluctantly chivvied his men into action. Here was the jeep they were expecting, at last and, with accustomed casuality, he motioned one man to his side and the other two towards the sandbagged MG position containing the .30cal machine gun. His eyes scanned the Americans approaching, but his mind had already turned to the thought of breakfast in a few hours time.

Perhaps it was the fact that they knew a jeep was coming.

Perhaps it was the witching hour at which it arrived.

Perhaps it was simply that the inept caporal-chef had taken away their sharpness.

Whichever way, no one questioned the fact that checkpoint#1 had not informed them of the approach. Their lack of alertness ensured that Makarenko's hopes were not dashed. The caporal-chef and his man died at close-range, taken by the HDM's and the other two took hits from the silenced Mosin rifles. Paratroopers emerged from the darkness, grabbed the dead men's berets and assumed their positions as the jeep started again on its way.

Makarenko nodded silently, a sign of satisfaction in the way his men were getting this all right and his confidence soared, even though he had spotted that these enemy troops were not military police, but combat soldiers. Whilst one part of his brain noted the battledress and tried to decipher the markings of French commandos, the other side argued that they did not appear to be good quality troops, so he pressed on with the plan as it was.

The General slid into the checkpoint sandbags and watched as his men silently advanced into the shadows.

A swift look at his watch told him it was 0512 hrs. Early, but one should never refuse an opportunity such as the one presented to him.

He observed the jeep slowly round the next corner on its way to the final checkpoint. He sent a platoon up the 'down' road, hugging the escarpment as they slowly moved off into the darkness. Swiftly looking around his new location, he became aware of a wired board with a raised red button, mounted centrally upon it. Obviously, that was for raising the alarm. He then also spotted a field telephone, sat silently on the low bench in front of him. His confidence evaporated as it squawked into life and the artificial sound probably became the death knell of his stealthy attack.

At checkpoint #3, adjacent to the Château's entrance, the Ensign in charge tried to raise the Caporal-chef. Why the imbecile man could not follow simple orders was a mystery to him. Standing instructions were to telephone through with the numbers of vehicle occupants, their names and purpose of their visit. It was simple enough and the man would get his ear bent whenever he picked up. None the less, the traffic list on his clipboard indicated only one expected arrival this morning, that being a US Major of paratroops and the approaching jeep was American. The phone rang on unanswered and he determined to ravage the idiot guards at #2 at his first opportunity. The jeep was almost at his checkpoint now and still the imbecile had not answered.

"Merde," was all he could say, but he promised himself that Capitaine de Frégate Dubois would be informed, the moment he finished with the new American arrival.

Controlling his anger, he put down the phone and turned to the now stopped vehicle.

He became aware of clacking sounds and flashes and that two of his men, positioned either side of the vehicle, were dropping to the ground like rag dolls. His other two men, their weapons jerking up from the relaxed positions of a second beforehand, suddenly blossomed into red flowers and collapsed, jelly-like, to the ground. He knew his death was coming, but still tried to make for the alarm button. Three more scarlet buds appeared and withered in a second, this time in his back as he turned, the silenced rifles doing their work.

He collapsed, glancing off the side of the sandbagged position and falling onto two ammo boxes that served as their table.

The noise of the breaking glass might just as well have been artillery to Makarenko, hiding only eighty metres away.

Many eyes swept left and right, up and down, scanning for threat and movement, but there was none.

No alarm was raised.

No shots rang out.

The attacking force froze until some, chivvied by seniors, rose to repeat the performance of secreting the dead and taking their positions. One of the paratroopers, grabbing at the dead Ensign's body, sliced a finger on the broken water bottle, but manage to stifle his yelp of pain.

The stealthy attack was still viable.

Frequently, Rettlinger simply could not sleep. His dreams simply would not permit rest, as they constantly threw up the faces of those family and friends he had lost and presented stark images of the things he had seen. Maybe it was he, not Treschow, with mental problems, he mused. He often walked around the ramparts of the Château and the commando guards had become comfortable with his nocturnal habits.

None the less, standing orders had required someone to accompany him, but, later on, someone walked with him out of choice, as he was popular companion. In any case, the security no longer looked inward as well as out and the Germans were universally accepted.

Rettlinger also had another advantage for, as a native Alsatian, he could converse with all the guards in their native tongue.

On this night, he and Capitaine de Corvette Fournier were strolling on outer walls of the Château, taking in the air, exchanging words on important gastronomic matters. For comfort, the German had foregone his suit jacket, whereas the dapper Frenchman was in his proper uniform and as impeccable as ever. Padding along behind them was a huge hound from the stock of guard dogs, complete with its handler.

The beast seem to enjoy the company, as well as the exercise, but Rettlinger knew it watched him constantly. He never touched the dogs without asking, for fear of losing something vital. They were fine once the word had been given by their master, in this case, a sunblasted little Algerian who could have been either eighteen or eighty, seconded from the 3e Division D'Infanterie Algérienne, along with three others and their dogs.

This beast was called Marengo, named for the decisive French victory that Napoleon's forces inflicted upon the Austrians in Italy, one and a half centuries before. Von Arnesen, the keen historian and wit, advised his comrades that the leviathan was actually named for Napoleon's horse Marengo, given the similarity in size. He got no arguments on that suggestion, as the solid Alsatian hound was far and away the largest of its breed that any of them had ever seen.

Walking round, the two officers had fallen into one of their traditional arguments about French and Alsatian food and wine. As a proper Frenchman, Fournier was defending the honour of the Bordeaux region, waxing lyrical about the combination of a good Garonne Sauterne and his mother's baked apple and honey pudding. As a gastronome second and soldier first, Rettlinger understood the value of alcohol whatever its place of birth, but hadn't always been such a philistine and he argued for a sweet Muscat that an uncle of his had experimented with, in Alsace, before the war, combined with the honeyed raisin pastries that made his mother money during harder times.

Both men halted their pointless verbal fencing with grins and took their normal station on stools within the small round tower, right above the main entrance.

They both leant back on the woodwork in satisfied silence, minds recalling times sat around family table's years before, mentally sampling the remembered delights of their argument, Fournier looking towards the half-open shutter, in anticipation of the first signs of an approaching dawn.

The inevitable cigarettes appeared.

A tinkle of breaking glass.

Followed by nothing but a low growl from Marengo.

Both men stopped for a few seconds, waiting to hear the unlucky person being berated by an officer or NCO, but nothing came; only silence.

Almost casually, they both opened the wooden shutters a bit further and looked out, gazing down towards the checkpoint. They had heard the jeep grinding up the slope as they talked, so were not surprised to see it in the road. The scene was vivid and obvious.

The two men had seen enough of war to know that the shapes on either side of the vehicle were dead men and that the flitting shadows moving up both sides of the road were not caused by trees lazily shifting in the breeze, but by concealed men, moving urgently and with deadly purpose. Men in uniforms, uniforms that only one of them recognised, were moving around the jeep and checkpoint, the two dead men in the road being swiftly pulled away as other shadows materialised with berets, moving to take their place.

More movement caught the eye and suddenly the whole area seemed alive, which it was.

Fournier reached for his .45 M1911 automatic and slipped off the safety. Taking rough aim, he fired three quick shots into the men at the checkpoint and then started running along the battlements, firing in the air as he went, shouting as he ran, almost overtaken by the diminutive Arab as he was dragged along by the huge dog attached to his left wrist.

Rettlinger dashed towards the sleeping area of his comrades, shouting the alarm at the top of his very considerable voice.

The Russians were coming.

The M1911 was an excellent handgun and had what was called 'stopping power'. The three bullets fired by Capitaine de Corvette Fournier were mainly to initiate the alarm, but he decided not to waste them and sent them flying towards the men at the second checkpoint.

The first bullet hit the Senior Lieutenant with the silenced pistol, taking him in the left side of the neck, ploughing downwards through windpipe, lung and liver, until it exited at thigh level, subsequently removing two toes from the soldier moving past his standing but already dead officer.

The second bullet passed through the roof of the jeep, clipped the steering wheel and buried itself in a sandbag.

The third bullet struck one of the men stooping to recover the dead guards, severing his spinal cord and wrecking his spleen in an instant. He flopped numbly to the roadway, his bleeding finger no longer a concern. He would die within a few minutes.

The alarm spread through the Château like wildfire, made more urgent as the fighting erupted. The duty guard inside rushed to their positions at the open entrance and engaged the attacking force, whilst others, roused from their slumber, dressed and tumbled out into the night, directed by the shouts of their NCO's and officers, not knowing who had come calling, but knowing that the killing had already started.

Capitaine du Frégate Dubois ran the short distance from the company office to assume command of the lower courtyard and was found there by a breathless Fournier.

His arrival coincided with the report from his Petty Officer Major, reporting that the phone lines were down and no one could be raised on the radio.

Therefore, for at least the moment, it seemed that 'Biarritz' was very much on its own.

A small group of commandos took position on the walls above the entrance and started to pour down fire and grenades, causing horrendous casualties to the elements forming for a second assault. However, a quick-witted Kapitan swiftly organised four sniper-rifle equipped troopers and they quickly silenced the French fire with well-aimed and mainly fatal results.

Another platoon of paratroopers was immediately directed to use their grapnels and gain the wall position under the covering fire of the sniper unit. The grapnels rose and all but two held first time. One landed harmlessly back on the ground and was recovered for another, again unsuccessful, throw. The other fell back and struck an unsuspecting young trooper on the head heavily, splitting his skull and dropping him senseless to the grass. His comrades ascended the taut lines, each second expecting the stinging impact of bullets.

At the north wall of the Château, two more platoons were already in the process of scaling the wall of the Little Bastion, having taken down three guards with silenced rifle fire before they could respond.

In the allied officer's sleeping quarters in the main building, pandemonium ensued as the alarm was shouted and then reinforced by the unmistakeable sounds of gunfire nearby.

Each allied officer had his pistol in his hand as they emerged on various floors, grouping up and deciding what to do.

Prentiss was senior rank in his group and he decided they should stay together and head towards the sound of the guns.

At the main entrance, the latest Russian assault had been more fruitful. Forty men had gathered on the pathway near the gate and rained grenades on the defenders, killing or incapacitating every man not in good cover.

A sudden surge brought success and the wooden gateway fell, its guards slain with no chance to close the wooden door. It was a matter of design that the defences should offer no protection to attackers, so the turret and wall positions were all open to fire from inside the Château. Paratroopers

315

surged inside, taking cover where they could, but all the time suffering casualties from the numerous firing points that could bear in the killing ground between the archways.

The next gate was closed and barred, obstructing the way into the Basse Cour. The Captain in charge ordered two men forward with satchel charges to resolve the blockage. Above the door were holes designed in a different age, defensive measures that had permitted defenders to pour pitch and oils upon any assault force. The old provision proved equally effective when used in conjunction with grenades and one per man arrived, shredding the two paratroopers before they could successfully deploy their explosives.

Reacting swiftly, the Russian officer sent forward one of his flamethrowers and in seconds, fire blasted through the same slits to fatally envelop the grenadiers, their screams rising above all the noise of battle.

The Captain ordered more explosives forward, but exposed himself in the doing, falling bloodily to the stone, his jaw shot away by a French rifle bullet.

The explosives set, Russian paratroopers scrabbled for cover as the fuses burned down and ignited the charges, turning the door into dangerous matchwood. Two French commandos and one paratrooper were struck down by large splinters, all three fatally.

Dubois had organised the defence of the lower courtyard, positioning the unit's .50cal heavy machine gun by a stone trough, ready to cover down the approach to the gateway and flay any attackers who got past the portcullis that he had ordered dropped.

Russian paratroopers charged into the smoke of the explosion and ran headlong into the medieval obstruction that barred their way.

Gathering in the areas between the two gates, more casualties were inflicted by the still active defenders of the living quarters, who shot down into the throng.

Makarenko pulled his men back into some sort of reasonable cover and ordered the portcullis destroyed. Three men dashed forward, one with explosives, the other two with rifle grenades. Meanwhile, support fire lashed the openings of the Basse Court Tower.

Both rifle grenades were fired through the portcullis and into the Basse Court itself, the first striking the door frame of the Alsatian House, killing three French officers who had posted themselves there. The other struck the rock path and sent deadly splinters into two commandos positioned on the corner of a low stone building.

The explosives set, the three paratroopers retreated at speed, finding safety at the precise moment that the portcullis disintegrated. A number of grenades bounced through the dust and smoke, causing casualties amongst the men who had been swiftest off the mark. Reloaded, the two rifle grenade men sent their deadly missiles through the gateway, again finding targets in the Alsatian House and beyond.

Makarenko ordered a charge and his men surged forward. The front runners dropped immediately, struck down as more grenades burst to their front. However, more men drove forward and through the gate, seeking refuge in the shattered doorway of the Alsatian House.

Two French commandos leant out of the gatehouse windows from the portcullis room, intent on shooting into the rear of the assault force, but were smashed back into the building by an accurate PPS burst from a watchful paratrooper.

The .50cal started up, its heavy calibre shells knocking lumps off the Alsatian House and anything softer that was unfortunate enough to get in the way.

The small assault force charged deeper into the officer's accommodation to evade the .50's deadly stings, finding dead and dying men in various states of dress. Some officers offered up resistance but were swiftly killed, the final deaths caused by a grenade thrown into a side room.

Makarenko sought refuge inside the tower's shadow, his mind working the military problem. His ability to control his unit had been reduced when the radio operator had been smashed by a burst of fire from the Château above, wrecking the precious equipment at the same time.

317

He had many men gathered behind him, most still outside the Château, but numbers did not matter when the approach was as narrow as the one that now challenged his professionalism and courage. Just over a metre wide, the gap between the stone building and the Alsatian House restricted his options and provided the defenders with a deadly choke point.

A further surge of men had gained the house to support the first party, at the cost of half their number.

Dropping to one knee, Makarenko wrestled with the problem, noticing, with horror, that the stone pathway was running red with the blood of brave men from both sides. Gravity was bringing gentle streams down the slope, seeking out the gaps between the stone and passing out into the charnel yard behind him, adding to the scarlet effusions from the many Soviet dead already lying there.

Momentarily distracted, he missed the initial sounds of more firing, but quickly focussed on the new sounds and he realised his north wall party must have come at the defenders from behind.

On his feet in an instant, he ordered his men forward and charged off up the path with gritted teeth.

Shouting "No grenades!" as he ran, he immediately shot down a wounded commando who was bringing his rifle up to fire.

A bullet tugged at his map case and severed the strap, carrying on to plant itself in the upper arm of one of his self-appointed bodyguards.

Looking up, he saw a figure on the battlements between the two towers and brought up his weapon, even though in the same moment his brain told him to hold his fire.

He recognised the Soviet uniform first and the bark of an SVT rifle second, as the two platoons who had scaled the north wall caught the defenders looking the wrong way.

The heavy machine gun team were already dead, as were most of the defenders of the Lower Courtyard. The dog pens were smashed and broken, two of their occupants red and bleeding inside the splintered cages.

Makarenko's troops had invested the Alsatian House and were lining up on the stone path, ready for the next attack. The north wall platoons assaulted the forge building, losing a handful of men on the run across the yard, before demonstrating their superior close-fighting skills, killing the defending commandos without loss.

The Senior Lieutenant leading the attack decided to launch a further assault, in the hope of carrying the stone staircase leading up to the Inner Courtyard.

He charged into the area at the bottom of the stairs and dove immediately to his left, as fire ripped down into his force. A wounded commando Petty Officer lay in what was obviously a administrative section, clutching an empty handgun, shot through both thighs and blinded by rock splinters in the eyes.

Two shots from a Nagant ended the Frenchman's life.

Behind the Paratooper officer, one of his junior NCO's had got a DP light machine gun positioned and was sending accurate bursts up the stairway, scoring the occasional hit, but mainly denying the defenders the ability to fire down.

A grenade skipped down from above, its metallic bounce heard by all who were immediately threatened. It flopped in behind the corpse of a body in civilian clothes before it exploded, distributing portions of the unfortunate 'Deux' agent all over the stairwell.

A shout attracted the attention of the Soviet officer and he understood his Sergeant's intent immediately.

Nodding to authorise the attempt and using his head to indicate the working DP, the Senior Lieutenant gathered himself for the lunge.

The Sergeant shouted instructions to the DP gunner and the man flayed the stairwell with every bullet left in his magazine, raising a haze of stone dust, as angry wasps ricocheted in all directions, two finding targets amongst the defenders clustered in cover all up the stairs and in the rooms leading off the north side.

Before the defenders reset themselves, the Sergeant brought up one of the panzerfaust's he had found in the forge and fired the projectile, rolling immediately into cover.

The Panzerfaust 100 was the most numerous of the panzerfaust family, carrying a twenty-eight ounce explosive load. They were extremely effective against vehicles and hard targets and, as the Germans found out on the Russian Front, equally effective against soft targets like the human body. Striking the corner of the right hand projection of wall, a few metres from the small drawbridge at the Lion Gate, the warhead exploded, sending deadly fragments of stone into three commandos gathered in the adjacent doorway.

The officer threw himself forward, closely followed by a group of his men, taking the stone stairs two at a time as they charged upwards, desperate to profit from the momentary shock and confusion.

The defenders opened up once more and paratroopers fell in the confined space of the stairs. Some made it to the first stage and ducked into cover within the rooms at the base of the keep, finding dead and wounded commandos littering the floors.

The Senior Lieutenant was tossed back down the stairs as a burst from a submachine gun struck him in chest and abdomen, the journey down ending his pain, as the fall broke his neck on first contact.

Capitaine de Frégate Dubois, changing the magazine on his Thompson SMG, ordered the drawbridge raised and two of his men surged forward to obey.

Beckoning Fournier to his side, he swiftly passed on responsibility for holding the approach, before doubling away up the next flight of stairs, where he encountered Prentiss and Ramsey organising orderlies and 'Deux' agents to defend the inner courtyard.

De Walle and Knocke strode briskly from the Hexagonal stairs, the former holding a plan of the castle and beckoning to Dubois.

Joined by Ramsey and Prentiss, the group of four took a rapid brief from Dubois, swiftly sketching his understanding of the tactical situation on the map that De Walle held out flat for all to see.

As he ended, both Knocke and Ramsey went to point at a spot on the map. The German deferred to the Englishman and Ramsey spoke loudly, rising above the growing sounds of battle.

"Here is a weakness for us. We need men here in numbers, or we are in trouble."

His finger described the northern enclosed area, the access to which was controlled by a single portal close by the forge. Once through that obstacle, the Russians would be able to make it to the Greater Bastion

"They may be through already."

Anne-Marie Valois arrived with three other 'Deux', each carrying three weapons and ammunition, taken from the secure lockers in De Walle's office. In one easy movement and without waiting for orders, she hoisted a Sten gun off her shoulder into Knocke's hands.

The other weapon, also a Sten, went to De Walle.

Valois set out her stall by retaining her own weapon.

As the remaining weapons and ammunition were distributed, Dubois summoned his senior NCO, issued brief orders and the man sped quickly away. He returned within a minute, a Bren gun team amongst the five men he had called to him.

Nodding at the swift response to his instructions, Dubois turned back to the assembled group, who were checking their weapons.

"The Petty Officer Major and his men, half of your party," he indicated Ramsey, who nodded his understanding, "And the Deuxieme, all will go to the Greater Battery and secure the northern door, here," Dubois tapped the map, indicating the base of the northernmost turret.

Turning to Knocke, he drew the German's attention to a blind return in the wall on the north side of the inner garden.

A flare rose from one of the high points, a commando tasked with sending the whole supply skywards at regular intervals. Turning back from the distraction, Dubois continued.

"Here they cannot be observed from the bastion. They might try to climb, so we need a small group there. Colonel Knocke?"

"I will take three of mine, but I will need more weapons."

321

Valois spoke decisively as she offered up her sten.

"Take this, I will bring up others and more ammunition."

An explosion from the Lion Gate approaches drew their attention, ending the meeting by mutual consent, the various groups speeding to their assigned posts.

Whilst the allied group had been sorting their hasty defence plans, Makarenko had organised an assault against the gate to the northern area and then launched his men against it.

The Commando defenders hacked down many paratroopers in the narrow confines, but were not immune to casualties themselves. The defensive fire slackened and then ceased, as they were overwhelmed.

He called Major Ilya Vidalevich Rispan to him, indicating first the northern gateway and second, the stairs to the Lion Gate.

"Ilya, I'm going to take a group through here, straight to the bastion. Keep up the attack there and get your men into the main building, regardless."

The wounded officer spat blood and a tooth fragment and summoned a reply, blood dribbling from the hole in his cheek.

"Yes, Comrade General."

"Are you well enough, Mayor?"

"I had worse in Vienna," Rispan countered, with an absence of humour.

Makarenko nodded, recalling the sight of Rispan's unusually nasty wood splinter wound, sustained when he slid down a damaged banister, in drunken celebration of the Viennese victory. Whilst the grenade fragment had knocked a few of his teeth out, the senior man thought it probably looked more nasty than it was.

"Press hard, don't stop, Ilya."

Slapping the man's shoulder, Makarenko moved off, gathering men to him as he angled towards the damaged gateway that led to the lists and the route to the Greater Bastion.

Rispan returned to the stairs and ordered his men forward.

At the Lion Gate, the explosion that had terminated Dubois' briefing had wrought great harm on the defenders.

Capitaine de Corvette Fournier lay surrounded by dead and dying commandos, victims of a satchel charge that had been tossed into their midst and exploded on the steps in the area to the west of the gateway.

His ears spilled blood from ruptured eardrums and more of the precious fluid seeped from the deep wound in his side.

Of more immediate concern was his left leg, attached to the rest of him by only a few strands of flesh and sinew, virtually severed below the knee.

Some freak of explosive force had caused the heavy door to jam shut into its frame, masking the shattered defenders from their bloodied attackers, providing some temporary respite from the butchery.

Rispan ordered another satchel charge placed to open the door, risking the wooden bridge. A young Lieutenant was detailed to find a suitable item to replace it, should the blast destroy the wooden structure and he returned before the charge had been prepared, smugly manoeuvring a solid table with the help of two of his men.

The charge was carried forward and laid at the base of the door, the frightened paratrooper Lance-Corporal pausing only to arm it before scurrying back to safety.

Every man in the Well room was killed, save the wounded Fournier, the blast tossing men aside like chaff in the wind.

Clutching his pistol, the French officer sensed more than saw the shape in the door and fired two shots, killing the Lance-Corporal, sending him flying back into the men behind him.

323

Two more paratroopers threw themselves forward, diving through the doorway into the cover of the stairs, only to discover, too late, that their executioner was lying amongst the bodies there, not at the top of the stairs as they had supposed.

Out of ammunition, Fournier dropped the pistol, wiped the blood from his eyes and snatched up a Sten gun that appeared in focus.

No man came into view, only a small round object, bouncing around, before settling against the body of one of the French commandos.

Its explosion decorated the inside of the chamber with more vivid colour and human detritus but, again, Fournier was not further harmed.

He dragged himself painfully up the steps a small distance and set his battered body into the window recess, taking advantage of the extra cover provided by a stone trough.

He took two spare magazines from the pouches of an unrecognisable comrade and set himself for the next assault.

The Sten rattled, messily downing the first man through the door. The second man hung back and risked a look around the shattered doorframe and was rewarded by a burst that blew the front of his temple off, sending him screaming into the shallow void behind him.

Rispan shouted at his men, but none chose to hear his orders. The attack was stalling badly.

Putting a new magazine on his PPS submachine gun, he braced himself for the run, mentally reciting some words of his faith, signalling his men to follow.

He rose and started up the stone stairs, but was overtaken by the young Leytenant who had obtained the sturdy table.

The two officers crossed the void, its occupant now permanently silent.

Fournier killed the younger man with a burst of fire, stopping the charging officer and dropping him to the floor on the spot.

The last three bullets in his magazine struck Rispan, two destroying his water bottle and the third passing through the flesh on the side of his stomach.

Gate. The Jewish Major's PPS ended the battle at the Lion

0535hrs Monday, 6th August 1945, Temporary Military Laager, Selestat, French Alsace.

In Selestat, what had started as curiosity had swiftly turned into genuine alarm and finally progressed into decisive action.

In and around the small Alsatian town were two companies of the 2e [Deuxieme] Regiment, Légion Étrangère Infanterie, on their way south to reunite with the 1e [Premiere] French Division, after performing ceremonial duties in Strasbourg.

Also, not by coincidence but by design, Colonel Christophe Lavalle was there, having arranged to meet with some old comrades as they passed by.

As senior officer present, he assumed command and ordered both companies to deploy towards the sound of fighting. The two companies were both mechanised with American halftracks and so made good progress, one having been tasked to advance through Kintzheim, the other through Orschwiller and St Hippolyte.

Lavalle rode with 3e [Troisieme] Compagnie's senior officer on the Kintzheim approach. He was anxious to discover what exactly was going on, the growing feeling that something extremely bad was happening being reinforced by the steady stream of flares being sent skyward from the Château.

Radio messages flowed to the Brigade headquarters and upwards, both informing, as best they could, and seeking information from higher command.

Over the sound of the half-track's 6.3 litre petrol engine came the sound of closer firing, followed shortly by a radio report from 2e Compagnie.

Lavalle listened in as the two radio operators exchanged information, the 3e Compagnie's Swiss commander, Commandant Albrecht Haefeli, waiting for his opportunity to speak.

325

It came as the other operator broke off in mid-sentence, his excited voice suddenly replaced by static.

Haefeli posed the question.

"Light machine gun fire at worst. But who is it?"

"Surely it has to be the Germans, Albi?" although, as he said the words, Lavalle gave them no credence whatsoever.

Haefeli slapped his operator on the shoulder.

"Get Isabella back. We need to know who the enemy is this day."

Using Haefeli's call sign, the operator sought out his counterpart in 2e Compagnie.

"Isabella-Zero-One, this is Achille-Zero-One, come in."

The static remained, almost challenging them.

A gentle tap from Haefeli encouraged the man on.

"Shall I stop the column, Sir?"

Lavalle shook his head.

"No," the decision immediately made, "We will push on to the Château, but we will be prepared to send forces down the road to St Hippolyte if needs be, Albi."

Haefeli nodded, sorting in his mind which of his units he would send into the rear of whatever was blocking 2e Compagnie's advance, once he knew what was happening. Retrieving a map of the area, he quickly consulted it, before drawing Lavalle's attention to a T-junction on their route of advance.

"Here, we should be able to drop down behind them, if 2e are on the right road."

Lavalle's response was drowned by the excited voice on the radio.

"Achille-Zero-One, Isabella-Three-One calling, Isabella-Zero is off air and burning. Request orders."

Both Haefeli and Lavalle ignored the probability that a comrade from the old days had just died.

"Three-one?" sought Lavalle, questioningly.

"Green officer. The name is Mardin, I'm sure."

Again the radio crackled into life.

"Isabella-Three-One, under heavy fire, request orders."

Taking the handset from his operator, Haefeli spoke calmly and deliberately, flouting radio procedure to get results. "Achille-Zero-One calling. This is Haefeli speaking. I need a situation report. How many, what weapons, where. Rely on your training, Mardin, over."

The silence of the radio belied the battles within a scared young man at the other end of the network, struggling to bring himself under control.

"Isabella-Three-One, sorry. Enemy infantry in platoon strength, sat astride primary advance route, three hundred metres north of St Hippolyte, oriented south. Light weapons only so far. We have lost three vehicles and crews. Mortars deploying for assault. Request orders."

The two experienced officers exchanged glances. The clearly shaken young officer had retained sufficient presence of mind to organise his mortars and was already thinking of attacking. If he survived the battle, he would have learned valuable lessons unavailable in the classroom.

"That puts them roughly here, I think, on this kink in the road."

Lavalle nodded his agreement and followed his friend's finger as it traced the roads to their own route of advance.

Haefeli voiced their shared thoughts.

"He's on his own for now, I think. Holding action would make sense, but we don't know what we are heading into. We may need his men."

Again, Lavalle's decision was immediate.

"Tell him to attack and force the road." The consummate legionnaire and leader paused a moment, weighing the situation. "Tell him we cannot assist him and he is in command there until relieved. He is responsible for the mission and his mission is to destroy the enemy force in front of him, reinforce our advance and to secure his own route, with minimal losses and at all speed."

3e Compagnie's commander grinned and quoted from a lecture the two had attended years ago.

327

"There is nothing like dropping extra problems and responsibility into a man's lap to help him deal with the pressures and indecisions of command."

Lavalle saluted Haefeli's memory with an inclined head.

The radio operator relayed the message, the calm acknowledgement from Mardin suggesting that the young officer had regained control of himself, giving weight to the sage words of a long-dead Legion training officer.

Haefeli switched to his own troops, the second operator issuing his Commander's orders for the advance, increasing the pace on the main road, but putting troops on the myriad of small tracks that were a feature of the route to the Haut-Kœnigsbourg.

The jeep at the point disappeared around the tight left hand bend ahead, reporting the road clear and also sounds of heavy fighting coming from the Château above.

The sounds of small arms fire and the low crump of exploding mortar shells, all growing in intensity from the 2e Compagnie area, informed Lavalle that Lieutenant Mardin had got his attack underway.

A brief radio message from the point vehicle confirmed no problems ahead, so the command track pressed on in response, following the hairpin bend all the way round as the road rose unerringly towards the Château.

Haefeli listened to a situation report from the now totally calm Mardin, content that the younger man was rising to the challenge.

Ahead of his halftrack, other vehicles of the company were fanning out into a small clearing, as directed by the hand signals of the NCO in the point jeep. Lavalle spotted a dismounted Sous-Lieutenant signalling at a tree beside the road and his eyes followed the man's frantic gestures.

In the early dawn light, he didn't quite believe what he saw, even when a yellow flare rose from the Château and illustrated the gruesome tableau.

He shouted an order to the driver to push forward, keen to get a closer look.

Haefeli, checking off Mardin's report against a map, looked up, startled by the urgency in the Colonel's voice.

He followed Lavalle's gaze and was similarly incredulous at the sight that was looming large, as the command track gained on the point jeep and its shattering discovery.

The radio again barked into life, Mardin's operator calling in information.

"Achille-Zero-One, Isabella-Three-One calling. Enemy identified."

Haefeli looked at the two bodies, battered and broken, hanging from a tree to the left of the road.

Exchanging looks with Lavalle, he heard Mardin's voice deliver confirmation to the evidence of his own eyes.

"Achille-Zero-One, Isabella-Three-One calling. Enemy are Russian paratroopers, confirm, Russian paratroopers, over."

The uniform was unfamiliar to both officers, although the two entwined parachutes that had been the cause of the young men's deaths, were obvious even to the uninitiated. None the less, each man possessed a PPSH sub-machine gun, a weapon synonymous with the Red Army.

Haefeli's operator automatically acknowledged the information and the radio fell silent.

Despite the years of experience, both officers were stunned, minds processing the ramifications of the message and the proof dangling before their eyes.

"Albi, send it in clear and keep sending it. Get the warning out. Russian paratroopers attacking Haut-Kœnigsbourg area. Unknown strength."

The operator heard and was sending the grim news before Lavalle's next set of orders formed on his lips.

"Well, whatever they are doing here, it is obviously important to them. Albi, get your men moving fast. Advance to contact with a priority to get to the Château as quickly as possible. We will need Mardin too, once he has sorted his own problems out."

329

Haefeli passed orders to the second operator, who sent them on to 2e Compagnie's newest commander, as 3e Compagnie picked up the pace and closed on their new enemy.

0555hrs Monday, 6th August 1945, Château du Haut-Kœnigsbourg, French Alsace.

In the Château, Makarenko was having problems with his attack. The thrust up the stairs into the lower courtyard was decimating his troops without great result, the defenders holding firm at the final threshold.

His own plan to push up through the north route to the Great Bastion had met with early success, until the lead section had been flayed in the choke point between the wall and the square projection of the living quarters.

Those eight men, plus another six, lay dead and dying in that small area, but his troopers had forced the path, killing the handful of French commandos who had barred the way.

The new point section was decimated as they neared the doorway in the bottom of the round tower, in the north section of the Greater Bastion.

His leading men had taken cover in returns in both the Upper Garden wall and the North outer wall, pinned down by accurate rifle and light machine gun fire.

He risked a glance around the corner of the stonework.

The increasing light of dawn would make the job all the harder on his men and he was also aware that time was not on his side, the sound of firing from outside the Château all too obvious.

The group concealed behind the Northern wall return were looking around them, seeking alternatives and options.

Makarenko watched as an old Sergeant gestured to two of his men, both of whom carried grapnels.

On his orders, they launched themselves from cover at speed, hoping to gain the wall on the other side of the killing zone before the defenders could bring them down, aided by covering fire from the NCO's PPSH.

Both men made it in safety and offered the suggestion made by their now dead Sergeant, shot down as he drew the enemy fire from his two young lads.

Makarenko regained cover and promised himself that the man's sacrifice would not go unrewarded. He also understood the dead man's plan perfectly and briefed a nearby Kapitan on what to expect, before slipping back to find out how Rispan was doing.

The defenders of the Greater Bastion had stopped the enemy attack by the North wall, inflicting great loss for no casualties of their own.

Having dropped the enemy sub-machine gunner, the Bren gun crew relaxed and reloaded their weapon, their position at the top of the tower guaranteeing them early warning of any further Soviet efforts.

A single rifle shot rang out and the view was temporarily obscured by the body of a commando plucked from the roof. The falling man screamed briefly on the way down, until he struck the rock at the base of the tower, the flare pistol springing from his grip as he bounced.

Yefreytor Nikitin, Hero of the Reichsbrücke, chambered another round and waited for the machine gunners to stick their heads up once more.

Rispan was in agony, a grenade fragment having carried away part of his left testicle in the last but one attempt to force the lower courtyard approach.

Makarenko found him below the Lion Gate, trousers down, a medic plugging the wound and trying to construct a bandage that would do the job of staunching the flow of blood.

"Ilya, can you go on?"

"The bastards just continued the Rabbi's work, Comrade General. I can still fight, but I won't be running anywhere for a while. I've sent men back to look for the flamethrowers."

Makarenko nodded as the wounded Major grimaced with pain, the bandage tightening around the wound.

"There are no more panzerfausts and we are out of grenades. I have men stripping the dead for more. I will not waste more of my men attacking until I have the tools I need, Comrade General."

With the Soviet Paratrooper General such talk was safe enough, especially as Makarenko knew his man well. None the less, the job had to be done.

"I will lead your men, Ilya. We have no time to wait and we risk being trapped here if the enemy gets organised. Outside, someone is already raising hell with our pickets."

His hand shot out to silence Rispan's protest.

"You said yourself, you cannot run, Comrade Mayor."

Men trickled up the stairs, distributing recovered grenades to eager hands, their own hands often contaminated with the blood and detritus of the former owners.

A familiar figure toiled up the stairs, weighed down with a flamethrower pack.

"Comrade General, this is the only one we have. We found another but it is unusable."

"It will have to do then, Starshy Serzhant. You too are wounded, Nakhimov?"

Egon Nakhimov held up his hand, displaying the gap where his little finger had once projected.

"Have no fear, I salute with my right-hand, Comrade General."

Such was the comradeship of the 100th Guards that the response elicited a laugh and a fatherly pat from Makarenko.

"Get them ready, Ilya."

Pulling up his trousers, the Major saluted formally and turned to the tired men around him.

At the barricade in the lower courtyard, the confidence of the defenders was high. Each assault had been bloodily repulsed at little cost, the narrowness of the approach restricting the options for their enemy, as well as negating their superiority in numbers.

Amon Treschow, late of the Luftwaffe, was apparently enjoying his first proper taste of ground action, despite its intensity. By his side, the sizeable figure of Rettlinger did not relish the return to close-quarter fighting, as he possessed intimate knowledge of its primitive nature.

Wolfgang Schmidt sat against the door frame of the converted cellar, a female French agent binding his wounded left forearm.

A commando Corporal tapped out his cigarettes and shared them with German and Frenchman alike. Bruno flicked his Calibri lighter and lit the young NCO's Gauloise.

A grenade arrived from the stairwell, bouncing back off the barricade and exploding.

Another caught the door frame, rolled along the threshold like a deadly ball, hit the other side of the woodwork and dropped back down the stairs, where the sound of the explosion mingled with cries of pain.

Grenades continued to arrive at regular intervals, only one lodging against the barricade. Fragments of red-hot metal penetrated gaps in the structure and one dropped the Corporal to the floor, the Gauloise still clamped between lifeless lips.

Two more followed, but with no result. Then there was the briefest of pauses.

Three grenades bounced against the wall and two of them settled perfectly against their barricade. Men scattered in expectation, none noticing their benign state, pins in place.

As planned, the assault party swiftly charged forward, flamethrower to the fore.

When the grenades arrived, Amon Treschow had reacted quickest, but travelled the least distance and so was closest to the barricade. On hearing the approaching enemy he stood, ready to cut down the attackers one more time.

The flamethrower stream took him in the upper chest, dropping him to the stone floor, his head and shoulders a mass of flames.

As he drew breath to scream, flames and hot gases seared and destroyed his throat and lungs, reducing his audible agony to little more than a high-pitched squeal.

Others were now screaming as fire sought them out, the barricade ablaze, both Treschow and the dead caporal being consumed by flames.

Rettlinger had thrown himself into the base of the Hexagonal staircase and found it perfect cover. He fired one shot that dropped the flamethrower operator to his knees.

The second shot he used on his friend, sending the mad Luftwaffe Hauptmann to a pain free afterlife.

Schmidt and the female agent were both wreathed in fire and were similarly mercifully dispatched by a commando's Thompson.

In all, half a dozen lay in flames around the lower courtyard. More Soviet grenades arrived and broke any hope of resistance there.

Prentiss, struggling to drag a wounded French officer to the staircase, was propelled through the air by two simultaneous explosions, striking his head on the roof supports of the stone cistern next to the kitchens. His insensible form lay draped over the cistern headfirst, his thighs and buttocks bloody from minor shrapnel wounds.

Soviet paratroopers rushed forward and into the converted cellar. The leaders were shot down quickly, but the rest swept into close quarter fighting with the handful of defenders.

A few of the allied survivors made for the stairs, knowing the courtyard was lost.

De Walle was the last to make it out of the kitchens before more Russians entered the courtyard. He and Rettlinger rushed upstairs as grenades arrived on their position.

In the cellar, the French tried to surrender and some succeeded without being struck to the ground. Jakob Matthaus, once Maior in the elite 'Großdeutschland' Division, had served many years on the Eastern Front and could not contemplate such a thing. His Wehrmacht uniform drew unwanted attention and most of the enemy in the room focussed on him. He swung his rifle at one paratrooper and missed, recovering his poise in time to parry a bayonet thrust. A rifle butt smashed into his throat and he dropped to the ground, where a frenzy of bayonets, butts and boots ended his life quickly.

The four surviving commandos were herded into a recess and summarily executed.

Fig#8

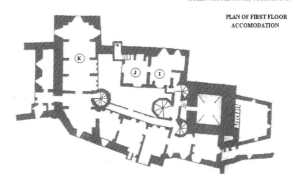

THE CHATEAU DU HAUT-KŒNIGSBOURG
FRENCH-ALSACE, 6TH AUGUST 1945.

PLAN OF FIRST FLOOR
ACCOMODATION

I - MENZEL'S RIFLE ROOM   J - VON HARDEGEN'S GRENADE ROOM
K - DUBOIS AND REITLINGER'S LAST STAND

The momentum was maintained and paratroopers moved quickly through the kitchens, killing some orderlies and more commandos.

Menzel, firing from a window in the Marshal's chamber, dropped two men in the courtyard, one shot through the head, the other through the chest. Behind him, Von Hardegen and a Commando opened a new box of grenades.

"Come on, Artillerie, make way for the Panzers", shouted Von Hardegen.

"Get your own window, Kuno," Menzel fired another shot and pointed into the next chamber.

Von Hardegen and the commando carried the box into the adjacent room.

335

An explosion cut down the Frenchman from behind, as a grenade blasted fragments into his back. The man dropped screaming to the floor.

The box of grenades went flying and cannoned into Von Hardegen's thigh, also dropping him to the floor.

Menzel lay unconscious across the threshold of the room, bleeding from a score of wounds, his breathing shallow and laboured.

The Panzer officer struggled to his feet and manhandled the box across to the window.

He pulled the pins and quickly dropped three grenades out of the window into the courtyard below. Explosions and screams followed, as the highly effective Mills bombs took a heavy toll on Soviet troopers gathering for an assault on the Hexagonal stairway.

The criss-cross diamond glass sections in the window disappeared as a savage burst of fire reached out in search of the grenade thrower. A grenade bounced off the ruined lead work and fell back to ground, adding to the slaughter below.

Von Hardegen moved into the first chamber, cradling six grenades.

Dropping the first two out of the window, he passed the remaining to Rettlinger at the top of the stairs.

On the return trip, he dragged the bleeding form of Menzel to the foot of the stone stairs that lead to the next level.

More Mills bombs followed, each claiming more lives in the courtyard, until each explosion brought only a display of blood and gore from those already dead, the living having sought safety from the terrible barrage.

The Soviet attack had stalled once more.

In the Greater Bastion, the Russians had not come again, although a sniper was causing casualties amongst the defenders.

Crisp, the ammunition for his pistol expended, had ascended into the large round bastion to search for more, only to find Ramsey struggling with a wounded man.

"For Christ's sake, hold the fellow down will you, Marion!"

A rifleman outside the Chateau had managed to shoot the 'Deux' agent in the face and the man was writhing in agony.

The American held the agent tightly as Ramsey attempted to reassemble the man's ruined face, removing loose teeth, pressing eyes and nose into rough shape before applying a rough bandage.

A French orderly arrived with two ampoules of morphine and dropped them on the floor next to Crisp before beating a hasty retreat, anxious to be away from the hideous sight.

Ramsey broke an ampoule and plunged it into the man's thigh. He picked up the second ampoule and hesitated, silently seeking out Crisp's opinion with his eyes.

A simple nod sufficed and the second ampoule deposited its relief into the Frenchman's system.

Ramsey lowered the shattered head onto a jacket that Crisp had quickly placed there.

Picking up the man's discarded Beretta35 pistol, Crisp checked the magazine and rechambered the weapon.

Catching the Englishman's look of disgust, he could only shrug.

"It will have to do until something else becomes available."

"Quite," commented Ramsey, with all the reserve of an archetypal Englishman.

Producing his Webley Mk 6 service revolver, Ramsey replaced the four spent cartridges. The Beretta carried eight rounds in a magazine, whereas the Webley cylinder held only six, but the .455 calibre rounds put people down a lot better than the lighter and less brutal .32 rounds of the Italian origin handgun.

Shaking off the strap from his shoulder, a Thompson was held out to the Paratrooper.

"No spare ammo I'm afraid, Marion, but that one's full. There's bound to be some more somewhere here."

337

Slipping the Beretta into his empty holster, Crisp grasped the sub-machine gun, checking the safety was on. He dropped the magazine out and tested it for weight.

"Thanks, John. What are you going to use?"

"Incisive wit and repartee, I should suppose."

The American laughed that laugh they save for the English, partially at the obvious humour, but partially at the inherent madness of those from the Old Country.

"Yeah right."

A heavy machine gun outside the walls broke the momentary awkwardness between them.

"That's a .50 cal. Relief is closing up, it seems."

As if in illustration of the likely fragility of their survival, heavy firing erupted from the north wall and lists, as well as renewed sounds of combat from within the living quarters.

"It appears our Russian friends agree with you, Major Crisp. They intend to finish the job right now."

Shouts came from all points of the Bastion, indicating enemy movements and threats.

"I suggest we hold the stairs. You take the North tower, I will take the main entrance. Best of luck, Marion, and keep your head down."

"Likewise, John, likewise."

Knocke and Von Arnesen and for that matter, even Anne-Marie Valois, had seen men die in strange and unfortunate ways, but what happened in front of their eyes was a new horror.

Positioned on the wall of the Upper Garden, directly above the return in which Soviet paratroopers huddled, they were covering any attempt to force a passage into the garden, either through the gateway in the north wall, or over the top, as had been suggested by the English Major.

Most of the battlement walkways were covered with a tiled roof, but a part of this section had seen one of only three hits sustained by the Château during a French artillery attack in early 1945. One shell had landed in the menagerie, killing an

338

old Alsatian herdsman. The second had struck the roof of the Grand Bastion, penetrating, but failing to explode. The third had struck the roof of the battlements above the return where Knocke and his party positioned themselves, removing it for a length of twenty metres and blowing away the stonework, leaving a marked elongated U-section removed, an area that was exposed and decidedly more easy to grapple than other parts of the ancient defences.

Olbricht concentrated on the scaling approach and kept taking quick looks through the portal, refusing to fire, in order to avoid drawing attention to himself and the others.

The grapnel sailed up unnoticed and dropped quickly down, striking the one-armed Engineer on his good shoulder. The metal tool then struck stone, a sound that prompted the paratroopers below to haul on the line.

The stunned Olbricht found his right thigh suddenly dragged from him, as it was pulled against the stonework by force applied from below. He was painfully pinned against the battlements, parallel with, but two feet from, the stone floor.

He resisted his pain until the paratroopers below pulled hard to test the line, causing two spikes to penetrate his flesh, before exiting the other side and biting into the battlements.

A second grapnel flew over the wall and down the other side, overthrown in the excitement of the soldier using it. He pulled swiftly to bring the device into play.

The grapnel bounced back up the wall and flew across the floor, catching under Olbricht's neck.

One spike penetrated the back of the skull at the base of the wounded man's neck.

The scream of pain was silenced as powerful arms below tugged hard, pulling the spike into the soft cavity of Olbricht's brain.

The dead man's head moved rhythmically, in time with the climbing pattern of the second paratrooper to scale the wall.

Von Arnesen shot the first Russian as he opened the shutter, sending the lifeless body to fall upon those gathered underneath the ropes.

The second paratrooper grasped the stonework and hauled himself over, two bullets from Valois' handgun smashing into his face. The impact threw the man off the battlement and into the lists below, striking soft flesh and causing more hurt to the attackers.

An object looped up over the wall and dropped into the Upper Garden. The explosion caught one of the French orderlies passing, penetrating his body with shrapnel and stone fragments. The man's screams attracted attention and two intelligence agents dragged him away towards the Bastion.

The cries of the wounded man decreased, as the noise from the Northern Ward increased, the Soviet paratroopers putting in an attack, encouraged by support from two DP machine guns. Knocke risked a quick look through an undamaged shutter and saw little by way of return fire from the Small Bastion.

Quickly realising the precariousness of their position, he shouted to Von Arnesen to move back from the gap and moved himself to cover the small entranceway from the Ward into the garden.

Before he was in position above, two paratroopers ran through and moved immediately to shoot down anyone on the wall, guarding the spot where their grapnels hung uselessly. Knocke brought up his Sten gun and pulled the trigger, only to be greeted by silence as the weapon failed. Two short staccato bursts sounded close in his left ear and the Russians were thrown back like rag dolls, their lifeless bodies testament to the accuracy and calmness of Anne-Marie Valois.

Quickly she grabbed at the German officer's weapon, removing the magazine and working the cocking lever before punching the magazine home again.

"Danke, Madamoiselle."

Anne-Marie dropped another paratrooper as he tentatively worked round through the entranceway, leaning over and firing into the top of his helmeted head.

A Russian grenade bounced through the opening and burst, quickly concealing the three dead bodies as its chemical smoke spread rapidly.

Fig#9

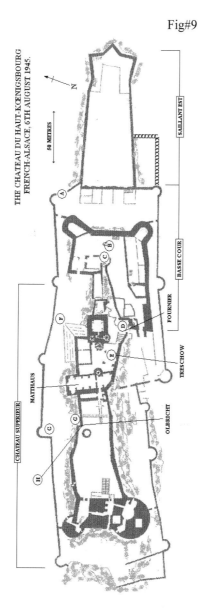

THE CHATEAU DU HAUT-KŒNIGSBOURG
FRENCH-ALSACE, 6TH AUGUST 1945.

50 METRES

N

A - GRAPNEL ASSAULT BY TWO PLATOON'S   B - .50 CAL MG POSITION   C - ENTRANCE TO STONE STAIRCASE LEADING TO INNER COURTYARD

D - LIONS GATE, DRAWBRIDGE AND WELL ROOM   E - BARRICADE IN INNER COURTYARD   F - CHOKEPOINT IN NORTH WARD

G - WALL RETURNS PROVIDING COVER TO PARATROOPERS   H - KNOCKE'S PARTY CONCEALED ABOVE RETURN

Both Knocke and Valois quickly repositioned, moving to the west of the opening, just in time to fire down into hazy shapes swiftly running into the garden. Most dropped, either instinctively or involuntarily, the former seeking cover as they rolled on the floor, the latter no longer caring.

A squeal came from Von Arnesen, hit in the act of killing two more paratroopers scaling the grapnel lines. One of them survived long enough to get a shot off with his heavy Nagant M1895 revolver, the 7.62mm bullet smashing Von Arnesen down as it clipped the femur on its path through his right thigh.

"I'll go", shouted the French agent and she dashed quickly along the battlements to Von Arnesen's side.

Swiftly unhooking the sling to her Sten, she wound the webbing around the German's thigh to create a ligature. Needing something rigid to tighten the tourniquet, she slipped the near empty magazine out of her submachine gun and inserted it in the knot, twisting it twice to tighten it further, much to the consternation of Von Arnesen, whose pain resistance level was already being tested.

A burst of fire from Knocke's position drew both their glances, but the man was still there; there were just more bodies in the dispersing smoke.

Slipping another magazine out of her waist bag, Anne-Marie primed her Sten.

"Danke, Mademoiselle."

"Keep it tight, Jurgen. Can you manage here?"

"Jawohl."

It was not a time for pleasantries and she scurried back along the stonework, leaving Von Arnesen propped against the wall, covering both grapnels and silently promising anyone a painful death if they showed themselves above the parapet.

Two more smoke grenades tumbled through the entranceway, both perfectly positioned to cover the Russian's next move.

A single arm jerked in the smoke and a more deadly object careened off the underside of the battlement roof, dropping between the two defenders.

Von Arnesen heard the shout and risked a look at his two comrades.

He saw a blur of movement through the smoke and then the flash of the explosion.

The other grenades continued to produce smoke, further obscuring the parapet where two bodies now lay.

Instinctively turning, he fired blindly at a noise he had almost missed, sending yet another young paratrooper to the ground, ten metres below.

Major Marion Crisp had been dragged away from the doorway, insensible, felled by the explosion of a grenade that did deadly work in the confined space at the bottom of the north stairs.

Enemy machine guns were lashing the defenders, permitting the assaulting party to make it into the stairwell without further casualties.

However, the confined space then worked against them, funnelling them forward one by one. A 'Deux' agent dropped the first three, two bullets a man, piling the corpses on each other, as momentum drove the dead flesh on.

Caught in the act of reloading his Beretta, the agent's head jerked back as a burst from a PPS took his life, his body slithering down the stairs and adding itself to the pile accumulating there.

The second agent, having dragged Crisp up the stairs, turned to help and was dropped by the same weapon, his lifeblood rapidly washing the stairs onto which he fell.

Crisp, the Thompson slung around his shoulder, groggily tried to get the weapon into action but could not disentangle himself. His hand sought and found the comforting butt of the Beretta pistol. Ears still ringing from the grenade's blast, he brought up the handgun and put four bullets into the men moving up the stairs. The lead man fell back into those behind and the advance stopped in an instant.

Shaking his head, the Paratrooper Major quickly released the fouled strap and found that the familiar shape and feel of the Thompson helped clear his mind.

343

It was the American sub-machine gun that stopped the next attempt to gain the stairs.

At the main staircase, Ramsey's Webley had been emptied stopping an assault, paratroopers suddenly able to enter the garden from the North Ward, the resistance offered by Knocke and Valois having been smashed aside.

Mounting the stairs, a few were picked off from behind, commandos and orderlies with rifles dropping men from safe vantage points in the accommodation part of the Château Supérieur. Twenty-five steps carried the survivors up to the drawbridge that lead to the Grand Bastion, but no further. A 'Deux' agent used his M3A1 Grease gun to good effect, emptying the thirty round contents of his magazine and killing or wounding the lead five troopers.

The garden was rapidly becoming a slaughter ground and the Russian paratroopers grew more desperate in their attempts to gain entry to the Bastion.

Every entrance was assaulted and mini battles raged, each the property of a handful of men from both sides.

The lower room was breached and paratroopers pressed in, the handful of defenders engaged in hand-to-hand combat around the stairs. Here, the Soviets had the advantage and the defenders were pressed hard.

The agent covering the main entrance, with Ramsey, took a round in the stomach and collapsed on the floor, rolling dramatically down the stairs before coming to rest against the inner door, writhing in pain and out of the fight.

Three paratroopers threw themselves through the main doors, bodies made small, but still expectant and scared.

One young Russian prodded the badly wounded agent in the throat with his SVT automatic rifle, the bayonet opening a nasty gash and silencing the Frenchman's moans.

At the top of the stairs, Ramsey was reloading his pistol, one round at a time, aware that he was about to become part of a race in which there was only one winner and losing had a price.

344

The fourth bullet slid home into the Webley's chamber as the SVT man saw the movement at the top of the stairs. The automatic rifle barked three times, each bullet missing the Black Watch Major, but each close enough to heighten Ramsey's fear.

The three paratroopers rose to their feet and sprang forward as the fifth bullet went home, their shouts of 'Urrah!' adding to the pressure of the situation.

All three Russians fired from the hip as they bounded up the stairs, one bullet passing through Ramsey's right armpit but leaving no trace on his body.

The sixth bullet went home and the Webley was closed, the two actions joined together by speed and urgency.

Ramsey brought the handgun up in an instant and fired.

The first .455 bullet took the SVT man in the chest, throwing him against the left–hand wall with the force of the impact, the second missed, chipping the stonework on its way down the stairs.

Switching to the second man, two more bullets took him down, dead before he hit the stairs.

The third man ducked low and left, intent on driving his bayonet into the British officer. Ramsey twisted as best he could to avoid the blade and, in so doing, missed with his fifth and final shot. The Russian barrelled into him and both crashed to the floor, Ramsey winded and pinned under the not inconsiderable weight of the larger man.

The Soviet paratrooper, benefitting from the softer landing, recovered quicker. One hand found Ramsey's throat and a knee pinned the Black Watch officer's right arm, as the Russian tried to retrieve a knife from his belt.

Ramsey started to see stars before his eyes as the pressure of the man's steel grip grew and his free arm, desperately trying to find a point of weakness on his assailant, started to lose power.

The weight suddenly lifted from the Englishman's body and he was able to draw breath, choking and coughing, eyes misty and blurred, but not so much that he hadn't seen the red spout as something burst out of the Russian's chest.

345

A French NCO, a Quartermaster 1st Class, had been fighting on the gun platform above the main entrance and had turned just in time to see the British officer's plight. One bullet from the Frenchman's Enfield rifle sent the paratrooper toppling off Ramsey and onto the floor, his breathing little more than a gurgling of bubbles as blood filled his damaged lungs.

The French NCO grabbed one of the 'Deux' agents and doubled round to Ramsey's position, in time to shoot down another paratrooper firing into the side room at the bottom of the stairs.

Ramsey shook his head and controlled his breathing, gradually returning to his senses, but remaining weak. He looked around for his revolver but could not locate it. The SVT lay nearby, so he retrieved it and removed three magazines from the quietly dying paratrooper. The SVT was a large weapon, four foot long and weighing over eight pounds; not ideal for a man still recovering from standing on the threshold of death just a few seconds beforehand.

He propped the automatic rifle against the stonework at the top of the stairs and sat on an ammo box, regaining more of his senses.

He became aware that the intelligence agent was looking at him, examining him from head to foot.

Normally smart and dapper, Ramsey was now anything but.

Blood from his nose gently leaked down his face, dripping onto his tie and jacket, the rupture caused by the impact of the Russian.

A painful cut on his hand made itself known, origin unknown this time, again adding its own red stain to Ramsey's attire.

His shoulder, the old sniper wound from Nordenham, stung and ached, but had not reopened.

Examining his right armpit, Ramsey discovered that the bullet had indeed missed him, but his probing fingers were met with ravaged cloth and he suspected the repair would prove a challenging job for his tailor.

Producing a handkerchief, he wiped blood and saliva away from his chin and mouth and started the process of composing himself.

As the agent looked on, Ramsey returned to some semblance of a British Infantry officer, straightening his tie, smoothing his hair into order, pulling and patting his uniform into some sort of presentability.

As he was doing it, the professional part of his brain was trying hard to relay a message and it was not until he accepted a cigarette from the French NCO that he realised what the inner voice was saying.

'They've stopped firing.'

No more paratroopers had come.

Technically, Ramsey was wrong; the firing had not stopped, it was just further away.

Whilst the attempts were being made to carry the garden and the bastions, Soviet paratroopers had pushed hard into the accommodation, fighting through chambers and hallways, across wooden balconies and up circular stairs.

The courage of the Russians was incredible, as they pressed the defence hard, urged on both by their commanding general and the sounds of heavy fighting outside the Château behind them.

Makarenko had sent Rispan to the Lower Courtyard, with orders to prepare for the assault force's exit from the Château. Firing from the road below had risen in ferocity since the first and only radio communication with the mortar group, who identified a solitary enemy vehicle coming from Selestat. The Major dispatched Nakhimov to the main gate, tasked to discover the facts, as he started to decide how best to evacuate the growing numbers of badly wounded men from the Château.

Heavy machine guns started to hammer away and Rispan understood that the situation was growing more precarious by the minute. He needed to see things for himself, so embarked on an extremely painful journey up the round tower in the southeast corner of the Basse-Cour, detailing a wounded Junior Lieutenant to continue with the evacuation planning.

Rispan was a brave man and a combat soldier of great experience and renown. It took but a few seconds for him to appreciate the perilous nature of the Soviet paratrooper forces' existence, as his eyes took in half-tracks pouring fire into his men's positions and disciplined infantry moving forward in large numbers.

He dismounted from the tower and received the report from Nakhimov. The situation was indeed dire, as the enemy armoured infantry unit was moving in close in an attempt to seal off any line of retreat.

Dispatching Nakhimov once more, this time to scout the north wall, Major Rispan limped off up the rising ramp, in search of his General. Rather than send a messenger, he decided this news needed to be given in person, lest Makarenko fail to appreciate its worth.

The assault force had set up a casualty area in the Inner Courtyard and he journeyed through it, mentally adding the numbers of groaning comrades there to those already gathered in the lower courtyard.

The temporary barricade continued to burn, its chairs, tables and barrels, feeding gentle flames. Other more horrible items around it continued to smoulder, adding a rich and sickly sweet smoke to the surreal montage in the courtyard.

Climbing the Hexagonal stairs, he met a group forming in the Marshal's chambers, preparing for an attack. Reversing his course, he moved back through bedrooms and found his progress blocked once more, as more paratroopers were readying themselves for the assault. As he went in search of Makarenko, it seemed that every stairway, room and hall contained dead comrades.

Ascending a stone spiral staircase to the second floor, he found the upper level littered with bodies, although he noted with satisfaction that the majority were not his own men.

He entered a room filled with feminine touches and collided with Makarenko, who was moving quickly in the opposite direction.

"Mayor Rispan, what news?"

348

"Comrade General, if the mission is fulfilled, we must now withdraw. The enemy has reinforced and our escape route is in jeopardy."

Hardly missing a step, Makarenko shepherded the Major back down the route, up which he had just painfully toiled.

"I can see much from up here, Ilya. They look organised and efficient. How long can we hold them?"

Such things were a matter of guesswork and both men knew it, but his General had asked, so Rispan ventured his reply.

"Twenty minutes absolute maximum, Comrade."

The two pressed on, the silence indicating only thought.

Makarenko broke it.

"I must launch this last attack, for we have not done all we set out to do here. How do you plan for us to leave, Ilya?"

Rispan's own moment of truth was now upon him and he delivered his verdict as evenly as he could.

"With our casualties, through the main gate. If we are bottled up, then over the north wall where our forces made their assault, but without our casualties, Comrade General."

The two officers were now moving through the first floor bedrooms Rispan had previously traversed, full of the dead and wounded of the paratroop battalion. As they passed by, each wounded man's face turned to them, silently seeking information, each set of dead eyes seemingly staring at them in accusation for what was to come.

Makarenko stopped so abruptly that Rispan cannoned into him.

"Those of our comrades who cannot move with us must remain here, Comrade Major. Formed as a rearguard, for those who are capable. There is no choice." The icy formality of his words masked the emotion of an officer who loved his men and understood the consequences of the decision he was making.

"One last attack and we will leave. Get it organised and start protecting that route out, Ilya."

He slapped his Major on the shoulder and turned away, immediately immersing himself in readying his men for the final assault.

Enemy troops were bottled up in the Armoury on the first floor. The last two attempts to crush them had been thrown back with heavy casualties. From his vantage point on the second floor, the General had observed how the assaults on the Bastion had withered.

His hasty plan allocated more men to aid those attacks. The support force was detailed to cross the small drawbridge leading from the apartments into the garden area, but only once the defenders of the Armoury were distracted by the new attack.

On the second floor, the enemy held a similar area, being pressed into the Kaiser's Hall and the two adjoining rooms.

After nodding to the wounded Kapitan who had volunteered to lead the Bastion assault party, the General closed his eyes and availed himself of a word with some higher authority, seeking hope amidst the hopelessness of death.

A whistle pulled him from his reverie and initiated the final attack.

0608hrs Monday, 6th August 1945, Approach roads to the Château du Haut-Kœnigsbourg, French Alsace.

Lavalle and Haefeli had executed their hasty attack to perfection, gaining good firing positions, from where their halftrack-mounted heavy machine guns started to cause casualties amongst the defenders and, more importantly, were able to provide good cover under which to manoeuvre.

Mardin's assault had overcome the resistance in front of him, his report citing the defenders as wounded men and medical orderlies, who had been organised into a roadblock.

His company had indeed wiped out the men who had been injured in the drop.

2e Compagnie was now pressing hard up the main road approach, driving the thin screen of enemy paratroops before it.

One platoon of Haefeli's men had overrun an enemy mortar unit before it had responded to the threat, the troops either dying or being driven off by the Legion's love of the bayonet.

Lavalle had remained with the command halftrack, in contact with other units moving swiftly towards the fighting, as well as coordinating the counter-attack. Haefeli had joined the vehicle belonging to his 2IC, bringing his company efficiently online to squeeze the Château from the south, leaving Mardin to do the same from the north road.

Four 6x6 'deuce and a half' trucks arrived, swiftly disgorging their troops, reinforcements courtesy of Lavalle's hasty planning. Normally comfortable transport for sixteen or so combat troops, each of these American-built GMC trucks brought over thirty men to the battle, each clad in the traditional brown and grey jellaba.

The Capitaine commanding the Tabor of Goumiers sought out Haefeli and took rapid orders, leading his men swiftly off towards the battle.

The Goumiers were Moroccan irregular troops, their courage and ferocity much respected by their allies, as well as their former German and Italian enemies. Their new Soviet adversaries would soon appreciate their courage and recoil at their ferocity.

A platoon of legionnaires was having a hard time at the main entrance, suffering casualties as they tried to overcome the same problems that had cost the Soviet paratroopers so dearly. Their advantage lay in the fact that the Russians were less organised for defence and were now low on ammunition. None the less, over a dozen men lay dead and wounded on the ramp leading to the main gate, including the platoon commander.

A second platoon mustered on the main road below the entrance, preparing to force the route by rapid storm. Suddenly, slipping quietly through them, came the Goumiers. They moved relentlessly forward, the sloped ascent seemingly effortlessly mastered by their ancient tribal skills.

Again, the Goumier commander paused, consulting with the Legion officer, before moving on after his men. Even

351

though a Frenchman by birth, his own climbing skills were no less impressive than those of his men and he was also soon swallowed up by the trees and bushes.

The legion platoon found the angled pathway and ascended at the double towards the next road level, already falling behind the nimble tribesmen.

From the west end of the plateau came the sounds of combat, proof that Mardin's legionnaires had engaged the enemy as they pressed hard to seal up the Château.

For the final time, the Capitaine in charge of the Goumiers halted to exchange information with a fellow Frenchman. The Legionnaire Sergent-Chef, a sunburnt African veteran seemingly old enough to be his grandfather, was newly installed as commander of his platoon, courtesy of the Russian rifle bullet that had slain his officer.

As senior, the Capitaine took the lead and quickly explained the brief.

With no hesitation, the Goumier officer stood and called to his men in their tribal tongue.

The Sergent-Chef had spent many years amongst the Berber peoples and understood the shouted exhortation perfectly.

"Come, brothers, these new enemies have not yet learned to fear us. Let us enlighten them!"

Bullets reached out and took lives amongst the heavily clad tribesmen, but less than before, despite the advantage of the increasing sunlight. Leaving half a dozen of their number on the stone, the Goumiers swept forward and into the South Ward, using both main and side entrances to good effect.

As the Sergent-Chef prepared to send his own men forward, he hesitated, the sound of a whistle and increased firing within the Château giving him a moment's pause.

0609hrs Monday, 6th August 1945, Château du Haut-Kœnigsbourg, French Alsace.

Two grenades bounced off the door and headed in different directions within the Armoury. One dropped at the threshold, causing the attacking paratroopers to dive for cover once more, losing the advantage they had hoped to gain by following up swiftly. The second rolled erratically into the room, causing the defenders to seek cover as quickly as they could.

Both exploded simultaneously.

Perversely, the one furthest away by the door, killed one of the defenders, a large piece of metal claiming the life of the Savoy orderly, punching into his heart as his slower reactions spelt his end.

The second nearer grenade took Von Hardegen out of the fight, the blast throwing him against the rounded arch support, knocking him senseless.

Rettlinger cut down the first Russians into the room, his newly liberated PPSH doing deadly work in the narrow doorway. A paratrooper positioned at the base of the door and obscured by bodies, poured fire into the defenders, claiming three lives.

Rettlinger and Dubois were the only men left standing, and the comatose Von Hardegen, the only other living man in the room. Both men dropped Russians, as a surge brought the paratroopers closer. Dubois ran out of ammo and was clubbed to the ground before he could react, a rifle butt smashing into his forehead and skinning the skull to the bone, the bloody flap of skin pushed up on his head like a flat cap.

Rettlinger shot the man down and two more besides and then his gun fell silent. A single paratrooper stood before him, panting, drawing air noisily in the way of a condemned man at the gallows.

Realising fate had spared him, he threw his own empty PPS at the huge German and lunged for the discarded rifle, butt sticky with Dubois' blood.

The PPSH remained silent, similarly empty and useless. DerBo threw it at the Russian, a man not much smaller than himself. It struck the hand scrabbling for the rifle, noisily breaking fingers and bringing a howl from the crippled man.

However, the paratrooper, veteran of the Eastern Front, quickly recovered and sought another weapon. By his other hand lay something from a different time; one of the classic swords from the medieval age that decorated the Armoury.

Sweeping it up, he ran at Rettlinger, roaring as much with the pain of his shattered fingers as with the intent to intimidate. Weaponless, the ex-SS Gebirgsjager officer could only roll out of the way.

The paratrooper breathed hard and gathered himself for another attack with the heavy blade. Again he missed, the metal clanging off the stonewall as he lunged past Rettlinger's twisting body. A rock hard fist smashed into the Russian's face, breaking his nose and bringing a watery mist to his eyes.

Unable to see properly, he dropped back and swung blindly, the tip of the sword flicking the German's shirt as he leapt aside in avoidance.

The paratrooper shook his head to clear his vision and the blood, flowing freely from his nose, splashed in all directions, decorating the living and the dead lying everywhere within the Armoury.

Rettlinger made a mistake, catching his foot on a corpse and losing his balance. He fell against the wall and the Russian saw his opportunity.

The ancient blade swung in an arc and bit into flesh and bone.

Slicing the muscle of Rettlinger's upper arm, the metal smashed into the bone, shattering the humerus at its mid-point. In olden days, such an attack would have severed the limb and gone further, probably to claim the life of the victim, but the blade's travel was suddenly arrested by the stonewall.

The ringing contact jarred the sword from the paratrooper's grasp and it fell to the ground. The Russian's left hand was broken and useless, his right now senseless and bereft of feeling, the heavy impact having robbed him of control.

His German adversary slumped to the ground, bleeding profusely from his wound and out of the fight.

The Russian moved purposefully to the doorway and picked up a PPS, recently dropped by his section Corporal, disentangling the sling from the dead man's bread bag with difficulty, his numb hand unable to properly function. The paratrooper halted and flexed his hand, bringing life back to numbed flesh. He slipped the weapon's strap over his head, less trouble now that his tingling hand was regaining its functions.

The man cocked an ear to the sounds of nearby fighting, rightly sensing that his comrades were withdrawing, deciding that he should follow them too.

However, the paratrooper had a debt to collect for his dead comrades.

Here.

Now.

Shaking his right hand to summon back more control, he turned to finish the German off. Rettlinger was conscious and pushing himself away with his feet, as his right hand worked to squeeze his terrible arm wound and restrict the blood loss.

The hate in the Russian's eyes was very real and DerBo expected to die. What he did not expect was to witness the paratrooper's death.

Both men sensed a presence, heard some sounds and feared the worst, as malevolence incarnate burst into the room.

As the paratrooper turned, the heavy weight smashed into his chest, propelling him backwards and onto Rettlinger's legs. The Russian's scream was silenced as soon as it began, throat ripped open from chin to chest.

Marengo.

Rettlinger had the most horrible experience of watching a man die three feet in front of his eyes, ripped apart in stages by the huge Alsatian. Lifeless eyes bounced in the savaged head as the beast worked on, opening cavities and stripping flesh from bone.

DerBo lost consciousness, his last vision being that of Marengo assessing him with merciless eyes.

The attack had mainly failed, at further great loss to the brave paratroopers, so Makarenko withdrew his forces, urging them to set fires, as he herded his weary and battered men towards the lower courtyard.

He paused quickly in the Upper Courtyard, exchanging quiet words with the medical orderly Serzhant who was responsible for the score of broken and crippled men that were to be left behind there. Embracing and kissing the man, a soldier from the very first days, an emotional Makarenko slipped away down the ramp towards the Basse Cour.

Despite the growing sounds of combat ahead of him, he was genuinely horrified at the sights he passed, his young troopers mixed with enemy dead, bodies riven and torn for seemingly no purpose.

In the Lower Courtyard, a repetition of the previous scene, with numerous wounded laid out as best they could be, tended by three orderlies and the only woman member of the Battalion.

Senior Lieutenant Doctor Stefka Kolybareva was hobbling between her charges, her own heavily bandaged thigh restricting her mobility, her bandaged left hand restricting her capability to provide care.

"Comrade General, I have told Mayor Rispan that I am staying. He refuses permission. You must grant me permission, Sir."

Behind the determined woman, an orderly pulled a blanket over the face of a Corporal whose suffering had just ended.

"I cannot agree to that, Stefka."

His decision given, Makarenko made to move on, but a firm hand stopped him.

"Forgive me, Comrade General, but you must."

Momentarily angry at being manhandled, Makarenko relaxed, despite the increasing intensity of fire coming from the main entrance behind him.

"I cannot walk and cannot hold a weapon. All I can use is my medical brain and that is best used here, Comrade. I am an officer of the Red Army. If I were not a woman, you would see this clearly. You must let me stay, Sir," her eyes strayed to the distraught man on the wall above, "And my Rispan must accept it."

Makarenko looked at the woman, her eyes moistening. She was a tough soldier who had killed her fair share of green toads; not a woman given to tears, or so he thought.

Instinctively, he looked up at the battlements. Rispan stood there, his strained face betraying him, his obvious emotion on the verge of overflowing.

'So the rumours were true, you two are an item.'

His thoughts only. He did not give them voice.

'There is no time for this,' his inner general shouted.

"On the Svir you told me that difficult decisions are the privilege of rank did you not, Comrade General?"

"Indeed I did, Stefka. You may remain. Look after my boys and look after yourself. I will see you when this stupidity has ended."

He hugged the Doctor, his peripheral vision seeing his Battalion commander sag in realisation at what had just come to pass.

"Goodbye, Stefka."

Makarenko called men to him and sent messengers to the main gate with orders to start disengaging. Two wounded paratroopers erected a white sheet with a large red cross in the centre, coloured by the most valuable commodity his soldiers had to give.

The surviving paratroopers started to exit the Château, retracing the grapnel route used during the two-platoon assault earlier. A French half-track had moved up and its .50cal downed a number of men as they moved across the road to safety in the woods.

Aleksey Nikitin, unscathed whilst most of those around him had fallen, brought his Mosin sniper rifle to bear, dropping the gunner into the half-track and forcing the vehicle to drop back.

Makarenko scaled the round tower and met Rispan.

The man's pain was wholly apparent, both in physical and mental terms, but there was nothing of value to be said.

"Bring the rest of the boys out this way, Ilya. I'll make sure we are set up to cover your withdrawal from the wood line. But we must hurry. I've pulled the main gate troops back now."

The Major nodded, not trusting himself to speak.

Makarenko placed his hand on the man's shoulder and made eye contact, sharing his friend's pain and anguish as best he could.

The moment disappeared in an instant, as running paratroopers appeared from the direction of the main gate, pursued by a burst of fire.

The General moved to the wall and grabbed a rope, quickly hoisting himself through the shutter and slipping down to road level.

Organising the men he found there, Makarenko pushed out a screen to keep the legionnaires at bay for as long as possible. His men were finding that the white kepis made excellent targets, the French troops being so equipped as a result of their ceremonial duties. As head shot casualties mounted, Mardin ordered his men to remove them, an order reluctantly but swiftly followed.

The young officer had learned valuable lessons since he had command forced upon him on the road from St Hippolyte, growing in stature and confidence as the battle raged.

Dragging the dying machine gunner into the back of his half-track, he ordered the vehicle to make a further withdrawal and raised his head to judge the distance.

Nikitin's bullet entered the base of his skull and Laurent Mardin was dead before it exited through the front of his neck.

Nakhimov moved between vantage points, taking in the growing pressure on the northern road and then the obvious advances of the enemy force pushing back his comrades in the lower courtyard.

"Comrade Mayor!"

Rispan jerked his head up and immediately looked to where the Starshy-Serzhant pointed. A few of his men were moving back from the North lists, most supporting a comrade unable to move by himself, funnelling past the now steadily burning forge.

The Major had a DP team set up in the Mill Tower window, covering down into the yard. The weapon started its chatter, indicating that the enemy were pressing hard, moving up from the main gate area.

Rispan, now equipped with an SVT, moved to the walkway above the casualty area and shouted down to a handful of paratroopers gathered around the fountain, pulling an enemy machine gun into position, in an attempt to use its firepower.

"Get ready, Comrades. We are leaving!"

A bloodied Corporal waved in acknowledgement and then hammered on the back of the man nearest him. As the soldier turned, he was thrown backwards, the impact of rifle bullets driving him against the wall, three metres behind. The Corporal moved quickly and the heavy hammer of the .50cal rang around the courtyard, a stream of bullets reaching out into the Goumiers, pressing up past the Alsatian House, dropping five bloodily to the stone path.

A movement in the doorway of the house caught Rispan's eye and he put six bullets into something that bled and disappeared.

Fitting the last magazine into the weapon, he looked around for other alternatives. It seemed that the dead commandos and paratroopers spread along the walkway had already been visited by others in search of ammunition and weapons.

Another look at the doorway.

Nothing.

He rummaged in a Commando's pouch and found nothing of value.

An enemy soldier suddenly appeared on the walkway and Rispan shot him down, sending the man over the balustrade, the strangely clad body sliding gently down the angled roof.

In the recess of a shutter, he caught the welcome sight of a pistol and a grenade, which he immediately stowed about his person.

Checking the situation below him, he saw the .50cal standing silent. The Corporal was hugging a shoulder wound as he harangued two other paratroopers, both encouraging the

359

reloading process and reporting the progress of the enemy soldiers.

His grenade was out and in the air before Rispan could shout.

"Move back now, Comrades! Now!"

The Corporal needed no second order and pulled his men towards the Mill Tower.

The grenade exploded amongst a group of Goumiers, halting the rush in an instant. Two more faces appeared at the Alsatian house door and Rispan switched his attention to them, sending one flying out of sight in a spout of blood and gore.

A burst of fire from the upper window of the house made him drop into cover, but the burst was not meant for him. The last surviving member of the Corporal's section disappeared into the Mill Tower, his two comrades lying desperately wounded behind him.

The SVT brought a body tumbling out of the window to fall onto the stone below.

"Stefka!"

His fiancée had rushed to the dying Corporal and was doing what she could for the man.

"Stefka!"

A rifle grenade exploded on the window frame, right where the DP was firing, silencing both weapon and crew instantly.

"Stefka!"

This time she heard and looked up just in time to see Rispan struck by a bullet that folded him double as it made its way through the stomach and out the small of his back. Blood gushed from his mouth and he dropped to the stone.

Kolybareva could not drag her eyes away from the still form.

An orderly with her started to stand and was suddenly a mass of scarlet, as a sub-machine gun hammered bullets into him at short range.

Another orderly went to run for the Tower door and was also mercilessly shot down.

Senior Lieutenant Doctor Stefka Kolybareva suddenly had stars before her eyes, the butt of an old French Berthier

M16 rifle caressing her head, hard enough to drop the woman, but not so hard as to deny her the full pleasures the Goumier had in mind for her.

Through misty eyes, Kolybareva saw her senior medic gutted on a wicked Arab knife, his entrails spilling as the sharp blade split his stomach open. The agony dropped the man to his knees. Grasping the dying man by his hair, the Goumier ran the blade up one side of the skull and back down the other, removing the trophies that would mark his prowess in battle around the campfires of his tribe in the years to come.

Throwing the screaming man to the stone, the tribesman moved on, joining others steadily working their way through the wounded men, so invitingly gathered for them to harvest.

Vision clearing, Kolybareva felt hands on her, dragging her across to the fountain, where other hands pulled and tore at her clothing.

Kusev, the youngest orderly in her medical section, was dragged up beside her, one of his ears dangling half sliced off, his lips split and one eye closed by vicious blows.

The young man had no moment to gather himself, as rough hands dragged him upright and threw him over the fountain trough. Both he and Kolybareva realised in an instant what the savages had in mind and the youth started to twist and writhe in an attempt to avoid the rape.

A 'gentle' blow stunned the orderly and he had little comprehension of his trousers being ripped off and a sweating Goumier penetrating him violently.

Finishing quickly, the tribesman moved away to other pleasures and was replaced by another, more sadistic, rapist.

His pleasures included violent rape of a kind that tore and ripped the young orderly, the pain clearing his stunned brain and permitting him to scream.

Lance-Corporal Nikitin was about to descend from the Mill Tower when the sound summoned him back. Risking a quick look through the shattered upper window, he was both horrified at what he saw and powerless to interfere, his rifle empty.

361

He checked the machine gun, but the DP was bent and useless.

Nakhimov found him there as he quickly looked for stragglers before escaping himself. He too risked a look, which drew fire from the men in the courtyard who were not wholly immersed in the intoxicating slaughter of the wounded.

"We must go, now."

Nikitin looked in disgust at his NCO.

"But Alexsey, we will remember these bastards."

The younger man teetered on the edge of a useless sacrificial gesture, a fact that Nakhimov was only too well aware of and something he was determined to prevent.

"We must go. Now! That is an order, Comrade Yefreytor!"

Discipline took hold and Nikitin moved towards the grapnel lines.

Sergeant-Major Nakhimov was the last man in the tower, so he swiftly moved to inform Rispan that the withdrawal was complete.

He stopped on the threshold leading to the battlements, the still body of his Major lying in front of him, still leaking blood on the stone.

"Govno!"

He turned and moved after Nikitin. Checking the situation in the road below, Nakhimov was encouraged to see Makarenko waving at him, signalling the all clear. Nikitin stepped away from the rope and moved off, as directed by a Sergeant who returned to the line, holding it tight to assist in Nakhimov's descent. The line rubbed his left hand badly, breaking the scabs and congealed blood that had sealed his finger stump, but the tough NCO lowered himself without complaint and touched down on the grass below.

Starshy-Serzhant Egon Nakhimov was the last member of Zilant-4 to evacuate the Château du Haut-Kœnigsbourg.

0620hrs Monday, 6th August 1945, North road approach to the Château du Haut-Kœnigsbourg, French Alsace.

The loss of their young commander had not stopped the 2e Compagnie from pushing hard and Makarenko had his work cut out to hold the legionnaires back. In truth, the Paratrooper General had not fully appreciated the disaster he was commanding and that he was recovering only a fraction of his force from the bloody battlefield.

He pushed his men hard, stopping the legionnaires in their tracks, holding open an escape route for his troopers.

He signalled to Nakhimov and moved to meet the man at the bottom of the line.

"How many more, Comrade? Time is short now."

"I am the last, Comrade General."

Makarenko felt like he had been struck in the stomach.

"Are you sure, Egon? Mayor Rispan is not yet here."

"He is dead, sir. They are all dead, including the wounded."

"Rispan dead?"

Nakhimov simply nodded.

"The wounded?"

"Butchered before my eyes, my General. Some dark-skinned bastards, cutting off ears with knives, slitting throats and stomachs. They are all dead, Sir."

His professionalism as an officer battled hard against the pain and despair of the losses of his comrades.

Professionalism won.

"Right, then let us get what is left of the battalion out of here. Get them moving north, now!"

The remnants of Zilant-4 fought their way north, killing legionnaires, being killed by legionnaires, finally evading the enraged French efforts to snare them.

General Makarenko, once commander of the 100th Guards Rifle Division 'Svir', once commander of Composite Force Zilant-4, became commander of fifteen shocked and battered survivors, all that was left from the assault upon the Château du Haut-Kœnigsbourg.

363

As he and his group found a place to rest, he learned more of what had happened in the final minutes. His shock and anger at the disaster was replaced by a hatred and loathing for the dark-skinned enemy in the striped dress, one which found equal station with the hatred and loathing he had developed for those who had sent him on the mission that had uselessly spent so many young lives. Young lives that were his privilege to command and protect, precious lives that he had led to nothing but pointless death, all on the orders of madmen.

He promised himself that there would be a day of reckoning on both counts.

0623hrs Monday, 6th August 1945, Lower Courtyard, Château du Haut-Kœnigsbourg, French Alsace.

Haefeli moved up quickly, partially because he was eager to get involved in the final stages, but mainly because he simply had to know who or what it was that Russian paratroopers had come so far to destroy.

Moving quickly up the ramp from the main entrance, he found the dying Goumier officer being tended by one of his men. The man had been hit in the stomach and thighs by a machine gun burst and the Goumier with him could do no more than comfort the Frenchman as he travelled into the darkness.

Haefeli motioned to his own medic, whose assessment was already made. A double dose of morphine was administered and the man's pain ceased forever.

Lavalle strode up, his face cherry red with the extra exertions of catching up, the grimace of pain from exercising his wounded thigh apparent.

"The area is not yet secure, Colonel. I have had no reports as yet, so we must be careful."

Lavalle, his face now under control, gestured to his friend.

"Then we must let you go first, Albrecht."

Smiling, the two moved forward, smiles that immediately disappeared as high pitched screaming reached their ears.

Neither was prepared for the sights before them.

Butchered Soviet paratroopers lay everywhere, the absence of ears bloodily apparent on each corpse.

At the fountain trough, a paratrooper, face down and bent double over the stonework, his backside exposed and bleeding, his most recent violator preparing for a second assault, oblivious to the two officers stood staring in disbelief at him.

To his side, female legs, held wide open by two grinning tribesmen, her arms pinned by two more as a fifth Goumier plunged himself vigorously into the screaming woman. She too was face down, as the unnatural violation ripped her painfully.

A sixth Goumier was displaying her bloody breasts, one in each hand, held out to any of his comrades who wished to inspect them.

What happened next was a blur, decent honourable men acting without thought, either for their own lives, or for the consequences of their actions.

Lavalle and Haefeli moved forward as one, producing their handguns.

As they ran, both officers shouted an age-old cry for assistance.

"A moi La Légion!"

Such a call could not be refused by any legionnaire who heard it.

The Colonel nearly blew the arm off the sodomiser of the unfortunate woman, his first bullet striking the man's shoulder. A second bullet took him in the stomach as he lay on the floor. Haefeli took the life of the other rapist, who collapsed over his victim, his ruined face spilling blood on the young Russian's corpse.

Lavalle's next shots struck the man holding the bloody trophies, his throat and chest exploding as he flew backwards into the stonewall.

The four men pinning the woman looked on in terror, knowing death was about to visit them. Haefeli's Sergent-Chef emptied his Garand into them, two bullets each, the heavy impacts throwing them into disarray. One man moaned, only wounded. Haefeli shot him in the crotch.

The legionnaires turned towards the larger group of Goumier's, comrades of those they had just mercilessly dispatched, expecting to die in turn.

The tribesmen seemed momentarily unsure of what to do, until one of their older NCO's spoke up, directing them to gather up their things and move on after the enemy.

The arrival of more legionnaires from the 3e may well have aided his decision.

The woman's screams had subsided to a low, continuous moan of pain and anguish, expressing suffering way beyond the thresholds of human tolerance.

The apparition pushed herself up on her arms, the bloody stumps of her breasts exposed, a knife in her side now apparent to the transfixed watchers.

Every essence of their being implored them to help her, but there was something about her struggle, something tangible to each of them, that instructed them to leave her, to let her make her efforts.

She slowly stood, the blood running freely from her mouth, chest, side and violated lower body. She took hold of the knife and pulled it slowly from her flesh, the pain making her eyes roll in her head.

Still the Legionnaires stood immobile, knowing that the woman needed to do this herself.

She dropped to her knees, her rapist groaning and bubbling, as red fluid gently seeped into his lungs.

She spoke to the Goumier, soft words in her native tongue, but they were not words of comfort, the venom and hate that they carried obvious to all.

Gathering herself for the effort, Stefka Kolybareva grabbed the man's genitals and twisted, the new pain washing over him in a wave. But it was as nothing compared to the extreme of suffering she visited upon him as she sliced away at his manhood, removing every tangible sign of his gender, before pushing open his scarlet thighs and using his rectum as a scabbard for the bloody blade.

Exhausted, both by her exertions and the huge blood loss, the hideously wounded woman toppled on top of her rapist, falling into merciful unconsciousness.

366

Haefeli's medic moved forward and the work to save her life began.

No one noticed the single Goumier turn and walk briskly forward, his target, the back of the senior Legion officer; the man who had shot his brother.

The arm rwas aised, knife about to plunge between Lavalle's shoulder blades, his revenge imminent.

When the shot rang out, all eyes immediately went to the source of the sound. A bloody hand on the battlements sagged and an automatic pistol fell from its grasp, bouncing on the stone floor of the Lower Courtyard.

Some intuitive sense made Haefeli check his men's fire, the wounded Russian clearly no longer armed or a threat.

Lavalle turned at the sound of a fall behind him, the headless corpse having dropped like a rag doll onto the dead Russian prisoner's.

The wound was immense, unusually removing everything from the lower jaw upwards. It was later discovered that the gun's former commando owner, against orders and all conventions, had converted his bullets into dum-dums with quartered heads. The destructive impact of Rispan's shot had put the Goumier down immediately and gave him no possibility of him fulfilling his act of revenge.

More men were sent to tend to the man who had saved Lavalle's life.

"A close call, Mon Colonel, a close call for sure."

Even the brave and the bold can be shaken by such things and Lavalle was no exception. He knew how close to death he had just been.

"Yes, Albrecht. I was very lucky."

Composing himself, Lavalle got his thought processes back on track.

Both men's eyes locked and silent communication took place.

"Yes. We will deal with these bastards later, Albi."

Lavalle did not mean the Russians.

"Now, let's get some information out to our superiors... and find out what the hell is going on here, eh?"

Nodding, Haefeli summoned a radioman.

"You do it, Albrecht. I think I will take some of the men and go on up."

He indicated the ramp that led up into the Château, the signs of battle evident, blood and bodies leading up into unseen places beyond.

0657hrs Monday, 6th August 1945, Château du Haut-Kœnigsbourg, French Alsace.

Within half an hour, the Château was declared safe, although armed legionnaires patrolled everywhere, in case some hitherto unsuspected hiding place disgorged enemy paratroopers.

2e Compagnie was still off pursuing the Russians, without much success, according to the reports filtering back via radio.

A senior French officer, a Brigadier-General no less, had arrived with the rest of the Goumier Tabor, gathered up the survivors, promising to keep the tribesmen employed in the pursuit of the enemy, as well as ensuring investigation and retribution in equal measure, horrified at the excesses his men visited on the Lower Courtyard.

Lavalle had forcefully ensured that the General understood that the matter would not be left dormant for long.

The commando barracks was now a makeshift field hospital, staffed by a group of doctors and nurses who had responded to the calls for assistance as they were passing by, on their way back from a detachment to the Red Cross in Geneva. They made no distinction between their charges, each man or woman receiving appropriate treatment, regardless of the uniform, although, perhaps unsurprisingly, Stefka Kolybareva received more personal attention than most, the women nurses drawn into her personal suffering by loyalty to their gender, as much as by their caring natures.

Lavalle took a close interest in the Russian officer who saved his life, slipping a note into the man's ID book and briefing the medical team on the man's actions.

Much as Ramsey had done a few hours beforehand, Lavalle reflected on the Château around him, fresh with signs

368

of slaughter, thinking on how a battle here would be fought or, at this particular moment, had been fought.

'No less a bloodbath than it would've been in the days of boiling oil and broadswords', was his sanguine conclusion.

Already, the butcher's bill was revealing itself in all its true horror. The 2e had lost nearly 20% of its men dead and wounded, the 3e twice as many, with more than two-thirds of those killed outright.

The Goumiers had lost forty men, including those who had not fallen in battle, but were none the less dead upon the field.

A groggy commando officer, sporting countless stitches in his head, was unable to confirm his unit strength, but the strangely familiar Général de Brigade seemed to think it was one hundred and twenty before the firing started, making the commandos' loss roughly one hundred casualties, also mainly dead.

Lavalle was trying to make sense of everything when a figure clad in black walked in carefully, a figure he recognised and who also recognised him.

Without intent to drop into cliché, Lavalle extended his hand.

"Herr Knocke, we meet again."

The slightly groggy German took the Legion officer's hand warmly.

"Oberst Lavalle. It is good to see you. Excuse me."

Wretching violently, Knocke spilled the contents of his stomach onto the floor of the Kaisers Hall.

Lavalle swept up some napkins from the table, passing one to Knocke and covering the vomit with the others.

"My apologies, Herr Oberst. I took a blow in the stomach and I can't stop doing it."

Steering Knocke to a chair, Lavalle acknowledged a new arrival, a man he now recognised as the shadowy intelligence officer he had once seen at Army Headquarters.

"Thank you for your timely arrival, Colonel Lavalle. I fear we would have all perished, had you and your legionnaires not got here so quickly."

Lavalle could do no more than shrug at De Walle, as it was undoubtedly true.

Given that the senior officers were now all within the Kaiser's Hall, it became the focus of activity, the place where reports went and people came in search of information.

Von Arnesen was next in, stopping the regulation distance in front of Knocke before clicking his heels and reporting in the old Prussian style, before he remembered the circumstances and place and his wounded thigh reminded him he needed to relax his posture.

"Sir, Mademoiselle Valois is now in the hospital. The medics say her wounds are painful, but not threatening. She asked me to thank you."

Knocke inclined his head, acknowledging De Walle's obvious joy, then turning back to Von Artensen and encouraging his stalwart to go on with his report.

"DerBo will live, although he may yet lose his arm. The doctors are unclear."

A nod acknowledged another comrade had been spared.

"Von Hardegen isn't scratched, but he does have concussion."

A moment's interruption as a Legionnaire walked in, saluted and presented De Walle with a report.

"Menzel may not survive. He is next to be operated on; they could tell me no more, Sir."

Knocke made a mental tick in the other column, as a white-faced De Walle passed the report to Lavalle.

"Confirmed dead are Matthaus, Olbricht and...," Von Arnesen paused and cleared his throat, "...Schmidt."

The mention of Schmidt's name brought a look of true sorrow to Knocke's face. A comrade of many years lost. One of many, for sure, but Schmidt had been there for what seemed like forever.

"We cannot find Treschow at this time, but it would seem likely that he has perished."

Lavalle silently sought permission to pass the report onto Knocke, which De Walle granted with a simple nod of his head.

"Herr Knocke, perhaps you would like me to read this to you?"

Haefeli burst into the room, his timing impeccable.

"Have you heard?"

De Walle held out a hand to silence the excited officer, permitting Lavalle to proceed with due gravity.

"We were asking ourselves what this is all about. Now we know."

Knocke rose to his feet, his need to be professional overcoming his present weakness.

"This is from SHAEF, the Allied headquarters, addressed to all units. What it roughly says is this. At 0530hrs, units of the Soviet Army, Air Force and Navy, launched mass attacks throughout Germany and Austria... and in the Baltic and North Seas. We are now at war with the Soviet Union."

In a Château filled with the freshly slain dead of both sides, the information seemed, at first, superfluous. Nevertheless, in the thoughtful silence that followed, all those present realised that here was just the start. Some of the minds present also worked the issue that someone on the other side had known of the colloquies and felt them important enough to target in a first wave attack. Two minds present suddenly wrestled with the prospect of fighting an old adversary once more. The same two minds then wondered how that would be politically accomplished.

Knocke broke the silence. As was his habit, he pulled his tunic into perfect place and moved his hand to pull out his side cap, suddenly remembering that it had been lost.

"I must see to my men. If you will excuse me, General De Walle?"

Saluting, Knocke left the room with a firmness of step that he ordered himself to find, suppressing the feelings of nausea that arose when he started to move.

"I meant to ask him what happened to Anne-Marie. Damn it."

Von Arnesen spoke with the authority and knowledge of a man who was there.

"He saved her life, Herr General. Threw himself on top of her to protect her from a grenade."

371

"Go on, Monsieur."

"She got some shrapnel in her shoulder and arm, nothing bad, just superficial, I think, but I'm no expert, Sir."

"And Herr Knocke? He seems unwounded."

"These things happen in war, as you will know. By rights, he should be dead, but not one fragment struck him, except for a lump taken out of the heel of his boot, that is. What you see now is the blast effect. It will pass, Herr General."

Major Marion Crisp strolled in, his uniform in good order, very little outward sign of the recent combat, until he opened his mouth.

His hearing damaged, he spoke, as he felt, in reasonable volume, whereas he shouted loudly.

The comedy of it was not wasted on the French officers and they took in it good heart. As the only American combat soldier present, Crisp had little by way of official duties, so had taken it upon himself to pick the remaining commandos up and get them back on the horse. His volume and pidgin French had both helped ease tensions with the French troopers and they were further lifted when it became clear that Dubois had survived the attack, with nothing more than a messy but relatively minor wound and the mother of all headaches.

Crisp concluded his report and the hall echoed with his words for a few seconds.

De Walle shouted his thanks back and indicated the jugs of water, placed there by the surviving orderly, to quench thirsts and drive away the dust of battle.

Exchanging nods with Von Arnesen, the American Major drank his fill.

The next man in had not been spared the signs of battle, despite a valiant attempt to pass the day off as any other.

Major Ramsey had two black eyes and there was nothing he could do to overcome that. His efforts to make his uniform presentable had failed and his spare uniform was elsewhere in the Château, somewhat charred. Noble efforts to remove the bloodstains from the tunic he wore had proven to be fruitless.

All in all, the normally smart Black Watch officer looked a total wreck, something that caused him more angst than it did those around him.

Forgetting himself, Crisp laughed.

"I take it the other fellah doesn't look so good either, John?"

"A fair statement, Major Crisp," using his reply to remind the American that they were no longer in relaxed company, a subtlety that Crisp missed completely.

"How's Cam?"

"Lieutenant Colonel Prentiss is in the hospital. He'll be fine, but I warrant he won't be comfortable sitting down for some weeks to come."

Ramsey gently tapped his own buttock and this time Crisp got the message, nodding and holding out a beaker of water to Ramsey.

"On the house, Major Ramsey."

"Thank you, Major Crisp."

Ernst-August Knocke had lost close comrades that day, men with whom he had endured the indescribable horrors of battle.

The awfulness of Olbricht's death.

Schmidt's corpse burnt almost beyond recognition, but not quite.

But as he went to the commando barracks to visit his men, in truth, all the men, it was the sight of the slaughtered Russians that moved him the most.

Disbelief.

Fury.

'This is not war!'

Something washed over the German, calming him, his anger abating as quickly as it had arisen.

Compassion.

Ernst-August Knocke, Waffen-SS soldier par excellence, enemy feared by every nation who fought him, moved silently amongst the dead men. As he moved, he recited something his cousin and best friend David had taught him,

373

long ago, in beautiful Königsburg. That was at a time when such non-aryan relationships were not frowned on and boys could simply be boys, in a happy time when the learning of such a text earned him a treat from Great Uncle Herr Doktor Jakob Steyn.

As he closed eyes and rearranged limbs, bringing peace to those who perished so violently, he spoke in his native German language, words that would never have passed his lips in the previous years.

"May his great name be exalted," a pistol still gripped in the hand of the dead boy, cocked and loaded, was retrieved and made safe, "And sanctified in the world which he created," and two young paratroopers, entwined in death, were separated and laid more easily.

"According to his will. May he establish his kingdom," a weathered and pock-marked face twisted in horror and pain was gently covered with a napkin from Knocke's pocket, "And may his Salvation blossom and His anointed be near," the next man's staring eyes were gently closed and his gaping mouth brought to a more comfortable position, restoring some dignity to the violated corpse.

Haefeli emerged from the ramp behind Knocke and halted, aware that a number of his men had stopped their work to watch a truly indescribable moment.

"During your lifetime," a blade reverently slid out from a chest and splayed arms brought to a position of repose, "And during your days, and during the lifetimes of all the House of Israel," this time three Soviet soldiers had rolled themselves tightly together and needed a more physical act of separation. Knocke looked up at the owner of the hands that helped, seeing Haefeli working with great tenderness.

He started Kaddish again.

"Speedily and very soon," the three were separated and laid out side by side, another legionnaire arriving and gently easing the last body into order.

"And say Amen," Knocke concluded.

"Amen" both Legionnaires spoke aloud before continuing.

374

"May his great name be blessed forever," Knocke looked confused at the two soldiers, who joined him in his prayer, voices firm, but soft.

"And to all eternity. Blessed and praised," they stood back as their work was being taken up by other legionnaires.

"Glorified and exalted, extolled and honoured, adored and lauded," the three men exchanged firm looks as they spoke in unison, the black German panzer uniform flanked by the olive green American kit of the Légion Étrangère.

"Be the name of the Holy one, blessed be he above and beyond all the blessings," Anne-Marie de Valois stopped instantly as she entered the courtyard, sensing the atmosphere, the crisp white sling on her arm catching the attention of her saviour.

Knocke nodded to the formidable agent, which nod was returned, accompanied unbidden by the genuine smile of a woman who knew she was witnessing something special from someone special.

"Hymns, praises and consolations that are uttered in the world," the three men's heads bowed as one.

"And say amen."

Every man, every throat in the courtyard, or looking on from the battlements, gave voice to end the Kaddish prayer.

"Amen."

The silence was perfect and heavy with symbolism.

Haefeli finally broke it.

"One day, Colonel Knocke. One day, I hope to sit down with you and listen to the story of what just happened here, if you will permit me to share it."

Knocke smiled disarmingly.

"One day, Maior Haefeli." Knocke turned to acknowledge the other man, an old legion caporal whose eyes were moist, the wonderful moment still working within him.

"Sir," the NCO cleared his throat to try to speak without emotion. He failed. "My name is Yitzhak Rubenstein and I am German and you, Sir, are a mentsch."

Ernst could do no more than pat the man on the shoulder and nod. No further words were necessary.

375

Bringing himself back to the moment and the purpose of his excursion into the lower Château, Knocke went to salute and curtailed his action, again conscious of his lack of headwear.

Removing his kepi, Haefeli extended it to Knocke.

"If you would so honour me, Colonel."

Hesitating for a moment, Knocke understood what a precious accolade the Swiss Officer was giving him.

"It will be my honour, Maior Haefeli. Thank you."

A dark blue officer's kepi of the 2e Regiment D'Infanterie, Légion Étrangère sat on the head of a man wearing the black panzer uniform and medals of the defeated German Reich. Those who examined the combination closely found it very much to their liking.

The Swiss grinned from ear to ear.

"It suits you, Colonel."

"I believe it does, Herr Maior!"

The smile was returned, along with a formal salute and, with a last glance at the Russian corpses, Knocke moved off to the field hospital to check up on the wounded.

Suddenly weary, Haefeli closed his eyes and raised his face to the sky, feeling the warmth upon his face, but could not enjoy it, for he knew that the sun, bright and strong in the early morning, was casting its rays on a very different world.

"Of all the branches of men in the forces there is none which shows more devotion and faces grimmer perils than the submariners."

Sir Winston S. Churchill

Chapter 39 – THE BALTIC

Traditional Naval Monday toast - "'To Our Ships at Sea"

0521hrs Monday, 6th August 1945, Aboard ShCh-307, Baltic Sea, 20kms East-South-East of Gedser Point, Lolland, Denmark.

Some time previously, a Soviet built Shchuka-class submarine, sweeping well ahead of a Soviet convoy transporting invasion troops to Denmark, had picked up indications of vessels gliding gently through the cold Baltic waters. The detection apparatus indicated that the sounds were fast screw warships and when Captain Third Rank Mikhail Kalinin took a swift look through his attack periscope, he was delighted to discover that there had been sufficient moonlight for him to identify the silhouettes.

Ceding the periscope to his First Officer, they agreed that the larger ships were the two British Cruisers they were informed of, one of the heavy County class and a light cruiser, probably Dido class.

Around them fussed four destroyers and they were preceded by what were probably a pair of minesweepers.

Kalinin was a successful Captain, already sporting the Red Star, so he quietly and calmly manoeuvred his submarine into firing position. Taking occasional snatched looks through his periscope, he was conscious of the need for restraint until the allotted time, but also very aware of the damage these cruisers could cause if they got in amongst his charges in such confined waters.

As the chronometer crept slowly towards 0530hrs, Kalinin maintained his firing solution, constantly updating with new headings and readings as the warships drove forward.

Inside, he was increasingly concerned, especially when the enemy group all increased speed. Perhaps, he agonised, the British radar operators had recognised the approaching invasion group for what it was, not the friendly naval flotilla with whom they had been invited to conduct exercises for the day, prior to putting into Rostock the night, to enjoy some comradely fraternisation. However, despite his own inner tensions, his outer calmness spread through his crew and settled all nerves.

All torpedo tube doors were already open, awaiting the order to fire.

A final solution adjustment, a snatched look through his periscope and he made a last check of the hour. Judging that running time would take any strike past the appointed hour, he ordered all four bow tubes fired. The First officer discharged his duty and ShCh-307 shuddered as each tube was emptied in turn.

Kalinin then ordered a dive to the bottom, some thirty metres down, to try to evade any prosecution by the escorts and to reload. Unfortunately for him and his craft, there was no good depth available to hide in here, like much of the Baltic.

Further orders were dispatched, encouraging the forward compartment crew to make the reload time the best yet.

As they headed deeper, the sonar operator reported other sounds of torpedoes fired nearby. Submarine K-56 had added to the impressive amount of high explosive that was running hot in the cold Baltic.

He sat down on the small commanders' perch and started to hum the 1812 Overture, loud enough that all in the control room could hear, eyes closed, dramatically building in volume on his way to the climax of the piece. This was his routine and undoubtedly, the crew always drew strength from it.

The Petty Officer Quartermaster with the stopwatch had made his calculations and was counting down the seconds.

He indicated first strike time passed, but no sound of an explosion echoed through the waters.

The humming continued.

378

Again, he counted down and on reaching two, all ears were greeted with a distant rumble and Kalinin's musical interlude was complemented with the sound of the explosion.

Cheers were quickly silenced and the count went on.

Four more hits were heard, two of which could not possibly have been ShCh-307's torpedoes, unless an escort had run foul of one of the weapons. Kalinin correctly deduced that K-56 had also scored.

Water is capable of transmitting sound over great distances and the sound of tortured metal is unmistakable to the submariners.

They could hear a ship dying, almost screaming like a wounded animal in its death throes.

A sudden huge explosion was heard, causing some of the less steadfast crew to squeal with fright.

Kalinin nodded to himself, devoid of any emotion, even though he had probably just killed hundreds of unsuspecting sailors.

He looked at the chronometer and reasoned that, after all, it was now war.

Messages of alarm flashed out from the escorting destroyers and HMS Dido as torpedoes struck home. There were actually seven destructive hits, which given the normal accuracy of Soviet torpedoes, or more importantly their inability to explode, was an unbelievable return as far as Kalinin was concerned. He did not realise that ShCh-303 had also joined the fight.

Above the water, all was blood, fire and chaos.

HMS Devonshire was gone.

Three of Kalinin's torpedoes had struck her starboard side, but by the fickle fortunes of war, it was one of those fired by K-56 which blew her up, striking precisely where the first of Kalinin's weapons had hit and already caused damage, penetrating deep inside the stricken vessel and instantly exploding her 'B' Turret magazine.

379

Seven hundred and eighty-one officers and men perished within seconds as the ship erupted and sank immediately.

HMS Dido was dying and already down in the water. She had taken two hits, one port, one starboard, diametrically opposite each other, between 'A' and 'B' turrets and her bow was already misaligned, nearly removed by the power of the explosions. Trapped within her jammed distorted front turrets men died, incinerated by the gathering inferno.

Two other torpedoes had ripped into her port side vitals and the large engineering spaces were already flooding.

Elsewhere on the stricken ship, the casualties were mercifully light. Her Captain, smashed and dying, gave the dreaded order and her crew moved quickly to escape the rapidly sinking vessel. Only three more men of her complement perished, two who were killed when other escapers dropped on top them in the water below the rising stern and the Captain, who observed naval traditions and stayed with his charge all the way to the bottom of the Baltic.

A few miles away, Kalinin was solely interested in self-preservation, as angry escorts commenced their search for the underwater killers. They did not come near the silent submarine, but instead started to prosecute other contacts to Kalinin's north and northeast. Their misfortune spelt continued existence for ShCh-307 and her frightened occupants.

Twenty minutes later, smashed by depth charges, K-56 and her sixty-five crew joined Devonshire and Dido on the bottom of the Baltic.

A short time after they were all joined by ShCh-303, struck down by a hedgehog anti-submarine bomb cluster as she drew her pursuers away from the invasion force. Her stern tubes had destroyed the bow of the Polish destroyer Piorun, which, despite supreme efforts at damage control, would become the last vessel sunk in the action that morning.

Some twenty-three days beforehand, four recently arrived submarines of the Soviet Baltic Fleet had quietly slid from their moorings in Gdańsk and disappeared beneath the waves, carrying the offensive hopes of the Soviet Navy. The crews had benefited from a few weeks of intensive training in their strange new craft, before being sent far away on their respective missions. The submarines also contained some German technical experts, who were less than happy to be press ganged into going on combat missions with the Soviet Navy.

The crew worked hard to learn how to properly handle the sleek thoroughbreds they had so recently 'inherited' and the unhappy Germans quickly reasoned that their prospects of survival were decidedly dependent on the newly acquired skills of their Russian 'colleagues'. They strove hard to ensure their Soviet pupils were the best that they could be.

Each pair of submarines was accompanied by two surface ships, one a minesweeper, the other a destroyer, whose jobs were to exactly mirror the movements of the submarines, to ensure little chance of detection, provide minesweeping capability and to overtly travel into the North Sea on their way to goodwill visits in faraway places.

To the experienced eye, the minesweepers and destroyers were not of Soviet design, but of American origin.

The former were small Admirable class vessels, being the T-112, ex-USS Agent and the T-116, ex-USS Arcade respectively. Both carried mines hidden below decks, but only those who knew what to look for would have wondered about the new openings towards the stern of both vessels. The latter were both old American WW-I vintage flush-deckers, subsequently British 'Town class' destroyers, worn out in the service of the Royal Navy under the lend-lease scheme and then sent onto the Soviet Union for further use.

The first of these, Doblestnyj, in its previous service known as HMS Roxborough, had orders to visit France, making landfall at Cherbourg and then to steam to Portugal to take the well-wishes of the Soviet People to the Iberian peninsula.

The second, Zguchij, formerly HMS Leamington, was tasked to make a brief stopover in Londonderry then sail on to New York.

These venerable vessels were employed on the expectation that they were so old and that allied naval personnel would be so familiar with them, that they would brook little attention or investigation and that sightseers would feel uninspired by their appearance.

They were also expendable.

Both 'Townies' had been modified by the Soviets in line with an idea by the British Navy used on other ships, removing torpedo tubes, one boiler room and two of the four smoke stacks in favour of cargo stowage. A sensible measure for England at a time when every piece of cargo landed kept the country alive and the U-Boats were more interested in sinking merchant vessels. Now the two destroyers carried the consumables of undersea warfare. Fuel oil, mines, battery sets, spare parts, engineering repair equipment and torpedoes, torpedoes, torpedoes.

The Allied Naval Authorities had been approached and accepted the proposed cordial visits between allies, even providing up to date information on possible drifting mine locations and promising a warm welcome.

The real Soviet plan was to clandestinely land the stores and personnel, establishing secret supply facilities to keep the submarines operational for as long as possible.

Doblestnyj was to use the dark of night to stock a covert base in an inlet on the south side of Renonquet Island, near Alderney, safe from prying eyes on an uninhabited shore.

Zguchij, using contacts born and bred before the start of WW2, was to meet with supporters from the Irish Republican Army and establish another site in a sheltered bay, just north of the isolated village of Glenlara, Éire. The IRA would ensure the security of the site and keep snoopers at bay.

The ship would then sail, with T-116, to the Americas. Fuel for the submarines destined for American shores was less of a problem, with Soviet agents in place to provide support.

However, a place to create a suitable clandestine supply site on the East Coast had not yet been established and the agents in place searched on.

Doblestnyj, with T-112, would sail on south from the Channel islands, after doing her brief flag-waving duties in

382

France. Both would leave some mines behind outside the French harbour and then sail to a bay north-west of Malpica on the north coast of Spain, clandestinely creating another site similar to Glenlara, this time set-up and policed by communists sympathisers, staunch veterans of the Spanish Civil War. Both vessels would then proceed to Portugal, where it was expected they would be interned when the war started.

Zguchij carried the engineers and service personnel who would maintain the secret bases, roughly the same numbers as were aboard Doblestnyj, but she also carried extra submarine crew. The IRA were so sure that they could provide a secure site that the Soviet planning even allowed for crew rest and substitutions, so that time on shore was available to sailors in facilities created by the Irish dissidents, which was hoped would ensure more time for the submarines to be at sea sinking allied tonnage.

Doblestnyj's subtle difference in cargo was a small group of dangerous men, who were to slip ashore near Malpica and make their way into the heart of Spain for a mission of extreme vengeance, close to Beria's heart.

T-112's Captain, Senior Lieutenant Vladimirov, had further orders known only to himself, but he doubted he would be able to proceed with them, as Gibraltar was such a long way and the time margins were thin.

Submarines B-27 and B-30, preceded by their surface consorts, swept through the Danish narrows and out into the North Sea. Both were intent on heading north between England and Norway, schnorkelling all the way to their operational assignment off the east coast of America, independent of their surface friends once open deep water was under their keel. Each also carried eight men to be put ashore on the continent of America itself, each group of four agents tasked with their own secret and important contributions to the Soviet drive.

The other two, B-28 and B-29, followed a similar route, six hours behind, but journeyed around the British Isles to position themselves on the approaches to the French ports.

The expectation was for two more submarines to join them in the coming weeks, once they had been passed fit for service.

All six were former Type XXI U-Boats, the so-called 'ElektroBootes'. The four now at sea had been handed over by the Western Allies under the Yalta Agreements and the latter two were amongst those found in the shipping construction yards during the liberation of Danzig, as Gdańsk had been known formerly, both vessels in an almost seaworthy condition. Even in March 1945, it seemed Germany could still produce quality weapons of war.

Each submarine could cruise underwater for days at a time, recharging its batteries via a schnorkel. They carried twenty-three torpedoes and housed up to sixty crewmembers. They were the very peak of submarine development, potentially mass ship killers with excellent survivability prospects and had the Germans put their keels and those of their sister ships in the water two years earlier, the impact of these sleek and efficient killing machines would have been immense and could have changed the course of the western war.

It was the Soviet Navy's hope that they would get the chance to show exactly what the XXI's could do, interrupting the flow of men and supplies that would inevitably come from America when the attack came and the reinforcements sailed for Europe.

Cry havoc and let slip the dogs of war.

William Shakespeare

Chapter 40 – THE ATTACK

<u>0522hrs Monday, 6th August 1945, Headquarters of Red Banner Forces of Soviet Europe, Schloss Schönefeld, Leipzig.</u>

In the Schloss' salon, which he had taken as his personal office, Marshal Georgi Zhukov, Commander of the Red Banner Forces of Soviet Europe, sat in quiet conversation with his Chief-of-Staff, Colonel General Mikhail Malinin. The planning was long over, the orders all sent, so the only real business they could attend to was to hurry up and wait, which was ever the lot of those who were sending men to their deaths.

Occasionally, a messenger would knock and enter with some piece of information for his attention, but orders prohibiting anything other than routine communications traffic meant he was little disturbed. All the usual messages would continue to be sent through Soviet-occupied Europe, so that all appeared normal, but no increase in volume of traffic was acceptable. Nothing was to warn the Allies of the impending storm.

One 'normal' report to fall beneath their gaze had been that referring to the Planá crash of a Li-2 transport aircraft and the death of a Lieutenant Colonel Potakov. Both men knew he was assigned to Zilant-4 and the loss was severe indeed, but both men were also comfortable that Makarenko's presence would ensure the success of the mission. In any case, the Zilant missions were not a priority for them, having been thrust upon them by the hierarchy. The greater shame was that the new requirement had meant the loss of 100th Guards as a valuable airborne reserve force.

Zhukov did not have the luxury of tobacco to fall back on to steady his nervousness; neither did he wish for alcohol by way of substitute. Instead, his orderly kept Malinin and he supplied with a steady stream of coffee, served strong and sweet.

As the young woman poured yet another cup for each, there was a knock at the door. Both men looked at each other, for the sound held something more urgent and promising than those that had preceded it.

Their eyes were then drawn to the French Ormolu mantle clock, whose insistent ticking both had found calming during hours of planning and discussion.

0526 hrs.

Malinin looked back at his Commander and shrugged slightly. They had always known that it was likely that some timing would go awry.

On invite, the door opened and an immaculate staff-Major entered, his face beaming with success.

The message form he passed to Zhukov was exquisitely simple and yet spoke volumes to the Marshal.

'Message sent in clear – Volga, Borodin 5'

This message indicated that the paratrooper unit codenamed Volga sent to attack the headquarters of British 21st Army Group had been successful. Borodin equated to Field-Marshal Montgomery and the code 5 indicated he had been liquidated.

Whilst Zhukov was not overly concerned with Montgomery's limited skills as a commander, he welcomed the confusion and disruption the death would bring to the British, Free and Commonwealth forces.

In actual fact, the report was at error and Montgomery was not dead, but he was severely wounded. However, the net effect was the same and 21st Army Group was temporarily leaderless.

"Very well, Major Yassin. We will move to the operations room now."

Zhukov and Malinin walked briskly from the salon as the clock moved remorselessly to 0530.

0531hrs Monday, 6th August 1945, Sterninghofen Bridge, US Occupied Lower Austria.

The message sent by General Clark had reached many ears in the all too short time between its sending and the Soviet attack. Unfortunately, some ears remained deaf to its message and many a young allied soldier died at his post for no other reason than his superior did not believe the report, or refused to act in a precipitous fashion.

Along the European divide, allied soldiers tumbled from their slumber as the Soviet attack rolled in close, often not preceded by artillery, in order to permit the infantry to get close without warning. Once contact ensued, then Soviet artillery was mainly used on rear-line and artillery positions.

Nothing the allied soldiers had experienced in their war with the Germans had prepared them for the intensity and ferocity of what the Soviet artillery could bring down upon them.

In some areas, American and British tanks received under the lend-lease scheme and marked up appropriately, led the Soviet advance, in an attempt to get through the first-line and onto an important second or rear-line location.

The tanks that had been seen by Uhlmann and Braun in the Persenbeug sidings were M-10 Tank Destroyers, marked as 1st US Armored Division, but which were actually crewed by experienced tankers from a company of 63rd Cavalry Division, 5th Guards Cavalry Corps.

They ground down the road from their staging area, west of Seitenstetten, heading west on the road to Steyr with all lights blazing and American-speaking personnel to talk their way through any roadblocks.

At the Sterninghofen Bridge over the Enns River, their self-propelled guns were waved through a checkpoint manned by American soldiers of 305th Combat Engineer Battalion, 80th US Infantry Division. Four Studebaker 6x6 trucks followed closely.

With perfect timing, the sky lit up as Soviet artillery commenced firing at its targets elsewhere. All awake American eyes were drawn to the display and none noticed the four trucks disgorge their malicious contents.

The assignment of this ill-fated platoon of the 305th had been to destroy the bridge, on receipt of orders, or under the initiative of the Officer in charge, as necessary.

That same Officer in charge was slumbering in his tent oblivious and only woke up briefly as a strong hand clamped over his mouth and a blade ripped his throat open.

As the tanks took up their defensive positions, the Soviet Cossacks moved swiftly on foot through the area, dispatching the sleeping men in a wide variety of ways whose only common factor was silence. The sound of artillery was now rousing the slumberers, but none offered any resistance and all were butchered where they lay.

Private First class Jan F. Podolski, one of the sentries on the prowl, had disappeared for a call of nature and so was missed by the systematic destruction of the engineer platoon. Emerging from behind a thick bush, he saw swiftly moving silent shapes.

Despite his youth and lack of experience, he immediately grasped what was going on and pulled his weapon off his shoulder. With remarkably steady hands, he took rough aim at the nearest figure, which was crouched down, back towards him. Podolski got off an eight round clip from his Garand before he was cut down by a hail of bullets from PPSH sub-machine guns. He had dropped Yefreytor Alexey Passov to the ground, where he bled his life out quickly, shot through the neck, groin and thigh.

Both were only nineteen years of age.

In the perverse way that history does these things, the 80th US Infantry Division had been credited with firing the final shots of the Second World War in Europe and it had now probably fired the first shots of the new ground war.

The bridge was inspected for explosive and the experienced Captain in charge ordered a second and third inspection before he accepted that none had been laid.

The discovery of a cache of explosives in the rear of one of the American trucks evidenced the omission.

With the bridge intact, the follow-up forces of 32nd Rifle Corps and 220th Independent Tank Brigade could drive straight into and through Steyr.

All along the thin lines, the Soviet forces broke through, sometimes with no resistance, other times, fiercely contested.

Advances were made on every assault, of which there were a total of twenty-one independent main attacks, from Sterninghofen in the south to Selmsdorf on the Baltic.

The Soviet plan departed from their standard tactics by utilising a general assault plan throughout Europe. Zhukov and his staff reasoned that the Allied soldiers would not be ready and that very little organised resistance would be found initially, so a broad front approach should yield more territory and offer the more opportunity for substantial penetrations at first.

The low opinion that the Soviet Military had for the Allies had translated into a rough expectation of about one week before any real organised counter-attacks came their way.

By that time, the picture should have developed more clearly and the large forces held in reserve would be employed to make the drives on their main targets through areas of weakness.

The Rhine beckoned to the Soviets as much as it had done to the Allies coming from the other direction a year before and so Soviet planning for the first phase of the assault expected a large drive on the Rhine, via the Ruhr and also via Frankfurt and on into Luxembourg and Saarland. Two major targets were the port city of Hamburg and nearby Bremen and, to a lesser extent, Cuxhaven. Of particular interest was the ability to operate submarines to interdict allied supply routes, much as the Germans had done in the preceding years and both Hamburg and Bremen has bunkers suitable for the task.

Soviet planning also required the destruction, or at minimum, negation, of the Allied fighter and ground attack capability throughout Europe so, from the beginning, artillery, saboteurs and aircraft, were fulfilling this element of the planning, in line with the requirements of Operation Kurgan, albeit with mixed results.

A six man observation force was landed clandestinely, from a Beriev MP1 seaplane, on Saltholm Island in the Oresund, sovereign territory of Denmark, tasked to observe shipping movement. The small group of naval specialists were concealed on the southern edge of the island, away from the farming community of Barakkebro to the north-west end.

Soviet naval vessels stood ready to converge on any allied naval force attempting to enter the Baltic.

Elements of the Baltic Fleet landed large Soviet forces on the islands of Lolland and Falster, also Danish territory, supporting the landings with ship's gunfire.

As soon as bridgeheads were established, auxiliary vessels began to unload heavy artillery pieces, that were to be sited to cover shipping routes around the island.

Aircraft flew in and established a fighter base at Marthasminde on Lolland and a combined bomber and fighter base at a larger field near Rødby. Ingenious use of the Sydmotorvejen road, running north from its junction with the Ringsebøllevej, adjacent to Rødby, permitted operations by 571st Assault Aviation Regiment, recently equipped with the new IL-10 ground attack aircraft. Three Tupolev TU-2t torpedo bombers, specially enhanced for maritime reconnaissance, completed the allocation on Lolland.

On Falster, a similar provision had been found on the Gedser Landveg road, angling north from the village of Gedesby and more aircraft arrived, this time IL-4 torpedo bombers of Soviet Naval Aviation. In fact, the Soviets had learned a great deal from the Luftwaffe's use of roads as airfields and had hidden air regiments the length and breadth of Europe in such a manner. All the better to evade any air raids by the Western Allies.

A smaller force, similarly equipped and tasked, landed simultaneously on the island of Mon. Fighters flew into Kostervig to complete the defence.

To all intents and purposes, the Baltic was closed and the Northern shores of Germany secure from interference.

To the south of the Austrian attacks, all would remain quiet for now. It had not been thought prudent for security to advise the Yugoslavs of their plans. Sometime after the first

Soviet units rolled forward into the attack, Russian liaison officers were being unceremoniously woken and virtually interrogated by their Yugoslavian allies, keen to understand what was happening and why they had not been informed. The delay also suited the Soviets as the Allies could not afford to ignore the large field forces of the Yugoslavian Army and their existence pinned numerous high quality allied divisions in place, divisions that could make a difference elsewhere.

GRU's report, endorsed by Pekunin, guaranteed that once Tito was onside, then the plan existed to carry Soviet and Yugoslavian forces into Northern Italy to the Mediterranean and beyond.

A high-level Soviet delegation, led by Deputy Minister of Foreign Affairs Andrey Vyshinski, was already on its way to Belgrade to seek cooperation and support in the coming months. The GRU report also indicated that the omission of Yugoslav forces from the planning and conception of the operation would be easily explained away by operational security needs and no harm would be done.

The first hitch in the Soviet planning occurred later that same morning. During the high-level meeting, Vyshinski was told, in no uncertain terms, that his Yugoslavian Communist Allies took an extremely jaundiced view of their exclusion from planning, or even being able to offer their views on this, as Tito put it, *'fucking lunacy'*.

There would be no Yugoslavian contribution to military matters.

Using extremely earthy language, Tito let Vyshinski know that the Soviets should be eternally grateful that the Yugoslav Army would stand its ground and remain a problem to affect Allied thinking. None the less, Soviet units were banned from overflying or setting foot on Yugoslavian soil until further notice.

The senior GRU officer previously attached to Tito's headquarters, accompanied the party back to Moscow under escort, where his report assuring his seniors of Tito's compliance was examined at painful length, before he succumbed in the cellars of the Lubyanka.

The great defence against the air menace is to attack the enemy's aircraft as near as possible to their point of departure.

Sir Winston S. Churchill

CHAPTER 41 – THE PILOT

0535hrs Monday, 6th August 1945, 182 Squadron, RAF, Rheine Airfield, Germany.

Andrew McKenzie had been in short trousers when Hitler's legions rolled across the Polish border. Admittedly, that was because the family had little by the way of spare cash, for his parents ploughed their money into the education of their three sons. His father and mother worked hard, long hours away from home, or taking in washing and sewing. Even though the Canadian education system was good, extra books and tuition went a long way towards their goal of giving the three apples of their eyes the best possible start in life and an opportunity to escape the poverty trap that had ensnared the parents.

From such a impoverished background sprang Mackenzie, a fresh-faced gangly Canadian youth of nineteen, who arrived in Europe with the rank of Pilot Officer and wings earned in basic training, when he had passed out top of his course by some notable distance.

Conversion to the brutish Hawker Typhoon followed and he arrived at 182 Squadron's RAF base nearby the German town of Rheine, eager to get to grips with the enemy. That he arrived on the evening of 6th May 1945 was, for him, a personal disaster that he felt nothing could ever overcome.

XM-F, his aircraft, was the latest refinement, with a four-bladed propeller and Sabre IIc engine. A fine weapon to take to war to be sure and he had managed one operational take-off, that following morning, but the mission was aborted and he returned having never fired his weapons in anger, touching down as peace descended over Europe once more.

For some time now, he had been the subject of much ribbing by his comrades, partially about his lack of combat experience, partially because he moved with the grace of the proverbial bull in a china shop and partially because he was blessed with a shaggy mass of ginger hair that defied all attempts to control it. It was all good-natured, because his seasoned comrades realised that in Andy McKenzie they were in the presence of a true phenomenon; a natural born flier, who could make the Typhoon do things they all considered unnatural at best and bordering on witchcraft according to the older lags.

His Flight Lieutenant, Johnny Hall, had woken him and the rest of the quarters with little ceremony some time previously, agitated beyond measure, ordering all to the briefing room.

182 Squadron had been alerted by the ripples of response to General Clark's message and was breaking out of its slumber to find a very different day developing around it.

As aircraft were prepared, the RAF Regiment personnel guarding the base readied themselves, not wholly aware of the circumstances surrounding their abrupt early morning reverie, but understanding enough to believe that something big was happening elsewhere.

In the early morning half-light, one patrolling section saw and challenged four men near one of the perimeter fuel storage bunkers and were brought under fire.

The nearby sound of automatic weapons gave urgency to the ground crews and it was not long before McKenzie and five others clawed their way into the developing morning, heading towards the headquarters of 21st Army Group at Bad Oeynhausen, from where frantic calls for help originated.

Behind them, one RAF Regiment Corporal and two German black marketers lay dead, their attempt to steal fuel terminated by the unexpected early morning mobilisation of base security personnel. The other two, wounded and bleeding, lay on the ground, at great risk from retribution, for the dead Corporal had been a very popular man.

No-one will know if they would have suffered at the hands of the irate RAF soldiers, for the entire group disappeared in a fireball of exploding aviation fuel, as the first of four Soviet manned P-39 D-2 Aircobras, devoid of any

393

national markings, swept over the field. The aircraft dropped five hundred pound bombs from home built fuselage-mounted racks, copied from American originals, aiming to crater the runway,, before going about the business of destroying the then stranded aircraft below.

The first bomb skipped off the runway and ploughed on through the controllers van, killing all inside, terminating in the fuel storage bunker where it finally decided to function as it was designed. Everyone for eighty yards in all directions died in an instant.

Bombs two and three hit the runway and created deep craters, scattering stone and earth in all directions, but did not deny its use.

Number four's bomb refused to drop and so the aircraft banked around for a second attempt to release the weapon. It stubbornly refused to go its own way, despite the pilot skilfully jinking the aircraft.

A 40mm Bofors gun on the edge of the strip started to hammer out its defiance, but the well-trained and experienced Soviet pilots soon silenced it. Other guns joined the defence, but the Aircobras worked over the field expertly, destroying aircraft at will, concentrating on anyone attempting to take off.

Parked on the western edge of the field, even the two defunct Me262's perished, curiosities retained for fun by the RAF base personnel, relics from the airfields Luftwaffe usage by Kampfgeschwader 51. The four aircraft retired after seven minutes of intense action that left the field cratered, fuel storage facilities wrecked, buildings burning and every aircraft smashed beyond repair. Casualties amongst the ground crew and flight personnel were severe.

Only a single hit had been inflicted on the attacking Soviets machines.

0559hrs Monday, 6th August 1945, 182 Squadron RAF, airborne over Bad Oeynhausen, Germany.

Circling at low level over the Bad Oeynhausen Headquarters, the Typhoon pilots of 182 heard nothing of the drama at their airfield, as Rheine's means of communication

394

had been smashed by the Aircobras attentions. Neither were they aware of the other numerous similar dramas being played out on RAF and USAAF airfields all over Europe.

Below them, they had all the drama they could cope with. Smoke and flames belched from the Hotel Konigshof, a former Gestapo HQ, now 21st Army Group Command building, the telltale flashes of heavy ground firing most evident.

On the ground, one quick-witted RAF liaison officer had grabbed a radio and worked his way through his frequency book, trying to find some way of communicating with the aircraft above him. He could see what they could not, which was a body of enemy troops retreating under the cover of the smoke, heading north for the forest.

A number of the locations he tried would never answer, struck down by either commando attacks or aircraft bombs. He was unable to raise Rheinbaden, the location of the headquarters of the British Air Forces of Occupation, formerly 2nd Tactical Air Force RAF and suspected, as was the case, that similar events had transpired there. US 9th Air Force headquarters in Wiesbaden had suffered the worst of all.

He managed to get through to an RAF controller in Bielefeld, who was able to establish contact with the circling typhoons and, after a few moments, connected the two.

Giving calm and precise instructions, the young Squadron Leader organised a strike on the retreating Soviet paratroopers, ignoring the pain caused by the grenade wounds in both legs. Wooden splinters, from what had once been chairs and tables, protruded from his flesh, like a myriad of porcupine quills.

Three of the Typhoons swept down, unloading their RP-3 rockets as directed, along the west side of the River Weser, slaughtering the retreating men in the gruesome ways that only sixty pounds of high explosive can manage. Pausing only to let the smoke from their ordnance clear, the three swept back down to low level and began to mercilessly grind up the survivors with their 20mm cannon.

Having taken heavy casualties during their assault on the Konigshof, these elite Russian paratroopers could take little of this kind of butchery and they scattered, discipline gone, not returning fire, just in an all out attempt to find personal safety and to hell with everyone else.

As the British infantry pursued them, they initially rarely took prisoners, killing without mercy, in the main. Soon, they became more and more horrified at the detritus of men that the RAF aircraft had spread around the ground. With their sympathy growing, shocked and dazed Russians were gathered up, almost compassionately, until only the occasional diehard required swift and decisive terminal force applied. Exactly one hundred and forty men had commenced the assault on Montgomery's Headquarters. Twenty-seven remained when the firing stopped, beaten, bloodied, but alive.

0608hrs Monday, 6th August 1945, 182 Squadron RAF, airborne over Bad Oeynhausen, Germany.

Whilst the ground attack section bore in, the remaining three typhoons automatically climbed higher, in order to protect their comrades better. No one knew what was going on yet, but it did not take a genius to work out that a shooting war had started, deliberately or not.

Flying in perfect formation, McKenzie fumed as he stole glances at the three tiffies attacking below him.

As the formation commenced a turn, something caught his eye and he focussed in on four aircraft skimming along at tree height, heading east and flying over the TeutobergerWald, north of Bad Oeynhausen.

The four American-looking craft seemed to be boring into the attack on his comrades, who were unaware, distracted as they were.

Training took over and the contact sighting was given.

Johnny Hall, the flight leader, immediately organised a dive to the attack and shouted a warning over the radio to the others.

The unidentified aircraft opened fire, a few pieces being visibly knocked off the rearmost Typhoon, but missing their enemies vitals as they had reacted just in time, thanks to the warning from above.

Hall was puzzled. "They're Aircobras. The yanks don't fly Aircobras anymore!"

Williams, the number two chipped in, his broad Scottish twang delivering a succinct response.

"No, but the fucking Russians do, Flight!"

That comment drew a second or two of silence.

"Oh fuck."

That just about said it all and the three Typhoons arrowed in, positioning to attack the Aircobras.

Hall opened fire first, missing badly and then jamming his cannon, pulling away from his attack and cursing for all he was worth.

However, his target Aircobra, Number 4, had dragged itself violently left when the first shells went past the cockpit, forgetting the bomb still attached and the problems that might have been caused by the thud he heard when attacking the airfield. The bomb's weight and its effect on aircraft performance, combined with the undetected damage to the bottom-most rudder hinge, meant that control was suddenly lost when the rudder came apart and the aircraft flipped sideways, condemning plane and pilot to plough into the TeutobergerWald at high speed.

Williams came in second as the surviving Aircobras evaded, going as low as they dared.

Latching onto one enemy plane, he fired three short bursts, but achieved only two shell hits with his 20mm. One hit the tail fin and did only superficial damage, the other hit pilot in the back of the head and decapitated him.

The Aircobra lazily lost height and spread itself through the treetops, pieces of the aircraft raining down like confetti.

The three ground-attack typhoons, organised and marshalled by Hall, from his position above, closed rapidly on the melee.

Turning to fight, the survivors must have known their chances were slim, but they did not lack courage.

Hall gained height again and tried to control the battle as best he could. Williams played chicken with one Russian and both were lucky to avoid collision. The skilful Soviet

397

airman turned his machine in a manoeuvre that defied the textbook and lashed out at Williams from a side angle. Shuddering under impacts, he dragged his aircraft around, feeling the G force build.

Unfortunately, fatal damage had already been done.

The Typhoon had always had a tail section problem, which had sometimes resulted in catastrophic frame failures.

Williams' tiffie had been modified to prevent this from happening, but the modification did not take account of direct hits from heavy machine guns. .50 cal bullets had bitten into the fuselage at the point of the modification and the high G turn finished the job. He didn't have time to scream before his aircraft disintegrated around him.

As Williams died, so did the other Russian.

Hall watched as the young protégé used textbook flying to get into a firing position. In the mess later, Hall claimed that McKenzie fired for about half a second, *'Half a sec, absolute maximum, chaps'*. However long he fired, it proved enough and another Soviet aircraft fatally succumbed to the laws of gravity, diving in an ever-increasing fireball and striking the green field below.

Again, the young pilot pulled his aircraft around and located his last quarry. He guided his aircraft into firing position, vowing revenge for Williams. This enemy pilot was clearly experienced and kept out of the line of fire, side slipping expertly, all the time getting nearer to safety. However, McKenzie was remorseless, Hall would later say *'fucking clinical'*, the young pilot waited for his moment until a single burst of fire ended the action.

Too low to bail out, the dying pilot rode his burning charge into the River Weser.

It was later discovered that eighteen rounds had been fired from each of the Hispano Mk II cannon, representing less than two seconds of finger on button time.

'Bloody Witchcraft' indeed.

The five remaining aircraft gathered themselves and headed back to their base, unaware that all was not how it had been when they left.

On arrival, they landed carefully and went about the business of finding their friends, dead or alive, preparing for the grim work that now, inevitably, lay ahead.

Operation Kurgan had enjoyed large-scale success and the allied air forces had been dealt crippling blows.

"A good run is better than a bad stand"

Irish proverb

CHAPTER 42 – THE COMMANDERS

0545hrs Monday, 6th August 1945, Headquarters, US Forces in Europe. I.G.Farben, Frankfurt-am-Main, Germany.

In the huge building, pandemonium broke out on receipt of Clark's message. Staff and intelligence officers were noisily awoken by subordinates needing orders and as the time elapsed, the higher was the rank of those whose rude awakening kick started the day from hell. Indecision piled on indecision, until someone decided to rouse Eisenhower from his slumbers, which decision was given impetus by the sound of explosions, as a Soviet air attack hammered one of the Frankfurt airbases.

Shaking the sleep from his eyes, the chain-smoking General of the Army lit the first cigarette of the day and started to organise the chaos around him, sending out the warning orders to his and allied commands. Even though he was now technically only responsible for the American zone in Germany, a contingency plan was in place for a reversion to the previous tried and successful SHAEF structure, in case of an emergency, which Eisenhower reasoned this was. He initiated the reversion process immediately.

Visiting his headquarters at the time was Lieutenant-General Sir Richard McCreery. Presently commander of the British Forces in Austria, he and a number of senior Allied officers were staying in Frankfurt overnight, ready for a round of conferences and steering groups that week. Business in a peacetime army is conducted at a different pace and in a different style, which explained why Army and Corps commanders from all the allied nations started to arrive in the main headquarters, hoping to receive that most vital of military requirements; information.

The staff officers started to assimilate reports coming through from commands all over Europe and information started to flow through channels all the way up to the Supreme Commander.

Maps were annotated with information and the observing generals started to appreciate what was going on through the length and breadth of occupied Europe.

Some Army commanders saw what was happening, turned to their subordinates, fired off a few quick orders and sent their corps commanders packing immediately.

Intelligence officers briefed and re-briefed Eisenhower and the Senior Commanders repeatedly, changing estimates and intents as more facts and reports came in.

It was certainly apparent that this was a designed general assault stretching from Denmark to the Alps, with widespread attacks on headquarters, air force and intelligence facilities throughout the occupied lands.

Losses in men and equipment appeared severe and control had, to all intents and purposes, been lost.

It was this that posed Eisenhower his biggest problem, especially as he started to wrestle with it at the same time as the shocking report about Montgomery came in from Bad Oeynhausen.

Eisenhower beckoned McCreery to a quieter corner and the British Cavalry Officer moved to the Americans side, displaying the limp he had acquired during his Great War service, when he had lost toes from his right foot, gained a hole in his leg and the MC on his breast.

"Monty is down, Dick. Not dead, but he's very bad."

McCreery was a professional soldier with an excellent reputation for steadfastness and command ability. He was also a quiet man and he mainly kept his thoughts to himself. He merely breathed deeply and pursed his lips by way of response.

"Can General Winterton handle Austria for us?"

The query was accompanied by eyes probing for truth in the reply.

"Indeed he is capable, Sir. Most competent."

Eisenhower nodded and tossed himself a cigarette from his pack.

401

"In which case, tell him he has Austria under Clarke. Priority is to preserve his forces intact, until we can organise and stop the reds. Keep tied in on his flanks and no holes. Take out his bridges as he goes. Give up nothing he doesn't have to, but keep casualties to a minimum. I stress, preserve his force."

A moment's thought.

"Better tell him we have lost most of our air for now."

Such a simple statement held so much meaning that was bad for the allies.

"I want you to take 21st."

McCreery started to speak, on his way to registering the fact that 21st Army Group was an appointment within the purview of His Majesty's Government.

Eisenhower smiled and stopped him short.

"We will sort out the niceties later. We need a commander in place, right now."

McCreery could not object to that reasoning.

"Same brief for you too."

Turning back to face the hive of activity, Ike gesticulated at the large situation map, already changed since they had moved away from it.

"If I'm any judge, the Reds are after Hamburg in your area. Make sure they don't get it. Hannover looks like it's a main target too. Do not give it up easily, but don't be cut off. No Bastogne's until I know what the heck is going on. They are already behind you in Denmark, but I doubt it is in significant numbers. Get on to that, firm up your Intel everywhere and get back to me, please. I will make sure your headquarters gets all my intelligence as soon as possible"

"And if they split my force at Hamburg? What then, Sir?"

Eisenhower considered that for a moment, lighting another cigarette from the stub of the one he then tossed into a plant stand nearby.

"The loss of Hamburg would be severe indeed, as I see it. If it happens, we'll survive, but I want you to make sure it doesn't. Even with Hamburg standing, we may well suffer a split at that point, as communications and supply would be difficult. Have a contingency drawn up for a separate command of all forces north of Hamburg if it comes to it."

Another thought crossed Ike's mind.

"I will cut orders placing the American Divisions of 13 Corps, north of Hannover, under your direct command."

That was not something done lightly, but it did make sense.

McCreery nodded accepting the gift of more fighting men with suitable British aplomb.

It went without saying, but Eisenhower felt the need anyway.

"I have every confidence in you. We will do what is necessary to prevail here."

Eisenhower held out his hand.

"Good luck, Dick. I shall inform your new command of your imminent arrival."

The shake sealed the appointment.

"Thank you, Sir, and good luck to you too."

A crisp salute and the new commander of British 21st Army Group went on his way to organise his command.

Gathering himself for a moment, Eisenhower looked at the demeanour of his senior men. Some agitated, some calmly absorbing the information that flowed in from all sources, coalescing either on the map in front of them or in written reports arriving by hand.

With his back towards Ike, Omar Bradley stood apart, hands on hips, observing the map and his area of command alter minute by minute, red arrows appearing to indicate an all-points assault by the armies of the Soviet Union.

He became aware that Eisenhower was stood silently by his side, more because the smoke started to sting his eyes than any sixth sense.

"Hell of a thing, Ike, hell of a thing. One day someone will ask why we didn't see this coming."

Eisenhower cocked a sage eyebrow at the commander of his largest field force.

"Let us hope and pray that we will be there to contribute to the discussions, General." He said in a light tone.

Bradley retorted, similarly lightly.

"And that they are not conducted in Russian."

That drew a light snort from Eisenhower, but his response to it was forever lost, as the calm exchange was interrupted by more reports from harried staff officers.

One Colonel, unruffled and competent, passed over a neat handwritten list. A visitor to the Headquarters, he was without responsibilities but had taken it upon himself to start compiling a list of units that had not made contact.

"Damn good thinking, Colonel. Hustle up some more manpower and develop that as far as you can. Update me when anything really major comes to light. Carry on."

A crisp salute exchanged and the bright Colonel went on his way.

The two generals exchanged satisfied nods and alone again, the businesslike talk of war took over.

"I've appointed McCreery to head up 21st. Monty won't be fit for a long time, if ever. Very bad, so I am told."

Bradley, being Bradley, said nothing. He had always coexisted with Monty reasonably well, but understood the man's complex ego issues had not helped at times. McCreery was a different man and the appointment was sound. In many ways, it worked out very well.

"I gave him 13 Corps. Seemed sensible to me. Bill Simpson won't be impressed, but I'm sure you will sweet talk him. Alvan Gillem has been under the British before, so he should be onside"

Bradley blew a soft raspberry by way of reply, as he cancelled off those units from his thinking.

"Sir, General Gillem was at the Schloss Kransberg. There is no news as yet. His deputy is in charge for now."

Issues with the possible loss of a Corps commander aside, Eisenhower knew his man was not happy, but hoped he would see the sense of it soon enough. Anyway, now was not the time for disagreement, as both men knew, so he moved straight into the task ahead.

"I'm sorry to hear that, Brad, and he's not the only fine officer we may have lost there today. I'm still waiting on the official list from Kransberg, but you can bet it won't make pretty reading."

He got no disagreement on that one.

Moving deftly onto the weighty matters of the new European war, Ike gestured at the map that was being updated by the army of staff personnel in front of their eyes, preparing to give a full briefing at the earliest possible moment.

"This is not what we expected from our understanding of Soviet doctrine. A broad front attack?"

Ike left that hanging, inwardly working out the why's and wherefore's of the Soviet's strategic departure.

His right hand shot out, complete with newly lit cigarette, selecting specific points to reinforce his words.

"Paratrooper attacks, sabotage, assassinations, throughout Germany."

Bradley grabbed his chin and awaited his turn.

When it came, he was his usual brief self.

"They intend to push us to see how far back we will go, while surprise and panic reign."

His hands prescribed fluid arcs over the map.

"You can bet the farm that they will revert to type when we can get organised and online. Then we will see the remaining breakthrough points heavily reinforced."

Bradley turned to look at Eisenhower.

"You remember what that German General Balck said? The Russians do what works and this works for them right now, but they will revert to standard doctrine once the thing shakes out, because that has always worked for them in recent years."

Eisenhower nodded, agreeing with an assessment he had already arrived at himself.

"What did the Germans call the method? Reinforce success in force with the OMG? Operation Manoeuvre Group wasn't it?"

Bradley sniggered.

"I believe Von Mellenthin said OMG stood for 'Oh Mein Gott'."

"I can understand that, Brad, I sure can understand that."

Eisenhower studied the map closely. He turned his head and whispered.

"Tell you what I think. This is contemptuous, almost like they have no respect for us, pushing everywhere at once, expecting us to fold and retreat."

Bradley nodded his agreement and whispered back.

"Well, they are right about one thing."

He looked at Eisenhower.

"Retreat is something we simply have to do, if we are going to preserve our capabilities. We must retreat, sort out this mess and then get organised to roll them back."

Eisenhower nodded slightly.

"Amen, General."

He snorted as a thought crossed his mind.

"You know something. I just thought, they never attacked us here. Why was that I wonder?"

Bradley narrowed his eyes in thought. Eisenhower continued.

"D'you reckon it's like we were with Rommel and they think they have the measure of us and don't want replacements they don't know?"

His general looked at his commander with a set in his eyes that Ike had rarely seen.

"Ain't they in for a big goddamned surprise then."

Eisenhower laughed and patted Bradley on the back.

What neither knew at that time was that Soviet units had tried to attack the headquarters, but faulty intelligence led them to attack the wrong I.G.Farben building, where things did not go well for them.

The interlude over, strategic appraisal recommenced, as a report on aircraft losses was handed to Eisenhower.

"Bad losses in air across the board, but some good news. A number of tac-air units, mainly Brits, had recently moved back ready to stand down. Unless I'm mistaken, they will get back online soon, but air command structure has taken some serious hits. So too radar."

Bradley acknowledged that but, whilst it was a help, what was needed was men in the field.

"Ike, we need to get our units back to Europe quickly."

406

Eisenhower nodded and beckoned a lurking signalman forward.

Swiftly dictating a general order to be sent to commands preparing to return to their homelands or already at sea, Eisenhower initiated the first stages of a return.

"That will get the ball rolling. We will get the details sorted out later. Now, let's see what we can do to sort out this mess and then we better let our leaders know that the world has changed overnight."

Both Bradley and Eisenhower strode forward and began the process of getting order back.

1030hrs Monday, 6th August 1945, Headquarters, US Forces in Europe. I.G.Farben, Frankfurt-am-Main, Germany.

A full briefing on the situation would not be possible for some time, so the allied commanders strove to make decisions as best they could. Finally, a formal time was arranged for a delivery of all that was known, before Eisenhower sent all his commanders on their way to their parent formations, hopefully with definite orders and a general plan.

At 1030hrs precisely, the large map was ready, a map that on the previous quiet evening had been solely appointed with corps zones, army locations and indications of the demarcation lines in Europe, but that now staggered under the weight of the intelligence garnered from a thousand reports from across Europe.

An American Brigadier-General started his work from notes.

Soviet attacking forces seemed to have penetrated the allied line at will, sometimes with subterfuge, using allied tanks sent to help the effort in the war against Germany to bluff their way through, sometimes using silent massed infantry to overwhelm defensive positions. Often no artillery was employed, so surprise was pretty much complete. Where the God of War did thunder, defenders reported barrages the like of which they had never experienced.

Working from top to bottom, there seemed to be little by the way of good news.

Reports from Danish authorities indicated Soviet troops had landed on some of the eastern islands. Combined with news of the sinking of three British vessels, it seemed the Russians wanted the Baltic door firmly closed.

Reliable reports from Lubeck stated that Soviet artillery was falling all over the city and infantry were already in the suburbs, attacking on two fronts.

More red arrows ran almost to Trittau, a short distance east of Hamburg.

Better news emanated from elements of the 82nd US Airborne division, who seemed to have held their ground, in the face of waves of Soviet infantry south of that route.

More disturbing was the combination of action reports at Melbeck and Grünhagen, south of Luneberg, where Russian paratroopers were reportedly in control of the road bridges and in heavy contact with elements of the 84th US Infantry division's 309th Engineer Battalion. Soviet tanks and infantry were hammering on the southern edge of Uelzen and the lack of response to any messages aimed at the 335th Regimental Combat Team of the 84th, known to be stationed in Uelzen and Bodenteich, meant that the divisional cavalry was having a hard time of it. 11th Guards Army had blasted its way through with artillery and rockets, before the tanks of the 1st Tank Corps relieved paratrooper units who had taken the canal bridge east of Uelzen. If this report was true, then Soviet units were already nearly ten miles beyond first point of contact and that report was timed at 0840 hrs.

Confusion reigned in the sector of the 102nd US Infantry division. Elements in and around Wolfsburg reported distant artillery fire, but nothing more. Other units spoke of tanks in large numbers hammering their way through, possibly already in Königslutter and Lehre.

British Guards near Wolfenbuttal reported Soviet tanks and infantry approaching from the south.

The 30th Cavalry Recon troops, who were positioned on that axis, were off the grid. 30th US Infantry Division, their parent formation, was holding Goslar and its environs and, by all accounts, inflicting heavy casualties on its attackers.

There were no reports of any ground activity for a distance of almost thirty miles south of Goslar, but allied troops were dying as Soviet artillery took them under fire.

The 4th US Cavalry Group had virtually ceased to exist, buried under an avalanche of fire and massive assaults, its few survivors falling back to new positions, as a very serious Soviet attack drove from Rittmannshausen towards Kassel.

Most surprisingly, 5th US Armored Division units seemed to be falling back before an attack aimed at Bad Hersfeld. No reports had been received from the division's command units, but the 5th was a prime formation and would have been expected to hold on for much longer. Eisenhower had already dispatched a Brigadier-General to assess the situation and do whatever was necessary to restore the divisions 'spine'. Ike was not to know that Major-General Oliver and most his staff lay dead in their command post, victims of a clandestine assault by Siberian infantrymen, well suited to stealthy attack. The 5th was leaderless and it showed.

An adjacent formation, the 6th US Armored Division, was faring no better, for its command structure had also fallen victim to ground assault, although this time the attackers were beaten off with heavy casualties. Whilst the Divisional Commander was still breathing, he was in no fit state to issue orders, concussed as he was by a grenade and, in any case, his ability to control his division had been destroyed with his main radio equipment. General George Windle Read Jr was a tough and decorated soldier, but he was out of the fight for some time and so his senior surviving officer took control, trying to ease the 6th into some sort of defensive order using runners and short-range radios, but instead caused a major gap to open in the lines.

Although still in possession of parts of North Fulda, the 6th had over adjusted and Soviet forces were already well on the road to the south-west, exploiting the positional error. Their target was obvious and of pressing concern to those in the very headquarters tasked with stopping them.

It was Frankfurt.

Further along the line, 89th US Infantry had been badly knocked about and was falling back to the south-west. No news of the 355th RCT had been heard since the intensive artillery barrage commenced. Some garbled reports of paratroops on the Säale Bridge, north east of Bad Neustadt, had come from a unit of the 340th Field Artillery stationed nearby. They were unconfirmed and no further contact had been made.

Another recent unconfirmed report placed units of 76th US Infantry Division in heavy fighting in Ebern, north of Bamberg, with other divisional units being forced back towards Hofheim, threatening the flanks of the 89th.

6th Cavalry in Coburg reported nothing, save the distant noises of combat. Neither did any of the formations in the curved defensive front from Coburg round to Weiden.

South of Weiden, the story was very different.

16th US Armored Division was an untested unit that had heard a few angry shots in Czechoslovakia at the war's end and the fury of the Soviet assault was more than many could stand. Some units just ran away, others just raised their hands, as waves of Russian infantry swept forward. According to a belligerent Brigadier General Pierce, cohesion was lost and, although some of his units were showing signs of resistance, he could not hold.

Information pieced together suggested that 64th Armored Infantry, with some tanks and artillery, was trying to retain a foothold on Wernberg, but with little success.

To Eisenhower and his Generals, there seemed to be a major breakthrough in the making east of Nurnberg and, combined with the issues north of the city, made this the most dangerous area of their front at the moment. The line from Coburg to Weiden, including Bayreuth, seemed to be in danger of being nipped off around the flanks.

This was compounded by the withdrawal of the 102nd US Cavalry Group from its blocking positions, northeast of Cham. It was already heading back as fast as it could, in the direction of Regensburg, closely pursued by what the reports described as hundreds of Soviet tanks. Not that anyone there or in the SHAEF Headquarters knew the Soviet units by name as yet, but as the Major in charge of the 102nd had quaintly put it, when asked for more information on the enemy units and why he was retreating, *'a tank's a tank, and hundreds of the fuckers, all painted green with red stars coming at you at speed are to be avoided at all costs, so we bugged out.'* In fact, 102nd Cavalry had been sitting astride the main route of advance of the huge 5th Guards Tank Army, so their resistance would have been extremely brief, had they stood their ground.

At Bayerische Eisenstein, units of the Soviet 29th Tank Corps, equipped with American Sherman tanks, had bluffed their way through the lines of the 90th US Infantry Division, driving hard for Regen and Deggendorf. Either side of the route of advance, Soviet artillery harassed the confused American troops.

Reports from the 26th US Infantry Division's Commander indicated Soviet formations approaching Passau, on the Donau, having already penetrated nearly twenty miles behind that morning's lines without any reported fighting.

Mixed news came from Kefermarkt, north of Linz in Austria. Soviet troops had again plunged deep into allied lines without any real combat but had stumbled into the early morning exercise of the 63rd Armored Infantry and 41st Tank Battalions of 11th US Armored Division, being supervised by their commander Major-General Dager. Casualties in tanks had been high, due to a surprise air strike. The Soviet 49th Army was tasked with this assault and its lead formation, 70th Rifle Corps, suffered grievous casualties, as the unsupported infantry were faced with alert and well-equipped experienced soldiers.

Dager's men had successfully executed a set-piece ambush and the Soviet assault was bloodily repulsed.

That action was ongoing, but it seemed the red arrows there had been stopped.

At Enns, the Russians had crossed the river and were fighting their way through the 317th Regt, 80th US Infantry Division, which was slowly giving ground as it fell back towards Asten. Elements of the 305th Engineers had blown the bridge at Enns as the attack started, but the enemy had crossed in boats and, unknown to the briefing officer, had already started work on a permanent structure capable of carrying tanks.

Other units of the 305th Engineer had been overrun near Sterninghofen and 318th Infantry Regt was falling back in front of a huge armoured assault, seemingly aimed at outflanking Linz to the south.

South of that, there were no reports of any activity whatsoever.

As the Brigadier-General finished and the next officer stood to speak, more reports arrived, condemning part of his outline to the bin as the situation changed yet again.

That would be the way of it for some time to come.

1035hrs Monday, 6th August 1945, Headquarters of Red Banner Forces of Soviet Europe, Schloss Schönefeld, Leipzig.

At Schloss Schönefeld, similar activity was taking place, although everyone was a lot more relaxed as, in the main, the attacks were going extremely well.

Zhukov received reports of the success of Operation Kurgan sceptically, encouraging Malinin to harry the air commander into firming up the figures his regiments were claiming.

None the less, he was pleased, for if the Kurgan reports from air and ground attack were only half-right, then severe blows had been dealt to the allied tactical air forces throughout Europe, with relatively light casualties themselves.

The destruction of the British warships had caused much celebration amongst his naval liaison team, but that was pretty much a sideshow to the Marshal. As long as they kept the allies off the North German shoreline, that was all he worried about.

It was the reports of ground successes that most interested him, particularly the low levels of resistance encountered, particularly in the southern part of Germany.

The feedback from the raids aimed at command and control was limited and there were few indications as to their

412

success, save for the obvious disorganisation in some allied units.

Nowhere on the map or in the reports were there indications of retaliatory air strikes, or even counter-attacks, so it was probable that the Allied command structure was paralysed by either incompetence, fear, or injury.

'Well whatever it is, it's fine by me,' mused Zhukov.

The plan ensured that the pressure would be kept on at all points of attack and that the Soviet air regiments would keep attacking the allied air forces, not permitting them time to recover, although new units arriving would be a problem in time.

Timed perfectly to the thought, Malinin appeared with the latest estimates of the destruction wrought upon allied air power.

The figures were larger than before.

Malinin replied to the question in Zhukov's eyes.

"Yes, Comrade Marshal, I think we can trust these to be a reasonable set of figures. The regiments have confirmed their submissions and understand the need for accuracy and the projections of success from the ground assaults are wholly reasonable, certainly not over-optimistic."

Zhukov studied the list again.

"In which case, Malinin, we have been extremely lucky today."

Handing the paper back to his deputy, Zhukov cast his professional eye over the map once more. Pointing at one place where things had not gone well, he gave Malinin instructions.

"Tell Rokossovsky to sort out his attack north of Linz or he will be counting trees."

Shifting his point of focus, Zhukov continued.

"And tell Bagramyan to get 43rd Army moving, or he won't get his Marshal's stars!"

Whilst the words were spoken with the normal bark of command, Malinin knew that the bite was not present, for the day was going very well indeed and his boss was a very happy man.

0530hrs Monday, 6th August 1945, Rittmanhausen, Germany.

Allied Forces - 'A' Troop, 4th Cavalry Recon Sqdn, 4th Cavalry Group, US 19 Corps, 9th US Army, US 12th Army Group.

Soviet Forces – 55th Rifle Division of 89th Rifle Corps, 189th Tank Regiment of 2nd Guards Cavalry Corps all of 61st Army, and 5th Guards Rocket Barrage Division, all of 1st Red Banner Central European Front.

Nothing the doughboys had experienced came close to the hell that was visited upon them that morning.

Veterans of D-Day and a score of actions on the drive across Europe, the troopers of 4th Cav rightly considered themselves skilled and solid soldiers.

From concealed positions, two and a half miles to the east, two Guards Rocket battalions from 5th GRBD employed ninety-six BM13-16 Katyusha mounts to deluge the American positions in Rittmannshausen and Luterbach.

That amounted to fourteen hundred and thirty-six rockets in the air at the same time, each with forty-eight pounds of high explosive at the business end.

Their arrival on target was devastating and many young men died without even knowing what had killed them.

German civilians also died, as their houses were swept aside in a wave of high explosive.

Divisional artillery guns from units of 89th Rifle Corps also joined in, initially firing a mixture of fragmentation and smoke, adding to the confusion.

Tanks of the 2nd Guards Cavalry Corps started forward, with tank riding infantry clinging to their sides, aiming straight down the road.

Infantry from 89th RC moved forward in the open to threaten Luterbach and Altefeld, as well as others, who slipped clandestinely through the woods between Rittmannshausen and Rambach.

414

Staff Sergeant Joshua Ravens was a tank commander and exceptionally proud of his M24 Chafee light tank, 'Lady Lucy', named for his fiancée back in New York.

On hearing the rocket strikes on the positions to his southeast, he immediately got his tank moving to support his colleagues in 'A' Troop, who were clearly under attack.

As 'Lady Lucy' moved cautiously forward, Ravens' attempts to bring up anyone else on the radio net failed.

Artillery was falling in front of them, in what looked like a combination of explosive and smoke rounds, so he commanded his driver to seek a position of cover off the road.

Immediately the driver swung the vehicle left and drew up adjacent to a small copse of trees, just off the road and about two hundred yards short of the village.

In between new explosions and the bursts of smoke shells, the crew could see the destruction being wrought on the buildings and people in front of them.

Emerging out of that destruction were a number of shell Shocked and dazed survivors, both military and civilian.

The nearest man was staggering around, oblivious to the fact that he had no arms, but he soon succumbed to his wounds and fell silent to the earth.

The falling artillery now seemed to be all smoke.

One or two unwounded men emerged from the village, gathering up the injured and creating a casualty station at the side of the road.

An M3 half-track drew up alongside the Chafee and Ravens went to seek orders and information in equal measure.

The young 2nd Lieutenant, so recent an arrival that Ravens could not recall his name, was no wiser than he and certainly less experienced in the arts of war.

Against Ravens' advice, he ordered the Chafee and his own vehicle forward into the village, the half-track immediately surging forward.

Ravens climbed aboard 'Lucy' in time to watch the M3 disappear into the smoke and immediately blossom into a deadly fireball.

With eyes fixed on the death pyre of the young officer and his men, Ravens tried the radio again, but stopped as he became aware that the half-track appeared to be backing slowly out of the smoke towards him.

It took a moment for him to realise that the destroyed vehicle was being pushed along by a tank coming out of the village.

Ravens, shocked into inactivity for a short time, watched as the half-track refused to be pushed in a straight line and started to swing its burning body off to the right as he looked. The tank pushing it helped it on its way and, in a scream of anguished metal, broke loose.

The tank's hull machine gun hammered out and the casualty station was no more.

"Tank action, front!" he yelled, dropping into the turret as fast as he could.

The gunner, another veteran, was on the ball, already tracking his target as the loader drove home a solid shot shell. Their target, actually a T34/85 of the 2nd Guards Cavalry Corps, was crewed by equally competent and experienced men.

Both tanks fired together and both hit.

The Chafee's gunner's 75mm was not noted for its armour piercing performance, so the gunner had tried for a turret ring shot. The shell struck the T34 on the right side of the turret and sped away to bury itself in the village beyond. On its journey, it wiped three tank riding infantry off the vehicle, leaving only bloody spray marks where men had once clung.

The Russian 85mm shell struck Lucy's front glacis plate and easily penetrated the thin armour in front of the driver's position. The rest of the crew were covered with the driver's remains, as the shell carved its way through, moving on to remove both of Ravens' legs at the hips, before it buried itself in the engine compartment at the rear and the vehicle started to burn.

By the time the shocked and dazed crew started to exit the vehicle, Ravens was dead.

The three survivors dropped to the ground and in their shocked state, were unaware of the approaching Soviet tank.

It swept on by as the riding infantry exacted revenge for their three dead comrades, killing the helpless American survivors as they passed.

With their deaths, 'A' Troop ceased to exist.

0810hrs Monday 6th August 1945, Neumarkt im Mühlkreiss - Kefermarkt Area, US occupied Lower Austria.

Allied Forces – 63rd Armored Infantry Battalion, 41st Tank Battalion, 11th US Armored Division.

Soviet Forces – 2nd & 3rd Btns, 440th Rifle Regt, 64th Rifle Division, 70th Rifle Corps, 49th Army, 3rd Red Banner Central European Front.

The two companies of the 63rd Armored Infantry had been there all night, as directed by the divisional exercise schedule. Set up on an east-facing line commencing on the Pernau side of Neumarkt, running along the heights all the way down until it curved to the east passing to the south of Wittinghof, terminating on the heights adjacent to the river Feldaist, with a strong reserve in Rudersdorf and a smaller force just to the north-east of Neumarkt.

The brief was for a narrow front dawn attack mounted by elements of the 41st Tank battalion, namely C & D companies who, along with C/63rd had laagered overnight in the fields south of Lasberg.

This was the 'enemy' force that was to attack and breakthrough the defence, needing to enter Matzeldorf to triumph in the exercise.

Languishing around Netzberg were the Shermans of A/41st, presently untasked, but slated to conduct a tank assault during the second exercise later.

B/41st was still on the northern outskirts of Linz, unneeded in the exercise and conducting maintenance, prior to the whole division being shipped back to the States for demobilisation.

417

None the less, in and around the exercise site, nearly one and a half thousand experienced US troops were wide-awake and loaded for bear.

Umpires from Corps Headquarters, who had quartered overnight in Lasberg , had been rudely awakened by the distant sound of artillery and, shortly after, by the arrival of a jeep containing soldiers with incredible news.

That news was soon handed to Major-General Holmes Ely Dager, a competent, capable man, born for combat. He had spent the night in the magnificent Schloss Weinberg and was well refreshed.

Immediately organising his units by radio, he pulled his formation into defensive order, moving to command them from close by a house on the six hundred metres line north of Rudersdorf, around which his armored-infantry were already arraigned.

Swiftly he pulled the 'enemy' units of the 63rd and 41st behind the lines drawn by the 63rd's 'friendly' companies, sending the infantry of C/63rd to extend the line across the front of the tankers at Netzberg and retaining some as a mobile reserve in the same area.

Making sure his tank companies had topped off on fuel at first light as instructed, the problem of practice rounds was addressed. Each vehicle had retained only mock main rounds to avoid any accidents, but each company had its own supply train close at hand with war rounds aboard. None the less, it was a long process and would take time to complete.

The infantry units had live rounds available nearby and the exchange went swiftly and without problems, a testament to the steady nature of the men, for all was conducted under the increasing noise generated by artillery moving its fire zones closer.

C & D/41st had withdrawn through the infantry lines and were rearming themselves, C/41st having made rendezvous with their ammunition trucks in the fields south of Neustadt, where they commenced the exchange of rounds. D/41st had met with their supply vehicles parked on an overgrown country road in the woods to the south of Rudendorf and were already well into the rearming process.

418

A new problem for the silent American defenders arrived overhead, as four Ilyushin-II's, the famous Shturmoviks, flew down the road line towards Linz.

Fig#10 Kefermarkt

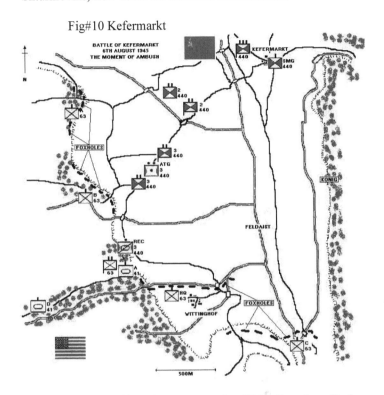

D/41st, although nearer to the flight line, benefited from the cover of overgrown road and was not spotted.

C/41st was not so fortunate.

Off to the right, one pilot saw tanks and lorries concentrated in a small open area, seemingly oblivious to their presence.

Amazed that they should find enemy tanks so exposed, they held off the attack whilst the leader radioed his contact report and the position of his targets, keen to avoid and mistaken attack on friendly forces.

419

No Soviet forces in the area possessed American tanks, so the order to attack was easy to give.

All four aircraft turned and drove hard and fast, aiming at the tanks gathered around the Neustadt-Matzelsdorf road.

Each carried a very successful Soviet tank-busting weapon, the PTAB, which was essentially a small bomblet with a shaped charge capable of penetrating the top armour of most battle tanks, as well as killing any men close enough to the point of explosion. Today, the PTAB's, each aircraft was carrying two hundred, were dropped like a carpet all over the tankers of C/41st, as they desperately toiled to load with ammunition.

The Sherman carried medium armour, designed to protect it in tank versus tank combat, but its roof armour of 25mm was not capable of resisting direct impacts from the PTAB's.

Of the sixteen tanks targeted, twelve were knocked out by either direct hits, or fires and explosions caused by strikes on the fuel tankers and trucks around them. The casualties were enormous and few capable men survived, effectively removing the whole company from action in a few seconds.

All four aircraft circled lazily to assess the damage, undertaking individual strafing runs on the site, before they flew back to re-arm, completely untouched and in celebratory mood.

The shock of that attack was felt in the headquarters tent of General Dager, but he quickly adjusted to the loss and reorganised his right, ordering A/41st nearer to the centre, into the woods to the south of Wittinghof and re-siting its supporting elements from C/63rd accordingly. D/41st would move as soon as rearmament was complete, secreting themselves in the woods to the east of Neumarkt.

Artillery was now starting to fall upon his infantrymen, but caused few casualties, as they were dug-in. In any case, the barrage quickly passed on, as it was supposed to be sweeping ahead of the advancing rifle corps it was supporting.

Overhead came the sound of an aircraft engine, immediately causing consternation, until it was recognised as an L-1 Vigilant Observation aircraft and, more importantly, friendly.

Within a few seconds, a radio burst into life, as a Colonel tasked as an observer in that aircraft and who had expected nothing more than a few hours flying over exercising tanks, called in a sighting report. He indicated infantry and light vehicles advancing towards Kefermarkt from the north. He reported no tanks and, on Dager's instructions, a confirmation was requested and received.

The Soviets were vulnerable.

This was something that Major Adam Yartsov of the 64th Rifle Division was only too aware of, despite the success of his mission so far. A handful of wounded was all his unit had suffered on its drive from Freistadt towards Linz and, even though one of those was his best non-com, he could not complain at getting away so lightly.

His 440th Rifle Regiment had not always been so lucky and leading an attack was pretty much always a poisoned chalice.

Prior to moving forward into the valley, Yartsov surveyed the ground. His route of advance took him between two heights, with the River Feldaist running down the eastern flank, with a few small brooks running off it towards the western heights. His prime route headed south-west, over two small bridges.

The ground was undulating, with hollows and raised areas in equal measure.

What troubled Yartsov was the scant cover available and he quickly decided to get through the potential killing zone as quickly as possible.

Mounting his men back into their vehicles, he summoned the recon force commander and gave him his orders.

He received the news of the Shturmoviks attack on the allied tanks with mixed feelings. If the Air Force had killed

421

them all as they claimed, then that would be just fine with him, but he knew how excitable fliers could get, so he expected tanks in his way very soon. However, more air support should be available to cater for that, if necessary, although the large column of smoke coming from behind the hills could even mean that the claims were correct, although it seemed closer than the location given by his regimental commander.

Which it was.

In their joy, the airmen had falsely stated that the destruction of the American tank regiment had been to the south-west of Gallneukirchen.

That error contributed much to what then came to pass, especially as Yartsov, unusually and fatally seeing what he wanted to see, wrongly attributed the presence of track marks on the road to the destroyed company withdrawing ahead of his advance. A view he supported with information gained from an Austrian police officer in Lasberg, regarding the swift movement south of a group of American tanks and by observing the hastily abandoned and churned up site where the 11th's troops had laagered overnight.

Sat in his Gaz67 4x4, he moved slowly along behind his lead elements as they pressed forward, taking the south-west road out of Kefermarkt.

His soldiers, preceded by a hastily designed artillery barrage, moved forward slowly in their hotchpotch of vehicles. American lorries and halftracks were mixed in with their own Gaz and Zis vehicles.

Two of his halftracks, SU-57's, mounted 57mm anti-tank guns and these were both immediately behind him, where he could more easily direct them.

As they moved further south, he was pleased to see that the barrage had not knocked out any of the bridges on his route of advance. He indicated that his driver should pull over at a junction, just in before the second of these bridges, surveying the heights to his right and left as the vehicle gently ground to a halt.

His lead recon element was halted at the Wittinghof road junction, the young officer standing bold and proud in the

422

turret of his BA64 armoured car. A second element was on the east road, level with the same road junction.

A perfect place for an ambush for sure, but air had reported nothing, except for the tanks and infantry they had savaged south of Gallneukirchen. The commanding general had been satisfied with that and refused permission for Yartsov to wait for armoured support, just in case the Americans still had fight, especially as Gallneukirchen was nearly ten kilometres away.

Like most general officers Adam had met in the last few weeks, his own commander was contemptuous of the Americans ability to fight. As a frontline soldier, he decided he would wait until the experience had come and gone before judging.

Still, orders were orders, so he did not halt his battalion's advance, despite his misgivings, although he did harry the new young officer, ordering the recon platoon on a surge forward, instructing the commanders to pay close attention to the silent heights on either side and the woods to their front.

Preparing to give the order to move forward, behind his two SP halftracks, Yartsov took one final sweep and almost missed a small movement on the corner of his vision as he ended looking east. Focussing his binoculars immediately on that spot, he saw nothing except a cleared area of woods and fallen tree trunks. As his eyes bored in on the spot he saw another movement and he suddenly he knew what was about to come.

He had no time to shout before the sound of an explosion rose above the sound of vehicle engines and all eyes were drawn to the BA-64 armoured car belonging to the young recon officer, now burning fiercely on the edge of the woods ahead. The second BA-64 was already reversing as fast as it could go and seemed to find safety in a small area of dead ground. American mortars found it in an instant and made it a victim of the previous night's preparations, for the American weapons were all nicely zeroed in on numerous points throughout the valley floor.

Machine guns started hammering from the direction of Wittinghof and the nearby woods and Yartsov's men started to go down. More mortars started to land to the east side of his strung out convoy, whereas the heights to his west stayed silent.

The east side recon element was not moving, thin wisps of smoke escaping the lend-lease scout car, betraying its fate.

Yartsov did not like it, but saw no option, as to stay was to die. He ordered his battalion to make for the trees to their west.

The two 57mm SP guns were directed to take the machine guns to his front under fire, just to distract and suppress them, whilst his infantry surged for safety. His mortar platoon was an ace up his sleeve and, under orders, it fell back quickly, setting up in a defile just south-west of Kefermarkt. It was joined by the mortar platoon of the second battalion, on the orders of 2nd Battalion's commander.

Firing smoke, they attempted to mask the 3rd Battalion's desperate move to the heights.

2nd Battalion's soldiers were already dismounted and moving west as fast as their legs could carry them, intent on achieving the heights before they were noticed.

The first of Yartsov's Su-57's ceased firing, as a direct hit from one of the armored-infantry's own 57mm anti-tank guns took the front off the stationary vehicle. The whole crew survived without a scratch and found refuge in a small hollow. The crew of the second vehicle threw smoke grenades and tried to withdraw, but only succeeded in throwing a track as they hit a large stone, making them easy meat for another 57mm. Only one man was killed in the vehicle, but none survived the withering bursts of MG fire that sought them out as they tried to escape.

None the less, they had deflected some of the American fire from Yartsov's men, fire that was again switched to the flanks of the 3rd Battalion, still toiling to find cover.

In war, timing is important. The American commander had timed his ambush to perfection. All the mortars were switched to the suspected location of the enemy mortars and within seconds, the Russians found themselves swept with high explosive equipped with surface detonating fuses. The carnage was immense and both mortar platoons ceased to function immediately, additional casualties being wrought by exploding Soviet ammunition.

At the same time as the mortar support platoons were smashed, the 57mm anti-tank guns sought out and found the Gaz containing the artillery officer, whose job it was to call in support from the batteries behind. No such support would be forthcoming until his replacement reached the scene, so the artillery continued to fire on his last orders, which were to drop smoke down the east side of the valley, in order to screen the troops from the heights there. The only eyes that looked down on Yartsov from the eastern heights were those of an Austrian woodcutter and his nephew, sat comfortably with bread, cheese and beer, intent on watching the mock battle they had heard was being staged that day.

The heights to the west, upon which the Russians had set their hopes of safety, erupted in fire and cut down soldiers from both Soviet battalions instantly. Having faced the German and his MG42 before, these men were used to extreme firepower but this was very different. Not only did the armored-infantry have numerous machine guns, from tried and trusted m1919 .30cal to the murderous M2 .50 cal, they also possessed the finest infantry rifle of the period, namely the M1 Garand, which gave American infantry units awesome fire power.

Hundreds of infantrymen were dug-in along the leading edge of the heights and they accurately poured round after round into the confused Soviet troops, who started to fall back, their expected refuge now so obviously a death trap.

Yartsov watched as his command was butchered, impotent, raging, unable to do anything but weep for his men. 2nd Battalion had fared no better and the survivors were falling back into Kefermarkt, the bridge over which they needed to pass now brought under fire by US mortars, causing more casualties.

Looking around him, the Soviet Major saw an abandoned half-track, engine still running. Ordering his own driver to accompany him, he determined to drive to the rescue of his men and get as many out of the death trap as he could.

The vehicle leapt forward and benefited from smoke drifting over from the west side, permitting it to proceed some distance before it was spotted. Yartsov served the .50cal on its pedestal mount and was rewarded with the sight of his rounds striking home on an anti-tank gun position, now visible on the heights. Shouting and beckoning to nearby survivors, he went back to the gun and emptied the whole belt into the woods.

He bent down to pick up a new box of ammunition at the moment a 57mm shell struck the vehicle, killing his driver and wrecking both the engine and machine gun mount. Yartsov dropped to the floor of the burning vehicle, trying hard to work out what had happened, trying to stand on ruined legs and wondering at the silence that suddenly enveloped him.

Mercifully, he was dead before the flames started to consume his body.

The commander of the 2nd Battalion, himself wounded in the stomach, reported back to his regimental commander on the destruction of his and Yartsov's commands.

The Soviet attack had been stopped dead in its tracks.

Major-General Dager was a satisfied man. He had undoubtedly destroyed the best part of two Soviet infantry battalions already, which, even though it did not balance with the terrible losses to one of his tank companies sustained in the air attack, did show that his boys could meet the Reds and beat them. His butcher's bill was remarkably light. One of the anti-tank gun crews had been killed and twenty-three of his armored infantrymen. Add one man from the mortar platoon, who had just dropped down dead whilst portering ammunition and his total of dead was twenty-eight, with forty-three wounded.

He fully expected it would be different the next time the Soviets pushed, for they would not come in so dumb a second time. He organised a situation report to be sent to his corps commander and then handed over command to one of his subordinates, recommending some reorientation of the defence for the next round. His place was rightly elsewhere and he left a capable Colonel with the responsibility of holding the line.

Up on the heights, Hans Konig and his nephew had been extremely impressed with the show.

At 11am Moscow time, a Soviet radio broadcast informed the world that the Red Army had responded to threats and intimidation on the part of America and Britain, acting to pre-empt a likely attack upon their territory by invading the remainder of Germany

Much play was made of the peace-loving nature of Soviet man and how no choice had been left but to attack, especially as the treacherous Capitalist Governments had cosseted German war-criminals, the agitated voice vehemently accusing the Allied leadership of substituting one sort of Fascist for another.

Minister Molotov, the speaker, soothed certain nations such as Sweden, Portugal, Spain and Switzerland, assuring their borders and confirming no aggressive intent against them, if they remained firmly neutral and unsupportive of the Allied forces.

His voice took on a different tone when warning others such as Mexico, Brazil and Italy, to immediately assume a neutral stance or suffer the consequences of their association with the Western Allies. Or as Molotov so eloquently put it, 'these Imperial fascist states, attempting to preserve their old order with their scheming, threatening the new world peace so recently won by the blood of the Soviet Union'.

Yes, it was just rhetoric, mainly designed for home consumption and for those easily influenced, but it also served the purpose it was intended for, which was to say to the world, 'You are either with us or against us... and there is no middle path.'

2102hrs Monday, 6th August 1945, Headquarters, US Forces in Europe. I.G.Farben, Frankfurt-am-Main, Germany.

The ambush of Yartsov's command had been an impressive yet simple affair, given the preparation that had occurred, some stupidity by the enemy troops and the nature of the ground on which it was fought. However, it would not be repeated. Events elsewhere meant that the position had to be abandoned before the defenders found themselves isolated, as Soviet forces were already knocking on the outskirts of Linz.

Kefermarkt had been one of a handful of successes on a day that went very badly for the Western Allies.

At SHAEF Headquarters, briefing officers delivered sobering reports from up and down the line, each of which acknowledged that another piece of Germany was now in Soviet hands. Some of the losses were important and, when cities like Passau held firm, it was a rare occurrence. It was not always good news, even then, as sometimes a prime defensive position was already outflanked and would have to be vacated in any case.

The clock had just pushed past 2100hrs when Eisenhower received the reports of the fall of Bamberg, fighting in the heart of Regensburg and enemy troops approaching Amberg. It became obvious that some American units, to the north-west of Nurnberg, were at great risk. Swiftly, orders were sent out to evacuate Bayreuth. Although regrettable, this would have the advantage of providing Ike with a reserve force in the area, of one armoured and one infantry division, the 9th in each case, both of which were prime formations.

The drive on Frankfurt, or more accurately one of the drives on Frankfurt, had reached Geinhausen, thirty kilomteres to the east, where it was blunted by elements of the 7th US Armored Division, already in place and determined to remain there.

6th US Armored, who had mistakenly moved aside and permitted the unchallenged incursion, started to filter back into Frankfurt and Bad Nauheim during the late afternoon and early evening.

Once the circumstances were known, no more was said, especially as the Brigadier-General responsible now lay dead on a stretcher in an aid station in Friedburg, victim of a strafing run by Yak fighters. The 6th's commander, George Windle Read Jnr, had recovered enough to re-establish command of his division and was appropriately inspired to 'kick some kraut ass', his white fury and rage preventing his staff from reminding him that it was the Soviets who were the enemy this time.

After some thought, the 6th was ordered back to Wiesbaden to regroup and prepare to act as an armored reserve.

All down the map of the frontline, the casual observer could see inroads into the allied positions.

Eisenhower was in deep conversation with Bradley when the latest estimate of air force effectiveness came through and, surprisingly, it made better reading than either had dared hope.

Losses in machines and pilots had been severe and a few airfields were damaged beyond immediate repair. Control facilities had been badly hit, but systems were being put in place for basic mission control over the coming days. It was not going to be perfect, but it would provide something by way of ground support.

Radar coverage had been badly hit, with losses in sets and trained staff quite high. These small installations seemed to have come in for particular attention from Soviet infiltrators and paratroopers.

Clearly, the Soviets saw reducing the allied air force capability as crucial, something neither of the two generals could deny.

Before the list had been fully read, another one arrived, delivered by the hands of a young and obviously nervous army officer. This one reflected losses in general supply, ammunition and POL. Ike gestured for the Captain to hand it directly to Bradley and continued reading the Air Force report.

Squadrons deploying home had been untouched and quite a number were still in France, all immediately available for the following day's actions. Others could be returned from the UK, to be ready for Wednesday.

The United States Army Air Force Colonel who stood waiting beside Eisenhower, was instructed to ask Tedder to work out a basing plan for all the squadrons that would return to his command, allowing for the further advance of the Soviet army for the next five days.

As the officer strode briskly away, Bradley's sigh got his full attention.

Eisenhower's lighter flared as Bradley indicated a piece of paper in his hand.

"You've seen the report from Kransberg, I assume?"

Eisenhower grimaced, as the list of the dead and wounded represented some stellar leadership talent lost to him.

"Yes, Brad. Shocking. They hurt us there."

A deep draw on his cigarette covered his emotions.

"Deputies in place of course. I shall be writing to the families, first chance I get."

Nodding his understanding, Bradley set aside that awful report, confirming the deaths of three US and one British Corps and four US Divisional, Commanders. Two more Divisional commanders, one each from the British and the French had also succumbed. Moving to a different file, Ike raised an eyebrow in enquiry.

"OK, Brad, let me have the good news."

"In short, there is little except to say that we have reasonable supplies throughout Europe; enough that will ensure we will be able to function. Attacks on the PLUTO facilities have reduced the supply of gas for everything, but we won't notice that for a little while, as we still have some stockpiles left. Some are gone, by air raid or commando attack. You will not be surprised to learn that air force supplies were a favourite target."

Eisenhower almost winced and motioned Bradley to go on.

"Aircraft munitions are greatly reduced. Airfields that received visits from the reds all seem to have their stockpiles prioritised for destruction and it seems few of our air units retain enough bombs, rockets and ammunition. We can get more to them all, but it will take time. We can get that firmed up, but I suspect that we will be told that, offensively, the air force is out for two-three days minimum, what with losses in machines and pilots as well."

Bradley read on, as Eisenhower informed him about the transit squadrons in France.

Nodding, Bradley quoted from the piece he was just reading.

"The report says we can do some offensive ops with the French based units, but to continue with them, we need to marry the aircraft up with stocks in munitions and POL."

Taking his eyes away from the report, Bradley paused for thought.

"If we can it, will be nice, but we will need to give the ground attack boys cover with fighters. Can't afford any more losses."

"We will find plenty of work for those poor boys tomorrow and the days to follow. And we will make sure they are covered. Arthur will be working on that, Brad."

Coffee arrived and the two sat, resting their legs in two comfortable chairs, drawn up facing the map.

"So, I don't think we were too far off the mark with our predictions this morning, do you, Brad?"

"No, sir," His comment was punctuated by a sip of scalding coffee, "Hamburg was an easy one to call. Cuts Denmark and a lot of the Brits off. Atlantic access too, so let's say Bremerhaven... and Cuxhaven possibly."

Gesturing with his mug, he described the lines in the centre of Germany.

"There they can go anywhere they want, but I will bet the farm that they are after the Ruhr... and the Rhine beyond that."

Eisenhower nodded, not yet courageous enough to sample his drink, but savouring the rich aroma none the less.

Taking the mug away from his face, he spoke in general terms.

"A countrywide attack to find weaknesses, push us back on as broad a front as possible, clog the roads with refugees and to burn up as much of our supply as possible as we manoeuvre backwards. Destruction of our ground-attack capability so we cannot interfere with them as much as we would like. No-one ever said the Reds were stupid, did they?"

"That they certainly ain't, Ike, but there are some questions here."

Ike ventured his lips to the mug and encouraged Bradley to carry on.

"They haven't touched the bomber force; maybe they couldn't, or didn't have enough assets. I would have tried at least. Why is that?"

His coffee mug placed on the period table set between the two chairs, Ike cleared his throat and then fed his nicotine habit once more.

"That's occurred to me too, Brad. Incredibly, I believe they don't see them as a huge problem. Their use tactically is limited, without planning and control, and we've lost so much of that control capability. Secondly, strategically, I am unsure if we can bomb the Urals or beyond, but you can bet your bottom dollar they have worked out what they are risking to our mainstream bomber force and that it's acceptable to them."

Bradley nodded, as this was the conclusion he had also arrived at.

"The Russians will have cities we can bomb and, sure as hell, we can bomb infrastructure like bridges and rail yards. I reckon they expect they can absorb the casualties, which we would have to say they can and, I can guarantee you, they already have their supplies stockpiled near at hand and they will be the very devil to find. Another reason for their big hit on tac-air, limiting our ability to interfere with their resupply. Main bomber force can hit these dumps, but I would be surprised if they are overly concentrated and not comprising smaller dumps nearer to the points of delivery."

Eisenhower's eyes narrowed, as if something had just illuminated his thoughts, which it had.

"Mind you, they don't actually have a bomber force of heavies like we have, do they?"

432

Bradley understood it was a rhetorical question and so left his commander to continue.

"You might think they would have learned a little from the use we got outta them during Normandy operations."

For a second or two, both men developed glazed eyes as their minds raced ahead.

"When we go back at them, then we can look at that, given time to get the control systems back online. In the meantime, I think we should scare up some plan to use them in support of defence as best we can."

"Or."

"Or if Intelligence can find us something worth bombing, then we will attack it. Command and control and the like."

Bradley commented mischievously.

"Tedder and his tribe will be busy."

Air-Chief Marshal Arthur Tedder was Ike's number two and was already snowed under, having been given responsibility for cleaning up the air mess, as well as developing allied offensive air capability as quickly as possible.

"We all will be, Brad, especially you I think. I have something in mind for you."

That obviously got the General's full attention.

"You and your army are the best I got and on you falls the bigger burden here."

Bradley drained the last of his coffee and waited.

"I think we know we won't be able to hold a solid front for some time to come and I want you to buy me as much time as you can so I can get some real defensive positions organised aways back, lines we can hold."

Nothing unexpected for the quiet general.

"We are going to have to relocate SHAEF soon, as I doubt we will hold Frankfurt for too long, even with you working a miracle or two."

It was not a stroke or flattery, just a statement of the trust one man had for the other.

"I will get someone on that straight away, but I am only going to move us once. We will nail our colours in place, wherever we choose to stand."

Bradley nodded, a little surprised at the pugnacious tone of his commander.

"What I need from you is your army intact at the end of it all. I see it as imperative that we preserve as much of our force as possible and always have done here."

Eisenhower continued rapidly.

"We will get more units in hand and quite soon from what I hear. But the resources of the Soviets are huge and they are all here, now, ready and able, whereas we are strung out from here to New York City."

In an act unlike any previously seen from the General, Eisenhower smacked his extended palm into his cupped left hand to emphasise his point, sending a shower of sparks from a new cigarette that had magically appeared.

"Even with what we have now and coming back, we are outnumbered badly, you know that. So you must preserve your force, Brad."

"I will do all I can to keep my soldiers alive, that goes without saying, but you will need time to get prepared and that will come at a cost and one we will regret for many years to come Ike."

Eisenhower, as if suddenly weighed down with that thought, dropped his shoulders.

"It will be hard, yes. And many mother's sons will not be going home alive. But we will prevail, Brad, for we must."

The moment passed and Eisenhower again stood resolute.

A moment to gesture for another coffee and he took Bradley's arm conspiratorially.

"I have an idea on manpower you might like to hear. Controversial for sure, but it will help us no end if we can pull it off."

Pausing only when the steward brought the fresh mugs, Eisenhower enlightened his man on the plan, interrupting his whispered conversation solely to order a new pack of cigarettes.

434

The normally calm Bradley was genuinely roused by the concept.

"Well ain't that a thing. Can it be done?"

"I will know tomorrow. I am having a little gathering in the music room at 1400hrs and I will press them hard. Our civilian masters will come onside once I explain the need and advantages," and casting a swift look at his wristwatch to check Ike grinned, "In fact, I am due some calls very soon."

Bradley smiled, unfolding a number of the usual facial lines and replacing them with others more rarely seen.

"Best of luck with that, Ike."

Brad stood after downing half his coffee.

"I must get to my command now. Need to be there by midnight."

The General stood to attention and threw up a salute, which was returned before Eisenhower stuck out his hand.

The two shook hands and the firm grips lingering meaningfully, as only handshakes between friends who face imminent dangers can do.

"You know there is a quote I heard a little while ago, which goes like this. 'History shows that there are no invincible armies.' It's true, Brad, it's true."

"That it is, Ike."

"And do you know who spoke those words?"

Bradley shook his head slowly.

"Joseph Stalin."

The two hands slipped apart.

"Amen."

I divide officers into four classes -- the clever, the lazy, the stupid, and the industrious. Each officer possesses at least two of these qualities. Those who are clever and industrious are fitted for the high staff appointments. Use can be made of those who are stupid and lazy. The man who is clever and lazy is fit for the very highest commands. He has the temperament and the requisite nerves to deal with all situations. But whoever is stupid and industrious must be removed immediately.

General Baron Kurt Gebhard Adolf Philipp Freiherr Von Hammerstein-Equord
Head of the Reichswehr [German Army] (1930-33)

CHAPTER 43 – THE BETRAYAL

0525hrs Tuesday, 7th August 1945, Headquarters, US Forces in Europe. I.G.Farben, Frankfurt-am-Main, Germany.

Eisenhower had permitted himself the opportunity to sleep for a few hours and was gently woken to the new day by his orderly, feeling more refreshed than most in his command.

A swift wash and change, punctuated by coffee and cigarettes, then he moved towards his command centre downstairs. Before his feet touched down, he was assailed by written reports from staff and his generals, as well as messages of enquiry from the political leadership.

He decided they could wait for now and strode into the centre to receive the news from the Brigadier-General tasked with collating and briefing on these things.

It was not all bad.

Lubeck was just about being held by the British 15th Division and 11th Armoured Division.

A number of Soviet spearheads were approaching Hamburg but, as yet, fighting was being kept away from the city.

Luneberg was being held by paratroopers of the 82nd US Airborne Division, but at high cost.

Braunschweig was being held without too many problems, but was in danger of being surrounded for the same reason that Hannover was threatened. That being because of a poor piece of judgement from the temporary divisional commander of the 2nd US Armored Division, who misconstrued his orders and withdrew his units rather than remaining in place and supporting 30th US Infantry Division.

Which unit was now separated from 2nd Armored and falling back towards the Gottingen-Hameln line, despite having roughly handled the attacking Soviet infantry. This also unseated the northern flank of 83rd US Infantry Division as it was withdrawing towards Gottingen itself.

This was not bad news in itself, as it meant that units that could have been trapped north of Gottingen were less likely to be threatened by the Soviet breakthrough towards Kassel, from where there were reports of heavy fighting. The 83rd had subsequently been ordered back into Kassel at top speed, primarily to help with the defence there.

4th US Cavalry Group had probably been destroyed, as there had been no contact with any of the units since mid-afternoon on the 6th, which also explained why Soviet tanks, infantry and, of all things, horsed cavalry, were in the south-eastern suburbs of Kassel itself.

Bad Hersfeld had fallen in the late evening and some reports had the Soviet advance units at Alsfeld, although other reports stated that the forces engaging south of Alsfeld were paratroopers, dropped to secure the road bridge. Either way, things north of Frankfurt were looking bad, as this Soviet spearhead had made a deep penetration of approaching sixty miles since the attack started.

6th US Armored's difficulties had opened up the road through Fulda and Soviet troops were already in combat in Geinhausen with the steadfast 7th US Armored Division, which was being pressed hard and preparing to fall back to a second line at Hanau. This was not an ideal defensive force, as tank units were better preserved for offence but, in this case, the need was great, as the attacking Soviet forces included a large number of armoured vehicles and the road to Frankfurt would be laid bare without the Lucky Seventh.

437

Eisenhower interrupted gently but firmly, calling a halt to the briefing and beckoning forward a one-armed infantry Colonel, whose chest indicated the booty and the baggage of many exchanges in the service of his country.

"Harry, we will be shifting our headquarters by tomorrow at 1800, handing over control to 12th Army Group, all personnel to be gone by 2300 latest. Get it sorted, advance party to get the new site prepared as best it can be. Organise some night air to shift us pronto. I want it to be up and running by 0300 latest. Any questions?"

None forthcoming, the Colonel departed to set the wheels in motion.

"My apologies. Carry on, John."

Matters around and south of Nurnberg were a lot trickier it seemed.

89th US Infantry had been pushed back to Schweinfurt, but was in good order, despite losing a full company of riflemen to Soviet flame-throwing tanks in the failed defence of Munnerstadt.

76th US Infantry had been battered back to Hochstadt and Erlangen, but had managed to keep a tenuous hold on the right flank of the 89th.

6th Cavalry had fallen back to Erlangen and 14th Cavalry was displacing to Altdorf, east of Nurnberg.

9th US Armored and 9th US Infantry had been withdrawing all night and many of the 9th Infantry's units were crammed into the defensive perimeter of Nurnberg itself. 9th Armored units were passed on through to reassemble around Ansbach to the south-west. The intention was to make the division available to hit back if possible.

In addition, Ike noted 12th US Armored units moving into a line centring on Bad Windsheim, probably for the same purpose.

16th US Armored had not managed to hold and was totally ineffective, its units split up and without proper leadership, resulting in disorganised but bitter clashes throughout the whole area east of Nurnberg. Some modest resistance seemed to be in place on the main highway, but Soviet troops were already through Amberg and fifteen miles further west, having relieved paratroopers dropped the day before, who had secured the bridges over the Vils, a major tributary of the Donau.

Regensburg was still the scene of bitter fighting, as elements of the 99th US Infantry, supported by stragglers from 16th Armored and 102nd Cavalry, strove to hold back the 5th Guards Tank Army driving in from the northeast, plus a portion of 2nd Shock Army that had sub-divided at Wernberg and was now hammering at the city from the north.

90th US Infantry were under pressure on the Donau line, just holding at Straubling and Deggendorf. 26th US Infantry were still bloodying the Soviet drive at Passau, but at a cost. It had been detected that Vilshofen, to the west, was undefended, so a reduced Regimental Combat Team [RCT] was being quickly switched to defend the river crossings there.

Linz was under immense pressure, with street fighting of great intensity going on all night in the southern suburbs. Units of the 65th and 80th US Infantry divisions were engaged in hard fighting and it was this and the situation south of Linz, that meant that the victors of Kefermarkt had to withdraw.

More than that, the corps commander was trying to disengage all of the 11th US Armored to act as his reserve, ready to prop up Passau, Linz, or Wels if needed, or as everyone thought, when needed.

Steyr had fallen in the night, but not without a serious fight with the 80th US Infantry, from which unit the report was that a Soviet Cavalry unit had been bled dry.

In general, there had been some night bombing by Soviet aviation regiments, but nothing of note. Mosquito NF30's from the Amiens based 219 Squadron RAF had had some rare success, getting in amongst some PE-3m night fighters and shooting down ten without loss.

At sea there was bad news and good news, in that another destroyer had been lost, as the Royal Navy tried to extricate itself from the trap it had been lured into east of Denmark and there were reports that a troop transport, recently turned back to France, had been torpedoed and sunk. That was yet to be firmed up but, if true, suggested that loss of life would be great and some quality units expected to be inserted back

439

into the order of battle would not be available. On the plus front, two submarines, believed to be Soviet, had been prosecuted and sunk off Norway, adding to the one sunk following the attack on the Devonshire.

A Soviet minesweeper that had been on a brief goodwill visit to Gibraltar had been bombed and damaged by coastal command aircraft operating from the same base. The stricken vessel beached itself on Spanish territory and the surviving crew of the T-112 were being interrogated by the Spanish Authorities, themselves no lovers of communism.

Eisenhower took everything in as the briefing was delivered, making a note here and there, but not interrupting.

After some discussions with his staff, orders were issued for various commands.

To McCreery, an update on the general position was attached to a reminder of the need to hold Hamburg and Bremen, as well as a request for information on the availability and intended commitment of the Polish and Canadian units in Holland. There was also a private message for McCreery's eyes only, which was sent by separate fast courier.

His staff was still working with Bradley's boys to decide where the line could be established, so Ike could not advise McCreery further.

Nurnberg was a problem with no easy solution and Ike feared that he would soon have to turn the city over to the Russians, to avoid huge losses by being outflanked and cut off.

Schweinfurt, Bamberg and Regensburg, were all key and their continued resistance bought time.

Linz was sticking out like a sore thumb now and he kicked himself for not seeing it yesterday, perhaps buoyed a little too much by the excellent defeat inflicted at nearby Kefermarkt. There was danger there and he made sure the Corps commander was aware of the big picture and the risks to his command.

His orders issued, Eisenhower attended to those who waited on further instruction, or needed his eyes on a report of importance. Ike took no break except the frequent pause to light a cigarette, or the rarer opportunity of a coffee.

One report covered the return of units that had been stood down and were on their way home, now being turned for the fast return trip back to a Europe once again at war.

"Too slow, Colonel, too damn slow. I want these units in France given all-priority to get forward. Bring me an update on our calendar as soon as you have it. And I mean all-priority, son."

The Colonel saluted and was on his way before Ike could return the formality.

The report also contained clearer information on the troop transport. It had been confirmed sunk and it now seemed likely that over thirteen hundred experienced US soldiers had been lost to a torpedo attack from an unknown submarine.

A Brigadier General had been waiting, already briefed by Eisenhower to await his signal before presenting his information. That signal came and Eisenhower took his first look at the full brief from the Pacific Theatre of Operations.

Far from being of little interest to him, he noted immediately that it contained some very bad news indeed.

"General, has this had time to reach my army commanders yet?"

A quick check of the watch and the officer confidently replied.

"I doubt it will have reached General Clark yet, but General Devers and the British will have it for sure... and General Bradley is on his way here directly, sir."

"Thank you, John. Make me up a further..." he paused doing the mental arithmetic, "...three and ten copies respectively by 1300, please."

A salute and the man was gone.

Eisenhower said nothing, reading every word and developing his assessment further.

So absorbed was he, that he burnt his fingers on the cigarette he was holding.

Licking the small blisters and then lighting another, he inhaled deeply, reading on and contemplating the implications as he went.

Bradley, looking extremely tired but in a pristine uniform, strode in quietly, acknowledging a man here and there.

Ike became aware of his arrival and waved a hand, inviting the General to take the weight off his feet in the comfortable chairs. No orders were needed to ensure coffee appeared for the two.

Bradley was holding his copy of the Pacific report.

Ike gestured angrily with his copy, "You read this then, Brad?"

"Yes, Sir, I have and if that is all true, we are worse off than I thought."

Eisenhower stubbed out his cigarette and started to address the issues raised.

"I haven't finished it yet, but we can do that together. OK, so firstly we have large units of Japs appearing out of the blue at Attu and Kiska in the Aleutians, the submarine base on Guam, the naval anchorage at Ulithi, the airfields on Saipan and many attacks on our forces in Okinawa, some of which are unusual in their nature and giving MacArthur the jitters"

He looked up, brow knotted.

"I wish they would be more specific on that. What do they mean by unusual in nature?"

Bradley shook his head slowly and offered a slight shrug. Ike continued.

"These attacks seem to originate from Soviet merchant and naval vessels on recognised business or goodwill visits. Even looks like some of our own freighters have been used, ones from the supply run into Vladivostok. So Soviet vessels transported Japanese troops into the heart of our defences and let them run riot. Attu and Kiska seem to be holding, but there are many casualties. Eniwetok and Ulithi Atoll have taken big hits. They are not naming names, but they seem to have lost at least a carrier, a battleship and two cruisers, plus change."

Eisenhower shook his head, knowing Guam was badly hit and submarines and experienced crews were lost. There were big losses in B-29's, as the Nips ran amok all over the airfields on Saipan, as well as appalling losses in air and

442

ground crew. Somehow they attacked Chengdu and did the same to the Chinese based Superforts."

Eisenhower gestured angrily at the report once more.

"And Okinawa, not so many losses indicated and nothing major ,but there's that damn 'unusual in nature' again, Brad."

Both men took hold of their coffee and savoured a moment's pause before plunging back into the meat of the report.

"Japanese units starting a huge offensive in China, tanks, infantry, the works. Chinese communist divisions moving aside and not resisting them?"

A cigarette appeared and was lit, breaking up Ike's flow.

"They don't have those kinds of resources, do they? No fuel to speak of, little armour of note."

Bradley looked straight-faced at his commander.

"You haven't read Colonel Gould's submission in the addendum have you, Ike?"

Bradley thumbed through the papers and found what he was looking for immediately.

"Permit me to read this. It's been cleaned up a bit and only has the salient information."

He cleared his throat and read it verbatim.

"Report from John F Gould, Lieutenant Colonel. US Army Air Force.

14th US Air Force, China, Attached –. ☐☐☐☐Fighter Group,☐☐☐ Fighter Squadron.

I must qualify my report by stating that I was a P47 Thunderbolt pilot engaged in ground attack and interdiction in the ETO from March 44 through February 45.

Whilst on aggressive operations in support of ground troops in the ☐☐☐ area, ☐☐☐ Province, China, I was directed to conduct ground strafing runs on infantry and tanks attacking friendly positions at ☐☐☐.

443

Casualties were successfully inflicted upon enemy ground troops, but the enemy attack was successful, as our flight did not possess weapons capable of stopping the enemy tanks.

The armoured vehicles I engaged were definitely German tanks of the Panzer IV and Sturmgeschutz type, and my flight was taken under fire by at least two self-propelled quadruple 20mm weapons mounted on German halftracks, and acting in close-support.

On return to our base, we encountered enemy aircraft returning from a raid. Lack of ammunition meant we could not engage, but these types were positively identified by Major Deng Ho as Petlyakov-2's in Soviet colours.

Signed,
J.F.Gould
Colonel.
Report ends."

Eisenhower looked physically shaken and did not speak, all the time looking down at the page in the report that he had found as Bradley started his recital and then followed word by worrying word.

Finally, he composed his thoughts.

"So that put's the fox in the hen house for sure. Damn, Brad. Goddamn."

Eisenhower tossed the report on the table, exchanging it for his pack of cigarettes and lighter.

Breathing in the calming smoke, he summarised his thoughts.

"The Soviets have this sown up, don't they? Obviously, they have a pact with the Nips, who are party to all of this. If they have given the Japanese all the German equipment they have captured, which is what I assume they have done, in one stroke they have eased their own logistics and massively increased the striking power of the Nip army. Want to bet they have lots of other hardware like artillery, anti-tank guns, machine guns, the complete works?"

444

Bradley had had the advantage of reading this report as he journeyed over from his own headquarters, so he was pleased his boss was on the same wavelength as himself.

Eisenhower paused, searching for information hidden in the deep recesses of his overworked mind.

"We have a Soviet document indicating a rough outline of their commitment to the Manchurian offensive somewhere, don't we? If I recall there were extensive forces involved and I bet they are removed from the ORBAT of their forces in Europe that we are working to at this time."

This suddenly took a direction Bradley had not gone as yet.

"I think we need to revise our estimates on what forces we are facing, Brad. Unless I'm way off, I suspect that the Reds have a whole lot more hardware opposing us than we first thought."

Eisenhower stood abruptly, clutching his jaw with one hand and flipping up a cigarette with the other as he continued, a disjointed humming sound coming from his throat, almost as if he was thinking out loud. He seemed to be staring at some distant horizon before humming and staring ceased.

He summoned an aide.

"Captain Horton, find the Soviet briefing document on their Manchurian Operation please. Quickly, Captain."

Turning to Brad, he continued without so much as an intake of breath.

"They will place some forces in the Pacific, to show willing and able to support their new friends, as well as protecting their back door. So figure that about...."

He suddenly became aware he was musing aloud and focussed on Bradley standing beside him.

"....about one-third of the force we expect to be committed there."

It was not a statement as such and Bradley quickly did the calculations from his memory of the report and nodded his agreement.

"That is a lot of hardware and manpower that we haven't allowed for."

Bradley ventured an idea.

445

"Assuming that they are not in position because of the risk we might discover them, then perhaps this is one which might interest Tedder and the bomber boys? The Reds have gotta move them somehow. Road, rail, whatever, the heavies might be able to keep them at arm's length if they are in transit and their march routes are vulnerable."

Eisenhower saw the sense in that and summoned an aide, gave him a verbal order to pass on, knowing he was just wrecking a whole lot of quality work done by Tedder and his staff ,who were creating a plan to govern air operations in the coming days.

"So, we also cannot guarantee extra resources coming from the States, nor from the Pacific, as the Nips are suddenly frisky and well-armed."

Bradley audibly sighed.

"You gotta hand it to them, they have worked this one out well, Ike."

There could be absolutely no disagreeing with that.

"Betcha one thing though."

Bradley nodded to himself as he searched for a memory and found it.

"There will be an opening, an omission, an error that we can exploit. After all, history shows us that there are no invincible armies."

Eisenhower's punctuated laugh stopped many a staff officer in mid-task, wondering what could possibly cause the supreme allied commander to laugh on such a black day.

"And we will find it, Brad," and with a rare display of open emotion, Ike slapped Bradley on the shoulder and turned to the first of a line of officers with paper in their hands.

During their conversation in the Secretary-General's office on the morning of 12th June, Beria had handed Stalin a document detailing 'DIASPORA - Intentions' and called his attention to Page seventeen, addendum F.

This addendum detailed the captured German equipment that could be transferred to the Japanese Army, for

446

their use against the Chinese initially and, subsequently, the Pacific Allies.

Throughout the war, the Red Army had captured significant amounts of Wehrmacht hardware of all types and it was these trophies of war that were now in the hands of the Japanese.

It was an impressive list indeed.

Moving such a large quantity of tanks, vehicles, weapons and munitions, would normally attract much attention, but the few Allied spies who were in a position to observe the broad gauge trains running to the Far East, solely reported numbers of tanks and carriages, not knowing that concealed under tarpaulins were German tanks, not Russian ones. It also suited the Soviet love of Maskirova, that the clandestine switch of captured axis equipment could be easily seen to be the intended move of the Russian Armies slated for the non-existent Manchurian Offensive.

A subsequent hand-written submission from an NKVD General indicated that the Tiger II B's, the so-called King Tigers, proved impossible to transport clandestinely and so they were being retained in Europe.

Operation Diaspora, the military plan for the Far East, was simple in its conception and beautifully crafted.

Initially, no Soviet ground forces would be employed. Sufficient training had been given to the eager Japanese to allow them to fight with their new acquisitions, although most of the vehicles required field modifications, for no other reason than the difference in size of your average German and your average Japanese.

Whilst the training was rudimentary, it was felt enough to overcome the light vehicles in the possession of the Chinese Nationalist Army, under Chiang-Kai-Shek. Battles would increase efficiency and by the time anything substantial from the American arsenal came their way, it was expected that the new tankers would be able to cope well enough. Some Soviet 'observers' went with Japanese ground units, just to provide some guidance on capabilities and use, until it was felt they could cope alone.

447

Vast tonnages of German ammunition had been captured during the four years of the Great Patriotic War and the Russians, being the Russians, had never thrown any of it away. Now most of it was here, stockpiled ready for the attack in China. Large numbers of German weapons were similarly handed over, increasing the firepower of Japanese infantry units tenfold. Sub-machine guns were a rarity in the Emperor's Army, but now they were numerous enough for every senior NCO and many officers to carry one. Tired and cumbersome Nambu machine guns were mainly replaced with tried and trusted MG34's and 42's; also, many riflemen were able to swap their modest Arisaka rifles for the efficient killing machine that was the Kar98K rifle.

A few hundred panzerfausts had made the long journey from Europe, but most were retained in Soviet hands, as they were a proven and effective anti-tank weapon.

Japanese artillery was limited, but now their units brimmed with German guns, from 75mm through to 150mm, all healthily supplied with ammunition.

Everything from the German arsenal seemed to have made its way east, in varying numbers and the Chinese Army would struggle to cope, undoubtedly failing, when it all rolled into the attack.

Diaspora also harnessed the Japanese willingness to die gloriously, as well as abused the trust between allies that tenuously existed in mid-1945.

Soviet freighters and warships did indeed transport large numbers of Japanese, who sweltered below decks in hot weather to avoid detection, only emerging at nights.

Such tactics enabled the attacks on Saipan, Okinawa, Eniwetok and Ulithi, to get close and use surprise to be disproportionately successful. At Okinawa, Eniwetok and Ulithi, the Soviet ships had transported Kaiten Human Torpedoes and it was these suicide weapons that had gutted the naval forces.

At Eniwetok, the light carrier USS Cabot CVL28 had rolled over and sunk, taking most of her hands down with her and the fleet carrier USS Wasp CV18 had also been badly damaged, having stopped off en route for Okinawa from the

States, after extensive repairs to kamikaze damage. Naval base personnel and supply facilities, especially fuel oils, had been badly damaged. One light cruiser and a number of fleet support vessels, were at the bottom of the harbour, each with heavy loss of life.

At Ulithi, another light carrier, the USS Langley CVL27, received two Kaiten hits and became an instant furnace, incinerating many of her crew and flight personnel before the fires were controlled. She was not lost, but would never fight again.

At Okinawa, the old battleship, USS Pennsylvania BB38, took a hit in her stern and flooded badly, but the old lady survived, being dragged to shallow waters and successfully beached. However, fleet Carrier USS Bennington CV20 and light carrier USS Belleau Wood CVL24, both lacked Pennsylvania's resilience and were sunk at their moorings, although fortunately, in both cases, few lives were lost. USS Monterey CVL26 took a direct hit from a Kaiten, which did no more than stove in a plate, as the warhead did not explode. In all cases, the freighters involved also disgorged Japanese naval marines, tasked to do grisly work ashore. Their orders were to kill and destroy until death overtook them, orders that they discharged extremely successfully.

1201hrs Tuesday 7th August 1945, Heiligenthal, South-West of Lüneberg, Germany.

Allied Forces – B Coy, 1st Btn, 325th Glider Infantry Regiment, Battery A, 320th Glider field Artillery Btn, Elements of 307th Airborne Engineer Btn, of 82nd US Airborne Division 'All-American', directly attached to British 21st Army Group.

Soviet Forces – 49th Guards Rifle Regt, 44th Guards Artillery Regt, of 16th Guards Rifle Division, of 36th Guards Rifle Corps, 285th [Independent] Tank Regt, 3rd Btn, 77th Engineer Bridging Brigade, 11th Guards Army, 1st Baltic Front.

Corporal Liam D. O'Malley had seen a lot of combat since his first taste at Salerno in 1943. The healthy respect he had developed for the German soldier was now being mirrored by the new enemy.

Courage in the man opposite can be admired and O'Malley had seen plenty of it that morning.

In front of his position lay the dead of two attempts to force a crossing over the Hasenburger Mühlenbach, a tributary of the Ilmenau River, that protected the route around the south of Luneberg.

He and his squad were positioned on the northwest bank of the Hasenburger, on a kink in the river that not only protected their flanks, but also gave them a lovely field of fire all the way to the woods, as well as covering the main vehicular approach from the south-west.

Soviet infantry had emerged from the woods on both sides of that track and made a rapid assault on the bridge, falling in their scores in the first failed attempt.

Falling back quickly, they took root in the tree line, from where accurate fire was brought down upon the defending glider infantry.

The new company commander had designated the old watermill as his CP, but was soon flushed out by accurate Soviet mortar fire as the building, already damaged from the fighting in April 1945, received more hits and started to burn fiercely.

O'Malley found himself smirking.

'Well, the sarge did try to tell him.'

The officer was not popular.

Artillery fire had not been brought to bear on the strong position, something each and every man was grateful for, although their gain was C Company's loss, as a rain of Soviet shells fell upon them in their positions within Oedeme, to the northeast.

The second assault, supported by a full company of Soviet mortars, had failed equally miserably, but only because of the timely intervention of 105mm's from 320th Artillery. With great skill, the 320th's Artillery Liaison officer dropped his shells as close as thirty yards in front of the defender's positions. One young Pfc was presently on his way to the aid station, bleeding and close to death, having been struck on the head by a portion of a Soviet rifle butt, blasted in his direction as the assault was stopped in a sea of shrapnel and high explosives.

The few Russians who struggled through were quickly disposed of and those fortunate enough to regain the woods prayed their thanks to a god few had paid heed to in calmer times.

Ammunition limitations prevented the Artillery Lieutenant from advising his battery commander to drop more artillery on the woods, but that did not stop the defenders from tossing a few 60mm mortar shells over, just to keep the Soviets on their toes.

The last rush had been over an hour beforehand and, as O'Malley figured, the damn Russkies were not going to go away, so they were definitely planning something more involved, something undoubtedly more dangerous, for him and his pals.

Captain [Acting Major] Vladimir Deniken swore loudly. The orderly was trying to be gentle, but the shrapnel tear in his arm hurt like hell and her ministrations agitated the wound.

His 3rd Battalion had been badly hurt in the assault on the bridge and he hated having his hands tied. Artillery would be such a help, but orders were orders. A reinforcement company from 2nd/49th Regt was on its way, sent to give him more men to achieve the rapid success required by his regimental commander.

In addition, having explained the tactical problem, the Colonel had promised tank support and it was the approach of these assets that first penetrated Deniken's veil of pain as the orderly finished up her work.

Thanking the woman, he walked back through the woods to a tight bend on the road where his reserve company was mustered [A] and where the newly arrived T34's growled gently at ease under the canopy of trees. As the Captain approached the tank unit's commander, he was greeted by the sight of an infantry unit doubling across the open field in his direction.

Assigning his Starshina to direct the new troops to a rest position off to the west, he briefed his own leaders, as well as the new infantry officers and the tank commanders, using a stick of chalk to draw a map on the glacis of the first tank.

The proposition was simple. Regiment wanted the bridge intact, so there was to be no firing on it. American paratroopers were dug in all along the far bank and had already destroyed the flimsy crossing point to the south-west.

To be honest, he thought, there is little opportunity for finesse here, but the tanks will help.

"Comrades, nothing complicated here."

An appraisal of the map confirmed that.

"These are good troops here. American paratroopers who know how to fight. I have lost a full company so far and they haven't moved one bit. So don't believe everything you have been told about easily walking over the allies."

There were a couple of haws, but it was not really a joking matter.

"There are no mines, but they do have artillery support and it's very accurate, so we must close with them quickly, no stopping to engage from safe distance."

The others were all experienced officers and NCO's who understood perfectly. Men would die.

"We have found two small boats, which I will use to get a platoon across the river, here," he tapped his finger on the glacis plate map, south of the bridge, where the trees met the water [B].

"That's our best chance of getting men on the other side. I will have another platoon in reserve if the boats can be used to reinforce, but they are flimsy craft, comrades."

What he left unsaid was that they were flimsy craft that would likely be riddled with bullets by the enemy on the opposite bank.

"I can't support them with mortars, as my main plan is to drop a smoke screen on the positions north and south of the

452

bridge," his hands described the dropping areas, the pain in his arm reminding him of the price of failure.

Deniken drew the roads, river, woods and bridge. Adding his recollections of the American positions, he drew back from his handiwork to form a tactical plan.

Fig#11

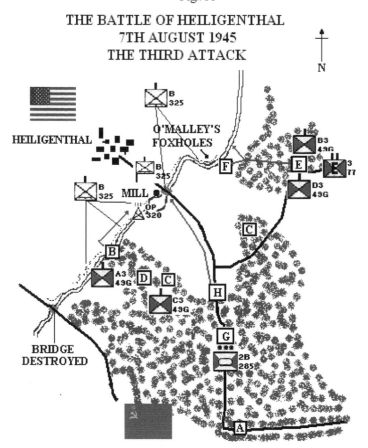

THE BATTLE OF HEILIGENTHAL
7TH AUGUST 1945
THE THIRD ATTACK

"I will position my heavy machine guns here, [C] to bring fire upon the defenders south of the bridge, with Grabin's remaining men as a reserve force[D]," the position he indicated in the wood line already contained spots of his blood from his soaked sleeve.

"My main force [E] will be gathered here", indicating the woods to the east of the bridge as he spoke, "And we will focus all our attention on swimming across on the bend of the river here [F]", he smudged the chalk on the point of O'Malley's foxhole position.

"That may seem a long way to move my troops but, from what I can see, it's better screened from fire out of Heiligenthal, than here, south of the bridge."

He indicated the newly arrived company commander.

"Your men will accompany the tanks in their dash up the road, straight for and over the bridge, dropping off men at the bridge and checking for charges immediately. The others wil move on up, establishing a position here in the village, facing front. Release at least one platoon to return to the river, to take any defenders left in the rear here, where I am attacking."

The infantry and tank leaders had exchanged looks and grimaced at the nature of their orders.

Deniken continued.

"Yours is not an easy task, comrades," he smiled, "But then, today, there are no easy tasks."

Pressing on quickly, Deniken selected the mortar officer, detailing the fire pattern and where to switch fire to, once the bridge had been crossed, but stressing the importance of dropping the smoke ON the enemy positions and switching fire at precisely the right moment.

"The tanks will be concealed at first, no further forward than here [G] and will remain so until Leytenant Grabin", he nodded at the hard-bitten old officer in whom he was entrusting so much, "Fires a green flare, which will be when my assault has commenced and made the river line, or earlier, if something unexpected occurs. Your tanks will then swiftly move up to this line [H]," he chopped a palm across the drawing, "And briefly take the bank, south of the bridge, also the mill, under direct fire, as much to announce yourselves and confuse the enemy as anything. That should be without risk, as I have seen no anti-tank guns, but move fast once you have

454

fired a few rounds. There is no shortage of their infantry tank killing weapons, plus I don't want you caught in a barrage."

The tank commanders nodded their understanding, never having heard of or seen a bazooka, but retaining painful memories of what a panzerfaust could do to a tank.

"What I want here is far too much happening for the defenders to respond to properly, lots of noise and lots of firing."

"Bravo, Deniken," the words were accompanied by a slow handclap.

The Regimental Commander and his entourage had arrived silently and caught most of the brief. Everyone stiffened to attention as the four officers strode into the heart of the briefing.

"Good plan, Comrade Captain."

Deniken saluted and the rest followed suit.

"Comrade Colonel, I didn't know you were coming."

"Well, we're stalled everywhere by these damned Amerikanski and as you're furthest west, it falls to you to lead the army, so I came to support you as needed."

Deniken also knew that the more sinister purpose was to relieve him on the spot if the assault failed for a third time.

"Indeed, Comrade Colonel."

He resumed the final part of his brief.

"Reserve formations will be committed as required, either on my command, or the initiative of the Reserve commander."

He took in Grabin with another look and he always trusted what he saw.

"Heavy machine gun troops to move up as soon as the defenders have been moved off the river line. Support my group, the boat group and defend the bridge from any counter-attack."

Addressing the badly scarred Engineer officer, Deniken sought a loan of equipment.

"Comrade Mayor, if you could let me borrow some spare rubber boats from you, then I can put more men across south of the river."

The Major and the Regimental Commander exchanged looks.

"Unfortunately, I have no spares, Comrade Kapitan. I have sent my spares to the 134th, to cover their equipment losses."

There was no more to be said.

He looked at his watch.

"Synchronise now, at 1215, on my mark," noting everyman, including his commander, ready with their watches, "3,2,1, mark."

"Mortars and support machine guns will start firing smoke at 1258, infantry will attack with the boats at 1300, I will commence the main infantry attack at 1305, tanks to roll on green flare from Grabin. Questions?"

Once the silence had confirmed that everyone knew the plan and their part in it., the Regimental Commander spoke.

"Comrades, I must stress that the bridge must fall into our hands intact. I have men from the Army engineer unit here", he indicated the scar faced Major of engineers who looked stonily at Deniken. Nods were exchanged.

"They have bridging equipment, but I would rather not use it. Understand me, comrades?"

They understood perfectly. The man who permitted the bridge to be brought down would not survive the day.

And with that thought, the orders group dismissed and the preparations for the attack got underway.

Divisional artillery was still pounding away at Oedeme for all it was worth, but the area around Heiligenthal was relatively quiet until two LA-5's fighters, one smoking badly, flew low over the bridge, heading southeast.

Some enthusiastic machine gunner sent a stream of tracer skywards, narrowly missing the wounded bird. The wingman lazily pulled off his guarding position and carried out one quick strafing run of machine gun and cannon fire, before returning to babysit his damaged companion back to their base.

Two men were hit by the strafing run and both were killed, as aircraft cannon shells tend to be hard on the human body.

One was the young machine gunner who had climbed on the jeep and sent .50cal rounds skyward. The other was the airborne unit's senior Non-com, the hard-bitten old Sergeant, who had run to the boy to drag him off the gun, determined to beast him for attracting such unwanted attention.

The Sergeant had been with the unit since it was formed and had seen O'Malley and his comrades through many tough scrapes, pulling them through with his skill and courage. Once the consuming fire of the burning jeep had abated, O'Malley promised himself he would bury Master Sergeant Thompson properly and mark his grave. It was the least that could be done.

Disturbed at the loss of the unit's senior man, O'Malley drew a camel from his pack and lit it, even though 1 o'clock chow time was approaching. The rich smoke wafted around him as he crouched in his foxhole, wondering who would give the mess call now that Thompson was in bits.

His thoughts were disturbed by distant coughing, not from the throats of men, but rather distinctly, from mortars.

The shells exploded all around his position, bathing the river and foxholes in choking smoke. No one needed to be told what was about to happen.

Machine gun fire could also be heard, but they were visiting their brand of hurt on someone else, so O'Malley kept his head up for now.

The wind was very low and so the smoke stayed pretty much where it was laid, occasionally wafting one way or another as a small gust pushed it around.

Steadying his BAR into his shoulder, he checked around him to make sure his section were up and alert, ready to do their jobs when the moment came. The BAR was not his normal weapon, but the squad needed the firepower and as its previous owner was back in the aid station having been clipped by a bullet in the second attack, O'Malley took the job.

More firing started, this time in the background.

457

A scream came from one of the men stationed just north of the bridge as he was struck directly between the shoulder blades by a smoke round. The unlucky man had bent over to pick up his helmet, dislodged by the previous explosive round to arrive. He was dead before anyone could move to his assistance, spine smashed, lungs and heart wrecked and bloody, the light smoke gently discharging from the unexploded shell, making the corpse a particularly ghoulish sight.

To O'Malley's left, a carbine stuttered and he turned to chastise his man. The wind wafted the smoke and created an arched clear zone in which Soviet soldiers could be seen running hard, straight at his position, holding wood, looted inner tubes, anything that would float.

No orders were needed and bullets reached out, dropping many at the full run.

The man nearest to O'Malley's right side grunted and slithered down lifelessly into his foxhole as a bullet effortlessly blew the back of his head off and sent his helmet careening off to the rear.

The smoke closed in again just as the Soviets reached the water's edge, but there was no respite in the fire from the defenders, who fired blind, killing and wounding the unseen enemy to their front.

O'Malley saw the flare reach its zenith before the smoke, moved by another breeze, engulfed his position completely.

Deniken grimaced as he ran, noting the bad luck as the smoke parted. His men were going down under accurate fire and there was little he could do except press forward with them.

Pausing to shoulder his rifle, he fired a shot and was rewarded with a helmet flipping away and the enemy soldier dropping into his hole.

Deniken was an officer and, as such, should not carry a rifle, but he was an excellent marksman and his skills had sent many a German to his grave.

458

Encouraging his second wave forward, he sprinted for the water, snatching an empty petrol can from the dead fingers of a Russian soldier lying at the water's edge.

He looked south towards the spot where Grabin was concealed and was immediately rewarded with the sight of a green flare lazily floating back to earth.

Try as he might, Deniken could not hear the roar of tank engines and he uttered a silent prayer to his mother's god that the unknown tankers were competent.

As he dove into the water, he heard the crack of 85mm guns and knew they had joined the battle.

With the rifle slung across his shoulders and using the petrol can as a buoyancy aid, he doggy paddled as best he could for the far bank and, all the while, bullets whipped like wasps around the struggling men.

He heard a distinct plop in the water beside him before his world went white and he was tossed skywards.

As the smoke concealed the attackers once more, O'Malley shouted at his men to throw grenades.

These flew from hands and dropped, some in the water and some on the banks.

One trooper was shot in the act of throwing, a random bullet emerging from the smoke and wrecking his wrist. The grenade dropped from useless fingers into the foxhole he shared with his buddy, neither of whom could escape before both died bloodily in a storm of shrapnel.

Screams could be heard as Soviet infantry endured similar deaths and mutilations in the smoke.

The wind started to gather strength and the smoke screen, no longer added to by mortars shells, moved at a walking pace to the northeast, thinning as it went.

Unfortunately for the defenders and attackers alike, the smoke from the blazing watermill now engulfed them, adding its acrid toxic fumes to those generated by weapons and high explosives.

A bullet fanned past O'Malley's head, kissing the helmet lightly.

He turned slightly left and saw an indistinct figure that he almost cut in half with a burst of .30 cal, the body immediately jerking backwards under the impacts. It was immediately replaced by another struggling shape that received the same treatment.

His eyes streaming from the mill smoke, O'Malley sensed rather than saw the grenade land adjacent to his foxhole and ducked as fast as he could. The man to his left did not hear his shout and was tossed against the side of his foxhole by the force of the explosion, surprisingly unscathed, except for a ruptured eardrum.

The young trooper calmly changed magazines on his carbine, launching more bullets into the shapes in the smoke, rewarded with the occasional scream.

O'Malley emerged from his hole in time to see the young trooper's death. He was amazed to see him alive, but his shout of congratulations was strangled, as a stream of sub-machine gun bullets reached indiscriminately out of the smoke and destroyed the man's face and neck.

Sprayed with blood, the Corporal continued his killing like an automaton, noting his dwindling supply of ammunition.

Deniken came to, staring at the grass, front teeth missing, lips split and nose bleeding from the impact as he came to earth face first, neatly scalped and leaking blood from where a lump of the grenade had come very close to ending his life.

The rest of his body was still in the water, bleeding from a number of small shrapnel wounds and bruised from the energy blow of the water displaced by high explosive.

Looking around, he saw others on the bank, lying low or firing back, depending on the bravery of the individual.

Behind him, others were struggling across the water as best they could and yet others were still, never to move again.

He had no weapon, his rifle probably consigned to the bottom of the river.

Searching around, he saw the remains of a Soviet soldier still clutching a Mosin-Nagant rifle with bayonet

460

attached. Moving sluggishly to his left, he acquired the weapon and pocketed some ammunition, not bothering to wipe the detritus of death from it.

He could hear the tanks on the bridge now, the distinct rattling of the track pins louder than the firing around him, their main guns still reaching out to kill the American paratroopers.

Attracting the attention of those around him, he steadied himself, ready to take them forward into the defending foxholes.

Rising to his feet, he yelled his small group forward and they plunged into the thinning smoke, even as some of them had the life plucked from them by American bullets.

O'Malley changed magazines but held his fire. It was the last one, after all. Ready to hand by the side of his foxhole were one grenade, his M1911 and a combat knife.

He automatically winced as a Russian tank exploded in a fireball, victim of a bazooka team to the south of the bridge.

His attention was drawn to four others moving towards his rear, infantry hanging on for all they were worth and other running figures fanning out in support.

The bridge had fallen and it was time to bug out. He wondered where the order was, but, unknown to O'Malley, the young inexperienced Lieutenant who should have provided it had broken down. He was mentally shattered and useless, cowering and crying loudly behind the watermill, where he was heard and dispatched by a compassionless Soviet sub-machine gunner.

The sounds to O'Malley's left changed now and he became aware that his squad was being overrun, soldiers grappling, stabbing and screaming, slashing and shouting, all in a frenzy of close quarter combat.

Suddenly to his front came a group of seven Russians, all seemingly intent on running straight over him.

They saw him too.

Weapons spat bullets in both directions and found their mark in American and Russian alike.

461

O'Malley did not feel his left arm break as two PPSH bullets struck home and shattered the lower bone structure, ruining his radial artery in their travel.

Neither did he feel his right ear nicked by another bullet.

He was aware of the bullets hitting the ground in front of him, throwing earth and pieces of grass into his eyes, reducing his vision.

Through his squints he finished his own work, putting down another Russian, the lifeless body flung backwards to join the three already cut down by fire from his BAR.

Three more enemy remained and he pushed the now useless Browning away and grabbed for his pistol, bringing it up and firing, simultaneously dropping another Russian as more PPSH bullets smashed into his right shoulder, wrenching him round like a rag doll even as he discharged the rest of his magazine uselessly into the ground.

O'Malley swung back round, suddenly aware of the tattered and bloody apparition standing over him and experienced excruciating pain as he was slammed against the side of his hole by an eighteen inch bayonet forcefully penetrating his upper chest. The blade travelled on and destroyed his trachea, blood pouring straight into his lungs in an instant. The unforgiving steel carried on, deflecting off his spinal column and out of his back and into the earth wall beyond.

It was stuck and no amount of twisting and pulling would free it, even with a boot planted firmly on O'Malley's chest, so the Russian holding it chambered a round and fired point-blank to blast the metal free, reloading the weapon as he quickly moved on to do more killing elsewhere.

O'Malley had but a few seconds of active thought before darkness forever overtook the mental pictures of family and home.

It was still there. Slightly damaged and scorched from the heat of the burning tank, but the bridge that had cost so many lives still stood.

462

Fighting continued in Heiligenthal, as the surviving four tanks and their accompanying infantry pushed hard for complete control.

Deniken sat beside the bridge, near a burning jeep, watching as his wounded were brought in to be treated as best they could be. The dead were also being reverently recovered and he could not take his eyes off the lifeless form of the young medical orderly who had bandaged his arm that very morning. No marks on her body, just a small trickle of blood from her mouth.

His newly acquired rifle lay propped by his side, its bloody bayonet testament to the hand-to-hand gutter fight that had resulted from the desperate charge.

They had died hard, these damned Amerikanski; as hard as the German to be sure.

The headache was extreme now and the bandage seemed to get tighter by the second, squeezing his head.

Grabin had reported to him but he could not remember what was said, except that he handed command of the battalion over to his old soldier.

The Regimental Commander's GAZ moved up the track, picking its way through the dead and dying, clearly on its way over the bridge.

Quickly, Deniken struggled to his feet to give his report and, just as quickly, dropped to the ground.

His fight was over for now, but he had done his duty and the line was broken.

It would be many hours before the newly-promoted Major and Commander of 3rd Battalion, 49th Guards Rifle Regiment, regained consciousness.

Some two hours after Deniken was taken back to the medical facilities, established outside of Bienenbüttel, one company of 3rd/77th Engineer Brigade was brought forward by the scar-faced Major Eltsov. He was keen to get his valuable bridging equipment secreted in the woods either side of Hauptstraße, running north out of Heiligenthal, now finally free of the enemy, who had been pushed back beyond Kirchgellersen.

The arrival overhead of three USAAF 405th Fighter Group Thunderbolts was perfect timing for the Americans and could not have been worse for the engineers.

A trio of quad-mount Maxim AA guns had been positioned to defend the bridge until more substantial assets could be placed and they engaged immediately.

Major Eltsov frantically signalled his trucks to scatter and seek refuge in the woods, but the previous artillery barrages had made the ground difficult to negotiate at the best of times.

Part of the briefing received by Soviet officers on the allied air forces capabilities concerned the use of rockets by ground-attack planes. For the Major, the claim that they were extremely inaccurate paled into insignificance when it came to being on the receiving end of a full salvo from a determined and experienced enemy.

The first P47 drove in hard and released all eight rockets at the scattering engineer vehicles.

Watching behind him as his Jeep rode up on the bridge, Eltsov winced as death was visited upon the troops he led, disproving the inaccuracy claims of the GRU Colonel who had briefed him.

In his rage, he screamed at his driver to halt, which the man did, bringing the jeep to a stop in a storm of pebbles and dust.

Eltsov slapped the driver on the shoulder and pointed off towards a smoking structure nearby. Grabbing his SVT automatic rifle, he ran back over the bridge, only to stop short as the second salvo of rockets arrived, more deadly than the first.

The vehicles carrying the inflatables had been in the centre of the column and it was these that had been received the brunt of it in the first strike. The second strike had been aimed at them as well, but had overshot and fallen, as accurately as could possibly be, upon the lorries containing most of the prime personnel, his best engineering troops, veterans of combat bridging operations from the Volga to the Elbe. Few of them survived intact as the soft-skin transports demonstrated their lack of resistance to high explosive.

The Major winced as bodies were tossed high, whole or in pieces, fire and smoke concealing the area from whence they sprang.

Shouting as loud as he could, he waved frantically at the front vehicles, desperately encouraging them to scatter for cover as he stood exposed on the bridge.

The fourth vehicle stalled, holding up those behind but first three vehicles sprang forward, almost propelled by the carnage behind them and reached the bridge, timed to the second with the arrival of the third aircraft's salvo.

Bridge and lorry disappeared together as the first pair of rockets struck precisely, the bridge decking units from the Studebakers load tossed and shredded by the blast. The next three pairs turned the east side of the bridge approach into a maelstrom, converting men and machines into pieces and spreading them for yards in all directions.

The planes were gone in the blink of an eye, pursued by lead from the two surviving, but impotent, Maxims.

In their wake, the carnage was complete, the bridging engineer company now consisted of thirty-seven wounded and shell Shocked men who would never be the same again.

Do what you can, with what you have, where you are.

Theodore Roosevelt

CHAPTER 44 – THE COUNCIL

1400hrs Tuesday, 7th August 1945, Headquarters, US Forces in Europe. I.G.Farben, Frankfurt-am-Main, Germany.

The first of them had arrived at 1325 and he was immediately shown to the elegant dining room where a modest buffet lunch had been provided and where sat General Dwight D Eisenhower in full uniform. The others arrived in short order and soon the ensemble was complete.

As quickly as was considered polite, the orderlies cleared away the side tables, provided coffee for the thirteen men and left.

The general hubbub of conversation dropped, conversation that had not been about the most pressing matter in the minds of the nine visitors, but had just been small talk of family and life. What they all wanted to know most was why they were here.

Eisenhower rose to his feet, two other senior allied officers remaining seated by previous agreement. A US Army intelligence Major took his cue from his General and commenced his brief, addressing both sides of the long walnut table equally, firstly in his native tongue and then in English, a courtesy not lost on the nine.

"Gentlemen, my name is Major David S. Goldstein," the Jewish officer could not help but leave his name hanging just for a split second, "And I am here to translate for both groups, which I will do honestly, literally and completely, to ensure full understanding."

Goldstein pulled out a small stack of V-shaped cards and walked towards his own grouping of officers.

"For ease, it has been decided that name indicators would be appropriate and so I will place them out now, by way of introduction."

466

He leant around Eisenhower, placing a name strip and, despite the General not needing any introduction whatsoever, named him, including the position of Supreme Allied Commander. Respectful nods were exchanged across the table.

Moving to Ike's right, the diminutive Major placed out the strip for Joseph de Monsabert, naming him as the representative of the French Government and General commanding French Forces in Germany.

Placing his own marker in the space he had recently vacated, to Monsabert's right, he moved to the other side of Eisenhower in order to complete the Allied ensemble with the naming of Brian Robertson, Baron of Oakridge, presently the British Deputy Military Governor of Germany and Britain's representative at these proceedings.,

Effortlessly, he moved around to the other side of the long table and commenced his introductions of the guests.

"Franz Von Papen".

More correctly known as Franz Joseph Hermann Michael Maria von Papen zu Köningen, his credentials were impressive. A former army Colonel, politician and one time Chancellor of Germany; Von Papen was a name that would be known to every German.

Leaning forward, the second strip was placed.

"Adolf Schärf."

Twice a political prisoner of the Nazis, Scharf was head of the newly formed Social Democratic Party of Austria.

Von Papen noted that with each name, nods from the Allied sides showed acknowledgement.

A strip for the provisional President of Austria.

"Karl Renner"

'*Nods of acknowledgement... and something else.*'

The old politician's senses lit up.

The Prime Minister of Bavaria received his name strip.

"Wilhelm Hoegner."

'*It isn't contempt.*'

No mention of his former military rank of GeneralOberst.

"Heinrich von Vietinghoff."

467

'*It isn't superiority.*'

Another's GeneralOberst status went unmentioned.

"Heinz Guderian"

'*It isn't hate.*'

The ex-minister of Armaments and War Production needed no introduction.

"Albert Speer"

'*It certainly isn't subservience.*'

Neither did the last leader of the failed Third Reich.

"Karl Dönitz."

'*It isn't even mistrust.*'

Finally, the last Chancellor of Germany, albeit briefly and not by that name.

"Johann Ludwig Graf Schwerin von Krosigk"

'*Grüß Gott! It looks very much like need.*'

Goldstein, having finished his introductions, strode to the main double doors and knocked on one, which was immediately opened, admitting two US NCO's bearing organised files and documents, one grouping of which was placed before each man present.

Each lay where they were placed, untouched by the recipient, as if by common agreement.

His work done, the First Sergeant left the room and the T4 Sergeant took her place at the stenotype in the corner of the room.

Eisenhower began and Goldstein translated into German.

"Thank you all for coming here at such short notice. I know some of you have been held awaiting investigations into your activities over the last twelve years and I must stress that such investigations will run their course and where there has been transgression, justice will surely follow. Today you should have been ten and now you are nine, because the individual concerned has been proved to be associated with unacceptable activities. What needs to be done cannot be done at any price. I hope that you will all understand that."

Ike waited until Goldstein had delivered the translation and deliberately prolonged the pause to let the words sink in. There was no hint of a reaction from those facing him.

"Gentlemen, by now you will all have heard of the events that commenced yesterday morning."

The pain on the faces of all of those across the table encouraged Eisenhower. His next words were deliberately chosen.

"This attack poses the highest possible risk to all our countries," indicating not only those before him, but also the two allied officers either side of him, "And will not be easily defeated and certainly not without great loss, even in the face of our unity."

That was noted loud and clear.

"Germany is without government, as is Austria, both controlled by our Military at this time."

As each word wormed its way into their minds of the Germans and Austrians and, to a man, both groups squirmed out of national embarrassment, as well as developing more understanding as to part of their purpose in being there.

"Each of you is a figurehead, a leadership icon to your people, to varying degrees and with appeal to different sections of your societies, from the military across the spectrum of your homelands political make-up."

Eisenhower's craving gave him a moment's pause. He coughed.

"I have today spoken with the President of the United States, the British Prime Minister and the French Head of State. They all support the view that we stand on the threshold of Europe... and indeed the World's darkest days and, I assure you, all three fully endorse these proceedings."

Ike could sense anticipation growing in the room.

"We have no time for democratic political processes. If we were to try to conduct such processes, events would overtake us and the ability to exercise such democratic rights would be lost to this continent forever."

Eisenhower opened the folder in front of him.

"The documentation within the blue folder in front of you contains the latest information on what is happening in

469

Europe, as well as intelligence estimates of how things may evolve."

Nine pairs of hands reached forward and opened their file.

Again clearing his throat, Ike pressed on.

"Also present, in the green folder, is a similar set of documents relating to events in the Pacific."

That caused a few heads to shoot up questioningly.

"Yes. I am afraid that your former allies have seen fit to throw in their lot with the Soviets and, as we speak, hundreds of Americans lie dead and dying throughout the Pacific Islands and Japanese soldiers are rampaging through China driving your tanks, firing your artillery and killing with your rifles."

Goldstein put the same emphasis employed by Eisenhower into each translation of 'your'.

A world at war once more, a thought which no-one present in that room could stomach, no matter which side of the artificial wooden divide they sat.

"I am empowered to constitute, here and now, the 'Council of Germany and Austria', consisting of all members here present, being of equal voice and with responsibility for governing domestic matters as detailed in the report within the red folder."

The sudden noise of paper and card being eagerly sought out and handled gave Eisenhower a moment's pause. Clearly some present spoke at least a little English as their eagerness to get at the information caused them to select the correct file before Goldstein had finished translating.

"Perhaps you would like to look at the proposals whilst we organise some more coffee here?"

Taking her cue, the Tech-4 exited the room.

Eisenhower sat down between his two companions and, as they were both doing, watched the reactions of the readers opposite as they digested the contents of the German language versions of what sat in front of him.

Monsabert sat rigidly, impassive, but not missing anything before his eyes.

470

Robertson shifted in his seat, drawing a glance from Ike. Their eyes locked, just for a second, men asking the same question of the other. Do they know what comes next?

Coffee arrived and with it came a selection of marzipan fingers and miniature pastries. Also, there was a special platter with a Smörgåsbord of tobacco products and the means to light them. Eisenhower was not a General for nothing and these, more than the sweet offerings, were homed in on by the visitors. Once one match flared from across the table, Eisenhower followed it with his own lighter and his craving was instantly satisfied.

The Tech-4 had resumed her seat unnoticed and silently waited for the resumption.

"The Council will need a leader and that man would be decided upon by you alone and he will be known as the Chancellor."

Interest was peaking.

"There will also be one representative from each of the governing allied powers present as part of the council, non-voting in matters relative to your domestic decision making. However, any two of these representatives may join together and veto any decision made on any matter."

Willing Goldstein to deliver that quickly, Ike started talking before the Major had finished.

"That is not a power that will be widely used, as we see it as imperative that the Council is seen by your countrymen as controlling domestic matters. It is also equally imperative that you understand, for yourselves, the responsibilities that are being placed in your hands."

The telltale creak of an antique French dining chair to his left told Ike that Robertson was fidgeting, preparing himself for what was coming.

This time he let the Major finish and found time to light another cigarette.

"Are there any questions at this point?"

He hoped there would not be, of course, as the documentation was quite inclusive. The translation complete, Ike watched what amounted to a silent ballet before his eyes, with looks, small shrugs and minute gestures, as the group

471

seemed to be sorting out a pecking order. He wondered who it was that would come out on top and be the one to speak.

"The outline of the proposal is most complete, Herr General."

So it was Von Papen. Damn, five dollars lost. He had been so sure it would be Dönitz,

"I believe that all of us here understand that our nations, having been conquered, cannot expect the niceties of freedom of self-determination at this time", looking around at his cohorts for a dissenting look or gesture and seeing none, he continued, "But this seems to go some way towards that goal."

He pursed his lips, lightly adjusting his small moustache.

"But at what cost to our nations, Herr General, what cost?"

Silence.

He dropped the file on the desk and it sounded like a gun shot.

"Would these niceties have been afforded us were the Russians not knocking on your door? I think not, so let us be free of the illusion that this is a philanthropic exercise on the part of any of your governments."

As Goldstein completed his words, Von Papen noted them strike home.

This time he took further stock of the attitudes of those around him and was satisfied to see that they seemed to understand his approach, his need to show that they were their own men, even though he knew, they knew, where this was going and what had to be done.

He adopted a more conciliatory tone and approach.

"Herr Generals," he deliberately addressed the three of them, "As we sit here, the Communist enemy Germany and Austria have been fighting since 1941 is knocking on your door, inflicting death and destruction upon the people and ideals you hold dear."

He looked around him enquiringly, searching each man for some sign of rebellion, some indication of discontent.

There was none to be seen.

472

"Our own people will suffer even more outrages and this time, without the hopes we had before."

Slowly he rose to his feet.

"How can I, as a German citizen, contemplate doing anything other than using every part of me, every effort, all my energy and dedicate myself to the preservation of my country and countrymen?"

He adjusted his waistcoat with a dignified tug.

"Personally... and I must speak solely for myself at this time," an unnecessary statement, but one appreciated by his comrades in the absence of formal discussions, "I will accept the proposal here as it stands, but understand that I am not a fool and neither is any man here. I know this comes with a price tag, but it is a price the German People will have to pay, no, will gladly pay to stand tall once more. It is the Army that you need and we old men are required to persuade our peoples of the correctness and necessity of it all, after six long years of blood and pain"

He gestured loosely at the documents in front of him, in a way bordering on contempt, certainly by way of total disregard.

"You may give us some rights to self-govern, but you and we all know they will be few and unimportant for now. Maybe later, when we have earned your trust and proved our worth, but not now. None the less, I will lend my support and ask my people to rise up again."

He looked around him.

"Kameraden?"

One by one, each of the men stood in agreement until no one save the stenographer was seated.

She had witnessed an historic moment.

"Now, Herr Eisenhower, what is it that you wish of our countries and peoples?"

Even in his wildest dreams, Ike had never foreseen that these men would throw their full support behind the Allied cause so readily and so easily. None of his concessions had been sought or offered and yet he had all he dreamed of from the Council.

"Gentlemen, I would ask that you inform your people of the contents of the documents in front of you."

Trying to ensure that his German allies felt in control in some small way he conceded.

"If and only if you all feel able to support it fully and with honour."

Eisenhower paused before the big one.

"We want the German Army," Goldstein translated Army precisely as he had been briefed, "Der Heer, Luftwaffe, und Kriegsmarine", the German words punched from his mouth in the Teutonic style, "To be placed under our command, under my orders and reconstituted as best can be done in the time available, to join us in defeating these attacks... and then..."

Their collective attention sharpened at the meaningful pauses.

"...And then forming part of the forces that liberate Europe, restoring all states, restoring all peoples and to put an end, once and for all, to the threat of a communist Soviet Union."

The group stood transfixed.

"Beyond the Polish Border, Herr General?" Von Papen posed the question that sat tantalisingly on everyone's lips.

"You bet your ass, Chancellor."

Von Papen looked at his group, taking each man's gaze in turn, understanding what lay behind each man's eyes and then, when all had been appraised, he turned to Eisenhower and nodded.

He moved around the head of the table, being met half way by an American General who believed he had just been handed the means to save Europe as easily as plucking a rose from its stem. Hands were grasped with a sincerity and comradeship that both sides appreciated there and then and came to fully understand in time.

The full documents prepared and presented to the Council members detailed how the German Wehrmacht, occupation forces and prisoners alike, would be formed and integrated into the allied structure, firstly as small units supplementing allied divisions and given time and resources in larger formations, albeit still under allied corps command.

The de-Nazification of the forces was to be undertaken before any units were committed, from the removal of the swastika from the uniform eagle through to scouring the same symbol from medals and awards. The national flag was to revert to the three horizontal colour bars of the years prior to Nazi rule, with a central device considered appropriate by all parties.

German forces of battalion size or above were to be commanded in the field by Allied officers, with German or Austrian officers of equal rank as liaison. Guderian and Von Vietinghoff could see the humour in that and assured the other members of the Council that such stupidity would not stand past first contact.

Specifically mentioned and excluded were the Waffen-SS, for whom there was to be no place, regardless of their élan and skill at arms. Their inclusion was deemed too much for the American and British public to accept, even in the face of adversity.

In return, the document reiterated stated Allied intents on the independence of the German State at some time in the near future, guarantees on national boundaries, alliances and support across the whole spectrum, in order to facilitate the return of Germany to as close to normality as was possible, post-apocalypse.

The document was fully endorsed by Truman, Attlee and De Gaulle and, for two of them, it was sincerely done.

And at the moment of their signatures, the Council was born.

That evening, orders were sent out to civilian and military posts throughout the western occupied area of Europe, warning of an important radio broadcast at 1500hrs on Wednesday, specifically for the attention of German civilians and POW's alike. Camp commanders were directed to ensure maximum audience for the transmission amongst their German charges and those officers dealing with civilian administrations were to ensure that as many high-ranking officials were able to listen as was possible in the available time.

A nation which makes the final sacrifice for life and freedom does not get beaten.

Kemal Ataturk

CHAPTER 45 – THE ANNOUNCEMENT

0656hrs Wednesday, 8th August 1945, Headquarters, Allied Forces in Europe. I.G.Farben, Frankfurt-am-Main, Germany.

Eisenhower was slightly buoyed by the first piece of news. At last, some organisation was coming on line for his air assets, or more accurately, what was left of them.

Some aircraft on their way home had been turned around, but his air force was still a fraction of what it had been prior to the attack.

None the less, it was a start.

The move to the new headquarters would be implemented in the late evening this very day, before the situation on the ground around Frankfurt became too difficult.

While he and his staff were on the move, Bradley would be in sole command from his army headquarters. That the new headquarters was in the Trianon Palace Hotel, Versailles, worried him a little, as it was the same place he had controlled the final defeat of Germany from in 44-45 and the Russians might come visiting if they understood that. However, its advantages were familiarity, facilities and proven working layout, so Ike went with it.

The loss of the Royal Navy battleship Queen Elizabeth, mined in the waters off Gibraltar, was unfortunate but, actually, not of immediate concern to the man trying to pull the proverbial coals out of the European fire.

Slipping the fifth cigarette of the day between his lips, he watched the bustle as the briefing officers prepared themselves and then grimaced, as he looked at the situation map behind them, current as of 0530, according to the markings.

Not so good, he thought.

"I need more men."

Not realising he had spoken his thoughts aloud, he was surprised to receive an answer to his statement.

"And you shall have them, Sir."

Ike turned around to find an Royal Navy officer stood at attention and in the act of throwing up an impeccable salute.

Responding in kind, or at least the best he could do holding coffee in one hand and a cigarette in the other, he let the man continue.

"Rear-Admiral Roger Dalziel, Sir, just flew in from Cherbourg."

Eisenhower took in the man's steady gaze.

"Good flight, Admiral?"

"Exciting, I admit. Prefer the water to the air for my jollies, Sir."

Dalziel left out the fact that his DC 3 aircraft was lying smashed and probably still burning on the Frankfurt runway, where it had pancaked after barely escaping pursuing Soviet warplanes. The American officer next to him had been badly wounded by bullets, but Dalziel's mission was too important to be delayed by such matters.

Eisenhower unburdened himself of his mug and butt.

Fishing in his brief case, which Eisenhower noted was extremely tatty, another sign of extreme Englishness, *'and that looks like blood?'*, Dalziel produced a sheaf of papers bound with neat ribbon hinges.

"The C-in-C suggested that you would want to see these straight away, hence the trip by aircraft."

Eisenhower could not help himself but stretch out a finger and sample the stain, examining the residue.

"Not mine, Sir, one of yours I am sorry to say but he should pull through."

Eisenhower nodded and produced a handkerchief to clean up with.

"So, what's so important that you risk yourself to fly here and share this report with me, Commander?"

478

"The report outlines the resources you can expect to receive that fall under our remit, either by way of army assets at sea or in port, or those that require our transporting to Europe from varying destinations, such as Stateside Sir."

"Ok, that would have been just fine by secure courier. I ask again, Admiral, what gives?"

The naval officer looked around to see who might be listening and, easing his collar, he took the plunge.

"I am from Naval Intelligence and we have discovered security issues within the facility at Station X, possibly Bletchley as a whole."

This Admiral had obviously taken a course in how to immediately get a superior's attention.

"Hence the need to relay matters personally."

The ramifications of a communications issue involving Bletchley Park were huge.

"What's compromised, Dalziel?"

"To be frank, Sir, we are unsure, but we appear to have at least two personnel who have prima facie impeccable credentials, but now appear to exercise poor judgement in the friends they keep, one of whom seems to have an awful lot of cash to spend."

Checking for listeners once more, Dalziel drew closer still.

"Stroke of luck really, one of our chaps was on holiday in High Wycombe and happened to see one of the blighters having a confidential with a Soviet attaché from their Embassy, who just happens to be the official NKVD Rezident."

He cleared his throat before continuing.

"We need to wring the offender, but first we simply have to know who else bats for the same side, if any. Our advice at this time is to keep high-level radio communications to an absolute minimum and use couriers where possible."

Eisenhower had a face like thunder.

"This will cripple my ability to react to events and control my forces. How long for?"

"Again, I am unsure, but I suspect no more than a week, Sir."

479

Even those deep in thought on the far side of the room heard Eisenhower's reaction.

"A goddamned week!"

Controlling himself and gesturing to his watching staff to get on with their own responsibilities, he took the Admiral by the shoulder and steered him to a nearby recess.

"So, because there is a commie spy in X, I lose full control of my communications for a week. Is that what you're saying, Sir Roger?"

The fact that Ike remembered his title was of no consolation to Dalziel; the man could not have been more uncomfortable.

"We simply must find out if she has accomplices, Sir, in order to ensure communications are safe once we have taken her out of the system."

Eisenhower nearly had a fit.

"You mean she's still working there?"

"For now, yes, but we have our best working this case and we hope to be able to give you back full radio communications sooner than a week."

Ike inhaled and exhaled deeply, composing himself.

"I think you should try very hard to do just that, Admiral. Europe depends upon it."

Lighting a cigarette, his offer to Dalziel having been declined, Ike thought for a moment.

"OK, I will look at these figures on troops as soon as I can. Please will you go and find the Headquarters Communications Officer, brief him in on the problems and your suggested temporary resolutions."

Dalziel saluted.

"Yes, Sir."

"Oh and Admiral, get me my radio back or we will be in deep trouble here."

The Admiral nodded curtly and strode off and with Ike's statement, a line was drawn under the matter, just for the moment.

480

GRU Lieutenant Colonel Ahbramov walked slowly to the bench seat in the well-tended gardens of the Schloss Gunsdorf, although the aromatic early morning air was wasted on him, as he was nursing the mother of all hangovers.

He had finally bedded pretty Alexandra Greshkova, partially because he had promised his little 'Anushka' a move to an easier post and partially because good Asbach in large quantities loosed her resolve.

That brandy was now eating its way into his consciousness and bringing on the mother of all headaches, which, in itself, concerned Georgi because he never got hungover.

'Maybe age is taking its toll?'
The thought worried him.

A drag on his cigarette produced a wave of nausea and he vomited, the spasm bringing on an almost unbearable pain in his head.

Again his vision misted and the headache surged, something he had been putting down to the pressure of work, whereas it was the pressure of blood from the Subarachnoid haemorrhage that was about to take his life.

Within a few seconds there was no way back and Ahbramov slumped on the bench, spending his last few minutes of life uncomprehending and alone.

The vacancy he left was too important to remain unfilled for long and before midday, Pekunin promoted Tatiana Nazarbayeva because of her competence, as well as his familiarity, creating the first female Lieutenant Colonel in Soviet Military Intelligence.

In the chess game of military intelligence, Nazarbayeva was a rising star indeed.

481

0721hrs Wednesday, 8th August 1945, Headquarters of Red Banner Forces of Soviet Europe, Schloss Schönefeld, Leipzig.

The briefing had been delayed by a false air-raid alarm, but was now about to start. Looking at his watch, Zhukov noted that the damn fool aviators had cost him twenty minutes. Damn them. To guard against the reoccurrence of such stupidity, a humourless staff major, equipped with a wide range of powers, was already on the way to the fighter regiment in concerned, having received a very precise brief from his irate Marshal, withregared to the futures of the two pilots in question.

There would be no second chances for them. Although reassured that his anti-aircraft defences were alert, aerobatic displays by imbeciles were guaranteed to incur his wrath.

Malinin, conducting the briefing that morning, waited patiently. Zhukov settled in his chair.

"Proceed, Comrade General."

Malinin turned to address the huge map behind him, extended pointer in hand.

"Comrade Marshal, there has been fierce fighting throughout the night as our forces press forward."

Engaging his commander's eyes, Malinin took advantage of their special relationship.

"Resistance has exceeded our expectations in a number of areas and our casualties have been higher than anticipated."

Zhukov remained impassive.

"The good news is that their air forces have been heavily disrupted by Kurgan and we have seen little organised operational direction from them and, what there has been, has been limited and we have inflicted some severe losses on those that have tried. We are winning the Air War convincingly."

It was a bold claim, but the facts could not be denied. Few allied sorties made any impact and a number were intercepted and put to the sword.

482

"Our Navy has lost a number of small vessels but has inflicted serious losses on the enemy, although it should be remembered that they have huge maritime resources to call upon. However, the Baltic is definitely closed and our Navy has started to interdict the reinforcement line, sinking one large ship and causing huge loss of life amongst the soldiers on board."

Malinin took a sip of his water to wet his throat.

"The naval war is not a war we can win, but our Soviet Fleets are performing magnificently and causing huge problems for the Allies, which will assist us in achieving our goals."

The General picked up a document, in order to precisely quote some important words.

"Pekunin informs us that Tito is extremely offended that he was not informed about our plans and has stated to both the Comrade General Secretary and the Allied leaders that he is remaining neutral until both sides *'come to their senses'*, at which time he will mediate between us."

Malinin looked up at his boss, who looked less than amused.

"Pekunin reports that Tito's submission also stated that his national borders are to be considered sacred and inviolable, either by land or air. Any violation will be met with force and the invader repulsed."

Malinin skim read, hurrying to get to the crucial part.

"Contrary to previous reports, it is now the Yugoslavian position to remain neutral, regardless, and to guarantee their borders to both sides."

Putting the report back in its rightful place, he spoke, almost as if to no one in particular

"It seems our General Pekunin has hitched his horse to the wrong sledge."

A staff Major hurried up and placed a document before the General, who took in its contents quickly and dismissed the officer.

"In the Far East, our forces and those of Imperial Japan, have been successful beyond all expectations, inflicting deep wounds on the American Navy, and they are already using the German equipment well in mainland China."

Addressing Zhukov directly, Malinin offered a shortcut.

"A briefing document on that operation has been prepared for later, so that we can concentrate on the situation in Europe."

Zhukov nodded his approval, especially as he had suggested the improvement to Malinin after the previous day's briefing.

"Fighting continues in Lübeck, with 21st Army launching a direct assault on the northern suburbs and 10th Guards Army flanking to the south. Last reports received placed elements of the 8th Guards Rifle Corps here, north of Kastdorf."

Looking down at his notes, he continued.

"We have identified enemy from the British 15th Infantry and 11th Armoured Division, as well as the American 82nd Airborne Division defending."

Moving his pointer down to just above Hamburg, Malinin moved on.

"Reinbek fell in the night and 4th Shock Army is in the eastern suburbs of Hamburg. 4th also sent a column north and they have reached and taken Bargteheide, hopefully relieving our surviving paratroopers at Ahrensberg before the morning is out."

"43rd Army has performed brilliantly, Comrade Marshal."

Zhukov noted Malinin's praise by placing an asterisk next to that part of the document, ready for his recommendations for promotion and awards at a later date.

"Not only have they broken through at Geesthacht and Bergedorf, but Major-General Lenskii sent 92nd Rifle Corps southwards to crush the defenders of Lüneberg, who were holding up 11th Guards Army. They are now driving hard south of the Elbe and were fighting in Winsen, at last report."

Zhukov placed another asterisk on his paperwork, as he could appreciate that Lenskii had done extremely well with his small army.

484

"A note of caution here. 11th has a wide-open left flank in its drive for Hamburg. Galitskiy has placed the paratrooper units he relieved as a guard force on the major roads, but he is vulnerable if the allies get organised."

Zhukov made a note to remind him to assess that more closely at the end of the briefing and gestured for Malinin to proceed.

"2nd Guards Tank Army encountered some problems with bridges, but that has been overcome now," he flatly acknowledged for Zhukov, "Not without cost in valuable bridging assets I must add, Comrade Marshal."

Zhukov made no note; he did not need to.

"On the upside, an American infantry regiment was crushed by 1st Mechanised Corps units overnight and 2nd Guards Tank Army has now outflanked Braunschweig," looking down at his notes once more, "And is now attempting to cross the canal at Wenden."

Malinin cleared his throat in an affected way, a sure sign to his commander that something bad was coming.

"In Braunschweig itself, 69th Army were stopped in their tracks by a British tank unit. Details are sketchy, but we believe that the 68th Tank Battalion was badly mauled by a British Guards Armoured Unit. This we did not have on intelligence and its appearance was a surprise. 69th is reorienting to push again, but I suggest that may not be necessary, given 2nd Guards Tank being past Braunschweig to the north already. I suspect the British will withdraw."

Zhukov considered that and agreed, especially as the Allies seemed to be avoiding any outflanking or encirclement risk to date, preferring to preserve their force.

'Very wise', he mused.

As Malinin's pointer moved slightly to the south, the briefing took an upbeat note.

"Here, 3rd Army has found that a huge hole opened up in front of them and Colonel-General Gorbatov pushed his tanks forward as fast as he could. They have now run into problems, here at Hildesheim, where the Amerikanski have rallied. However, we appear to have struck on the hinge

485

between two US divisions. 2nd Tank has folded back to the north-west and the 30th Infantry to the south-west."

Slapping the map on Göttingen, he continued.

"Here, we appear to have an opportunity to exploit. We can bite off north and south here and destroy one infantry and one tank division in situ. If Malinovsky releases more assets now"

No more needed to be said and he waited as Zhukov thought through the matter.

"Very well, comrade. Tell Malinovsky to release 1st Guards Tank Corps and one of the First Red Banners' spare rifle corps to Gorbatov's command. Order him to exploit the gap opening between Hildesheim and Göttingen ..." pausing to study the map, "...With either Paderborn or Minden in mind, but closing the rear door on Göttingen. Tell him also I will be moving some reserve assets up closer, so that if he finds favourable conditions, he's to exploit it in the knowledge that substantial reinforcements will be close at hand."

Zhukov made a suitable notation on his paperwork, already mentally ticking off which units he would move up ready. He looked up once he had thought through the list, Malinin taking his cue.

"At Kassel, our units are embroiled in heavy street fighting in some areas and in tank battles to the north and south."

The General's concern was obvious.

"We have identified parts of the 8th American Tank Division here at Witzenhausen, where they badly mauled one of our tank regiments."

He was unable to recall the designation, but progressed anyway.

"South of Kassel, one of their tank-destroyer units reduced 1315th Guards SP to flames inside one hour. American Jackson Tanks with big guns; very nasty. In the end, they were driven off with artillery and our forces are holding until a heavy tank regiment arrives to support the advance."

Again, the pointer contacted the map with a clear slap and all knew more good news was coming their way.

"Between Bad Hersfeld and Fulda there is nothing. Intelligence previously slated the Amerikanski 5th and 6th Tank Divisions, but they seem to have melted away, with very few units standing to fight."

"We believe that the 6th tried a stand north of Fulda but was already outflanked, so withdrew before it was tested."

Prescribing an area bounded by Kassel, Giessen, Hanau and Fulda, Malinin spoke of no palpable resistance.

"13th Army relieved the paratroops at Alsfeld and is already fighting in Giessen itself!"

Dropping the tip of the pointer down the map, the triumphant voice continued.

"3rd Guards Army is approaching Offenbach, just west of Frankfurt. Resistance is heavy and losses are increasing but progress is still being made. However," he sought out the newly arrived document and read it aloud, "Colonel-General Gordov reports a set-back on the Nidderau – Hanau axis, where an enemy tank attack is in progress as we speak, seemingly aimed at trapping the units west of Hanau. Gordov is moving 22nd Rifle Corps and 87th Guards Heavy Tank Regiment into line to prevent this and roll them back. He has postponed his attack on Offenbach until he is clearer on the situation."

Zhukov knew Gordov well and understood the man knew his business. He would leave it to him and, after all, 3rd Guards was a huge formation. Still, as he made a small note on his report, a word to Konev of Second Red Banner to watch and prepare to reinforce would not go amiss.

Malinin waited until his boss was back concentrating on the briefing.

"Here we have an issue."

He circled the area between Frankfurt and Würzburg, drawing Zhukov's attention to the nothingness it contained.

"We believe that elements of the US 42nd and 63rd Infantry are falling back through this area, but I have concerns over their ability to cause problems in the rear of either 3rd or 5th Guards."

"Agreed," said Zhukov instantly, "Send warnings to Konev and ask him what he has done to address the matter."

Zhukov held no love for Konev, but expected the man to have seen the problem and resolved it already. Still, just in case.

"5th Guards Army is fighting hard in Würzburg and the situation is not wholly clear. From what we understand, Lieutenant-General Paramzin has been badly wounded, but this area, above all others, lacks the specific information we need."

More scribbling meant more work for Konev.

"Our drive to Bamberg suddenly moved forward as the Amerikanski defenders seem to withdraw at speed. Bamberg fell late yesterday evening and our lead units are now fighting on the outskirts of Erlangen. Not without cost, as the bridges over the Main at Hallstadt were blown and American artillery unluckily savaged the bridging engineers while they were at work."

Malinin thumped the centre of Bayreuth.

"The allies worked out what was happening here too quickly. It seems the units in and around Bayreuth will escape our trap. However, air force ground-attack regiments harried them yesterday and will do so today."

"65th Army is pushing onwards towards Nürnberg, pursuing an Amerikanski tank division in full flight. This has been confirmed as the 16th Tank's, an untested new unit. This was not identified as being in the area and 65th has no tanks. Rossokovsky informs us that he has sent one of his reserve tank corps to back up 65th, in case the enemy starts showing some fight."

Zhukov expected nothing less from one of his best generals.

"In Regensburg, 2nd Shock Army has taken heavy casualties trying to prevent destruction of bridges over the Danube and the Naab. They have been, in the main, unsuccessful. General Fedyuninski has relieved one corps and two Divisional commanders and requests more bridging assets for his advance."

Zhukov looked at a separate list on the table in front of him.

488

"No, not from me. Tell Rokossovsky, it's his mess to sort out and no engineers will be coming from me. I need all of mine. Make that very clear, General."

Another order issued and the briefing ploughed on.

"5th Guards Tank Army," the name never failed to give everyone in earshot a buzz, for it was a huge and extremely powerful formation, "Reached Straubling to find the bridges down, so deflected north-west, crossed the river at Wörth and is also fighting inside Regensburg, but on the south side."

That was good news.

"5th Guards Tank's southern prong surprised the defenders at Deggendorf and captured the Danube bridges intact."

That was good news indeed.

"29th Tank Corps has reached Landshut, where it has run into the 4th US Tank Division. However, Volsky has managed to send part of 8th Mechanised Corps northwards, towards Regensburg, which should relieve the pressure on 3rd Guards as well as his own units there."

"Fighting at Passau is intense."

Malinin searched for a document.

"Lieutenant- General Romanowsky states that the defenders, the 26th Infantry, are fanatics and must be an elite unit. He reports that his 134th Rifle Corps is all but destroyed and that the bridges are down, so no progress can be made."

Zhukov's pencil descended, ready to condemn the man, but was halted as Malinin continued.

"However, Romanowsky formed a Special Group, outflanked the position, forcing and capturing the crossings at Vilshofen, destroying an American infantry unit in the process, caught on the march and attacked by aircraft and tanks in turn. He is moving this Special Group round to take Passau in the rear and he thinks it will fall today."

The pencil was stayed, as was the execution.

"At Linz, we are engaged in heavy fighting, 49th Army pressing from the north and 70th from the east. The enemy are well-handled and good quality troops. However, it appears that 5th Shock Army can seal their fate, as it is already

489

past Linz to the south, pressing here at Gmunden... and here at Wels."

A casual observer would be able to see that Wels was the back door to Linz and that the units still defending there were all but cut off.

"Berzarin has turned some of his forces north to strike at the escape route of the capitalist troops. We have identified their 11th Tanks and 65th Infantry. They should be destroyed in situ."

"Tolbukhin, Chuikov and Yeremenko are holding as previously ordered, but seek confirmation."

Zhukov cut over the end of his deputy's words, showing his irritation at this unexpected and wholly unnecessary problem.

"Confirm their orders, hold in position for now but be ready. Saturday's meeting will decide much."

Changing gear slickly and moving to a new subject, an excellent ability Malinin demonstrated well when his chief was aggravated, the facts and figures of the Pacific war were brought out and reviewed, also seemingly showing superiority and victory throughout the region.

1131hrs Wednesday 8th August 1945, Office of the NKVD Chairman, the Lubyanka, Moscow, USSR.

The messages dispatched from London on the 4th August were the last to leave before the flow dried up for good.

Contained within the bag was one message destined for NKVD headquarters and marked 'eyes only chairman', which arrived into Lemsky's care.

It was a short note and easily decoded with the right knowledge.

In its readable form, it now sat on Beria's desk, informing him that, as directed, the Rezident had met in a public place with asset 'Baron'.

What the message clearly did not say or ask was why the NKVD Chairman had certainly deliberately blown the cover of 'Baron' and revealed the existence of this valuable agent within Britain's most secret establishment.

490

Beria was extremely satisfied with his work and penned a swift note to Zhukov assuring him that he had crippled Allied higher level communications for at least four days, possibly as long as two weeks.

He smugly thought that at the cost of one female agent, not an ideological person or one who spied through conviction, but one who worshipped solely at the altar of money, no-one in Bletchley would trust anyone and the allies would use slower, less effective means to relay orders for some time to come.

It all worked out very nicely.

Beria rose from his desk and decided to surprise Danilov in his own lair with a request for his car.

1210hrs, Wednesday 8th August 1945, Geesthacht, Germany.

In Geesthacht, two worlds were about to collide.

General Lenskii was ecstatic and with good reason.

His 43rd Army had the allies on the run and he was ahead of schedule.

Spreading the latest map across the bonnet of his jeep, he made a few swift appreciations and then started to issue his orders, sending out the tentacles of his rifle corps to exploit the fluidity of the situation as much as possible, fingers making movements over the paper and giving life to his words. The officers gathered round him made records of their own on maps or in notebooks, ready to translate his needs into operational orders. Lenskii paused as a rattle of sub-machine gunfire overcame his thoughts and he sent a Lieutenant to investigate.

Life was sweet and the rewards of a professional soldier when things went well were great.

At the other end of the scale was Helga Dein, who was still in a state of shock, after seeing her family destroyed before her young eyes, a few hours beforehand.

Her father, her rock and her idol, had survived six years of European War, only to fall this day, victim of a Soviet grenade tossed into the basement of their home in Krumme Straße. The family had taken refuge here during the brief

491

fighting and had not moved since the town became silent, some time beforehand. Herr Dein's attempt to cover the blast with his body failed and the grenade claimed not only him, but also her mother and sister.

Her grief and upbringing both determined that life was now pointless and Helga resolved that her's would end this day, but not before her family were avenged.

With tearful eyes, she had taken up the weapon her father had dropped and, as he had shown her, braced herself, pressd the trigger and destroyed the two Soviet infantrymen who ventured into the cellar after the grenade.

The MP40 jerked in her hands again and over half the bullets were on target as a third man charged in, only to be thrown back bloodily into the entrance.

Scrabbling at the packing around the small window, she snatched up a magazine lying on a box and wriggled her way out, in the end, half propelled by the force of three more grenades exploding behind her.

Running for all she was worth, Helga found the small air-raid shelter at the junction of her street and Hafenstraβe and dived in quickly, narrowly avoiding a running Soviet Lieutenant heading back the way she had come.

Changing the magazine on her weapon, just as her father had demonstrated, she was calm, belying her nineteen years.

Now was the time.

She moved silently out of the bunker and turned right.

On the junction of Hafenstraβe and Schillerstraβe, a small group of soldiers were gathered round a vehicle, oblivious to her presence.

Russians.

She gathered herself and struggled for control as fear suddenly washed over her. Her bladder let go as she moved forward, tears in her eyes, but still focused on the hated enemy to her front, her fear subjugated by her desire to kill.

One man looked up and realised the danger, snatching for his weapon but knowing he was too late.

492

The German sub-machine gun burst into life, sending twenty-one 9mm bullets in the direction of the Soviet officer group.

Only the first six were on target and the petrified Russian officer made contact with his weapon, bringing it on target and pulling the trigger.

The PPS43 sent its stream of bullets in return but all missed.

Again, both weapons lashed out and this time both were on target.

Helga Dein was dead before she hit the ground, metal ripping through her stomach, heart, liver and head.

The Captain, her target, sank slowly to the ground as his own throat wound spilled his lifeblood over the roadway in front of him.

Two of the men had remained untouched and cautiously rose from their position of cover on the other side of the jeep. One even put another burst into the immobile girl, causing parts of the ruined corpse to disintegrate and spread themselves on the roadway.

The Colonel, 43rd Army's Senior Artillery Officer, had taken four of the six bullets to strike flesh and lay dead, sightless eyes still carrying indignation at the mechanics of his end.

Major-General Boris Lenskii lay where he had been dropped by the two impacts, knowing that he was badly injured. The wound to his rectum was painful indeed, the metal having ripped through his anus and then moved on, removing most of his manhood. The second projectile took him under the right shoulder and, hitting bone, disintegrated into a number of small but devastating pieces, each one reducing sections of his liver to paste as they moved inexorably through his body.

As he slipped into merciful darkness, he knew his end was approaching.

Troops of his headquarters defence unit gathered up his shattered form and carried it into St Salvatoris Kirche, where a small aid post had been established. He died four hours later, to the minute, never having regained consciousness.

493

His vengeful troopers visited themselves upon the civilian populace and the small ruined town was bathed in the blood of innocents until darkness fell.

1500hrs Wednesday 8th August 1945. Former Headquarters of SHAEF, Trianon Palace Hotel, Versailles, France.

At three o'clock precisely, radios across Europe first went silent and then burst into life with an announcement, made first in English, then French, then German, calling for all citizens of Europe to be attentive and standby for an important message.

Listening to that broadcast, from prison of war camps to small farming communities across the full range of continental Europe and beyond, nations held their breath, expecting the very worst.

A detached voice announced General Dwight D. Eisenhower, Supreme Commander of SHAEF.

A long pause.

The tape rolled.

Eisenhower's voice cut the silence.

"People of Europe, the last six years have been dark indeed and, in May of this year, we came to the end of a gigantic conflict, a conflict that cost many lives on all sides. Those lives were needlessly lost in a false cause; the pursuit of power and sovereignty by a small group of men."

The extended pause was in place to permit translators to do their work, French and German over the radio, other languages done in the huddled groups listening all over the continent.

"I have no doubt that each of you has, as I have, made an oath to do all in our collective powers to ensure this never happens again in our lifetime, or that of our children, or of their offspring."

"We are now called upon to discharge that oath, as Europe finds itself again threatened by a small clique bent on extending their power and imposing their will upon the free."

As the German speaker moved through his words, a keen ear could detect light coughing in the background.

"America stands with you in this struggle and, as we speak, her sons are dying to preserve you, your nations, and your ethnic groups, be you French or German, English or Austrian, Romany or Jew."

"Forces of the Russian Empire, at the direct bidding of Dictator Joseph Stalin, have attacked along a broad front from the Baltic to the Adriatic."

Not wholly accurate, but it made better listening.

"We are striving to stop their progress but you should all know that, for now, we are striving in vain. More farms and villages are coming under their control, towns and cities falling within their domain."

"Now, more than ever, Europe... no... the World needs her citizens to come together as one, joining to defeat this aggression and ensure that our nations, yours and mine, stay free. I say the world and mean the world, for this will not stop here in Germany, nor on some distant Atlantic or Mediterranean shore, but it will spread across oceans and engulf continents until the World as we know it has gone."

"Separately, entrenched in our recent divides, we will fall. Together, we will stand proud and destroy this menace forever. Thank you."

Once the translation had finished the listeners were regaled with the distinctive voice of Churchill, taped in England the previous evening and played at the newly reactivated communications centre at Versailles, delivering a speech as only he could, enshrining every virtue of man in his stirring words and focussing his audience on uniting in the coming struggle.

By the time that De Gaulle commenced, the only allied leader to speak live from Versailles, sixteen minutes had passed. The French leaders address was short and seemed more leaning to stirring his own compatriots to stand tall, perhaps recognising that his country, of all the Allies, needed most inspiration and resolve.

De Gaulle concluded and there was a silence, seemingly designed to build tension, but actually no more than

495

a hitch at the radio base as the next speaker sat down at the microphone and waited his turn.

A monotone voice announced Von Papen as the next speaker.

A silence descended, heavy with the static of expectation, until a single steady voice spoke in his native tongue.

"Meine Herren, kinsfolk of Europe. Germany and her allies have endured much these past six years and we have been beaten in a war, enduring beyond the barriers of human endurance, giving all for our country and state, our nation and folk."

"That we endured so much, gave so much and invested so much blood and sweat in such a faulty cause will be our national burden for generations to come."

"The leadership of our nations, Germany and Austria, was faulty, but these leaders were followed too readily, obeyed too easily, for any of us to avoid the national guilt we now feel."

"I speak to you at this hour as an appointee of the conquering powers, without mandate or common assent from my nation, placed at the head of a governing body, the Council of Germany and Austria. This body consists of leaders, political and military, known to you all these last few years."

Pausing, Von Papen referred to his list, reciting the names in order of entry and including the military ranks where appropriate.

"These men have agreed to serve on the Council, in order to commence the process of returning our lands to the control of those who have lived and died here for generations."

"I have been given the position at the head of this table, as Chancellor, to make some decisions, small admittedly, but ones made for Germans and Austrians by Germans and Austrians."

A throat cleared and on he plunged.

"These last few years, our countries have visited aggressive war upon our neighbours and that is a burden we must carry to the next millennium and beyond."

496

Von Papen's voice was rich with both pain and resolve.

"Crimes have been committed and those crimes must be atoned for by those responsible; there can be no other way."

"Regardless of whether you pulled a trigger, drove a tank, or stayed at home enduring the bombs, our peoples have a collective responsibility to make amends for these excesses, to fully atone for our national actions before we can move forward as nations, without the burdens of our past."

"We come to this now, the start of our national atonement, at the moment of Europe's darkest need and when we are least capable of answering the call."

Those in the radio room witnessed him stiffen as he gathered himself.

"In line with the request the Council has received from General Eisenhower, on behalf of the governments of the United States, United Kingdom and France, I now instruct the …"

A silence descended, one that should not have been and, across the continent, millions of eyes bored deeply into radio sets, willing the speaker to press on.

Gathering himself, Von Papen pressed on.

"In line with those requests, the Council requests that all capable persons, be they free living or presently detained, with the exception of ex-members of the SS, make themselves ready to serve in the military struggle to preserve Germany, Austria, Europe and the World."

"Identify yourselves to the nearest allied personnel and do as you are instructed, observing your moral conscience at all times, representing your nation and state and acting as a soldier and citizen of Europe."

"As nations we, Germany and Austria, now have an opportunity to make good some of the harm we have done and to be in the vanguard that delivers freedom to our world."

"To you all, I say this. Stand tall, proud of your national identity and know the man next to you, be he white or black, Christian or Jew, stands with you through choice in a great crusade for freedom."

"Thank you and good luck."

497

In the I.G.Farben building in Frankfurt, Eisenhower looked at his staff and whistled.

"Well if that doesn't do the trick, nothing will."

1528hrs Wednesday, 8th August 1945, Headquarters of Red Banner Forces of Soviet Europe, Schloss Schönefeld, Leipzig.

The reception at the Schloss Gunsdorf was completely different.

Zhukov nodded gently, dissecting the broadcast, exploring the possibilities.

'Quicker than expected but practical? Resources? Organisation? Usefulness?'

Malinin put both their thoughts into words.

"GRU and NKVD will be squirming, Comrade Marshal. Not quite as they predicted is it?"

For two generals who had just been told that the enemy forces were likely to be receiving reinforcements in seven figures, both men seemed reasonably calm.

Calm with good reason, as Malinin continued, thinking aloud.

"Provided we continue to push and keep them on the run this will not get off the ground on a large scale. There are intact German units in Norway and the French ports and those in Denmark could be a small problem, but the Western Allies do not have the resources for even their own forces at this time."

Zhukov pondered some more and then spoke.

"We will proceed without change, but delays will not be tolerated. We must press forward incessantly. Tired units must be rotated out and replaced with fresh ones and we must push, push and push. Inform all commanders. Also, seek information from the GRU and NKVD on their assessment of the impact of this call to arms and what forces the new Germany can field, reasonably field, I mean."

With a wry smile between comrades, Zhukov added.

498

"And tell them to get it right this time."

He then recalled something extra from the broadcast.

"They have held back from using the SS bastards though. That will be their loss and our gain, Malinin. There may be some things that the NKVD can design to cause friction in their cosy little camp, disrupt the new brotherhood, eh?"

Malinin grinned, confident once more.

"Yes, Comrade Marshal. Their enterprise will die a death soon enough, at our bayonet point, or their own."

Soviet Aviation has been desperately searching for their number one target without success, ever since the ground attack planned upon it had failed. Photo recon, acquired at great expense by 193rd Guards Reconnaissance Aviation Regiment, had demonstrated the fact that the wrong target had been assaulted in any case, so a considerable amount of effort was being directed at locating it so it could be visited by bombers as soon as possible.

Photos were compared against possible location lists and three possible locations in the Frankfurt area presented themselves. Without assets on the ground to confirm or disprove, it was decided to hit all three and the sooner the better, as Soviet ground forces would surely cause the enemy to displace in the near future.

22nd Guards Bomber Division was given the task and assigned one full bomber regiment to each of the targets, with each bomber regiment given its own fighter regiment for cover, with an additional fighter regiment held back to reinforce as needed. A formidable force indeed, which was already airborne and crossing no-man's land.

At the conclusion of the broadcast, Eisenhower took further briefs from his staff and issued whatever instructions were required.

Then, checking in with Bradley, dead on 1800hrs and finding the General ready as expected, SHAEF temporarily handed control of Europe to Bradley's Twelfth Army Group Headquarters.

Taking a final look around, Ike ordered the move to commence and was immediately rewarded by bustling staff officers and earnest looking soldiers, brought in to speed up the loading process.

Some personnel and items would be going by road overnight. Key personnel and important records had places booked on a number of C-47 flights out of Frankfurt and, in order to ensure the safety of the valuable personnel, USAAF fighter squadrons were in the air already, ready to keep the Soviet aircraft away.

1820hrs Wednesday, 8th August 1945, Airborne over Frankfurt-am-Main, Germany.

On his way south to the airfield, Eisenhower was shaken from deep thought by the hammering of anti-aircraft weapons nearby. First looking at the firers, he saw a number of stationary M-15 Anti-aircraft gun halftracks firing furiously skywards. The unit had been on its way to Frankfurt's main airfield to stiffen up defences but the enemy was here and here right now. Turning his head, he was startled to see Soviet aircraft heading for the same airfield, preparing to bomb one of their suspected targets into submission.

In the last few days, Soviet pilots had developed a healthy respect for the quadruple .50cal mounts carried on the M-16 halftracks, or on trailers, quickly learning to stay out of MG range to avoid taking punishing hits.

The aircraft flying overhead belonged to the 11th Guards Bomber Red Banner Air Regiment and were all experience pilots who had learned this lesson well.

However, the M-15 was a different animal altogether, possessing a sting that had cost many a Luftwaffe pilot his life. Having learned the range of the .50cal and then learned to stay out of it, a large number of German pilots had been shocked to find their aircraft disintegrating under the impact of 37mm cannon shells. Experienced US M-15 gunners often only used the two machine guns until the target came closer, then

500

surprising it with burst of 37mm shells from their triple gun mount.

11th Guards acquired this extra knowledge the hard way, as three Shturmovik were flayed from the skies in under a minute, with no chance for any of the crews to escape.

Eisenhower's driver pulled the car over into a place of safety, from where her charge could observe the air battle.

Fighters came flitting overhead and, with eyes shielded, both driver and General could see Soviet and allied aircraft engaged in a twisting low-level dance of death in which there were losers on each side, marked by the black of smoke, the red of fire, or the orange bloom of an explosion.

At the airfield itself, the Shturmoviks pressed home their attack, desperate to destroy the hangars and office buildings that were considered a possible SHAEF location.

More fell victim to a new arrival on the European battlefield, the M19 GMC, a converted M24 Chafee tank sporting twin 40mm cannon. Two such weapons were situated at each end of the main runway and each claimed a Soviet bomber in short order. Unfortunately, having broken through the fighter cordon and into the IL-3's, an American P-51D Mustang was hacked from the sky in a tragic case of mistaken identity, the wreckage ploughing into an air-raid shelter on the perimeter and claiming another eight allied lives.

Of the fifteen aircraft the 11th had committed to the attack, only nine released their bombs over the target. The tenth, commanded by the Regimental Commander himself, carried its bomb load remorselessly on, further into allied territory, unusually steadily, dead hands holding the controls in perfect balance.

The strike was very accurate and much damage was done to the facilities they targeted, as well as to two parked C-47 transports being refuelled nearby, both of which were transformed into infernos before the regiment turned for home.

The 339th Bomber Air Regiment attacked their allocated Frankfurt target with eleven remaining IL-3's, successfully tumbling much of the building to the ground and raining death and destruction on the poor unfortunates within. This target had been selected on the basis of the number of

501

vehicles going back and forth rather than military certainty. That it was the St Elisabethen Krankenhaus was of no concern to those planning the raid and the aircrew executing those plans were not aware of the fact that they were bombing a civilian hospital.

The bombs sent over three hundred innocents to an early end.

The 220th Guards Stalingrad Red Banner Air Regiment were most successful and actually hit their intended target of SHAEF, spreading their high explosive over both the I.G.Farben building and the nearby Gruneberg Park prison camp, used as a transit centre and troop accommodation, as well as still containing a few ex-POW US aircrew, waiting their turn to go home.

Casualties in the park were heavy, in the I.G.Farben building even heavier, as fire took hold and carved its way through the whole structure. A building preserved from destruction by the Allied bomber fleet, on Eisenhower's express direction, burned for three days before the US Air Force and local Frankfurt fire fighters could extinguish the flames.

Many members of SHAEF staff were killed and wounded, as few had run for cover, most staying to finish their preparations for the move to Versailles.

The 220th did not enjoy its success for very long. Their fighter cover was still busy keeping USAAF aircraft at bay and failed to spot the arrival of another four P-47's, that immediately set about the retreating Ilyushin's. On the 6th August, these P-47's had been in transit to the French coast, from where they were to fly to England, prior to the pilots returning to their homeland. Now, having been recalled to active service with the blessing of their government, four Brazilian pilots of Green Flight, 1st GAVCA of Força Aérea Brasileira, fell upon the Soviet aircraft and started to tear them from the sky.

1° Teniente-Aviation Alberto Morales made three passes and downed an enemy craft each time. His number two put two into the ground, three and four destroyed one each.

502

Morales, officially now an ace with six kills in total, swept back into the attack, as the eight surviving Shturmovik's desperately flew low and fast, screaming for their fighter cover to return.

Another pass saw Morales knock lumps off the rearmost enemy, causing it to lose speed, but the Brazilian ran out of ammunition before he could complete the job.

He rose higher to observe the rest of the attack and saw the damaged aircraft felled by his number two.

As his number three charged in, Morales became aware of the sound of metal striking metal, the smell of hot oil and an indescribable pain, as his aircraft shuddered under hammer blows from a vengeful La-7's Berezin cannon. 20mm explosive shells chewed their way through oil and fuel lines, instruments and flesh. The cockpit became a furnace and Morales died quickly, but horribly, his aircraft slowly rolling away and crashing into the Main River below.

The remaining fighters, both Brazilian and Russian, drew apart as if by silent agreement and went in opposite directions, one side with no ammunition and the other side running light on fuel. Returning to their bases without further incident, one damaged Shturmovik skilfully landed wheels-up, saving the crew, but reducing the 220th Guards to only five serviceable planes.

All together, St Elisabethen apart, the day had been another huge success for Soviet air regiments the length and breadth of Europe, consistently meeting Allied aircraft with a numerical advantage and maintaining their undoubted air superiority.

Eisenhower watched the smoking P-47 disappear below his sightline, feeling true pain at the death of the young pilot he had watched destroy three enemy aircraft. He promised himself he would ensure the man's efforts went rewarded and that his memory was suitably honoured.

Climbing back into his staff car, he went on his way to the airfield, only to find more delay, as his allocated aircraft was a smouldering heap and a replacement needed to be brought in.

Waiting and feeling helpless, removed as he was from his staff and communications, Ike sat in his car chain-smoking his way through his thoughts, inevitably drawing the conclusion that the war was being lost and things needed to change.

The hour spent waiting was not wasted and by the time the replacement DC-3 touched down, Eisenhower had a change firmly set in his mind.

2019hrs Wednesday 8th August 1945, 12th US Army Group Headquarters, Wiesbaden, Germany.

In Bradley's headquarters, the task of overseeing the Allied Forces went smoothly, or as smoothly as it possibly could do.

The General was catching forty winks in his campaign chair when he was awoken by a Colonel bearing bad news.

"Sir, you need to see this."

Bradley stretched himself awake and accompanied the staff officer to the map table.

"OK ,Colonel. What's got you so fired up?"

The officer pointed at the map and spoke one word.

"Gottingen."

An experienced eye followed the pointing finger and took in the dire situation in a minute.

Bradley winced at the thought of American units surrounded and surrendering, his mind reaching into its dark recesses to summon the spectre of the 106th Infantry during the Battle of the Bulge.

Quickly firing a few questions at his staff, he determined that getting the doughboys out was not going to be easy.

"OK, we've some work to do here."

He paused, grabbing his chin, contemplating, then acting.

504

"Looks like the new boys of the 15th will have to learn on the hoof. Please get General Simpson on the horn, straight away."

One officer scurried away, to be replaced by another waiting for his instructions.

"Please inform Air that we are counter-attacking here, at Fritzlar," the finger tapped the map, "And here, at Bad Driburg," this time the finger almost caressed the spot, betraying some inner struggle in the man.

Whatever the thought process was, it abruptly stopped as the phone rang.

"Bradley."

A tinny voice could be heard at the other end of the line.

"Yes I know, Bill and before you ask, I don't have anything else to send you at this time. I want you to relieve the situation. Seems to me the best way is a hit at Frankenberg with 3rd Tank-destroyer and the 79th Infantry."

Clearly that was received without issue, as Bradley continued.

"I'm looking at the 15th Armored hitting through Brakel and regaining the Diemel River line. Should help with getting your boys out of the mess at Göttingen."

That drew a response and then some, Bradley raising his eyebrows. as General Simpson went into a lengthy diatribe.

"Hold on, Bill, hold on." Bradley's voice was rarely raised, so he drew a few looks from those working around him.

"It's not a question of blame, Bill, so get that straight right now. We just have to sort the mess out as best we can and get back on line."

A short response and Bradley continued.

"My intel gives me only infantry and SP's from the Red's 3rd Army. You tally that, Bill?"

As Bradley listened to the response, he checked a small marking on the map.

"Yes I know, but they should cope well enough, especially if you give them some help."

Squinting at the map, he retrieved the details he needed.

"You got some of Baade's boys at Gütersloh, 320th RCT. Send them up with the 15th as some back-up."

The reply was swift and acceptable. Then came an enquiry.

"Absolutely, in fact I have given Air the heads up to give you all possible support, within the limitations obviously."

That was very clearly well received.

"Ok then, please let me have your plan as soon as you can. Nothing complicated, but I think it'll need to be done as soon as possible."

A swift reply did not bring the answer Bradley sought. None the less, he accepted what Simpson had said.

"Provided you can hold where you are, then Friday morning will have to do, General."

Simpson was right. It would take time to get the plan ready, units prepped and supplies in place. None the less, the delay was a huge risk and Bradley had demonstrated his irritation.

'*Let the man do his job*,' he thought.

"I know you'll do the best possible, Bill."

Final words exchanged.

"Thank you... and good luck to you too, Bill."

"I hold it to be of great prudence for men to abstain from threats and insulting words towards any one, for neither the one nor the other in any way diminishes the strength of the enemy; but the one makes him more cautious, and the other increases his hatred of you, and makes him more persevering in his efforts to injure you"

- Niccolo Machiavelli

CHAPTER 46 – THE GENERALISSIMO

0520hrs Thursday 9th August 1945, Rear-line positions, 'B' Btty, 60th Field Artillery Btn, 9th US Infantry Division at Neunkirchen am Sand, Germany.

The 9th Infantry Division had set up a loose screen to protect retreating units on their way to the comparative safety of Nurnberg.

On the northern edge of Schnaittach, a company of the 2nd/39th Infantry Regiment held the line, backed up by a battery of 105mm howitzers from 60th Field Artillery, positioned to their rear, just outside of Neunkirchen.

No attack had developed and 'B' Battery was preparing to fall back through the next screen to their allotted positions at Malmsbach, just northeast of Nurnberg.

The Captain in charge, new to the unit, having shipped in from the States that very week, was finally satisfied that all guns were hitched and he gave the order for the battery to move out, relaying their departure to the infantry commander they were leaving behind.

Rattling down Hauptstraße, 'B' Battery drivers became aware of a tank column approaching from their left, five Shermans intent on using the same route to Nurnberg.

Captain McDaniels was half-inclined to give the order to accelerate and try to beat the tank column to the junction, but he figured he would let it pass, especially as his high-speed tractors already seemed to have lost the opportunity.

He leant out of the window, signalling to the vehicles behind to slow down. Flopping back into his seat, he was

507

extremely surprised to see the rearmost tank explode into a fireball, running off the road into the verge and coming to a halt, as the next Sherman in line took another killing hit and stopped dead on the road, crewmen bailing out and coming under small arms fire

Mind racing, head turning in all directions, McDaniels indecision meant his battery moved closer to whatever it was that was reaching out and killing the tanks.

As the lead tank spewed flame, McDaniels noticed the telltale smoke trail of a bazooka shell running from the trees on the south side of Hersbrucker Straße.

The second tank reversed, panicked and blind, crunching into the third vehicle and broke its track, which immediately uncoiled its full length as the drive sprocket rotated at full reverse. A panzerfaust sailed almost leisurely past its turret, hitting a telegraph pole and bringing it down on top of tank number three, which had stalled on the impact of the reversing tank. The desperate driver, trying to restart his vehicle, suddenly found himself alone as his crew deserted him abandoning the sitting duck in search of safety.

McDaniels' driver halted the M5 HST without orders and the Pfc manning the .50cal started lashing the crewmen abandoning the Shermans, who were running in all directions as more small arms fire reached out from the woods, dropping men hard to the ground.

Shocked, McDaniels shouted at his gunner to cease fire, his voice reaching a crescendo of despair as a burst flayed two men into butcher's meat before his disbelieving eyes.

"They're our men! Cease fire, they're our fucking men!"

Shouting at his men, the desperate officer ran towards the tanks, waving his hands, screaming for a halt to the firing.

The handful of surviving tank crew chose two courses of action. Some put up their hands and sought safety in surrender; a few others chose valiant resistance and blazed away with sub-machine guns or pistols.

Either way, fire from the HST's and the force in the woods could not discriminate between a coward and a brave man and soon all of them were stilled and bloodied.

508

McDaniels, the only American casualty of the ambush, never felt a thing as a single bullet from a Soviet Nagant revolver took him in the forehead and ended his life.

Stopping to recover the body of their dead commander, a few gunners found time to loot trophies of pistols and medals from the dead Soviet tank crew. 'B' Battery then swept past the fire-savaged lend-lease Shermans, leaving the junction to the dead men, destroyed tanks and the engineer platoon from 15th Combat Engineer Battalion, responsible for the ambush and destruction of the over-confident advance guard of the 65th Soviet Army.

0800hrs Thursday 9th August 1945, The Kremlin, Moscow, USSR.

At 0800hrs precisely, Beria placed before Stalin his plan for reacting to the intended German mobilisation. In truth, he admitted to the General Secretary, most of the legwork had been done some time before. There would definitely be some small delay before the plan would start to bear fruit but with the assets available, numbers that silently impressed Stalin with the foresight and diligence exhibited by his NKVD Chairman, he had no doubt that the plan would be very effective.

Beria, as usual, maximised his presentation to take the kudos, not informing his leader that the assets had not been placed for this task but another, completely different one.

The plan was approved and within a few hours messages had been sent to sympathisers within the International Red Cross, from where it would slowly reach the assets.

As with many things devised by Beria's mind, the plan was simple but the dividends could be huge. Time would tell.

0830hrs Thursday 9th August 1945, Headquarters of SHAEF, Trianon Hotel, Versailles, France.

It had been hoped that SHAEF would be able to retake control at approx 0400hrs, but the disruption caused by the air attacks on both the airfield and the I.G.Farben building played havoc with the timetable.

Valuable personnel had been killed or wounded and it took extra time for Eisenhower to get his headquarters online.

It was not until 0830hrs that SHAEF again took control and commenced the normal everyday processes associated with controlling a shrinking army in a losing war.

Towns and cities that had lain in friendly territory yesterday, were now behind a line that was relentlessly marching westwards, occasionally checked, occasionally blooded, but presently unstoppable and inexorable.

The first concept of a halt line had never got off the ground, vital sections already having fallen to Soviet advances.

Whilst some new formations were coming online, there were still not enough assets in place to be able to do anything meaningful to, in some way, wrest the initiative from the Russian armies.

Clearly Hamburg was vital and McCreery would hold it against whatever the Russians threw at him.

One British Corps commander had stated that it would be a second Stalingrad and was reminded, very succinctly by McCreery, that the Russians had won the first rather convincingly.

Canadian and Polish divisions had moved up and stiffened resistance on the North German plain and Eisenhower felt sure the Soviet timetable was being wrecked there, which it was. British engineers had developed a penchant for destruction, dropping most of the bridges behind them as they retreated, slowing the Russian advances.

For now, the German divisions in Denmark, complete and ready for battle, were tasked with defending the coastline and probing the Soviet landings in Lolland to the east.

Eisenhower left his political masters to soothe the ruffled Swedish feathers, feathers agitated by the thought of armed Germans and armed Russians a few kilometres from their border. A fair portion of the Swedish Army stood to, watching events and ready to lash out if anyone should forget national boundaries.

Allied airpower was concentrating on a protecting brief for now, ensuring moving units were not seriously attacked, watching air bases being reconstructed although, where possible, belligerent commanders undertook aggressive incursions to harry the enemy formations with surviving ground attack assets. In basic terms, exchange rates were pretty much one for one, although many allied pilots were recovered as the air war was mainly fought over Allied territory.

Plans to use the bomber force had been decided upon, in principle, but it was felt important that sufficient fighter escorts were available before they were fully implemented.

However, Tedder had put forward one or two low-risk ideas that whetted the appetite for things to come.

At sea, things were not looking so good, with a troop transport mined as it slipped into Cherbourg and the talisman that was the liner Queen Mary, torpedoed within sight of the Statue of Liberty. Whilst loss of life on her was much less than at Cherbourg, her loss to the reinforcement machine was immeasurable and certainly counted as a huge success to the Soviet navy.

On the plus side, two Soviet submarines had been sunk off Norway and a Soviet minesweeper destroyed when discovered hiding in a small bay near Savannah, South Carolina. Apparently masquerading as an American vessel, the Russian ship had been there for days quite openly.

On land, the Russians were winning and winning convincingly, although Eisenhower remained equally convinced that resistance was more than they had anticipated and that it was having an effect upon their plans.

Ike drained another coffee and drew down another cigarette, all the time taking in the situation map as it was updated with newly arrived information.

The loss of Lubeck was grave indeed, placing more pressure on Hamburg's defenders, as well as opening up Southern Denmark.

Soviet forces had immediately pushed forward and taken another bloody nose. British 11th Armoured Division had manhandled the Soviet 22nd Army at Timmendorfer Strand, taking considerable numbers of prisoners for the first time.

For now it seemed that the Soviet advance into Southern Denmark had been stopped, but Eisenhower did not celebrate too much, as he watched red markings outflanking Timmendorfer and worryingly, starting to appear on the eastern and southern suburbs of Hamburg, indicating small but important inroads by Russian forces.

The 82nd US Airborne had all but ceased to exist in bloody defensive battles north and south of the Elbe.

Ike's attention was drawn back to the area north of Hamburg, as a Corporal placed new red markings at Bad Segeberg, heading west from Lubeck. That they went through an area apparently held by the British Guards was a concern and he beckoned a Major forward to send off a message to McCreery for more information.

Once done, he returned to his observations, noting that the advances into the southern environs of Hamburg appeared stalled for now.

Elements of the famous 51st Highland Division had been moved up and were engaged in fierce fighting south of the Elbe, around Harburg. Lighting another cigarette, Eisenhower smiled to himself as he also noted the steady progress of 1st Polish Armoured Division, crossing the Weser and assembling at Bremervorde and Stade.

Ike gave himself a moment's pause and wondered if he was producing a smile or a grimace, for the move was not without risk if Bremen came under direct attack. He liked McCreery's style though and it looked like the British General was planning to hit back, driving the enemy back from below Hamburg and relieving the pressure on the city.

In fact, the more Ike looked at the northern sector, the more he felt that a stabilised line was possible in short order, provided no more huge surprises came his way.

Braunschweig had fallen and enemy units were heading to Hannover but were presently stalled at Peine, where the 405th RCT of the 102nd US Infantry, receiving timely assistance from elements of the British 8th Armoured Brigade, defeated and bloodied a strong force of the Soviet 69th Army.

Eisenhower remembered reading a report of that action, where the US Commander described the Soviet artillery as incredibly powerful, a string that was repeated across the front. What the Soviets lacked in technology and finesse they made up for with weight of shell and dealing with the massed artillery assaults was a problem for which no immediate solution was apparent.

Making a mental note to find out what progress had been made on that issue, another cigarette armed him for the mental journey down the front line.

Hildesheim.

Still holding.

There, an RCT from 30th US Infantry Division, part of 2nd US Armored, plus stragglers from a number of units, were battling against the Soviet 3rd Army and doing exceptionally well.

'*Need to know more,*' and accompanied the thought with a gesture to Colonel Samuel V. Rossiter USMC, officially a USMC officer attached to Ike's staff to fly the flag for the Corps, which he did ably, but in reality a senior member of OSS who briefed Eisenhower in on special ops when needed.

"What's the situation at Hildesheim, Sam?"

"Very strange, Sir. Nothing happening at all except nuisance artillery fire. It seems the boys gave the commies a good working over yesterday and maybe they are sat back, licking their wounds. We have recon working on it, but no reports back as of yet."

Moreover and unknown to either man, there would be no further report today. The photo-recce Spitfire had long since been struck from the skies.

"2nd Armored has got set on the Hameln-Springe line, but we have confirmed sightings of Soviet vehicles at Blomberg. Not sure what numbers or type and it could just be a small recon force. General Collier has switched some 2nd Armored assets to cover his southern approaches, just in case.

"Excellent."

Rossiter was looking directly at his commander and noted the pained look that suddenly developed.

"We still have a huge issue with Göttingen. General Bradley has ordered them out, I understand?"

513

"Yes, Sir. There is a difficulty with the route of escape."

Rossiter tapped the Weser River line, which ran across the path the trapped units needed to use.

"I believe the Soviets have managed to trap most of the 83rd Infantry and part of the 8th Armored east of the Weser."

Fishing in the sheaf of papers he held in his left hand, he extracted the report he was looking for.

"Major General Macon of the 83rd states he can't disengage as he is pressed on all fronts and fighting every foot backwards. Recon elements of the 8th are trying to find a way across the Weser. Unusually, the Reds are bombing the bridges, something they've singularly avoided doing so far. Options for withdrawal over the Weser are becoming less by the hour. General Bradley's ordered a stand on the west bank of the river opposite these forces, to try and give them the best chance of escape and engineers are putting extra bridges across."

Eisenhower had recently discussed this with Bradley and, whilst he was content to let the old warhorse do his work, the risk to both the trapped units and those ordered to hold the Weser line was great.

Gesturing with his smoking right hand, Ike pointed out a Soviet drive that was moving north-west from Fritzlar.

"Actually, Sir, we have garbled reports of enemy activity just south of Istha."

"Where's that?"

Rossiter walked to the map and his finger pointed out a small town, positioned west of Kassel.

Eisenhower's face was a mask of horror.

Returning, the Marine Colonel hastily continued.

"We're trying hard to firm that up but we've now no contact with the unit from the 79th that gave us the heads up. We have a cavalry battalion en route at this moment, Sir."

"OK," an angry finger waved in the general direction of the map, a voice slightly raised, "But we do need to stay on top of that one, Sam."

"Yes, Sir."

514

Coffee arrived on cue and gave a natural break, permitting one man to retire feeling chastened and the other to drink, feeling that he just displayed a little too much emotion for a Commander-in Chief. A word of apology later would be needed. The Colonel was good at what he did and did not deserve his boss's anger, leastways not for that.

It was not getting any better by the time he resumed his observations. Kassel was holding and holding tough, but the Soviets looked like they were trying to bypass to the south. Frankenberg had stopped them, or rather the Eder River through it had, 75th Infantry's Commanding officer reporting the bridges down and his front stabilised in a very recent report.

Giessen was also holding, having been assaulted very early on in the conflict, the Soviet advance being unexpectedly deep, mainly because of the positional problems experienced by 5th and 6th Armored Divisions.

An enemy move to the south, aimed at Butzbach, had been anticipated and blunted. The Soviets didn't know that the paratroopers dropped on Kransberg were all dead or captured. It had been an easy call to anticipate a relief attempt, so when they peeled south-east and then drove back into Bad Nauheim the Americans were ready again, although the fighting was hard and casualties heavy on both sides.

Frankfurt was still friendly, but that was very finite, as the eastern suburbs now belonged to the enemy and probes were being thrown out north and south in an attempt to surround.

A southeast aimed thrust had taken Aschaffenburg in a bloodless advance and that element seemed to be turning south-west.

'*Looks to be aiming at Darmstadt,*' he proposed, in discussion with himself.

'*Too close to the Rhine for my tastes,*' he conceded.

Beckoning Rossiter over again, he did not forget what he owed the man.

"My apologies, Sam. Forgive me."

"Think nothing of it, Sir; it's a hell of a day, that's all."

No harm done, plus one very serious and competent officer thinking that his Boss was actually a good man.

"Darmstadt?"

"Third herd in situ and Grow is itching for them to come in harm's way."

Eisenhower laughed aloud.

"OK, that will do for me. They will hold. Thank you, Colonel."

"Sir."

'Third Herd' was the nickname of 3rd US Armored Division, an outfit that was as tough as they came. The unit's commander, Bob Grow, was a fighting General, with a reputation for bravery and steadfastness.

South-east of that and more trouble, as 42nd and 63rd Infantry were being pressed hard on a north-west to south-east line, either side of Bad Mergentheim. They were struggling to create a holding barrier on the Main and Tauber Rivers, acknowledging the main line would be on the Neckar behind them and making their left flank fast to the 28th US Infantry, who had moved up to Mannheim and Heidelberg.

Ike noted the French in the picture, with the tough 3rd Algerian Division turning Stuttgart into a fortress to the 63rd's rear.

Aggressive intent revealed itself, as he noted the 12th US Armored moving up to around Bad Windsheim, to the west of Nürnberg. The Soviet left flank looked vulnerable and it would be a shame not to take the opportunity offered, especially as Tedder had added a surprise to the pot, with fighter squadrons in relative abundance to cover the attacks, at the cost of cover elsewhere admittedly, but worth the risk.

12th and 9th Armored will give the Reds something to think about.

'Hooah.'

Tomorrow.

Nürnburg would hold.

So would München, but the area was rapidly becoming a machine, consuming men and equipment in large numbers. Bombing raids and artillery by themselves were

516

causing casualties enough, but the Soviets were now pressing on the ground.

A thin salient was developing, where the 45th US Infantry's 180th RCT was defying all efforts to shift them from the Bavarian township of Moosburg.

Attempts to outflank the 'Thunderbirds' were stopped short at Erding in the south and Allershausen in the north, but both thrusts reduced the corridor from Moosberg to München to a worrying ten miles width, all of which was under artillery fire.

4th US Armored was forming the southern defences, together with the 157th RCT, with bit and pieces of the 99th Infantry coming together to the northern side, finally becoming organised after their flight from Regensburg.

As Eisenhower studied the whole München situation, his view was obscured as three agitated officers started running fingers over the map, voices raised, not in anger but in concern. One turned to Eisenhower, catching his eye and pointing at Ingolstadt.

And there it was; the hole.

The dam had burst, even as he had sat looking at the map, making his plans, assessing, whilst all the time the goddamn Russians were through.

When the French had taken back their country, the members of the FFI became redundant virtually overnight, as the Germans were soon back beyond their borders. Some were patriots of the Maquis, long standing fighters from the early days, but many others were recent arrivals to the cause, having been less than active under occupation, but now suddenly keen to be involved.

Eisenhower always suspected that the employment of FFI in line divisions would not bode well, but they had done enough, fighting as they were against a hated foe on his shrinking territory.

Somehow, the 14th French Infantry Division had become relatively isolated in the line at Ingolstadt and their right flank had caved in completely, melting away in front of what was believed to be the Soviet prime attack force, namely the 5th Guards Tank Army.

He had missed it, his Generals had missed it, but the Soviets clearly had not and now they were flooding through the front line at Manching. Their right flank on the Donau, with nothing between them and Augsburg.

All across Germany and Austria, Allied forces were retreating under orders, holding where required, occasionally having to react to appalling problems like Göttingen and the developments around Kassel.

However, this was different. There was little beyond to stem the flow and it had caught everyone by surprise.

The rest of the map could wait because this needed his personal attention and he strode forward to take charge of what was rapidly becoming a pantomime scene, as concerned staff rushed around brandishing reports and messages.

It was a question of assets and the immediate one to hand was 2nd French Armoured Division, in and around Memmingen, which could be quickly backed up by two modestly equipped US cavalry groups; the 115th near Kempten and 101st at Ehingen.

Ike could get the Cavalry moving quickly and he did so, calming his subordinates with his unruffled approach and steady voice, dictating his orders to the 7th Army commander, General Patch. Under his direction, the staff group came back to order, once more efficient and functioning at 100%.

He could also alert 1st US Infantry Division, 'The Big Red One', who could look to their southeast flank and stiffen it with some armor, in case the Soviets turned to the north to undercut Nürnberg.

As he pondered more moves, another report indicating continuing resistance in Ingolstadt from part of the 14th helped a little, but he could not trust them anymore.

Now he had a French General to order forward and, ever the diplomat, he considered how he would present the abject French collapse to the proud Frenchman.

518

0845hrs Thursday 9th August 1945, Curau River crossings, South of Malkendorf, Germany.

Fig#12 - Malkendorf.

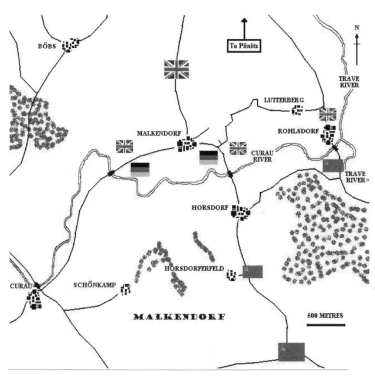

Allied Forces – 'C' Sqdn, 3rd R.T.R., D Coy, 8th Battalion, The Rifle Brigade, 119th Battery, 75th Anti-Tank Regt RHA, 2 Battery, 13th [HAC] Regt, RHA, 2nd Independent Machine gun Company, Northumberland Fusiliers of 11th Armoured Division, British 8th Corps, British 2nd Army, British 21st Army Group, plus Horsdorf Defence Unit [Kommando Horsdorf], Malkendorf Defence Unit [Kommando Malkendorf].

519

Soviet Forces – 1013th Rifle Regt, 1015th Rifle Regt, 1017th Rifle Regt, 835th Artillery Regt of 285th Rifle Division, 27th Guards Heavy Tank Regt of Soviet 21st Army, 1st Baltic Front.

Lubeck had been a bitter pill indeed, but the Soviet 21st Army had subsequently made steady progress, pushing a handful of British troops before them, driving inexorably northwest. Then the call for help came from 22nd Army, halted by obdurate British defence at Timmendorfer.

Swinging north, 21st Army intended to drive in the direction of Pönitz, using the river Trave as a secure right flank, before turning east and compromising the defenders of Timmendorfer with a swift rear attack.

Earlier that morning, 1017th Rifles of 285th Division had been leading the way until they were stopped dead at Rohlsdorf, the bridge blown in front of their eyes and then, to add insult to injury, they were swept with accurate and frequently fatal, artillery fire. Lacking bridging assets to continue with his planned advance, the 1017th's Colonel requested orders.

The Divisional Commander called his artillery into action at once, replying in kind on the defenders of Rohlsdorf, at the same time swinging the 1013th Regiment westwards, looking to cross the Curau-Malkendorf bridge and sending his reserve regiment, the 1015th, up the middle and over the Horsdorf Bridge.

Under his orders, just for this advance, was the 27th Guards Heavy Tank Regiment, whose IS-II's were a very welcome addition to his force.

The 1017th left one battalion opposite the destroyed bridge at Rohlsdorf and pulled the rest back to the south-west to form a reserve force.

The 285th Division had seen little combat in the war against the Fascists but it was a professional unit, well drilled and confident, so its regiments adapted to the new orders immediately, swiftly closing on their allotted routes of advance.

The ground was flat and relatively featureless, marked only by the occasional knot of trees, clump of hedgerows and small depression.

Fortunately, that was enough good cover for the British commander to conceal his self-propelled guns and tanks, although most of the tanks were held back to the north-west of Malkendorf ,enjoying cover in the extensive woods.

With the services of the excellent 13th Honourable Artillery Company to call on, Lieutenant Colonel Julian Fairbairn-Banks felt confident, despite his limited infantry.

Fig#13 Malkendorf First Assault.

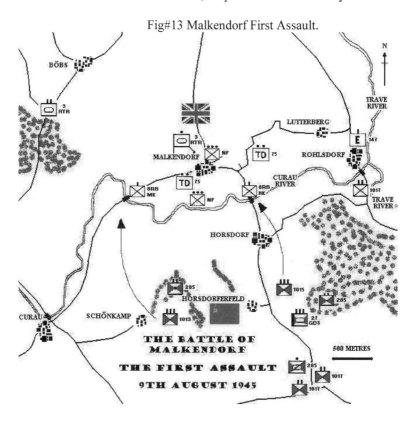

521

On which subject his thoughts immediately leapt to the Germans.

Within an hour of the broadcast made by the new German Leadership, ex-German soldiers, some with their uniforms and, more alarmingly, some with weapons, reported for duty with units under his control.

For now, he had organised each of them under the command of a British Officer and had them placed adjacent to and covering a bridge. The 'Horsdorf' group of fifty-two men covered the main bridge to his centre left. The 'Malkendorf' group, consisting of forty-four men, covered the right flank bridge, each German force closely supported by a platoon from his infantry company; 'supported' was the word he had carefully chosen anyway.

The rest of his infantry were concealed, in reserve, between the river and Malkendorf.

One platoon of the machine gun company was placed centrally, able to support either or both bridges, a second platoon again in reserve, this time in Malkendorf itself.

Topping off his defences was an experienced artillery observer positioned in the church tower, ready to bring fire down on whatever the Russians threw at them.

Every one of his troops was dug in and well concealed, although he grudgingly admitted that the Germans had completely disappeared. Lessons to be learned when time permitted he told himself.

Fairbairn-Banks was a professional soldier, long in service and drenched in combat experience, from his early days in the BEF through to the surrender of Germany.

He was by far the tallest man in the 11th Armoured, standing a full 6'9" in his stockinged feet. His men knew him as 'Barney', drawn from the barn door analogy, for he was also as wide as a rugby prop forward. His Brigadier cynically called him 'Sniper's Heaven' because of his obvious disadvantages when it came to hiding under fire.

Even sat down in his Humber scout car, vast areas of his upper body were visible, unless he really tried hard to bend himself out of shape.

522

He now sat in that scout car, radio handset in one hand, binoculars in the other, watching and waiting, counting the yards as the Soviet infantry moved closer.

Judging the moment to perfection, he gave the order and the killing commenced.

Using only the German and British units at the bridges, he kept the other units silent for now, believing, quite rightly, that the Russians would be stopped with just those he alerted.

The combination of Bren guns and Vickers heavy machine guns did deadly work, with Lee-Enfields and Kar98k's adding their barks to the noisy chaos that descended upon the lead Russian units.

The Malkendorf unit had found an MG42 from somewhere, but were obviously conserving the small amount of ammunition that came with it.

Leaving many dead on the field, the two lead Soviet companies withdrew to await the next attempt.

Colonel Leonid Shvpaghin was beside himself with rage.

His two precious T-60 reconnaissance tanks had previously covered the same ground as was now littered with his dead men, reported nothing and then had withdrawn to refuel.

Seeking permission from the Army Commander, his plan being to move around the river at its source, some 4 miles west near Dakendorf, he anticipated the expected refusal and developed his plans for attack in situ.

Ordering the artillery officer to lay smoke when the time came, he radioed an order to the Major commanding the 1013th, preparing them for a frontal assault, but also to send one company to probe westwards towards Curau, just in case.

The commanding Leytenant from the recon troop was demoted to private on the spot and replaced by his Starshina, who was ordered to support the 1013th's attack as closely as possible with the machine guns of his tanks.

During combat in Lubeck, Shvapagin's men had liberated a British Cromwell and he sent this forward to provide heavier support for his troops.

1015th would let their brothers close and take advantage of the moving artillery to storm forward in the centre, sweeping the way clear for the heavy tanks to cross the river.

Fig#14 - Malkendorf Second Assault.

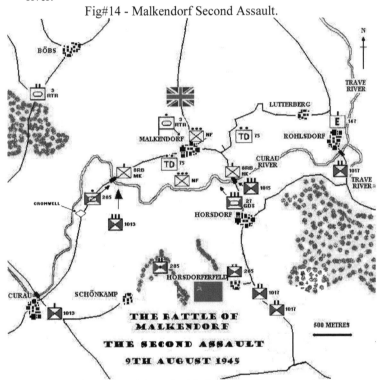

The Colonel brought his heavy tanks nearer the front line, ready to cope with any surprises and to more quickly develop the attack once 1015th had captured their objective.

Mounting the two battalions of 1017th in their trucks, he prepared to use them either as reinforcements should they be needed, or close support infantry for the 27th's Tanks once they got to Malkendorf itself

524

He would have liked more artillery, but his artillery regiment had suffered one of the few successful allied air strikes the previous evening and valuable guns had been lost.

Finally, he deployed his mortars in the thin strip of dense woods, west of Horsdorferfelde.

He knew his Army Commander well and Major-General Gusev's reply was no surprise. On receipt of both the refusal of the move to the west and the usual exhortations regarding the price of failure, he ordered the attack to commence at 1215 hrs.

At the allotted time, the 1013th's soldiers charged forward, unable to see their objective for smoke, which had been dropping since 1210 hrs. Whilst 1013th's attack was closing, the artillery switched, the first smoke shells burst off target, needing correction, before the infantry and tanks started forward.

The defenders of the Malkendorf Bridge started to engage, dropping the advancing Russians to the ground as they desperately sought cover, some never to rise again. An additional heavy machine gun, then another, cut into their right flank from across the river, herding the desperate soldiers closer together around the road and to its western edges.

Shvpaghin screamed at his battalions, urging them not to bunch up, urging his mortars to hit the machine gun positions. The divisional communication's personnel desperately punched his orders out into the radio waves.

The Colonel let out a low moan as the unmistakable whine of incoming artillery upstaged the noise of the infantry battle and he winced as accurate fragmentation shells from the 25-pounders of the H.A.C. ripped whole platoons to shreds.

The 25-pdr, in expert hands, was a very capable artillery piece, as he was now learning, witnessing his lead battalion gutted in front of his eyes, casualties made worse by bunching together, herded as they were by the machine gun fire.

As Shvpaghin watched his own mortars ineffectively seeking out the heavy machine guns, he saw his left-flank attack go to ground, totally out of steam.

He ordered the supporting three tanks to press forward.

The Cromwell tank slewed off the road, track broken by some erratic driving. The crew abandoned the stranded vehicle with gusto.

The two T-70's moved forward, inevitably crushing the dead and the living alike, as they jinked to avoid anti-tank weapons.

The 25-pdr's fell silent and, encouraged both by the absence of shrapnel and the valour of their tank crews, the 1013th's soldiers rose up again.

Ordering the mortars to increase their rate of fire, Shvpaghin ensured that the artillery bathed the Horsdorf Bridge with smoke. 1015th were then ordered forward, with the IS-II's in close support.

A small trail of smoke reached out from a previously unseen position on the north bank, adjacent to the bridge, touching the lead T-70 and transforming it in a hearse, the occupants killed instantly as the panzerfaust struck home.

The second light tank fired down the line of the smoke and was rewarded with demostrative strikes on enemy soldiers, as pieces of bodies flew in all directions.

They were still firing as a second smoke trail terminated accurately on the front of their turret, killing the commander and gunner instantly.

The attack stalled once more.

In the centre, the 1015th fared much better. The mortars had beaten down much of the machine gun fire initially directed at the infantry and the smoke barrage was very effective in masking them from enemy fire.

However, 25-pdr fragmentation rounds started to arrive and casualties again mounted.

Shvpaghin's joy disappeared as swiftly as it arrived, when the report from his artillery officer stated that the smoke rounds would be consumed within three minutes.

He looked through his binoculars and weighed up the ground.

It could be done.

'It must be done!'

"Order Banov to charge, full tilt. Smoke is nearly gone and he must close. He must close now!"

The order was dispatched straight away and the Colonel saw a discernable increase in speed spread through the attacking lines of infantry. The heavy tanks put on a spurt and drew level with the rear of their infantry comrades.

Gripping his binoculars tightly, Shvpaghin watched as the first wave of infantry started to melt away, victims of desultory fire from the other bank. Enemy artillery was still killing, but it was not as accurate as before.

It was working.

"Smoke expended, Comrade Colonel," came the report, but he did not hear it, watching, concentrating, as his second wave ran over the first and reached the riverbank.

Checking his mortars were still giving the enemy machine guns hell, he switched back at the time that the smoke first started to dissipate. Within a minute, the enemy artillery was more accurately directed and a direct strike from a high-explosive shell wrecked the lead IS-II's engine, starting a fire that produced oily black smoke to add to the fading smokescreen. The driver staggered out to be shot down by a grinning German youth wielding a Kar98k.

In the Colonel's vision, he could see the men of his second wave, dead and dying, struggling in the water, or hugging the earth, in whatever scrape in the ground they found themselves. Grenades were being thrown back and forth, doing the Grim Reaper's work without distinction.

Conscious of the fate of the two T-70's, the heavy tankers were holding back.

He ordered the commander of 27th Tanks to press on regardless, to support his infantry and continue to close Malkendorf. The order was not acknowledged, causing him to turn and examine the burning IS-II more closely.

The destroyed vehicle had radio aeriels.

"B'lyad!" he shouted and spat with all his might after delivering his favourite expletive.

"Contact the tank regiment's deputy. Get them fucking moving!"

527

The third and fourth waves were bunching up, repeating the error of the failed flank attack, but this time there was less MG fire to herd them and the artillery caused fewer casualties.

The HAC, positioned just north-west of Rohlsdorf, had been spotted by Soviet air-reconnaissance and counter-battery fire was arriving, forcing both of the troops to relocate, not without loss in men and guns.

The IS-II's started forward again, first company deploying into formation ready to cross the bridge, the second company moving to the left to provide support, if needed, with the third taking the right-hand position with the same brief.

Each of the companies had lost two tanks for various reasons whilst en route to Malkendorf and so a total of fifteen 122mm guns prepared to destroy anything that opposed them.

Behind the lead company came the 2-I-C's T34, the rest of the regiment's support troops remaining well out of harm's way.

Fairbairn-Banks wiped the blood from the lenses of his binoculars and tried not to look at the padre, whom the finger of God had selected as the sole casualty of a short shell from the HAC's guns. The pious man had been kneeling in prayer in the churchyard, when a defective charge propelled a high explosive round from a 25-pdr barrel a considerably less distance than intended, dropping it neatly in front of the padre, just as the Lieutenant Colonel was moving position.

'Barney' could not help the wry thought.

'Perhaps it's a miracle that there is enough of the man left to carry in a blanket.'

None the less, he had been a likeable man and a popular replacement for old Father O'Reilly, whose heart had given out in Normandy.

No time for further reflection, Fairbairn-Banks turned over the battle to the young Major commanding the twelve concealed Achilles tank destroyers, suitably arranged to cover their intended killing grounds around the bridges.

528

Some of the IS-II's were firing big HE rounds at his infantry and clearly causing casualties. A panzerfaust leapt from underneath the Horsdorf Bridge, detonating against the turret side of the least cautious member of third company.

Apart from a scorch mark on the turret, the vehicle seemed none the worse for the encounter, but it took no further part in the battle, the crew placed beyond the skills of the surgeons already snowed under with wounded carried back to their aid station.

First Company took the bridge area bit by bit, clearing the tenacious defenders from its environs, rushing over the wooden structure in support of the tanks. Many fell, victims of grazing fire from the no longer subdued machine guns.

Those who made it across the bridge fell headlong into a position manned with Germans dressed in all manner of attire, wielding weapons from bayonets to medieval broadswords taken from the nearby Schloss. The slaughter was atrocious, hands clutching at throats, fingers gouging out eyes, the blood, faeces, urine and bile of the dead mixing with the vomit of the living as a hundred men became feral beasts in the name of self-preservation.

The fighting was so intense that no-one paid any attention to the heavy crack of big guns and the resultant clangs, as missiles burrowed into metal and converted expensive killing machines into just so much scrap metal.

The young British Major had timed his shoot well, waiting until most of First Company's tanks were across the bridge and the Second Company had turned side on to follow them. As a bonus, Third Company had their field of fire reduced by their living and dead comrades.

Only one IS-II of First Company was still in full running order. A PIAT shell struck the leviathan, but it shrugged the hit off, the turret swivelled, two accurate bursts slaying the British AT gunners as they desperately reloaded. Exerting more than enough pressure on an anti-tank mine, the heavy tank shuddered as the mine exploded. The right track flopped uselessly away and the crippled beast slewed to the right, exposing its left side to a second round of shots. Five were targeted upon the IS-II and the nearby British infantry had

529

a first-class view of a real tank brew-up, so much so that the heat forced them to relocate, at the cost of several wounded as vengeful Soviet infantry sought recompense for their dead tank.

Second company had now lost four tanks, although one of those could still fire.

The Achilles' 17-pdrs were a weapon to be feared and more shells traversed the battlefield in search of victims.

The 27th Tanks was an experienced formation, but even those men could not stand such losses and the survivors turned to run, creating what smoke they could and carving a bloody trail through the friendly infantry that had naturally migrated to them, seeking safety behind their metal bulwarks.

Having had the satisfaction of watching the lone Soviet spotter aircraft crash in flames, victim of the attentions of a De Havilland Mosquito hunting party, the relocated HAC gunners set up their artillery as quickly as they could and reported in their readiness to join the fray again.

The observer had a nice plum target ready and waiting.

Shvpaghin watched silently, bereft of any emotion, save total shock. His eyes saw but did not understand, the visuals of the destruction of his command not digested until he was shaken from his doldrums by the arrival of accurate artillery on his infantry reserve, all nicely laid out in trucks for the killing.

As the two battalions were butchered and more of the retreating IS-II's fell victim to whatever monster guns the British were using, he became aware of his second in command approaching, grim faced.

Not taking his eyes away from the continuing slaughter in front of him, he merely requested the officer's report.

"Comrade General Gusev orders you to his headquarters immediately, Comrade Polkovnik."

Shvpaghin turned to his subordinate, with whom he had served since the early days.

"And what else, Alexander?"

"I am to place you under arrest and relieve you of your weapon."

"I see."

He turned back to face his destroyed division, now strangely calm, assessing perhaps 60%, or even 70% casualties in men and all but two IS-II's immolated.

"So, what will you do, Comrade", his eyes remained glued to the binoculars that he was now using to cover his tears.

Tears not for himself but for the men he had led for so long.

"I will come back in a little while, my friend."

Shvpaghin nodded gently and turned to shake the hand of the man who was his friend.

No words came.

No words were necessary.

The Colonel turned back for one last look at his command and saw Major Banov, bloodied and dirty, staggering back up the road.

'Another of the old team,' thought Shvpaghin and he saluted the apparition smartly, which salute was returned as best as the severely wounded Major could accomplish.

Taking his treasured Walther P38 pistol from his holster, he looked skywards to a hot sun, partially obscured by the smoky products of his ruined heavy tank regiment, aiming his final words at a God he hated beyond measure, as he put a bullet in his brain.

"B'lyad."

The casualty figures were truly disproportionate.

In all the combat that morning, the 27th Guards Tank Regiment ceased to exist, solely one running heavy tank to its name, supported by twelve shattered and traumatised survivors. All but two of the other tank crew remained permanently on the field.

285th Rifle Division was removed from the Soviet order of battle. Its artillery, mortars and support services, all absorbed into the Army reserves and the remnants of the three rifle regiments formed into one shocked battalion and sent rearward for security duties.

Each of the three regiments had sported over two thousand men before the commencement on the 6th. A few had fallen along the way, but Malkendorf had been a slaughter akin to the early days of 1941. German civilians, pressed into action to help clear the field, four days later, insisted that over three and a half thousand bodies were recovered and interred in five mass graves, west of Horsdorf.

A day later, Colonel Leonid Borissovich Shvpaghin was buried by his friend, Alexander Bissanov, where he was placed alongside his long time comrade, Major Alexei Vassilevich Banov and thirty-seven of his men. They were interred adjacent to the bridge, north of Horsdorf, forever occupying the southern bank, directly opposite the burial place of their German adversaries.

The Malkendorf Kommando, as they called themselves, suffered twenty-three dead and an equal number wounded. They were buried next to the bridge they had defended so valiantly.

The Horsdorf group suffered grievous losses, mainly in the hand to hand fighting at the north end of the bridge. Seven men were left standing, none unwounded. The Rifle Brigade helped them bury these brave men on the evening of the battle, similarly, adjacent to their last post.

One Achilles had suffered a hit. Lightly armoured, a 122mm shell was always going to be the winner and the five crew members were buried in a hasty ceremony, interred in the convenient hole created by the short drop in the churchyard.

Along with them went the padre, eleven members of the Northumberland Fusiliers, one unlucky tanker from the 3rd RTR, who broke his neck falling off his tank and twenty-seven riflemen from the 8th Battalion.

The last body laid reverently in the grave was that of Lieutenant Colonel Fairbairn-Banks, his life extinguished by a mortar shell, heart stilled by the smallest piece of hot metal slicing through his aorta.

Contrary to his gleeful statements in life, the grave was long enough.

1028hrs Thursday 9th August 1945, Headquarters of the French First Army, Baden-Baden.

Eisenhower's urgent phone call overrode the instruction not to be disturbed, as issued by the Commander of the First French Army to his Aide.

The Colonel begged forgiveness and informed his commander of the urgency of the situation.

Général d'Armée Jean de Lattre de Tassigny accepted the man's nervous interruption and dismissed him, then apologised to his guests as he picked up the simple bakelite phone and had his world turned upside down by the American General.

The men watched him closely, imagining the words that the General was hearing, judging their severity by the expression on his face. The woman poured a second glass of Perrier and gently flexed her wounded muscles; left shoulder and arm swathed in bandages as a result of fragments from a grenade. Nothing serious, but very painful.

The phone call was already coming to an end, with everyone by now aware that something had gone badly wrong.

De Lattre replaced the receiver carefully, his own shrapnel wounds stiffening his right arm. He addressed the group, favouring the most senior man.

Having quickly outlined the details of the 14th Infantry disaster and the moves ordered by Eisenhower, he begged the group's indulgence and picked up the phone once more, instructing the 2nd Armoured Division forward as requested.

That done, he sat back in his chair, ready to hear the rest of what de Walle had to say and, more to the point, what De Gaulle's reaction was going to be to it.

Even with both of them in the room and the extremely pretty agent Valois to examine at length, as attractive as ever,

533

despite not wearing any make-up whatsoever, her charms unobstructed by the bandages and scratches on her face, De Lattre spent more time looking at the fourth person, sat directly opposite him.

Such was the presence of Ernst-August Knocke.

1215hrs Thursday 9th August 1945, Headquarters of the French First Army, Baden-Baden.

The meeting concluded shortly after midday and De Lattre had secured the full support of De Gaulle for the proposal brought to him by De Walle and Knocke. In the way that adversity sometimes assists in the plans of men, Eisenhower's information about the 14th Division's collapse solved one major hurdle of the plan and De Lattre would address that when the time was right.

De Gaulle left the Baden-Baden headquarters openly and with his normal flourishes.

The other three took their leave of De Lattre and left less theatrically, departing through the kitchens.

Anne-Marie de Valois' natural beauty drew admiring glances from the kitchen staff, as well as from the Major making his coffee just the way he 'liked' it; fresh ground beans in a glass mug with boiling water added to brew in the cup. It was the Polish way and he had taught himself to do it with enthusiasm he did not feel. Information was his business and kitchen staff the world over know all the gossip and do not mind who they share it with, so drinking the disgusting brew was a small price to pay.

Sipping the coffee, he admired the sensual lips, thrusting bosom, perfect hips and shapely legs of the pretty woman striding past. His eyes swept up and down, from head to toe. Almost in spite of itself, his brain announced something important, and his eyes reluctantly gave up the vision of beauty, to be drawn to the polished military boots and immaculate gaiters on the otherwise nondescript figure behind her. Wrapped in an old raincoat, the man's very existence was easy to overlook in the presence of such beauty. His senses lit off all at once.

534

'*She's supposed to draw attention,*' said one side of his brain as the other side shouted, '*Look at the man*'!

Snatching a half-second as the figure disappeared through the door, Kowalski saw a face that he felt he ought to be able to put a name to.

At 2240, it came to him.

His recent temporary attachment as a Liaison Officer with the 3rd Algerian Division in Stuttgart had disrupted his reporting methods, but now he was back with the French First Army, Moscow would know that the French were courting the SS swine soon enough and he might even learn specifics by then.

'*Ernst Knocke.*'

"Skurwielu", the Polish word for bastard slipped easily from his tongue.

'*Govno*', He thought in his native language.

2135hrs Thursday 9th August 1945, Headquarters of SHAEF, Trianon Hotel, Versailles, France.

Eisenhower waited in his private chamber, his orderly somewhere else, in an earnest hunt for a pack of Ike's cigarettes, the main portion of which seemed to have disappeared in the move to Versailles.

A knock on the door and a relieved Corporal provided a more relieved General with a stack of six packs to keep him going, which became five and a bit before the orderly reached the exit. So important was Ike's habit that a Major was now tasked with ensuring that a steady supply was obtained from the PX.

Having finished telephone discussions with Bradley and Devers some minutes beforehand, covering the next staged withdrawals, Eisenhower wanted to drop back down to the main intelligence room, just to take one last look at the map, in case anything needed his attention prior to the intended relieving attacks slated for dawn on Friday morning.

Settling back in his chair to savour the rich smoke, his quiet solitary world was interrupted by urgent knocking on his door, which then opened without the customary niceties. Ike

535

was about to chew the Colonel out but he stayed himself, noting the excited and beaming smile on the man's face. The older officer was a true Southern gentleman, never flustered and always correct, so something had well and truly got his dander up and Ike wanted to know without delay.

"Sir, my apologies to you this fine evening. I have a gentleman outside whom I believe you will want to see without delay."

No amount of movement of mouth and chin could shift the smile.

"Judging from your grin, Thomas, I believe you may be right. Enlighten me."

Colonel Thomas Bell Hood, who was always at pains to state he was no relation to THE General Hood, composed himself and, although failing somewhat to remove the whole smile, spoke formally and with great precision.

"General, outside is Lieutenant-General Agustín Muñoz Grandes, official representative of the head of the Spanish State, His Excellency Generalissimo Don Francisco Franco y Bahamonde, Caudilo de España, por la Gracia de Dios."

Eisenhower was impressed with Hoods' perfect recall, as well as the impact of the name itself.

"He seeks an audience with you immediately, in order to relay information of vital importance to the Allied cause."

Now Ike understood why Hood's composure had evaporated.

Reaching for his cap, he shared Hood's smile.

"Then I will see him without delay... and once you conduct the Caballero in, please contact Generals Bradley, McCreery, Devers, Alexander and Clark and let them know to stay by the phone."

Hood conducted the Spanish officer into Ike's quarters, where he stood at parade attention, resplendent in his countries uniform and, very noticeably, sporting a German Knight's Cross with Oak leaves around his neck. These were honours earned on the steppes of Russia, as leader of the 250th German Infanterie Division, more famously known as the Spanish Blau Division.

536

Eisenhower returned his immaculate salute and immediately extended his hand, which was firmly grasped and warmly shaken.

As Ike showed Grandes to a chair he knew he was about to get some good news at last.

"You have come a long way, General. I hope you have had some refreshment?"

"Thank you, General. I have been afforded the opportunity to eat and drink. Once I have given you my brief, I would be grateful if you could order your staff to allocate me a modest room, where I might catch up on my sleep before I return with your reply."

"Consider it done, General," and he leant across to the telephone, organising comfortable quarters for the tired looking Spaniard.

Grandes inclined his head in thanks as Ike replaced the receiver.

The Allied general settled back in his chair, his eyes inviting the Spaniard's information, although all he wanted to do was sit on the edge in anticipation of the words to come, much like a child at the end of a good fairytale.

Grandes spoke firmly and with a lilt only those from Mediterranean climes have perfected.

"General Eisenhower, I am here, on behalf of Generalissimo Franco, to give you the official and irrevocable position of the Spanish nation."

Eisenhower nodded, but did not interrupt the flow with pleasantries.

"The Soviet broadcast on the 6th August made clear the position the Communists have adopted regarding Spain and other countries. My Generalissimo wishes the Allied nations to be very clear on the position Spain has adopted regarding the Soviet Union and her allies."

A light cough broke his flow.

"Spain believes that America, Great Britain, France and all the other Allied nations intend to resist this communist aggression. Is that correct, general?"

Eisenhower nodded and reinforced the message.

"Since that broadcast on Monday, I can tell you that all nations who were committed to the Allied cause in May 1945 have reaffirmed their commitment to opposing this violent incursion into free Europe. As well as additional commitment being made by both the Brazilian and Mexican governments, we have received overtures from Argentina on offering assistance. You, Generalissimo Franco and the Spanish nation may rest assured that we and our league of free nations will resist this with all our might… and we will not stop until Europe is no longer under threat."

Eisenhower made sure that Grandes would get the real importance of what he was about to say.

"We all will not stop until nation states, since absorbed or made puppets by the Soviet advances, are returned to their rightful leaders and peoples, all the way to the borders of Russia herself and that the Soviet Union is made incapable of further acts of aggression for generations to come. That is the position of my government, the British Government and that of France, a position supported by every other member of the alliance that is presently building."

Grandes looked genuinely shocked to learn of the political position of the allied governments and wondered why it had not been announced.

Eisenhower answered the unspoken question.

"General, we will prevail, that is a given, for the Peoples of the World are stirring to our cause. But much as Abraham Lincoln could not announce the emancipation of the slaves without a signal victory, any such words on our part will appear hollow without a victory, our Gettysburg."

Realising that in his efforts to explain the political position he might have strayed into a part of American history unfamiliar to his audience, Ike apologised.

"Sorry, General, not everyone is interested in that part of our history. Allow me to explain a different way."

Grandes smiled.

"I understand perfectly, General Eisenhower. Until you can do something to the communists and they have tasted a defeat of note, then no threats, no announcement by you, will have standing, either in their eyes or the greater world."

538

Eisenhower inclined his head in a gracious acceptance of the Spaniard's understanding and eloquence.

"General Eisenhower, Spain is with you."

Four words with much meaning.

"As we speak, the Blau Division is reconstructing and will be ready to be placed at your disposal within the month. The Spanish Army will prepare an Expeditionary Force, which will constitute a full Corps of four divisions. This will be made available, under Spanish Command of course, once the position is made clearer to us regarding what direct threats exist to our homeland."

Eisenhower had just been given an extra division of troops, not a huge force in the greater scheme of things, but the prospect of a corps of troops from a new ally filled him gave him a huge boost.

"Our ambassadors in the Allied countries are delivering our promise of support and commitment to the Allied cause as we speak. The specifics of the military support remains solely with me, for you to use as you see fit, given the difficulties experienced by your intelligence services of late."

In this case, the Spanish eyes in question betrayed nothing of what was known, but the mere fact he had raised the matter made Eisenhower aware of more than a passing suspicion on his new ally's behalf.

Grandes continued, aware he had been indelicate but not regretting it.

"I have in my possession a tape made by the Generalissimo himself. As you have the facilities here to broadcast it, he asks if you would do so tomorrow at the earliest appropriate time."

Eisenhower's question, forming on lips that had not touched a cigarette for a record time now, was unnecessary.

Grandes continued, fishing in his briefcase.

"Here is a translated transcript of its contents, word for word, General."

Eisenhower returned to his phone and requested coffee.

He was only vaguely aware of its arrival, so engrossed was he in what he was reading.

Unconsciously, he reached for a cigarette, sliding it between his lips and was startled from his trance as the Spaniard's lighter flicked into life.

Grandes smiled and gestured lightly, dismissing Ike's embarrassment, lighting his own with a flourish.

"Well, General, these are fine words and will inspire not only your country but all the countries aligned with the cause you join."

Eisenhower arranged the document neatly and placed it on the exquisite cherry wood table, grabbing the arms of his chair. Both generals stood, as if on a silent cue, shaking hands firmly.

Reseating himself, Ike picked up a scalding coffee and grimaced as he noticed a mark on the otherwise pristine surface.

Both men drank in comfortable silence.

"We will have to sort out much by the way of logistics, chain of command, a great deal in fact, General."

"Once I have returned to Madrid to reflect our conversation to the Generalissimo, I believe he intends to dispatch me here to assist you and act as Liaison, if that is acceptable to you?"

"General Grandes, that would be most acceptable to me indeed."

Both men grounded their empty cups, drained simultaneously and shook hands for the third and final time that evening.

"Colonel Hood will see to your needs, General. I hope you sleep well. I certainly will."

"Thank you, General Eisenhower."

"Thank you, General Grandes."

Once the Spaniard had gone, Eisenhower flopped into his chair, lit another celebratory cigarette and commenced a number of phone calls to his closest generals.

Any coward can fight a battle when he's sure of winning, but give me a man who has pluck to fight when he's sure of losing.

George Eliot

CHAPTER 47 – THE NIGHT

0215hrs Friday 10th August 1945, Headquarters, US Forces in Europe, Trianon Palace Hotel, Versailles, France.

The atmosphere was markedly different in SHAEF, partially because news of the Spanish commitment had been a positive boost, but mainly because this morning they were going to do something substantive to the enemy for the first time.

Despite the euphoria brought on by Grandes' words, Eisenhower had slept soundly for a few hours, waking refreshed and focussed, content that all was how it should be.

Exchanging a quizzical look with Tedder across the grand room, he received a nod of confirmation.

Reaching for his cigarettes, the Supreme Commander closed his eyes briefly and imagined what was about to occur some five hundred miles east of where he stood and in a number of other places marked in red on his map.

He smiled.

0257hrs Friday 10th August 1945, Airborne over Leipzig, Germany.

Flight Lieutenant Lawrence Saul watched as another of the friendly predators did its work. The cover they had received so far was excellent and only one of his squadron's aircraft had succumbed to the Soviet night-fighters.

Approaching the start of his run-in, the sky was perfect for his job that night.

Anti-aircraft fire reached up but was wholly ineffective, clearly badly calculated and exploding beneath the Lancaster Mk III's of 460 Squadron R.A.A.F.

The plan was for them and their sister squadrons to make their visit on the Russians and then land at various airfields in Northern France, ready for round two, the following night.

Lancaster AR-S was the design culmination of years of bombing experience and it served no purpose other than to destroy. Despite the protestations of the Squadron Adjutant, Saul and his crew had humorously nicknamed their bird after the Squadron letters and his own name. The Squadron Commander let it ride and calmed the Adjutant's ruffled feathers. It was good for morale and Bomber crews had it tough.

Tonight, S for Sugar was once more in the skies over Germany, having normally carried bombs to wreak havoc on a German City, but this time for a wholly different purpose.

Gently easing the huge craft in accordance with the calm instructions of his bomb-aimer, Saul watched as the anti-aircraft fire grew more accurate and he gripped the stick more firmly in case something burst nearby.

His mid-upper gunner swore loudly and shouted at his Skipper to look to port.

Saul turned and saw the stricken Lancaster AR-N lazily roll over, nose gone, removed by a flak burst. Every member of the crew that could watch did so, until the aircraft containing their friends and colleagues fire-balled on impact with the ground, fifteen thousand feet below.

Everyone except the bomb aimer, who remained fixed to his bombsight.

"Steady."

"Call that in, Sparks. Confirm N for November gone."

"Roger skip."

"Steady."

A burst on the port side close in moved the bomber to starboard in a small surge.

"Left, left, steady."

Another Lancaster was hit, this time more spectacularly, main spar giving way, smashed by the explosion within her fuselage, four distinct pieces of aircraft slowly separating and falling to earth.

542

A pained voice spoke a single word.

"Aaron."

As the severed rear section fell, the tail-gunner's voice lost its emotion, sounding mechanical and detached.

"That's C for Charlie going down, Skipper."

Silence, oppressive silence, as oppressive as only silence containing real horror and pain can be.

Saul swallowed hard and keyed his mike.

"Roger, Den. I'm sorry mate, really sorry."

A short delay, enough for a man to steady his voice and get control of his emotions once more.

"Roger, Skipper. I'm ok."

Saul looked at the flight engineer, automatically correcting as the bombardier's instructions came in. They nodded at each other.

"Want a spell there, Den? Give you some time? Wally will come back."

No delay this time.

"Negative. I'm fine Skip. Let's get it done."

Wally shrugged and resumed his position.

"Roger that, Den."

Saul wasn't too sure what else he could usefully say to a man that had just watched his twin brother die.

"Bombs gone!"

The aircraft leapt and Saul cursed himself for not hearing the bomb-aimer's warning as the weight difference caused the bomber to gain height rapidly.

On the target, three different colour flares had been set by the Pathfinders, Mosquitoes of 163 Squadron.

S for Sugar's crew was an efficient group and their bomb-aimer was one of the best in the business. So provided the 163 Squadron boys had done their job right then the bombs would be on target.

Both groups were on top form and S for Sugar put her cookies right on the money.

543

0259hrs Monday, 6th August 1945, Headquarters of Red Banner Forces of Soviet Europe, Schloss Schönefeld, Leipzig.

Whilst the Soviet night-fighters had proved ineffective and the Flak little better, those on the ground had reason to be thankful for their advance warning and preparations for such attacks.

Had there been none, then the loss of life would have been extreme. As it was, whilst many soldiers and civilians were killed, key personnel were almost unaffected, although the disruption to Soviet military affairs would be considerable.

Schloss Gunsdorf disintegrated under the pounding of eleven bomb loads, each of twelve thousand pounds of high explosive.

Admittedly, the headquarters of the Red Banner Forces of Europe had planned to move to its forward location the following evening and so some personnel and accoutrements had already moved out, but it could not be denied that the loss of the Schloss was a setback.

Zhukov sat in a special radio truck with his communications staff, briefing his Front commanders on events in Leipzig, receiving news of similar occurrences at half a dozen places behind Soviet lines and, more importantly, sorting out how the following day's military affairs were going to be managed.

Finally, before returning to the air raid shelter to grab a few hours sleep, he and an NKVD Colonel discussed the untenable position of the Front's Air Force Commander, Major-General Boris Komarov.

Zhukov was woken from his slumber at 0600.

Anna Komarov had been a widow for just over an hour.

0535hrs Friday 10th August 1945, Vendeville Airfield, France.

The flight back from 'stonking' Leipzig was quiet, far quieter than normal. Another kill occurred briefly but

544

spectacularly close by, the ever-present NF30 Mosquitoes of 141 Squadron pouncing on an enemy, aircraft type unknown, which was a threat and then it was dead.

Approaching their temporary airfield, designated B51, at Vendeville near Lille, the banter was absent and as they touched down the standard derisory comments about a bumpy landing were not forthcoming; nothing.

S for Sugar came to a halt near a newly erected blast screen, bulldozed into place so recently that the shrubs that had been removed in its favour still stuck haphazardly skywards, some roots first, others branches uppermost.

Engines off and shut down complete, the crew made their way out of the aircraft.

The six men looked at each other. Wally moved to the fuselage door and called down towards the tail-gunners position.

"Den? Come on mate. Den?"

As he did so, Saul walked slowly around the tail-plane and came to an abrupt stop, knowing what he might see and shocked to confirm his suspicions.

The rear turret was fully turned to port and the break out hatch in its rear was gone, exposing the workings of the guns to the elements.

It was empty.

As Saul looked on in disbelief, Wally's ashen face appeared.

"He jumped, Wally. The poor bastard bloody jumped."

Wally said nothing, holding Dennis Riley's parachute up for Saul to see.

"The poor bastard."

0320hrs Friday 10th August 1945, Advance Headquarters of 12th US Armored Division, Bad Windsheim, Germany.

12th US Armored Division, the Hellcats, was itching to go. Having force marched over two nights and hidden during the daylight hours, they had displaced from Heidenheim and

Augsburg northwards, nearly eighty miles to their staging area around Bad Windsheim.

Both the 152nd Signals Btn and 56th Armored Infantry sustained some casualties due to Soviet air attacks but, in the main, the move had gone off without a hitch for them.

The unit commander, Brig. Gen. Willard A. Holbrook Jr as was on the 7th August, but who was now a temporary Major General, went over the plans for the relieving attack with his Combat Command leaders and Regimental CO's.

The part to be played by his three field artillery commanders in tandem with Lieutenant Colonel J.M.Welch of the 573rd AAA Btn was relatively unique and would hopefully pay dividends in the battles ahead.

To their east side, elements of the 9th US Armored, recovered from the Bayreuth Pocket and reinforced by the 16th RCT of the Big Red One, were preparing to relive the pressure on the northern side of Nurnberg, aiming a thrust from Neustadt-an-der-Aisch north-east, towards Bamberg.

The 12th's job was to buy time for the 42nd and 63rd Infantry on the Tauber River and possibly drive back up towards Würzburg.

For both the 10th and the 12th, the job was also to minimise casualties in both men and equipment.

The Black Widow was her name and she was designed for a number of tasks from bombing to reconnaissance. Tonight three P61-C's of 416th Night-Fighter Squadron USAAF were roaming the skies at night, locating prey with their radar and using deadly Hispano cannon to end resistance. Until very recently, the 416th had been stationed at Schweinfurt but, having been singled out for Soviet attention, they had withdrawn to a new home near Günzburg. The rest of the squadron, eleven in all, were off accompanying bombers on offensive operations, but these three survivors of the twenty-two on the squadron strength on 6th August were special.

Recent arrivals from Northrop, they possessed higher performance. In case the Soviet air force got lucky and shot one down, examined it and gleaned the secrets, they were forbidden

546

from flying over enemy territory, in case their modifications were copied.

As München had been receiving a number of night bomber attacks, they were tasked with its defence that night.

And what a night it would be, for the Black Widows were not the only lethal ladies aloft and heading to München.

A casual observer at their airfield might have wondered if he was looking at a serious military unit. Starting with the planes, even a rudimentary knowledge of aircraft would make someone think he was back in the First World War. The Polikarpov PO-2 was a wood and canvas biplane, designed in 1928, for purposes like training and crop-dusting. With a maximum speed below the stalling speed of its German adversaries, the aircrews who used the PO-2 found that lack of speed was their saviour in the Patriotic War.

The aircrew had consistently distinguished themselves from 1942 and Taman, through to the end in May 1945. Taman particularly, for the unit had been honoured and renamed as the 46th "Taman" Guards Night Bomber Aviation Regiment, respectfully known by friend and foe alike as the Night Witches, for all the air crew were female.

The full Regiment normally consisted of twenty aircraft, but on the third mission of the night only thirteen were aloft, returning to bomb the army holding camp on the outskirts of München, a facility that was steadily growing larger,. Two of their number remained within the perimeter of that camp, knocked down by anti-aircraft fire on the first mission. The second mission had been a bloodless success, until the return when one of the PO-2's flipped on landing, killing both crew members. Two other aircraft were being repaired, having taken damage during the week's fighting. Thus far, 25% of the Witches had been killed in less than a week, but during the Patriotic War there had been no shortage of replacements waiting and the 46th was rarely below strength for long.

On this mission, they were accompanied by three Yak-9M PVO's, adapted for night fighting from the basic Yak-9.

None of the three pilots had fired a shot that night and neither did they expect to, as the Soviets ruled the air, or so they were told.

0325hrs Friday 10th August 1945, Airborne over München, Germany.

There it was, a smudge on the screen, not very distinct, but certainly something worth chasing and killing. Nothing in the air over Munich that night was friendly, except the two aircraft operating five thousand and ten thousand feet above "Night Reaper", the Northrop Black Widow of Captain Lassiter and his crew.

He had bottom station, at ten thousand feet, where things were about to get lively. According to the radar operator, there were a number of slow moving aircraft at about nine thousand five hundred feet altitude, some eight miles ahead.

A matter-of-fact statement in his ear told him that one of his group, Radowski, had three contacts in the air space above, joined by an eager French-Louisianan voice confirming that the third Northrop also had acquired and was attacking the three higher targets.

Lassiter slowed his airplane with perforated air brakes, part of the modification they wished to keep secret, but still he found he was gaining on what ever it was that was in front of him.

Making the decision to keep back, he manoeuvered 'Reaper' in a lazy circle as he let his comrades do their work.

He was facing directly away from the group he had discovered when his gunner informed him of a kill.

Completing his turn, he was able to watch the night sky dissected by an orange line, marking the death plunge of an aircraft.

Within a second, another similar line started, almost prescribing a fiery cross in the sky, but terminated early as the aircraft exploded before reaching the ground. The first aircraft had buried itself into the hallowed soil of the Friedhof Perlach, killing the gravedigger, who was out preparing for the following day's business.

548

"Antoinette has a confirmed kill", Lebel transmitted, his Cajun voice betraying his excitement at a first ever shoot down.

"Scratch one for Warsaw, on number three" the New York Pole's voice clinical as ever when killing enemies of his country, particularly those who had betrayed and violated her in 1939.

Going round once more, Reaper's pilot again missed the death of an enemy and this time there was no streak of flame to mark its death, just the toneless Radowski claiming his second kill for his aircraft "Warsaw's Revenge", named for his home City and his general outlook in war.

Now that was over, Lassiter could do his work.

The loss of two of her top cover fighters disturbed Major Ludmilla Perkova, leader of tonight's mission. She was a Hero of the Soviet Union, as were two others in the air with her that night and you did not get the award for being timid. She was disturbed because no night fighters had been encountered before and her own cover was reduced from three to one in as many seconds.

Ordering her regiment to be vigilant, she began her run in on the target, the Forstenneder Park, where a tented city was springing up and growing daily.

As per the usual tactics, distance between aircraft was important, especially as on the run-in the engine was turned off to glide, creating a soft whooshing sound, which was all that normally betrayed the presence of death in the sky above.

Perkova reached for the engine switch and died in the same instant, a burst of 20mm cannon shells ripping through her position and exploding, destroying her completely and killing her navigator outright.

The following PO-2's saw only the briefest flare from the night-fighter's guns, but realised that something was very wrong.

Taking over, Perkova's next senior officer dived her aircraft, trading height for safety... and failing.

549

The Black Widow, flying as slow as Lassiter dared, curved lazily round onto the biplane's tail. The navigator saw or sensed the approaching shape and fired her ShKas machine gun, the tracer merely giving a more accurate steer-in for Lassiter. Despite this, he missed with a small burst but Washington the gunner, controlling the quad .50cal remote turret, did remarkably better. Heavy bullets messily killed both aircrew and inflicted structural damage, causing the airframe to disintegrate.

Lazily circling around again, 'Reaper' was confronted with an enemy regiment, seemingly in panic, aircraft splitting in all directions and diving for safety. The Night Witches were doing as they were trained; two even deciding to press on with their attack. Lassiter focused on these two and ordered his other aircraft to concentrate on those attempting to escape.

Acknowledgements from the others followed, but he still felt the need to remind them of the air safety zone and how close they were going to go to it. Friendly Flak isn't friendly; a maxim for pilots the world over.

The rearmost PO-2 seemed on autopilot, almost stationary, not attempting to sideslip or do anything to avoid the pursuer. This was the Regiment's junior pilot, whose bravery in pressing on was not matched by either her composure or her flying skill under pressure.

Concentrating hard, Lassiter managed to register radio calls recording success for both his fellow Northrops, all the time trying not to stall as he gained on his quarry.

The PO-2 died and this time there was no swift death for her occupants. Both crew were hit, but not killed, both wounded but conscious, they rode their burning craft into the ground, mercifully ending their ordeal.

Seeing the last one directly in his sights, he pulled the trigger once more and was greeted with nothing more than silence, as the weapons were empty or jammed.

Cursing, he swung lazily by the PO-2, encouraging his gunner to take a shot on the way past.

He did, as did the navigator of the PO-2. No bullets hit the vulnerable biplane. Seven hit the Black Widow; or rather, five hit her and two hit flesh.

Whilst not dead, Washington had a very nasty and prodigiously bleeding head wound and was not in a position to contribute further that night, collapsed senseless on the floor of his gunner's station as he was.

The other was in Lassiter's right shoulder and it damn well hurt.

Considering it had been a wild burst, the female gunner had done a good job, as flares suddenly erupted next to Mackenzie. Fire invaded his position, damaging the radar, destroying his maps and burning his legs. The fire extinguishers did their work as he battled to beat down the flames, choking himself and the unconscious gunner with the toxic fumes. In agony, the plucky operator twisted and tried to put the oxygen mask on his gunner, as flames fired up again, adding burns on top of burns on his legs.

The PO-2 had missed its target, over flying in an attempt to evade the Black Widow and now turned, heading for home directly over Forstenneder Park.

'Night Reaper' weighed nearly twenty-three thousand five hundred pounds in her stockinged feet and was built to American specifications; heavy and robust.

For Lassiter, the decision was instant and irrevocable, cutting through the pain and focusing him.

He dropped his starboard wing and described a curve, judging his approach perfectly, accelerating and calling out to McKenzie to hold tight.

A point approximate five feet from the end of 'Reaper's' starboard wing came into high speed contact with the rim of the PO-2's rear crew member's cockpit area. Metal versus canvas and wood. Metal won, carving through the position and separating what was left of the navigator from the front of the aircraft, which fell from the sky and blossomed into a fireball on the ground, as bombs armed for dropping exploded on impact.

That was not something Lassiter had considered and the thought left him cold.

One bullet had hit the radio and the Radar Operator was desperately trying to fix it, despite the fact that he had dislocated two fingers on his left hand when the impact happened. Try as he might, transmitting was beyond them, although they could hear more successes from their comrades.

Feeling sick, cold and bleeding like a stuck pig, Lassiter turned for his new home, leaving the Cajun and the Pole to finish the job, which they did very efficiently and at no cost. The pair left only two PO-2's to return to relate the horrors endured by the Night Witches.

In three years of combat against the Luftwaffe, many of them had died, but never had they suffered such losses in one single night and it would take them a long time to recover.

None of their highly decorated female officers in the air that night survived the encounter with the 416th.

Lassiter executed what he considered to be a passable landing on return, considering McKenzie was not feeling too confident in his navigation and his own vision was not all it could be.

His commanding officer begged to differ and rode out in a jeep to chew the Captain out for such a poor landing.

They had been unable to make any transmissions to warn their base. They had no red flares left to fire off, the normal warning of wounded onboard. So it was much to the Colonel's surprise that he was greeted with a burned McKenzie needing help with an unconscious Washington. His rollicking forgotten, the Colonel grasped the gunner's inert form, soiling his pristine Number One uniform with blood and soot.

Shouting for help, the Colonel laid Washington on the ground and then helped McKenzie down, trying not to touch his badly burned legs.

Smoke gently wafted from the open door, as something started to burn once more.

The Colonel may have been a martinet but he was no coward and he plunged into the aircraft to get Lassiter as the flames started to build.

The airfield fire crews arrived and tackled the internal fire and both men were assisted to safety, one choking and coughing, the other unconscious from his loss of blood. Lassiter's shoulder wound had akmost killed him.

552

Base medics were all over them in seconds and the four were rushed away to the hospital tent on the north side of the strip.

Working hard, the docs got bloods and fluids into all three aircrew. By the end of two hours hard labour, they were satisfied enough to assure the smoke blackened Base Commander that all three would live and two would fight again, McKenzie the probable sole exception.

Wheezing and taking his fill from the oxygen at his side, the Colonel wondered what the hell had gone on that night and couldn't wait to hear the story of 'Night Reaper' in full.

Some of what had happened had been filled in by an excitable Cajun pilot, who was in sickbay having his hand stitched after cutting it climbing out of his aircraft, but there was clearly so much more to hear.

When the Colonel eventually learned of the full events of that night from Washington, Mackenzie and a surprisingly lucid Lassiter, he was amazed and congratulated them all.

On reaching his office later, he firstly composed himself, then composed his formal recommendations for the Medal of Honor.

0423hrs Friday 10th August 1945, Battle lines of the 15th US Armored Division, Bad Driburg, Germany.

Having recovered from their appalling exercise in front of the Russians, the mainly untried personnel of the newly formed 15th US Armored Division had finally regained their haughty swagger. Few had seen action and most of those that had were the product of their former commanders moving on problem people, rather than sending quality personnel to provide example and experience.

Removing the inept Divisional Commander had been a first step and the 15th were also boosted by a sprinkling of talent from the 13th and 20th Armored Divisions, both now back in the States for training for the Invasion of Japan.

The inclusion of some ex-POW tank crew made the most difference, as a handful of experienced men from the

553

prime US Armored formations took their place alongside the greenhorns.

Not a moment too soon, as the 15th was handed a difficult mission.

Their task was to attack the Russian 3rd Army to their front and push them back to the Diemel River, relieving the pressure north of Kassel. The Soviets had already been in action for four days and had been hammered at Hildesheim, so were probably ripe for plucking.

Major Nathaniel Parker may have been a prize fool but he was looking forward to the Friday dawn attack, commanding his own company of Pershing Tanks in the 361st Tank Btn, 15th Armored Div.

Clad as he would be, in forty-two tons of mobile armour, armed with a devastating 90mm high-velocity gun, his excitement about charging through enemy positions kept his sleep unrewarding for most of the night, as dreams of medals and glory took over the night.

Soon he would show that old kraut what it meant to be a tanker.

Elsewhere during the night, British and Commonwealth bomber crews visited a range of locations with varying degrees of success.

The railway junction at Prague was totally obliterated, where as the important junction at Dresden was hardly touched.

Both missions cost the British and Commonwealth bomber force six aircraft apiece.

In Vienna, squadrons from North Italy caused great destruction. Once known as the Reichsbrücke, the newly renamed 'Red Army Bridge' was dropped into the Donau by a wave of high-explosive that left the city completely cut in two as other bridges, the work of many hours by Soviet engineers, were similarly destroyed.

Just as dawn was rising, the world-famous brick-built Göltzsch Railway Viaduct was visited by three specially equipped Lancasters. None of the huge tallboy bombs actually hit, but the explosions and shock waves were enough to topple the magnificent structure.

Whilst no military headquarters, other than Zhukov's, was directly hit, many a Soviet Marshal and General got little sleep as high-explosive fell from the skies nearby.

The rest of the allied plan went well.

Up and down Europe, a maximum bomber effort put over thirteen-hundred aircraft into the attack, destroying railway lines and bridges, road junctions and bridges, airfields and bridges. All in an attempt to ruin Soviet logistics and to prevent free movement of the Red Army's superior numbers.

Soviet night bombers passing in the opposite direction were often intercepted by allied night fighters, using radar to hunt down their prey, although one notable and unfortunate Soviet success was the destruction again inflicted upon Frankfurt's main airfield, closing it for the foreseeable future.

Every night fighter the Allies possessed went up and enjoyed remarkable successes, gutting numerous Soviet night fighter units sent up by the enemy. So much so that for that night and the nights that followed, it was the Allied Air forces that owned the skies in darkness.

Having received reinforcements from the disbanding units in the UK and those on their way home, ground attack squadrons threw themselves into one huge attack, one massive effort to claw back the inequality that faced them in daylight operations, mirroring the Soviet effort of 6th August but with less success.

Valuable pilots and aircraft were lost pressing home attacks through intense anti-aircraft fire or swarms of Soviet fighter planes. The savaged allied fighter's flying escort were occasionally overwhelmed and on three occasions whole squadrons ceased to exist.

Both sides could recover, bringing new pilots and aircraft into action. The question was who could do so faster and, for now, it could only be the Russians.

American bombers then rose to do their work in daylight, repeating many of the targets from the night before.

Escorted by weary Mustangs, the Flying Fortresses and Liberators dropped thousands of pounds of high explosive

555

on communications routes the length and breadth of Eastern Germany, Czechoslovakia, Austria and Poland.

American bomber losses were modest, but the mission was yet again heavy on the fighters, whose second mission of the day cost more lives than the first.

When the evaluation was done by intelligence, it was felt that Soviet Night aviation had been dealt a crippling blow for some time to come. Communications and logistics would definitely be disrupted and the effect of that should shortly be felt in a positive way by those facing the Soviet armies in the field. Higher than predicted allied losses, particularly in ground-attack and fighter aircraft, meant there could be no repeats and, as Eisenhower and Tedder firmly believed, should be no repeats.

The purpose had been to hit back, not lose their offensive air capability.

Washington did not receive the Medal of Honor for his actions that night, receiving the Silver Star instead. Lassiter and McKenzie attended the White House in November that same year, having recovered reasonably well from their wounds, and were the first US aviators to be recommended for, and awarded, the Medal of Honor, in the extended conflict that had become known as World War Three.

They wrote in the old days that it is sweet and fitting to die for one's country. But in modern war there is nothing sweet nor fitting in your dying. You will die like a dog for no good reason.

Ernest Hemingway

CHAPTER 48 – THE RIPOSTES

0545hrs Friday 10th August 1945, 12th US Armored Division and other Assault formations of the US Fifteenth Army, Ochsenfurt- Goßmannsdorf, Germany.

Allied Forces – 494th Field Artillery Battalion, B Company, 92nd Cavalry Reconnaissance Battalion, 2nd Platoon 152nd Signals Company, all of Combat Command 'A', 495th Field Artillery Battalion of Combat Command 'B', all of 12th US Armored Division, 573rd AAA Btn [Mot] temp attached to 12th US Armored Division, all of US Fifteenth Army, US Twelfth Army Group.

Soviet Forces – 3rd Battalion, 912th Rifle Regiment, 2nd Battery 975th Artillery Regiment, 243rd Rifle Division of 34th Guards Rifle Corps of 5th Guards Army and Special Grouping Nautsev, 1st Regiment, 3rd Guards Rocket Barrage Division, both of 2nd Red Banner Central European Front.

In this instance, the cavalry had a dangerous job, but a job they did well and with minimal casualties.

Pushing out, using the Main River as a secure right flank, they dashed towards Soviet infantry drawn up in cover in woods to the south of Goßmannsdorf, units that seemed to be preparing to move out in their own advance.

M5 Stuart tanks and M3 halftracks fired into Soviet troops about to embuss in their British-made universal carriers, causing chaos amongst the weary soldiers, chaos that was added to by the sound of artillery dropping to their rear. The bridge southeast of Goßmannsdorf had been destroyed two days previously.

Causing casualties with their fire, the cavalry darted in and out, braving anti-tank rifle and machine gun fire, but little else of note.

Captain Bortsov, the officer in charge of 3rd Battalion 912th Rifle, noted the obvious inexperience of the Amerikanski, clustered together in one killing zone to his front, moving, most certainly, but confined to an area no more than five hundred metres across.

'Perfect.'

His artillery support officer received his orders and calmly relayed the coordinates to the officer in charge of the unit designated as support for this day's bloody work.

Curiously, the enemy force to his front slipped to his right flank in one graceful movement, clearly meaning his riposte would fall on unoccupied ground.

Revising the orders and reorienting his own troopers to meet the possible attempt to outflank, he received with stoic acceptance the news that the radio was not functioning properly. His country had never been at its best when producing quality electrical items, although he suddenly remembered that the artillery officer was very proud of his new Canadian built Type 19 set, the same radio set his own command vehicle had enjoyed until it had been destroyed in the American air strike.

Bortsov was not to know that communications were being jammed by a twenty year old bespectacled American Corporal, sat in a halftrack a kilometre away.

He watched with some annoyance as a regiment's worth of Katyusha rockets arrived, ploughing up ground and bushes, but doing no damage whatsoever to his intended target.

Standard artillery rounds also arrived, 76.2mm he estimated, meaning that some of the divisional artillery had joined in the shoot.

Meanwhile, free from interference and harm, the American reconnaissance troops were presently flanking him towards Darstadt.

With typical Russian black humour, he congratulated himself on passing the problem to Drinkov's 1st Battalion, who were presently positioned there, but the moment passed as he reminded himself that he would be accountable to the Colonel for wasting artillery ammunition.

However, his more immediate problem now was sorting out his own battalion after the disruption, confirming his orders in the light of this changed American threat and silencing the artillery. The latter two would prove difficult without a useable means of communication, so he swiftly moved to his command carrier, where he was found a perplexed radio operator trying to do something useful with an uncooperative radio.

The urgency of the situation became more apparent as more artillery joined the barrage, brought in by officers who believed that the silence meant that the 279th Rifle Division was in trouble.

Which of course it was, but did not yet know it.

573rd AAA Btn [Motorised] was an unremarkable anti-aircraft unit that had enjoyed a reasonably low risk and trouble-free war through to May.

This morning, it made history.

For some time, it had been known that the radar sets used to monitor low-level aircraft raids, such as the ones 573rd was designed to repel, had another unsuspected capability.

They could read mortar round trajectories and, by a relatively simple process, calculate the point of origin of a round in flight.

Artillery had not been trackable, but today they tried a new combination of radar information and experienced artillery personnel, using maps and good old intuition.

The batteries of 494th and 495th Artillery Battalions were locked and loaded, just waiting for the right coordinates to visit hell upon some 'Stalin's Organs,' and hopefully start hitting back heavily at one of the Soviets greatest assets; their artillery.

2nd Lieutenant Rodney W. Chambers watched as his operators did their work and he then passed their accurate data to the 494th's Captain Maynard, seconded to the radar section.

559

Based on the number of radar tracks, the Captain's decision was to put down a twelve round barrage from all forty guns on the location identified by the radar.

Twenty-six M7 Priests spat their 105mm HE shells in the direction of the fields, west of Erlach.

Accompanying them were 155mm VT fused shells from M40 gun Carriages, specifically for airbursts over the target, designed to kill valuable artillerymen.

1st Regiment, 3rd Guards Rocket Barrage Division was an experienced unit and no strangers to combat casualties, having more than once picked up their rifles for closer combat work against the Germans, the last example of which had been the day before, when they suffered seven wounded in a guerrilla attack outside of Estenfeld.

However, the casualties visited upon them on the morning of 10th August 1945 destroyed them as a fighting unit.

The men and women were struggling to reload their charges, humping around ninety-two pounds of high-explosive and propellant in rocket form, at sixteen reloads to a vehicle, twenty-three vehicles in total to be serviced, Mixed in amongst them were the ammunition trucks and the officers and non-coms, chivvying their crews into greater efforts.

American shells arrived and took lives by the dozen as shrapnel cut into bodies and explosive shells did their horrible work. Secondary explosions from rockets and vehicles added to the slaughter and, in truth, the final four salvoes did no great additional damage, as there was little left of note.

Every launcher was useless, ranging from unserviceable through to completely destroyed. Less than twenty personnel struggled through the smoking carnage, recovering their wounded comrades. Given the previous evening's combat strength of two hundred and eight personnel, the maths suggested more dead and wounded than were actually recovered from the field.

The second part of the shoot was trickier and required judgement and intuition on the part of the experienced Artillery Officer attached to the 573rd.

Fig#15 - Reichenberg/Rottenbauer battleground.

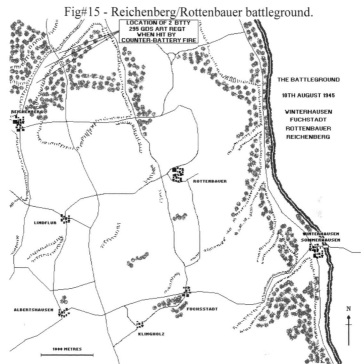

As the 76.2mm shells continued to rain down on the churned ground in front of Goßmannsdorf, radar tracked as best it could. Artillery shells had a different type of trajectory, one not dealt with easily by the sets.

However, it did offer up enough information to get a flight direction and so the artillery officer waited for some input, armed solely with a map and a ruler.

Chambers carefully recorded the details and double-checked the results, not that he didn't trust his Corporal.

Moving over to the Captain's map table, he annotated it with a single line. Commencing at the point of shell arrival and departing in the direction indicated by the radar.

He then stood back and let Maynard do his part.

It took a few seconds before the Captain found what he looked for and he marked a simple X on Chambers' contribution, in an area just off road, north-east of Reichenberg.

Calling in the coordinates to his battalion, he could not help himself but check and recheck the possibilities.

The battery of guns he controlled fired four salvoes and a very satisfied Maynard noted the reduction and then cessation of shellfire on the now silent approaches to Goßmannsdorf.

The arrival of 105mm shells was a very unpleasant experience for the Soviet gunners. However, only a few fell close enough to do harm, killing four artillerymen and wounding two more.

None the less, the unit seemingly panicked and started to hitch up guns without proper orders, hence the lessening in incoming fire witnessed by Maynard and Chambers.

Losing only one gun and two prime movers, the battery withdrew in ragtag order, finally coming to a halt on the southern approaches to Würzburg, where the young Junior Lieutenant in charge was summarily executed by the NKVD officer who intercepted the withdrawing unit.

The Junior Lieutenant had, without his knowledge, been instantly promoted to battery commander by the arrival of a 105mm shell on the previous incumbent and his second in command, neither of whom were recovered from the field.

0858hrs 10th August 1945, American Counter-attack, Vicinity of Rottenbauer, Germany.

Allied Forces – 23rd Tank Battalion, 17th Armored Infantry Battalion, C Company, 92nd Cavalry Reconnaissance Battalion, all of Combat Command 'B', 12th US Armored

Division and 2nd Battery, 573rd AAA Btn, all of US Fifteenth Army, US Twelfth Army Group.

Soviet Forces – 2nd Battalion, 179th Guards Rifle Regiment, 59th Guards Rifle Division of 34th Guards Rifle Corps of 5th Guards Army of 2nd Red Banner Central European Front.

Fig#16 - Rottenbauer,US Counter attack.

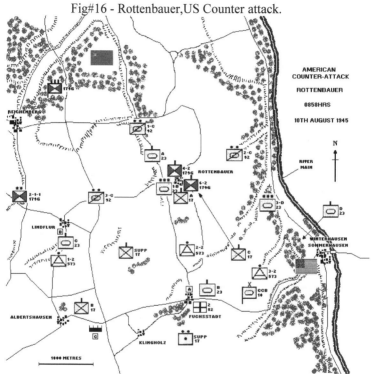

Over three hours had passed since the first shots had been fired and the 12th Armored had made excellent progress.

Plunging on nearly five miles into Soviet lines, fighting steadily and with purpose, the advancing US force drove the 906th Rifle Regiment of 243rd Rifle Division before it, killing men by the score.

Initially, the advance had been slowed by dogged resistance from 3rd/912th in Goßmannsdorf, but they had been forced to withdraw to the south-west, leaving Combat Command 'B' of the 12th Armored to plunge further towards Würzburg.

Arriving at Winterhausen-Sommerhausen in a blaze of fire, the lead elements of the 92nd Cav, supported by a platoon of M4A3[76mm] tanks from A/23rd, made short work of a retreating mortar platoon and surprised a bridging engineer unit that was striving to make good the damage to the bridges.

Pausing only to destroy the engineer's good work, CC'B' moved forward, only to be taken under fire by Soviet anti-tank guns positioned on the east bank, losing one half-track from the 92nd and one Sherman from A/23rd.

CC 'B's commander quickly switched his artillery to suppress the enemy guns, whilst temporarily redirecting his forward elements away from the river line, pointing them west towards Fuchsstadt, ready to drive north on the parallel roads between Eibelstadt and Reichenberg.

Fuchsstadt was swiftly overcome, but at the cost of the cavalry company commander and his vehicle [A], victims of a panzerfaust hit as the Captain drew his vehicle to a halt, turning his back on the modest firefight behind him to concentrate on his next leap forward to Rottenbauer.

Again, the lead platoon of A/23rd swept forward, reducing some of the buildings on the edge of the town to rubble and flames with their HE shells and allowing a dismounted platoon from the 17th Armored Infantry to move into Rottenbauer and start clearing it completely.

The rest of A/23rd's lead platoon then moved through the position, preceded by a platoon of the cavalry and both were immediately brought under fire from positions at the rear of the town.

C/23rd continued through, heading towards Albertshausen, before swinging north once more, running into no resistance until taken under fire from their left flank, near Lindflur.

A platoon of cavalry reached the crossroads between Rottenbauer and Lindflur without any problems, as did another group, making it to the end of a cut, northeast of the disputed town.

CC'B's commander intended that nothing would escape from Rottenbauer.

As both sides sought each other out at long distance, the 12th's luck started to run out.

The limited fighter cover given them for the attack had been hugely successful and nothing had got through to harm them, until ten Shturmoviks finally arrived over the battlefield and received orders from a ground director.

Each of them carried four RS-132 rockets and four of the ground-attack aircraft delivered them accurately on the tanks of C/23rd.

Two Shermans were destroyed in the attack [B] and both immediately burned fiercely, living up to their gruesome reputation, despite the new ammo stowage and additional onboard fire precautions.

One commander stuck rigidly to his .50cal MG and was rewarded with noticeable hits on one of the aircraft, which limped away trailing smoke.

His joy was short-lived and he provided a lesson to all his fellow commanders on their vulnerability in the turret, when a rifle bullet, fired from a hidden position around Lindflur, took him in the head,.

The other six aircraft fell upon C Coy of the armored infantry, as well as the juicy target of three platoons of 57mm AT guns, one from each of the 17th's companies, waiting together under the supposed protective watch of B Coy.

The armored-infantry, well disposed and taking advantage of trees and buildings on the outskirts of Albertshausen, suffered few casualties.

The AT platoons were ravaged by rocket fire and most of the guns knocked out, along with many of their trained servants.

Return fire from a pair of half-track mounted machine guns was ineffectual, encouraging the Shturmoviks to return for a strafing run.

More US casualties occurred and still no rounds hit the attackers.

Two M-16's from the 573rd had more joy and they knocked an Ilyushin from the sky, causing it to crashland south of Fuchsstadt, where the dazed crew fell victim to vengeful civilians before soldiers of the armored-infantry managed to get to them.

While C/23rd sorted themselves out, the CC'B' Commander plunged his troopers on into Rottenbauer, where sudden stiff resistance caused the set-piece deployment of a full company of armored infantry, complete with mortar support from the M21's in the support company.

The rest of A/23rd put down fire on the town as they moved forward and past Rottenbauer, deploying halfway between the crossroads and the village, approximately two hundred yards north of the fighting. Professionally, they partially oriented to their rear, in case Soviet forces tried to withdraw, with the rest of the unit watching their front, using small but adequate hillocks as hull down cover, paying specific attention to likely ambush spots ahead.

Occasional rounds from Soviet PTRD anti-tank rifles hit home, fired from the village they had passed, having little real effect, but excellent as a distraction and for nuisance value.

Resistance in Rottenbauer was unexpectedly fierce and a platoon of tanks from B/23rd was sent forward to assist, the remainder of B Company sitting in reserve at Fuchsstadt.

Most of D/23rd's light tanks remained at Winterhausen, keeping well hidden from the anti-tank guns across the river, whilst a platoon pushed up half a mile to act as an early-warning if the Russians returned, happily screened from the same anti-tank guns by trees.

Casualties amongst the armored infantrymen were mounting, as they battled house to house against quality Russian fighting men, experienced soldiers of the 59th Guards Rifle Division, or to give it the full honorifics due, the 59th 'Order of the Red Banner, Order of Suvurov, Order of Bogdan Khmelnitskiy' Guards Rifle Division, named for 'Kramatorsk', 'Nikopol', 'Budapest' and 'Lower Dneistr'.

They had been in almost constant combat since March 1942 and were veterans of a thousand battles against a competent and deadly foe.

Levering them out of Rottenbauer's quaint houses was time consuming and costly, both in lives and the necessary chattels of war, as huge quantities of grenades, bazooka rounds, mortar shells and small arms ammunition, were being expended.

In open combat, the American units had a real advantage with the M1 Garand, but in close combat fighting, they were rapidly acquiring a healthy respect for the capabilities of the PPSH sub-machine gun.

4th and 6th Companies of 2nd Btn, 179th Guards Rifles had quite a lot of them, accompanied by the skill and bravery to use them to full advantage.

The armored infantry push started to grind to a halt as casualties ate up their effectiveness and resolve, requiring closer support from the tankers of B/23rd, which exposure cost two more tanks, both knocked out by hand thrown anti-tank grenades.

In an effort to kick-start his advance again, the Colonel sent in 'C' Company of his armored-infantry.

A vicious fight took place in the Schloss itself and an armored-infantry platoon, attempting to establish itself there, was forcefully ejected from the main building, seeking refuge in the stable block to the west side.

Before they could properly set themselves, the guardsmen threw themselves forward, taking casualties as they charged across the open yard.

Hand to hand combat ensued, at which the Soviets excelled, so the Americans were further displaced, as much by the extreme shock of the assault and violence of the gutter fight visited upon them, as by the casualties they started to sustain.

Many of the Russians employed sharpened spades as cleavers, slashing down in the manner of a chopper, aiming for vulnerable neck flesh where head met torso. More than one blow went the full distance, separating the parts.

Whilst most of his comrades recoiled from such bestiality, one American saw, for the first time, his natural element. Or rather, the raw natural element of his tribal ancestors.

Tsali Sagonegi Yona of the Aniyunwiya Tribe, named as Cherokee by the Creek Indians, named as Corporal Charley Bluebear by the US Army and known, both jokingly and seriously, as Moose, was that man. The 6'5" frame had all the litheness and flexibility associated with his tribe, but accompanied by a body tone, solidity and strength rarely seen in combination.

Add to the mix courage beyond measure, offer up an enemy disposed for close quarter fighting and the recipe for untold savagery and slaughter was in place.

What happened next was a blur of metal and blood.

Bluebear discarded his BAR and reached around his waist belt, extracting his heirlooms, ready to fight in the manner of his ancestors and with their weapons, treasured items entrusted to him by his family before he left for the war. A tomahawk and a battle knife that had last seen enemy blood in the Argonne Forest during 1918, when wielded in his father's hands against the German. Uttering his father's name, he plunged forward. As he struck out and killed, he bellowed the battle cry his father had taught him, once for each enemy who fell under his blades.

"Tsuhnuhlahuhskim!" for which the English translation would be, "He tries, but fails."

The US platoon officer went down, stunned by a rifle butt, the attacker shaping to plunge his bayonet deep into the senseless man while another guardsman drew back his entrenching tool, also intending to end the officer's life.

In a blur, the Cherokee stepped over his insensible leader and struck out, his tomahawk curving in a backhanded stroke, from right to left, smashing through the eye sockets of the rifleman, bodily detritus flying from the awful wound. The tomahawk had barely completed its stroke before the knife was slammed, low and hard, into the groin of the other attacker.

The screams were awful, as much for the horror of those witnesses on both sides, as they were for the pain of the two hideously wounded soldiers.

"Tsuhnuhlahuhskim!"

568

Bluebear stood in defence as others grabbed the unconscious officer and pulled him clear.

Another bayonet lunged, but missed.

The brave Russian soldier ducked the intended hatchet blow, only to have the battle knife driven powerfully and terminally into the side of his neck.

"Tsuhnuhlahuhskim!"

Gushing blood over his killer, the dying Russian stuck on the blade, pulling the Cherokee to one side with his body weight.

Another soldier, with the courage of youth, that courage the young possess that makes them feel invulnerable, saw his chance and leapt to the attack, thrusting a bayonet forward and penetrating the jacket of his target.

Initially, Bluebear did not notice the blade slice his flesh, although pain caused by the swift movement of it down his rib could neither be ignored, nor overcome by his adrenalin.

He backhanded his tomahawk into the young soldiers' neck, a glancing blow because of his lack of balance, penetrating, but not enough to kill by itself. However, the blow caused swelling to such an extent that the airway virtually closed up in an instant.

Letting go of his rifle, the youth fell to the ground, not aware of Bluebear's yelp of pain, as the unsupported Nagant rifle dropped away and caused the bayonet to rip out his side.

Focussed by pain and anger, the Cherokee spared a second to stamp on the back of the head of the dying boy, breaking the neck instantly and, although not his design, releasing the soldier from the longer and more painful journey.

"Tsuhnuhlahuhskim!"

Men who had stood the rigours of a Stalingrad winter, who had been in close combat in a score of skirmishes, paled before the deadly whirling apparition.

An experienced Corporal managed to slice through Bluebear's left forearm with a spade cut, but received a blow to his left temple that stove his skull to his brain stem and dropped him dead to the floor.

The battle knife dropped from Bluebear's useless fingers, but the killing went on.

569

All around the stable block, men scrambled away from the death giver, friend and foe alike, recognising the bloodlust that had overtaken him. No longer using his war cry, simply screaming as hard as his capacious lungs permitted, the Cherokee moved like lightning, slowed neither by the wounds or by the efforts he had already expended in his frenzy.

Panic is a virus that spreads at speed. Self-preservation took over and the surviving guardsmen escaped as best they could, more than one screaming in fright as they ran.

One Guards Sergeant turned and, without aiming, fired off every round left in his pistol, in panic and desperation, virtually closing his eyes to blot out the apparition he was running from.

Bluebear, in the act of pulling his hatchet from the head of another victim, felt the stings, as two bullets hit him in the right thigh.

Anyone else would have gone down immediately, but not the Indian. Bluebear managed the ten yards or so to the Sergeant, who had tripped over a dead comrade in his terror.

Charley Bluebear claimed his last victim of the battle when he sunk his weapon into the man's forehead.

The remaining guardsmen could be heard shouting warnings to their comrades in the Schloss as they ran for their lives, some splashing through the moat in their blind panic, not knowing that the Devil had collapsed from exhaustion and blood loss behind them.

A shaking armored-infantry medic quickly bandaged the bloodied thigh wound, applying a tourniquet and squeezing the femoral artery virtually shut, saving Charley Bluebear's life.

The Soviet reverse really did not matter in the greater run of things, as the shocked American troops decided to withdraw, led by a wide-eyed Sergeant, who would need treatment for his traumatic experiences until the day he died.

After the battle, reports from the survivors who escaped the day's slaughter were incredulously assessed. Conservative estimates suggested a total of twenty-two men personally slain by Tsali Sagonegi Yona of the Aniyunwiya Tribe, named as Cherokee by the Creek Indians, named as

Corporal Charley Bluebear by the US Army and known, both jokingly and seriously, as Moose by his comrades.

Except those comrades who witnessed that day at first hand and those enemy who escaped the stables and lived, for whom, be they Armored-Infantry or Guards, he was forever named Death.

Despite the horrors in the Schloss, the balance seemed to perceptibly change in favour of the defenders and when weary Guards retook St Josef's Church for the third time, it did not change hands again.

One older guardsman committed himself to the attack with a liberated bazooka, wrecking a Sherman that had strayed too close, but setting fire to religious trappings, hanging behind him, with the unexpected back flash from the weapon.

A teenage guardsman started to bayonet the American wounded who lay bleeding on the pews, standard fare for the German war of course. A bloodied Starshina stayed his hand before he could send a third American boy to a better place. The young man shrugged and moved off to a firing position in a damaged window. Within half an hour he would lie dead with his victims, slain by a jagged lump of stone blasted from the wall by a tank shell.

As the fight for the village became more and more stagnant, the US Commander began to realise that he was nearly as far as he was going to go unless more infantry support was available. One battalion from the 63rd Infantry division had been freed up as an infantry reserve and he made a case for its deployment with his command. He got one company allocated under his orders and it was immediately sent forward from its reserve area, ten miles to the rear. Until it arrived he would have to make do with what he had.

Rottenbauer was a stalemate, both sides having fought themselves to a bloody draw, but still the killing went on, although neither side was trying to expel the other anymore. The Russians were exhausted, having been fighting since midday on Monday.

The Americans were tired but, more than that, they were shocked at their full initiation in the rigours of modern infantry combat. The 12th's soldiers thought they had acquired good experience against the German in 1945, even though they were already defeated and lacking in supplies.

By a coincidence, the 12th had captured Wurzburg in the first week of April 1945, some four months previously, sustaining a handful of casualties in the doing.

These Russians had first been committed to action in the hardest combat school ever known to man, in December 1942, on the Volga, at Stalingrad.

The 12th Armored's experiences at Herrlisheim, the Colmar Pocket and subsequent romps through Southern Germany were as nothing compared to that Friday morning's initiation ceremony in Rottenbauer, District of Würzburg.

Moreover, it was not yet complete.

It had taken over two hours to progress roughly two miles and casualties had mounted as enemy resistance stiffened, Soviet commanders drawing on years of combat experience gained at the hands of the world's counter-attack specialists.

Ambulances and adapted jeeps from the 2nd/82nd Medical Battalion extracted the American wounded from the hellhole, unknowingly under the gaze of the observing Russian gunners who, faithful to their orders, remained silent behind their weapons.

The 179th's Regimental Commander, Colonel T.N. Artem'yev, Hero of the Soviet Union, had stayed his hand thus far, all the time knowing his troopers in Rottenbauer were bleeding and dying in close combat with the armored infantry and tanks of this American Division. A very necessary sacrifice to persuade his enemy to orient themselves as he wanted, which his enemy had now obligingly done.

Of course, he did so with regret, for he was an officer who valued the lives of his men, but it was necessary as he waited for the elements of the capitalists' destruction to assemble on the battlefield, which they were very close to doing.

'Why is it always the damn tanks that mess things up?'

572

He mused, all the time watching the to-ing and fro-ing of American vehicles, bringing fresh meat to the grinder and taking away that which the grinder spat out, maimed and crippled.

A BA-64 arrived to his rear and he received word that 'armour' had finally deigned to arrive.

Taking one last look at the open ground he had spent over an hour reading and understanding, he nodded in satisfaction and went to speak to the assembled senior officers', the men of four different arms of service, each commanding one of the units about to immolate the capitalist legion on a killing ground of Artem'yev's choosing.

As senior Colonel, he laid out his plan for destroying this Amerikanski tank force, coordinating with the newly arrived Colonel of Tank troops, Popov of the Army anti-tank unit and a Captain from his own divisional Artillery regiment.

He explained the plan to them and it was a thing of simple beauty, requiring only one act of cooperation from the Americans to succeed.

Looking at his watch and judging how much time the tank Colonel would need to get back to his unit and brief them, he designated 1240hrs as the start time for his plan.

1239hrs 10th August 1945, Soviet Ambush and Counter-attack, vicinity of Reichenberg, Germany.

Allied Forces – 23rd Tank Battalion, 17th Armored Infantry Battalion, 495th Field Artillery Battalion, C Company, 92nd Cavalry Reconnaissance Battalion, all of Combat Command 'B', 12th US Armored Division and 2nd Battery, 573rd AAA Btn, all of US Fifteenth Army, US Twelfth Army Group.

Subsequently arriving - 2nd Battalion, 255th Infantry Regiment, 63rd US Infantry Division, detached from US XXIII Corps, US Fifteenth Army, US Twelfth Army Group

Soviet Forces – 2nd and 3rd Battalions, Anti-Tank companies 179th Guards Rifle Regiment, 127th Guards Artillery Regiment, 59th Guards Rifle Division of 34th Guards

Rifle Corps, 242nd Tank Brigade of 31st Tank Corps, Special Anti-tank gun Battery Popov,1317th Anti-Tank Regiment, all of 5th Guards Army of 2nd Red Banner Central European Front.

Fig#17 - Reichenberg, Soviet counter-attack

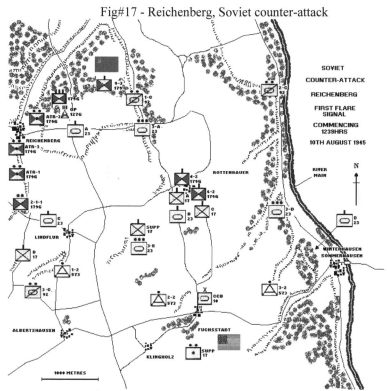

Simple orders issued and understood, Artem'yev had but to fire three flares to fully implement his plan.

In his right hand he held a battered but functional Model 26 flare pistol, his left arm crooked so he could count down the seconds on his father's wristwatch, an inner whispering from his subconscious registering the newly cracked glass. At three seconds to time he pulled the trigger, sending one red flare skywards and setting in motion the death of many a young man.

Flare number one was the signal for PTRD's and 45mm anti-tank guns to open fire on the tanks, north of Rottenbauer. Neither type were of much use when targeting the Sherman tanks nearest them, but some sought out the more vulnerable Stuarts and half-tracks, scoring hits and taking lives, causing 3-C/92nd troopers to displace south-west, searching for a way round the southern flank of the enemy.

The CC'B' Commander responded quickly and aggressively to the challenge, noting the ground between him and the Russian firing line on the other side of the railway track was sound, both to the military eye and on the map.

C/23rd were ordered to move immediately north with their armored-infantry component, to take a left turn into line when level with Lindflur, orienting to the north-west, with a view to reaching the BahnhofStraße and turning north to Reichenberg.

B/17th moved west and north to come in behind them, ready for an assault, once the AT guns had been beaten down.

A/23rd were to take their cue from C/23rd and move forward to the crossroads, before turning left to descend upon Reichenberg from the east. As a precautionary measure, one platoon of tanks was to set up at the crossroads, oriented north, screened by a recon platoon in the tree line ahead and the armored-infantry's support companies were moved up to an off-road position between Rottenbauer and Lindflur, ready to react as directed.

The cavalrymen were immediately drawn into a close-quarter firefight with Soviet guardsmen stationed in the woods to their west.

A further tank platoon of B/23rd was added to the mix in Rottenbauer, the rest joining the support companies off-road as a mobile reserve. The Colonel set up his mobile command post adjacent to the destroyed cavalry M24, having decided that Fuchstadt was suitable for his command needs.

He climbed to the attic room of the modest private house on the village's northern edge to test the view, the occupants having long taken to their heels when the Soviets returned.

575

As he steadied himself and took everything in through his field glasses, he caught sight of a hit on one of C Company's tanks that flipped the track off in an instant. The tank fought back, even though immobilised and it was noticeable that his tank crews had already done good work amongst the camouflaged Soviet gun positions, where barrels stuck skywards, or scars in the earth indicated positive hits and definite kills.

A half-track disintegrated under two simultaneous hammer blows, body parts and weapons thrown in all directions, momentum driving the burning hulk forward, a fiery hearse containing a dozen young men.

An M5 Stuart light tank was halted, the furthest forward vehicle in the advance, smoke gently drifting from open hatches. The impetuous cavalrymen who had crewed it bolted in all directions, trying hard to find cover before Soviet machine gun bullets found them and, in all but one case, failed.

A second flare rose from the Soviet position. The Colonel had no time to think before the crack of more powerful weapons were heard and tanks began to die in earnest.

The Soviet 179th's Regiment's TOE contributed four Zis-3 76.2mm guns to the fight, but the ace played by Artem'yev was the battery from the Army's independent anti-tank regiment, consisting of one additional Zis-3 and a pair of 100mm BS-3 guns.

A late addition to the Soviet war inventory, the penetrating capability of the 100mm was awesome and nothing on the field that day was going to be able to resist its shells.

To the American Commander, it seemed that the Grim Reaper was at work on the field in front of him. Clearly, the answer was for his tanks to press closer, supported by whatever mortars and artillery he could lay his hands on. To close and use weight of shot and shell to overcome the defenders, for to withdraw meant an end to his attack and probably an end to his unit. He added the B/23rd reserve force to the headlong charge.

Fig#18 - Reichenberg, Soviet second flare attack.

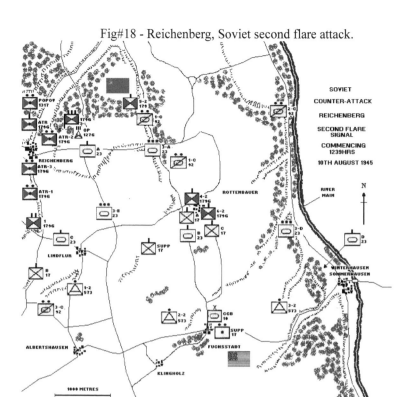

Three knocked-out Shermans became five before his gaze, his binoculars remaining glued to his face as he rapped out orders, orders intended to save his command from being butchered, but which only hastened its end.

His artillery officer called in vain to the 495th Artillery supporting them. The American unit was on the end of a severe aerial attack and unable to save themselves, let alone contribute to the debacle developing nine miles away.

The Armored Infantry's self-propelled M7 battery, stationed adjacent to Fuchstadt, waited on orders from a dead fire-controller whose OP vehicle had long since been destroyed. The three M7 SP guns failed to open fire when it might have made a difference.

577

Once Artem'yev saw the American tanks driving harder at his lines, he prepared the third flare and, when they had reached the most advantageous position, launched it and initiated the final phase of the plan.

The twenty T34/85's of 1st and 2nd Companies, 242nd Tank Brigade had been concealed in dead ground, in exactly the same position occupied some hours beforehand by the ill-fated 2nd Battery of the 975th Artillery Regiment.

They burst from cover, to be confronted with the unprotected right flank of an under fire and under pressure American tank battalion.

The American tank platoon at the crossroads engaged them as quickly as they could, but it did not save many of their fellow tankers. Seven A Company Shermans received telling hits in as many seconds.

Fig#19 - Reichenberg - Soviet third flare.

In any case, that covering platoon was suddenly confronted by a further Russian tank company and headquarters unit, with infantry support, coming from further north. Twelve armoured green beetles spewing fire, seemingly intent on running over the top of them and on into Rottenbauer, already sweeping the demoralized remnants of the 1st Platoon's troopers in front of them.

The third flare also had another purpose and its ascent cued in the supporting artillery battery, whose 122mm shells descended on the troops in Fuchstadt. The three M7's took the opportunity to displace according to their interpretation of standard doctrine, withdrawing from the field in disarray.

The six 120mm mortars of the 179th Regiments heavy battery targeted Albertshausen and 'killed' an M-16 half-track from the 573rd with their first salvo.

23rd Tank Battalion and its supporting elements were on the precipice and only firm resolute leadership would save them from disaster.

The American Colonel snatched the radio mike from the hand of his operator, his response prepared and ready to pass on to his dwindling force.

A Soviet OF-471H standard issue HE-fragmentation round contained 3.8 kilos of high-explosive and the whole projectile could arrive on a target nearly twenty thousand metres away, delivering twenty-five kilograms of fragmentation power.

The particular round in question had left gun no2 of the Divisional Heavy Battery some seconds beforehand, lovingly wiped clean and slid into the breech of his A19 122mm field gun by a leathery old man, who wished for no more than a swift return to his modest existence in the Ural mountains.

In truth, most of the OF-471H's destructive power was wasted, as a fraction of it was all that was needed to eradicate the entire mobile command group of the 12th's Combat Command 'B'.

The round struck the apex of the dormer roof above where the Colonel was stood, radio handset at the ready. It did not explode, instead carrying on and obliterating the radio operator before surrendering up its destructive force at bedroom floor level.

If nothing else, it was quick.

The Shermans were fighting back, some reversing, keeping their front to the enemy. A few others turned tail and ran, quickly falling victim to anti-tank guns or T34's, who lapped up kills on tanks displaying their weak areas of armour. The half-tracks fared badly, falling victims to the complete range of Soviet weaponry, one limping home with its full nearside bogie set removed by a 100mm shell.

More casualties were sustained as tanks and transports strayed into artillery and mortar zones, fire being shifted expertly by the Artillery Officer, who was already on Colonel Artem'yev recommendation list, along with more than a few others in this wondrous victory.

Switching the rest of the 2nd Battalion to go to the aid of their beleaguered comrades in Rottenbauer, he watched in satisfaction as the 242nd Tank Brigade swept the field clean.

He witnessed the sight of one vehicle transformed into an instant fireball by a bazooka hit and then watched the dead tanker's comrades avenge themselves by first machine gunning then crushing the group responsible.

A pair of B Company Shermans dropped in behind shallow ridges to the north of Fuchsstadt and tried to cover the disorganised retreat.

Both scored hits, the first bounced off the tank unit commander's vehicle, having given the crew a huge fright, the second struck the vehicle behind him, contacting on the driver's hatch, flat on the vision slit, just as the tank dipped into a depression.

It did not emerge into sight again; instead, the view became clouded with a rich oily smoke, marking the loss of more sons of Mother Russia.

Vengeful comrades hurled shell after shell at the brave Americans, occasionally hitting but not causing terminal damage.

Another T34 shuddered to a halt, this time one from the outflanking force descending from Rottenbauer in the north. No fire, no smoke, no life.

An American half-track [D] burst from the village behind them, bouncing along in their wake, unseen by those closest, recognised by others more distant, but immune from harm because of the nearness of their comrades.

Against all the odds it escaped, dropping into a small cut that took it northeast towards the river.

An M-16 ran from Albertshausen, its quad .50 mount lashing out at anything in range [E].

It died, victim of the fog of war, in this case smashed by a friendly bazooka round, hastily aimed by a terrified infantryman virtually blinded by smoke. Three men escaped, two more ran around, thrashing in their agony, as flames slowly consumed them.

The Soviet Artillery Officer switched his radio to a different channel and sent information to the tanks, which started to perceptibly slow.

122mm shells started to arrive, accurately dispatched onto the point of dogged resistance.

Neither Sherman was hit but no further shells came from them. They were later recovered for use as spare parts by Soviet tank maintenance crews. The Americans who rode the Shermans into battle either died from blast or concussion within their chargers, or perished in a sea of metal and explosives trying to escape them.

Combat Command 'B' had been swept from the field with huge loss of life.

Soviet casualties amongst the 242nd Battalion's armoured units were evenly spread, with each of the three medium companies losing four tanks, some of which were salvageable. Other gaps were made up with three Shermans salvaged from the field. 4th Company lost only one vehicle and crew, inexplicably driven over a ridgeline and turning over, killing all inside.

The most notable Soviet tank casualty was the commanding Colonel, victim of an excellent shot from Belinda's Bus.

One of the 100mm guns had been hit, losing a wheel, but a jury rig was in place to keep it operational.

No Zis-3's had been hit and none of the gunners touched during the exchange.

Losses in 45mm AT guns were much worse, with seven destroyed with nearly all their crew members.

Anti-tank riflemen had also sustained large casualties and over thirty lay dead on the field, with as many bleeding in the aid stations set up in Reichenberg.

1st and 3rd Battalions of the 179th Guards counted less than forty casualties between them, mainly because they had not been heavily targeted during the battle.

The 4th and 6th Companies that had fought in Rottenbauer were finished as effective formations. Of the two hundred and eleven officers and men alive that morning, barely a third responded to roll call that afternoon and those seventy-two shattered men and women included walking wounded and those upon whom deeper wounds were not yet apparent.

2nd Battalion 179th Guards Rifle Regiment was effectively finished as a fighting force, given that 5th Company, already roughly handled in fighting north of Würzburg on the 8th August, had been dealt heavy blows by the US cavalry troopers in the wood line skirmish, adding just another fifty-eight effectives to the roster. They were formed into some sort of order as a single entity, albeit unusable for the foreseeable future.

Artem'yev gathered the living of 2nd Battalion in Rottenbauer, where the medics had converted the Schloss into a hospital. He moved amongst his men, tears falling for their pain and sacrifice, not caring to celebrate his complete victory, bought at the cost of their blood.

For the Americans, the reaper's bill was immense.

Whole tactical units had disappeared from the order of battle.

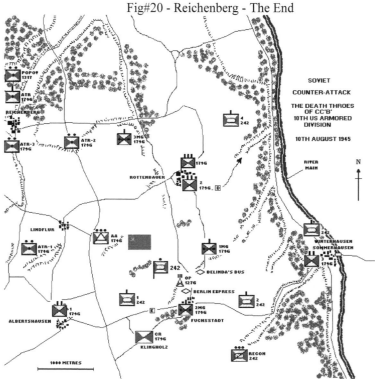

Fig#20 - Reichenberg - The End

Of the four tank companies comprising 23rd Tank Battalion, only D Company, the light tanks, existed as a useful fighting force, having lost only one of their number during the day's combat, that being an M8HMC, abandoned due to engine failure on the retreat back to Goßmannsdorf.

Each of the medium companies had been at decent strength, with 12 M4A3 [76]'s and 1 M4A3 [105] close-support tank. Four C Company tanks escaped the field, as did one each from A and B, although the B Company vehicle broke down south of Sommershausen and was abandoned.

Astonished staff officers, assembling as news of possible tragedy spread, firstly refused to believe and then surrendered to despair as a tank battalion that had mustered forty-one running tanks at the start of the day now could bring

583

just five to the field, those crewed by men who were exhausted and shocked beyond measure.

17th Armoured Infantry Battalion, support elements and all, had gone into action with precisely one thousand and one personnel to its name.

It now could muster only two hundred and twelve equally exhausted and shocked men, although that number swelled to three hundred and two in the night, as stragglers made their way back to the relative safety of the front line.

C Company, 92nd Cavalry was gone, its sole living representatives occupying six beds in the divisional aid station.

Three men died in the night and by the next time the sun rose, one more had succumbed.

573rd's Battery had lost all its vehicles, but eighteen men had escaped the Devil's cauldron that had been created in the fields before Reichenberg.

As a fuller picture of events was assembled, it rapidly became convenient to blame a long dead Colonel for the defeat, much to the disgust of those who fought in the action.

Amidst the horror and the suffering, tales surfaced of the two tanks, 'Belinda's Bus' and 'The Berlin Express', the staff starting to build up a picture of their valiant stand in the face of overwhelming odds. Reliable information from the AAA Lieutenant and a Captain from the armored-infantry, who had both escaped because the brave tankers had sacrificed themselves, filled in most of the blanks, with other witness testimony embellishing the whole.

The family of eight crew members from the two tanks, both 'B' Company, 23rd Tank Battalion, attended the White House in November 1945, to receive posthumous DSC's for their loved ones. Alongside them were the proud but emotionally wrecked parents of 2nd Lieutenant Jurgen Knapp, German-American commander of 'The Berlin Express' and Belinda Montoya, grieving wife of Tech5 Antonio Montoya, mother of the young son he never saw and for whom the Medal of Honor was a poor substitute for a loving son, husband and father.

For the family of Charley Bluebear, there was no prouder moment than that when President Truman requested

584

permission to hold the legendary weapons, which had accompanied them to the presentation ceremony. Except possibly the moment when their son had to dip his huge form slightly to enable the President to slip that most precious of medals over their son's head. That being the moment Tsali Sagonegi Yona, of the Aniyunwiya Tribe, named as Cherokee by the Creek Indians, named as 2nd Lieutenant Charley Bluebear by the US Army and known, both jokingly and seriously, as Moose by his comrades, became the holder of a Medal of Honor, earned as a brave warrior of the Great European War and a legend and example to his people, to be spoken of for generations to come.

The tank regiment, supported by rider infantry supplied by Artem'yev, closed on Winterhausen, securing the town and taking up defensive positions whilst replenishment of fuel and ammunition was organised.

Artem'yev received orders to form a line, starting on Winterhausen and then west to Maisenbach, as the 12th's Combat Command 'A' had been considerably more successful, dealing heavily with his comrades from the 243rd Rifle Division, who had had neither the benefit of tanks and heavy anti-tank support, nor of favourable terrain.

The Colonel smiled to himself, only just now noticing the bloodstain where a wood splinter had slashed his left thigh.

It also helped that the Americans had been overconfident and inexperienced; a very bad combination.

However, he had seen enough to know that they would learn and know that when they got it right, there would be hell to pay.

All warfare is based on deception. Hence, when able to attack, we must seem unable; when using our forces, we must seem inactive; when we are near, we must make the enemy believe we are far away; when far away, we must make him believe we are near. Hold out baits to entice the enemy. Feign disorder, and crush him.

Sun Tzu, the Art of War

CHAPTER 49 – THE WEAKNESS?

1355hrs 10th August 1945, Headquarters, US Forces in Europe, Trianon Palace Hotel, Versailles, France.

"Dear God."

Apart from the normal analysis post-battle, there was little else to be said that made sense that afternoon.

It would be necessary to know what went wrong so that there were no repeats and early reports suggested some leadership and support failings.

Combat Command 'B' of 12th Armored had ceased to exist in all but name and, regardless of where the blame lay, the loss of life was appalling. As usual, Ike took the weight fully on his own shoulders.

The proposed counter-attack at Fritzlar had gone forward as planned and blunted Soviet efforts, retaking Fritzlar, or more accurately, what was left of the town.

However, the drive had only gained one mile beyond the ruins before being halted in turn.

He had spent some of his morning chewing out his officers over the new 15th Armored failure to move forward and attack.

He now held in his hand a report detailing what had happened to one of his formations that had discharged its orders to attack that morning and it made appalling reading.

'*Perhaps the Almighty's showed his hand and stopped the green division from receiving similar treatment?*'

In the main, the air support promised by the USAAF and RAF had proven excellent. Allied fighters had protected

586

the armored columns well, inflicting palpable losses on the Russian air regiments who tried to get through them. This enabled Combat Command's 'A' and 'R' of the 12th Armoured to discharge their function and inflict great damage on enemy forces, south of Wurzburg, all at a small cost in lives and equipment.

9th US Armored's more modest attack had also achieved all it set out to do and at an even lower cost in lives, the most valuable of a General's assets.

The air attacks slated for the cancelled Göttingen operation went ahead and resulted in modest casualties for Eisenhower's valuable ground-attack assets, consider as fair exchange for huge disruption to the Soviet drive on and around Göttingen. An overnight RAF bomber raid on Northeim had been confirmed as having successfully wrecked every crossing point on the Rhume River, including the two recently constructed by enemy engineers.

Running north and west from Northeim, every crossing point on the Rhume and Ilme Rivers had now been dropped, all in an effort to hinder movement and logistics on the northern side of the pocket.

The Russians were doing the same to the bridges to the west of the trapped troops, destroying or damaging every bridge on the River Weser between Reinhardshagen and Gieselwerder.

Fortunately, their efforts to destroy the crossing at Lippoldsburg had failed, partially because of some excellent work by USAAF Mustangs in defence, partially ensured by the presence of two full AAA battalions, whose only purpose in life was to shoot down anything in range wearing a red star.

Again, the failures of the 15th Armored could be seen as fortuitous, as the changing situation now meant that a thrust aimed at Beverungen would be more productive. In addition, one of the few successful photo-reconnaissance missions of late had confirmed an absence of significant armored forces on that possible advance axis. A second mission to establish enemy forces around Boffzen and Holminden had similarly turned up nothing of note, making the whole area appear ripe for a more involved counter-thrust when assets permitted.

US Intelligence presently slated only the Soviet 3rd Army in the area, part of which had been given a bloody nose at Hildesheim. Intel also credited the formation with only rifle corps and a single tank regiment, the latter being identified as away from the area of immediate interest.

The news about the radar capability test was excellent and the information was already spreading through his Commanders, cascading down to where it could be employed usefully.

All in all things could be worse, although Eisenhower did not feel that was an appropriate thought for a Commanding officer.

He was comforted by the fact that the units that had broken through at Ingolstadt had inexplicably halted, stopping short of moving into contact with the cavalry, or the French Armored division rushed to seal the break.

Overnight bombing claimed modest returns, although there was the one report being evaluated, even as Ike discussed the matter with himself.

'Fuel? Is that their weakness?'

'Could it be true?'

More and more, he found himself mentally fencing with his thought processes.

'Maybe the shrinks would have a field day with that one.'

He rapidly looked in his own pile of reports, in search of the USAAF general submission for the previous night's operations.

Eisenhower found and read it to himself, urging impartiality and no pre-judgement.

He found the section he sought and lit up.

'669th Bombardment Squadron reports state that whilst bombing enemy communications at Höfartsmühle and Oberwöhr they came under anti-aircraft fire and returned fire, causing an explosion and fire on the ground to the south of Oberwöhr.'

The report also stated that one A-26 Invader was lost on the mission, but Ike did not read further, his mind working, arguing against himself.

588

'This isn't for you to work out, Give it to your staff.'
A reasonable statement.
'Yes, you're right. But what if it's true?'
'Then we know how to stop them.'

Eisenhower dragged himself out of his thoughts and beckoned an Air Force staff Major forward.

The man was new and there had been no time to get acquainted informally. The previous incumbent had yet to be recovered from the I.G.Farben building.

"Major, I want you and your team to work this 669th report and anything that ties in with it. I'm looking at enemy fuel supplies, their guarding of them, their response when we attack them. I specifically want to know which enemy areas have been affected by successful attacks on fuel supplies. Tie in with Colonel Wright and Lieutenant Colonel Rossiter on this."

"Yes, Sir," the young officer, given clear directions by his commander, saluted and turned.

"Oh and Major, quickly please."

"Sir."

The new arrival was now in possession of clear directions and a clearer indication of the importance of his project and he hurried off to find the two officers in question.

The next report covered action in Denmark; or rather, inaction, as the Germans had the Soviets nicely bottled up. McCreery was content with the two units used and anticipated no problems, especially as they were fully intact divisions from the Danish Occupation.

Preparing to accept more reports from a steadily growing line of staff officers, he noticed his European Marine pushing his way through and noted with an inner laugh that no one disputed his rite of passage.

The Colonel's report was simple.

"Sir, I can now confirm that Berlin surrendered yesterday at approximately 2100 hrs. I am unable to furnish more detail at this time."

Not unexpected, obviously, as Eisenhower had given the commander of the beleaguered garrison permission to make whatever call he felt was right.

589

To be frank, militarily, its resistance had been of little value, especially as there was no ground attack, just a relentless barrage of artillery shells and bombs to which the defenders had no reply.

Civilian casualties had mounted along with the military losses as the hours went past.

Obviously, the enclave had pinned some enemy assets in place that could now be released, but not many.

Of more concern was the effect on the German people.

"Sam, please ensure this message and any relating to it are passed to the Council immediately and request that we hold a meeting to discuss the effects of it as soon as is possible."

Rossiter smiled.

"Yes Sir. For your information, Generals Guderian and Von Vietinghoff are in this building as we speak and receiving a brief on the military situation. The rest of the council is on its way already. I have been asked to request a full meeting with you."

Eisenhower pursed his lips.

"Well no-one ever accused them of being inefficient, did they, Sam?"

The Marine shook his head slowly, understanding the deeper thoughts involved, which Ike put in to spoken word anyway.

"So, how did they know I wonder eh?"

With nothing to say on that point, Rossiter wisely said nothing.

The General looked at his watch.

"Set it up for 1630 and we will start with the gentlemen who are here, although I suspect it will be all of them."

"As do I ,Sir."

"Anything else, Sam?" enquired Ike with a casualness he did not feel.

"Sir, the Spanish broadcast was successfully transmitted at 1330hrs, as you instructed. No reports of reaction as yet," and to confirm the answer to his commander's initial enquiry, the Colonel continued, "There is nothing else to report that I am aware of, Sir."

"Thank you, Sam," and appreciating the dark circles under the man's eyes Ike added, "Have a break, Colonel, that's an order."

"I will, Sir."

Saluting, the Marine did a parade turn and made way for the next in line.

Ike looked at the next young officer as a father to a child.

"OK, Anne-Marie, what's happening with our French Allies?"

2056hrs 10th August 1945. Headquarters, US Forces in Europe, Trianon Palace Hotel, Versailles, France.

Grabbing some quiet time in his room to eat his evening meal, Eisenhower pondered the afternoon's events.

The German Council had met as planned, with all members except the two allied officers present, something not wasted on either Eisenhower or the Germans.

By the time the brief meeting was complete, the American Commander-in-chief was in no doubt that the fall of Berlin would not affect the resistance and spirit of the German, unless it was in a positive way.

Information on volunteers from amongst the ranks of German POW's showed a very high rate, much higher than the acceptance rate, for many had been kept in appalling conditions since capture, partially because of the huge numbers placing strain on a creaking supply system, but also because of some highly regrettable examples of man's inhumanity to his fellow man. One day there would be an investigation into all that and no one in authority would avoid blame, that he knew.

Meanwhile, marrying the volunteers with equipment and then creating a useful field force would take time, but the overall input was encouraging throughout the twenty-nine minute assembly.

There was also a part of the General, actually, more honestly, the basic soldier, to whom the concept of controlling German soldiers in the field appealed, which it definitely did, but he was not totally sure he wanted to know why.

591

When he raised the matter of the SS and the French, there was no adverse comment and, after the meeting, Eisenhower was not sure if he thought there would have been some, or even, should have been some. None the less, that hurdle never existed, except in his and De Gaulle's minds, so the decision was now his to make.

He would discuss that with his senior commanders on the telephone this very evening.

He looked at his watch, coming up to 2100hrs, confirming that now was the time for his call to McCreery.

A knock on the door received his normal invitation to enter and in stepped Rossiter and Hood, both very clearly men on a mission, albeit he sensed separate ones.

Both men came to attention and stood silently, expecting their General to make the decision for them.

Eisenhower smiled and gave a small laugh, enough to take the small tension out of the situation.

"OK, rank has its privileges, spit it out Thomas."

Both visitors relaxed.

"Sir, General McCreery reports severe Soviet activity on his front, around and to the north of Hamburg. His initial interpretation is a focussed attack on the city with diversions to the North. He is unable to confirm facts at this time and needs to get a hold of the situation. He will ring you as soon as he has firm information, but he requests the normal call be set aside for now."

Eisenhower had to concede that was quite reasonable and McCreery did not strike him as a man easily roused, so there must be something to this report. Again Ike's inner humour made itself known as the thought that McCreery would not get roused even if his house were on fire and burning down around his ears at four in the morning; he would probably just stroll out immaculately dressed as always and holding a cup of tea.

"OK, Thomas, thank you. Keep me informed."

Hood turned and left the room.

Eisenhower had chosen Hood to go first so that he could be gone, in case the Marine officer was here on OSS business.

He was not.

"Sir, the matter of the raid on Oberwöhr you asked us to look at. We have found some more information. I confess that it was all missed initially."

Ike's silence drew him further in.

"A matter of geography unfortunately. One report says 'south of Oberwöhr', the next says 'East of Höfartsmühle'" and producing a folded sheet of paper, he continued, "Or more importantly in this case, the important report states 'South-west of Münchsmünster'."

Passing the paper to his General like it was solid gold, which in a way it was, he spoke to illustrate further the words Ike was reading.

"A Black Widow of the 425th was searching around his designated area, centred on Landshut. He became aware of enemy aircraft and pursued them, shooting both down. This receives a great deal of coverage in his report, as you will see. However, he also speaks of the large ground fire south-west of Münchsmünster and of witnessing additional explosions on the ground during his observations. Admittedly, he didn't stay long as the light from the fire would not have been welcome, but his report is timed at 0250hrs, when he claims shooting the last of the two Soviets down, whereas the 669th attacked their designated target at 0200hrs on the button and place the secondary attack at approximately 0208 hrs."

"So something was burning and causing secondary explosions."

It was not a question, just a General thinking aloud.

'Is there more?,' he wondered.

There was and a second piece of paper was handed over.

"This report was delayed because it's an RAF report, complicated by being of Polish origin."

Eisenhower understood, as it was ever thus in his cosmopolitan forces.

"A Halifax of 301 Polish Squadron was returning from bombing Nabburg when it suffered damage, losing radio, compass, everything of note except good old Mark 1 standard eyeball."

Out of respect, Rossiter completed the section.

"They also lost the radio operator, flight engineer and navigator."

Both officers gave a respectful moment of silence, naturally and unbidden.

"They were already running late, as you can see and, according to the report, the pilot just needed some sort of ground reference so they could make sure they were going to go the right way home. They saw a big fire and steered towards it, hoping to catch sight of something on the ground to direct them. He and his gunner are adamant that they made a positive identification and they support their statement well, as they were both on missions to nearby Regensburg in the last war."

He stopped for an instant.

'Is this a new war or just a continuation of the last one?'

Rossiter set the matter aside and continued.

"They identified the bends on the Danube near Kelheim and were able to orient themselves and return without further problems."

Eisenhower checked the timings on all three reports and then looked up as a signal for the Marine to press on.

"They state that there was still a considerable fire, with visible explosions, at 0330hrs, positively identified as the Dürnbucher Forest."

"The Dürnbucher Forest?"

Rossiter's feature took on a wry smile that persisted through his words. Placing a map on the round table, he tapped his finger on the Durnbucherforst.

"Yessir, the Dürnbucher Forest."

The Marine continued, accompanying each statement with an imaginary line to the Forest, "The Dürnbucher Forest... south of Oberwöhr... east of Höfartsmühle... and south-west of Münchsmünster."

Each line terminated in the same spot, namely, the Dürnbucher Forest

Eisenhower felt the man's discomfort and took up the trail.

594

"So we have bombers reporting fire and explosions at 0208hrs, continuing through to last witnesses, the Poles, at 0330 hrs."

Rossiter nodded.

"Explosives or fuel."

Not a question as such, just a statement in the first instance.

"You've gone somewhere with this already, haven't you Sam?"

Ike knew his man.

"Yes, Sir. I figured you'd want to know, so I've done some rooting around. The Soviet tank force that has stopped dead the other side of Ingolstadt has not been meaningfully engaged, period."

"Meaning, Sam?"

"Meaning, Sir, it's a fresh unit and it's not attacking. There has to be a reason for that, as it doesn't seem to be a military one that we have imposed."

"Meaning?"

Eisenhower felt he knew why, but wanted confirmation from a man he trusted.

"Meaning, in my view, it could be fuel, Sir. It isn't ammo because they haven't fired any, pretty much the only thing they are consuming when advancing is POL and foodstuffs."

"We discussed this quickly downstairs and not one of us felt that Ivan would pause because he didn't have his K's."

Not that the Soviets had K ration packs, but it illustrated the point he was making.

'POL?'

Petrol, oil and lubricants, to the uninitiated.

Eisenhower closed his eyes for just one moment, enough for two inner voices to congratulate themselves, before opening his eyes to reality once more.

"We've a team working on their military fuel reserves right now, but I guess we could be looking at an Ardennes repeat if we can interdict appropriately."

Ignoring the fact that his cigarette had just deposited ash all over the remainder of his meal, Eisenhower took a deep draft of his coffee.

"Excellent work, Sam and don't be too hard on yourself. Things get missed and the team picked it up before harm was done. Thank you and stay on it."

Mentally terminating the discussion, Ike suddenly wondered if there was something else and refocused.

"Oh, anything else, Sam?"

A question with unspoken meaning.

"Not at this time, Sir."

A reply addressing the concerns voiced.

"Keep me informed, Sam and thank you again."

Salutes were exchanged and Eisenhower was alone once more.

A cigarette dealt with his craving, but his stomach still felt light and it had nothing to do with the half-eaten meal.

'History shows that there are no invincible armies, General.'

The two sentries stood outside Eisenhower's door swore later that they heard uncharacteristic laughter from within.

'Amen, General, amen.'

He commenced his telephone discussions with his senior commanders making his last call to Field-Marshal Harold Alexander.

After getting a report and passing on his own situation, he discussed the possible fuel issue with his British commander in the Mediterranean.

"Yes, Ike, I do understand and wouldn't it be absolutely marvellous if it were true?"

"Harry, you think I'm holding the wrong pig here?"

"Let me just say that my own staff have done work on this. I will get copies to you by pip-emma tomorrow. Obviously, I was interested in knowing how far our Red friends could drive if they chose to go sightseeing."

Ike had heard the substitution of pip-emma for p.m. before from Alexander, so did not lose the meaning. However, he would never get used to the British way of talking in riddles.

596

"Our conclusion was they have no shortage of fuel whatsoever, unless some local depletion is achieved, such as you might have seen with this instance."

"Others seem to think we may have something to work with here, Harry."

"Well yes, we maybe, but I actually think not, certainly not on what my staff generated, Sir."

Negative input from one of his seniors made all Eisenhower's other positive feelings fade a little.

Sensing the moment correctly, Alexander pushed a bit harder.

"If I might offer a few words of Kipling, General. His boy was in my Regiment in the First War, don't you know; tragic loss. You are familiar with 'If', I trust."

"I have read it, but familiar may be too much of a claim Harry."

"Understood, Sir," Alexander chuckled.

"There is more than a little that is pertinent there."

Eisenhower tried to summon the words for himself.

Alexander recited the poem by memory. For an ex-Irish Guards officer, it was an easy enough task.

Ike found himself nodding.

"Thank you for that, Harry. The message there is loud and clear. Keep my feet on the ground while those about me get carried away and don't dream something into a fact that it isn't."

"I think that puts it rather well, General."

"You are right, of course. I will wait on more information before I start imagining the ticker tape parade through New York."

Alexander laughed sincerely at that one. Remembering something important, he curtailed his response.

"By the way, Sir, Mr Attlee was none too pleased that McCreery was popped into place without so much as a by your leave. It's the province of His Majesty's Government etc etc. Just so you know. He is ok with it now, but I think he felt circumvented, which of course, he was. I don't think he understood the necessity of immediate action, despite my

597

championing the appointment. You know what I mean. Maybe a little bit of careful handling for a while, Sir?"

"As you say and thank you again, Harry."

"My pleasure Sir, Good night... and good luck."

"And to you."

Eisenhower went to his bed feeling less buoyant than an hour beforehand, but slept reasonably well for the second time since the lead had started to fly once more.

None the less, in his initial slumber the dreams were uneasy, raising doubts and questions.

As he slipped into deeper less turbulent sleep he wrestled with one final session as Devil's Advocate to his own mental processes.

'Is Alexander right and there isn't a fuel problem for the commies?'

Lots of fuel?

'But that tank corps has stopped.'

No fuel?

'But that could be local loss, not theatre-wide.'

Lots of fuel but just not there?

'Wait until the morning.'

Enough fuel?

'Why would they not have?'

How much fuel?

'It can't be that simple can it?'

And, of course, it wasn't.

1422hrs 10th August 1945, Durnbucherforst, Germany.

Having arrived at the site of the attack during the early afternoon, the 10th Tank Corps' commander was being briefed on what exactly had befallen his supplies. One of his Staff Colonels, sent on first thing that morning, was imparting the bad news. Henceforth Major-General Sakhno was in a blue funk. His Chief-of-Staff, NKVD KomBrig Davydov, was even worse, having summarily executed both the trigger-happy Sergeant who brought the destruction down upon the supply train, as well as the Captain who spoke in the man's defence.

598

The forest around the site had been incinerated, along with over 75% of the 10th Tank Corps' fuel supply and a modest 25% chunk of the corps' ammunition. Losses in service manpower were extreme and Sakhno had yet to find any officer from his supply units above the rank of Lieutenant, except for the burnt and shocked man shot dead by his incandescent Chief of Staff.

It was also reported that most of the protecting AA battalion from 1701st AA Regiment had also been ravaged.

Valuable assets that had been equipped with the highly effective German 20mm Quad weapons mounted on trucks, one of the few German weapons that had not completely and strangely disappeared from the Soviet order of battle in Europe that summer.

Mikhail Gordeevich Sakhno sat down on a fallen tree and ran his hands through his hair, or more accurately, where his hair had once been, the balding patch emphasised by the bushier growths on either side of his crown.

As he sat, Davydov strode up, muttering oath after oath.

Sakhno indicted a space on the fallen trunk next to him.

"Let us sit and take stock, Nikanor Karpovich. I must think how best to present this disaster to Savelev, or the pair of us will be counting trees."

Davydov looked at his superior, surprised.

"The Army Commander is aware of the situation, Comrade General. His Supplies section is working on how to get us moving again as we speak."

It was Sakhno's turn to look at his companion with surprise.

Indicating a camouflaged truck, drawn up on the edge of the devastated zone, the NKVD officer spat smoky oily phlegm and rummaged for a cigarette with which to freshen his mouth.

"Our valiant comrade, Polkovnik Rassov from Army Command, with a radio truck, reporting back as we speak, Mikhail Gordeevich."

Both men spat on cue for the same reason, a disgust and fear of Rassov they both shared.

Colonel Rassov was an asshole but, unfortunately a powerful one who had the Army Commander's ear. Throughout the Red Army he was known as 'The Weasel'.

Both men lit up and inhaled, coinciding with the first spots of rain dropping on the General's balding pate.

"Well that's just fucking great! Now it simply can't get any worse," chuckling in the way that people who have had a sense of humour failure chuckle in the face of great adversity.

"There is more, Comrade."

Reluctantly, Davydov drew his commander's attention to a previously anonymous set of wrecks lined up on a woodland path, deliberately parked close together and hidden from aerial view, until such time as the fireballs consumed vehicles, occupants and protective forest canopy.

"According to Rassov, that is apparently the illustrious 2nd Battalion of the 8th Pontoon Brigade, sent here last night to fuel up before moving forward behind the attack we have just failed to make, because of our lack of fuel."

Sakhno screwed his face up, concentrating on the numerous wrecks that were now apparent to his gaze, making out the remains of vital bridging equipment as he moved his eyes up and down the charred lines.

"Well that's just fucking great."

Davydov could do no more than nod at that. Going through the options in his mind, the General was unaware of the approaching figure until his companion stiffened at his side.

Casting a swift look, he saw the diminutive figure of Rassov, marching in their direction, clearly filled with purpose.

The two comrades exchanged a knowing look.

As the NKVD officer stood, he leaned naturally, allowing him to whisper in his general's ear.

"I'd love to shoot the little bastard but I think it would only make matters worse, my friend."

Sakhno, remaining seated, spoke his thought rather more openly.

"Well, if it looks like going bad for us, the fucking weasel will be the first to bite a bullet."

Davydov gestured to the approaching Rassov and spoke with a lightness he did not feel.

"Comrade Polkovnik Rassov. Please join us."

1748hrs Friday 10th August 1945, Ainauwald, Germany.

Rassov had insisted on accompanying Sakhno back to his mobile headquarters at Starzhausen, just over a mile north of Wolnzach.

The five-vehicle convoy was led by a BA64 armoured car, acting as the advance screen, with the security section in an American Studebaker truck that led the main group, consisting of the 10th Tank Corps' Commander's GAZ staff car, Rassov's jeep and finally, the signal vehicle, from which Rassov had sent his damning reports, bringing up the rear.

The BA64 driver, anxious to be back to his unit by mealtime, moved his vehicle forward above the agreed speed, his vehicle commander failing to notice the error, as he was engrossed in examining in detail some interesting photos, recently 'liberated' from a ladies salon in Straubling.

Quite often in life, where there exists one error, another arrives to make matters worse.

The driver of the security section vehicle, having lost sight of the armoured car, made an assumption and, instead of carrying on down the same road, turned his lorry left, just past Ainau, heading down a woodland track to nowhere.

The three senior officers, deep in conversation in the GAZ behind, noticed nothing, the last two vehicle's drivers would not have recognised the error in any case.

One large lorry, a signal truck and two staff 4x4's make quite a lot of noise, especially when driven in the Russian style, down unmade roads.

Without that warning, things might have been different.

However, the racket the four vehicles made ensured that the matter was never in doubt, as the Ainauwald contained nothing but a swift death for anything with a Red Star.

Davydov had just finished remonstrating against Rassov's accusation about the possible effects on his health of

601

the obvious deviation from standard procedures regarding positioning of battle fuel stocks. Angry, he turned away and slowly became aware of his surroundings. He started to question the driver, an extremely average looking leviathan called Anasimova, picked for her driving ability and nothing else.

The security lorry disappeared in a wall of flame as it drove straight over a teller mine chain, three devices exploding virtually in unison.

The radio truck and crew lasted less than three seconds more, as two panzerfausts arrowed in, one from each side, obliterating the cab.

The rattle of small arms fire exceeded the screams from the dying and the air was filled with deadly metal insects, each capable of taking a life.

Three, fired from an ST44 assault rifle, took Olga Anasimova in the chest, stopping her heart in an instant.

The vehicle continued forward, losing momentum and came to a halt by bumping into the rear of the burning Studebaker.

The front seat passenger, Colonel Rassov, was hit by the same burst that killed Anasimova. Eyes wide open in shock and horror, he was conscious but unable to move, his spine severed by one strike, both his arms broken by three more and his chest penetrated by the five others. Unable to move, Rassov's death was noisy, protracted and excruciating, as the flames advanced.

Davydov and Sakhno had bailed out, each already hit and bleeding, firing with their pistols at imagined shapes in the undergrowth.

Nodding at a thicker clump of bushes to their rear, the two gathered themselves for a superhuman effort.

They burst from behind their cover and made for relative safety that the thicker undergrowth behind them offered, from where suddenly emerged an armed middle-aged man, wearing an SS camouflage smock.

"Sieg Heil!"

Instead of attacking that morning and exploiting the break in the line caused by the collapse of the French division, 10th Tank Corps was paralysed by the loss of its allocated fuel supply and the loss of its two key senior commanders.

Commander of 5th Guards Tank Army, Lieutenant-General Mikhail Ivanovich Savelev stepped in, reorganising the hierarchy of the 10th, mourning the loss of two competent veteran officers and spared no thought whatsoever for the weasel he had despised.

The hiding place of Kommando Lenz had been well and truly blown and the armed group, led by the former SS Hauptsturmfuhrer of Fallschirmjager, had long disappeared.

1959hrs, Friday 10th August 1945, The Kremlin, Moscow, USSR.

Leaning back into his comfortable chair and drawing deeply on a simple pipe, the General Secretary read the military intelligence estimate compiled following the Spanish radio message that same day, something that they had been forewarned of by agents in Spain.

Beria sat similarly comfortably polishing his glasses, enjoying the fact that Pekunin was in the limelight. Of course, he had himself been quizzed, but the NKVD had already done some of the basic footwork, so his report had been examined and accepted some time before the GRU one arrived.

It was delivered by a strikingly attractive GRU female Lieutenant Colonel, in itself a novelty.

Beria made a mental note to check out this Nazarbayeva more thoroughly, as she must have achieved her status by clever use of her obvious charms and, to his mind, that meant leverage and compliance with any proposition he might put to her in future.

As she stood there, he studied how she favoured her left leg whilst stood at attention and amused himself with reaching into the recesses of his mind for the details he must have read on her at one time or another.

603

The shiny star on the upper left chest helped prod him in the right direction as he recalled her report on the French symposiums and then brought forward details of her service.

'You have a husband too,' he reflected, smiling inside but not out,

'All the better for what I have in mind, Tatiana.'

Catching her eye accidentally, he was immediately aware of a strength and resilience in her gaze and part of him spoke a warning, whereas another part relished the challenge.

His warped thought process was interrupted.

"So, Comrade PodPolkovnik, you conclude that this new development will interfere with our schedule?"

Nazarbayeva, inwardly feeling slightly overwhelmed at her present company but outwardly cool and composed briefly replied.

"Most certainly, Comrade General Secretary, I can see no other conclusion."

Both Stalin and Beria knew that the NKVD report agreed with that but anticipated only a modest effect throughout the run of Kingdom39.

Stalin, referring to the document, challenged the GRU officer.

"I see here that this report originated from you, authored from start to finish by you, delivered to my hands by you. Why is that, Comrade?"

"Comrade General Pekunin was wounded in an air attack on our Headquarters, not seriously, but enough to place him in hospital for the moment, Comrade General Secretary. Comrade Leytenant General Kochetkov is in temporary command and it was on his order that I compiled the report and presented it to you."

Neither man said a word, but both thought that Kochetkov was keeping his neck off the block and setting up his Colonel for the fall if things went wrong.

In actual fact, he had directed Nazarbayeva to do the work because of her ability, something that never occurred to either of them.

"The NKVD disagrees with you, Comrade PodPolkovnik."

604

"Perhaps they have seen information that I have not Comrade General Secretary? Maybe the GRU has information that the NKVD does not. My report is based on all information available to the GRU, Comrade General Secretary. "

She stood her ground, something not lost on either man.

"Very well, you may explain yourself, PodPolkovnik."

Drawing heavily on his pipe, he relaxed his frame back into the chair.

"Comrades, the Spanish Army presently consists of no more than twenty-five understrength divisions under arms, with the possibility of mobilising a maximum of two hundred-thousand more men, making their existing divisions properly constituted within a minimum of forty-eight days of any decision."

Beria was mentally ticking off the points contained within his report and, thus far, Nazarbayeva was mirroring the NKVD submission. He had not seen the GRU document, but expected no surprises.

"The Blue Division, whose membership is experienced, as we know, is being mobilised right now and it is anticipated that it will start to move forward within fourteen days. It is also possible that extra personnel may be found amongst veterans of the unit, sufficient to form an additional smaller formation, possibly of brigade size."

Tatiana was relating all from memory and had just scored one point over Beria's report.

"This force will be deployed under American command and we understand is most likely to enter Germany, north of the Swiss border, into an area of some interest to our Generals."

Another tick.

"This force is unlikely to pose a huge problem for our armies, but will have significant propaganda value to the Allies."

And again.

"It is our assessment that this unit, or pair of units, would most likely be equipped with captured German weapons

605

from allied stocks in the south of France, with no need for huge training, as most members would be familiar with whatever equipment they are given."

'Keep going PodPolkovnik, you are doing very well,' came the thought, the spectacled face betraying nothing.

"Estimate that these Spanish soldiers will be capable of deployment into combat by the end of the month."

'Close enough.'

"The remainder of the Spanish Army is of little import at first look, ill-equipped, poorly officered and lacking in spirit."

Again, from memory she summoned accurate figures as she carried on.

"Documents recovered from the Spanish Embassy in Berlin indicate that they officially received twenty Panzer IV tanks and ten self-propelled guns from German production."

Coughing gently, she moistened her mouth with saliva and pressed on.

"GRU interviews with German prisoners who served in the south of France indicate that they may also have acquired some French Army equipment, circa 1940, ranging from armour through to small arms. Also, there are also unsubstantiated rumours of some Panther and Tiger tanks crossing the border to safety during the Allied landings in 1944."

'Really?'

"None the less, relatively insignificant amounts of materiel for our Army to get concerned about."

'Agreed.'

"All in all, it appears that the Spanish Army could contribute a great deal of manpower, but not a lot of substance."

This was precisely the conclusion of the NKVD report.

"However, Comrade General Secretary, I believe there is more to be concerned about."

Stalin gestured with his pipe stem for Nazarbayeva to continue, quiet and strangely content to just observe and listen.

"The embargo of Spain has been lifted, which will engender popular support for the Spanish commitment. The previous years of government have been spent in division, with two different camps vying for power."

Beria studied her closer, waiting.

"Those two groups are now united and fully behind the commitment. That removes some of the political shackles that could have prevented proper military development. The Spanish spend huge amounts of their wealth on arms and now they are united and can proceed efficiently"

'Very good, Comrade PodPolkovnik, not just a pretty face after all, are you...are you?' This time his nods were noticed and appreciated by Nazarbayeva.

"We anticipate that Spanish troops will start to receive military supplies in the near future, if they haven't already started to be delivered."

"I think you go too far now, Comrade PodPolkovnik," interjected Beria, continuing forcefully.

"It is the NKVD position that the allies will not have sufficient military hardware for their own needs, let alone to supply to an ally of dubious worth."

Stalin chuckled, which immediately made both intelligence officers wary, one with direct knowledge of his master, the other on her instinct.

"Go on, Comrade PodPolkovnik," and he flashed a look at Beria that was fully understood.

"We have two reports of shipments crossing from Africa into Gibraltar yesterday, both then moving on into the Spanish interior. One of those reports suggests armaments as a possibility."

Beria did not know of this and that was written on his face for both the others to see. He wanted to speak but remembered the veiled warning he had just been given.

"When the Axis powers surrendered in Africa, they left behind considerable stocks of equipment, as did the Vichy forces, equipment which is redundant and which could now be on its way to Spain."

"How much?"

Replying directly to Stalin, Tatiana accessed her memory banks.

"That is not something that is known for certain, Comrade General Secretary. However, it is a matter of record that over two hundred and seventy-five thousand prisoners were taken in 1943 alone."

Stalin leaned forward, his posture encouraging further information.

"That represents a huge amount of modern effective weaponry, cheaply available and immediately ready for disposal."

"These weapons will be ones that most Spanish soldiers will be familiar with and, if the Allies are indeed sending them across to Gibraltar, then it is feasible that the entire Spanish Army could possess effective equipment within two weeks."

Nazarbayeva continued.

"Given that the Allies have acted so swiftly in lifting the embargo and moving cargoes into Southern Spain, it is reasonable to assume that they believe the effort is worthwhile and that Spain will contribute to their cause."

Again, Beria itched to speak up but remained mute.

"The availability of Spanish ports will change the allied logistics, but will offer them limited improvement and we believe there will be a negligible effect for our forces. Spanish airfields will be of some use to them, most certainly, but only as we push further into France."

"Of concern will be the ability to deploy reinforcement units from Africa through Gibraltar and into Spain. I can see no reason why the Spanish would refuse that, given their new political stance."

Pausing to gather her thoughts before proceeding, Nazarbayeva started to feel real discomfort in her left foot. Having lost everything from the heel forward, the only way her left leg could keep her upright was by use of the metal ankle strap, an 'L' shaped piece that replaced the foot. Prolonged standing made it very sore and she had been on her feet for nearly an hour.

608

The pause was misinterpreted and Beria shifted, enquiring of his leader.

Stalin silently gave his NKVD chief his head.

"Comrade PodPolkovnik. In matters of intelligence, it is always possible to interpret matters in more than one way. We agree in most areas, but is there any substantive evidence to support your view that a properly equipped Spanish force would be able to take the field, or indeed, if the political will actually exists to do so?"

Turning to address Stalin directly, he made a valid point.

"After all, Franco did much posturing during his relations with Germany and still only sent one division to fight for a cause he apparently supported wholeheartedly."

And addressing Nazarbayeva directly, he continued.

"A posturing that he undertakes again and proposes providing the same single division to further his cause."

Beria's eyebrows rose, feeling he had scored a point over the GRU submission.

'Check.'

He sat down and looked up at the woman, expecting to see turmoil, but instead saw only calm.

"This afternoon, just before I left to deliver this document, we received a report from our agent within the Spanish Government."

Beria also had his agents in place and none of them gave any indication of a difference to Spanish physical commitment to the Allied cause. Unfortunately for him, they simply were not in the right place.

Tatiana had left the best until last, for no other reason than reinforcing her report with a juicy fact, whereas she had actually drawn Beria into nailing his colours to the mast of a sinking ship.

"Our agent informs us that the Spanish Army is already undertaking planning for a Spanish Expeditionary Corps consisting of," and for this her memory failed her and a glance at the last page of addendum was required, "One armoured division, six infantry divisions, one mountain division and the Spanish Legion from Morocco, Franco's old unit, specifically asked for by Franco himself. In order to participate in and I quote, 'the World Crusade against Communism'."

Check-mate.

'You fucking bitch.'

Stalin appreciated that the woman Colonel had given her honest appreciation and had made her point well in support of the GRU report. Unlike her, he also appreciated that she had just made an enemy for life.

"Thank you, Comrade PodPolkovnik. Excellent work. You are dismissed."

Nazarbayeva sat at a table in the waiting room as her flight was not yet ready to go.

As was her practice, she slipped off her left boot, unnoticed by the other occupants of the room, bringing instant relief to her aching limb.

Consuming the coffee provided by a one-armed veteran of Kursk, she re-examined her time in Stalin's private office.

Beria.

He had not devoured her lustfully with his eyes like most men, but none the less, she had felt them upon her.

Assessing.

Calculating.

Planning.

Malevolent.

Her thoughts were interrupted by a gruff Air Force Captain calling for passengers to load on the Lisunov-2 ambulance plane that was to be her ride home.

The lascivious gaze of the Kursk veteran avidly examined the form of the GRU Lieutenant Colonel from head to toe, obviously superb despite the lack of tailoring in the uniform, but even then he failed to spot her efficient off/on boot routine.

On the flight back to Leipzig she slept hard, drained by her encounter with those at the centre of power.

As Nazarbayeva left the room, Beria was already preparing his defence.

Stalin knew it and trashed it out of hand.

"GRU seem to have assessed this correctly, Comrade Marshal. I agree with their assessment."

He illustrated his point by leaning forward and dropping the NKVD document into Beria's lap.

It lay there, a mark of NKVD intelligence failure, weight increasing, seemingly pressing Beria down into the chair.

The silence made it even heavier.

'Fucking bitch.'

Stalin knew his man.

"Plot your revenge later, Lavrentiy, for now I need a solution."

Focussing on the main issue, Beria immediately realised he had a possible solution already, a matter of personal revenge which could now be turned into something that would resemble incredible foresight and planning.

Buoyed by the thought, he removed the redundant report from his lap, slipping it into his briefcase and searched for another small file, successfully.

He passed it to the General Secretary, exhibiting a genuine smugness that Stalin easily noticed.

"This NKVD contingency operation will solve the problem Comrade."

And as Stalin took the document, Beria started speaking of a ship called Doblestnyj, a town called Malpica and committed men on a mission.

Our greatest glory is not in never failing, but in rising up every time we fail.

Ralph Waldo Emerson

CHAPTER 50 – THE PLAN

0255hrs 11th August 1945, Headquarters, Red Banner Forces of Europe, Kohnstein, Nordhausen, Germany.

Outside it was raining, but that was not something the occupants of tunnels thirty-eight to forty-five were aware of, given the protection offered by the Mountain above them.

Driven into the rock, initially in the mining search for anhydrite, the tunnels were then expanded after being taken over by German Industry and used for storing important petroleum products, chemicals and poisons. However, the tunnels, finally amounting to forty-six in number, were mostly notorious for the underground production of the V2 Rocket and their association with the Nordhausen Concentration Camp.

Regardless of the dubious lineage of the premises, Soviet planners had been unable to ignore the protection offered and so had prepared tunnels thirty-eight to forty-five as the controlling centre for all military action within Europe, with other tunnels converted as areas for food preparation, barracks, sleeping accommodation for headquarters staff, in fact, everything a self-contained facility required. Even with prior notice, the facilities were Spartan but ,having seen what visiting heavy bombers were capable of, very few grumbled and even fewer were prepared to exchange carpeted hallways and fine art for the protection offered by a few hundred feet of solid rock.

Zhukov had been woken by his orderly and, having completed his ablutions, he now sat with most of his senior officers and Front Commanders, already present for the crucial meeting.

The rest of the officers in the room were the permitted Deputies, who all engaged with their own circle, be it by rank or post.

Tea, strong and sweet, was the order of the day and the men sat drinking steadily, sampling basic fare from platters spread before them. Sliced sausage, ham, boiled eggs, salted cucumbers and marvellous breads of different ilks. A soldier's meal had been the request and a soldier's meal it was, albeit of a higher culinary standard than the average Soviet soldier in the frontline.

Chuikov, the Colonel General commander of the unengaged 1st Alpine Front, was sat alone, concentrating on taking healthy bites of bread, ham and cucumber.

Marshals of the Soviet Union Malinovsky and Rokossovsky, 1st and 3rd Red Banner Central European Front's respectively, were in animated conversation regarding the upcoming planned phase two and if it was yet appropriate.

Zhukov debated entering the discussion but felt it would keep.

Sokolovsky, Colonel General of the sidelined Polish Army, was in more quieter and less agitated discussion with the Armenian General Bagramyan, his de facto superior as commander of 1st Baltic Front.

Zhukov laughed inwardly as he realised that Colonel Generals Yeremenko, of 1st Southern European Front and Malinin, his own Chief of Staff, were both cornered by Marshal Tolbukhin and his legendary rendition of the camel joke.

Whilst the joke itself was of average quality and had been in Tolbukhin's armoury for more years than Zhukov cared to remember, no one who witnessed the delivery could fail to be impressed by Tolbukhin's application and spirit in the telling.

Bringing himself back from the lighter moment, Zhukov told himself that Tolbukhin, as commander of the 1st Balkan Front, would need all his good humour to deal with the delicacies of being adjacent to an upset and sizeable Yugoslavian army.

Zhukov looked at the clock.

'Where is the fool?'

A thought he could not give voice to.

Malinin caught sight of his commander's unspoken question and followed his gaze to the wall clock that had ticked

613

past 0330hrs, the allotted time for the meeting. He shrugged almost imperceptibly and nodded, taking his leave of Tolbukhin, who was in full swing.

He exited the room, which was what it really was. Walls, ceiling and floor, all constructed of wood, the whole box like structure sitting in a cavernous space.

He almost collided with an agitated Soviet officer.

About to reprimand the man, he realised that he had nearly come into contact with Marshal Konev, the late arrival, which officer was in a state of some disrepair. Apart from being soaked, his greatcoat was torn, muddy and rent down one side.

There was more than a hint of blood on his left ear and he looked particularly unhappy.

"I hope you're not hurt, Comrade Marshal?"

A very disgruntled Konev merely grunted, handing his dirty coat and cap to an orderly. There was no need for any cleaning instructions; the two would both be sorted by the time the Marshal came out of the meeting.

Konev, commander of 2nd Red Banner Central European Front, strode in, nodding here and there and finally at Zhukov, before apologising generally and grabbing some tea and food.

A large black smudge across Konev's bald pate and a noticeably bloody left ear made those present realise that there was more story to his delay than a missed turning or a flat tyre.

Zhukov tried hard not to be irked by the man, but failed miserably. There was no love lost between the two since the race for Berlin and, in truth, there was little prior to that for more than one reason.

Stalin had assigned the capture of Berlin to Zhukov but, some said deliberately, had not laid out defined borders between the two Fronts. Konev, being Konev, had oriented his forces in such a way as to ensure his forces made it into Berlin. His forces arrived some time ahead of Zhukov's because of the relatively successful German defence of the Seelow Heights, which slowed the advance of Zhukov's forces.

Such things are unrepeatable milestones in a military career and Zhukov saw his milestone as permanently tarnished.

Calling the meeting to order, Zhukov beckoned to one of his aides, who removed the drapes concealing a map of the Far East.

Addressing one matter that all wanted cleared up first, he directly addressed Konev.

"Comrade Marshal, are you wounded?"

Konev picked at his ear and inspected the red smear on his fingers.

"Shall I just say that a journey by air at night is not safe, even behind our lines, Comrades."

Konev, being Konev, had decided to leave as late as possible and fly to Nordhausen's airfield, having been led to believe it was safe enough and also being given the promise of a fighter escort.

He witnessed the destruction of three of his escorts, before being singled out for attack by whatever it was that was out there.

"Flying back will be easier in daylight I'm assured, provided I can get another pilot."

The previous airman was presently being bandaged in the headquarters aid station, hopeful that the loss of four toes would not prevent him from flying again.

"None the less, we're glad you are relatively unscathed, Comrade."

Which, in essence, Zhukov was, but probably only because of the disruption that the loss of a Front Commander would cause to his military progress.

Drawing a line under the matter, Zhukov pressed on.

"Comrades, before we progress into the purpose of this gathering, can I confirm with all of you that you've had opportunity to read this document," holding up a copy of Vasilevsky's report on progress with Operation Diaspora, he turned the cover towards him reading aloud, "Version B, dated 10th August?"

It wasn't a question as such, because every man there was required to be totally aware of Diaspora, in case a change in leadership came about due to unforeseen circumstances.

"I must say, Comrade Marshal Vasilevsky is performing brilliantly, hand in hand with our Japanese Allies."

615

He smiled broadly.

"It seems our new friends have adapted well to the gifts we sent and all of us here know how effective they could be in the hands of the green toads."

Dropping the '*Diaspora -B-10/08- MRBF- Chief Intelligence Office - AMV*' report like it was a hot coal, he snatched up another small report.

"However, you'll probably not be aware that the Americans are sending a considerable number of units to the Chinese mainland, as listed in appendix 'B' of this document."

Waiting hands eagerly grabbed this new report from a young Major tasked with issuing out the copies.

"Appendix 'A' deals with naval allocations and, as such, is of limited interests to us, except to say that Diaspora is doing exactly what we hoped and more so."

Chuikov, the roughest by nature of the gathered Commanders, speed-read and gave vent to his surprise.

"Govno!"

"I think you'll find I am correct, Comrade Polkovnik General."

There was a general ripple of laughter, especially as Marshal Zhukov was rarely given to public displays of humour.

Chuikov started to rise to his feet.

"Apologies, Comrade, I was just surprised by this," he indicated Appendix 'B'.

Zhukov gestured the man back down into his seat, knowing that Chuikov may well be rough by nature, but he had stood his ground when no other had stood; Hero of the Mamayev Kurgan in Stalingrad.

He liked the man immensely.

"I think Comrade Chuikov expresses it well. The list of units they're sending to China will definitely inconvenience Vasilevsky, but is undoubtedly of advantage to us."

There was no intended humour in that and, in any case, Rokossovsky stood requiring the floor.

"Comrade Zhukov, is this information accurate? Has it been tested?"

The man, never given to excessive verbiage, resumed his seat.

616

Zhukov nodded, accepting the sensible question.

"Comrade General Pekunin has received this through his own agents and assures the General Secretary of its factual nature."

A small rumble of positive noises needed to be quelled before he could press on.

"In fairness, our beloved Marshal Beria," such talk was safe amongst military men, even Konev, "Has not been able to verify this list, but then you wouldn't expect him to, would you?"

The rivalry between GRU and NKVD was the stuff of legend.

"I think we must look at this report with a view to believing it to be true. After all, Pekunin's lot have done well for us so far."

Chuikov stood and was given the floor by Zhukov.

"I note from this list that a number of formations that we anticipated would be deployed in my area of operations are no longer slated for Europe. If this second phase of our attack proceeds as we have planned, then the front opposite me will be weakened by the Allied movements we anticipate into Southern Germany and Austria."

That was window dressing for his next question, actually, statement.

"In that case, are we planning to initiate phase three earlier and also proceed with the Iberian option?"

Holding out his palms in surrender, Zhukov cut straight in before others could get a word in.

"Wait, Comrade. I appreciate your aggressive intent, but we can't yet be sure what assets the Allies will move northwards from Italy when we unleash our armies. Let's not get ahead of ourselves."

Zhukov paused.

"And while we're on the subject, NKVD seems to feel that the Spanish change of position will be of little effect, a view I'm inclined to agree with."

There was no contrary view put forward, although there certainly would have been had Nazarbayeva's report been to hand.

Indicating the next covered area on the rear wall, Zhukov stepped aside, as the orderly repeated his unveiling.

"This is the situation you're all aware of."

Sitting down, he gave the floor to his deputy, Malinin, who stepped forward, ready armed with long handled pointer.

"Comrades, our progress has, for the main part, been less than we would have hoped. However, the purpose has been served and served well."

As he started speaking, another staff officer was distributing the latest figures on losses and strengths.

"I can't recall the figures from memory, but you will see that overall we're not suffering casualties as we expected, either in manpower or equipment."

Clearing his throat, he added a cautionary note.

"Except for air, where the losses have been murderous. Operation Kurgan was a brilliant success and their ground attack assets were decimated. Huge casualties were inflicted upon their command and control facilities, as well as their early-warning sites."

He noted that the officers were all consuming the figures in front of them, so paused to draw their attention back to him.

"The air regiments have suffered grievous losses in maintaining our command of the daylight airspace, for that IS what we have, Comrades. Night time is a different matter and, as you will all know, we're suffering problems with logistics because of deep penetration heavy bomber raids on rail and bridge facilities."

He added as evenly as he could.

"I've no need to remind you of the potential effects of that problem, Comrades."

Konev choked silently on a piece of chewy ham and Malinin took advantage of the respite to swallow some water.

"Our night capabilities are greatly eroded; fighter squadrons have been reduced to well below 50% strength in the vast majority of cases, night-bombers…"

Night Bombers; well they all knew that story.

"The Comrade General Secretary has ordered a review of our night air provisions, as a matter of urgency."

618

That this review was not to be conducted by the commander of Soviet Air Forces Europe was because the man was already in his grave, a result of a visitation from an NKVD squad.

"On the ground, we're looking extremely healthy."

Slapping the pointer against Denmark, he started his full brief.

"The Germans have two divisions, their former garrison troops, sat opposite our forces in Denmark. No aggression, except patrolling. No problem for us, although note that the Fascists went over in record time and as complete units."

That was a monkey on everyone's back.

"Comrades Beria and Pekunin have means to ensure that such cooperation between the Fascists and the Allies will not be so smooth elsewhere and will, in fact, further undermine their capability and capacity to fight."

No one asked because they all knew Malinin didn't know either.

"The purpose of our controlled, broad front attack was to draw enemy forces into disposition as early as possible and to conceal our intentions as best we could."

"It was also felt that it was important to permit Diaspora to get underway and affect Allied strategic thinking before we showed our complete hand.

Everyone there knew that and not everyone had agreed with it. However...

"This seems to have worked exactly as was planned, as can be witnessed by the document Comrade Marshal Zhukov has just discussed with you." Not so much of a discussion they all thought, but the list was impressive none the less and, if those soldiers were going to the land of the slant-eyes instead of Europe, then that was all the better for them.

"Our attacks on their command and control weren't as successful as we were first told. We discovered this very morning that Montgomery is actually alive, but incapacitated. The other major players, we did not hurt. Losses amongst our paratroopers and special personnel were extreme, as we expected."

Wishing to be upbeat, he ventured into an area initially of little concern to the military minds there.

"The Zilant operation was wholly successful, with the four locations purged as was hoped. Not of great significance for us of course, but with the bonus of many dead experienced allied officers, including some Corps and Divisional commanders of key American and British units."

There was no point in mentioning casualties.

"The Allies in defence are quite stubborn, although some units are better than others. Intelligence officers in your respective headquarters have compiled a list of fighting qualities based on combat reports and, in general, those divisions that arrived in Europe within the last six months of the fighting, tend to be less capable than those that arrived before."

"In general, it was how we were expecting. The Americans are more aggressive than their British Allies, but generally not as competent in the attack, making many basic errors which have been punished by our forces."

A hubbub of agreement from those whose forces had engaged.

"A word of caution, Comrades. Our initial assessments of the Allies fighting abilities may have been slightly inaccurate. We cannot underestimate either of these nations' forces. The British may not be aggressive but, as Hamburg and Northern Germany have already demonstrated, they are the devil to shift."

Many eyes shifted to Bagramyan, who could only move his weight uncomfortably in his chair by way of agreement.

"Some American units are fanatics. Their paratroopers for one and some of their infantry units stand when even the German would probably have moved back."

Most there knew that and grudgingly admired their adversary because of it.

"There is a report from Comrade Marshal Konev's Front of American Red Indians going wild, breaking a Guards unit in hand to hand combat"

Konev stood with purpose.

"I received that report and immediately investigated it. No substance whatsoever. Examples have been made for loose talk."

Malinin nodded.

"We stand corrected, Comrade Marshal," and by using the 'we' ensured no further wrath would come his way.

Moving quickly on.

"Then there is the French Army."

Tapping Ingolstadt, he turned back to the assembly.

"We broke a whole division of them here. Ill-fortune prevented a full exploitation of the hole and more American and French units have since plugged the hole."

Tapping his way across Southern Germany, he pointed out French divisions that seemed to be moving back to their homeland.

"The purpose of our scaled attack we all know here. The need to get our enemy to commit his forces forward, where our logistics and support is better, bringing him on so we can concentrate upon him in crushing force. It has succeeded, Comrades, although the front lines buckled, his reserve forces moved forward, in blocking positions with very little now left in his reserve to worry us."

He checked a note on his paper.

"We estimate no more than four divisions presently untasked within the allied plans, available as reserves when we break through."

There was no 'if'; there never had been.

"However, this backward movement of the French is unexpected and we do not know what it is."

"Division? A rift in the allies' structure?"

The question came from Bagramyan.

"Not according to Pekunin. He has agents close to matters here," not needing to say within SHAEF and the French Army, "And his information is that relations between Eisenhower and De Gaulle are extremely good and there is no hint of political disunity."

A low animal like sound emanated from Bagramyan.

A growl possibly? Certainly the sound of a man with concerns.

621

He spoke.

"We set much store by the words of our General Pekunin. Do we set too much?"

Zhukov pondered that, as he had pondered it a few times of late. They must trust their Intelligence officers.

Standing up, he took the pointer from Malinin as a sign he had the floor.

"Pekunin is always clear about what he knows and what he suspects. Comrades, so far his intelligence in military matters has been wholly accurate, the Yugoslavian matter apart. The idiot responsible for that has since been dealt with."

Many nodded, some did not.

"We can't always know everything is as it should be. Sometimes, we must go on our gut. Look at what we do know and it all ties in."

A fair point, but still, much faith was being placed in the GRU's intelligence system.

"We cannot get bogged down on this point and we must proceed here."

Passing the pointer back to Malinin, he spoke words to focus his Commander's minds.

"Our question here today is not do we instigate the great attacks of Kingdom39. It's just a question of when."

By sitting down, he made it quite clear that further discussion on that point was not going to take place, leastways not that day.

They moved onto the initiation of second phase and the discussion was fierce.

More tea and food was ordered and staff bringing the samovars and platters into the meeting room were surprised to find relaxed general officers discussing family and friends with each other.

When those not rated for the proceedings had left, Zhukov gestured towards the food and drink.

"Quickly if you please, Comrades. We all have much work to do this day."

In record time, all were seated again, not without a few laughs at Chuikov's expense, as he carried the largest plate of food away to his place.

Zhukov took centre-stage.

"So, in brief, Comrades. Marshal Bagramyan can be ready by 1800hrs today."

He nodded in military deference to a man who knew his business inside out.

"All but 2nd and 3rd Red Banner's can be ready by 1200hrs on Sunday."

Looking at the two without rancour, he continued.

"Marshals Konev and Rossokovksy cannot be ready before Monday morning and, as they have the larger forces and the most engagement so far, we can understand that."

A statement meant to assure both that no slight was to be made of the timing, although Konev did not quite see it that way.

"So again, we come to a Monday, this time the 13th. 0300 hrs."

The time was Zhukov's requirement and had been the subject of much verbal jousting.

Nevertheless, he got his way.

The discussion was at an end.

"Very well, Comrades."

As befitted the moment everyone stood.

"Phase two of Kingdom39 will be initiated at 0300hrs on 13th August."

His monotone delivery scarcely did justice to what he had just ordered and, for the Allies in Germany, it would make all that had gone before look like a fistfight under Queensberry rules.

0951hrs Saturday 11th August 1945, Office of the NKVD Chairman, The Lubyanka, Moscow, USSR.

He had been early into his office, as usual.

Beria sat reading the report, drinking tea and humming quietly to himself. It always paid to be prepared in his business. Even though Marshal Zhukov was travelling to

623

Moscow that very day, to bring the General Secretary and GKO the latest information and planning, Beria was in possession of a document that outlined the discussions and decisions made in the Nordhausen headquarters, just a few hours beforehand.

He noted the mocking comment Zhukov made about him and stowed the information in the deep recesses of his mind, for use on another day.

'That day will come,' Beria assured himself.

He leant back in his chair, savouring the expectation of that moment and found his mind moving once more to Nazarbayeva.

Puzzled by that, he concentrated more on why the offence she gave should be felt more deeply than others who committed worse and more regularly.

'Was it intuition?'

'Sexual discrimination?'

'Revenge I can take any time in any way.'

He looked at the top drawer that held the recent report from Geneva and frowned.

'Why am I now taking a detailed interest in the woman?'

He was no closer to fully understanding the problem when his reverie was interrupted by a powerful, almost excited, knock on his door. A swift eye cast at the clock confirmed that it was still not quite time for his ten o'clock meeting with Pekunin's deputy.

Inviting entry, an NKVD Captain handed Beria two reports marked urgent. One was from a no-nonsense Colonel in the Headquarters intelligence assessment unit, listing its contents as a forwarded report from an NKVD unit in Königsberg, coded for an intelligence gathering operation now being resurrected, as well as a general report on the overall progress of same.

The other, from Deputy Kobulov, reporting on plans for the planting of agents within the forming German forces.

Beria simply cast an eye over the former's file jacket before pulling out a lower drawer and adding it to a modest file he extracted and returned.

624

'Later,' he thought, mentally downgrading the priority on German soldier's families for the moment, but making a firm commitment to ensure the two projects were aware of each other and exchanged information.

He quickly wrote out an order to that effect and set it aside for proper typing up later.

Relaxing back into his chair, he read the contents of the latter report with great care, finding much to celebrate there and reminding himself to ensure that Kobulov didn't take all the credit.

The GRU officer arrived to the second and, to Beria's surprise, it was Pekunin himself. A small plaster was the sole external sign of any wound and further enquiries revealed no long lasting effects on the GRU Chief, making Beria wonder if the previous briefing really had been deliberately ducked by the GRU general.

'Hmmm, an interesting thought, I shall test it later.'

Giving no sign of his inner conversation, Beria gestured Pekunin towards a large chair.

Taking seats either side of the desk, the two exchanged the normal Russian pleasantries of enquiries about wife and children before getting down to the business of Intelligence.

The meeting was scheduled to run for an hour, but surprising both men, the business of the day had run its course shortly after 1040am.

Tea seemed the only reasonable course to take and Beria ordered some immediately.

Settling himself back in his chair, he eyed Pekunin directly, preparing his words.

"Your PodPolkovnik gave a full briefing yesterday, Comrade General, very full indeed."

Pekunin was too old a horse not to know that Beria wasn't praising Tatiana. He could imagine how she might have ruffled a feather or two with the NKVD boss, so he fenced a little.

"She is extremely talented, Comrade. I don't doubt that both you and the General Secretary will have had honest and forthright answers from her. She doesn't do frills and she is

625

not a political animal such as we, Comrade Marshal. I promoted her to PodPolkovnik because she was the best man for the job."

The tea arrived and, leaning around the orderly placing out the accoutrements, Pekunin smiled disarmingly, "You know what I mean."

Beria ceded the point to Pekunin, as well as the post of pourer.

The conversation halted whilst tea was prepared.

Sipping his tea gently, Pekunin continued.

"She is a holder of the highest bravery awards, as you will know. She also has a husband and four sons in military service to the Motherland."

Beria replaced his cup in his saucer.

"Three."

"Three?"

Pekunin knew what Beria meant.

"Three."

Beria knew he had been understood, but it made him feel good to say it a second time.

'Bitch.'

He pulled open the top drawer and extracted a copy of a Red Cross document, obtained by and relayed back through, his vast ring of agents.

"This is a document relating to casualties sustained by Soviet airborne forces engaged on a special operation in Alsace last Monday. I speak of Zilant-4, Comrade General."

The report made its way over the desk and Pekunin was able to see that the Red Cross officially reported interring the remains of *'Vladimir Yurevich Nazarbayev – Senior Lieutenant – 100th Guards Airborne Division'*, along with three hundred and seventeen other members of the Division.

Whilst horrified for Nazarbayeva, the clinically professional side of him continued through the document, reading the listings of healthy and wounded prisoners and he noted the absence of one name from the list.

"He's not here?"

"Quite so, Comrade Pekunin. It seems that Comrade General Makarenko has the devil's own luck, unless he ranks amongst those unidentified bodies. There seem to be at least twenty of our men unaccounted for."

Bringing himself back to Nazarbayeva's loss, the GRU General spoke aloud, for himself as much as for Beria.

"She doesn't know," said Pekunin.

"It seemed the wrong thing to do last night, Comrade General. Perhaps you should have the pleasure?"

In any other man, Pekunin might have put the words down as a slip of the tongue, an incorrect word, or an attempt at black humour. In Beria, he recognised it as decidedly meant and, in that sense, a very real and worrying indication of ill will.

He must find out what had happened during that meeting, but he had not yet had a chance to see her report or speak with her.

Feeling concerned for his protégé, Pekunin changed the subject to something lighter, to enable his mind to work in parallel.

"Talking of Zilant-4, one of our agents picked up a face in Baden-Baden on the 9th. Have your agents supplied you with the names of the Allied and German dead?"

Beria resisted leaning back and retrieving another page of the Red Cross report from his desk drawer. It did not pay to show all one's cards, especially those that don't reflect total success.

"I have some information on which of the green toads escaped, although I am informed they are out of the fight for some time to come."

Reluctantly, Beria reached for the drawer and passed over the brief report.

The GRU General examined the list and realised it was inaccurate.

He savoured his small moment.

"I fear you're misinformed then, Comrade Marshal, for Knocke was seen in the French Baden-Baden Headquarters, intact and unharmed, on the following Wednesday."

For Beria it was of no real significance, in itself, but the fact that the GRU had knowledge he didn't always rankled.

627

"News indeed, Comrade, but of low importance to us I think. We got all the big fish at their Frankfurt base. This Knocke was just a Colonel."

Pekunin started to object.

"Yes, I know, a competent one for sure, but Colonels are twenty to the rouble and Colonels don't win wars, Comrade."

Was that a general statement or yet another warning sign for Tatiana; Pekunin could not decide.

Time brought an end to the proceedings, as the phone rang to let both men know that their cars were ready. One to spirit the GRU head away to a meeting with the General Secretary, the other to take a satisfied NKVD Marshal to his Dacha. Beria intended to have a 'quiet' day with whatever woman would later be procured for him by his trusted NKVD bodyguards, Colonels Sarkisov and Nadaraia.

Beria was a serial rapist, coercing women with talk of freeing loved ones from Gulags, or using just plain basic force to have his way.

The thrill of it excited him beyond measure, as his Packard Limousine took him out of Moscow.

'Perhaps,' he wondered, then finally realised why Nazarbayeva had got so deep under his skin.

'Ah yes, Tatiana,' and he leant back in the deep seats and smiled the smile of a man imagining a future that would definitely come to pass.

'Fuck you.'

Arriving back in his headquarters just before midnight, General Pekunin took his deputy aside and informed him of the heart-rending task he was about to perform. A bottle of vodka was located and, with it in hand, Pekunin sought out Nazarbayeva's office and found her hard at work as usual.

He entered and dismissed her staff.

The next few hours he spent with Nazarbayeva, the woman and mother, in his guise as Pekunin, friend and comforter.

He shared her grief and held her close and they drank vodka together until morning came.

The small matter of Beria's wrath he left for another time.

*The bravest are surely those who have the clearest vision of
what is before them, glory and danger alike, and yet
notwithstanding, go out and meet it.*

Thucydides

CHAPTER 51 – THE HORRORS

<u>0341hrs 11th August 1945, Units of the 1st Guards Tank Army at Stammen, South of Trendelburg, Germany.</u>

Fig#21 - Trendleburg

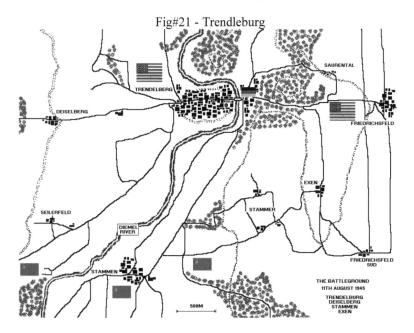

It was an awful night, bringing rain, thunder and
lightning in equal severity, for which the Soviet Commanding
officer was extremely grateful.

Pounding rain and thunder masked the sounds of his
armoured vehicles as they moved forward behind the screen of
skirmishing Siberian infantry, advancing closer to their
objective.

Colonel Fedor Iosifovich Serov stood on the flank of a two hundred metre hill, from where he could overlook his forces in Stammen and those of the enemy in Trendelburg to the north. His binoculars could see no sign of either, but he knew both were there.

Units of the 1st Guards Tank Army had been advancing in relative silence since 2230hrs the previous evening, leaving their positions, west of Hannoversch-Münden. Stealthily leading the way were the men of the nondescript 415th Rifle Division, temporarily attached to 1st Guards for their expertise, a deadly expertise learned from birth in the harshest of environments and finely honed since the Division was sent to the Front from its home base in Vladivostok, Siberia.

Normally more at home in winter, their ability to move swiftly and silently was equally comfortable in the dark of night and on the roads north to Hofgeismar and Reinhardshagen lay the many bodies of those who were their unwitting victims.

Following hard on the heels of the men of the 1323rd Regiment's 2nd Battalion came a company of valuable bridging engineers, tasked with a record time repair of a downed bridge over the River Diemel, just south of Sielen, itself four kilometres south-west of the assault's objective, Trendelburg.

Units of 3rd Army were performing a similar thrust, aimed at driving south and occupying Helmarshausen and Wülmersen.

A simple look at a map would reveal the consequences of Soviet success. One possibility trapped all American forces from the Gottingen area east of the Weser, in which case they would be easily mopped up. The other confined them to an area west of the Weser, but bottled up by the Diemel River, meaning the sole focal point for their escape would be the bridge at Deisel.

This was chosen because the river funnelled the approach into a sock roughly two hundred metres wide, a sock into which desperate enemy forces would flood to reach the safety of the west bank and into which the artillery of two

631

Soviet armies would pour death and destruction on a huge scale.

Into this sock would come the tankers of the 8th US Armored Division, infantry from 83rd US Infantry Division and a swarm of specialists from numerous other units of engineers, artillery et al, all trapped east of the Diemel.

Serov and his special detachment of units from 1st Guards Tank Army were to close the bottom route by occupying Trendelburg and preventing its use. His army commander openly stated the STAVKA order regarding blowing bridges, for the benefit of any NKVD informers on the staff.

As he saw Serov off, he made it absolutely clear that the bridge could go if it was a choice between it and the Americans escaping. None the less, the Colonel understood that the longevity of the bridge and his neck were intimately related.

Knowing the engineers of the 6th Brigade had done a superb job in record time, he had ordered the planned assault for 0400, safe in the knowledge that he was already both sides of the river.

0351hrs 11th August 1945, Soviet attack, Stammen & Friedrichsfeld-Sud, south of Trendelburg, Germany.

Soviet Forces - 11th Guards [Independent] Heavy Tank Regiment, 14th Guards [Independent] Engineer Sapper Battalion, II/2nd Btn, 7th Pontoon-Engineer Brigade, 12th Guards Motorcycle Battalion, 399th Guards Self-Propelled gun Regiment, 22nd Penal Company, all of 1st Guards Tank Army, 1323rd Rifle Regiment of 415th Rifle Division of 89th Rifle Corps [temp attached] Penal Company Zin, of 61st Army, all of 1st Red Banner Central European Front.

Allied Forces – A & C Coys, 1st Btn 330th US Infantry Regiment, C Battery, 453rd AAA Battalion, C Coy, 308th Engineer Battalion all of 83rd US Infantry Division, A & B Troops, 125th Cavalry Squadron, 113th Cavalry Group, 2nd Platoon, A Battery, 226th Searchlight Battalion, C Battery,

554th AAA Battalion, 2nd Platoon, B Company, 247th
Engineer Combat Battalion, C Company, 736th Tank Battalion,
all of US XIX Corps, US Ninth Army, US 12th Army Group.

The thunder and lightning were building in intensity,
adding to the pre-attack nerves of the Russians moving around
south of Trendelburg.

Fig#22 - Trendelburg - Stealthy Attack

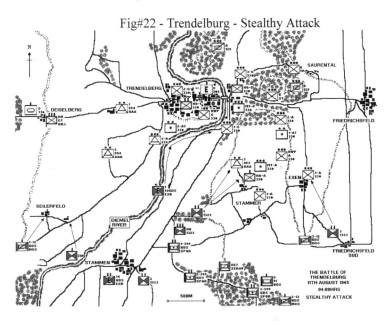

Normally, a Brigade Commander should not be at the
front of his troops, but this was not normal; far from it.

1st Company, 14th Guards Engineer-Sapper was
going in harm's way and Chekov fully intended to be with his
men when the difficult business of the day started in earnest.

The former engineer brigade commander had died two
days previously, probably of untreated appendicitis and its
attendant complications, leaving the popular young Lieutenant
Colonel Chekov in command.

In their own rubber boats and those taken from the rest
of the Brigade, supplemented with small craft 'liberated' from

633

along the river, plus anything that could be sat on that floated, or, in some cases, hanging onto the sides of one of the above, the reinforced company of sappers rode the steady current towards their objective.

Trendelburg had one solid bridge standing and they were to take and hold it, preventing its destruction at all costs.

Chekov checked his watch and silently signalled around him for some extra pace in their advance, paddles and rifle butts digging into the water, adding more energy to the boats northward advance.

Unseen shapes moved in the darkness all over the area that night, in many cases bringing silent death with them before moving on to new victims. A young American sentry taking shelter under his cape, hiding from the fury of the downpour, had his life taken by a soaked apparition. He went without a chance to scream, or even recognise that he was dying on a wicked blade.

Blade and man moved inexorably on into the night, seeking further victims.

The advance group of the 1st Rifle Battalion was tasked to steal quietly into Stammer. 3rd Rifle Battalion was given Exen. On the other side of the Diemel River, 1st Company, 12th Guards Motorcycle Regiment, without their bikes, bore silently down upon Seilerfeld with murderous intent, accompanied by the assault platoon of Zin's Penal Company on their right.

All did bloody work in the driving rain, but none more than 1st Battalion, who butchered the entire 3rd Battery of 453rd AAA Battalion as they slept, moving on to do exactly the same to the headquarters group of A Company, 330th Infantry Regiment.

Two shots split the night.

They were fired by the A Company Headquarters Warrant Officer as he walked in on the deadly business and who managed to pull his trigger twice before was spitted on a long bayonet. However, it seemed that the sound of the Colt was lost in the ferocity of the thunderstorm and their quiet and deadly work continued.

1st Battalion's Siberians had killed sixty-four men in silence.

0352hrs Saturday 11th August 1945, US Front Lines, Stammen, south of Trendelburg, Germany.

Mortar Platoon, A Company, 330th Infantry, had long since acquired a reputation for their ability to scrounge anything anywhere and to cope with the extremes that life, nature and the war, could throw at them.

That was why Major Buck G. Brennan Jr had chosen to venture out into the night, rather than stay in his own miserable, partially dry headquarters.

Accompanied by 1st Lieutenant H.H.Brown and Warrant Officer Frazzoli, he had arrived at the mortar platoon's position and experienced a moment of disbelief, followed by wonder, substituted by suspicion, replaced by panic and finally coming to rest in admiration.

'Sonofabitch'.

Brown laughed quietly and confided to no one in particular.

"You have to hand it to old Caesar, but he sure as shit knows how to get his outfit comfy."

Brennan could not disagree and turned back to examine the view, helpfully illuminated by some sustained lightning.

His mortar platoon had four 81mm mortars and four 60mm mortars, each firing position was covered over with a watertight roof, some of which looked suspiciously like rubber dinghies, although the camouflage tended to disguise the shapes that the lightning tried hard to reveal.

Grinning mortar crew were observing his approach, one or two waving their commander into cover.

Criminals and thieves they may be, thought Brennan, but they are goddamn efficient.

He had the sudden vision of Captain Catesby of the 308th Engineers going mad looking for his equipment and somehow the thought made him grin widely, for he didn't like the man personally.

He then became further distracted by a large irregular shape sat behind the positions.

If it were not for the green colour, he would have sworn it was the USO entertainment tent used by Jack Benny and Ingrid Bergmann some days back.

He took advantage of more of nature's illumination and looked again.

It was.

'Sonofabitch.'

Frazzoli chuckled, saluting Brennan.

"Guess I shouldn't really see this, so I will take off back to the office, Major."

Brennan grinned and slapped his non-coms shoulder as he passed.

A mortar man in a long cape was pointing his Garand at them, determined to follow company standing orders, even if it meant keeping his CO out in the rain a few more seconds.

The niceties were observed and both officers ducked into the shelter, which from the inside could not have been anything else but the show tent.

"Sonofabitch!"

He hadn't meant to say it aloud but it was too late now, he had been heard, as the grins of those warm and dry soldiers lying on warm and dry beds attested to.

A cursory look around told him that everything soldierly had been attended to, from foot inspections through to weapons cleaning. The smell of cooking still hung in the air too, something that had been a disaster for his HQ group that evening.

The mortar unit CO's half-track had been backed up to the rear entrance, from where a US army radio played Glenn Miller and similar, providing background music for a poker school that was reaching its conclusion.

The Major's eyes were drawn to the superbly painted laurel leaves and Roman soldier painted on the rear of the vehicle.

Unable to help himself, he mouthed the familiar words intertwined there.

'We came. We saw. We blew it away.'

Whenever Brennan saw the unit's unofficial insignia, he could never quite work out if he should ban it or not, but mortar platoon was a top-notch outfit, so he cut them plenty of slack.

2nd Lieutenant Finch was lying fast asleep in a cot nearby, oblivious to his commander's presence.

Master Sergeant Julius Augustus Collins looked across to his own boss snoring softly, then up at his company commander, who shook his head in understanding and then gestured comfortably so that Collins knew he didn't need to interrupt his game.

Collins passed the Major a bottle and pointed him at an ammo box stack where he could take the weight of his legs.

Concentrating on the hand, the bald non-com carefully counted out $20 in $1 bills and pushed it forward, announcing a raise.

Cards were thrown down in disgust, until the only other player holding was Lopez, the swarthy little Mexican.

Pulling deeply on a cigar nearly as large as himself, the card player contemplated the Sergeant with apparent disdain.

The Master Sergeant similarly drew heavily on his Cuban, knowing that that Lopez had taken three cards and safe in the knowledge that his own ace-queen flush was good.

After a delay, during which Brennan took a slug of the cool coca-cola and passed it on to Brown, Lopez pushed all his money forward and dropped his cards face down in front of him, staring unblinkingly at Collins.

"All in, muchacho."

The Master Sergeant laughed loudly in triumph, pushing his own stack forward, laughing harder as he threw down his flush in spades and stopped laughing only as Lopez slowly leant forward and started to arrange the pile of bills, his full house of eights on tens, sat proud for all to see.

"Sonofafuckingbitch! You Mexican bandit!"

Lopez was the card king and Collins really though he had him there.

637

Laughter was a good indication of a happy unit and, even in the face of the casualties and defeats of late, this group were high on morale.

"Good morning, Major, Lieutenant Brown. Want me to wake him up?" He indicated the still snoring Finch.

Brennan did need to speak to the officer and was debating the point inside when something registered in his mind, the same thing that was registering in a few minds within his field of vision.

'That wasn't thunder.'

A sentry was through the tent flap within a few seconds.

"Gunfire, two shots, Sir. Perimeter secure."

The man disappeared as quickly as he had arrived.

Finch would have had a gentler awakening a few minutes earlier, but now the tough as nails non-com known as Caesar roared his troops into business at the top of his voice, startling the sleeper into life, then being startled some more when his CO stood over him.

"No time, Finch. We just heard two shots. Some distance away I think. None the less, get your unit ready for bear a-sap. Send a runner to heavy weapons platoon next in line and get them to hustle up here with some extra support."

Leaving the startled lieutenant to gather his wits and his uniform, Brennan cast his eye around the controlled mayhem before him.

Pointing at an old Corporal.

"Watkins, get on that horn and inform all company call Signs that we may have infiltrators and to stay alert."

The Corporal was on the job within seconds.

"Master Sergeant, I want three of your men."

Collins, fully dressed and armed, clicked his fingers at three men, putting them to the duty and ran out into the driving rain.

Major Brennan followed him out and immediately saw that the mortar positions had lost their dinghy protection and were ready to go.

Collins was in conversation with one of his Corporals, taking in the man's information and agitated pointing.

"Major, Runcieman reckons it came from the direction of your hooch."

Brennan nodded.

Collins understood the needs of the moment too.

"More security, Sir," and he gestured to a squad to follow on the heels of the CO's group, steadily picking its way towards the headquarters location.

Safety catches were off.

0400hrs Saturday 11th August 1945, Trendelburg, Germany.

Chekov's men had reached the bridge undiscovered and they quickly moved off the water and into the surrounding undergrowth to wait for the signal.

A special party stole silently under the bridge.

From the darkness under the structure, a red torch flashed twice. The special party received ten further engineers to help them cut wires and make safe the demolition charges prepared and laid by the American defenders.

The designated security force stood watch and was forced to act immediately, pulling a wandering American soldier into the darkness, where his life was ended, all for the want of a pee in the river.

A young sapper took his place, Garand rifle in hand, cape and helmet in position. To any distant observer he looked pretty much the same as any other American doughboy in the storm.

The special party continued with its urgent work, the moment of the attack growing closer.

0412hrs 11th August 1945, US Front Lines, Stammen, Germany.

Brennan and his group approached the farm buildings that comprised his company headquarters, taking in every sight and sound, despite the unrelenting thunderstorm.

It was Brown who saw the boots, or rather the soles. He signalled for a halt and the detail went to ground, watching, listening, tense.

The Lieutenant pointed and eyes followed the direction of his gesture. Drag marks in the grass and US Army issue soles facing them, attached to god knows what, but none the less a warning that something bad was happening.

Collins gestured one of his men forward and the man slipped away, appearing adjacent to the boots some minutes later, making the universal gesture of a finger pulled across the throat, telling them all they needed to know.

Gathering his force together into a defensive perimeter, Brennan discussed options with Brown and Collins.

The thunder grew in intensity until they all realised that it wasn't thunder at all and the flashing away to the north was artillery, not lightning.

Lopez hissed a warning as numerous swiftly moving shapes could be seen running parallel to their position heading northwards.

Whirling around to face east, some of the detail became aware of the sound of engines, both light and heavy.

They did not know that a company of Soviet motorcyclists and armoured cars was hammering past the heights, intent on mischief to the north, or that heavy self-propelled guns were moving up to position themselves on the ridge, east of Stammer.

Roughly where they were presently positioned.

Brennan made a decision to bug out and took his men back the way they had come, all the way to the mortar platoon positions.

The change was marked, with firing positions fully cleared and ready to go, dinghies nowhere to be seen and just a faint suggestion of a collapsed marquee on the ground.

Two .50cal MG teams had arrived from the Heavy Weapons Platoon and these were set up to guard the route from which Brennan emerged, as well as the ridge line to their front.

Caesar immediately spotted a flaw and detailed a half-squad to positions watching the western approaches.

Small arms fire was building to a crescendo, seemingly from locations to the east, punctuated by thunder and dramatised by lightning.

Brennan detailed Brown to investigate whilst he made his way to the halftrack, where Addison Watkins was still working the radio.

"Give me the good news, Corporal."

Watkins tossed off the headset and examined his notes, water dripping off the greaseproof pen notations.

"1st and 3rd Platoons are under attack, big attack, infantry and armour. I just finished on the horn with 3rd and they're bugging out right now, heading this way."

Brennan made his mental changes to the positional map.

"No contact with company HQ, Sir."

"They are off the net, Watkins. The 453rd?"

Watkins checked his notes.

"Nothing heard, Sir."

No more than the Major had expected, given the rush of Soviet infantry they had seen.

"Heavy weps, the anti-tank platoon and 2nd Platoon all report noise but no contact as yet."

Was that good news, Brennan asked himself?

"Battalion HQ is screaming for a sitrep. I just told them what I know, but the Colonel and General Clough both want you on the horn a-sap, Major."

Brennan composed his report in silence, but Brown arrived to trash his preparations before he had even delivered a word.

Taking his commander aside so as not to be overheard, Brown passed on his information.

"Jeez, Buck, but we are in deep shit."

No arguments there.

"We lost 1st and 3rd."

"What the fuck, Harold?"

"3rd Platoon were flushed out of Exen by a horde of reds, figure at least two companies worth on foot and a whole lot more in armoured cars and on motorcycles."

641

Brown had his map in his hand and described the enemy movement with a wet and bloodied finger.

"They headed west, towards Stammer and 1st Platoon."

Buck looked at the painful finger and gave Brown a questioning look.

"I slipped," was the sole explanation forthcoming.

Brennan's mental map was redrawn in an instant.

"1st Platoon moved out of Stammer and bugged out east towards Exen."

So, two platoons, bereft of cover, were moving towards each other in darkness and in the full knowledge that the night held the enemy, but without the faintest idea that the another friendly unit was on the move.

"Great. Go on."

"They engaged each other, from what I could see. No idea on casualties because some huge Russian SP guns turned up and brought fire down on the boys."

"So what happened?"

Brown was embarrassed.

"They surrendered, Buck, the whole two platoons."

Brennan took off his helmet and ran his fingers through his hair.

Taking the moment to compose himself, he worked out his plan.

"Right Harold, get this lot ready to move, except don't break down the mortars yet. Get Caesar onto finding us a route that isn't full of commies. I'm gonna dial in the bad news to the Colonel. Don't get outta sight."

Throwing a cursory salute up, Brown went efficiently about his orders.

Brennan turned to a worried looking Watkins.

He grabbed his shoulder firmly.

"Don't worry, Addison, I'll see you home to your porch in Mobile, come what may. Now get the Colonel on the horn please."

642

0513hrs 11th August 1945, Trendelburg, Germany.

Lieutenant Colonel Chekov's men had not finished their dangerous work by the time the attack started in earnest, but it appeared that the Americans had no orders to blow the bridge in any case. His men, now combat infantry rather than specialists, moved into firing positions, from where they could defend the bridge from all sides.

Fig#23 - Trendelburg - Sound of shots

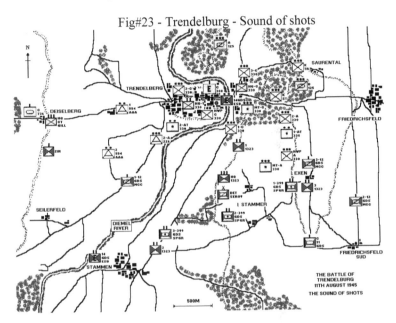

Chekov's orders were to maintain fire discipline and to not reveal their presence unless they were attacked.

A squad of running men clattered over the structure and headed off to the east of the bridge, carefully watched until out of harm's way.

Machine guns started to hammer out their staccato song off to the southeast and, shortly afterwards, mortars closer by began to add to the noise.

As dawn's light began to make itself known, the thunder and lightning started to abate but no one noticed, as man was creating his own type of noisy storm on the Diemal Plain.

Chekov worked out that the 1st Battalion of the Siberians must be attacking enemy positions somewhere near the road from Stammen.

A red-faced and soaking engineer emerged from the water close by, coughing his way up the bank to where the command post, such as it was, had been set.

"Comrade PodPolkovnik, Kapitan Smina requests permission to attack the Amerikanski mortar positions," the dripping man turned and pointed, "Which lie roughly one hundred metres east of the bridge."

A deeper cough to remove the detritus of his swim and the young soldier continued.

"Kapitan Smina states that he believes he can easily destroy the position with the twelve men he has ready and awaits your reply, Comrade PodPolkovnik."

Chekov smiled. Of course it would be Smina who wanted to attack.

And of course, he would let him.

"Tell your Kapitan that he may do so, but he mustn't get involved in anything else, He's to return back once his mission has succeeded, or if it isn't possible. Is that clear, comrade?"

"Yes, Comrade PodPolkovnik. I'll return immediately."

The engineer ran back to the bank and plunged into the river once more.

A figure that Chekov recognised as Smina met the exhausted man at the water's edge. A swift discussion took place before the Captain raised his hand to his CO and organised his section for the attack.

The Engineer commander watched as the group all but melted into the ground beyond the bridge.

All around, the firing was increasing in volume and intensity.

644

Looking at his watch, Chekov correctly calculated that the main advances would now be approaching Deiselburg from the south and Trendelburg from the south-west and southeast.

Whilst Deiselburg was too far away from him for now, he looked out for more opportunity to get involved with the fighting and help his comrades in the infantry and tanks.

His attention was suddenly focussed on intense firing closer at hand, as Smina launched his attack. There was no doubt that it had an immediate effect, the distinctive mortar sounds ceasing within seconds, replaced by the unmistakable sound of PPSH sub-machine guns hard at work.

He suddenly remembered the engineer who had donned the American uniform and looked for him, but the man was experienced enough to have already cast off the enemy trappings.

'No sense in getting shot by your own side.'

A new sound emanated from the south-west, a sound unlike anything he or his men had heard before; a low ripping of cloth. Whatever it was, Chekov suspected it was bad news for someone.

The sound came from an M16 quad .50cal AA mount that was visiting hell upon the motorcycles and armoured cars of the 12th Guards, cutting them down as they tested the Seilerfeld road approach to Trendelburg.

The noise at the mortar position was abating and Chekov was watching carefully for signs of his men returning.

Eleven men had gone forth and the first of them scurried back, carrying a second senseless over his shoulders.

The next two men were supporting another, whose screams rose over the increasing sounds of nearby battle. He had no legs.

Four more men slid into view, one of them favouring a wounded side.

'No more?'

Turning to question his trusted Starshina, he saw that the man was already on his way to the water, preparing to swim across and find out what had happened, in company with another NCO he didn't recognise from the back.

Chekov noted with grim satisfaction that the mortars had not started again.

A Mosin rifle on his side of the river fired and was joined by other weapons as his troops engaged a small group of American infantry that was falling back down the eastern bank of the river. Most were successfully dropped to the ground and the others ran back to where they had come from, only to fall back into the hands of the advancing 1st/1323rd Rifles.

As the sunlight began to spread further, the welcoming shapes of BA64 armoured cars and ISU-152 self-propelled guns became evident on the southern approach road.

More enemy soldiers emerged from the north-west side of the bridge, some of whom were immediately killed by the nearby engineers.

However, this new enemy was a full company of American engineers from the 308th Engineer Battalion, now galvanised by orders to protect the bridge, coincidentally defended by Soviet engineers of the 14th Guards Sappers with the precise same instructions.

A modest fire started from the buildings to the west of the bridge, which began steadily increasing, as more American troops were set to the task.

It now seemed to Chekov that a severe battle was taking place to the south-west of Trendelburg, as well as on his own doorstep.

A panting Senior Sergeant, the NCO he had not recognised, arrived with a report, rivulets of water running off the shivering man.

"Comrade PodPolkovnik, the attack was successful and the mortars have been destroyed with grenades or by smashing sights. Comrade Kapitan Smina was wounded in both legs and he ordered his men to withdraw while he covered them."

Chekov would have expected no less from Smina.

"Serzhant Iska saw him disarmed and taken alive."

'*Good,*' thought Chekov, '*The Motherland will have need of such men when this abomination is concluded.*'

"Starshina Neltsin says that, with your permission, he'll remain on the east bank to assist."

646

"Agreed. Thank you, Abramov."

He considered that news.

Neltsin wouldn't do that unless there was good reason.

'Good luck and stay safe, Mikhail, my old comrade.'

Bringing himself from his thoughts, he grabbed a blanket from the pile next to the ammunition boxes and passed it to the NCO, who had done the river there and back in record time.

"Thank you for your effort, young Abramov. Get yourself dry, Comrade. There'll be hot work here for you, soon enough."

The firing immediately next to his position took on an almost desperate quality and he saw his men rise to receive a charge.

Abramov threw aside the blanket and fell, all in the same motion, the grenade exploding behind him, killing him instantly, punctured by a score of hot fragments.

Chekov was aware of two thumps on his right side but felt nothing, as a mixture of courage and fear drove him forward to repel the assault, his men grabbing their close-combat weapons.

He fumbled for his Tokarev automatic.

Shouting for reinforcements, he charged up the bank into what had instantly become a whirling mass of bodies.

Standing back from the throng, he careful selected target after target, dropping each American engineer with an aimed shot, turning the tide single-handedly and allowing his men to gain the upper hand.

One wounded enemy Sergeant rushed at him, bayonet lunging, but Chekov sidestepped it, allowing momentum to carry the exhausted American down the bank. He shot him in the back of the neck, dropping him into the water to drown in a combination of blood and river water.

One of his own men cartwheeled dramatically away, the top of his head distorted by the impact of a bullet fired from vengeful Americans supporting from the buildings, who had witnessed the massacre of the assault party.

647

Another wounded sapper was dragged into cover before both sides recommenced a steady exchange of fire at distance.

Suddenly feeling his own aches and pains, Chekov examined himself. A lump had been taken out of his right calf. Painful now the adrenalin was abating, but no more than that.

The pain in his hip was worse and required him to drop his waist belt to examine the area.

His PPSH had been struck by a grenade fragment and the wound in his hip was actually caused by splinters from the sub-machine gun's wooden stock. He pulled out three obvious ones and felt instant relief, but the sharp stabs of pain told him there were more present.

His PPSH was of no use, neither was his Tokarev, as he had no more ammunition for it.

Looking around, he took up the rifle and bayonet his recent attacker had carried.

With no qualms, he grabbed the legs of the dead body, lying half in, half out of the water, dragging it ashore.

Undoing the belt containing the rifle's ammo, Chekov tried to remember how to use the impressive weapon. Loading an eight round clip, he shouldered the rifle and moved around his bloodied engineers getting reports, encouraging the living and noting the dead.

Smina was in pain, but he reasoned that at least he was alive to feel it.

Gritting his teeth, he dragged himself up on a sandbag position and surveyed the scene of his attack. Dead Americans were everywhere, his assault force's only fatal casualty peacefully at rest, arms strangely but neatly folded, lying where he had been dropped by a single rifle bullet.

Smina nodded at the familiar corpse, acknowledging the man's bravery in the attack, remembering the veteran in happier times and promising the stilled heart that he would recommend him for the valour award he deserved for his actions.

The sun was rising and the Kapitan turned his face upwards, smiling, half in wonder at seeing a new sunrise and half in pleasure at ensuring his men escaped.

His smile was not well received by his enemy.

"What the fuck are you smiling about, you bastard?"

Smina did not speak a word of English, but he didn't need to, understanding by the tone alone that his last sunrise had come.

The 1st Lieutenant who, until eleven minutes ago, had commanded the mortar platoon of C Coy 330th Infantry, had survived his men, but only just.

Dragging himself upright, blood running freely from his shattered left arm, he unbuckled his holster and walked slowly over to the wounded Russian.

"Smile at this, you murdering son of a fucking bitch."

The first bullet was enough, but he discharged all seven to assuage his anger.

0512hrs Saturday, 11th August 1945, Exen, south of Trendelburg, Germany.

Brennan's 1st and 3rd Platoons were rounded up by a platoon of Guardsmen from the 12th Guards Motorcycle Battalion and chivvied along at the point of a bayonet.

The Junior Lieutenant in command selected a brick outhouse on the west side of Exen and directed his men to secure the prisoners inside.

The space would probably have comfortably housed a dozen men, but thirty-nine survivors were shoehorned into the derelict structure, the wounded, as well as the fit.

Leaving a section of twelve men to guard them, he took the rest off to perform a tragic duty.

Quickly, they buried the twenty-one dead that his 3rd Company had suffered during the assault on Exen, including the company commander, an extremely popular officer, who was his friend, and the unit's female radio operator, who was his lover.

The Lieutenant spoke words of farewell over the graves of his comrades and then he spoke no more. Taking up a flamethrower, he strapped it on and transformed the derelict building and its human contents into a sea of fire.

As both screams and flames rose higher, his shocked men watched as he cried and, stricken with grief, blew his own brains out.

0512hrs Saturday,11th August. Trendelburg, Germany.

Chekov was now in a desperate position, under attack from both sides. On the positive side was the fact that his infantry comrades were nearly up to his positions on the east side of the river, the SP guns firing in direct support.

On the other side, the battle was obviously hotting up to the west side of the town, but he was under increasing pressure from the engineer enemy and what appeared to be some infantry reinforcements.

As he watched the east bank, one of the SP's took a hit on its flank, followed by three others, that transformed it into scrap metal and immolated the crew.

The SP unit oriented to face the threat from the other side of the river and the support they offered was temporarily lost.

However, some of the Siberians bravely pressed forward and linked up with his troops on the east bank.

None the less, the situation remained grim there, as the enemy launched a determined counter-attack at the same time.

Whether coordinated or not, the west side increased its rate of fire and more Americans swept forward. Small calibre mortar shells had been landing in and around the Soviet position for some time now, but these stopped, for fear of causing friendly casualties.

A vehicle, the like of which Chekov had previously only seen from a distance, rattled round the corner immediately opposite the bridge and the world exploded.

Such vehicles had been supplied to the Red Army under lend-lease, but he had never seen them in action and certainly never been on the receiving end.

650

The quad .50cal mount was being used to good effect, eating away at the edge of the rise where his men were in cover. In horror, the Lieutenant Colonel watched as the heavy calibre bullet stream chewed the earth and stone apart, reducing the cover to a nothing in seconds, moving on to savage the soft flesh beyond.

Within a heartbeat, the deadly fire transformed five of his men into bloodied lumps of meat.

The lethal gun mount switched to the other side of the road and repeated its butcher's work there.

Chekov's shocked engineers recoiled from the attack, ceding the edge of the rise to the attackers and, in doing so, placing themselves in the utmost danger.

Chekov acted quickly.

He had seen the Garand used when his unit had a shooting competition with some American troops during the celebrations in May, a contest his troops had won very convincingly. It was then he had seen the loading process he had already performed. However, each weapon has its own distinct characteristics, which he would have to learn in combat.

He pulled the unfamiliar weapon into his shoulder and took aim at the fraction of the halftrack gunner that he could see.

Discharging the rifle's eight rounds completely, he shouted to his surviving men.

"Prepare grenades!"

Those retaining their senses grabbed grenades and readied themselves.

The fire from the AA halftrack had stopped, but only because the ammunition had run out. Chekov had missed his target.

However, the loaders were vulnerable and he fumbled for another clip as he watched the enemy assault wave close.

He caught an inexperienced finger as he pushed down, yelping as metal sliced flesh. The shock and surprise, more than the pain, caused him to drop the eight round charger on the muddy ground.

651

He reached for another, successfully drove it home and brought the weapon up.

Some of the attackers saw him too. Bullets sprayed from bouncing weapons fired by frightened running men with heaving chests, all inaccurate. Chekov remained unscathed.

However, a rifleman at a window supporting the attack was better placed and fired a bullet that struck Chekov's left arm. Fortunately for the Lieutenant Colonel, it was an M1 Carbine, which penetrated without doing major damage.

"Grenades, throw!"

His men launched their explosives up and into the assault force, causing carnage.

Despite his arm wound, Chekov managed to get off aimed shots at the reloading crew and dropped one to the floor of the halftrack.

His men regained the edge of the rise and fired into the surviving attackers, receiving casualties in turn from the supporting infantry.

The bodies were mounting up and nothing was being gained by either side.

The AA halftrack backed off, probably to re-ammo out of sight.

A few Americans reached the defenders and again desperate close fighting ensued.

An American, armed with a Thompson sub-machine gun, was felled by a single shot from across the river. Chekov quickly turned to see a casual wave from a grinning Starshina Neltsin, who chambered another round in his Mosin-Nagant rifle and turned back to his own problems once more.

One bloodied US Corporal continued gouging out the eyes of the sapper unit's youngest soldier, even as others were bayoneting and hacking at him with spades.

He fell dead onto his blinded enemy, the young boy screaming with pain and fear as they dragged the mangled corpse off him.

The combination of Siberians and engineers on the east side of the bridge were heavily engaged by infantry, both American and German from reports.

Chekov's position was precarious, as it seemed that the south-west prong of the Soviet assault had been blunted and the southeastern thrust was heavily engaged.

One moment of relief was brought when an ISU-152 spotted the returning AA halftrack. The vehicle had fired less than a second's burst before it and the crew were struck by a heavy 152mm shell, flesh and metal immediately converted to small pieces and driven sideways and backwards into the adjacent house, causing further casualties amongst the infantry firing from there.

His position on the east bank was now in great jeopardy, as two M5 Stuart light tanks and a half-track rushed into sight.

More Siberian infantrymen had siphoned up the bank into the defence, but it seemed only a matter of time before the position was broken.

Chekov thought the situation through. He had to hold no matter what.

Looking at the heavy self-propelled guns, he worked the problem.

'The ISU's can't engage the enemy light tanks, but it's the infantry that's more of a threat.'

In that he was wrong but didn't realise it at that moment.

'Obviously the enemy wants the bridge intact too or mortars and artillery would be falling on our heads.'

'Can't radio the ISU's to fire at the enemy positions on the west bank and they obviously won't fire unless they have a recognised target.'

A soaked engineer Kaporal interrupted his thought process.

"Comrade PodPolkovnik, the enemy have been driven back once more, but we are very low on ammunition. Leytenant Munin has stripped our dead and that of the enemy for weapons and ammunition, but he says it's unlikely that we can hold another attack."

There was little to be said by way of positive response.

Gripping the Kaporal's shoulder, he responded with all he had to give.

"Tell Leytenant Munin that the rest of our battalion is on its way. We've but to hold for another quarter of an hour, clear?"

"Yes, Comrade PodPolkovnik, clear."

"Go back now... and thank you, Comrade."

The Kaporal rushed back to the river and dived headlong into it, returning to pass on the news of impending relief.

Chekov hated himself for it, for he doubted that the rest of his unit would arrive within that time scale.

As it happened, they were already over the river and had been sent into the fighting south-west of Trendelburg, where the Americans had been more than holding their own.

Returning to his thoughts, he concluded that, barring a miracle, there was little to prevent the loss of his command and the bridge.

'If only the radio hadn't been lost in the river, maybe.....'

Standing upright, he tugged down his tunic, ending such self-pitying thoughts.

Speaking aloud, he summoned his inner-strength.

"You are a PodPolkovnik in the Red Army. Now act like one."

He laughed and summoned a nearby Yefreytor, instructing the man to get a section together to strip arms and ammunition from friend and enemy alike, ready for the next assault.

Polkovnik Serov had moved forward from Stammen, too far forward for his staff's liking, taking up a position on the edge of the heights, some two hundred metres north-west of Stammer.

From there he could add visual images to the flow of reports that were bombarding his staff, or more precisely add visual images ruined by the heavy rain, which was still descending unabated.

Behind him, to the southeast, lay the detritus of a destroyed enemy AA unit, all done with the silent edged weapons carried by his Siberian troops.

Clearly a lot was going wrong on the west bank and he had spent a few heated minutes on the radio to the commander of the bridging engineers near Seilen to ensure the tanks could get across very soon. The Kapitan of Engineers understood what was at stake for the army and was now under no illusions as to what was at stake for him personally.

Sweeping the battlefield, Serov was appalled to see some American tanks on the Deiselberg Rise taking his troops under fire in the valley below, although he appreciated the fact that they were not deploying to Trendelburg, which might have caused serious problems.

None the less, it was hard on the Guards and Penal troops, who had already suffered greatly at the hands of enemy AA weapons in the valley.

He had been able to help with removing that American force and the destruction of a nearby enemy anti-tank unit, by use of some well placed artillery.

Soon he hoped to have some airpower to back up his under-pressure force.

Moving his glasses and scanning Trendelburg, his eyes were drawn to its most noticeable landmark, the Rapunzel Tower, which was aflame after receiving the attention of one of his ISU gunners.

He could not see the bridge, obscured as it was by smoke, but that smoke meant that someone was still fighting and he knew that Chekov would not let him down.

The infantry of 1st Battalion, 1323rd Rifles had taken murderous casualties from enemy mortars and then dug-in infantry, firing from south-east of the bridge.

The American mortars seemed to have switched their fire elsewhere, for now. The enemy infantry had been driven back in disarray, but 1st Battalion was a spent force.

One unit of SP's from 2nd/399th had been ordered to take the American armour west of the river under fire, the other to proceed on orders to cover the approaches from the east.

655

That latter unit had recently reported that they had crushed an American counter-attack on the heights to his northeast.

Guards motorcycle troops and the 3rd Battalion of Siberians had overrun American units on the heights and joined battle with another enemy infantry group in the woods, on the northern edge of the high ground.

They had been attacked on their eastern flank by American light tanks and half-tracks, which were repulsed.

Serov assumed this was the same attack as the SP's of 2nd/399th had reported driven off.

He had edged his reserves forwards, but had already committed the remaining engineer-sappers of Chekov's brigade to get over the river and help drive into Trendelburg.

That left him with 3rd/399th's ISU-152's and the infantry of 2nd Btn/1323rd Rifles.

He hated not having anything left in his bag but there was no choice, as 1st Battalion simply did not have the strength any more.

"Order the 2nd Rifle Battalion to advance at top speed into Trendelburg, priority to support the bridge defenders, keeping to the east bank at all times. Order C Company of the 11th Guards Tanks to drive at high speed to support 3rd Battalion. Warn both about the enemy tanks at Deiselberg."

He waited as the Kapitan finished taking his notes.

"Order 3rd/399th to move up to...." Serov stepped back under the rough shelter his staff had erected and hurriedly camouflaged, grabbing the edge of the map table, his finger prescribing the river shape, ending up at the bulge two hundred metres south of Trendelburg, "Here... and engage the Amerikanski at Deiselberg."

Pausing for a second, he added.

"Tell them also to be aware of friendly tanks from 11th Guards coming up on the east bank. No accidents."

The Kapitan saluted and moved to the radio operator. The messages were relayed in good time and Serov received a report that all units were moving.

656

Ackowledging the information, one thought was all-consuming, as he stood desperately probing the smoke with his binoculars.

'Where is Chekov?'

Major Brennan and the survivors of A Company had collectively held their breath as enemy infantry and armour moved past them on all sides.

The huge SP guns, although they came closest of all, failed to realise they had driven through the hiding place of a large number of desperate men.

Forty-eight desperate men to be precise.

Holding a quick meeting with Brown, Finch and Collins, the matter was laid out in easily understood terms.

There would be no surrender.

Equally, it was pointless to stay and fight for a position already behind enemy lines.

It was swiftly decided that safety lay the other side of the Diemel River.

After all, Mortar Platoon had the means and three usable dinghies were ready to be dragged from under their camouflage.

The half-tracks would be left in place after being wrecked, an escape on foot being most likely to succeed.

A heated exchange on the perimeter behind them interrupted their conversation.

Collins stepped off smartly to sort it out whilst the officers continued.

Brown was finger tracing his suggested route to the river when he became aware of the look on his Major's face.

Following the direction of Brennan's gaze, he saw Caesar, or rather Caesar looking like he had never looked before.

For once, the man seemed lost for words.

There was no time for sensitivity and so Brennan prompted the man.

"Go on, Caesar?"

657

They sensed that Collins was composing himself, which made the three officers very wary indeed.

"Two boys from 3rd Platoon just blundered past and we pulled 'em in quick. Seems they have a story to tell, Major."

This time no one interrupted the man.

"The bastards killed the boys who surrendered, torched them up in a building with a flamethrower, every last man of them. Over forty from 1st and 3rd, so these two say."

Brennan and Finch had no words.

"Mother of God, that has to be a mistake, Collins!"

The tough non-com shook his head.

"No mistake, Lieutenant. These two are steady doughs, good soldiers who bugged out and didn't surrender. They know what they saw."

Brennan took an audible deep breath.

"OK, this changes nothing, but we sure as shit ain't gonna surrender no matter what."

He got no argument on that score.

"Let's go with what we have, pick up what we can equipment wise as we travel and use this damn rain to our advantage while we can."

A chorus of 'yessir's' marked an end to the group and they split up to get their troops moving.

At Trendelburg Bridge, the end was in sight.

The west bank had held, but only just. This time the attack was broken up with small arms and phosphorous grenades and the smell of roasted flesh was all-pervading, as Chekov scurried amongst his men, checking their wounds and encouraging them to one final effort.

Even though this last attack had been pressed home hard, it seemed to falter more quickly than the others and Chekov used that as a sign to his exhausted men that their relief was close at hand.

He surveyed the scene in front of his positions, risking attracting enemy fire in order to assess the situation.

Despite the downpour, two bodies were burning fiercely, probably Americans, both victims of the same phosphorous grenade. They were lying in an X shape, one on the other.

As he ripped his gaze away from the awful sight, a grenade on one corpse exploded and caused further indignity to the dead men.

Fig#24 - Trendelburg - The Fall

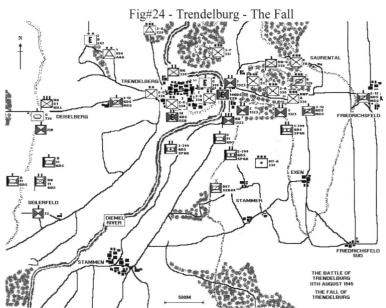

There seemed no sign of any of the covering infantry force in the buildings and, in fact, no sign of any life whatsoever in Trendelburg itself.

Detailing a reliable old sapper to keep watch, he sat down and stared across at the east bank.

Unfortunately for his beloved engineers, there was no sign of life there either.

Involved in his own battle for survival, he had only managed snatches of the sights of that action, seeing only a portion of what had happened to the east, but it had been horrible enough as it was.

659

A group of A Sqdn 125th Cavalry had struck hard into his men.

He remembered a quick vision of the American light tanks being stalked by the Kaporal who had swum the river.

When he looked around again one of the tanks was burning fiercely, but of the Kaporal there was no sign.

"I must find out about him," he vocalised the thought in his weariness, knowing full well the man was dead.

The other M5 Stuart had got through to the bank, its track marks not yet fully washed away by the rain.

Driving up and down, it had either run over the sheltering engineers, forced them into the river, or up and over the edge of their safe haven.

Its silent hulk was partially in the water adjacent to the bridge, where a Siberian rifleman with a liberated panzerfaust had stopped it, but not before it had wrought havoc on his engineers.

Chekov winced at the memory of the gun firing and his men being mown down, not knowing that the 37mm carried by the Stuart could fire a canister round, which acted like a high powered shotgun, carving swathes through the defenders on both sides of the river.

More friendly forces were now arriving on both sides of the bridge and Chekov was buoyed when a platoon of his own engineers rushed in, looking for their comrades.

Their relief at finding some alive turned to shock and anger at the number of their comrades that had been killed and wounded.

Fighting was still going on to the east and further to the west, but Trendelburg itself had fallen silent.

Medical orderlies started to bring relief to the wounded. Chekov waved away one who approached him, deciding to go in search of survivors on the east bank.

He walked the bridge as best he could, sharp pains in his hip and with a stiffening leg, looking down, eyes flitting from abhorrence to abhorrence, seeking the living amongst the piles of dead and finding none.

There was Leytenant Munin, laid open by canister shot, the man who received news of becoming a father on the night of the great attack.

As if the corpse could hear him, Chekov gave him his promise.

'Your son will hear of the man that was his father, Andrey. Thank you.'

His men lay everywhere he looked and it was more than he could bear.

Moving to the south edge of the bridge to avoid the scrutiny of the medics working amongst his dead, he leant on the wooden rail and his watery eyes found the body of Neltsin.

'Not you too, Mikhai,l my old comrade?'

He literally sagged onto the side of the bridge, his sight filled with the horrible vision of his senior non-com and fighting comrade of many battles lying disembowelled on the bank.

He became aware of a presence and turned to see a smoke-blackened Serzhant standing next to him, taking in the same vision as he.

"Is there anyone left, Comrade PodPolkovnik?"

Chekov turned again to the man, eyebrows wrinkled in concentration.

"Iska? Serzhant Iska?"

"Yes, Comrade PodPolkovnik, it is me, minus a bit here and there."

Chekov now noted the new bandages in place.

"Can you walk, Pavel Stefanovich?"

Even after everything that had happened since they reached the bridge, Iska was taken aback by his commander's use of his names.

"Yes Comrade PodPolkovnik, I can walk."

With one last look at the remains of Neltsin, Chekov turned and headed east.

"Come Iska, let us see what mischief our Comrade Smina visited upon the Amerikanski."

The two walked silently, both suffering from leg wounds and by the time they had reached the US mortar positions, six more east-bank engineer survivors had joined them.

With professional eyes, they looked at the work of Smina and his assault force.

It was Iska who found the body, features unrecognisable, rank markings and bodily size alone giving voice to the identity.

Chekov and the others were alerted by the animal like sound that was escaping Iska's mouth.

"Noooooooo!"

The Lieutenant Colonel hobbled to Iska's side.

"What's this, what's this?"

Chekov was stunned.

Iska had fallen silent.

"You saw him captured you said, you saw him taken alive you said."

It was not an accusation, even though it sounded like one. It was a man avoiding the bitter truth crafted by his own eyes.

"They fucking killed him, fucking executed him!" howled Iska, "Bastards!"

The Lieutenant Colonel, not for the first time that day, drew deeply on the sodden smoky air and took hold of himself.

"No, Comrade Serzhant Iska."

He pointed sharply at the river behind him.

"THAT.... back there....that was killing, THAT was execution. THIS..." he turned back and swept his hand over the corpse of his best officer, "THIS was murder!"

Moving forward to where a dead enemy officer lay, still with pistol in hand, Chekov grabbed the man's jacket and rolled the corpse over, the badly damaged left arm flopping grotesquely, shattered bone protruding through the material of his jacket.

Chekov produced a knife and pulled on the divisional insignia, tainted with the dead man's blood.

He separated it from the jacket with a few twists of his blade.

662

"Comrades, each of you take one of these. There are plenty about here. We will meet these men again and when we do, there will be a bloody vengeance for our comrades."

He looked more closely at the black triangular patch, with a strange pattern of golden orange straight lines and circles and spat on it with real venom and malice.

As far as any observer could see, it was to the bloody inanimate patch he spoke, but in his mind he spoke to Kapitan Smina, to Leytenant Munin, to his dead engineers at the bridge and to Starshina Mikhail Neltsin, his friend.

"We will meet them again… and there will be a reckoning."

0620hrs Saturday, 11th August 1945, Stammen Heights, Germany.

The American defenders of Trendelburg had melted away, helped in their escape by a renewed downpour.

That same surge in rainfall prematurely concluded the exchange between the Shermans on the rise at Deiselberg and the IS-II's's and ISU-152's on the east bank of the Diemel.

Both sides had scored hits and Serov had to concede that the American gunnery had been better, four ISU's and three IS-II's lost in the exchange. His vision was obscured, but at least five distinct columns of smoke rose from where the US tanks had stood to exchange shots.

That increased to seven in one second as the remaining two companies of the 11th Guards Heavy Tank Regiment arrived on the flank of the defending US armored unit.

The Colonel expected the defenders to withdraw and turned his attention elsewhere.

Reports from Penal Company Zin placed them on the outskirts of Deiselberg. Mentally correcting himself, Serov reduced Zin from a company to about a full platoon strength.

According to reports, Zin's unit had suffered horrendously at the hands of the automatic AA weapons they faced on the plain.

663

14th Guards Sappers had taken full control of Trendelburg and he had not been able to contain his relief that Chekov had survived the battle.

1st Battalion of the 1323rd Rifles had been hit very hard and was being pulled back into the east bank part of Trendelburg and given time to sort itself out as best it could.

2nd and 3rd Battalions had pushed hard and dislodged the defenders from their positions in the woods and pressed them back beyond Saurenthal. Two units of Germans, more militia than proper soldiers, had been the very devil to shift and many of his men had been killed in the wooded valley to the east of Trendelburg.

Earlier, the 2nd Battalion of the Guards Motorcyclists had taken Friedrichsfeld without loss and had been bolstered by the subsequent arrival of the 3rd Battalion.

The 7th's Bridging Engineer officer had saved himself just in time, but had been presented with a new problem as the last IS-II from A Company had partially collapsed the bridge. Efforts were in progress to extricate the forty-five tons of Soviet heavy tank from the structure and effect repairs.

Ever the martinet, Serov had no intention of letting up on the unfortunate Kapitan, even though the Trendelburg Bridge was safely in friendly hands.

He smiled at that thought, but the smile disappeared as quickly as it arrived, when he remembered the first casualty reports from the scene. He had ordered Chekov's battered company back to the relative safety of Stammen, partially to ease their burden, but partially so he did not have to look Chekov in the eye this day. His Leytenant had asked how many trucks would be needed.

The answer had said a great deal.

One.

'Not this day,' Serov repeated to himself, imagining the pain present in the younger man.

Another report from the 1323rd's senior medical officer stated that a casualty station had been established near the burning Rapunzel Tower and that it was already overflowing with wounded.

Serov had radioed back for more medical assets and was surprised to receive them without having to fight for them.

It had been the same when he had requested more infantry reinforcements. 22nd Penal Company was already on the field and there were more troops coming.

Clearly, the Army Commander was a happy man.

"Time to move. Five minutes, Comrades."

A sudden flurry of activity showed he had been heard and understood.

"Kapitan Fleurov, contact 14th Guards and request a suitable location for us to set up in the town... and get directions."

The Kapitan saluted and changed direction smoothly.

The Colonel sauntered off to the rear of the slope that overlooking Stammer and sampled one of his stash of captured American cigarettes as his staff broke down the mobile HQ.

Enjoying the cigarette away from the hubbub of command, he closed his eyes and dreamt of himself at home with his wife, playing his accordion as she sung her songs. Startling himself from his reverie, he checked his watch.

According to his calculations, he had run slightly over the five minutes, so he fully expected his staff to be ready when he walked back.

He became aware of a dull insistent ache and his brain reminded him that his bladder only had so much capacity.

In the time honoured tradition of man, regardless of nationality, he sought a convenient spot to relieve himself and located a patch of scrub just off to his left.

Manoeuvring his trousers as needed, he let relief flood over him.

The ecstasy of the moment was interrupted.

"Sonofabitch!"

He looked down into the scrub in time to see a bayonet thrust upwards and stop just short of his pride and joy, whilst another hand, containing a pistol, emerged into view, attached to an indistinct shape in the undergrowth.

No words were necessary and he moved as directed by the waved directions of the pistol, rounding the scrub and finding himself in the middle of about twenty American soldiers.

'I'll have Haganski's hide for this,' he thought, failing to appreciate his predicament.

There was muted conversation amongst his captors, but nothing that seemed threatening.

The large soldier, 'is he a Sergeant', spoke to two others, whilst the majority of the Americans kept their eyes firmly on his headquarters group.

Had he known of the events at Exen, Serov would not have been so calm.

"Ok then boys. He's yours. Silent and quick."

Collins sidestepped to let the two survivors of 3rd Platoon do the job.

The older man walked up to Serov and launched his rifle butt straight into the Soviet officer's mouth, smashing teeth and breaking his jaw, blood flying as the man's head recoiled from the blow.

Still conscious, the Soviet Colonel fell to the ground.

The soldier carefully placed the butt of his rifle on the terrible wound and pushed hard, stifling any sound Serov was capable of.

Brennan and Collins watched dispassionately. It was not to the Geneva Convention, but neither of them cared a damn.

The younger soldier slid his bayonet into Serov's open flies and destroyed his penis and testicles in a rapid sawing motion.

The rifle butt pressed harder as a high-pitched squeal tried hard to escape.

Withdrawing the bloodied bayonet, the emotionless young soldier planted his left boot on the awful wound and pushed his weight down hard, steadying himself for a powerful lunge.

That lunge caught Serov in the upper chest and mercifully extinguished the pain instantly.

666

His corpse never felt the rain turn warm as his killers relieved themselves in a final act of vengeance.

It was Brown's group that went in first and the few shots fired were probably lost in the general hubbub of the battlefield.

Seventeen men and women had stood before the charge. Ten now faced the attackers, pawing at the sky in surrender.

Each was forced to their knees and, in turn, bayoneted to death. The two women were first to die and were quickly dispatched. However, after them, each death became more creative as the killers tried to outdo each other.

Brennan, Brown and Collins were stood together observing, when the horror of it all clearly broke through the red mist.

"What have we done?" asked Brennan, an appalled and pained look distorting his face.

"Jesus Buck, we've become animals."

Collins said nothing, but couldn't disagree with Brown, especially as he could see the same thought processes going on in the minds of his soldiers. So much so that the last man on his knees was not executed, the horrified GI who had stood in judgement on him having unclipped his bayonet and slid the virgin blade back into it's scabbard very deliberately.

The old soldier from C Coy took his place and, with an already bloody stock, stove in the back of the last Russian's head, but he did not delight in the killing and ensured the man died instantly.

The survivors felt cold and tired, their motivation and energy all consumed by the anger that had died at the same time as the Russian prisoners.

It seemed that only Collins wasn't paralysed by it all. He walked into the middle of the disorganised group and started to rap out orders, waking them from their malaise and bringing them back into some semblance of a fighting unit.

Brown shook the party out into new squads. Brennan, jolted from his own personal waking nightmare by a steady

667

encouraging hand gripping his shoulder, was now accompanying the owner of that hand in a search for Finch and it was Collins who found the officer, some thirty yards from the Soviet position.

"Reckon he musta tripped and fallen during the run in, Major. Neck's broke."

Brennan thought for a few seconds.

"Get his body put in one of the dinghies and we'll use it as a stretcher."

Collins started his objection but was cut off short by a tried and stressed officer.

"I am not leaving him here, not," and he pointed squarely at the line of murdered Soviet soldiers, "Not with that nearby. We owe him more than that, Caesar."

There was no more to be said, so Collins doubled away to organise the recovery of his officer.

Prudently, Brennan moved his group on swiftly, moving down the line of trees towards the river beyond.

0655hrs Saturday 11th August 1945, Stammen, Germany.

Chekov actually had more men left than would fit in a lorry comfortably, but he still managed to shoehorn thirty-three men, himself and cargo into a space more readily used by twenty-four.

The battered lorry slowly carried him and the survivors away from Trendelburg and towards the promised peace and quiet of Stammen.

A working suspension had long since become a distant memory for the ancient weather beaten driver, but that didn't stop him from hitting nearly every dip and pothole on the road back.

Even the cessation of the rain didn't ease the pain of the journey, as potholes filled with water looked very much like puddles unless you looked closely. In any case, Chekov was convinced the old fool was blind.

Finally, the lorry drew up outside a large undamaged building in North Stammen and the weary engineers dismounted and were chivvied into line by Iska. Under orders from his commander, Iska organised the removal of the boxes and crates from the back of the lorry and he gave orders to clean weapons and replenish ammunition.

Without a single word of complaint, his men set about the task. Chekov swelled with pride and walked amongst the men as they professionally went about their soldierly craft.

As Iska wandered around, handing out grenades and magazines, Chekov strolled to the edge of the village and lit up a Sobranie. The rich Turkish tobacco made him feel extremely light-headed and he leant against the badly rusted wreck of a steam tractor, long since become engulfed in grass and creepers.

From his comfortable position, he could see the Rapunzel tower billowing smoke and flame. To the naked eye it now seemed that much of the rest of the castle was burning fiercely too.

He took out his binoculars, only to find that they too had been damaged during the battle. Fragments of one glass lens fell out, tinkling onto the ground around his feet.

Chekov suddenly felt so tired and hoped that the men would soon complete their task, although he knew only too well that he would remain awake for the first sentry turn to show example to his weary sappers.

A sound developed more and more in his subconscious, until it was identified as aero engines.

Scanning in the direction of the growing roar, he spotted a flight of Shturmoviks heading north-west and flying almost directly over his head.

He craned his head, following the flight.

'Off to cause the Amerikanski more grief,' he mused, too tired to really care.

His gaze lowered, the further the aircraft flew on.

Just as he was about to look away, he spotted the movement, brief, vague, but none the less, very real.

Gently but purposefully stretching, apparently unconcerned, he strolled back round the building to where his men were finishing up their cleaning and rearming.

He needed to ask for one final effort from them and quickly brought them to order.

669

Serzhant Iska would take a cover group of the two DP machine guns and six of the best riflemen into the building that was to be their billet.

As Chekov had walked back from the abandoned tractor, he decided that building's field of fire would be good enough, if the movement was what he thought.

A cover force of six men, placed under a steady Yefreytor, was set to watch the right flank of Iska's group.

Chekov, with the remaining eighteen men, would move west to the riverbank and then move northwards in its cover.

Now that action seemed likely, Chekov's lack of a suitable weapon needed addressing. He had sixteen rounds left for the Garand, so decided to discard it.

Iska went to one of the unloaded crates and fished out two weapons. The first was an SVT-40 automatic rifle, showing signs of damage, similar to that which had rendered his PPSH useless at the bridge. The other was a pristine Mosin-Nagant sniper's rifle. Whilst Chekov loved shooting, his head won over his heart and he took the SVT, along with a bag of magazines retrieved by an engineer at Iska's direction.

The sniper's rifle went with Iska's unit and was quickly given to the unit's best shot.

Chekov moved his men out and, using the cover of buildings and undergrowth, quickly reached the river.

It was agreed that if Iska saw enemies on the loose, then the lorry's horn would be used, three times to confirm and then once for every five or so men seen.

It was simple but should prove effective, thought the Serzhant, who stifled a laugh as he realised the rifle protruding from the window he was sneaking a look out of was in the hands of the elderly truck driver.

"Make sure you point that in the right direction, granddad. You know which way that is don't you?"

The old man looked at the NCO with something approaching disdain and hawked deeply, spitting the product out of the window,and nearly reaching the derelict beyond.

"Have no fear; I've had cause to use one before, Comrade Serzhant."

Iska laughed softly.

"Such as where and when, old man? I'm keen to know the metal of the man I fight next to."

"I joined the Army in 1928 and became a rifleman in the 87th Rifle Division."

Iska, speaking the truth but intent on mischief, probed further.

"Never heard of them. What did they do? Convoy duty on the Caspian Sea?"

"Bit of this, bit of that, Comrade. Finland for the Winter War and, of course, Kiev. That's all the 87th did really."

Enjoying his baiting, he searched for more dismissive lines.

"That's not a lot. Why didn't you 87th do anything impressive and brave then?"

"Because they changed our unit designation and the 87th was no more, Comrade Serzhant."

"Oh, you were disbanded then?"

"No, Comrade Serzhant. Just renamed."

Part of Iska's mind sounded warning bells, but they were overridden by his attempts to wind up the old man. From the grins on the faces of his riflemen, he was providing glorious entertainment for them, grinning to a man as they were.

"Oh really? What was that to? 1st Guards Kitchen Division, Comrade?"

With all the skill of a striking snake, the old man put Iska in his place.

"Close enough, Comrade Serzhant. 13th Guards Rifle Division. You may've heard of them."

There was not a man in the Red Army who hadn't heard of the 13th Guards, mainly for their heroics at Stalingrad.

The grins had vanished and the awkward, yet extremely respectful silence, encouraged more from the old soldier.

"I was with Leytenant Dragan at the railway station and, later on, I served on the Mamayev Kurgan."

After a moment's silence, the Serzhant ate his humble pie.

671

"My apologies, Comrade Driver. Had I known I would not have...", embarrassment overtook him, "You know... sorry."

Against all convention, the old man slapped Iska's arm robustly.

"Think nothing of it, Comrade Serzhant. From what I saw of that mess at the bridge, you boys've been 'there' too."

A hissed warning from the sniper brought everyone back to the task in hand.

"I count... eight...no....twelve.....no....govno!"

He slid his eyes away from the scope and looked unaided at a rapidly moving group of Americans, well over thirty strong, a sight that everyone there, even the old guardsman, could see unaided.

Rushing across the landing to the window at the front of the house, he called down to one of the cover group, stood by the lorry with precise orders.

"Three and six, Boris, three and six."

As he moved back to the rifle group, the sound of honking in the required pattern reached his ears.

"Wait for the PodPolkovnik to engage and make sure of what you're aiming at."

With that, he visited the other rear bedrooms to say the same to the two DP gunners and their loaders.

Chekov had moved his party speedily and when the contact report sounded, he checked his party and moved up to the edge of the rise. One look told him that he was nearly in a direct path with the enemy group's advance, having actually gone about fifty yards too far.

Taking a few seconds to shake his men into line, he ordered them up to the ridge of the riverbank and started to fire.

The first bullets took the lives of Brown and Lopez, each man taking two rounds from Chekov's SVT. Other rifles and sub-machine guns opened up from the riverbank and more men dropped, never to rise again. Brennan immediately took his men left, away from the threat and nearer to the haven offered by the buildings.

This haven transformed into Hades, as Iska ordered his men to open fire.

Two DP machine guns poured fire into the group, one into the front end, one the rear, causing the troops to bunch more.

The riflemen calmly fired and reloaded, sweeping the centre ground.

Some eighteen enemies were already lying motionless and more were moving with difficulty because of wounds.

However, enemy fire was now coming back and one DP ceased firing amid animal like screams.

Iska ran into the room and recoiled in horror. The loader was dead, shot through the centre of the forehead.

The gunner was rolling on the floor in agony, blood pouring through the fingers that clutched at his shattered face, portions of which had been displaced by two bullets striking the magazine of the machine gun, causing vicious metal fragments to fly off. Sharp pieces had flayed his face open, shredding his eyes and opening his jawbone to view. Steady spurts of lifeblood, leaking from his jugular, drained his strength with each pulse.

The screaming was awful, a comrade in pain.

Not for the first time, a merciful bullet from a friend was preferable to the agony of wounds and Iska dispatched the poor soldier with a single shot.

There was no time to dwell on the matter and the tough Serzhant returned to the rifle room, only to be smashed in the shoulder as soon as he walked through the door. The impact dashed him against the solid door frame, causing further hurt.

His rifle dropped to the ground and all he could do was clutch his painful wound and watch on as his men fought.

Considering they had the advantage of cover over the Amerikanski, they seemed to be taking too many casualties.

Iska suddenly realised that there was another enemy group, presently unengaged, that was firing at them unhindered.

673

Stepping up to the firing line again, he got the attention of both the sniper and the old driver, pointing with his bloody hand, issuing his orders to engage the new enemy group through gritted teeth.

This group was also in the act of setting up a .50cal machine gun, which could well have changed the balance.

Iska's quick thinking meant otherwise and both of his men killed their targets, the old soldier calmly directing the fire of the younger sniper.

When the firing had first started, the enemy were about four hundred yards away, but Iska realised that they were closing his position, being half that distance and at the full run.

Disaster had struck the Americans and there seemed little to do except fight it out and die. Brennan prepared to do just that, dropping to a knee, bringing up his Garand and taking out two enemy on the river line.

Suddenly he became aware of a drop in fire volume from the village and realised that his cover force had engaged and scored hits.

"Caesar, get the fuckers moving to the village now! I'll cover! Go, go, go!"

Collins' huge voice rose above the sounds of battle and not a single member of the group failed to hear the instructions.

They ran helter-skelter for Stammen.

Dropping down next to his Major, the bald NCO took down at least one man with a controlled four rounds from his Garand.

"The boys're moving, Sir. We can buy 'em some time."

The Master Sergeant looked quickly around and saw what he needed, pulling his Major into the relative safety of a shallow depression, exactly halfway between the two roads.

Both men fired constantly, more intent on keeping the riverbank enemy focussed on them, not on the backs of their running men.

674

Collins tried a long throw with a fragmentation grenade but came up short, getting nicked on the upper arm for his trouble.

"Goddamn it," he growled as he dropped back into cover and tested the wounded limb.

He risked a quick look at the men's dash for the village and was appalled to see how few were left. Even as he watched, two more went down hard.

A low groan and a weight fell heavily against him, snapping his right leg at mid-calf in one hideously painful instant.

Brennan had taken a round through the shoulder and it had knocked him off his feet.

Collins, tears of pain in his eyes, pushed the Major back up and watched as the officer tried to fire his Garand one handed.

The Master Sergeant picked up his own weapon, discharged the last two rounds skywards and inserted another full charger.

"Drop me your ammo and rifle. I'll reload, Buck."

Also in great pain, Brennan laughed the laugh of the half-mad.

"Did you just call me Buck, you bald bastard?"

"Guess I did at that, Major. Bust me when we get out of this ok?"

"Reckon I might at that Julius! Anyway, that was my last clip."

Looking around, Brennan saw a corpse with Garand ammo, lying a few yards behind their position.

"I'm gonna get some more ammo. Be right back."

Despite his shoulder wound, Brennan rolled out of the hollow and shuffled over to the body.

It was Addison Watkins.

He pulled at the webbing, but his injuries betrayed him.

He had not even begun to get the ammunition when the IS-II shell arrived.

"Idiot man!" yelled the tank commander. "Wait until the tank stops before you fire. What a waste."

He looked again at the target his gunner had engaged, a single American soldier, rolling around, clearly dazed and confused by the near miss.

"Driver, forward."

He looked at the small group of Americans running into the village and decided they were worth a shell.

"Driver, halt. gunner engage infantry to front, high-explosive, range eight hundred."

"Ready."

"Fire."

The commander stuck his head out to better observe the carnage.

The huge 122mm lashed out another high-explosive shell, this time better aimed, and it arrived where it was intended.

The two leading figures in the American group disappeared, vaporised in the explosion. Four other were tossed like rag dolls, smashed and broken by the blast.

A bazooka shell reached out from a position close on the left and exploded on the side of the turret, just below the commander's cupola.

The gunner screamed in horror as a headless corpse flopped into the tank, spraying the insides with copious amounts of blood.

Self-preservation took over and he rotated the turret, flaying the bazooka operator, even as the man struggled to reload his weapon.

A group of infantry beyond caught the crazed gunner's attention and he called for H.E. The loader, completely rattled by the death of his commander had dropped one part of the shell on the turret floor and was still trying to retrieve it.

The machine gun spoke again and bowled two of the group over with impacts. A BA-64 armoured car swept past the IS-II, aiming bursts into the survivors and scoring hits in turn.

The gunner looked around for more enemies and again saw the stunned American, now on his knees.

676

"Driver, forward."

Chekov had escaped without further injury, but how he didn't know. Another eight of his men were dead and two wounded, all but one of the casualties being head shots.

He took in the failure of the American rush with satisfaction and turned his attention to the forlorn figure of the stunned American officer to his front.

Checking that the other group of Americans had been beaten down by the armoured car, he rose from his position and beckoned his men into loose line behind him.

The SVT was nearly out of ammo so he took up a PPS sub-machine from one of his dead engineers, grabbing two more magazines and stuffing them in his tunic pocket.

As he walked forward, he determined to shoot the American out of hand.

He waved casually at the approaching heavy tank, before its true purpose was clear.

That moment of realisation converted him back from an avenger into a reasonable and honourable man and he rushed forward in an attempt to save the unknown enemy.

His wounded leg gave way, partially through its own weakness from the calf wound and partially through a grass clump that Chekov clipped hard.

He fell headfirst, bringing him to the same level as the glassy eyed American.

From about twenty yards distance, Chekov screamed at man and tank in turn, until the unforgiving tracks pressed across the back of the American's thighs, reducing them to a bloody pulp.

The engineer blazed away at the still living, screaming rag doll, its flesh and bone inextricably joined with the metal tracks. He missed and the submachine gun fell silent. In horror, Chekov fumbled with a spare magazine as the awful apparition was lifted up at the back of the tank and fed into the top running gear legs first.

The track dragged the squealing American through the gap between hull and track, carving, peeling and snapping

677

unrelentingly. Chekov fired the whole magazine and bullets struck home, the suffering mercifully ended, the mangled remains falling away at the front of the tank.

The IS-II drove on, heading for the Americans who had charged the village.

He watched as five of his men ran forward waving their arms, the distinctively tall Iska amongst them waving just the one good arm. They were trying to obstruct the leviathan's progress, risking their lives to turn it aside to save the petrified wounded men on the ground.

It did turn, heading off down the road it had come up earlier that morning.

Chekov recovered his feet and reloaded. He could not take his eyes off the gory remains of the officer destroyed by the IS-II.

Nothing he had ever seen was more awful.

His men moved on, checking every body.

One of them stood over a shallow depression and started calling his comrades, slipping more rounds into his rifle as he shouted.

Chekov called for him to wait and he painfully hobbled over to where his man had found a survivor.

The large bald-headed American soldier was clearly in excruciating pain, his right leg snapped at mid-calf and virtually at right angles to its proper position, sharp bone protruding from the open wound.

Other obvious injuries included the upper right arm and a superficial but messy chest wound.

The IS-II's HE shell had done the extra work on Collins.

Chekov looked down at the man and decided that there had been enough killing for today.

As more soldiers arrived to assist in the fight, a medical unit was called over and the American placed in their hands.

As the wounded man was lifted carefully onto a stretcher, he turned his head to Chekov.

"Spassiba, Comrade."

Chekov smiled. *'Close enough, Amerikan, close enough.'*

"Dosvidanya, Amerikan."

Fig#25 - Trendelburg final positions.

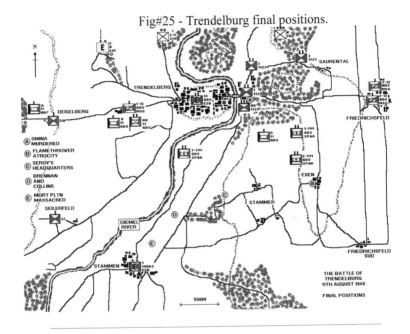

Chekov stumbled and limped over to the village, where he noted Iska and the ancient truck driver in animated conversation about the battle, occasionally interrupted by the medics trying to do their work on the pair. The former was receiving medical attention from a male doctor and his companion seemed to be relishing having his head bandaged by a wonderfully attractive young nurse.

Their laughter was infectious so, by the time Chekov got to them, he was smiling for no reason whatsoever.

Clearly the two had acquired a bond somewhere along the line and he would enquire later but, for now, he had to look after his men.

Iska formally introduced him to the old soldier and made light of Chekov's concern at both their wounds. After making sure that both Pavel Iska and Pyotr Harunin were fine, for that was the old man's name apparently, the commander did the rounds of his battered troops.

'13th Guards Rifle Division? Who would have thought that?'

Silence fell across the valley and the gutter fight that had been the Battle of Trendelburg came to a final close.

Deception, in order to be fully effective, must be practised upon friend and enemy in equal measure.

Georges De Walle

CHAPTER 52 – THE FRENCH

1001hrs Saturday 11th August 1945, Headquarters, US Forces in Europe, Trianon Palace Hotel, Versailles, France.

Eisenhower had been awake for some time, woken from his light slumber by an agitated orderly, intent on summoning him to a crisis in the making.

Without shaving or washing, he had responded and discovered that his enemy had not slept and had used the worst thunderstorms in a hundred years to mask assaults along a broad front.

The phone lines were humming as his senior commanders called in with progress reports, more often than not negative reports describing enemy progress and allied units being pushed back.

Now, as morning really took hold, there seemed to be a surreal pause in operations. Almost as if the enemy were collectively taking a breather and gathering themselves for another effort.

Up to the lull, there had been little good news and a lot of bad. The recently confirmed loss of Trendelburg meant that the American units on the Weser had only one route of escape and Eisenhower confirmed with both Bradley and Tedder that this route would be preserved and defended at all costs.

The new numbers on ground attack aircraft were encouraging, with disbanded and dispersing squadrons pulled back together in record time. Nothing like the power he had at his disposal a few months back, but better than it was last Monday and getting better every day.

McCreery's brief call told Ike all he needed to know about the ongoing assault on Hamburg and he sensed it would be a close run thing, despite the heroic efforts of the Allied forces defending the city.

Eisenhower took advantage of the quiet and made himself presentable, following his ablutions with a proper breakfast.

Before he succumbed to sleep the previous evening, he had been given the definitive intelligence estimate on the Soviet fuel situation.

He had been wrong. It was not their Achilles heel.

"Damn!"

Ike remembered his curse faintly echoed around his bedchamber, almost taunting him, but after a reasonable sleep, he had put the disappointment behind him.

Relaxing back into his chair, he received the first written reports from the night's actions. Ground attacks up and down the front line, one where the Air Force continued its good work in interdicting enemy fighters and bombers and another in which the bomber force reported being on target on all of its objectives. That was nothing unusual as the Bombers always claimed that. The erosion of his photo-recon capability was of great concern to the General, as so much that was claimed went unconfirmed.

As a resolution, more Mosquitoes were being temporarily converted and allocated to air-recon work, but their losses were great too.

Sucking greedily on his cigarette, Ike looked at a passing orderly and gave her the universal hand signal for coffee.

The smile that came back made Ike's morning nearly as much as the coffee when it arrived.

Perfect.

Bringing his mind back to the problems at hand, he started at the top of the map as usual.

As he examined the British positions, he received a brief note from McCreery's headquarters. Hamburg had been held by a thread but, by all accounts, the commies had pushed very hard. Reinforcements were being moved in, but such levels of combat could not be sustained indefinitely and

682

withdrawal was an increasing possibility, if only to preserve his force.

Ike nodded to himself, understanding that if such a decision had to be made it was McCreery's to make, at least in the first instance.

As he put down the British report, he decided on another cigarette and a general appreciation of the front before the rescheduled main briefing, or rather the second main briefing of the day.

Across the towns and villages of Germany, the Red flags flew, more now than earlier, showing the successful advances of the Soviet Army.

On the 6th August, Eisenhower's first decision had been a preservation of his force, something that had been reasonably successful to date. He winced as he reflected on Gottingen and the events that resulted from the issues there, hoping above hope that his units could escape. Gottingen was a mistake, an error of judgement by both himself and Bradley, for which historians would criticise them well into the next millennium.

The relative failure of the spoiling attacks had wasted some valuable assets and that lesson was learned.

Ike leant forward and examined a one page listing on major ground units on their way to Europe.

Outwardly, he exuded confidence that the Allied line would hold until the new forces arrived, at which time they would start rolling back the enemy.

Politically, the US Government appeared totally committed and had swung its industry back fully into wartime production, or at least had stopped the process that was converting factories back to peacetime production.

Materiel wise, he did not expect shortages, nor were problems anticipated with the very necessary liquids of war, although Soviet sabotage had caused a blip for two days.

It was in manpower and, more specifically, trained manpower where his problems would come.

A man can be trained to hold and fire a rifle quite quickly, but to understand military manoeuvre and tactics was a longer process. Specialist troops took even longer and losses in those had been quite high in the last few days.

Without a doubt, there would be an issue with pilots for a while, but the training programmes had not been reduced as many other programmes had, something that Ike hoped would prove advantageous.

Lighting up another cigarette, a new line of thought developed.

'Specialists?'

If it was going to be a problem for the allies, would it be a problem for the Reds?

His brain sought an example. The Red Army was full of artillery troops, but it was known that literacy levels were low and that the units were run by officers who were the only ones who understood the mechanics of war. The soldiers were there just to discharge their orders and not perform technical duties, over and above those learned by rote and performed like automatons, or at least that was the belief.

'So, is that the same for others units?'

An interesting thought.

Ike stubbed out his cigarette, using his free hand to beckon a newly arrived Hood to his side.

"Good morning, Sir. How may I be of service?"

"Good morning, Thomas. I hope your trip was successful?"

Colonel Hood had spent a day away liaising with the French at their new headquarters in Nancy.

"Yes, Sir, it was. I will have the report ready for your evening brief."

Unusually for Hood, he drew closer to his Commander and whispered conspiratorially.

"I will also prepare a separate report on a matter I became aware of. Someone was indiscrete within my earshot, Sir. I believe you may wish to know of it, but not officially."

"Intriguing statement, Thomas, I shall look forward to it. Thank you. Now, for this moment, I want you to scare me up some information on the Soviet specialist units, artillery, engineers and the like."

"For what specific purpose, Sir?"

"I'm looking to get a feel of their deployment and use, which are performing as they should, or as expected and which are not."

The Colonel made a note on a small pad, his pencil working furiously. Ike sensed rather than saw that the man needed further focus.

"I see our forces having difficulties with specialists, from pilots through to drivers, Thomas. I want to know if the Red Army has similar issues, ok? The more information I can get on them at the moment the better."

"I understand fully, General."

The Colonel came to attention and went on his way, seemingly ignoring, but actually just not hearing, Eisenhower's parting words.

"And I will look forward to your reports later, Thomas."

Ike took another cigarette and turned to the head of the small queue that had formed.

"Good morning, Anne. How are you this morning?"

Receiving the normal response, a report changed hands. There was a contrite apology and covering explanation as to how some parts of it had been missed for the last few days.

General Clark had sent a message regarding the extraordinary visit he had received from an escaping officer of the Waffen-SS and the intelligence the man had passed him, enabling some sort of early warning to go out, saving many lives.

USAAF Intel had done some work on the information therein and generated some interesting possibilities. Using the escaping prisoner's debriefs, cartographical interpretation and civilian reports, Intelligence had identified five other possible sites for the same sort of concealment, all of which were in central and southern occupied Germany.

RAF Air Recon and British Military Intelligence had picked up twitches at three of the locations, but found nothing conclusive.

Photos taken by a Spitfire reconnaissance aircraft over the forest south-east of Gardelegen, showed what looked like smoke from a fire in the woods, but as the annotation stated, it could as easily be a steam train, but that there was evidence of increased road traffic to the area to add to the potential of the site.

The large wooded area between Suhl and Schmeidefeld had drawn attention because of the ferocious AA fire that greeted some passing Thunderbolts, who were driven off by the swift arrival of Soviet fighter aircraft. Both photo-recon aircraft sent out had not returned, in itself a possible pointer.

The final possibility was underlined and emphasised in Red.

'Where the hell is Ceske Kubice?' enquired Eisenhower of himself and then aloud of the Captain.

"Czech border region, approximately fifty miles north-east of Regensburg, Sir."

Most significantly, this was intelligence from an on the spot source, albeit more negative than positive input.

'Villagers cannot use this road; this area of woodland is now restricted and guarded by army and NKVD units. Curfew imposed, commencing two hours before dusk.'

Ike read and reread the next line.

"Increase in train traffic, particularly at night time. Tuesday night 12. Wednesday night 17."

He looked at the Captain encouraging her response.

"Contact has been lost with the informant. No messages since Thursday, Sir."

As Ike read on he felt his senses start to sharpen, hairs prickling on the back of his neck, wondering if the clandestine Manchurian units had actually been located.

"Anne, make me another copy and then pass it onto Marshal Tedder. Ask him to provide me with a strike plan to hit these targets tonight. Please tell him I consider this a matter of the highest priority."

Impressed with the importance of her mission, the pretty young officer fairly skipped away to do her commander's bidding.

Eisenhower moved to the next offering, reports on submarine attacks in the Atlantic. One particularly unwelcome paper recorded the sinking a full troopship, one returning to Europe with veteran soldiers and, with its loss, an entire tank-destroyer group was struck from the Allied inventory.

As he read the painful pages, his attention was suddenly piqued by a highly polished pair of shoes that halted a respectful distance from his chair.

He finished the paragraph and slid his thumb into position to show him where he had to start reading from and then looked up.

His eyes took in the immaculate vision of Rear-Admiral Sir Roger Marais Dalziel and he immediately knew that something good was about to happen.

Standing, he responded to the naval salute offered up by Dalziel and then extended his hand.

"Excellent timing, Sir Roger, I need to speak to you about the Atlantic." Moving his head slightly to address the waiting officers.

"Unless anything is particularly urgent, please give the Admiral and I fifteen minutes, gentlemen."

A chorus of mutters indicated nothing of epic importance and the space suddenly belonged solely to Ike and the British officer.

Extending his hand to the adjacent chair, Eisenhower resumed his seat and poured coffee for both of them.

"Actually, I do want to speak about the Atlantic, but by the look on your face you have something you want to tell me, Sir Roger?"

"That I do, Sir. Hopefully I'll brighten your day."

Reaching into his ancient briefcase, the intelligence officer extracted a report laden with the external paraphernalia of utmost secrecy.

"Your eyes only for now, Sir, if you please."

Eisenhower nodded his understanding.

"Want to give me the précis, Sir Roger?"

"I thought you'd never ask, Sir," he smiled the words as much as spoke them, "Rather proud actually. We found two more communist agents at Bletchley, bringing the total to four."

"And this is good news, Admiral?" Eisenhower was imagining the horrors these agents, well placed in his communications, could have wrought.

"I understand your angst, General. There has been damage, but it has already been done and we'll learn the lessons of that. What is more interesting is the future and how we may profit from this debacle."

"We'll profit by not making the same mistake again, I would imagine," Ike spoke abruptly, not in irritation, but aware that there was something else.

"Ok, Admiral, hit me with it."

"They all now work for us, Sir."

That statement opened a very intriguing line of discussion.

1910hrs Saturday 11th August 1945, Headquarters, US Forces in Europe, Trianon Palace Hotel, Versailles, France.

Eisenhower had eaten heartily of his evening meal and felt as full as he had done for a long time.

He had gone back out into the main room to sit and look at the situation map as he enjoyed a large coffee.

Colonel Hood approached carefully, similarly stuffed with beef and onion stew, potato cakes, turnip and carrots, all covered with the finest thick gravy.

"Good evening, Sir."

"Colonel Hood. Dinner lies heavy on you too, eh?"

Gestured to the adjacent chair, he placed a report on the table in front of his General.

Eisenhower, drinking the last of his coffee, inclined his head to read the cover and screwed up his face at the title.

"Assessment of French Military Capability – 11th August 1945."

More coffee arrived and Colonel Hood was graced with his own china mug, although he was considered a total philistine for indulging in sugar.

"It's been a heck of a day, Colonel."

"That it has, Sir."

688

"OK then, Thomas, gimme the bottom line on our Gallic Allies please."

Drawing deeply on his cigarette, Eisenhower was treated to Hood's appraisal of the present French capability, as supplied by the US Liaison Officer to the French 1st Army, as well as the French staff themselves. All of which was tempered with his own eye for the things, things that some may have wished to be kept hidden.

"We know the regular and colonial formations can do the job, Sir. Heck, they did magnificently in Italy and beyond."

Hood took a quick gulp of his coffee.

"All the prime formations are at good strengths and maintain their fighting ability."

The Colonel leant across and flicked open the folder, producing a list of units that were not so blessed.

"These formations were pretty much all built out of FFI forces and, to be blunt, using General De Lattre's own words, are about as much use as a Sunday school coach party."

Eisenhower raised an eyebrow.

"Well actually, he added some extra words; I cleaned it up a bit, Sir."

Eisenhower grinned, imagining exactly what the dapper French officer might actually have said.

"Oh do go on, Thomas."

"Only the Alpine Division is going to be retained for possible front-line duties, the rest of the FFI based units will be withdrawn to France for re-training and security duties, freeing up some more experienced forces for your disposal."

That certainly made sense and was very welcome to a General who needed quality manpower badly.

Colonel Hood sensed that and quickly moved before his Commander got too carried away.

"One General on the staff there told me that, in the short term, he expected no more than three worthy divisions to come out of that process."

Eisenhower did the maths and still figured he was in profit on the deal.

"The French participation in the mobilisation of German soldier prisoners is extremely good."

689

Eisenhower nodded.

"Extremely good, Sir, so much so that it is almost embarrassing in its swiftness and completeness."

That seemed a strange statement and it was not going to go unchallenged.

In response to his General's question, Hood continued.

"As you are aware, the French offered to take responsibility for all of our SS prisoners. They are already moving them into the interior of their country in large numbers, relieving all our troops who were guarding them and freeing up even more bodies for our units."

"So they're doing what needs to be done for the Allied cause and quite right too, Thomas."

"I understand that, General, but it's being done at a pace that is unusual for our allies plus…"

"Plus?"

"Plus, it is being done against a back drop of total compliance with every request we've made and every order we've issued. With one exception only."

"I take it this is the bit that isn't in your report, Colonel Hood?"

Eisenhower adopted a more formal tone, fencing with his trusted staff officer, indulging him as he enjoyed the moment.

"Yes, Sir. As you know, we're all presently re-arming the German ex-POW's with captured weapons, stockpiled since the capitulation in Africa. Even the Brits, who are not known for their swiftness, have started to ship captured weapons from Rommel's Army to the continent, through Gibraltar, some of which are intended for the Spanish, but much is marked for German Formations to be formed in Southern France. Despite a tentative start, they're fully onboard with the arming of German soldiers now."

A new cigarette lit, Eisenhower was still none the wiser on where Hood was going.

"So out with it, Thomas."

"Our French Allies have not handed over one single bullet from the stocks they control. One of the first duties their

FFI units took over, when they returned to France, was to relieve Allied forces guarding enemy stores and munitions dumps."

Eisenhower took a second to think on that.

"Strange I agree. Nothing handed over at all?"

"Nothing, Sir, except at Tilly, where some of our engineers were building running German tanks out of all the damaged stock. Our troops were attached to their work and refused to give them up. But that is it."

Hood ploughed further on.

"It is also the fact that they have handed weapons to our new Spanish allies as was agreed. Those weapons do contain some German rifles, but are mainly old French stocks from Vichy supplies, pre-1940. No machine guns or assault rifles, no mortars, or artillery pieces, save old French stocks or equipment we have supplied to their FFI units."

"So what are they playing at, Thomas? What does this mean?"

The moment of truth had arrived and Colonel Hood checked that no one was within earshot.

"I overheard a conversation in their headquarters. I was indisposed at the time. Two officers came in and didn't realise I was in the stall."

Again the conspiratorial check of surroundings.

"The French intend to make a full military contribution to this war at last, with new French divisions within a powerful Corps, filled with experienced troops, tasked with attacking, defeating and throwing back the Red Hordes."

Ike's silence drew him forward.

"They retain the weapons and stores to arm their own private army of experienced soldiers, an army that'll be organised into French units and carry the flag of France in combat."

Eisenhower's eyes narrowed, searching for treachery.

He was unprepared for the truth.

"At this time, plans exist and are in motion for the forming of a French Foreign Legion Corps, with one Tank, two motorised infantry Divisions and numerous smaller formations,

691

all consisting of German ex-prisoners, fighting under the banner of France."

The General lit another cigarette from the stub, exhaling deeply as he conjured with the thoughts.

"I can't see that. Why would the Germans do that when they can fight under their own German Republic Flag in German units?"

Hood coughed politely.

"They'll do so because our politicians prevented them from fighting under that German Flag and in their own national divisions."

'Oh my Lord!'

Someone switched the light on in Eisenhower's brain.

"The French can't do that? I mean, they wouldn't do that, would they?"

Hood looked his General steadfastly in the eye.

"They can and they are, Sir. It all makes sense when you look at the whole picture. They are pragmatists, for sure, so, to them, something carrying the Tricoleur will be French and that's the way it'll be painted."

Eisenhower inadvertently lit yet another cigarette and smoked each in equal measure.

Automatically, he stated the default position.

"I think this is one for our political masters to sort out, Colonel."

"Yes, Sir."

Hood extracted an envelope from his inside jacket pocket, sealed and unmarked, nothing to betray its contents.

"So, Sir, do you want me to give you an official written report, or do I say nothing."

The brain was working hard on that. The French were not the only pragmatists about.

'If I have a report then I must act and we could have a political meltdown. I'm sure the Germans would be the least of our worries. It would be the Poles and the Brits who'd make the most noise.'

The brain was nearly at its point of decision.

Eisenhower spoke conspiratorially.

692

"If I don't have a report, then I can just plead ignorance. That'll also mean that the French plan will succeed."

Hood continued the spoken thoughts in his own words.

"In which case, I've no doubt that they'll present SHAEF with a large field force of experienced and capable soldiers, all under the guise of the French Foreign Legion and with nice new French Flags in abundance; soldiers who would be an asset to the Allied efforts."

Eisenhower nodded emphatically, putting his decision into words.

"I won't burden you with unnecessary report writing, Thomas. Keep an eye on the situation and report verbally to me on anything I might find of interest."

Hood grinned widely.

"Yes, Sir, it will be my honour, Sir."

Hood stood, saluted and left, all in one slick flowing movement, leaving Eisenhower seated alone, with his cigarettes, coffee and thoughts, the sudden flare of burning paper on the log fire noted by his peripheral vision.

Only the Europeans would have a fire burning brightly in the hearth on hot summer's afternoon. Apparently it added ambience.

It was also convenient for destroying unwanted paperwork, the flames from which were now dying down.

'*French Foreign Legion? Jesus.*'

Eisenhower had to hand it to them; it was quite elegant in its simplicity, although the duplicity of his French Allies was there for all to see.

The French even had an agreed protocol that they could recruit Germans into the Legion, including Waffen-SS, a protocol agreed amongst the Western Allies, solely for the purpose of fighting Communist Guerrillas in Indo-China.

Wracking his memory, he could not recall the exact wording. He challenged himself with a bet.

'*Care to speculate on whether they've that bit of paper ready to quote when tackled and that it doesn't prohibit recruitment for other areas?*'

693

A moment's pause.

'No takers on that on, General.'

None the less, politically acceptable to his masters or not, extra experienced soldiers would be most welcome.

"Jesus."

Speaking aloud as he stood, he drew the attention of the passing Rossiter.

"May I help, Sir?"

Thinking quickly, Ike excused his language by complaining of a twinge in his back.

Rossiter moved away.

This time, ensuring he kept his thoughts to himself, Eisenhower picked up his cigarette pack and headed to the telephone for his regular chat with his senior commanders.

'Goddamn, the SS are going to go back to war.'

"When men find they must inevitably perish, they willingly resolve to die with their comrades and with their arms in their hands"

-*Flavius Vegetius Renatus*

CHAPTER 53 – THE RATHAUS

0437hrs Sunday 12th August 1945, 'Haus der Zufriedenheit', Baltische Straße, Metgethen, East Prussia.

Less than four months ago, it would have been the fear of the Gestapo that would have troubled the woman, all the way from her bed to the front door.

Now the heavy insistent knocking summoned up images of the NKVD, who had similar habits to the GeheimeStaatsPolizei, with pretty much the same end result.

People went missing.

It had been difficult for the residents of Metgethen. Occupied by the Red Army, retaken by the Wehrmacht and then reoccupied once more. There had been atrocities visited upon the German populace. Unspeakable atrocities that had become world knowledge, although in truth, many who heard them merely shrugged and mentally balanced the reports against the actions of German and other axis soldiers in other faraway places.

A number of visitors from the International Red Cross had been and gone and, with their departure, the enthusiasm of the world's press waned, so the village was once more settling back into a life of obscurity.

However, insistent loud knocking on a door at half four in the morning is never a good thing, but more especially if it is your door.

A match was struck and a candle lit, throwing its eerie light on the hallway.

"Open up," came a voice, clearly used to instant obedience, "Open up or I will break the door down."

She reached the front door, calling out her approach, reaching down to slide back the bottom bolt, the noise of which confirmed her presence to those outside.

Undoing the top bolt, she opened the door.

There stood the local policeman and an NKVD soldier, side by side, illuminated by the headlights of the car behind them.

"What on earth do you want at this time in the morning, Karl?" she said, asserting her strong community position and addressing the policeman.

There was no reply.

The two callers folded back as if hinged like double doors, opening and revealing a black silhouette.

"Guten morgen, gnädige Frau."

Some voices carry venom and hate no matter what words they speak and this voice, speaking a cultured yet clinical German, was such a voice.

"I am Major Savitch, gnädige Frau, Major of NKVD. You and your family have five minutes to dress. Then you will all come with me."

"On what charge?" rallied the woman.

The NKVD officer laughed dismissively.

"No charge whatsoever. Come now, you're wasting time," and he clapped his hands, trying to chivvy the confused woman along.

"No charge? If there's no charge, why must I come with you? To be interrogated? I know nothing." The woman's two daughters were now visible on the stairs and she gestured at them, "We know nothing."

Again Savitch laughed, this time in real amusement.

"I do know that, gnädige Frau. It is not what you know but who you know that interests us."

He made a great play of checking his watch.

"Three minutes now."

Confused by the early awakening, the lack of sleep, the car headlights and the threat to self and family, the woman swept up her children and grabbed what she could.

The three men waited in silence on the porch, two smoking American cigarettes, the policeman hoping above hope to be offered one from the pack of either of the NKVD officers,

Savitch allowed her an extra five minutes, which he considered extremely generous.

Knocking on the doorframe, he waited for her to appear.

The silence from inside was deafening and he exchanged looks with his subordinate.

His growing anxiety was soon assuaged as an NKVD Serzhant marched round the corner, heading a party consisting of four troopers surrounding the mother and her two daughters. A swift explanation from the Serzhant detailed how they had apprehended the family sneaking out the back door.

Savitch stood there, legs apart and hands on hips, looking down on the family.

"Now, now, gnädige Frau. Why do you run away from us. We just want to talk."

The woman brought herself up to her full height, defiance apparent in her gaze, fear present in her words.

"Herr Maior, I do not know anyone or anything of interest to you. We keep ourselves to ourselves."

Savitch stepped down to ground level and shepherded the group towards a large Mercedes, the back door of which stood open ready to accept them.

The girls both slipped inside easily, but the woman was a more reluctant entrant.

"Please," he encouraged her to enter, "You and your family will come to no harm. We just wish to ask a few questions and to have you somewhere that we can ensure your safety, Frau Knocke."

She reluctantly took her seat.

With the door shut, the car and occupants moved slowly away, never to return.

1439hrs Sunday 12th August 1945, Altona, Hamburg, Germany.

Soviet Forces – 215th Rifle Regiment, 259th Rifle Regiment [less 1st Battalion], 619th Artillery Regiment, all of

179th Rifle Division, 938th Rifle Regiment, 3rd Btn, 992nd Rifle Regiment of 306th Rifle Division, both of 1st Rifle Corps, 2nd Btn, 39th Guards Tank Brigade, 2nd Btn 28th Engineer-Sapper Brigade, all of 43rd Army, 283rdHowitzer Artillery Regt, 376th Howitzer Artillery Regiment, both of 64th gun Artillery Brigade of 21st Breakthrough Artillery Division, 10th Guards Mortar Battalion, 1st Coy, 106th Pontoon Bridge Battalion, 134th Knapsack Flamethrower Company, all of 1st Baltic Front.

Allied Forces [Llewellyn Force] – A, C and D Coys, 4th Royal Welch Fusiliers of 71st Infantry Brigade, B Coy, 1st Manchester Regiment [MG], C Battery, 71st[t] Anti-Tank Regiment R.A., 83rd Field Regiment, R.A., Ad-hoc section, remnants of 555th Field Company, R.E., all of 53rd Welch Division, B Coy, 7th Black Watch, 154th Infantry Brigade, 51st Highland Division, C Sqdn, East Riding of Yorkshire Yeomanry, 33rd Armoured Brigade, all of British XXX Corps, British 21st Army Group. 4th Hamburg Defence Unit, also known as Fallschirm Batallione Perlman [formerly III Btn/22nd Fallschirmjager Regiment, 8th Fallschirmjager Division.]

1439hrs Sunday 12th August 1945, St Georg Krankenhaus, Hamburg, Germany.

Lieutenant-General Afanasii Pawlantevich Beloborodov was a worried man and not without justification.

He had seen a great deal of action during his time, not the least of which was the bitter fighting around Memel the previous year, through to January 1945, but this action was proving to be his most difficult yet.

Getting to Hamburg had been far easier than moving through it and far less costly, save for the loss of the man he had replaced as commander of 43rd Army.

Beloborodov had started the assault with three Rifle Corps under his command. Two, the 1st and 92nd were roughly at 90% strength, the third one at about 50%, that being the 60th Rifle Corps.

The last few days of hammering against the defences of this huge German city had altered all that.

Fig#26 - Hamburg street plan

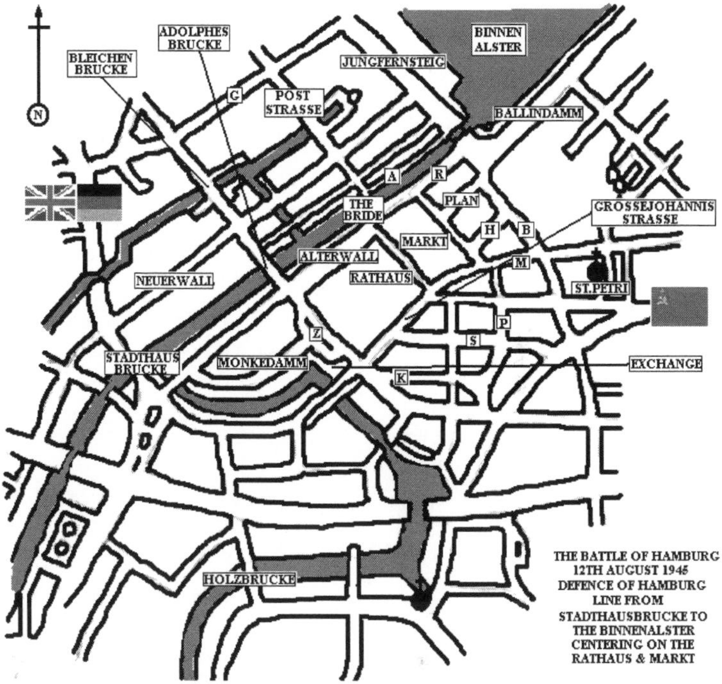

G- GroßeBleichen. A- Alsterarkaden. R- Reesendamm
Z- Adolphesplatz H- Hermannstraße. B- Bergstraße.
M- Mönckebergstraße. P- Pelzerstraße.
S- Schauenbergerstraße. K- Börsenbrücke.

92nd Rifles were out of the fight temporarily, losses in officers and command structure making the unit combat ineffective. The 60th had all but ceased to exist, having bravely thrown itself onto the English defences, albeit in vain, dying in their hundreds.

Beloborodov's problem was manoeuvre, or rather, the inability to do so.

Hamburg is a city of canals that run alongside streets, separating city blocks and neighbourhoods, almost parcelling them into individual islands.

He was sure that in peacetime it was a beautiful place, but in time of war it was a military nightmare to move through, especially if the enemy removed the bridges as they retreated, destroying option after option for the attacking forces.

He pored over the map with his C.O.S., the leadership of 1st Rifle Corps and his Army Artillery Commander, all looking for something that had been missed, all willing themselves to find an alternate route, but knowing there was none.

43rd Army was just about dead on its feet, its offensive capability all committed to this one last throw of the dice.

"There is no choice, we must breakthrough here, Comrades."

His finger struck the map on the point of the last slaughter, ended just after 12pm by his order, when he ordered the withdrawal of the bloodied remnants of the 60th's 235th Rifle Division and the tanks of 39th Guards Tank Brigade.

"Marshal Bagramyan has promised me the 22nd Guards Rifle Corps to replace our casualties, but only if we can break the English here, now, today."

Looking up from the map, he addressed the trio from 1st Rifle Corps.

"You will take the Rathaus and unlock this sector, Comrades. The Rathaus is the key."

The Army Artillery Commander was next.

"64th Artillery Brigade and 10th Guards Mortars will both be dedicated to this attack. Use them wisely, Comrade."

Used to his General's style, the artilleryman merely nodded and remained silent.

The Colonel commanding 39th Guards Tanks was next.

"Your tankers have performed superbly these last two days, Comrade Polkovnik Zorin, but I must ask more. Your remaining full company must support the 1st's attack; closely, very closely."

Beloborodov said that as much for the 1st's officers as for the exhausted young Colonel of tank troops, who had less than half the unit he had entered Hamburg with three days previously.

Fig#27 - Hamburg - Soviet positions

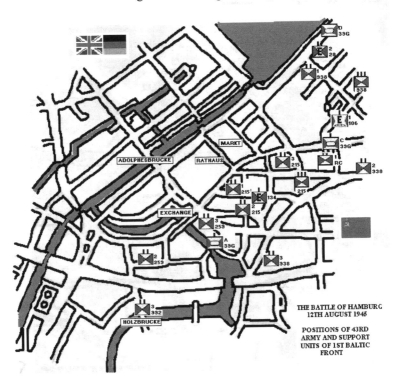

THE BATTLE OF HAMBURG
12TH AUGUST 1945

POSITIONS OF 43RD
ARMY AND SUPPORT
UNITS OF 1ST BALTIC
FRONT

"Right then, Comrades, this is how we'll get this done."

Leaning back over the map once more, he used a pencil to describe the intended movement, marking crosses or circling stop points, rally points, or targets. "1st will bring themselves up to the same start line used by the 60th, here."

He looked up at the relevant officers to make sure they had understood.

"Artillery and mortars will fire on this line of buildings until the attack starts. At that time they will shift to the other line here," he ran the pencil along the building lines in DüstenStraße and WexStraße, two watercourses further up from the Rathaus.

"This worked before, but enemy reinforcements were still able to get through to the Rathaus once the attack got underway."

Circling a number of points on the waterways north of the Rathaus, he continued.

"These crossings are down, every one of them, except the Adolphesbrücke here... and the AlterDamm cross bridge here... both of which we have avoided bringing down for obvious reasons, Comrades."

Throwing the pencil on the map, he pulled off his Ushanka and ran his fingers through his thinning hair.

"To hell with the bridge now, we will bring it down if we must, but no-one will reinforce the Rathaus this time, so be prepared to drop your artillery support closer to the front line positions," his eyes bored into the Artillery Commander, "Is that clear, Comrade?"

"Yes, Comrade General."

Picking out a street name after a quick look at the map, the General pressed home his point.

"Neuer Wall and no closer to our troops."

"Yes, Comrade General."

Picking up the pencil once more, he beckoned everyone closer.

"The infantry attack will not be on a broad front, although I expect you to allocate a battalion for a diversion south, near the Elbe."

Having circled KatharinenStraße and the Holzbrücke, his preferred spot for the diversion, he brought their attention back to the Rathaus and its environs.

"This area must be taken, the English driven out and it must be done in this attack, Comrades."

"Once 1st breaches the defences, then the 134th will move up and burn them out."

At the mention of his unit, the horribly scarred Kapitan moved forward to scrutinise his part more closely.

"I don't care if the whole lot burns, just make sure you shift them all out before nightfall, Comrade."

"Yes, Comrade General."

All those present had heard the Kapitan speak before, but that didn't make him sound any less sinister now. The man's vocal chords had been damaged at the same time as his body, all victims of a German Flamethrower in 1942.

That Kapitan Scelerov was alive was, in itself, a miracle. That he returned to active duty was remarkable. That he chose to adopt the flamethrower as his weapon of choice was incomprehensible, until you listened to the hate that drove him on each day, through the pain barrier.

Then you understood.

Revenge is a powerful force.

"And so to the tanks. Close support, paying particular attention to machine guns obviously. Tanks and infantry will remain together at all times; no-one gets isolated."

Directly addressing the infantry officers, he expanded on their role.

"Your own mortars will support your attack obviously, but make sure they can be redirected to take out the anti-tank guns which hurt 39th the last time," he looked at the tank battalion commander, stating with honesty, "That was an oversight on my part. I will not have it repeated."

"Thank you, Comrade General," said the Colonel of Tank Troops, although his inner self wondered why the 60th's mortar units had not done so as a matter of course.

Dug-in anti-tank guns could be a real bitch, but plunging fire tended to be an excellent remedy.

"Here, at the end of RathausMarkt, is where 106th will do their job," he indicated where the Schleusenbrücke had once stood, "And where I want you to ensure that you have sufficient tanks and riflemen in place to cover them while they construct a crossing for us."

His commanders understood perfectly, but it would not hurt to remind them.

"The 106th is extremely valuable and cannot be frittered away, so take great care to make sure they can do their job unhindered, Comrades, or we may all be counting trees before the week is out!"

Again, the pencil hit the map as he stood upright.

In the silence, all eyes were drawn to the gentle sound of the pencil rolling steadily and inexorably to the table's edge before it dropped onto the floor.

"Comrades, we'll not stop until we've moved over these obstacles and are beyond them. Push on and on. Once it's dark we will stop and not until then. All units will defend their positions when they halt."

He pulled up his sleeve and signalled for a time check.

"On my mark it will be 1514 hrs. 3,2,1, mark."

Fingers pressed down and watches were synchronised as required.

"I think you can all sort out your liaison and pass on your orders in good time. 1st Rifles will take about an hour to get into position, so the attack will commence at1645hrs exactly. Artillery will commence in earnest at 1630 hrs."

He dropped his left arm, shaking his sleeve down.

"Get the job done and let's kick these bastard English back to their little island. Good luck, Comrades."

1515hrs Sunday 12th August 1945, The Rathaus, Hamburg, Germany.

Actually, they weren't English at all.

Some five hundred and thirty years beforehand, these men's ancestors had provided the backbone of Henry V's Army at the Battle of Agincourt. To the inexperienced eye, they looked like the standard British infantryman, pudding bowl helmet, khaki uniform, boots, gaiters and all sporting either the SMLE, Sten, or Bren. To call them English was an insult.

They were Welsh and proud of it.

704

For two days, the 4th Royal Welch Fusiliers had stood in the face of huge enemy attacks, side by side with actual Englishmen in the form of men of the 1st Oxford and Buckinghamshire Light Infantry.

That ravaged battalion had endured such heavy casualties that it had been withdrawn and 4th RWF had spread out to cover the full front, which was why they now found themselves in the strange position of being integrated with jocks of the Black Watch, who had arrived just in the nick of time during the previous attack.

A quick officer's orders group had decided to wait for a definite lull before shaking the two different units out and so, for now, men with names such as Jones and MacDonald shared the same positions in and around the Hamburg Rathaus.

Over one-half of the Welch battalion's officers were either dead on the field, or bleeding in aid stations behind the lines. Even the Lieutenant Colonel commanding the Royal Welch had been carried from the field, torn and bloody, leaving a young Major in command.

He was inexperienced, but led his men well, turning up at the hottest points of contact and directing his meagre reserve forces to critical points in order to stave off defeat.

None the less for him, the sight of the 'Legend' rushing in with his men had been truly inspirational, which feeling quickly spread through his whole unit, as word spread that Ramsey VC was fighting alongside them.

7th Battalion, The Black Watch, had been temporarily detached from its parent formation to bolster the southern area of Hamburg. Each of its companies was sent to a different hotspot. In the case of the Rathaus, it was B Company, under the command of Major John Ramsey VC, that arrived in the nick of time and helped drive off the surviving Russian troops.

Major Llewellyn automatically deferred to Ramsey but, as was his style, Ramsey made sure the young man knew that the Black Watch was there to assist and that the Welshman was firmly in command.

The few junior officers left were scurrying around the positions, ensuring wounded were either tended to or evacuated to an aid station and that replacement ammunition was distributed as needed.

Another orders group was called for 1530hrs, convening, without any intended humour, in the Bürgerschaft, the meeting chamber of the Hamburg Governing body.

Eight attendees represented the CO's of the units defending the area defined by JungfernSteig to the northeast and StadthausBrücke in the south-west, encompassing the Rathaus, Hamburg's Exchange Building and all the area within the northern confines of GroßeJohannisStraße; all in all an area of less than half a square kilometre.

Major Llewellyn introduced himself and then went round the group, asking each to identify themselves in turn.

Ramsey had already attracted a great deal of attention, as much for the kilt he sported and the cane he carried, as for who he was and what he displayed on his chest. He needed no introduction, not even to the German officer commanding the 4th Hamburg Defence unit, as Maior Perlman's 8th Fallschirmjager Division had fought the 51st Division in the Reichswald.

His unit was a true anomaly, an intact throwback to the Wehrmacht of May 1945. Originally the 3rd Batallione, Fallschirmjager Regiment 22, it had been captured and disarmed, then rearmed on 9th May and employed by the British at Bad Segeberg, sweeping the forest for armed Soviet foreign workers who were causing mischief amongst the local populace.

Perlman was not the only man there who found it a little bizarre that a decorated Major of German paratroops, in full uniform, was stood in a briefing with British officers.

Captain Arthurs of the 1st Manchesters certainly did, for he had lost a brother at Dunkirk and an uncle on the arctic convoys. Forgive and forget was not in his nature, but he understood the needs of the present crisis, so bore the hated German's presence as best he could.

The artillery observation officer, 1st Lieutenant Ames, had already proven that he was top-notch at his job, despite being tapped by a piece of shrapnel that made it hard for him to sit down.

706

1st Lieutenant Ramsey, attempting humour, confirmed he was no relation to the great man and apologised for the absence of the anti-tank battery commander, who could not be located.

CSM Richardson, senior rank in the ad-hoc platoon comprised of survivors of the 555th Field Company, R.E., was not cowed by being the only NCO in the room. In the last few days, a lot of people he had spent years with had died, safely coming through the German War, only to fall like dominoes in the latest conflict. He and his men were there to even the score and he had made sure that the officers all understood that.

Finally, clad in the giveaway one-piece tank crew oversuit, Acting Major Frederick Brown QC, Cambridge Blue and Olympic Polo silver medallist from the 1936 Berlin Games, capped the introductions with a flourish.

A tray of corned beef sandwiches was strategically placed to one side and it had been drawing the attention of hungry men, the nearer the man, the more obvious the attention.

Llewellyn decided that they could work and eat. The nearest man to the prize was Ames.

"Grab a sarnie, Lieutenant, pass the plate on."

There was no need to repeat that order and the plate moved swiftly anti-clockwise, ending up with Llewellyn and offering a choice from the three left.

In an almost surreal display, all heads slowly swivelled towards the sound of one of the number enjoying the feast with a little grunt here, a contented 'mmmm' there.

Perlman suddenly became aware that he was the centre of attention.

He grinned widely, displaying teeth covered with the detritus of his meal and spoke in accented schoolboy English.

"It is beating horse, my man!"

They could not help but laugh and the moment of levity eased the tensions of their situation. Major Ramsey later argued that it was a pivotal moment in the brief existence of what became known as 'Llewellyn Force', despite his own run-in with Perlman later.

Fig#28 - Hamburg - Llewellyn Force positions

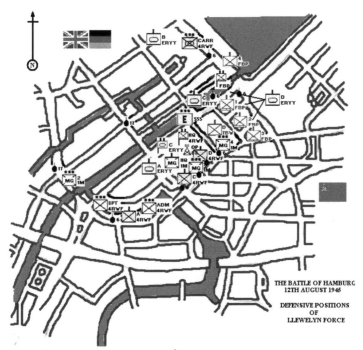

1M- 1st Manchesters, 4RWF-4th Royal Welch Fusiliers, FBP-Fallschirm Batallione Perlmann, ERYY-East Riding of Yorkshire Yeomanry.

Moving to the rough hand-drawn map on the rear wall, the Welch's commander quickly ran through the defensive positions, fields of fire, artillery and mortar support available. He updated the new arrivals on the previous Soviet tactics, pointing with his left hand, taking hurried bites of his doorstep in between sections of his briefing.

Llewellyn was adamant that each company should provide a reserve force to counter-attack any position lost, or to reinforce another under extreme pressure.

Richardson strongly resisted the use of his platoon as a tactical reserve, seeking a position in the front line where he and his vengeful engineers could kill their fair share of commies. John Ramsey said nothing, but prepared to intervene if it proved necessary.

It didn't.

Major Tewdwr Llewellyn would not be moved, but assured the belligerent NCO that his men would get all the action they could stand when the Soviets came again.

Ammunition was a problem, but he had sent his RSM back with a party to get more, even for the German weapons of Perlman's unit.

Once he had finished, he sought questions from the group. Perlman and Ramsey sought clarification of where the counter-attacking forces would be positioned, but there were no other questions or suggestions as the defence was pretty straightforward. There was nowhere to run to, no room for manoeuvre, so it was a case of stand or die.

The group broke up, dispersing swiftly, inadvertently leaving Llewellyn and Ramsey with the remaining sandwiches.

Both eyed the tray and each other.

The Welshman led the way.

"Can't let these go to waste now can we?"

Offering up the tray to his companion, he grinned.

"Be rude not to," the end of which was slightly distorted as sandwich went from tray to lips in one easy movement.

The Welshman's eyes strayed to the ribbon on his fellow officer's breast.

"Well, we Welsh are used to this, of course. This will be the new Rourke's Drift, but without the singing."

Meeting the young man's humour with his own, the Englishman swallowed his last mouthful.

"Singing may be all we can hold them back with if the ammunition doesn't arrive. These buggers don't use assegais, old chap."

Not willing to be bested, Llewellyn fought back in the traditional way.

"My boys'll keep quiet and let you strangle that cat, which should keep the Reds at arm's length."

709

Even though he was an English officer, Ramsey appreciated the value of the pipes to the Scottish soldier. He considered continuing but decided against it, ceding the last word to the younger man with a decidedly mischievous grin.

Both left and immediately separated, heading out to their different units as the Hamburg Council Chamber clock moved silently to 4.15.

It was nearly time.

1615hrs Sunday 12th August 1945, The Rathaus, Hamburg, Germany.

Ramsey strode purposefully out of the main entrance, deep in thought, nearly colliding with a stationary Perlman.

"I do apologise, Herr Maior," the words were out of his lips even as he brought himself back upright

"Alles klar Englander," was Perlman's dismissive response, distracted as he was. The British officer looked at the inscription above the door that had held the paratrooper's attention so much that he had not noticed Ramsey's impending arrival.

Perlman weighed up his British counterpart.

"Do you know what it is saying, Herr Maior?"

"I'm afraid your ability with my language is far better than mine with yours, Major Perlman. If you please?"

The paratrooper tugged his camouflaged jacket formally, ensuring it was properly in place before he spoke.

"I was born in this city, so I am lived with the knowledge of this words since I can remember."

Ramsey remained quiet, aware that the German was strangely emotional.

"I have just fight a war, a loosed war and during those six bloody years I never really knew this words and what they mean, until today."

Perlman coughed gently, more to buy him a moment to compose himself than for any other reason.

"It says 'May the descendants look to maintain the freedom that was winned by our fathers.' "

710

Ramsey nodded in understanding, drawing out more from the German.

"How is it that I never knew what this words mean until today, ...this hour, ...this minute?"

Considering his words carefully, the British Major spoke softly and with feeling.

"In truth, Herr Maior, I suspect that when you fought for the Nazi cause you didn't understand the words because they **had** no meaning," emphasising the word 'had' brought the point home, "Whereas now that meaning is crystal clear and very real for you and all Germans, is it not?"

Perlman considered the words for a few moments, his face screwed up in thought, frowning as he worked it through.

An onlooker would easily have imagined the men as enemies, both by posture and atmosphere.

"Do not think for any moment that most of we Germans fought for anything but our country, Herr Ramsey."

The tension mounted in seconds.

"Do not think that you are the only ones having honour, the only ones fighting for freedoms for six years."

Ramsey found his body gently buzzing as the presence of threat transformed him.

Perlmann took a half step closer, bringing the men to within arms reach of each other.

"Do not think for a first second that I do not hate you, Herr Maior, that I do not remember those you killed and do not remember the places of my youth you army destroyed."

Ramsey's eyes narrowed but he held his tongue, conscious of, but not seeing, the additional gathering presence of soldiers, German and British alike.

The paratrooper officer was breathing hard.

"I hate all of you, but today I fight side to you because I hate the communists more and I am ordered by my Government."

"Just remember that, for when we have kicked the red bastards back to the Urals, Herr Maior, well, just remember that."

Whilst none of the Welch present understood the language, none of them was ignorant of what was being said by

711

the big German, as his demeanour and tone carried all he intended. The paratroopers understood only too well.

Weapons were held with less relaxation and eyes warily scanned for the first hint of action.

Perlmann and Ramsey suddenly realised they had created a situation where a mix of their troops now stood at close quarters, eyeing their former enemies with suspicion and anger.

A few murmurs from the spectators seemed to awaken something in both officers.

The gap between them widened perceptibly.

Perlmann was a professional soldier and a damn fine officer and demonstrated it.

"You are right, of course, Herr Maior. I apologise." The tone of the words was as important as the words themselves and his softer voice immediately had an effect on all present.

"The meaning ist klar for us Germans and today we will show that we understand these words," he cast a hand at the doorway, drawing a number of people's attention to the improbable cause of the confrontation.

He relaxed slowly into a smile that did not look totally forced.

Unclipping the famous Fallschirmjager helmet from his belt, he placed it firmly on his head and tightened the strap.

"Now, I go prepare my unit."

Extending his hand, he took hold of Ramsey's. Both men gripped firmly for their own different reasons.

"You and I fight in the Reichswald as enemies. Now, in mein home city, we fight together as Allies, ja?"

All Ramsey could suddenly see were nine fresh graves filled with his young Scots. Unconsciously, his grip tightened as the anger washed over him again and then it disappeared as quickly as it had come.

The momentary change had not been lost on Perlman.

"Major, we all lost good man in that place. I write words to the parent and sweetheart of thirty of my boys once we out of there. And for what?"

The hands drifted apart, almost reluctantly, remaining hovering in the limbo between handshake and lying at ease.

Ramsey cleared his throat with a low rumbling cough, inadvertently permitting Perlmann to continue.

"We fight alongside as each other as Kameraden today. I wish you and your man luck," the German Major extended his hand, picking out a single word from the inscription and waving his finger at it, "And let us all make sure that all our fathers is proud of what we do here today."

Ramsey smiled ruefully as he watched the disappearing figure lead his small escort away, hopping from cover to cover now he was out in the open and away from safety.

He spoke softly, saying only "Good luck", finding himself sincere in thought, but never being more certain that he would not see someone alive again.

Llewellyn Force did not have a huge remit. The only requirement of the adhoc unit was to stand and fight. In the event that withdrawal became absolutely necessary then there was only one reliable exit point, that being the AdolphesBrücke, between the Alter and Neuer Wall.

Charges had already been laid on it and it was not to fall into enemy hands intact.

Much of the area they defended had been ravaged by allied bombing over the previous years. Some structures were partially collapsed, offering the godsend of the rubble protection from which to fight. Some damaged buildings seemed more precarious and the stability of those less hardy structures was of great concern to those positioned within them.

Amazingly, the Rathaus had withstood all the RAF and USAAF had thrown at it relatively unscathed.

The StadthausBrücke to the south-west was the border of their zone, even though most of it had been long since dropped into the water.

At the northeast end of their area of responsibility was the JungfernSteig, or rather the remains of the crossing point where it met the BallinDamm.

713

A rough wooden structure, suitable only for a few men to cross at a time, ran across to the back of the Rathaus from the end of PostStraße. None of the officers would acknowledge the flimsy structure as a complete and proper bridge, much to the initial chagrin of Richardson, whose men had laboured long and hard to construct it from available wreckage. The humour of the running gag had brought a little light relief to command meetings over the last two days and Richardson now played to his audience in the role of indignant 'Father of the Bride' as the structure became colloquially known.

The left flank of their position hung onto the Binnen-Alster, a lake that provided a formidable barrier to the advancing Russians, forcing them to move around and into the positions occupied by Llewellyn Force.

This flank was the responsibility of the battered Fallschirmjager, now supported by a machine gun section from the Manchesters. 1st and 4th Kompagnies were the largest and Perlmann had the 4th on the Jungfernsteig and the 1st backstopping on the Reesendamm, with 2nd forward between Plan and Hermannstraße and two platoons of the 3rd Kompagnie pushed right up to the junction of Bergstraße and Monckebergstraße. The remaining half-platoon of 3rd and a full platoon from each of 1st and 4th provided the German reserve. Additionally, the surviving two Shermans of the Yeomanry's 'B' Troop were secreted in GroßeBleichen, ready to move out, should enemy forces move up the BallinDamm.

Another two tank unit, 'C' Troop, was secreted in piles of rubble along the Alsterarkaden, on the opposite bank to and level with the RathausMarkt. 'D' Troop was on the edge of the RathausMarkt, covering the approaches up HermannStraße, Reesendamm and Plan.

'A' Troop was positioned to cover the approaches to AdolphsBrücke and finally, the Squadron HQ's four tanks remained in hiding on the AlterWall south-west of the Rathaus.

Most of the Royal Welch's transport was the other side of the water, guarded by a handful of lightly wounded men.

'A' Company had been severely reduced by the last two attacks, so it was bolstered by the pioneer and admin

714

platoons from the Welch's support and Headquarters companies respectively. The combined group defended the ruins stretching from the Stadthausbrücke to the Exchange Building.

'C' Company, less a platoon held in reserve near the AdolphesBrücke, defended the next block to just short of the Rathaus.

Again, less a platoon dedicated to reserve duties, 'D' Company defended the Rathaus and immediate area. Their reserve platoon policed the 555th's 'Bride' from rubble bunkers on the AlterWall.

The battalion 6-pdr anti-tank guns were spread out between the defending Welch, covering junctions and approaches.

The mortar platoon was established just off the north end of the AdolphesBrücke, plenteously supplied with ammunition and a good fire support plan for when the Russians started it all up again.

The members of the carrier platoon, or at least the survivors who had survived a pitiless artillery strike two days beforehand, were drawn up in buildings on the JungfernSteig facing the Binnen-Alster.

Battalion HQ was established in the north-west corner of the Rathaus.

The 71st had also suffered badly and now 'C' Battery's troops had only 2 guns each, of which only two were the lethal 17-pdr's. These were stationed, one each, to cover the partially destroyed StadthausBrücke and the intact AdolphesBrücke.

The other four, all 6-pdrs, had been dispatched to the north side of the battleground with orders to dig in to cover routes of approach and to get more ammunition, as most of their supply had been distributed amongst the Welch's AT guns.

The 71st's missing Battery commander was found by the Welch's mortar men, floating face down in the canal, placing command responsibility firmly on the shoulders of the younger Ramsey.

1630hrs, Sunday 12th August 1945, Altstad, Hamburg, Germany.

Soldiers around the world had learnt that time milestones were important marks in military affairs and tended to sharpen their awareness on hours, quarters and halves.

Experienced men saw the second hand clicking towards 4.30 and took a firmer grip on whatever it was they would do their killing with that day. The moment came and went with nothing more remarkable than the squeal of a diving seagull, until the moment that banshee wail of approaching Soviet rockets took over the defenders senses. The rockets, joined by artillery and mortars shells, fell on the allied troops all along the northern edge of Mönckebergstraβe.

Two short platoons of Fallschirmjager, from the already greatly reduced 3rd Company, were immolated in a storm of high explosive and then crushed by falling masonry, as the already damaged buildings between Mönckebergstraβe and Hermannstraβe collapsed.

Seven men struggled through the barrage, choking on the dust, trying to find safety. Two Black Watch privates dashed out and led the confused men into the relative safety of a sandbagged position on the edge of the Rathausmarkt.

One 'A' Sqdn Sherman took a direct hit from a 122mm shell and was transformed to a blazing junk pile, setting light to the adjacent building in Mönkedamm. The other 'A' Sqdn tank lost its nearside track to an adjacent burst in Adolphsplatz.

One section of the Welch's C Company was set up to cover a 6-pdr defending the Borsenbrucke approach. Men and weapon disappeared in the blink of an eye, as five Katyusha rockets contrived to land within a few feet of each other.

'A' Company of the Welch lost its commander and CSM, both killed as a massive 152mm howitzer shell punched through the roof of their building and arrived in the room they had selected as a headquarters. Although it did not explode, the projectile obliterated both men, leaving little evidence of their existence.

716

The dud shell proceeded on to bury itself deeply in the buildings foundations.

Admin platoon lost half their number to Katyusha rockets, the survivors either leaving their positions in a quest for safety or burrowing deeper in the rubble. More casualties were inflicted on those trying to flee as a second wave of shells arrived.

Apart from those killed covering the anti-tank gun, 'C' Company was remarkably unscathed, its sole other casualties being a lance-Corporal who took a large concrete splinter in the left ear and the young fusilier who was subsequently hit in the face when it exited the NCO's right ear.

The screaming, blinded teenager was quickly carried away to the aid station on the other side of the Adolphesbrücke.

The Black Watch lost men too, although few rounds seemed to come their way. One Katyusha rocket obliterated a Bren gunner and his team in the centre of the Rathausmarkt and a mortar shell blew the company runner into the canal where, rendered unconscious by the blast, he sank like a stone.

The Rathaus was burning, having received huge quantities of incoming fire. The defenders were not occupying the upper floors and so the rocket and mortar strikes killed no one, solely damaging the upper structure and starting fires that developed quickly, producing vast quantities of thick smoke.

The same could not be said of the heavy artillery fire.

In the first volley, four 122mm shells plunged down and penetrated deeper into the building, the first transforming the chamber of the Bürgerschaft into a ruin. It killed four fusiliers, including the RWF's chief medical officer, who was setting up a triage station with three of his men. The other three inflicted casualties on the Manchesters and fusiliers equally.

The newly-fledged commander of the 71st Anti-Tank Regiment's 'C' Battery, 1st Lieutenant Ramsey, was not struck by the last projectile, but was propelled by its irresistible explosive power and slammed into the adjacent stone window frame with such violence that he remained hanging ten foot up, welded into the stonework by the force. Whilst the sight was extremely gruesome, more than one man who passed by the

717

barely identifiable mess remarked on the presence of gaiters and the odd absence of boots and trousers.

High explosive can do strange things.

Fig#29 - Hamburg - Soviet artillery

At A - Two 'platoons' of Fallschirmjager lost when buildings unexpectedly collapse under bombardment.

At B - 'A' Sqdn Sherman killed by direct strike from a 122mm Shell.

At C - 'A' Sqdn Sherman disabled by near miss.

At D - 6-pdr Anti-tank gun and section from C/4RWF lost in Katyusha strike.

At E - OC 'A' Coy 4RWF and CSM killed by artillery.

At F - Admin Platoon 4RWF receives high casualties from artillery.

At G - 4RWF Chief Medical Officer and orderlies killed by artillery fire.

At H - Lt Ramsey killed by artillery fire.

At J - 'D' Sqdn ERYY Sherman killed by artillery fire.

The incoming rounds were relentless, covering the whole defensive area with smoke and dust in equal volumes.

Most allied casualties were sustained in the first few minutes, although the destruction of the Yeomanry's D Sqdn tank in Reesendamm occurred in the very last salvo, immediately before the Soviets switched their attention to the other side of the canal.

Despite the fact that every fusilier and rifleman was fully focussed, the first warning of an attack was the roar of a Russian tank exploding in Bergstraβe, after a Fallschirmjager panzerfaust had sought it out. This was closely followed by the sound of a Sherman's 75mm, as D Sqdn engaged Soviet T34's flanking Rathausmarkt.

A Vickers from the Manchesters, positioned in the Rathaus, started hammering out as Soviet troopers came into and disappeared from view in swirls of dust and smoke, pouring out from behind St Petris' and beyond.

The gunner knew his job and few bullets were wasted, .303's tearing great swathes in the Russian infantry of III/215th Rifle Regiment and the support companies of the 1st Rifle Corps.

As the dust grew less and vision improved, other weapons reached out and touched the attackers, adding to the growing piles of dead and dying all along Llewellyn Forces' front line.

The Black Watch worked their Enfield bolts mechanically, shifting target when the target man dropped, taking a steadier aim if the bullet went wide.

Corporal McEwan, relieved of his driving duties, was doing what he knew best and his sniper's rifle dealt death with every pull of the trigger. Positioned on the first floor of the Rathaus, he had a superb field of fire down Mönckebergstraβe. Methodically the Corporal destroyed the visible command structure of III/215th Rifle Regiment as it hurled itself down the highway, intent on gaining the Markt and beyond.

Talking to himself, as was his habit in the stress of combat, McEwan showered himself with plaudits for taking the cap off one officer who was stood back encouraging his men forward.

719

That the bullet took the life of the IIIrd's commander was incidental to the pleasure the slightly mad Scotsman derived from seeing the headgear roll away.

Fig#30 - Hamburg - First Soviet assault

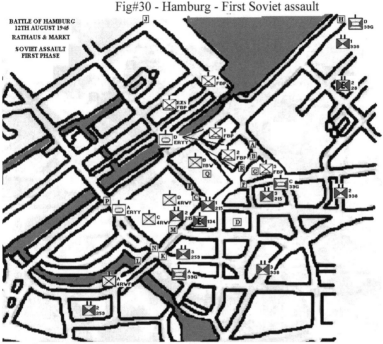

At A - T34 killed by Fallschirmjager Panzerfaust.
At B - Sherman 76mm concealed in Hermanstraße kills a T34.
At C - Cpl McEwan's sniping position from the first floor of the Rathaus.
At D - Defensive artillery strike area.
At E - 6-pdr Anti-tank gun engaging Soviet T34's misfires.
At F - Disabled T34.
At G - Fallschirmjager counter-attack drives out Soviet troops.
At H - T34 killed by 71st Regt 6-pdr gun. [at J]
At J – 6-pdr Anti-tank gun killed by T34's firing from Ballinndamm.
At K - III/259th Regt attack.

At L - Scene of bitter fighting between Admin Platoon,arriving reinforcements of A/4RWF and Soviet infantry.

At M - 6-pdr position, focus of heavy fighting between Soviets and C/4RWF.

At N - T34 advances believing both sides secured by own infantry.

At Q - The Rathaus fighting.

At R - M4 Sherman, which previously killed a T34 disabled by infantry with mines.

A consummate professional, 1st Lieutenant Ames again judged the artillery support just right and brought its accurate and deadly fire down in the area of Pelzerstraße and Schauenburgerstraße, the lethal 25-pdr's causing heavy casualties with a mix of HE and Fragmentation shells and giving the two lead battalions of the 215th a very hard time.

One of the 71st's 6-pdr's reached out at a T34 pushing up towards the Markt and succeeded in damaging it, as well as killing the driver. However, the tank crew did not lack courage and engaged the anti-tank gun, missing with their first shot but killing one of the Manchesters in the window beyond.

The anti-tank gun then misfired, causing panic amongst the crew, who screamed at each other as they started the procedure to clear the weapon.

A second shell from the tank again missed but was close enough to cause the crew to bolt from their useless weapon, all seeking cover within the Rathaus.

A PIAT round arrived on the Soviet tank and removed the offside track, causing casualties amongst the infantry who were supporting the T34.

Mortar rounds were now dropping on the anti-tank gun position, ensuring that the crew did not have second thoughts and try to re-man their gun.

The Lieutenant commanding the T34 stuck his head out to assess the damage and left it there for enough time to attract the attention of a number of Black Watch, who opened fire. Even as he ducked back in, angry wasps clanged off the tanks armour, ricocheting in all directions, one of which caught the III/215th's oldest soldier in the back of the head, killing him instantly.

Howling with rage at the death of their talisman, the younger men threw themselves forward but were beaten off, falling back to seek cover in the ruins that had collapsed on the Fallschirmjager.

Doing what the Germans did best, an ad hoc force of Perlman's troopers counter-attacked violently and threw the Soviet infantry back with heavy loss of life, recovering the lost ground.

'A' Company RWF still received incoming mortar fire but was generally fine as only II/259th Rifles were opposite them, with nothing more than a holding brief.

RWF's mortars were dropping accurate fire to the east of the Rathaus, denying the area, rather than killing in numbers.

Down Ballindamm came a mixed force of infantry, engineers and tanks, the latter of which were three survivors from the previous attack, intent on surviving this attack as well. Remaining outside panzerfaust range, they proceeded to pound the Fallschirmjager defensive positions with accurate HE rounds, causing some casualties

A 6-pdr shell streaked across the water, catching the nearest tank on the turret ring and boring inside, destroying mechanics and flesh with equal efficiency.

Only the hull gunner and driver escaped. Both fled down Gertrudenstraße, uniforms smouldering.

Enraged, the other two tanks turned their guns on the anti-tank gun and destroyed it in turn, complete with its entire crew and four members of the RWF carrier platoon who were nearby.

The Soviet artillery was still killing, a salvo of shells arriving near the Bleichenbrücke destroying four of the RWF trucks and killing the fusiliers set to guard them.

III/259th Rifles made a sudden surge, charging recklessly through the smoke in Große Johannisstraße, losing considerable numbers of men to grenades and small arms fire in the process.

A large group broke into the ground floor of the Exchange, having mistakenly crossed the junction, missing their intended target. Close combat with the RWF's 'A' Company ensued.

A short platoon of battle-hardened Russians burst upon the already unsteady survivors of the Admin platoon and virtually wiped them out in close combat, the clerks and drivers being unprepared for the horror of bayonets and sharpened spades, both wielded by a enemy filled with hate.

Two sections from 'A' Coys 2nd Platoon were swiftly thrown into the fray and managed to beat the Russians back into the corridors and rooms from which they had emerged. The reserve platoon was summoned and the Captain, now commanding the depleted company, held his ground until they arrived and he could throw the Russians back out into the street. Very few Soviet soldiers lived to retreat back across the road.

In the initial rush across the open ground, a larger group had managed to reach their intended target and, as with 'A' Coy, the Fusiliers of 'C' Coy found themselves in fighting where the hand grenade and sub-machine gun ruled as a king until the closer bestial work required less sophisticated weapons.

A 6-pdr position became the focus of much fighting, with the Soviets determined to capture the weapon and the Welch equally determined to retain it. The gunners had succumbed in the first rush and lay dead around their weapon.

A T34 pushed forward, encouraged by signs of friendly infantry in the buildings on either side of Adolphsplatz. Another survivor of the previous attack, this commander, an experienced and decorated Starshina, had got through his war so far by skill and luck and, by his own admission, more of the latter than the former.

His hull gunner was on the ball and a short burst killed a 'C' Coy Corporal intent on setting up a PIAT to their front. A quick glimpse through the smoke and another burst took the lives of two stretcher-bearers rushing forward through Adolphsplatz as they searched for ruined bodies to transport to the Aid post.

The same hole in the smoke gave the tank commander his own glimpse of another enemy to his front and he knew his luck had finally run out.

An 'A' Sqdn Sherman had him targeted and he watched as the white blob reached out towards him. The solid shot struck in a shower of sparks and then whined away off the mantlet, failing to penetrate.

Ordering his gunner to return fire, he got his driver to manoeuvre to the right, moving the T34 into the lee of the building where 'C' Company was fighting for its life against his supporting infantrymen.

The 85mm barked and the shell streaked past the enemy tank, striking the bridge beyond and ricocheting skyward.

The Sherman fired again, hitting the side of the building and bringing down brickwork, adding more dust to the smoke and immersing the T34 in a cloud of particles and smoke, shutting off all sight of the enemy.

Opening his hatch and holding the half-moon section forward to provide cover for his upper body the Starshina deployed his PPS, in case enemy infantry took advantage of the cover offered by the smoke and dust to try and get close in.

The Sherman, having no target registered, decided on a speculative shot and fired another AP shell.

The Starshina's luck had indeed run out and his was an unusual death.

The solid AP shell would have missed the tank but the vertical commander's hatch increased the height by a short distance. Even then, the Sherman's round only lightly kissed the top side of the hatch on its way past and into the buildings beyond. That 'kiss' was enough to slam the heavy cast metal hatch into the NCO at a speed that destroyed his chest in a micro-second, leaving him trapped in the hatch and hanging down inside the turret. His crew were oblivious to his death until the smell of blood, urine and faeces overtook them. They withdrew immediately, the turret gunner firing parting shots from main and coaxial weapons as they went.

It was 'D' Company RWF who had the hardest fight to date, with scores of Soviet troopers breaking into the ground floor of the Rathaus and forcing the fusiliers back. This permitted more Russian troops to charge across Große Johannisstraße relatively unhindered.

Major Llewellyn immediately ordered the 555th Engineers forward and made efforts to push the stubborn Soviets out of the Rathaus.

A runner was dispatched to bring forward 'D' Coys reserve platoon and this arrived within minutes, less two men, both wounded in the Soviet artillery and mortar barrage.

As Allied reserves plunged into the fight, the 134th Flamethrower Company was sent forward to expand on the success of the ravaged 215th Rifles.

Yells accompanying Welsh and English success were soon replaced with screams in the universal language of fear and pain as Scelerov's men set to their grisly work.

CSM Richardson's valour went unnoticed, the fate of many acts of bravery in wartime. He charged a flamethrower group preparing to launch a flank attack through a corridor and offices. With absolutely no expectation of surviving the experience, he fired short bursts with his Sten until all bullets were expended and his life's blood was draining from his body, his legs and stomach ravaged by a dozen wounds. In the full knowledge of what he was doing, he drew his Webley pistol and exploded the fuel tank on a dead sapper, setting fire to the corridor and a number of attacking engineers, saving the situation with his own sacrifice. The flames reached him and started to consume his flesh, so he used the Webley one last time.

The Royal Welch were good troops, but there are few soldiers who will stand their ground when concertedly attacked with the flamethrower. They gave ground slowly, inflicting losses upon engineers and infantry alike, but the screams of the horribly burnt, wounded and dying started to have a psychological effect upon the defenders.

The Rathaus was now alight on every floor, but still the fighting and dying continued, men struggling for and escaping burning areas at the last minute.

A section of Soviet engineers found an undefended staircase and moved up a floor, intent on going over and coming down behind the defenders.

Only McEwan heard them coming, having been driven back from his perch on the Rathaus' first floor when accurate Maxim fire started peppering the position. Quickly, the indomitable little Scot exchanged his sniper's rifle for the PPSH sub-machine gun he had taken from a dead Russian the previous day.

The Soviets came on, oblivious to his presence and he easily wiped the group out with two long bursts of fire.

Two of the knapsacks were leaking fuel product so he decided to withdraw after quickly grabbing a round PPSH magazine from the nearest corpse. He tossed a grenade into the pile of dead and wounded for good measure, transforming the stairwell into a maelstrom of flame and preventing further enemy sallies as the resultant fire cooked off more fuel and grenades. He had no sympathy for the wounded enemy who screamed as they were consumed by his efforts, simply reasoning that they had brought the flamethrowers to the party so they deserved everything they got.

Reloading his PPSH, he set it aside again and took up the rifle, spotting a group of enemy all over the disabled Sherman in Hermannstraβe. Prioritising the two carrying what looked like teller mines, he took steady aim and dropped the first man to the roadway. Missing the second man, he gave himself a stiff reprimand and chambered another round, hitting the running figure in the left knee.

Puzzled, he relaxed the rifle away from his body, swiftly examining every inch of the beautiful Standard 4 Lee-Enfield, seeing nothing to disturb him and, blowing away an imaginary speck of dust, placed his cheek into the modified stock and held his breath.

This shot took his target perfectly in the chest, slamming 'him' to the ground instantly.

The woman's dying screams reached his ears, high-pitched and penetrating.

Holding his breath for another shot, McEwan relaxed, as again the paratroopers counter-attacked and drove the enemy back, one German pausing to sink his bayonet into the screaming woman and end her suffering.

Below him, on the ground floor of the Rathaus and in the Markt to his front, things were not going quite so well for the defenders.

Major Llewellyn, singed and black, had finally rallied his fusiliers, clinging onto the last few rooms on the north side of the ground floor of the Rathaus. So much of the building's upper floors was a sea of orange flame that he had considered abandoning the position entirely, but dismissed it immediately as his men fought on in the positions either side.

That the next target in his sights was a woman gave him an unusual moment of pause, but he pulled the trigger and she went to her maker just the same, the impact throwing her against the tank she was circling as she exhorted the others to greater efforts.

Precious few of the 555th's engineers had survived and Richardson was nowhere to be seen. D Company was down to about a quarter effectives and few of them were unscathed.

In the Markt, the Black Watch had finally stopped the Soviet advance, holding a line of shell holes, sandbags and ruined vehicles roughly halfway across the open area.

The Scots reserve platoon, led personally by Ramsey, had mounted a bayonet charge, which saved the Fallschirmjager from being outflanked as Soviet infantry surged into the Markt end of Plan and Hermannstraße. Joined by the paratroopers from the headquarters platoon, the former antagonists fought side by side, virtually wiping out the enemy force that had reached towards Reesendamm.

Those Red Army soldiers now isolated at the end of Plan stood their ground and fought back, dropping Scot and German alike with accurate fire.

The Fallschirmjager rose up as one and drove forward, taking casualties but gaining ground.

Ramsey could see Perlman leading his men forward, taking hasty aim with the Walther P38 pistol in one hand and throwing grenades with the other, his supply seemingly inexhaustible, as he produced English Mills bombs from a heavy bag around his neck.

Ramsey shouted his men to their feet and plunged forward, noting the big German go down as an enemy grenade exploded in front of him.

Angling his run towards the paratrooper, he saw the injured German officer struggle gingerly to his feet and wave his troopers on to greater efforts, again moving forward himself, albeit with the favoured gait of a wounded man.

Having fallen a few feet behind his first line of men, Ramsey witnessed a scene more fitting of the First World War, as defending Russian infantry rose to meet the charge of the Black Watch and Fallschirmjager.

The two Allied forces, approaching on different axes, started to blend into one as they merged on the enemy position.

An SVT automatic rifle put down a Scottish rifleman and a German paratrooper running side by side.

Two Russians were swept away in a short-range burst from Perlman's senior NCO, the Stabsfeldwebel's ST44 almost decapitating both men as they rose to their feet.

One eager young trooper jumped into a group of Russians and drove the bayonet of his FG42 through the neck of a Soviet officer trying to rally his troops. Discarding the empty weapon immediately, he threw himself on to another enemy, the pair rolling across the ground. Coming to a halt on top of the screaming man, he ripped off his own helmet and smashed it repeatedly into the face of his Russian foe.

All around him men were dying, Scots, Germans and Russians, in every way possible. The young paratrooper bellowed in pain as a Russian bayonet sliced into the middle of his back and emerged bloodily from his belly. His pain ended in an instant as the Soviet Yefreytor blew the blade free and, chambering another round, moved on to bloody his blade further.

Ramsey, his Webley pistol now empty, snatched up a Kar98k rifle and worked the bolt, firing and missing, succeeding only in attracting the attention of a light machine gun crew setting up to one side of the main position. The two-man DP team considered him a threat and they reoriented the gun, its tripod skittering across the rubble to point his way. Chambering another round, he took careful aim and shot the gunner in the left eye, throwing him backwards.

His rifle empty, he could do no more than charge forward, as the loader ripped her eyes from the fallen gunner and overcame her shock, grabbing at the weapon.

Ramsey won the race and the young woman squealed as he dived and landed on top of her, winding the pair of them, the DP thrown to one side, the Kar caught in a cobblestone and bent.

The commando knife slid from its scabbard and two rapid and deep strikes took the woman's life silently and swiftly.

The hand to hand combat in and around the end of Plan was no more than a huge confused rolling mass of soldiers and Ramsey momentarily halted to make an assessment. His eyes were drawn to a group of about forty Russian soldiers emerging half way down the street, intent on reinforcing their comrades.

He half rolled to the DP and looked at the unfamiliar weapon, assessing his chances.

Knowing that the previous owners had just set it up, it seemed reasonable to expect a full magazine. He had no choice but to expect that as the enemy force had already covered half the distance to the melee and no other options existed.

Flipping the weapon onto its front bipod, he determined to take the leading section first and to fire short bursts to reduce the chance of jamming. Something was wrong and the weapon just did not feel right. Ramsey spotted that the bipod was broken and couldn't support the weapon so he lodged it across the chest of the dead woman and started firing.

The DP was a primitive looking weapon, with a large round magazine mounted on the top. However, it was extremely effective and reliable and, more importantly at this moment, easy and forgiving in its use.

The first burst flayed the leading enemy group as they ran at full tilt, dropping all but one. Similar success followed as first two and then four enemies were shot down. The Russians responded and Ramsey was immediately put off his aim, missing the next group completely.

Two bullets struck the woman's corpse and splattered him with her blood, one more rammed into the ammunition pannier, jamming the weapon and hammering it back into his right shoulder. The Nordenham wound made itself known and Ramsey felt a wave of nausea wash over him.

The Russians, apparently thinking they had killed the British officer, accelerated forward into the fray, with just three men detaching themselves in Ramsey's direction.

A Fallschirmjager Oberfeldwebel dropped all three with a single burst of his MP40 without realising he had saved Ramsey.

The Black Watch commander fell back towards his struggling men, seeking out a weapon so he could rejoin the fight. For want of anything else, he pulled the stick from his belt.

The noise of heavy fighting in the Rathaus grabbed his attention for a moment and he dropped into cover to observe as a wave of Russians fell back from the burning building, encouraged by the bayonets and bullets of the Welch counter-attack. It seemed that Llewellyn had summoned every single spare man to retake the focal point of the Russian assault.

Content that his rear was secure, Ramsey turned to his own predicament once more.

They were losing.

The Fallschirmjager and Black Watch were back on the edge of the defensive position, with nowhere left to fall back to other than back into the Markt from whence they had come. The influx of men that Ramsey had tried to stop with the DP had made the difference after all.

Bullets pinged off the wrecked Volkswagen behind which Ramsey had taken cover, betraying the presence of more Soviets that had been cautiously moving into the corner of the Markt, directly opposite the Rathaus. Ramsey slid the stick back into his belt and picked up an Enfield rifle sat propped up, almost by design, against the vehicle. Checking it automatically, the weapon seemed fine; it was just empty.

730

Taking some ammo from the dead former owner, he prepared to intervene.

However, before he could commit himself the problem was dealt with in a more dramatic fashion, as two tanks from the Yeomanry's headquarters rounded the Rathaus and took the new threat under fire.

One of the Sherman's was the HQ close support tank, armed with a 105mm howitzer and its explosive shells did deadly work in short order, once again snuffing out a Soviet threat.

A shell struck the CS tank but did not penetrate, rather carrying away the nearside drive sprocket and smashing the track. The companion tank sought out the enemy and engaged what it thought was the right target, setting fire to a T34 that had been knocked out the previous day.

The concealed operational T34 fired again and penetrated the hull front of the CS Sherman just underneath the machine gunner's position, cutting the luckless gunner in half before moving on to destroy the main gun loader as he was in the act of sliding a shell home.

Whatever happened in that split second turned the tank into an instant inferno, immolating both the dead and living. Within seconds, the vehicle was 'brewing up', a typically British understated term for the way some tanks burn like furnaces, firing flames in hard straight lines from openings and loudly whooshing like a boiling kettle.

Those in and around the Markt who had not seen the phenomenon before could not help but spare it a horrified gaze, the more so when the awful fate of the crew occurred to them.

Finally locating the enemy tank, the other British vehicle, a Firefly, put three shells into the now silent hulk. The 17-pdr's sabot rounds had a high penetrative performance but lacked the punch of larger shells once inside. In this instance it hadn't mattered, as the first shell had killed three of the crew, the last two succumbing to the second impact.

Much to the regret of the Firefly crew, the enemy tank did not burn as their friends had burned.

They moved forward into a sandbagged position to assume a cover position up the Mönckebergstraβe and

731

immediately destroyed another T34 manoeuvring its way past its dead comrade. This time the Firefly gunner was rewarded with the sight of flames and a satisfactory imitation of CS tank behind him.

In Ramsey's position it was total chaos. Some of the Scottish and Germans soldiers exchanged fire with the majority of the Russians, who had temporarily dropped back to regroup for another attack, satisfying themselves with grenades and bullets over the thirty yards that separated the two forces. The remainder were engaged in close quarter fighting with the score or so enemy who had not fallen back with the others.

The sudden squawk of the pipes being winded penetrated the sounds of fighting.

B Company's piper had taken a bullet in the leg as he ran across the Markt and had only just managed to crawl to his instrument to contribute as best he could to the fight.

Setting himself against the dead body of an unknown paratrooper he started his repertoire, 'Scotland the Brave' building in volume as he set about his task.

The effect upon Ramsey's Jocks was electric and they renewed themselves to greater efforts, especially as their Major had rejoined them, unharmed and in fighting mood.

Ramsey could sense the difference and, for that matter, so could Perlmann twenty yards away to his left.

Turning around to shout at the Piper, the very English Ramsey drew a number of grins from his men for behaviour less than that expected of a gentleman.

"Piper Sinclair!"

The piper played on.

"Sinclair!"

Affecting his finest Scottish accent, Ramsey tried a different tack.

"Sinclair, ye deaf bas!"

Picking up a piece of brick, Ramsey tossed it at his piper who thought that it was a grenade and rolled over the body of the German with the speed of a gazelle.

Sheepishly looking over the corpse, he noted his Major grinning and shouting in his direction.

Ramsey, confident he now had the undivided attention of his piper, issued his orders.

"Black Bear, Sinclair, give the lads Black Bear!"

Putting wind in his instrument once more, the pipes started to belt out Ramsey's choice, which the company always played when they went on the attack.

The Scots braced themselves and waited on Ramsey's order.

That order came and the Watch rose up, charging forward, screaming like banshees, closely followed by the strangely yet equally inspired Fallschirmjager.

The Soviet force also chose to attack at the same time and the two groups met in the middle area, clashing at the charge.

A hideously ugly Russian leapt up off the ground, intent on staving Ramsey's skull with his rifle butt. As he descended he changed direction in mid-air, the force of bullets from a paratroopers MP40 sending him flying into the Soviet rifleman to his left.

There was no time for thanks as that man, regaining his balance, threw himself at the Black Watch commander, bayonet surging towards his unprotected belly.

Ramsey fell, his feet tangled in the straps of a discarded Soviet rifle. The thrust missed its target and skidded off Ramsey's canteen.

Winded by the force of his fall, Ramsey twisted as best he could, narrowly avoiding a second thrust which hit the road and snapped the bayonet of his enemy.

The Russian stupidly looked at the broken blade and Ramsey took advantage, swinging his Enfield round and slamming it into the side of the man's head sending him flying, the impression of the front sight clear on the side of his forehead.

Ramsey moved quickly, as he sensed rather than saw another threat and felt heavy pressure as his rifle was almost forced from his hands. As he had turned, the bayonet had become a spike onto which the attacking Soviet officer had propelled himself with his own momentum.

The dead body slid easily off Ramsey's steel and he turned to quickly shoot the other unconscious man in the head before taking a moment to assess the situation.

Many of the Russians were down, over half their number had perished in the ferocious counter-attack, but there were also a large number of his own men who would never see the glens again.

The Fallschirmjager had fared better, possibly because they had run in slightly behind the Scots.

'Black Bear' had stopped. Piper Sinclair had been sought out by a rifleman and shot in the head.

Over a hundred more Soviets flooded out of the ruins and into the fight, throwing everything into the balance again.

Ramsey knew the moment had come.

Shouting encouragement to his men, he waded into a group of Soviets, angling in from their left side. He ran the first through with his bayonet, screaming with pain as a rifle butt hammered against his wounded shoulder, dropping him to his knees. A Soviet soldier loomed over him, raising his entrenching tool to maximum height and then falling away as a line of crimson flowers appeared out of his chest.

Recovering his own rifle, Ramsey suddenly found himself isolated and the sole target for three enemy soldiers.

A moment's pause was all he needed, triggering the Enfield and dropping the centre man with a round to the stomach. Rushing left, he caught the next man by surprise and bundled straight into him, sending him flying. Turning to the third man, he felt the sear of pain as a bullet flicked his thigh. The man worked the bolt on his rifle quickly but Ramsey ended his life with a powerful thrust through the throat.

Turning to the second man, he saw that no further action was needed. The force of Ramsey's impact had propelled the Russian onto a wicked wooden spike that stuck out from the rubble. The man was face down on it, twitching and mumbling incoherently as his life drained out of him.

Re-chambering his own rifle, Ramsey shot down a Soviet Officer who was exhorting his men forward. The man was the III/215th's Commander and the sight of their leader screaming his last few seconds away proved to be a turning point and the fight went out of the Russian troops in an instant.

Turning and running, they lost a number of soldiers shot in the back as they tried to regain friendly cover.

The Fallschirmjager pursued them relentlessly and, in the process, again recovered most of the ground previously lost.

Ramsey organised his men, aghast at how few could still stand. He had led the sixty men forward and only twenty-eight could answer the call. Not all the rest were dead and some could fight again that day, but precisely half would never move again.

At his feet lay a young Scot, James Munro, his belly ripped open by some unknown blade and a bayonet wound in his shoulder, in excruciating pain but resolutely silent, despite his approaching death.

Ramsey knelt at the young soldier's side knowing that all he could do was share the boy's final moments. Holding his right hand tightly he placed his left hand on Munro's forehead, stroking the boy's head and encouraging eye contact. The medic rammed home three doses of morphine and James Munro died pain free.

More Fallschirmjager arrived, released from their defence of Jungfernsteig after they and the Yeomanry had drubbed the attacking force. These set about evacuating their injured comrades and the wounded jocks, as well as setting a strong defensive position in place.

Four of the paratroopers reverently removed the insensible body of their commander, Perlmann having fallen unnoticed amongst a pile of dead, alive, but bleeding from a dozen wounds.

The arrival of Russian small calibre mortar rounds ended the brief lull and Ramsey determined to reform his reserve and to find out what was going on across the front of Llewellyn Force.

In essence, Llewellyn Force was holding but only just.

The Rathaus was again more Soviet than British as extra troops pressed forward, exhorted by their officers.

The Soviet diversionary effort had run into an allied counter-attack to the south as 71st Infantry brigade sought to throw the Soviet moves off-balance. 1st Battalion, Highland Light Infantry, supported by more of the Yorkshire Yeomanry's armour had struck back, threatening the Holzbrücke, so Beloborodov had been forced to switch one of his reserve battalions to assist. This left solely the III/938th Rifles uncommitted.

II/259th Rifles had been ordered to probe the positions in front of them, not by the Army Commander, but by the Regimental Commander, who just couldn't believe the British could be strong everywhere.

This was a huge mistake and his pinning force suffered huge casualties charging A Coy/RWF and the support platoon. He was only saved from the vengeance of his General by a Welsh bullet. It also meant that the dead Lieutenant Colonel would be an excellent scapegoat for what was to come.

'A' Company's commander realised the tactical situation had changed in his favour and released the support platoon and one section from each of his own platoons, creating a reserve force, which he immediately sent to the aid of his Battalion Commander in the Rathaus.

'C' Company had held their own at great loss of life, helped by the arrival of armoured support in the shape of the rest of the Yeomanry's headquarters troop, which had forced into the Soviet flank at a crucial time. Not without loss, as was attested to by Acting Major Brown's body hanging half in, half out of his command tank, slowly being consumed by the lazy fire inside.

In the Rathaus there was a stalemate. Scelerov and his men had burned everything and everyone they could and had run out of usable flamethrowers. A fuming Scelerov has sent ten men back for more and contented himself with throwing phosphorous grenades as he waited to be rearmed. He was unaware that he would wait in vain, as the party had been vaporised by a 25-pdr HE shell as they were returned laden with fresh cylinders.

The situation in the Rathaus was unclear to the Russians, so the Commander of 1st Rifle Corps committed his

736

final reserve to where he could see there was an opportunity and where they could be directly supported with tanks.

Shouting out his orders, his left hand, formed into a fist, marking out the tempo of his words on the map table and his right hand gesticulating wildly, the General got his officers moving.

There were only seven running tanks left in 2nd Btn after fierce exchanges with British tanks and anti-tank guns but they were ordered to go forward once more.

Ordering the 106th Pontoon Engineers to be ready, the Rifle Corps commander sent his men forward.

A number of things happened at once.

Ramsey reconstituted his reserve force at the rear of the Markt, bolstering the numbers with a stiffening of Fallschirmjager and a handful of Manchesters.

Llewellyn's 'A' Company reserve force arrived at the Rathaus.

The Yeomanry's D Sqdn lost its last tank to a mortar round which started an engine fire.

Adolphesbrucke dropped into the canal, victim of Soviet artillery fire.

Losing no time, Major Llewellyn organised a counter-attack that started to push back the Soviets on the ground floor of the Rathaus again.

Charging forward, the Welsh threw the Russians back all the way to the main lobby before they turned and held their ground.

Sub-machine guns and grenades did their deadly work and Llewellyn's life was saved when one of his young fusiliers threw himself on a grenade that had landed at his side. The young man died, the officer lived. Llewellyn promised himself and the boy that he would record the brave act appropriately.

Another grenade landed close and was plucked up and thrown in an instant, returned from whence it had come to good effect, screams of pain marking its effectiveness.

Sensing the need to push hard again, Llewellyn shouted his troops forward and charged, dropping an enemy rifleman with a burst of Sten.

737

An enemy officer rose and fired his pistol, missing with his first two shots but hitting soft flesh with his third and fourth. Llewellyn, dropped to the ground by the impacts, pressed the trigger of his Sten and put a burst into the disfigured man.

Scelerov was thrown backwards by the impact of five bullets, losing his pistol as he hit the wall hard.

A group of fusiliers ran past him, intent on mischief further down the hallway.

Bleeding and in pain, Scelerov pulled himself onto his knees, extracted a fragmentation grenade and pulled the pin, intending to toss it into the middle of the fusiliers who had been forced to ground fifteen yards away.

As he raised his arm, a huge weight descended upon him, rugby tackling him and pinning him to the ground with the deadly charge still in his grip under his body.

In the last second of his life, Scelerov screamed, not in fear, but in anger, his revenge incomplete and all those months of pain borne for nothing.

The grenade exploded, eviscerating the Russian instantly.

Llewellyn received a fragment through his right wrist, which damaged his tendons. The blast lifted him off the distorted body of Scelerov, throwing him to the left and stunning him as he hit his head on a lump of stone.

Carried forward by the momentum of the charge, the Welch continued to drive the Soviet engineers and riflemen before them, reclaiming most of the Rathaus.

Combined with the successful recapture of the old defensive positions, now occupied by the Fallschirmjager, this created a shallow U-shaped area into which the 1st Rifle Corps was inadvertently committing its last force of note.

Without orders, the Hauptmann now commanding the Fallschirmjager secured the southernmost corner of his position and deployed two MG42's on the right flank of the Soviet attack.

Simultaneously, the Welch Captain who found himself temporarily in charge in the Rathaus, stiffened the southern wall defences and then organised a firing line in the

Rathaus, looking across into the Markt. Three Vickers .303's, two from RWF and one from the Manchesters, bolstered the defence.

In the Markt itself were the Black Watch, with their own Vickers and three more from the Manchesters.

The T34's of 39th Guards Tank Brigade pushed forward, firing wildly as they advanced. One lucky shell reduced a Welch Vickers to scrap metal in short order.

The Russian tanks opened their formation as they moved into the southern edge of Markt and were brought under fire by C Sqdn of the Yeomanry and the last 71st 6-pdr, positioned at the end of Reesendamm.

Fig#31 - Hamburg - Finale

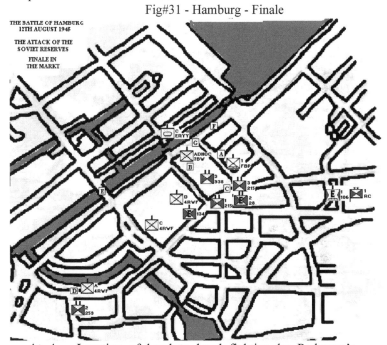

At A - Location of hand to hand fighting by Perlmann's Fallschirmjager and the Black Watch.

At B - Point from which the Yeomanry's two headquarters tanks engaged the Soviet tanks and where the CS tank was destroyed.

At C - Deployment zone for T34's supporting the Markt attack.
At D - II/259th's probing attack that failed.
At E - Adolphesbrücke struck by Soviet artillery and drops into the canal.
At F - Last 'D' Sqdn Sherman knocked out by Soviet mortar fire.

.

Light mortars sought out and killed the anti-tank gun but the tanks still died, as the Yeomanry Firefly opened up, killing three in quick succession.

A T34 shell struck the 17-pdr gun barrel and deformed it, forcing the crew to evacuate their vehicle.

Four T34's now remained, spitting death from their machine guns, bullets flying in all directions, keeping the enemy's heads down as their own infantry reached the Markt and plunged forward.

The Russian 'Urrah' leapt from five hundred and fifty throats as they charged headlong into the Markt.

Fire erupted from the Rathaus and a huge audible sigh went up from the Soviet ranks as metal met flesh and bone, sending man after man to the ground.

Instinctively, the waves of Russians moved to their right, away from the withering fire that claimed more lives every second.

Again the collective anguished gasp as two MG42's and other weapons spat death from the right hand side of the Markt.

1st Lieutenant Ames, Royal Artillery, was not to be outdone and dropped his shoot on the money, wiping out a score of Russians with every burst.

It was the nearest thing to mass murder Ramsey had ever seen.

In less than five minutes, an assault force of over five hundred men had been reduced to a few witless survivors trying to scrape holes in the ruined road or sitting glassy eyed amongst the bloody wreckage that used to be their comrades and friends.

Some Soviets closed with Black Watch and Manchester firing positions in the Markt, more for the protection offered by getting close than for aggressive intent.

Swiftly the battered and shocked men were either shot or bayoneted, even those surrendering, for this was no time to be encumbered with prisoners. Once dealt with, the Scots and Mancunians went back to the business of killing at range.

The slaughter was soon over and the infantry withdrew, leaving piles of corpses behind.

The 39th Tanks had been wiped out in all but name, one running tank withdrawing, its crew taking the young wounded Colonel back to the aid post to be either saved or to die in peace.

1930hrs Sunday 12th August 1945, Altstad, Hamburg, Germany.

The Battle of the Rathaus ended at roughly 7.30pm, although there was sporadic firing and men died from then until night descended and the area became quiet.

The Allied camp licked its wounds and took stock of whom and what had been lost.

Young 1st Lieutenant Ramsey's body was recovered as best could be done and wrapped in a canvas for evacuation. His battery of the 71st had suffered appallingly and would contribute very little on the morrow.

Brown of the Yeomanry still hung from his turret, it being too dangerous to do any more than watch the glowing hull grow cooler in the late evening air. Half the tanks had been lost, but they had given a fine account of themselves and were still high on morale.

555th Engineers had nil effectives now, those who were not dead on the field having been evacuated over the Bride, now the sole means of communication, rearming and reinforcing left open to Llewellyn Force. CSM Richardson's burnt body had been recovered and was removed to the west bank with those of his dead men.

The Manchesters had done well; very well. Captain Arthurs could not be found and the credit for the defence went to his second in command.

Fallschirm Batallione Perlman had suffered modest casualties in comparison, those units that had been situated on the Jungfernsteig relatively unscathed, whilst those adjacent to the Markt had been savaged badly. Perlman has refused to be evacuated, remaining in his command post to be fussed over by the battalion doctor.

For the Royal Welch Fusiliers, it was a mixed day. Support and Admin platoons illustrated this well. Support platoon had done fine work, moving on to counter-attack within the Rathaus, sustaining surprisingly few casualties. Admin platoon had three men left standing, the rest either on stretchers or in the lines of dead arranged at the Alterwall, adjacent to the Bride.

'A' Coy had sustained the fewest casualties, mainly because of the Russian tactics, but the dead company commander had been very popular and would be missed.

'C' Coy had lost 50% of its effectives, but with a high proportion of wounded men.

'D' Coy had suffered the most, now with only thirty-four effectives and too many of those absent lying dead.

The Black Watch had arrived the day before with one hundred and twenty-seven men.

Ramsey stood back as Sgt MacFarlane went through the roll call, smiling at the humour in McEwan's voice, sighing with emotion as Young Munro did not reply to his name and imagining the faint sound of the pipes when Sinclair failed to answer the roll.

Himself included, 'B' Company, 7th Battalion, The Black Watch, now consisted of forty-six effectives.

Dismissing the parade, Ramsey turned and looked over the Markt, sensing rather than seeing the heaps of enemy dead, knowing that they had suffered more losses than he had, but finding no consolation in the thought.

Ramsey wept, silently and stiffly, as only a man battling with his inner self can do.

For the Russians, the reaper's bill was higher than could ever have been expected and without success to sweeten the bitterness of so many deaths.

179th Rifle Division was combat ineffective now. None of the five battalions committed had their commander, four being dead and one missing vital parts of his body, removed by grenades as he led his men forward at the Exchange. The five battalions, consisting of one thousand seven hundred men just a few hours ago, now mustered less than six hundred and many of those were unfit but refused to go to the aid stations.

The three battalions of 938th Rifle Regiment had done no better. I Btn had been hammered in their advance up Ballindamm, II Btn savaged as they went to the support of the under-pressure diversionary attack force, III/992nd Rifle Regt. III/938th had been the main force that blundered into the Markt, complete with companies from the 215th Rifles and the sappers of the 28th.

II Btn 28th Engineer Sappers had been pulled from the Ballindamm attack, preserved for the Markt assault and had suffered the most casualties of any battalion in the field, there being only twenty-four men left from a unit which boasted three hundred and sixty at the start of the day.

Second to them came the III/215th Rifles, which had been the opponents of Ramsey and the Fallschirmjager during their wild counter-attack. They had started the Battle of Hamburg with two hundred and ninety-nine effectives, ending with forty-seven capable of holding a weapon.

39th Guards Tanks had worked wonders and now had a total of eight running tanks, its mechanics scrounging from wrecks to make whole. Casualties amongst the crews had been less than the norm, as many had escaped back to their own lines. However, their morale was shot away, lowered further by the grievous wounding of their much-loved commander.

10th Guards Mortar had been badly hit by radar-guided counter-battery fire and the 64th Gun Artillery Brigade had been given a nasty going over by allied ground-attack aircraft, appearing unopposed over the Hamburg skies.

743

Last on Beloborodov's list were the 134th Knapsack Flamethrower Company of ninety-four men and one mad disfigured Kapitan. Simply put, there was no one left.

True to form, Beloborodov blamed the actions of the II/295th's commander for the whole failure and was, surprisingly, believed.

He never did get the Guards Rifle Corps and 43rd Army was withdrawn from front-line action to reform.

2300hrs Sunday 12th August 1945, Adjacent to the 'Bride', Altstad, Hamburg, Germany.

Llewellyn organised a command group on the quayside adjacent to 'the Bride', where a large sandbagged position provided protection from the Soviet artillery fire that had been redirected onto the front line positions shortly after the failure of the attack.

No lighting was necessary as the burning Rathaus adequately illuminated the entire area.

As he waited for his officers, an orderly finished tending to his day's wounds, a clean shot through the left arm muscle, a flesh wound to the right side of his belly and the nasty wrist wound that presently denied him the full use of his right hand.

The two bullets from Scelerov's pistol had hit nothing vital and the new bandages on calf and arm protected wounds that bled a lot, stung like crazy, but were not serious.

First to arrive was Schuster, the competent Fallschirmjager Hauptmann now sporting his own mark of honour; a head bandage. He was closely followed by 2nd Lieutenant Maitland of the Manchesters, Captain Jones of RWF's A Company and CSM Price, the senior man left standing in the savaged D Company.

Next came Angell, Lieutenant of Yeomanry, his uniform stinking of petrol, his eyes speaking volumes of the horrors he had faced that day, deep in whispered conversation with C Coy's Captain Anwill, who favoured a wounded leg.

Lieutenant Reece arrived, his uniform immaculate by comparison with the others, his mortar unit not having

744

sustained a single casualty thus far, having joined in with the defeat of the Ballindamm assault and added to the misery of those slaughtered in the Markt from a distance only. Accompanying him was the less than pristine Ames, who had taken up a rifle in the Rathaus resistance, closing with an enemy face to face for the first time. Blackened by soot and with smoke-reddened eyes, he hoped never to repeat the experience.

Last to join the group was John Ramsey, none of his wounds of any great note but, none the less, stiff and aching from his exertions.

Welcoming everyone and permitting smoking, Llewellyn swung into organising the defence for that night and the following day, formally and efficiently discharging his function, not referring to the horrors of the day they had just shared.

As he wound up proceedings, a panting Lance-Corporal runner arrived, bearing orders from the Brigadier. The man disappeared as soon as Llewellyn acknowledged that he understood and would comply, a process that took slightly longer as he had to open the envelope one-handed.

Staring at the back of the runner, very obviously a man who had pressing business in safer areas, the Welshman composed himself.

"I'm sure you can imagine what this is?" holding the message pad out towards his officers.

"Attack orders?" quipped Ramsey with a lightness he did not feel, his comment drawing weary chuckles from the assembly.

"Forget all I just said, gentlemen. We are pulling back to the other side of the canal. The Brigadier doesn't want us cut off. Nice of him really. Just a little late."

It was a sensible order to a man some miles away, but the impact of paying so high a price to defend ground and then to retreat was galling to every officer present.

Unfolding his map once more, Llewellyn drew his commanders closer and under the flickering orange light they planned.

Smearing the map with a combination of blood, sweat and ash, he ran his finger over the positions, illustrating his words.

"Hauptmann, part of your unit will evacuate back over the Bride, positioning opposite the breach here. You will be first to move your men at," looking at his watch and making a quick decision, "2330 hrs."

Schuster checked his own timepiece and nodded.

"The first group should be able to resite within thirty minutes?"

This time the Hauptmann smiled wearily.

"Twenty minutes, Herr Maior. No more than that."

Llewellyn appreciated the man's enthusiasm and national pride, but there was something vital that needed to be said.

"We will allow thirty minute, Hauptmann. The Bride is a flimsy lady and we mustn't rush her."

Schuster could not help but concede that point.

"At the same time, A Coy will start evacuating over the remains of the Stadthausbrücke, same procedure, covering force behind, force over the water and set for defence."

And Llewellyn went piece by piece through the withdrawal, allowing a few minutes here and there as a safety margin until he got to the end. Firing orders for the mortars and artillery were confirmed, Reece and Ames taking notes, the artilleryman's constantly shaking hands drawing more than one sympathetic look.

"Black Watch will be next at 0120 and will set up right opposite the Bride, covering the rearguard sections of D Company."

Llewellyn stood upright, almost challenging his officers to disagree.

"D Company will move over the Bride commencing at 0140... and I shall be last to cross."

There was no dissent. The young Major had, without question, earned the right.

The moment had arrived and Llewellyn took it head on with all the emotion of his celtic race.

"Today we have lost many a good man. Friends have fallen," the slight crackle in his voice betraying the exhausted man's angst.

"I can only say that it was a privilege to fight with all of you on this day, for we've done our duty to the fullest degree."

In a remarkable moment of leadership, he repeated the phrase, his eyes boring into the disconsolate Reece, words spoken for him and his predicament, "To the fullest degree."

The young Welshman tightened his jaw and accepted the gift his Major offered. Honour was satisfied.

"Thank you all and please pass on my admiration and thanks to every man under your commands."

Bringing himself back from the emotional edge, Llewellyn looked across the assembly.

"I will not expect your written reports until after we have relocated."

The look on his face carried the intended humour and the comment was well received.

"If there are no further questions, gentlemen?"

There were none and the group broke up.

A meaningful look from the Welshman had stayed Ramsey's departure and, once again, the two found themselves alone.

The younger man struggled for his words.

"I know, lad," the soothing voice of the Black Watch Major cut through the emotional silence.

"You did extremely well today, extremely well."

Coming from the legend, Llewellyn could accept that as praise indeed.

"Thank you, Major Ramsey. Everyone did well today I think."

A brief moment's pause, during which the RWF officer's stance softened, his face reflecting how his mind was dragging up the day's demons.

"They came on and on… they didn't stop."

"No one said they aren't brave soldiers, did they?"

"No… and they are very brave; very, very brave."

747

"Valour knows no national boundaries, Major Llewellyn."

The tired Welshman nodded wearily.

"Many a brave man died here today and that's a fact, Major Ramsey."

To bring an end to the maudlin moment, the Black Watch officer brought himself to the attention.

"Major Llewellyn, it has been a privilege to serve with you."

He saluted the younger man and went to take his leave.

He stopped, considering something, and turned back again.

"One day, when all this is over, someone will write a book about today, Lieutenant Chard."

The reference to the commander of Rourke's Drift brought a dry laugh from the Welshman.

Affecting a posh English accent, he quipped back, feeling a lot better than he had done for some time.

"See you on the other side of the water, Bromhead, old chap."

0040 Monday 13th August 1945, Altona, Hamburg, Germany.

Llewellyn Force successfully completed its relocation as planned and without major incident, reforming the defensive line, a line that still spread unbroken across the whole of the city, which good news Radio Hamburg hammered out to a frightened population.

Reece and Ames put down their covering fire, as much to create noise as to disrupt any enemy moves.

Ames, with the uncanny ability to sense the right action, altered his fire plan, ordering a three round battery shoot on the area around St Jacobi, where the Soviets had gathered for the attack that afternoon.

His instincts proved correct.

748

1st Company, 106th Pontoon Engineers had sustained no casualties that day, being held back ready for when the infantry did their job.

Under cover of darkness, they were moving their equipment up ready for the assault the following day. The command group was being briefed by the shocked General whose 1st Rifle Corps had bled out in the attack.

Twelve rounds of HE landed in a tight area, testament to the skills of the British gunners.

The screams of the dying were mixed with the shouts of rescuers who rushed forward as the fire shifted to other areas.

Many of the 106th's personnel lay broken and bleeding with their equipment wrecked beyond use.

The engineer command group and that of the 1st Rifle Corps were unidentifiable, two shells having landed a few feet either side of them as they worked.

They were the final casualties of a bloody day.

In 1879, at the Battle of Rourke's Drift in Natal, South Africa, the defenders were awarded eleven Victoria Crosses and numerous other awards, two of the VC's falling to Lieutenants Chard and Bromhead, the officers commanding.

In 1945, Llewellyn submitted a long list of recommendations for his men, all of whom deserved an award many times over.

In 1879, the British Government had been keen to reduce the impact of the disastrous Isandhlwana battle and played up the defence of Rourke's Drift, hence its place in British Military history and the numerous awards of medals for such a small action.

In 1945, Llewellyn Force and its stand in Hamburg was historic because of the huge losses the modest British and German Force inflicted on the enemy.

It was also historic because it was the first battle of the new war in which two Victoria Crosses were awarded.

Llewellyn's report laid over forty names before his commanding officer and only three were downgraded from the original recommendations of the proud Welshman. Ranging from a Military Medal for CSM Price to a DSO for Maior Perlmann of the Fallschirmjager, a bar to the Military Cross for the dead Frederick Brown to a DSO for Captain Daffyd Jones of A Company.

Last on Llewellyn's list was the recommendation for the award of a Victoria Cross to a young fusilier, the one who had sacrificed his life so that others could live, fulfilling the promise he made over the boy's corpse in the burning Rathaus.

The commanding officer of 43rd Welch Division also received a report submitted by a British Officer, not of his division, counter-signed by all but one of the leadership of Llewellyn Force. This document put forward another name for the highest award, a report given much weight by bearing the signatures of a number of experienced and decorated officers, not the least of which was Major J Ramsey VC, DSO and 2 Bars, MC and Bar, The Black Watch, the author of the recommendation.

Which meant that, on 3rd January 1946, Major/Acting Lieutenant Colonel Tewdwr Llewellyn, stood in the Throne Room of Buckingham Palace, alongside the proud sister of Private Euan Jenkins, where both received Victoria Crosses from a grateful King and Country.

2045hrs Sunday 12th August 1945, Curau River Bridge, south-west of Heiligenthal, Germany.

Nazarbayeva had once again come very close to death and she knew it, Allied aircraft the offenders this time, in the shape of thunderbolts intent on mischief. Her driver and security officer were poring over the GAZ, trying to mend the radiator damage resulting from the crash, which itself had been caused by hard manoeuvrings as they avoided the attentions of the fighters attacking the bridge she was just about to cross.

She checked her watch.

It was precisely 8.45pm on a lovely summer's eve and she immediately decided that a Lieutenant Colonel's rank had to have some privileges

Looking around her, she decided against the ruined watermill as a starting point, instead looking north towards the meadow.

Leaving the vehicle and would-be mechanics to the job, she decided to go for a walk, as this was the first time she had stretched her legs since leaving the military hospital at Kirchgellersen, where she had interrogated a severely wounded British Intelligence Colonel. Pekunin's decision to send her personally had been the correct one as the man had died this very evening, but not before Tatiana had garnered some interesting and important information.

As she walked, Nazarbayeva watched the small unit of bridging engineers at work, having already placed out barriers to prevent anyone from using their bridge while they set to repairing the damage from the air attack.

Nazarbayeva paused to scrutinise them more closely, assessing their skills and the time they would take. Moving on, she walked past the stubs of a larger wooden bridge that had been knocked down during the fighting a few days beforehand.

All around her, the detritus of war was still randomly spread, plainly marking the location as one on which blood had been prodigiously spilt.

Rough graves containing Soviet soldiers lay close to those where the enemy were obviously buried, all committed near to where they fell.

A blackened hull of a destroyed T34 tank stood silently guarding the watercourse and a ruined burnt-out jeep, clearly pushed from the roadway, half in, half out of the nearby bushes.

On the other side of the river stood a number of large trucks, smashed and rent, each with its own crop of burial markers recording the unfortunates who had died.

All around the site the ground had been scarred by high-explosives, the fields seemingly despoiled by the work of huge moles.

Tatiana walked along the bank of the river, picking her way around the shell holes, trying to read the battlefield.

She followed the bend, finding ammunition, belts and helmets in large quantities.

In a large shell hole, the obvious signs of a temporary aid post, with blood stained bandages and torn clothing in thick piles.

A shattered rifle, obviously American, lay sundered on the rim.

She followed the river round to where the visible indications of multiple grenade bursts covered the ground.

A very obvious corpse lay in the bushes on the other side, a cloud of flies rising and descending, feeding on the decaying flesh. The uniform was that of the Red Army. She promised herself that she would order the engineers to remedy the situation and bury this unknown hero of the Motherland once she returned to the bridge.

She stopped and looked around her, recognising the shallow depressions as filled-in trenches and foxholes. She concluded that this was the American defensive position and decided to walk it with a professional eye.

As she strode past the first foxhole, her good foot connected with a stone in the grass. She bent down to pick it up, intending to send it into the water.

However, this 'stone' was manufactured in the US of A, as it was a Mk II Fragmentation grenade, placed ready for use beside the foxhole by the former American occupant.

Inspecting the grenade, Tatiana could see no problems with it and slipped it into her pocket as a deadly souvenir.

She continued her walk, her veteran's eye assessing the signs of intense combat, interpreting the marks of violence, imagining a rush of feet here and a last stand there, until her reverie was broken by shouting from her security officer, beckoning her to return to the vehicle.

Pausing only to commend the Mladshy Leytenant for his speedy repair and apprise him of the unrecovered remains, she mounted the GAZ and continued the journey back to GRU Headquarters.

1807hrs Sunday 12th August 1945, Headquarters of SHAEF, Trianon Hotel, Versailles, France.

Eisenhower was worried, or more accurately, concerned, because he wasn't worried as much as had been the case the past week. Across the whole front, Russian attacks had now stopped, with the sole exception of Hamburg. Report after report from frontline units spoke of enemy units halting, as if exhausted. All except Hamburg. The situation was unclear and a report from McCreery was due at any time.

The plan to bomb the potential enemy reserve sites had been put together well and received Ike's wholehearted endorsement, although Soviet night fighters had been in the air in large numbers the previous night and the British had sustained unusually heavy losses, damaging the intended operations for that evening. None the less, the brave crews would go out again, bolstered by bomber training squadrons and every night fighter unit in the Allied inventory.

The arrival of more operation ground-attack assets was another fillip to a General under great pressure.

However, as always, there was a balance.

A Soviet submarine had sunk another troop carrier off the south coast of Eire, with great loss of life. She was the Empire Windrush, formerly known as the Monte Rosa of the Hamburg-Sud Company, carrying over two thousand young replacement troops to the British and Canadian armies in the field.

A mine had taken out a large tanker off Cherbourg that very evening, bringing to three the number of fuel deliveries lost to the Allied armies in as many days.

Allied anti-submarine deployments were being doubled, but it was taking time to get the assets in the right places.

None the less, more units and supplies were coming, from the States, from the United Kingdom and her dominions, from Spain, from South America and from…

Eisenhower's flow of positive thoughts was interrupted by a knock on the door of his private office, a small and cosy room, a place he rarely went but had chosen for this brief encounter.

Standing, he crushed his cigarette into the overflowing brass ashtray and stroked his uniform jacket into place, checking his appearance in the tall mirror. Adopting an authoritative tone, he invited entrance.

Hood looked round the door.

"Shall I show the gentlemen in now, Sir?"

Eisenhower nodded and Hood's head retreated to be replaced by a procession of three men in uniforms of uncertain parentage, most certainly a mix and match of mainly American, but all with German boots and gaiters mixed with US Army trousers in one case, belt and helmet comforter in another and two with German side caps.

The pistol holsters drew Eisenhower's eye, even though he knew the weapons had been surrendered at the security point. Such measures were now considered necessary and there were no exceptions allowed.

There was no doubt that all three men had made efforts to sharpen their appearance.

'Professionals are always professionals,' the General reminded himself.

Bringing up the rear was Colonel Samuel V. Rossiter USMC, whose holster was very obviously filled and who was there ostensibly to interpret.

In spite of the deliberate informality of the setting and the purpose of the meeting, there seemed to be a definite tension in all six men.

'Hardly surprising,' thought Ike.

The present military alliance between the two countries was still young and raw and the last four bloody years were not so easily set aside.

It fell to Eisenhower to break the awkwardness.

"Gentlemen, good evening. Welcome to the Headquarters of Allied Armies in Europe. I have requested the three of you come here this evening so that I can thank you personally for your efforts."

Rossiter translated. Eisenhower clucked at himself.

754

"My apologies, we haven't been introduced. I am Dwight D. Eisenhower, Commanding Officer, Allied Forces."

The middle man of the three took a small step forward and indicated the man to his right, nearest the General.

Braun, speaking English, took the initiative.

"If I may, Sir, this is Rolf Uhlmann, formerly Sturmbannfuhrer with 5th SS Panzer Division," stepping back and extending his hand to his left-side.

"And this is Ostap Shandruk, a Ukrainian national, formerly Obersturmfuhrer with 14th SS Grenadiere Division."

Each clicked their heels in deference as they were introduced, receiving a smile and a nod from the Allied Commander.

"For myself, I am Johannes Braun, formerly Sturmscharfuhrer with 5th SS Panzer Division and all of us were prisoners of the Russians at Edelbach."

"Thank you, Master Sergeant Braun. I regret that we must be brief and I hope you will all understand that time is limited to me at the moment."

This time Braun took up the translating.

"I know General Clark has already thanked you for your service but I wanted to add to that, as now we know that you saved many lives and gave some of our units the early warning they needed."

Braun shared the words with the men either side of him equally, his head moving from side to side almost rhythmically.

Eisenhower waited, eyeing his cigarette pack longingly.

"I would very much like to know why you undertook this perilous journey and then risked your lives again to bring us the information."

The translation ended and a swift exchange in German between Uhlmann and Braun followed. Eisenhower didn't understand but Rossiter did. The Marine smiled and pursed his lips in amusement.

Uhlmann spoke slowly so that Braun could translate his words as he went.

"Herr General, until recently we were enemies but my country has capitulated and that war is ended. What we saw was a new war about to start, one in which the Russian would be the common enemy. It was our simple duty to report what we saw, because we could not believe that our country would do anything but ally itself with the anti-communist cause."

Eisenhower nodded his way through the translation, a serious look on his face. This was what he had been told but it was something else to hear it from the horse's mouth, although Rossiter could attest to the fact that Braun was not repeating exactly what the former SS officer had said. Very wise as it never paid to swear at a General.

Uhlmann had not yet finished.

"We Eastern Front soldiers had already seen the Red Army at work, destroying, raping, looting and murdering."

The ex-SS officer punched out the last words, adding the emphasis of passion.

"Part of Germany lies in their control, we could not see more of it invaded, Herr General."

Eisenhower went to speak but Uhlmann suddenly whispered to his comrade, so the General bided his time.

Braun coughed and sought permission to continue.

"Sturmbann... sorry...Herr Uhlmann says that, in truth, it would have been more difficult to sit and do nothing."

'An honest point made by an honest man', thought Ike.

"I understand, Gentlemen, so again I must thank you for your efforts. Now, how may we best reward you?"

Braun translated and Eisenhower saw the confusion on their faces.

"All our ex-SS prisoners are being transferred to France under the care of the French Army."

Whilst Eisenhower had made the decision that he would not admit any knowledge of the French plan for the time being, he had impulsively decided to trust these men. What he had to say would not be news to Rossiter.

"I know that they intend to form Foreign Legion units from ex-SS personnel to fight the Soviets. I tell you this in good faith and request that you never speak of this to anyone as I do not 'officially' know this."

Braun spoke his words and the three chorused "Zu Befehl, Herr General," indicating their observance of his wish.

No translation was necessary to the American.

"Thank you. I can offer you your freedom and a release from military service, as all German personnel have been placed under my command. Your Council have been consulted and fully endorse this offer. I understand General Clarke has provided you with safe conduct papers in any case."

It was time to deal with a delicate subject.

"The SS are not to form part of the regular German forces because of their reputation for war crimes and association with the camps and other excesses. The French have found a way round that for the common good and, I'm sure, also for their own means," he added lightly.

Returning to a more deliberate style, he continued.

"I must tell you that you have been investigated and we have not found any reason to detain any of you for war crimes, but do understand that if evidence is found then you will be brought to trial for any matter in which you are implicated. It cannot be otherwise, gentlemen."

Eisenhower felt uncomfortable saying it, Braun likewise translating it and Uhlmann and Shandruk listening to it.

Quickly the General moved on.

"I do not doubt that the honour you showed by your actions is indicative of the way you conducted yourselves during the hostilities."

Braun stumbled on 'indicative' but Rossiter rescued him with a prompt.

"The alternate is to return you to French custody, with General Clarke's and my own endorsement, of course, where I suspect your only choices will be to remain in a camp or fight under the flag of France for the European cause."

Eisenhower sought a decision and indicated the three towards a 17th Century sofa as Rossiter, on cue, poured coffee for all.

757

A knock on the door was quickly accompanied by Hood's head reappearing, eyes enquiring silently of his General and receiving the reply he sought in equally noiseless fashion.

Within a minute he reappeared with six boxes, three odd sized and three small rectangular ones, placing three stacks containing one of each sort on Ike's desk.

The General flicked his lighter and drew in the pungent smoke, realising his guests were eyeing his packet.

Rossiter stepped forward and the three were soon drawing on their own cigarettes.

Eisenhower sucked his down in record time, conscious of the importance of what he was about to do as well as reminding himself he was on a time limit, a time limit already exceeded according to the mantlepiece clock.

He stood, initiating a similar response from the three ex-prisoners.

Braun spoke, not as interpreter, but as spokesperson for the group.

"Shandruk cannot go home, for his home is the Ukraine and it is not yet liberated. Herr Uhlmann and I cannot go home because our country still needs us. We do not really understand why it is the Foreign Legion and not the German flag we would fight under, but fight we will, Herr General."

Eisenhower nodded and smiled broadly.

"I never doubted it, gentlemen. Colonel Rossiter."

Sam Rossiter, for all his serious nature, had been waiting for this bit.

"Achtung! Stillgestanden!"

Automatically the three men froze in rigid poses, mirrors of each other, stood at parade attention.

"Colonel Rossiter, if you will translate my words please."

"Major Uhlmann, Lieutenant Shandruk, Master Sergeant Braun, on behalf of the free States of Europe and the United States of America, thank you." To emphasise the moment, he looked at each man in turn. "Sincerely, I thank you."

A moment of pause and then forward again.

758

"As a token of our appreciation, we restore to you the awards of your former enlistment."

Hood passed over the boxes one at a time, in descending rank order and Eisenhower presented it to the appropriate man. Each one of the irregular boxes was marked with solely their surname.

The recipients did not look at the contents until prompted by Eisenhower. Each contained their listed gallantry and service awards, de-nazified by the removal of swastikas as agreed with the Council and accompanied by an 'authorisation to wear' document very boldly signed with a signature that could open doors in a very real sense, originating from the office of the Supreme Commander.

Whilst such things are a matter of pride for combat soldiers, there was an amount of confusion apparent on their faces.

"Our understanding is that those who serve in the Legion will be permitted to wear their bravery awards, so wear these with pride gentlemen."

Confusion was replaced by surprise, tinged with not a little pride.

"Additionally, on the recommendation of General Clarke and fully endorsed by myself," Eisenhower turned and picked up the first small box, removing its contents.

Eisenhower smiled and spoke, almost as an aside.

"This is one of the advantages of having German forces under my command."

He stood in front of the senior German who automatically stiffened.

"Major Uhlmann, for bravery and sustained courage in the face of the enemy, you are awarded the Silver Star."

The medal was pinned in place, despite Uhlmann's confused look.

"The Council of Germany and Austria has approved the award and granted you permission to wear it and indeed any and all awards that will come to your fellow countrymen, now and in the months ahead."

Uhlmann suddenly realised that the American leader was extending his hand and his confusion arrested his own response.

Eisenhower's hand stayed, firm and steady, until Uhlmann regained his senses.

Some years later, Eisenhower would record how he suddenly wished he had made not arranged a private affair, wasting the symbolism of the moment in a small office, witnessed solely by six people. However, the secrecy issues remained, hence the absence of even a photographer.

'Maybe when it's all over a repeat for public consumption?' he mused.

And with that, Ike repeated the process with Shandruk and Braun, each ready for the moment the American offered his hand.

Passing over the medal boxes for inclusion in the larger ones, he beamed broadly at the three men, each sporting the shiny new award.

"Wear this award with the same pride as you wear all your others."

Once more Rossiter barked a command and once more it drew instant disciplined response.

"Congratulations and thank you once again gentlemen. May you all stay safe in the difficult times ahead."

On receipt of the translation, all three clicked their heels but were again disarmed immediately by Eisenhower, released from the moment of formality, moving forward with his hand extended, grasping Uhlmann's, which reciprocated automatically this time.

Shaking all three men's hands warmly, Eisenhower glanced at Hood who took his cue and opened the door.

"Gentlemen, my apologies, but I must now go to work. Stay safe and do your duty. God go with you all."

Once the meaning of his words had been laid out to Uhlmann and Shandruk, the three responded by coming to parade attention and throwing immaculate salutes to Eisenhower, who responded, strangely proud of himself and the men in front of him.

Without further ado, the three left the room to go to France as legionnaires in the new French Foreign Legion Corps D'Assault.

1844hrs Sunday 12th August 1945, The road to Calvados, France.

Waiting to be taken to a French Reorganisation Camp, Uhlmann and Braun sat in the back of the 4x4 Dodge eyeing each other whilst they waited for Shandruk, for whom a visit to the latrine had been a priority.

Having occupied some of their wait with rummaging in the boxes of awards, both discovered that their tank destruction badges were omitted. None the less, the two set about restoring the marks of their service, asking advice about positioning here, offering input on adjustments there.

With their own uniforms it would have been much easier but eventually the awards were in position and, bizarrely, did not look out of place on the uniforms they wore.

Braun looked up just in time to see Shandruk shake an unseen hand in the doorway before bounding down the steps.

Strange.

He swung himself up into the back of the small vehicle and whistled softly at his comrade's appearance, nodding his approval. Braun wanted to ask but for some reason stayed his hand, the furtive look the little Ukrainian cast at the disappearing Hotel preventing open discussion.

As the vehicle departed, the American congratulated himself on a piece of quick thinking. He was never wrong about a man and Shandruk fitted his needs precisely.

'We can work on the English later', he reminded himself of the one shortcoming he was aware of.

Realising the man's qualities and attributes too late in the day, there was no opportunity to organise matters as he would have wished, retaining Shandruk close at hand.

Still, the Colonel knew where the Ukrainian was heading and would use the time to do some extra checking before spiriting him away for special deployments. All in all, a very successful seven minutes spent with a young man who could make instant decisions on his future.

And, as was instilled in every man who served in his unit, such success was punctuated with some basic Latin.

'Semper fi'.

The Dodge bounced down the road, hindering the process of restoring Shandruk's awards, even drawing blood from his finger as the close combat clasp fought back.

He had noticed Braun's expression and answered it with a silent but meaningful look of his own, ending it with a nod towards the two Americans in the front seats.

Once the arrangement of his awards was complete to everyone's satisfaction, he held a cautionary hand up to his comrades and moved forward, dipping his head between the two US soldiers.

"Comrades, do you have a cigarette please?" the German precise and slowly spoken.

"Don't speak Kraut" was all the driver could say, concentrating on avoiding the continuous line of US supply trucks heading in the other direction.

The other man turned his head and encouraged a repetition.

Shandruk did so and the man shook his head.

Braun said nothing, observing the Ukrainian.

This time he accompanied his words with the universal hand gestures and finally received understanding. A pack flipped cigarettes in seconds, generously being passed round all three Germans before returning to its owner's blouse pocket.

The three leant back in their seats sampling the rich tobacco, Uhlmann also now aware that something was up.

Shandruk spoke gently and unexcitedly, in German.

"I had a strange encounter back in their headquarters, Kameraden."

Still watching the front passengers for any sign of cognition, he continued.

"The American Colonel, the German speaker, he is not what he seemed."

Braun's coughing gave him a moment's pause. The watery-eyed man held up a hand of apology as the smoke sent him into another convulsion, drawing the gaze of the co-driver.

Addressing Uhlmann, the young Ukrainian took advantage of his comrade's plight, shaking his head in sadness.

"Schiesse, German NCO's are not as tough as they used to be, Herr Sturmbannfuhrer, veritable pussy cats nowadays," which comment brought more spasms from Braun as he struggled to counter-attack, as well as new coughs from the amused Uhlmann.

And in the way that such things often spread, the driver ended his own short burst of hacking by spitting a large gobbet off to the side.

"Anyway, I will not be with you for long, or so it appears. My Russian language skills mean I will serve in other ways."

Flicking his dog end from the rear, he leant forward, bringing the now recovered pair closer.

"There was little time to decide but the man seemed sincere and I made a snap decision. If it is not for me then I will come back, or maybe just disappear eh?"

That statement had two meanings which was not lost on the listeners.

"Did he say what he wants of you, Ost?" Braun ventured, having now recovered.

"He said it would be dangerous work, but that it would be important and will hurt the Russians very badly."

Leaning back once more, Shandruk drew a line in the proverbial sand.

"He said a little more, but asked I say nothing to you and I will honour that as I gave my word."

Both men could understand that and so there was no pushing the point further, although Uhlmann had to ask why the Ukrainian was travelling with them.

"Simply put, he said he had no time to organise anything with the French and he doesn't want to attract attention. I am to go with you until he brings me back; that is all I know for now."

Probably it wasn't, but neither German pressed their comrade further.

The rest of the journey was filled with small talk, mainly about what they expected from the French. It was of little interest to 'Corporal Higgins', who had finally stopped being angry with himself for laughing at the Ukrainian's joke and, at the same time, congratulating himself for covering it with feigned coughing, embellishing the deception with a flourish of spit.

He would have little positive to report to Rossiter when he got back, although he could say that the one thing that Shandruk had been asked not to repeat had remained concealed.

If he had spoken of it then he and his two comrades would have quietly disappeared, silver stars or no silver stars; that had been the Marine Colonel's express instruction. Offing the two SS bastards would have been easy enough but there would have been regret over the Ukrainian.

'*Well probably*', thought 'Corporal Higgins', or as he was known in darker circles, Lieutenant Solomon Meyer, formerly of Munich, more lately a member of the Jewish Brigade Group and now a member of OSS.

As was his co-driver, Sergeant Michel Wijers, Dutch citizen, former Royal Dutch Army, resistance fighter and current OSS operative, master of many Slavic languages and aboard in case Shandruk and the Germans had other unsuspected communication options.

2213hrs Sunday 12th August 1945, French Foreign Legion Camp, Sassy, France.

The journey to their destination took three hours to the minute and it was rapidly approaching 2200hrs when they were dropped off and placed in French hands.

The French had chosen an area in the Calvados region for the holding and training camp, centred on the commune of

Sassy, with no comprehension of the amusement their selection caused to the extremely few allies in the know.

Their own Army HQ was set up within the Benedictine Monastery in nearby Saint Pierre-sur-Dives and different secure holding areas established to the south-west.

French military and police units secured the area, even going so far as to evacuate the residents of Sassy, Olendon and Emes, creating a large 'military-only' area.

In actual fact, the area was chosen for its proximity to the stockpiles left over from the Normandy campaign and the ability to effectively isolate a large area, rather than for any other reason.

Already the fields, which had yielded their crops prematurely, were sprouting tents and temporary structures in large numbers.

French engineers had swiftly constructed a modest runway, control tower and two hangars to the south-west of the commune, adding a large two storey wooden building on the edge of Sassy, which was to serve as the nerve centre of the effort.

The same engineers now lent their assistance to the inhabitants of St Pierre and the rebuilding of the fire ravaged Halle de Saint Pierre helped ease some of the tensions that arose with the arrival of the hated Boche.

Before the three arrived at the camp, they had been preceded by over seven thousand of their comrades from across the spectrum of the Waffen-SS, but mainly members of the 5th, 6th and 12th SS Divisions so far.

A leavening of German NCO's from the Legion had been quickly brought in to ease the transition and to start passing on some of the Legion's ethos and character. Traditions such as the motto 'Legio Patria Nostra', which translated from the Latin means 'The Legion is our Fatherland'. A concept not unfamiliar to the ex-soldiers of the Waffen-SS, who based much of their élan on the unit and comrades.

Many field and senior officers had been culled from the group on the basis of fact or suspicion and there were few leaders above the rank of Captain in the camp.

An exception to that had been placed in charge of attracting ex-SS soldiers to the Legion cause and had been promised a command role in the use of units formed.

The large room contained two tables set with five chairs in a simple V shape, opening towards the door, with an empty chair set for any new arrival

The man sat on the opposite wing to Knocke was the former SS-Obergruppenfuhrer Willi Bittrich, commander of the divisions that resisted at Arnhem and recently released from French custody, where he was absolved of wrongdoing in the matter of the deaths of the seventeen Nîmes resistance workers.

Still in his field grey German Officer's uniform, he cut a dashing figure, despite his fifty-one years. His medals also having been restored to him, he perfectly balanced the black-uniformed Knocke seated across the table from him.

Next to him was the imposing figure of Bruno Rettlinger, head still bandaged after his close encounter with the stonewall and left arm protruding from a simple uniform shirt, cut open to accommodate the frame that held the badly broken bone in place. The nasty deep sword wound was stitched tight, yet obviously red and angry.

Adjacent to Knocke, Lothar Von Arnesen sat, or more accurately, leaned, favouring his painfully wounded right thigh.

Seated centrally, clad in the crisp new uniform of a Général de Brigade in La Légion Étrangère, Christophe Lavalle presided over the theoretical construction of a powerful force for his Legion.

Working late, the five had quickly set aside their work and restructured the room when informed of Uhlmann's arrival. Instructions that arriving ex-SS officers of Captain or higher rank should be brought to the headquarters building ensured that Uhlmann was stood at attention before the five men in short order.

Gesturing the man to a seat, Lavalle took up the running as usual.

"Welcome, Commandant Uhlmann. You come with an enhanced reputation," and brandishing a pristine document bearing Eisenhower's signature, "And with impeccable credentials."

"Thank you, Herr General."

Uhlmann had decided to say as little as possible when he arrived at this place, but was greatly put at ease by the presence of both Bittrich and Knocke, obviously in a trusted supervisory role.

He did not know the other two officers.

"Apparently, you had the chance to walk away and chose to come here on very little information. Why is that?"

Uhlmann did not need to consider his words.

"For the same reasons as I went to the Amis with my information. It was the right thing to do, Herr General."

Conforming to their practised technique, Bittrich spoke next, in a clipped tone intended to establish authority and provoke memories of former times.

"Explain, Sturmbannfuhrer."

"Sir, I am here to fight for Germany first and Europe second. If I cannot fight as a German soldier then I will fight in the costume of the Folies Bergère, if it provides me with the opportunity to liberate my fatherland."

Bittrich tried but could not help smiling and his eyes flicked swiftly to Knocke who obviously had similar problems.

The ball was back in Lavalle's court.

"So, Commandant, you understand that you would be fighting as a Legionnaire under French command, acting under French orders and wearing French insignia?"

Uhlmann had already noticed the altered eagle, which now bore coloured wings, one of French and one of German national colours, the body constituted by some strange unfamiliar device which he would soon understand as the grenade insignia of La Légion Étrangère. It had been decided to create an insignia that covered completely the area previously occupied by the SS eagle and every man present carried it on his upper left arm and, strangely to Uhlmann, even Lavalle was so adorned.

"Herr General, I understand perfectly and will serve with honour until the Soviets are gone from my homeland."

Knocke leant forward.

"And beyond, Sturmbannfuhrer?"

The meaning of that was loud and clear.

767

"To the gates of Moscow if need be, Herr Standartenfuhrer."

It was a good answer and with it, Sturmbannfuhrer Rolf Uhlmann ceased to be, becoming, with five handshakes, Commandant Rolf Uhlmann of the newly forming 1st Legion Brigade de Chars D'Assault 'Camerone'.

The British message arrived just before midnight, bringing some excitement to an otherwise unusually uneventful evening. Suspicious commanders had organised and sent out patrols but nothing seemed amiss as, aircraft excepted, Europe enjoyed its quietest night for a week.

Eisenhower was awoken by a staff major clutching a report from McCreery. Grabbing his glasses, Eisenhower swiftly read the few lines, exhibiting real relief at the report.

Hamburg had held.

It is only the dead who have seen the end of war.

Plato

CHAPTER 54 – THE STORM

0258hrs Monday 13th August 1945, The Frontline, Europe.

From the smallest to the largest, each weapon was tended by a silent and expectant crew. Poised with shell in hand or firing cord taught ready for the order, the length of the Soviet front line concealed artillerymen with their mortars, howitzers, rockets and field artillery, in numbers undreamt of in modern warfare.

All bent for a single purpose.

Officers concentrated on their watches, tense with the expectation and understanding of what was about to come to pass.

The constant drone of enemy bombers overhead only served to increase the tension felt in a million hearts, although the sound of distant muffled explosions was unheeded by those preparing for battle.

The seconds advanced, bringing closer the moment of action until it arrived in an instant of unprecedented noise, light and fury.

Hundreds upon hundreds of weapons barked, spitting shells into the night sky, only for them to fall upon their targets, killing and maiming thousands of allied soldiers in a few minutes, stunning some into shocked inactivity and destroying some units as effective formations.

Opposite the assault formations, the biggest concentrations of artillery did their awful work, psychologically as well as physically destroying men in a few minutes of fiery hell.

The Soviet spearhead formations charged forward and, meeting very little resistance, broke through the front lines and rushed onward.

Europe lay bare before them.

This is not the End.

List of figures.

Bibliography

Rosignoli, Guido
The Allied Forces in Italy 1943-45
ISBN 0-7153-92123

Kleinfeld & Tambs, Gerald R & Lewis A
Hitler's Spanish Legion - The Blue Division in Russia
ISBN 0-9767380-8-2

Delaforce, Patrick
The Black Bull - From Normandy to the Baltic with the 11th Armoured
Division
ISBN 0-75370-350-5

Taprell-Dorling, H
Ribbons and Medals
SBN 0-540-07120-X

Pettibone, Charles D
The Organisation and Order of Battle of Militaries in World War II
Volume V - Book B, Union of Soviet Socialist Republics
ISBN 978-1-4269-0281-9

Pettibone, Charles D
The Organisation and Order of Battle of Militaries in World War II
Volume V - Book A, Union of Soviet Socialist Republics
ISBN 978-1-4269-2551-0

Pettibone, Charles D
The Organisation and Order of Battle of Militaries in World War II
Volume VI - Italy and France, Including the Neutral Conutries of San Marino,
Vatican City [Holy See], Andorra and Monaco
ISBN 978-1-4269-4633-2

Pettibone, Charles D
The Organisation and Order of Battle of Militaries in World War II
Volume II - The British Commonwealth
ISBN 978-1-4120-8567-5

Chamberlain & Doyle, Peter & Hilary L
Encyclopedia of German Tanks in World War Two
ISBN 0-85368-202-X

Chamberlain & Ellis, Peter & Chris
British and American Tanks of World War Two
ISBN 0-85368-033-7

Dollinger, Hans
The Decline and fall of Nazi Germany and Imperial Japan
ISBN 0-517-013134

Zaloga & Grandsen, Steven J & James
Soviet Tanks and Combat Vehicles of World War Two
ISBN 0-85368-606-8

Hogg, Ian V
The Encyclopedia of Infantry Weapons of World War II
ISBN 0-85368-281-X

Hogg, Ian V
British & American Artillery of World War 2
ISBN 0-85368-242-9

Hogg, Ian V
German Artillery of World War Two
ISBN 0-88254-311-3

Glossary

.30cal machine gun — Standard US medium machine gun.

.45 M1911 automatic — US automatic handgun

.50 cal — Standard US heavy machine gun.

105mm Flak gun — Next model up from the dreaded 88mm, these were sometimes pressed into a ground role in the final days.

39th Kingdom — See Kingdom39

6x6 truck — Three axle, 6 wheel truck.

Achilles — British version of the M-10 that carried the high velocity 17-pdr gun.

Addendum F — Transfer of German captured equipment to Japanese to increase their firepower and reduce logistical strain on Soviets

Alkonost — Creature from Russian folklore with the body of a bird and the head of a beautiful woman.

Anschluss — The 1938 occupation and Annexation of Austria by Germany.

BA64 — Soviet 4x4 light armoured car with two crew and a machine gun.

Battle of the Bulge — Germany's Ardennes offensive of winter 1944

Bazooka	Generic name applied to a number of different anti-tank rocket launchers introduced into the US Army from 1942 onwards.
Bletchley Park	Location of the centre for Allied code breaking during World War two. Sometimes known as Station X.
Blighty	British slang term for Britain.
Boyes	.55-inch anti-tank rifle employed by the British Army but phased out in favour of the PIAT.
Branden burghers	Rough German equivalent of commando, who were trained more in the arts of stealth and silent killing.
Bund Deutsche Madel	The League of German Girls, young females' organisation of the Nazi Party.
Camel	US cigarette brand
Cavalry	The German army had cavalry until the end, all be it in small numbers. The SS had two such divisions, the 8th and 22nd.
Chesterfield	American cigarette brand.
Combat Command [CC]	Formation similar to an RCT, which was formed from all-arms elements within a US Armored Division, the normal dispositions being CC'A', CC'B' and CC'R', the 'R' standing for reserve.

Colibri	High-class men's accessories producer, initially specialising in cigarette lighters.
Colloque Biarritz	The fourth symposium based at the Château du Haut-Kœnigsbourg.
Deuxieme Bureau	France's External Military Intelligence Agency that underwent a number of changes post 1940 but still retained its 'Deux' label for many professionals.
Douglas DC-3	Twin-engine US transport aircraft, also labelled C-47. [Built by the Russians under licence as the Li-2]
DP-28	Standard Soviet Degtyaryov light machine gun with large top mounted disc magazine containing 47 rounds.
Edelzwicker	Alsatian wine that is a blend of noble and standard grapes and, as a result, is sometimes hit and miss, sometimes superb.
Fallschirmjager	German Paratroops. They were the elite of the Luftwaffe, but few Paratroopers at the end of the war had ever seen a parachute. None the less, the ground divisions fought with a great deal of elan and gained an excellent combat reputation.
Fat Man	Implosion-type Plutonium Bomb similar in operation to 'The Gadget'.

FBI	Federal Bureau of Intelligence, which was also responsible for external security prior to the formation of the CIA.
FFI	Forces Francaises de L'Interieur, or the French Forces of the Interior was the name applied to resistance fighters during the latter stages of WW2. Once France had been liberated, the pragmatic De Gaulle tapped this pool of manpower and created 'organised' divisions from these, often at best, para-military groups. Few proved to be of any quality and they tended to be used in low-risk areas.
FG42	Fallschirmgewehr 42, a hybrid 7.62mm weapon which was intended to be both assault rifle and LMG.
Firefly	British variant of the American M4 armed with a 17-pdr main gun, which offered the Sherman excellent prospects for a kill of any Panzer on the battlefield.
Fizzle	Failure of a nuclear device to properly explode, but which can result in radioactive product being distributed over a sizeable local area.
Gamayun	Creature from Russian folklore with the body of a large bird and the head of a beautiful woman.

GAVCA	Grupo de Aviação de Caça [Portuguese] Translated literally means 'fighter group', the 1st GAVCA serving within the Brazilian Expediationary Force.
GAZ	Gorkovsky Avtomobilny Zavod, Soviet producers of vehicles from light car through to heavy trucks.
Gebirgsjager	German & Austrian Mountain troops.
Gestapo	GeheimeStaatsPolizei, the Secret Police of Nazi Germany.
Gitanes Mais	French cigarette brand
GKO	Gosudarstvennyj Komitet Oborony or State Security Committee, the group that held complete power of all matters within the Soviet Union.
Großdeutschland	Literally, 'Greater Germany', the elite Grossdeutschland Division was not an SS formation although it wore a cuff title on its right arm.
GRU	Glavnoye Razvedyvatel'noye Upravleniye of Soviet Military Intelligence, fiercely independent of the other Soviet Intelligence agencies such as the NKVD.

Hapsburg	European monarchy that ruled Austro-Hungary amongst other European states.
Hauptmann	Equivalent of captain in the German army.
Hero of the Soviet Union award	The Gold Star award was highly thought of and awarded to Soviet soldiers for bravery, although the medal was often devalued by being given for political or nepotistic reasons.
Hitler Youth [Hitler Jugend]	Young males' organisation of the Nazi Party.
Hohenzollern	Noble house of Germany, Prussia and Romania.
IS-II	Soviet heavy tank with a 122mm gun and 1-3 mg's
IS-III	Iosef Stalin III heavy tank, which arrived just before the German capitulation and was a hugely innovative design. 122mm gun and 1-2 mg
Jeep	½ Ton 4x4 all terrain vehicle, supplied in large numbers to the Western Allies and the Soviet Union.
Kalibr	Codename of David Greengrass, US Army Sergeant who was a Soviet Spy.

Katyn	1940 Massacre of roughly 22,000 Polish Army officers, Police officers and intelligentsia perpetrated by the NKVD, Site was discovered by the German Army and much propaganda value was made, although in reality there was no sanction against the USSR for this coldblooded murder.
Katyusha	Soviet rocket artillery weapon capable of bringing down area fire with either 16, 32 or 64 rockets of different types.
Kavellerie	German translation of Cavalry.
King Tiger tank	German heavy tank carrying a high-velocity 88m gun and 2-3 machine guns.
Kingdom 39	The Fairytale Kingdom in Russian Folklore.
Kradschutzen	Motorcycle infantry, term also applied to reconnaissance troops.
Kreigie	US slang for a German prisoner of war.
Kreigsmarine	German Navy
Kriegsspiels	Wargames
LA-7	Single-engine Lavochkin fighter aircraft, highly thought of despite poor maintenance history.

Leutnant	German Army rank equivalent to 2nd Lieutenant.
Liebfraumilch [Liebfrauenmilch]	German semi-sweet white wine.
Lisunov Li-2	Soviet licenced copy of the DC-3 twin-engine transport aircraft,
Little Boy	Uranium based fission bomb.
Luftwaffe	German Air Force
M-10	Known as the Wolverine, this US tank destroyer carried a 3" gun with modest performance. It was subsequently upgunned in British service and the many potent 17-pdr equipped vehicles became known as Achilles.
M13/40	Italian light tank with a 47mm gun and 3-4 machine guns.
M-16 half-track	US half-track mounting 4 x .50cal machine guns in a Maxon mount. For defence against aircraft at low level it was particularly effective against infantry.
M1Carbine	Semi-automatic carbine that fired a .30 cal round, notorious as being underpowered.
M20	US 6x6 Armoured utility car, which was basically an M8 without the turret.

M21	M3 halftrack with an 81mm mortar mount, providing mobile fire support.
M24 Chafee	US light tank fitted with a 75mm gun and 2-3 machine guns.
M26 Pershing	US Heavy tank with a 90mm gun and 2-3 machine guns. Underpowered initially, it had little chance to prove itself against the German arsenal.
M3 Halftrack	US standard half-track normally armed with 1 x .50cal machine gun and capable of carrying up to 13 troops
M3A1 sub-machine gun	Often known as the Grease gun, issued in .45 or the rarer 9mm calibres with a 30 round magazine.
M5 HST	Based on the M5 Stuart chassis, this was a high speed tractor, used as ammunition portee, crew transport and prime mover for US artillery units.
M5 Stuart	Light US tank armed with 37mm gun, mainly used for recon work.
M8 greyhound	6x6 Armoured car with 37mm main gun and 1-2 machine guns.
Maior	German Army rank equivalent to Major.

Manhattan Project	Research and development project aimed at producing the first atomic bomb.
Market-Garden	Montgomery's failed plan to drop paratroopers and secure river crossings into Northern Germany, thus ending the war by Christmas.
Maskirova	Soviets have a fondness for deception and misdirection and Maskirova is an essential of any undertaking.
Mauthausen	More properly known as Mauthausen-Gusen Concentration Camp, the camp grew to oversee a complex of Labour camps throughout the area. The high estimate of persons dying within the Mauthausen camp system is 320,000.
Maxon mount	A single machine gun mounting which could be installed on a half-track of a trailer, by which means 4 x .50cal were aimed and fired by one man.
Metgethen	Scene of a successful German counter-attack in 1945, where evidence of Soviet atrocities against the civilian population was uncovered.
MG34	German standard MG often referred to as a Spandau.

MG42	Superb German machine gun, capable of 1200rpm, designed to defeat the Soviet human wave attacks. Still in use to this day.
Mills Bomb	British fragmentation hand grenade.
Minox	Gained notoriety as the first 'miniature' spy camera.
Mlad	Codename of Theodore Hall, Nuclear Physicist and Soviet Agent.
Moscow Crystal Vodka	Highest quality triple distilled vodka.
Moselle	Mainly white wine originating from areas around the River of the same name.
Mosin-Nagant	Russian infantry rifle.
Mosquito	DH98 De Havilland Mosquito was a multi-purpose wooden aircraft, much envied by the Luftwaffe.
Mustang	P51 Mustang, US single seat long-range fighter armed with 6 x .50cal machine guns.
Nagant pistol	Standard Soviet revolver, very rugged and powerful using long case 7.62mm ammunition.
Natzwiller-Struhof	Concentration camp in Alsace.

NKGB	Narodny Komissariat Gosudarstvennoi Bezopasnosti, the Soviet Secret Police, separated from the NKVD in 1942 and absorbed once more in 1946.
NKVD	Narodny Komissariat Vnutrennikh Del, the People's Commissariat for Internal Affairs.
OFLAG XVIIa	Offizierslager or OfLag No 17A, prisoner of war camp run by the Germans for officer detainees.
Operation Anvil	August 1944 landing in Southern France.
Operation Apple Pie	US project to capture German officers with specific knowledge about the Soviet Union's industry and economy.
Operation Kurgan	Soviet joint-operation to employ paratroopers, Naval Marines, NKVD agents and collaborators to attack and neutralise airfields, radar, communications and logistic bases throughout Europe. Subsequently enlarged to include assassinations of Allied senior officers.
Operation Paperclip	OSS project to recruit German Scientist to the Allied cause post May 1945.
Operation Sumerechny	Soviet plan to remove German leadership elements from their prisoners.

Operation Unthinkable	Study ordered by Churchill to examine the feasibility of an Allied assault on Soviet held Northern Germany.
Panther Tank	German heavy-medium tank carrying a high-powered 75mm gun and 2-3 machine guns, considered by many to be the finest all-round tank of World War 2.
Panzer IV	German tank, which served throughout the war in many guises, mainly with a 75mm gun.
Panzer V	See Panther Tank
Panzer VI	See Tiger Tank
Panzertruppen	The German tank crews.
PanzerVIb	See King Tiger Tank
PE-2	The Soviet Petlyakov PE-2 was a twin-engine multi-purpose aircraft considered by the Luftwaffe to be a fine opponent.
PIAT	Acronym for Projector, Infantry, Anti-tank, the PIAT used a large spring to hurl its hollow charge shell at an enemy.
Plan Chelyabinsk	Soviet assault plan utilising lend-lease equipment in Western Allies markings.

Plan Diaspora	Soviet overall plan for assaulting in the East and for supporting the new Japanese Allies.
Plan Kurgan	Soviet joint-operation to employ paratroopers, Naval Marines, NKVD agents and collaborators to attack and neutralise airfields, radar, communications and logistic bases throughout Europe. Subsequently enlarged to include assassinations of Allied senior officers.
Plan Zilant	The Soviet paratrooper operations against the four symposiums, detailed as Zilant-1 through Zilant-4.
PLUTO	Acronym for 'Pipeline-under-the-ocean', which was a fuel supply pipe that ran from Britain to France, laid for D-Day operations and still in use at the end of the war.
P.O.L.	Petrol, oil and lubricants.
PPD	Soviet submachine gun capable of phenomenal rate of fire. Mostly equipped with a 72 round drum magazine but 65 rounds were normally fitted to avoid jamming. It was too complicated and was replaced by the PPSH.
PPS	Simple Soviet submachine gun with a 35 round magazine.

PPSH	Soviet submachine gun capable of phenomenal rate of fire. Mostly equipped with a 72 round drum magazine but 65 rounds were normally fitted to avoid jamming.
Pravda	Leading newspaper of the Soviet Union, Pravda is translated as 'Truth'.
PS84	Passenger Aircraft built at factory 84, the initial designation of the Li-2 transport aircraft.
PTAB	Each Shturmovik could carry four pods containing 48 bomblets, or up to 280 internally. Each bomblet could penetrate up to 70mm of armour, enough for the main battle tanks at the time.
RCT	Regimental Combat Team. US formation which normally consisted of elements drawn from all combatant units within the parent division, making it a smaller but reasonably self-sufficient unit. RCT's tended to be numbered according the Infantry regiment that supplied its fighting core.[See CC for US Armored force equivalent.]
Red Star	Standard issue Soviet military cigarettes.
Rodina	The Soviet Motherland.

Sherman [M4 Sherman]	American tank turned out in huge numbers with many variants, also supplied under lend-lease to Russia.
Shturmovik	The Ilyushin-2 Shturmovik, Soviet mass-produced ground attack aircraft that was highly successful.
Skat	German card game using 32 cards.
SMLE	Often referred to s the 'Smelly', this was the proper name of the Short, Magazine, Lee-Enfield rifle.
SS-Hauptsturm fuhrer	SS equivalent of captain.
St Florian	Patron saint of Upper Austria, Linz, chimney sweeps and firefighters.
ST44 [MP43/44]	German assault rifle with a 30 round magazine, first of its generation and forerunner to the AK47.
Standard HDM .22 calibre pistol	Originally used by OSS, this effective .22 with a ten round magazine is still in use by Special Forces throughout the world.
Starshina	Soviet rank roughly equivalent to Warrant Officer first Class.
Station 'X'	See Bletchley Park entry.
STAVKA	At this time this represents the 'Stavka of the Supreme Main Command', comprising high-ranked military and civilian members. Subordinate to the GKO, it was responsible for military oversight

and, as such, held its own military reserves which it released in support of operations.

Sten	Basic British sub-machine gun with a 32 round magazine. Produced in huge numbers throughout the 40's.
Stroh rum	Austrian spiced rum.
Studebaker	2.5 ton truck built in USA and USSR [under licence] and often used as platforms for the Katyusha.
Stuka [Junkers 87]	Famous dive-bomber employed by the Luftwaffe.
SU-76	76mm self-propelled gun used as artillery and for close support.
SVT40	Soviet automatic rifle with a 10 round magazine.
Symposium Biarritz	Utilisation of German expertise to prepare wargame exercises for allied unit commanders to demonstrate Soviet tactics and methods to defeat them.
T/34	Soviet medium tank armed with a 76.2mm gun and 2 mg's.
T/34-85 [T34m44]	Soviet medium tank armed with an 85mm gun and 2 mg's.
T-70	Soviet light tank with two crew and a 45mm gun.

Thompson	.45 calibre US submachine gun, normally issued with a 20 or 30 round magazine [although a drum was available.]
Tiger Tank	German heavy tank carrying an 88m gun and 2-3 machine guns.
Tokarev	Soviet 7.62mm automatic handgun [also known as TT30] with an 8 round magazine.
Trimbach	Quality Alsatian wine.
Type XXI submarine	The most technologically advanced submarine of the era, produced in small numbers by the Germans and unable to affect the outcome of the war.
Typhoon	RAF's most successful single seater ground attack aircraft of World War Two, which could carry anything from bombs through to rockets.
USAAF	United States Army Air Force.
Ushanka	Fur hat with adjustable sides.
Venona Project	Joint US-UK operation to analyse Soviet message traffic
Vichy	Name of the collaborationist government of defeated France.
Vitruvian man	Da Vinci's sketch of a man with legs and arms splayed.

Wacht am Rhein	Literally, 'Watch on the Rhine', a codename used to mask the real purpose of the German build-up that became the Ardennes Offensive in December 1944.
Waffen-SS	There will always be much debate over these troops. Ideologically driven, politically inspired, pathological killers with an unshakable faith in the superiority of the Aryan race or highly motivated troops with an incredible 'esprit de corps'? Whatever your point of view, the military achievements of the SS Soldiers were without parallel in WW2. That others wore the same uniform as they tended the camps and satisfied the despicable agendas of the Nazi party has, in many ways, tarnished the Waffen-SS. None the less, they have their own crimes to pay for, as do all who wore a uniform in WW2, for no side came away with clean hands.
Walther P38	German 9mm semi-automatic pistol with an eight round magazine.
Wehrmacht	The German Army
Yakolev-9	Soviet single-seater fighter aircraft that was highly respected by the Luftwaffe.
Zilant	Legendary creature in Russian folklore somewhat like a dragon

ZIS3   76.2mm anti-tank gun in Soviet use.

Extras available on the website
www.redgambitseries.com
Please register and join the forums.
Remember only to visit the areas relevant to your
book or you may pick up spoilers.

About the Author.

Colin Gee was born on 18th May 1957 in Haslar Naval Hospital, Gosport, UK, spending the first two years of his life at the naval base in Malta.

His parents divorced when he was approaching three years of age and he went to live with his grandparents in Berkshire, who brought him up.

On 9th June 1975 he joined the Fire Service and, after a colourful career, retired on 19th May 2007, having achieved the rank of Sub-Officer, Watch Commander. Or to be politically correct for the ego-tripping harridans in HR, Watch Manager 'A'.

After thirty-two years in the Fire Service reality suddenly hit and Colin found himself in need of a proper job!

As of today, Colin is permanently employed doing night shifts for NHS Out of Hours service.

At this moment in time Colin has a wife, two daughters, one step-daughter, two step-sons and two grandsons, Lucas and Mason-James, who are both avid Manchester United fans, although they don't know it yet.

Two turtles and four cats complete the home ensemble.

He has been a wargamer for most of his life, hence the future plans for a Red Gambit wargaming series.

In 1992 Colin joined the magistracy, having wandered in from the street to ask how someone becomes a beak. He served until 2005. The experience taught him the true difference between justice and the law, the former being what he would have preferred to administer.

Red Gambit was researched initially over ten years ago, but work and life changes prevented it from blossoming.

Now it has become many books, instead of one, as more research is done and more lines of writing open themselves up.

Colin writes for the pleasure it brings him and, hopefully, the reader. The books are not intended to be modern day 'Wuthering Heights' or 'War and Peace'. They contain a story which Colin thinks is worth the telling and to which task he set his inexperienced hand. The biographies are part of the whole experience that he hopes to bring the reader.

Enjoy them all and thank you for reading.

'Stalemate' - the story continues.

Read the first chapter of 'Stalemate' now.

Artillery is the god of war.

Iosef Stalin

Chapter 55 – The Wave.

0255hrs Monday, 13th August 1945, Europe.

Whilst not as big a bird as the Lancaster, or as potent a weapon in general, the Handley Page Halifax Bomber had seen its fair share of action and success up to May 1945.

NA-R was one of the newest Mark VII's, in service with the Royal Canadian Air Force's 426 Squadron, presently flying out of a base at Linton on Ouse, England.

Tonight the mission was to accompany two hundred and forty-one other aircraft and their crews to area bomb woods to the south-east of Gardelegen.

The Halifax crew were relatively inexperienced, having completed only two operations before the German War ended, added to four in the new one.

The night sky was dark, very dark, the only light provided by the glowing instrument panel or the navigators small lamp.

Until 0300 arrived, at which time night became day as beneath the bomber stream thousands of crews operated their weapons at the set time. Across a five hundred mile front Soviet artillery officers screamed their orders and instantly the air was filled with metal.

From their lofty perches, the Canadian flyers witnessed the delivery and arrival of tons of high explosive, all in total silence save for the drone of their own Bristol Hercules engines.

They watched, eyes drawn to the spectacle, as the Russian guns fired salvo after salvo.

Their inexperience was the death of them, as it was for the crew of K-Kilo, a Lancaster from 626 Squadron RAF.

Both crews, so intent on the Soviet display, drifted closer until the mid-upper gunner in UM-K screamed in shock and fear as a riveted fuselage dropped gently down towards him. The Halifax crew were oblivious to their peril, the Lancaster crew resigned to it as contact was made with the tail plane and rudders, the belly of the Halifax bending and splitting the control surfaces.

The Lancaster bucked slightly, pushing the port fin further up into the Halifax where the ruined end caught fast, partly held by a bent stay and partially by control wires caught on debris.

The Halifax pilot, a petrified twenty-one year old Pilot Officer, eased up on his stick, dragging the Lancaster into a nose down attitude and ruining its aerodynamic efficiency. The young pilot then decided to try and move left and, at the same time, the Lancaster pilot lost control of his aircraft, the nose suddenly rising and causing the port inner propeller to smash into the nose of the Handley Page aircraft.

Fragments of perspex and sharp metal deluged the pilot, blinding him. His inability to see caused more coming together and the tail plane of the Avro broke away, remaining embedded in the belly of the Halifax.

Both aircraft stalled and started to tumble from the sky. Inside the wrecked craft aircrew struggled to escape, G forces building and condemning most to ride their charges into the ground.

Halifax NA-R hit the ground first, with all but two of its crew aboard. Fire licked greedily at one of the NA-R crew's parachutes, taking hold and leaving only one man to witness his comrade's fate, plunging earthwards, riding a silken candle into the German soil.

The explosion resulting from NA-R's demise illuminated the area enough for many Russian soldiers to watch fascinated as the ruined Lancaster smashed into the ground some five hundred yards north, four parachutes easily discernable in the bright orange glow which bathed the area.

The Bomber stream tore the Gardelegen Woods to

797

pieces, destroying acres of trees and occasionally being rewarded with a secondary explosion. Seventeen more bombers were lost but they reported success and the obliteration of the target.

Unfortunately for them, or more importantly the British and Canadian units in the line at Hannover, the units of 6th Guards Tank Army which had occupied hidden positions in the target area had moved as soon as night had descended.

Apart from a handful of supply trucks and lame duck vehicles, nothing of consequence had been destroyed.

At Ceske Kubice the results were far better, with the Soviet 4th Guards Tank Corps and 7th Guards Cavalry Corps still laagering hidden and believing themselves safe.

Lancaster's and Mosquitoes bathed the area in bombs, destroying tanks, horses and men in equal measure. It was an awful blood-letting and the survivors were in no mood to take prisoners when the New Zealand crew of a stricken Lancaster parachuted down nearby. Vengeful cavalry sabres flashed in the firelight, continuing on when life was long since extinct and the victims no longer resembled men.

On the ground the results on the Allied units were quite devastating as the Soviet Armies resorted to their normal tactic of concentrating their attacks on specific points.

Whole battalions were swept away in an avalanche of shells and rockets.

On each of the five chosen focal points breakthrough was achieved swiftly, the leading Soviet units passing through a desolate landscape tainted by the detritus of what a few minutes beforehand had been human beings and the weapons they served.

Occasionally a group of shell Shocked troops rallied and fought back, but in the main only the odd desultory shot greeted the advancing Red Army.

The reports of advances were immediately sent back and within twenty minutes Zhukov knew he had all five breakthroughs ready to exploit and ordered the operations to go ahead as planned.

Ten minutes after Zhukov's orders had gone out, a bleary eyed Eisenhower, woken from his much needed sleep to swiftly throw on his previous day's shirt and trousers, learned that he no longer had an intact front line and that a disaster was in the making.

Swift conversations with his Army Commanders took place, each man in turn receiving a simple order.

"Reform your line General, reform your line."

Each was different, for McCreery had problems contrasting those of Bradley, who had worse problems than Devers et al.

Eisenhower felt like Old Mother Hubbard. He already knew that he had probably just lost the best part of three divisions of good fighting troops and he sought replacements.

The cupboard was all but bare.

Some units were coming ashore in France, some in England. A few were already moving forward to their staging areas near the Rhine, ready for operational deployment.

Setting his staff to the problems of logistics he let them take the strain whilst he sucked greedily on a cigarette and watched the disaster unfold.

Report followed report, problem heaped on problem as the Red Army moved relentlessly and surprisingly quickly forward.

Ike stubbed out number one having lit number two from its dying butt, spotting the normally dapper but now quite dishevelled Tedder approach, half an eye on his Commander in Chief and half a horrified eye on the situation map.

So shocked was the Air Chief Marshal that he stopped, mouth open wide, watching as blue lines were removed to be replaced by red arrows.

Eisenhower moved to the RAF officer who seemed rooted to the spot.

"Arthur, they've hit us bad and we're in pieces as you see."

The Englishman managed a nod accompanied by a grimace as arrows, red in colour, appeared moving north of München .

"I want maximum effort from you, maximum effort.

799

Get everyone in the air that can carry a bomb or a machine gun. I will get you my list of target priorities within the next hour. Send everyone, Arthur, even those who have been out tonight."

That drew a dismayed look from Tedder, this time aimed at Ike.

The complaint grew on his lips but withered under Ike's unusually hard gaze.

"Arthur, I know your boys will be tired and I know the casualties will reflect that. Send them in later if you must, but send them in, come what may. Are we clear?"

Tedder stiffened.

"Yes, General, we are clear. There will be a turnaround time in any case, so I can rest them but it is a long time since many of them have done day ops."

Eisenhower, both hands extended palms towards his man, spoke softly.

"I know, Arthur. I am asking a lot of them but I think much will be asked of many of us this day, don't you?"

The Air Chief Marshal couldn't buck that at all, especially as he caught the stream of arrows around München grow further out the corner of his eye.

"Very well, Sir. I will get them ready for a maximum effort. Target list will be with me by five?"

"I will do my very best, Arthur."

The man sped away, his mind already full of orders and thoughts of incredulous RAF officers reading them as tired crews touched down at bases all over Europe.

No one was going to be spared on this day.

Four Mosquitoes of 163 Squadron RAF had been tasked with destroying a Soviet engineer bridge laid over the Fuhse River at Groß Ilsede, the main road bridge having been dropped into the water by British demolition engineers some days previously.

The plan was for the lead aircraft to illuminate with flares to permit the rest of the flight to drop accurately.

Squadron Leader Pinnock and his navigator Flying Officer Rogers both knew their stuff inside out and the Mk

XXV Mosquito arrived on time and on target, releasing its illumination.

Flight Lieutenant Johar, a Sikh and the squadron's top bomber was confused. The landmarks were quite clearly right; the parallel railway, the watery curve, both present and yet it wasn't there.

Johar streaked over the target area, his bombs firmly on board, closely followed by three and four, equally confused. Navigators did checks and came up with the same result.

"This is the right place, dead on Skipper, no question" Rogers holding out his handwork for his boss to examine.

"Roger Bill," Pinnock not bothering to go for the normal play on Rogers name and radio procedure that whiled away hours of lonely flying for the pair.
Thumbing his mike he spoke to the others.

"This is Baker lead, this is Baker lead. Mission abort, say again mission abort. Take out the rail track rather than dump ordnance."

The bombs rained down, savaging the track running to the east of the Fuhse, rendering it useless for days to come.

163's professionalism was such that no more was said over the radio until they touched down at Wyton some hours later.

The base adjutant, debriefing the crews, insisted that there must have been a navigational mistake until all four navigators produced their documentation, setting aside his first possibility.

Which raised a rather interesting second one.

[Book Two of the Red Gambit series 'Breakthrough' is available now on Amazon Kindle as a download and createspace.com as a book.]